ZANE GREY COMBO EDITIONS

Great way to get the books you want for a lower overall price! Excellent reading.

D1605327

ZANE GREY COMBO 1

THE BORDER LEGION

THE CALL OF THE CANYON

DESERT GOLD

ZANE GREY

CreateSpace
2013

Zane Grey Combo #1

The Border Legion originally published in 1916
The Call of the Canyon originally published in 1921
Desert Gold originally published in 1913

The First Omnibus Edition

This CreateSpace edition prepared in 2013

ISBN-13: 978-1492111306
ISBN-10: 1492111309

THE BORDER LEGION

1

Joan Randle reined in her horse on the crest of the cedar ridge, and with remorse and dread beginning to knock at her heart she gazed before her at the wild and looming mountain range.

"Jim wasn't fooling me," she said. "He meant it. He's going straight for the border... Oh, why did I taunt him!"

It was indeed a wild place, that southern border of Idaho, and that year was to see the ushering in of the wildest time probably ever known in the West. The rush for gold had peopled California with a horde of lawless men of every kind and class. And the vigilantes and then the rich strikes in Idaho had caused a reflux of that dark tide of humanity. Strange tales of blood and gold drifted into the camps, and prospectors and hunters met with many unknown men.

Joan had quarreled with Jim Cleve, and she was bitterly regretting it. Joan was twenty years old, tall, strong, dark. She had been born in Missouri, where her father had been well-to-do and prominent, until, like many another man of his day, he had impeded the passage of a bullet. Then Joan had become the protegee of an uncle who had responded to the call of gold; and the latter part of her life had been spent in the wilds.

She had followed Jim's trail for miles out toward the range. And now she dismounted to see if his tracks were as fresh as she had believed. He had left the little village camp about sunrise. Someone had seen him riding away and had told Joan. Then he had tarried on the way, for it was now midday. Joan pondered. She had become used to his idle threats and disgusted with his vacillations. That had been the trouble—Jim was amiable, lovable, but since meeting Joan he had not exhibited any strength of character. Joan stood beside her horse and looked away toward the dark mountains. She was daring, resourceful, used to horses and trails and taking care of herself; and she did not need anyone to tell her that she had gone far enough. It had been her hope to come up with Jim. Always he had been repentant. But this time was different. She recalled his lean, pale face—so pale that freckles she did not know he had showed through—and his eyes, usually so soft and mild, had glinted like steel. Yes, it had been a bitter, reckless face. What had she said to him? She tried to recall it.

The night before at twilight Joan had waited for him. She had given him precedence over the few other young men of the village, a fact she resentfully believed he did not appreciate. Jim was unsatisfactory in every way except in the way he cared for her. And that also—for he cared too much.

When Joan thought how Jim loved her, all the details of that night became vivid. She sat alone under the spruce-trees near the cabin. The shadows thickened, and then lightened under a rising moon. She heard the low hum of insects, a distant laugh of some woman of the village, and the murmur of the brook. Jim was later than usual. Very likely, as her uncle had hinted, Jim had tarried at the saloon that had lately disrupted the peace of the village. The village was growing, and Joan did not like the change. There were too many strangers, rough, loud-voiced, drinking men. Once it had been a pleasure to go to the village store; now it was an ordeal. Somehow Jim had seemed to be unfavorably influenced by these new conditions. Still, he had never amounted to much. Her resentment, or some feeling she had, was reaching a climax. She got up from her seat. She would not wait any longer for him, and when she did see him it would be to tell him a few blunt facts.

Just then there was a slight rustle behind her. Before she could turn someone seized her in powerful arms. She was bent backward in a bearish embrace, so that she could neither struggle nor cry out. A dark face loomed over hers—came closer. Swift kisses closed her eyes, burned her cheeks, and ended passionately on her lips. They had some strange power over her. Then she was released.

Joan staggered back, frightened, outraged. She was so dazed she did not recognize the man, if indeed she knew him. But a laugh betrayed him. It was Jim.

"You thought I had no nerve," he said. "What do you think of that?"

Suddenly Joan was blindly furious. She could have killed him. She had never given him any right, never made him any promise, never let him believe she cared. And he had dared—! The hot blood boiled in her cheeks. She was furious with him, but intolerably so with herself, because somehow those kisses she had resented gave her unknown pain and shame. They had sent a shock through all her being. She thought she hated him.

"You—you—" she broke out. "Jim Cleve, that ends you with me!"

"Reckon I never had a beginning with you," he replied, bitterly. "It was worth a good deal... I'm not sorry... By Heaven—I've—kissed you!"

He breathed heavily. She could see how pale he had grown in the shadowy moonlight. She sensed a difference in him—a cool, reckless defiance.

"You'll be sorry," she said. "I'll have nothing to do with you any more."

"All right. But I'm not, and I won't be sorry."

She wondered whether he had fallen under the influence of drink. Jim had never cared for liquor, which virtue was about the only one he possessed. Remembering his kisses, she knew he had not been drinking. There was a strangeness about him, though, that she could not fathom. Had he guessed his kisses would have that power? If he dared again—! She trembled, and it was not only rage. But she would teach him a lesson.

"Joan, I kissed you because I can't be a hangdog any longer," he said. "I love you and I'm no good without you. You must care a little for me. Let's marry... I'll—"

"Never!" she replied, like flint. "You're no good at all."

"But I am," he protested, with passion. "I used to do things. But since—since I've met you I've lost my nerve. I'm crazy for you. You let the other men run after you. Some of them aren't fit to—to—Oh, I'm sick all the time! Now it's longing and then it's jealousy. Give me a chance, Joan."

"Why?" she queried, coldly. "Why should I? You're shiftless. You won't work. When you do find a little gold you squander it. You have nothing but a gun. You can't do anything but shoot."

"Maybe that'll come in handy," he said, lightly.

"Jim Cleve, you haven't it in you even to be BAD," she went on, stingingly.

At that he made a violent gesture. Then he loomed over her. "Joan Handle, do you mean that?" he asked.

"I surely do," she responded. At last she had struck fire from him. The fact was interesting. It lessened her anger.

"Then I'm so low, so worthless, so spineless that I can't even be bad?"

"Yes, you are."

"That's what you think of me—after I've ruined myself for love of you?"

She laughed tauntingly. How strange and hot a glee she felt in hurting him!

"By God, I'll show you!" he cried, hoarsely.

"What will you do, Jim?" she asked, mockingly.

"I'll shake this camp. I'll rustle for the border. I'll get in with Kells and Gulden... You'll hear of me, Joan Randle!"

These were names of strange, unknown, and wild men of a growing and terrible legion on the border. Out there, somewhere, lived desperados, robbers, road-agents, murderers. More and more rumor had brought tidings of them into the once quiet village. Joan felt a slight cold sinking sensation at her heart. But this was only a magnificent threat of Jim's. He could not do such a thing. She would never let him, even if he could. But after the incomprehensible manner of woman, she did not tell him that.

"Bah! You haven't the nerve!" she retorted, with another mocking laugh.

Haggard and fierce, he glared down at her a moment, and then without another word he strode away. Joan was amazed, and a little sick, a little uncertain: still she did not call him back.

And now at noon of the next day she had tracked him miles toward the mountains. It was a broad trail he had taken, one used by prospectors and hunters. There was no danger of her getting lost. What risk she ran was of meeting some of these border ruffians that had of late been frequent visitors in the village. Presently she mounted again and rode down the ridge. She would go a mile or so farther.

Behind every rock and cedar she expected to find Jim. Surely he had only threatened her. But she had taunted him in a way no man could stand, and if there were any strength of character in him he would show it now. Her remorse and dread increased. After all, he was only a boy—only a couple of years older than she was. Under stress of feeling he might go to any extreme. Had she misjudged him? If she had not, she had at least been brutal. But he had dared to kiss her! Every time she thought of that a tingling, a confusion, a hot shame went over her. And at length Joan marveled to find that out of the affront to her pride, and the quarrel, and the fact of his going and of her following, and especially out of this increasing remorseful dread, there had flourished up a strange and reluctant respect for Jim Cleve.

She climbed another ridge and halted again. This time she saw a horse and rider down in the green. Her heart leaped. It must be Jim returning. After all, then, he had only threatened. She felt relieved and glad, yet vaguely sorry. She had been right in her conviction.

She had not watched long, however, before she saw that this was not the horse Jim usually rode. She took the precaution then to hide behind some bushes, and watched from there. When the horseman approached closer she discerned that instead of Jim it was Harvey Roberts, a man of the village and a good friend of her uncle's. Therefore she rode out of her covert and hailed him. It was a significant thing that at the sound of her voice Roberts started suddenly and reached for his gun. Then he recognized her.

"Hello, Joan!" he exclaimed, turning her way. "Reckon you give me a scare. You ain't alone way out here?"

"Yes. I was trailing Jim when I saw you," she replied. "Thought you were Jim."

"Trailin' Jim! What's up?"

"We quarreled. He swore he was going to the devil. Over on the border! I was mad and told him to go.... But I'm sorry now—and have been trying to catch up with him."

"Ahuh!... So that's Jim's trail. I sure was wonderin'. Joan, it turns off a few miles back an' takes the trail for the border. I know. I've been in there."

Joan glanced up sharply at Roberts. His scarred and grizzled face seemed grave and he avoided her gaze.

"You don't believe—Jim'll really go?" she asked, hurriedly.

"Reckon I do, Joan," he replied, after a pause. "Jim is just fool enough. He had been gettrn' recklessler lately. An', Joan, the times ain't provocatin' a young feller to be good. Jim had a bad fight the other night. He about half killed young Bradley. But I reckon you know."

"I've heard nothing," she replied. "Tell me. Why did they fight?"

"Report was that Bradley talked oncomplementary about you."

Joan experienced a sweet, warm rush of blood—another new and strange emotion. She did not like Bradley. He had been persistent and offensive.

"Why didn't Jim tell me?" she queried, half to herself.

"Reckon he wasn't proud of the shape he left Bradley in," replied Roberts, with a laugh. "Come on, Joan, an' make back tracks for home."

Joan was silent a moment while she looked over the undulating green ridges toward the great gray and black walls. Something stirred deep within her. Her father in his youth had been an adventurer. She felt the thrill and the call of her blood. And she had been unjust to a man who loved her.

"I'm going after him," she said.

Roberts did not show any surprise. He looked at the position of the sun. "Reckon we might overtake him an' get home before sundown," he said, laconically, as he turned his horse. "We'll make a short cut across here a few miles, an' strike his trail. Can't miss it."

Then he set off at a brisk trot and Joan fell in behind. She had a busy mind, and it was a sign of her preoccupation that she forgot to thank Roberts. Presently they struck into a valley, a narrow depression between the foothills and the ridges, and here they made faster time. The valley appeared miles long. Toward the middle of it Roberts called out to Joan, and, looking down, she saw they had come up with Jim's trail. Here Roberts put his mount to a canter, and at that gait they trailed Jim out of the valley and up a slope which appeared to be a pass into the mountains. Time flew by for Joan, because she was always peering ahead in the hope and expectation of seeing Jim off in the distance. But she had no glimpse of him. Now and then Roberts would glance around at the westering sun. The afternoon had far advanced. Joan began to worry about home. She had been so sure of coming up with Jim and returning early in the day that she had left no word as to her intentions. Probably by this time somebody was out looking for her.

The country grew rougher, rock-strewn, covered with cedars and patches of pine. Deer crashed out of the thickets and grouse whirred up from under the horses. The warmth of the summer afternoon chilled.

"Reckon we'd better give it up," called Roberts back to her.

"No—no. Go on," replied Joan.

And they urged their horses faster. Finally they reached the summit of the slope. From that height they saw down into a round, shallow valley, which led on, like all the deceptive reaches, to the ranges. There was water down there. It glinted like red ribbon in the sunlight. Not a living thing was in sight. Joan grew more discouraged. It seemed there was scarcely any hope of overtaking Jim that day. His trail led off round to the left and grew difficult to follow. Finally, to make matters worse, Roberts's horse slipped in a rocky wash and lamed himself. He did not want to go on, and, when urged, could hardly walk.

Roberts got off to examine the injury. "Wal, he didn't break his leg," he said, which was his manner of telling how bad the injury was. "Joan, I reckon there'll be some worryin' back home tonight. For your horse can't carry double an' I can't walk."

Joan dismounted. There was water in the wash, and she helped Roberts bathe the sprained and swelling joint. In the interest and sympathy of the moment she forgot her own trouble.

"Reckon we'll have to make camp right here," said Roberts, looking around. "Lucky I've a pack on that saddle. I can make you comfortable. But we'd better be careful about a fire an' not have one after dark."

"There's no help for it," replied Joan. "Tomorrow we'll go on after Jim. He can't be far ahead now." She was glad that it was impossible to return home until the next day.

Roberts took the pack off his horse, and then the saddle. And he was bending over in the act of loosening the cinches of Joan's saddle when suddenly he straightened up with a jerk.

"What's that?"

Joan heard soft, dull thumps on the turf and then the sharp crack of an unshod hoof upon stone. Wheeling, she saw three horsemen. They were just across the wash and coming toward her. One rider pointed in her direction. Silhouetted against the red of the sunset they made dark and sinister figures. Joan glanced apprehensively at Roberts. He was staring with a look of recognition in his eyes. Under his breath he muttered a curse. And although Joan was not certain, she believed that his face had shaded gray.

The three horsemen halted on the rim of the wash. One of them was leading a mule that carried a pack and a deer carcass. Joan had seen many riders apparently just like these, but none had ever so subtly and powerfully affected her.

"Howdy," greeted one of the men.

And then Joan was positive that the face of Roberts had turned ashen gray.

2

"It ain't you—KELLS?"

Roberts's query was a confirmation of his own recognition. And the other's laugh was an answer, if one were needed.

The three horsemen crossed the wash and again halted, leisurely, as if time was no object. They were all young, under thirty. The two who had not spoken were rough-garbed, coarse-featured, and resembled in general a dozen men Joan saw every day. Kells was of a different stamp. Until he looked at her he reminded her of someone she had known back in Missouri; after he looked at her she was aware, in a curious, sickening way, that no such person as he had ever before seen her. He was pale, gray-eyed, intelligent, amiable. He appeared to be a man who had been a gentleman. But there was something strange, intangible, immense about him. Was that the effect of his presence or of his name? Kells! It was only a word to Joan. But it carried a nameless and terrible suggestion. During the last year many dark tales had gone from camp to camp in Idaho—some too strange, too horrible for credence—and with every rumor the fame of Kells had grown, and also a fearful certainty of the rapid growth of a legion of evil men out on the border. But no one in the village or from any of the camps ever admitted having seen this Kells. Had fear kept them silent? Joan was amazed that Roberts evidently knew this man.

Kells dismounted and offered his hand. Roberts took it and shook it constrainedly.

"Where did we meet last?" asked Kells.

"Reckon it was out of Fresno," replied Roberts, and it was evident that he tried to hide the effect of a memory.

Then Kells touched his hat to Joan, giving her the fleetest kind of a glance. "Rather off the track aren't you?" he asked Roberts.

"Reckon we are," replied Roberts, and he began to lose some of his restraint. His voice sounded clearer and did not halt. "Been trailin' Miss Randle's favorite hoss. He's lost. An' we got farther 'n we had any idee. Then my hoss went lame. 'Fraid we can't start home to-night."

"Where are you from?"

"Hoadley. Bill Hoadley's town, back thirty miles or so."

"Well, Roberts, if you've no objection we'll camp here with you," continued Kells. "We've got some fresh meat."

With that he addressed a word to his comrades, and they repaired to a cedar-tree near-by, where they began to unsaddle and unpack.

Then Roberts, bending nearer Joan, as if intent on his own pack, began to whisper, hoarsely: "That's Jack Kells, the California road-agent. He's a gun fighter—a hell-bent rattlesnake. When I saw him last he had a rope round his neck an' was bein' led away to be hanged. I heerd afterward he was rescued by pals. Joan, if the idee comes into his head he'll kill me. I don't know what to do. For God's sake think of somethin'!... Use your woman's wits!... We couldn't be in a wuss fix!"

Joan felt rather unsteady on her feet, so that it was a relief to sit down. She was cold and sick inwardly, almost stunned. Some great peril menaced her. Men like Roberts did not talk that way without cause. She was brave; she was not unused to danger. But this must be a different kind, compared with which all she had experienced was but insignificant. She could not grasp Roberts's intimation. Why should he be killed? They had no gold, no valuables. Even their horses were nothing to inspire robbery. It must be that there was peril to Roberts and to her because she was a girl, caught out in the wilds, easy prey for beasts of evil men. She had heard of such things happening. Still, she could not believe it possible for her. Roberts could protect her. Then this amiable, well-spoken Kells, he was no Western rough—he spoke like an educated man; surely he would not harm her. So her mind revolved round fears, conjectures, possibilities; she could not find her wits. She could not think how to meet the situation, even had she divined what the situation was to be.

While she sat there in the shade of a cedar the men busied themselves with camp duties. None of them appeared to pay any attention to Joan. They talked while they worked, as any other group of campers might have talked, and jested and laughed. Kells made a fire, and carried water, then broke cedar boughs for later camp-fire use; one of the strangers whom they called Bill hobbled the horses; the other unrolled the pack, spread a tarpaulin, and emptied the greasy sacks; Roberts made biscuit dough for the oven.

The sun sank red and a ruddy twilight fell. It soon passed. Darkness had about set in when Roberts came over to Joan, carrying bread, coffee, and venison.

"Here's your supper, Joan," he called, quite loud and cheerily, and then he whispered: "Mebbe it ain't so bad. They-all seem friendly. But I'm scared, Joan. If you jest wasn't so dam' handsome, or if only he hadn't seen you!"

"Can't we slip off in the dark?" she whispered in return.

"We might try. But it'd be no use if they mean bad. I can't make up my mind yet what's comin' off. It's all right for you to pretend you're bashful. But don't lose your nerve."

Then he returned to the camp-fire. Joan was hungry. She ate and drank what had been given her, and that helped her to realize reality. And although dread abided with her, she grew curious. Almost she imagined she was fascinated by her predicament. She had always been an emotional girl of strong will and self-restraint. She had always longed for she knew not what—perhaps freedom. Certain places had haunted her. She had felt that something should have happened to her there. Yet nothing ever had happened. Certain books had obsessed her, even when a child, and often to her mother's dismay; for these books had been of wild places and life on the sea, adventure, and bloodshed. It had always been said of her that she should have been a boy.

Night settled down black. A pale, narrow cloud, marked by a train of stars, extended across the dense blue sky. The wind moaned in the cedars and roared in the replenished camp-fire. Sparks flew away into the shadows. And on the puffs of smoke that blew toward her came the sweet, pungent odor of burning cedar. Coyotes barked off under the brush, and from away on the ridge drifted the dismal defiance of a wolf.

Camp-life was no new thing to Joan. She had crossed the plains in a wagon-train, that more than once had known the long-drawn yell of hostile Indians. She had prospected and hunted in the mountains with her uncle, weeks at a time. But never before this night had the wildness, the loneliness, been so vivid to her.

Roberts was on his knees, scouring his oven with wet sand. His big, shaggy head nodded in the firelight. He seemed pondering and thick and slow. There was a burden upon him. The man Bill and his companion lay back against stones and conversed low. Kells stood up in the light of the blaze. He had a pipe at which he took long pulls and then sent up clouds of smoke. There was nothing imposing in his build or striking in his face, at that distance; but it took no second look to see here was a man remarkably out of the ordinary. Some kind of power and intensity emanated from him. From time to time he appeared to glance in Joan's direction; still, she could not be sure, for his eyes were but shadows. He had cast aside his coat. He wore a vest open all the way, and a checked soft shirt, with a black tie hanging untidily. A broad belt swung below his hip and in the holster was a heavy gun. That was a strange place to carry a gun, Joan thought. It looked awkward to her. When he walked it might swing round and bump against his leg. And he certainly would have to put it some other place when he rode.

"Say, have you got a blanket for that girl?" asked Kells, removing his pipe from his lips to address Roberts.

"I got saddle-blankets," responded Roberts. "You see, we didn't expect to be caught out."

"I'll let you have one," said Kells, walking away from the fire. "It will be cold." He returned with a blanket, which he threw to Roberts.

"Much obliged," muttered Roberts.

"I'll bunk by the fire," went on the other, and with that he sat down and appeared to become absorbed in thought.

Roberts brought the borrowed blanket and several saddle-blankets over to where Joan was, and laying them down he began to kick and scrape stones and brush aside.

"Pretty rocky place, this here is," he said. "Reckon you'll sleep some, though."

Then he began arranging the blankets into a bed. Presently Joan felt a tug at her riding-skirt. She looked down.

"I'll be right by you," he whispered, with his big hand to his mouth, "an' I ain't a-goin' to sleep none."

Whereupon he returned to the camp-fire. Presently Joan, not because she was tired or sleepy, but because she wanted to act naturally, lay down on the bed and pulled a blanket up over her. There was no more talking among the men. Once she heard the jingle of spurs and the rustle of cedar brush. By and by Roberts came back to her, dragging his saddle, and lay down near her. Joan raised up a little to see Kells motionless and absorbed by the fire. He had a strained and tense position. She sank back softly and looked up at the cold bright stars. What was going to happen to her? Something terrible! The very night shadows, the silence, the presence of strange men, all told her. And a shudder that was a thrill ran over and over her.

She would lie awake. It would be impossible to sleep. And suddenly into her full mind flashed an idea to slip away in the darkness, find her horse, and so escape from any possible menace. This plan occupied her thoughts for a long while. If she had not been used to Western ways she would have tried just that thing. But she rejected it. She was not sure that she could slip away, or find her horse, or elude pursuit, and certainly not sure of her way home. It would be best to stay with Roberts.

When that was settled her mind ceased to race. She grew languid and sleepy. The warmth of the blankets stole over her. She had no idea of sleeping, yet she found sleep more and more difficult to resist. Time that must have been hours passed. The fire died down and then brightened; the shadows darkened and then lightened. Someone now and then got up to throw on wood. The thump of hobbled hoofs sounded out in the darkness. The wind was still and the coyotes were gone. She could no longer open her eyes. They seemed glued shut. And then gradually all sense of the night and the wild, of the drowsy warmth, faded.

When she awoke the air was nipping cold. Her eyes snapped open clear and bright. The tips of the cedars were ruddy in the sunrise. A camp-fire crackled. Blue smoke curled upward. Joan sat up with a rush of memory. Roberts and Kells were bustling round the fire. The man Bill was carrying water. The other fellow had brought in the horses and was taking off the hobbles. No one, apparently, paid any attention to Joan. She got up and smoothed out her tangled hair, which she always wore in a braid down her back when she rode. She had slept, then, and in her boots! That was the first time she had ever done that. When she went down to the brook to bathe her face and wash her hands, the men still, apparently, took no notice of her. She began to hope that Roberts had exaggerated their danger. Her horse was rather skittish and did not care for strange hands. He broke away from the bunch. Joan went after him, even lost sight of camp. Presently, after she caught him, she led him back to camp and tied him up. And then she was so far emboldened as to approach the fire and to greet the men.

"Good morning," she said, brightly.

Kells had his back turned at the moment. He did not move or speak or give any sign he had heard. The man Bill stared boldly at her, but without a word. Roberts returned her greeting, and as she glanced quickly at him, drawn by his voice, he turned away. But she had seen that his face was dark, haggard, worn.

Joan's cheer and hope sustained a sudden and violent check. There was something wrong in this group, and she could not guess what it was. She seemed to have a queer, dragging weight at her limbs. She was glad to move over to a stone and sink down upon it. Roberts brought her breakfast, but he did not speak or look at her. His hands shook. And this frightened Joan. What was going to happen? Roberts went back to the camp-fire. Joan had to force herself to eat. There was one thing of which she was sure—that she would need all the strength and fortitude she could summon.

Joan became aware, presently, that Kells was conversing with Roberts, but too low for her to hear what was said. She saw Roberts make a gesture of fierce protest. About the other man there was an air cool, persuading, dominant. He ceased speaking, as if the incident were closed. Roberts hurried and blundered through his task with his pack and went for his horse. The animal limped slightly, but evidently was not in bad shape. Roberts saddled him, tied on the pack. Then he saddled Joan's horse. That done, he squared around with the front of a man who had to face something he dreaded.

"Come on, Joan. We're ready," he called. His voice was loud, but not natural.

Joan started to cross to him when Kells strode between them. She might not have been there, for all the sign this ominous man gave of her presence. He confronted Roberts in the middle of the camp-circle, and halted, perhaps a rod distant.

"Roberts, get on your horse and clear out," he said.

Roberts dropped his halter and straightened up. It was a bolder action than any he had heretofore given. Perhaps the mask was off now; he was wholly sure of what he had only feared;

13

subterfuge and blindness were in vain; and now he could be a man. Some change worked in his face—a blanching, a setting.

"No, I won't go without the girl," he said.

"But you can't take her!"

Joan vibrated to a sudden start. So this was what was going to happen. Her heart almost stood still. Breathless and quivering, she watched these two men, about whom now all was strangely magnified.

"Reckon I'll go along with you, then," replied Roberts.

"Your company's not wanted."

"Wal, I'll go anyway."

This was only play at words, Joan thought. She divined in Roberts a cold and grim acceptance of something he had expected. And the voice of Kells—what did that convey? Still the man seemed slow, easy, kind, amiable.

"Haven't you got any sense, Roberts?" he asked.

Roberts made no reply to that.

"Go on home. Say nothing or anything—whatever you like," continued Kells. "You did me a favor once over in California. I like to remember favors. Use your head now. Hit the trail."

"Not without her. I'll fight first," declared Roberts, and his hands began to twitch and jerk.

Joan did not miss the wonderful intentness of the pale-gray eyes that watched Roberts—his face, his glance, his hands.

"What good will it do to fight?" asked Kells. He laughed coolly. "That won't help her... You ought to know what you'll get."

"Kells—I'll die before I leave that girl in your clutches," flashed Roberts. "An' I ain't a-goin' to stand here an' argue with you. Let her come—or—"

"You don't strike me as a fool," interrupted Kells. His voice was suave, smooth, persuasive, cool. What strength—what certainty appeared behind it! "It's not my habit to argue with fools. Take the chance I offer you. Hit the trail. Life is precious, man!... You've no chance here. And what's one girl more or less to you?"

"Kells, I may be a fool, but I'm a man," passionately rejoined Roberts. "Why, you're somethin' inhuman! I knew that out in the gold-fields. But to think you can stand there—an' talk sweet an' pleasant—with no idee of manhood!... Let her come now—or—or I'm a-goin' for my gun!"

"Roberts, haven't you a wife—children?"

"Yes, I have," shouted Roberts, huskily. "An' that wife would disown me if I left Joan Randle to you. An' I've got a grown girl. Mebbe some day she might need a man to stand between her an' such as you, Jack Kells!"

All Roberts' pathos and passion had no effect, unless to bring out by contrast the singular and ruthless nature of Jack Kells.

"Will you hit the trail?"

"No!" thundered Roberts.

Until then Joan Randle had been fascinated, held by the swift interchange between her friend and enemy. But now she had a convulsion of fear. She had seen men fight, but never to the death. Roberts crouched like a wolf at bay. There was a madness upon him. He shook like a rippling leaf. Suddenly his shoulder lurched—his arm swung.

Joan wheeled away in horror, shutting her eyes, covering her ears, running blindly. Then upon her muffled hearing burst the boom of a gun.

3

Joan ran on, stumbling over rocks and brush, with a darkness before her eyes, the terror in her soul. She was out in the cedars when someone grasped her from behind. She felt the hands as the coils of a snake. Then she was ready to faint, but she must not faint. She struggled away, stood free. It was the man Bill who had caught her. He said something that was unintelligible. She reached for the snag of a dead cedar and, leaning there, fought her weakness, that cold black horror which seemed a physical thing in her mind, her blood, her muscles.

When she recovered enough for the thickness to leave her sight she saw Kells coming, leading her horse and his own. At sight of him a strange, swift heat shot through her. Then she was confounded with the thought of Roberts.

"Ro—Roberts?" she faltered.

Kells gave her a piercing glance. "Miss Randle, I had to take the fight out of your friend," he said.

"You—you—Is he—dead?"

"I just crippled his gun arm. If I hadn't he would have hurt somebody. He'll ride back to Hoadley and tell your folks about it. So they'll know you're safe."

"Safe!" she whispered.

"That's what I said, Miss Randle. If you're going to ride out into the border—if it's possible to be safe out there you'll be so with me."

"But I want to go home. Oh, please let me go!"

"I couldn't think of it."

"Then—what will you—do with me?"

Again that gray glance pierced her. His eyes were clear, flawless, like crystal, without coldness, warmth, expression. "I'll get a barrel of gold out of you."

"How?" she asked, wonderingly.

"I'll hold you for ransom. Sooner or later those prospectors over there are going to strike gold. Strike it rich! I know that. I've got to make a living some way."

Kells was tightening the cinch on her saddle while he spoke. His voice, his manner, the amiable smile on his intelligent face, they all appeared to come from sincerity. But for those strange eyes Joan would have wholly believed him. As it was, a half doubt troubled her. She remembered the character Roberts had given this man. Still, she was recovering her nerve. It had been the certainty of disaster to Roberts that had made her weaken. As he was only slightly wounded and free to ride home safely, she had not the horror of his death upon her. Indeed, she was now so immensely uplifted that she faced the situation unflinchingly.

"Bill," called Kells to the man standing there with a grin on his coarse red face, "you go back and help Halloway pack. Then take my trail."

Bill nodded, and was walking away when Kells called after him: "And say, Bill, don't say anything to Roberts. He's easily riled."

"Haw! Haw! Haw!" laughed Bill.

His harsh laughter somehow rang jarringly in Joan's ears. But she was used to violent men who expressed mirth over mirthless jokes.

"Get up, Miss Randle," said Kells as he mounted. "We've a long ride. You'll need all your strength. So I advise you to come quietly with me and not try to get away. It won't be any use trying."

Joan climbed into her saddle and rode after him. Once she looked back in hope of seeing Roberts, of waving a hand to him. She saw his horse standing saddled, and she saw Bill struggling under a pack, but there was no sign of Roberts. Then more cedars intervened and the camp site was lost to view. When she glanced ahead her first thought was to take in the points of Kells's horse. She had been used to horses all her life. Kells rode a big rangy bay—a horse that appeared to snort speed and endurance. Her pony could never run away from that big brute. Still Joan had the temper to make an attempt to escape, if a favorable way presented.

The morning was rosy, clear, cool; there was a sweet, dry tang in the air; white-tailed deer bounded out of the open spaces; and the gray-domed, glistening mountains, with their bold, black-fringed slopes, overshadowed the close foot-hills.

Joan was a victim to swift vagaries of thought and conflicting emotions. She was riding away with a freebooter, a road-agent, to be held for ransom. The fact was scarcely credible. She could not shake the dread of nameless peril. She tried not to recall Roberts's words, yet they haunted her. If she had not been so handsome, he had said! Joan knew she possessed good looks, but they had never caused her any particular concern. That Kells had let that influence him—as Roberts had imagined—was more than absurd. Kells had scarcely looked at her. It was gold such men wanted. She wondered what her ransom would be, where her uncle would get it, and if there really was a likelihood of that rich strike. Then she remembered her mother, who had died when she was a little girl, and a strange, sweet sadness abided with her. It passed. She saw her uncle— that great, robust, hearty, splendid old man, with his laugh and his kindness, and his love for her, and his everlasting unquenchable belief that soon he would make a rich gold-strike. What a roar and a stampede he would raise at her loss! The village camp might be divided on that score, she thought, because the few young women in that little settlement hated her, and the young men would have more peace without her. Suddenly her thought shifted to Jim Cleve, the cause of her present misfortune. She had forgotten Jim. In the interval somehow he had grown. Sweet to remember how he had fought for her and kept it secret! After all, she had misjudged him. She had hated him because she liked him. Maybe she did more! That gave her a shock. She recalled his kisses and then flamed all over. If she did not hate him she ought to. He had been so useless; he ran after her so; he was the laughing-stock of the village; his actions made her other admirers and friends believe she cared for him, was playing fast-and-loose with him. Still, there was a difference now. He had terribly transgressed. He had frightened her with threats of dire ruin to himself. And because of that she had trailed him, to fall herself upon a hazardous experience. Where was Jim Cleve now? Like a flash then occurred to her the singular possibility. Jim had ridden for the border with the avowed and desperate intention of finding Kells and Gulden and the bad men of that trackless region. He would do what he had sworn he would. And here she was, the cause of it all, a captive of this notorious Kells! She was being led into that wild border country. Somewhere out there Kells and Jim Cleve would meet. Jim would find her in Kells's hands. Then there would be hell, Joan thought. The possibility, the certainty, seemed to strike deep into her, reviving that dread and terror. Yet she thrilled again; a ripple that was not all cold coursed through her. Something had a birth in her then, and the part of it she understood was that she welcomed the adventure with a throbbing heart, yet looked with awe and shame and distrust at this new, strange side of her nature.

And while her mind was thus thronged the morning hours passed swiftly, the miles of foot-hills were climbed and descended. A green gap of canon, wild and yellow-walled, yawned before her, opening into the mountain.

Kells halted on the grassy bank of a shallow brook. "Get down. We'll noon here and rest the horses," he said to Joan. "I can't say that you're anything but game. We've done perhaps twenty-five miles this morning."

The mouth of this canon was a wild, green-flowered, beautiful place. There were willows and alders and aspens along the brook. The green bench was like a grassy meadow. Joan caught a glimpse of a brown object, a deer or bear, stealing away through spruce-trees on the slope. She dismounted, aware now that her legs ached and it was comfortable to stretch them. Looking backward across the valley toward the last foot-hill, she saw the other men, with horses and packs, coming. She had a habit of close observation, and she thought that either the men with the packs had now one more horse than she remembered, or else she had not seen the extra one. Her attention shifted then. She watched Kells unsaddle the horses. He was wiry, muscular, quick with his hands. The big, blue-cylindered gun swung in front of him. That gun had a queer kind of attraction for her. The curved black butt made her think of a sharp grip of hand upon it. Kells did not hobble the horses. He slapped his bay on the haunch and drove him down toward the brook. Joan's pony followed. They drank, cracked the stones, climbed the other bank, and began to roll in the grass. Then the other men with the packs trotted up. Joan was glad. She had not thought of it before, but now she felt she would rather not be alone with Kells. She remarked then that there was no extra horse in the bunch. It seemed strange, her thinking that, and she imagined she was not clear-headed.

"Throw the packs, Bill," said Kells.

Another fire was kindled and preparations made toward a noonday meal. Bill and Halloway appeared loquacious, and inclined to steal glances at Joan when Kells could not notice. Halloway whistled a Dixie tune. Then Bill took advantage of the absence of Kells, who went down to the brook, and he began to leer at Joan and make bold eyes at her. Joan appeared not to notice him, and thereafter averted; her gaze. The men chuckled.

"She's the proud hussy! But she ain't foolin' me. I've knowed a heap of wimmen." Whereupon Halloway guffawed, and between them, in lower tones, they exchanged mysterious remarks. Kells returned with a bucket of water.

"What's got into you men?" he queried.

Both of them looked around, blusteringily innocent.

"Reckon it's the same that's ailin' you," replied Bill. He showed that among wild, unhampered men how little could inflame and change.

"Boss, it's the onaccustomed company," added Halloway, with a conciliatory smile. "Bill sort of warms up. He jest can't help it. An' seein' what a thunderin' crab he always is, why I'm glad an' welcome."

Kells vouchsafed no reply to this and, turning away, continued his tasks. Joan had a close look at his eyes and again she was startled. They were not like eyes, but just gray spaces, opaque openings, with nothing visible behind, yet with something terrible there.

The preparations for the meal went on, somewhat constrainedly on the part of Bill and Halloway, and presently were ended. Then the men attended to it with appetites born of the open and of action. Joan sat apart from them on the bank of the brook, and after she had appeased her own hunger she rested, leaning back in the shade of an alderbush. A sailing shadow crossed near her, and, looking up, she saw an eagle flying above the ramparts of the cañon. Then she had a drowsy spell, but she succumbed to it only to the extent of closing her eyes. Time dragged on. She would rather have been in the saddle. These men were leisurely, and Kells was provokingly slow. They had nothing to do with time but waste it. She tried to combat the desire for hurry, for action; she could not gain anything by worry. Nevertheless, resignation would not come to her and her hope began to flag. Something portended evil—something hung in the balance.

The snort and tramp of horses roused her, and upon sitting up she saw the men about to pack and saddle again. Kells had spoken to her only twice so far that day. She was grateful for his silence, but could not understand it. He seemed to have a preoccupied air that somehow did not fit the amiableness of his face. He looked gentle, good-natured; he was soft-spoken; he gave an impression of kindness. But Joan began to realize that he was not what he seemed. He had something on his mind. It was not conscience, nor a burden: it might be a projection, a plan, an absorbing scheme, a something that gained food with thought. Joan wondered doubtfully if it were the ransom of gold he expected to get.

Presently, when all was about in readiness for a fresh start, she rose to her feet. Kells's bay was not tractable at the moment. Bill held out Joan's bridle to her and their hands touched. The contact was an accident, but it resulted in Bill's grasping back at her hand. She jerked it away, scarcely comprehending. Then all under the brown of his face she saw creep a dark, ruddy tide. He reached for her then—put his hand on her breast. It was an instinctive animal action. He meant nothing. She divined that he could not help it. She had lived with rough men long enough to know he had no motive—no thought at all. But at the profanation of such a touch she shrank back, uttering a cry.

At her elbow she heard a quick step and a sharp-drawn breath or hiss.

"AW, JACK!" cried Bill.

Then Kells, in lithe and savage swiftness, came between them. He swung his gun, hitting Bill full in the face. The man fell, limp and heavy, and he lay there, with a bloody gash across his brow. Kells stood over him a moment, slowly lowering the gun. Joan feared he meant to shoot.

"Oh, don't—don't!" she cried. "He—he didn't hurt me."

Kells pushed her back. When he touched her she seemed to feel the shock of an electric current. His face had not changed, but his eyes were terrible. On the background of gray were strange, leaping red flecks.

"Take your horse," he ordered. "No. Walk across the brook. There's a trail. Go up the cañon. I'll come presently. Don't run and don't hide. It'll be the worse for you if you do. Hurry!"

Joan obeyed. She flashed past the open-jawed Halloway, and, running down to the brook, stepped across from stone to stone. She found the trail and hurriedly followed it. She did not look back. It never occurred to her to hide, to try to get away. She only obeyed, conscious of some force that dominated her. Once she heard loud voices, then the shrill neigh of a horse. The trail swung under the left wall of the canon and ran along the noisy brook. She thought she heard shots and was startled, but she could not be sure. She stopped to listen. Only the babble of swift water and the sough of wind in the spruces greeted her ears. She went on, beginning to collect her thoughts, to conjecture on the significance of Kells's behavior.

But had that been the spring of his motive? She doubted it—she doubted all about him, save that subtle essence of violence, of ruthless force and intensity, of terrible capacity, which hung round him.

A halloo caused her to stop and turn. Two pack-horses were jogging up the trail. Kells was driving them and leading her pony. Nothing could be seen of the other men. Kells rapidly overhauled her, and she had to get out of the trail to let the pack-animals pass. He threw her bridle to her.

"Get up," he said.

She complied. And then she bravely faced him. "Where are—the other men?"

"We parted company," he replied, curtly.

"Why?" she persisted.

"Well, if you're anxious to know, it was because you were winning their—regard—too much to suit me."

"Winning their regard!" Joan exclaimed, blankly.

Here those gray, piercing eyes went through her, then swiftly shifted. She was quick to divine from that the inference in his words—he suspected her of flirting with those ruffians, perhaps to escape him through them. That had only been his suspicion—groundless after his swift glance at her. Perhaps unconsciousness of his meaning, a simulated innocence, and ignorance might serve her with this strange man. She resolved to try it, to use all her woman's intuition and wit and cunning. Here was an educated man who was a criminal—an outcast. Deep within him might be memories of a different life. They might be stirred. Joan decided in that swift instant that, if she could understand him, learn his real intentions toward her, she could cope with him.

"Bill and his pard were thinking too much of—of the ransom I'm after," went on Kells, with a short laugh. "Come on now. Ride close to me."

Joan turned into the trail with his laugh ringing in her ears. Did she only imagine a mockery in it? Was there any reason to believe a word this man said? She appeared as helpless to see through him as she was in her predicament.

They had entered a canon, such as was typical of that mountain range, and the winding trail which ran beneath the yellow walls was one unused to travel. Joan could not make out any old tracks, except those of deer and cougar. The crashing of wild animals into the chaparral, and the scarcely frightened flight of rabbits and grouse attested to the wildness of the place. They passed an old tumbledown log cabin, once used, no doubt, by prospectors and hunters. Here the trail ended. Yet Kells kept on up the canon. And for all Joan could tell the walls grew only the higher and the timber heavier and the space wilder.

At a turn, when the second pack-horse, that appeared unused to his task, came fully into Joan's sight, she was struck with his resemblance to some horse with which she was familiar. It was scarcely an impression which she might have received from seeing Kells's horse or Bill's or any one's a few times. Therefore she watched this animal, studying his gait and behavior. It did not take long for her to discover that he was not a pack-horse. He resented that burden. He did not know how to swing it. This made her deeply thoughtful and she watched closer than ever. All at once there dawned on her the fact that the resemblance here was to Roberts's horse. She caught her breath and felt again that cold gnawing of fear within her. Then she closed her eyes the better to remember significant points about Roberts's sorrel—a white left front foot, an old diamond brand, a ragged forelock, and an unusual marking, a light bar across his face. When Joan had recalled these, she felt so certain that she would find them on this pack-horse that she was afraid to open her eyes. She forced herself to look, and it seemed that in one glance she saw three of them. Still she clung to hope. Then the horse, picking his way, partially turning toward her, disclosed the bar across his face.

Joan recognized it. Roberts was not on his way home. Kells had lied. Kells had killed him. How plain and fearful the proof! It verified Roberts's gloomy prophecy. Joan suddenly grew sick and dizzy. She reeled in her saddle. It was only by dint of the last effort of strength and self-control that she kept her seat. She fought the horror as if it were a beast. Hanging over the pommel, with shut eyes, letting her pony find the way, she sustained this shock of discovery and did not let it utterly overwhelm her. And as she conquered the sickening weakness her mind quickened to the changed aspect of her situation. She understood Kells and the appalling nature of her peril. She did not know how she understood him now, but doubt had utterly fled. All was clear, real, grim, present. Like a child she had been deceived, for no reason she could see. That talk of ransom was false. Likewise Kells's assertion that he had parted company with Halloway and Bill because he would not share the ransom—that, too, was false. The idea of a ransom, in this light, was now ridiculous. From that first moment Kells had wanted her; he had tried to persuade Roberts to leave her, and, failing, had killed him; he had rid himself of the other two men—and now Joan knew she had heard shots back there. Kells's intention loomed out of all his dark brooding, and it stood clear now to her, dastardly, worse than captivity, or torture, or death—the worst fate that could befall a woman.

The reality of it now was so astounding. True—as true as those stories she had deemed impossible! Because she and her people and friends had appeared secure in their mountain camp and happy in their work and trustful of good, they had scarcely credited the rumors of just such things as had happened to her. The stage held up by roadagents, a lonely prospector murdered and robbed, fights in the saloons and on the trails, and useless pursuit of hardriding men out there on the border, elusive as Arabs, swift as Apaches—these facts had been terrible enough, without the dread of worse. The truth of her capture, the meaning of it, were raw, shocking spurs to Joan Randle's intelligence and courage. Since she still lived, which was strange indeed in the illuminating light of her later insight into Kells and his kind, she had to meet him with all that was catlike and subtle and devilish at the command of a woman. She had to win him, foil him, kill him—or go to her death. She was no girl to be dragged into the mountain fastness by a desperado and made a plaything. Her horror and terror had worked its way deep into the depths of her and uncovered powers never suspected, never before required in her scheme of life. She had no longer any fear. She matched herself against this man. She anticipated him. And she felt like a woman who had lately been a thoughtless girl, who, in turn, had dreamed of vague old happenings of a past before she was born, of impossible adventures in her own future. Hate and wrath and outraged womanhood were not wholly the secret of Joan Randle's flaming spirit.

4

Joan Randle rode on and on, through the canon, out at its head and over a pass into another canon, and never did she let it be possible for Kells to see her eyes until she knew beyond peradventure of a doubt that they hid the strength and spirit and secret of her soul.

The time came when traveling was so steep and rough that she must think first of her horse and her own safety. Kells led up over a rock-jumbled spur of range, where she had sometimes to follow on foot. It seemed miles across that wilderness of stone. Foxes and wolves trotted over open places, watching stealthily. All around dark mountain peaks stood up. The afternoon was far advanced when Kells started to descend again, and he rode a zigzag course on weathered slopes and over brushy benches, down and down into the canons again.

A lonely peak was visible, sunset-flushed against the blue, from the point where Kells finally halted. That ended the longest ride Joan had ever made in one day. For miles and miles they had climbed and descended and wound into the mountains. Joan had scarcely any idea of direction. She was completely turned around and lost. This spot was the wildest and most beautiful she had ever seen. A canon headed here. It was narrow, low-walled, and luxuriant with grass and wild roses and willow and spruce and balsam. There were deer standing with long ears erect, motionless, curious, tame as cattle. There were moving streaks through the long grass, showing the course of smaller animals slipping away.

Then under a giant balsam, that reached aloft to the rim-wall, Joan saw a little log cabin, open in front. It had not been built very long; some of the log ends still showed yellow. It did not resemble the hunters' and prospectors' cabins she had seen on her trips with her uncle.

In a sweeping glance Joan had taken in these features. Kells had dismounted and approached her. She looked frankly, but not directly, at him.

"I'm tired—almost too tired to get off," she said.

"Fifty miles of rock and brush, up and down! Without a kick!" he exclaimed, admiringly. "You've got sand, girl!"

"Where are we?"

"This is Lost Canon. Only a few men know of it. And they are—attached to me. I intend to keep you here."

"How long?" She felt the intensity of his gaze.

"Why—as long as—" he replied, slowly, "till I get my ransom."

"What amount will you ask?"

"You're worth a hundred thousand in gold right now... Maybe later I might let you go for less."

Joan's keen-wrought perception registered his covert, scarcely veiled implication. He was studying her.

"Oh, poor uncle. He'll never, never get so much."

"Sure he will," replied Kells, bluntly.

Then he helped her out of the saddle. She was stiff and awkward, and she let herself slide. Kells handled her gently and like a gentleman, and for Joan the first agonizing moment of her ordeal was past. Her intuition had guided her correctly. Kells might have been and probably was the most depraved of outcast men; but the presence of a girl like her, however it affected him, must also have brought up associations of a time when by family and breeding and habit he had been infinitely different. His action here, just like the ruffian Bill's, was instinctive, beyond his control. Just this slight thing, this frail link that joined Kells to his past and better life, immeasurably inspirited Joan and outlined the difficult game she had to play.

"You're a very gallant robber," she said.

He appeared not to hear that or to note it; he was eying her up and down; and he moved closer, perhaps to estimate her height compared to his own.

"I didn't know you were so tall. You're above my shoulder."

"Yes, I'm very lanky."

"Lanky! Why you're not that. You've a splendid figure—tall, supple, strong; you're like a Nez Perce girl I knew once.... You're a beautiful thing. Didn't you know that?"

"Not particularly. My friends don't dare flatter me. I suppose I'll have to stand it from you. But I didn't expect compliments from Jack Kells of the Border Legion."

"Border Legion? Where'd you hear that name?"

"I didn't hear it. I made it up—thought of it myself."

"Well, you've invented something I'll use.... And what's your name—your first name? I heard Roberts use it."

Joan felt a cold contraction of all her internal being, but outwardly she never so much as nicked an eyelash. "My name's Joan."

"Joan!" He placed heavy, compelling hands on her shoulders and turned her squarely toward him.

Again she felt his gaze, strangely, like the reflection of sunlight from ice. She had to look at him. This was her supreme test. For hours she had prepared for it, steeled herself, wrought upon all that was sensitive in her; and now she prayed, and swiftly looked up into his eyes. They were windows of a gray hell. And she gazed into that naked abyss, at that dark, uncovered soul, with only the timid anxiety and fear and the unconsciousness of an innocent, ignorant girl.

"Joan! You know why I brought you here?"

"Yes, of course; you told me," she replied, steadily. "You want to ransom me for gold.... And I'm afraid you'll have to take me home without getting any."

"You know what I mean to do to you," he went on, thickly.

"Do to me?" she echoed, and she never quivered a muscle. "You—you didn't say.... I haven't thought.... But you won't hurt me, will you? It's not my fault if there's no gold to ransom me."

He shook her. His face changed, grew darker. "You KNOW what I mean."

"I don't." With some show of spirit she essayed to slip out of his grasp. He held her the tighter.

"How old are you?"

It was only in her height and development that Joan looked anywhere near her age. Often she had been taken for a very young girl.

"I'm seventeen," she replied. This was not the truth. It was a lie that did not falter on lips which had scorned falsehood.

"Seventeen!" he ejaculated in amaze. "Honestly, now?"

She lifted her chin scornfully and remained silent.

"Well, I thought you were a woman. I took you to be twenty-five—at least twenty-two. Seventeen, with that shape! You're only a girl—a kid. You don't know anything."

Then he released her, almost with violence, as if angered at her or himself, and he turned away to the horses. Joan walked toward the little cabin. The strain of that encounter left her weak, but once from under his eyes, certain that she had carried her point, she quickly regained her poise. There might be, probably would be, infinitely more trying ordeals for her to meet than this one had been; she realized, however, that never again would she be so near betrayal of terror and knowledge and self.

The scene of her isolation had a curious fascination for her. Something—and she shuddered—was to happen to her here in this lonely, silent gorge. There were some flat stones made into a rude seat under the balsam-tree, and a swift, yard-wide stream of clear water ran by. Observing something white against the tree, Joan went closer. A card, the ace of hearts, had been pinned to the bark by a small cluster of bullet-holes, every one of which touched the red heart, and one of them had obliterated it. Below the circle of bulletholes, scrawled in rude letters with a lead-pencil, was the name "Gulden." How little, a few nights back, when Jim Cleve had menaced Joan with the names of Kells and Gulden, had she imagined they were actual men she was to meet and fear! And here she was the prisoner of one of them. She would ask Kells who and what this Gulden was. The log cabin was merely a shed, without fireplace or window, and the floor was a covering of balsam boughs, long dried out and withered. A dim trail led away from it down the canon. If Joan was any judge of trails, this one had not seen the imprint of a horse track for many months. Kells had indeed brought her to a hiding place, one of those, perhaps, that camp gossip said was inaccessible to any save a border hawk. Joan knew that only an Indian could follow the tortuous and rocky trail by which Kells had brought her in. She would never be tracked there by her own people.

The long ride had left her hot, dusty, scratched, with tangled hair and torn habit. She went over to her saddle, which Kells had removed from her pony, and, opening the saddlebag, she took inventory of her possessions. They were few enough, but now, in view of an unexpected and enforced sojourn in the wilds, beyond all calculation of value. And they included towel, soap, toothbrush, mirror and comb and brush, a red scarf, and gloves. It occurred to her how seldom she carried that bag on her saddle, and, thinking back, referred the fact to accident, and then with honest amusement owned that the motive might have been also a little vanity. Taking the bag, she went to a flat stone by the brook and, rolling up her sleeves, proceeded to improve her appearance. With deft fingers she rebraided her hair and arranged it as she had worn it when only sixteen. Then, resolutely, she got up and crossed over to where Kells was unpacking.

"I'll help you get supper," she said.

He was on his knees in the midst of a jumble of camp duffle that had been hastily thrown together. He looked up at her—from her shapely, strong, brown arms to the face she had rubbed rosy.

"Say, but you're a pretty girl!"

He said it enthusiastically, in unstinted admiration, without the slightest subtlety or suggestion; and if he had been the devil himself it would have been no less a compliment, given spontaneously to youth and beauty.

"I'm glad if it's so, but please don't tell me," she rejoined, simply.

Then with swift and business-like movements she set to helping him with the mess the inexperienced pack-horse had made of that particular pack. And when that was straightened out she began with the biscuit dough while he lighted a fire. It appeared to be her skill, rather than her willingness, that he yielded to. He said very little, but he looked at her often. And he had little periods of abstraction. The situation was novel, strange to him. Sometimes Joan read his mind and sometimes he was an enigma. But she divined when he was thinking what a picture she looked there, on her knees before the bread-pan, with flour on her arms; of the difference a girl brought into any place; of how strange it seemed that this girl, instead of lying a limp and disheveled rag under a tree, weeping and praying for home, made the best of a bad situation and unproved it wonderfully by being a thoroughbred.

Presently they sat down, cross-legged, one on each side of the tarpaulin, and began the meal. That was the strangest supper Joan ever sat down to; it was like a dream where there was danger that tortured her; but she knew she was dreaming and would soon wake up. Kells was almost imperceptibly changing. The amiability of his face seemed to have stiffened. The only time he addressed her was when he offered to help her to more meat or bread or coffee. After the meal was finished he would not let her wash the pans and pots, and attended to that himself.

Joan went to the seat by the tree, near the camp-fire. A purple twilight was shadowing the canon. Far above, on the bold peak the last warmth of the afterglow was fading. There was no wind, no sound, no movement. Joan wondered where Jim Cleve was then. They had often sat in the twilight. She felt an unreasonable resentment toward him, knowing she was to blame, but blaming him for her plight. Then suddenly she thought of her uncle, of home, of her kindly old aunt who always worried so about her. Indeed, there was cause to worry. She felt sorrier for them than for herself. And that broke her spirit momentarily. Forlorn, and with a wave of sudden sorrow and dread and hopelessness, she dropped her head upon her knees and covered her face. Tears were a relief. She forgot Kells and the part she must play. But she remembered swiftly—at the rude touch of his hand.

"Here! Are you crying?" he asked, roughly.

"Do you think I'm laughing?" Joan retorted. Her wet eyes, as she raised them, were proof enough.

"Stop it."

"I can't help—but cry—a little. I was th—thinking of home—of those who've been father and mother to me—since I was a baby. I wasn't crying—for myself. But they—they'll be so miserable. They loved me so."

"It won't help matters to cry."

Joan stood up then, no longer sincere and forgetful, but the girl with her deep and cunning game. She leaned close to him in the twilight.

"Did you ever love any one? Did you ever have a sister—a girl like me?"

Kells stalked away into the gloom.

Joan was left alone. She did not know whether to interpret his abstraction, his temper, and his action as favorable or not. Still she hoped and prayed they meant that he had some good in him. If she could only hide her terror, her abhorrence, her knowledge of him and his motive! She built up a bright camp-fire. There was an abundance of wood. She dreaded the darkness and the night. Besides, the air was growing chilly. So, arranging her saddle and blankets near the fire, she composed herself in a comfortable seat to await Kells's return and developments. It struck her forcibly that she had lost some of her fear of Kells and she did not know why. She ought to fear him more every hour—every minute. Presently she heard his step brushing the grass and then he emerged out of the gloom. He had a load of fire-wood on his shoulder.

"Did you get over your grief?" he asked, glancing down upon her.

"Yes," she replied.

Kells stooped for a red ember, with which he lighted his pipe, and then he seated himself a little back from the fire. The blaze threw a bright glare over him, and in it he looked neither formidable nor vicious nor ruthless. He asked her where she was born, and upon receiving an answer he followed that up with another question. And he kept this up until Joan divined that he was not so much interested in what he apparently wished to learn as he was in her presence, her voice, her personality. She sensed in him loneliness, hunger for the sound of a voice. She had heard her uncle speak of the loneliness of lonely camp-fires and how all men working or hiding or lost in the wilderness would see sweet faces in the embers and be haunted by soft voices. After all, Kells was human. And she talked as never before in her life, brightly, willingly, eloquently, telling the facts of her eventful youth and girlhood—the sorrow and the joy and some of the dreams—up to the time she had come to Camp Hoadley.

"Did you leave any sweethearts over there at Hoadley?" he asked, after a silence.

"Yes."

"How many?"

"A whole campful," she replied, with a laugh, "but admirers is a better name for them."

"Then there's no one fellow?"

"Hardly—yet."

"How would you like being kept here in this lonesome place for—well, say for ever?"

"I wouldn't like that," replied Joan. "I'd like this—camping out like this now—if my folks only knew I am alive and well and safe. I love lonely, dreamy places. I've dreamed of being in just such a one as this. It seems so far away here—so shut in by the walls and the blackness. So silent and sweet! I love the stars. They speak to me. And the wind in the spruces. Hear it.... Very low, mournful! That whispers to me—to-morrow I'd like it here if I had no worry. I've never grown up yet. I explore and climb trees and hunt for little birds and rabbits—young things just born, all fuzzy and sweet, frightened, piping or squealing for their mothers. But I won't touch one for worlds. I simply can't hurt anything. I can't spur my horse or beat him. Oh, I HATE pain!"

"You're a strange girl to live out here on this border," he said.

"I'm no different from other girls. You don't know girls."

"I knew one pretty well. She put a rope round my neck," he replied, grimly.

"A rope!"

"Yes, I mean a halter, a hangman's noose. But I balked her!"

"Oh!... A good girl?"

"Bad! Bad to the core of her black heart—bad as I am!" he exclaimed, with fierce, low passion.

Joan trembled. The man, in an instant, seemed transformed, somber as death. She could not look at him, but she must keep on talking.

"Bad? You don't seem bad to me—only violent, perhaps, or wild.... Tell me about yourself."

She had stirred him. His neglected pipe fell from his hand. In the gloom of the camp-fire he must have seen faces or ghosts of his past.

"Why not?" he queried, strangely. "Why not do what's been impossible for years—open my lips? It'll not matter—to a girl who can never tell!... Have I forgotten? God!—I have not! Listen, so that you'll KNOW I'm bad. My name's not Kells. I was born in the East, and went to school there till I ran away. I was young, ambitious, wild. I stole. I ran away—came West in 'fifty-one to the gold-fields in California. There I became a prospector, miner, gambler, robber—and road-agent. I had evil in me, as all men have, and those wild years brought it out. I had no chance. Evil and gold and blood—they are one and the same thing. I committed every crime till no place, bad as it might be, was safe for me. Driven and hunted and shot and starved—almost hanged!... And now I'm—Kells! of that outcast crew you named 'the Border Legion!' Every black crime but one—the blackest—and that haunting me, itching my hands to-night."

"Oh, you speak so—so dreadfully!" cried Joan. "What can I say? I'm sorry for you. I don't believe it all. What—what black crime haunts you? Oh! what could be possible tonight—here in this lonely canon—with only me?"

Dark and terrible the man arose.

"Girl," he said, hoarsely. "To-night—to-night—I'll.... What have you done to me? One more day—and I'll be mad to do right by you—instead of WRONG.... Do you understand that?"

Joan leaned forward in the camp-fire light with outstretched hands and quivering lips, as overcome by his halting confession of one last remnant of honor as she was by the dark hint of his passion.

"No—no—I don't understand—nor believe!" she cried. "But you frighten me—so! I am all—all alone with you here. You said I'd be safe. Don't—don't—"

Her voice broke then and she sank back exhausted in her seat. Probably Kells had heard only the first words of her appeal, for he took to striding back and forth in the circle of the camp-fire light. The scabbard with the big gun swung against his leg. It grew to be a dark and monstrous thing in Joan's sight. A marvelous intuition born of that hour warned her of Kells's subjection to the beast in him, even while, with all the manhood left to him, he still battled against it. Her girlish sweetness and innocence had availed nothing, except mock him with the ghost of dead memories. He could not be won or foiled. She must get her hands on that gun—kill him—or—! The alternative was death for herself. And she leaned there, slowly gathering all the unconquerable and unquenchable forces of a woman's nature, waiting, to make one desperate, supreme, and final effort.

5

Kells strode there, a black, silent shadow, plodding with bent head, as if all about and above him were demons and furies.

Joan's perceptions of him, of the night, of the inanimate and imponderable black walls, and of herself, were exquisitely and abnormally keen. She saw him there, bowed under his burden, gloomy and wroth and sick with himself because the man in him despised the coward. Men of his stamp were seldom or never cowards. Their lives did not breed cowardice or baseness. Joan knew the burning in her breast—that thing which inflamed and swept through her like a wind of fire—was hate. Yet her heart held a grain of pity for him. She measured his forbearance, his struggle, against the monstrous cruelty and passion engendered by a wild life among wild men at a wild time. And, considering his opportunities of the long hours and lonely miles, she was grateful, and did not in the least underestimate what it cost him, how different from Bill or Halloway he had been. But all this was nothing, and her thinking of it useless, unless he conquered himself. She only waited, holding on to that steel-like control of her nerves, motionless and silent.

She leaned back against her saddle, a blanket covering her, with wide-open eyes, and despite the presence of that stalking figure and the fact of her mind being locked round one terrible and inevitable thought, she saw the changing beautiful glow of the fire-logs and the cold, pitiless stars and the mustering shadows under the walls. She heard, too, the low rising sigh of the wind in the balsam and the silvery tinkle of the brook, and sounds only imagined or nameless. Yet a stern and insupportable silence weighed her down. This dark canon seemed at the ends of the earth. She felt encompassed by illimitable and stupendous upflung mountains, insulated in a vast, dark, silent tomb.

Kells suddenly came to her, treading noiselessly, and he leaned over her. His visage was a dark blur, but the posture of him was that of a wolf about to spring. Lower he leaned—slowly— and yet lower. Joan saw the heavy gun swing away from his leg; she saw it black and clear against the blaze; a cold, blue light glinted from its handle. And then Kells was near enough for her to see his face and his eyes that were but shadows of flames. She gazed up at him steadily, open-eyed, with no fear or shrinking. His breathing was quick and loud. He looked down at her for an endless moment, then, straightening his bent form, he resumed his walk to and fro.

After that for Joan time might have consisted of moments or hours, each of which was marked by Kells looming over her. He appeared to approach her from all sides; he round her wide-eyed, sleepless; his shadowy glance gloated over her lithe, slender shape; and then he strode away into the gloom. Sometimes she could no longer hear his steps and then she was quiveringly alert, listening, fearful that he might creep upon her like a panther. At times he kept the camp-fire blazing brightly; at others he let it die down. And these dark intervals were frightful for her. The night seemed treacherous, in league with her foe. It was endless. She prayed for dawn—yet with a blank hopelessness for what the day might bring. Could she hold out through more interminable hours? Would she not break from sheer strain? There were moments when she wavered and shook like a leaf in the wind, when the beating of her heart was audible, when a child could have seen her distress. There were other moments when all was ugly, unreal, impossible like things in a nightmare. But when Kells was near or approached to look at her, like a cat returned to watch a captive mouse, she was again strong, waiting, with ever a strange and cold sense of the nearness of that swinging gun. Late in the night she missed him, for how long she had no idea. She had less trust in his absence than his presence. The nearer he came to her the stronger she grew and the clearer of purpose. At last the black void of canon lost its blackness and turned to gray. Dawn was at hand. The horrible endless night, in which she had aged from girl to woman, had passed. Joan had never closed her eyes a single instant.

When day broke she got up. The long hours in which she had rested motionlessly had left her muscles cramped and dead. She began to walk off the feeling. Kells had just stirred from his blanket under the balsam-tree. His face was dark, haggard, lined. She saw him go down to the brook and plunge his hands into the water and bathe his face with a kind of fury. Then he went up to the smoldering fire. There was a gloom, a somberness, a hardness about him that had not been noticeable the day before.

Joan found the water cold as ice, soothing to the burn beneath her skin. She walked away then, aware that Kells did not appear to care, and went up to where the brook brawled from under the cliff. This was a hundred paces from camp, though in plain sight. Joan looked round for her horse, but he was not to be seen. She decided to slip away the first opportunity that offered, and on foot or horseback, any way, to get out of Kells's clutches if she had to wander, lost in the mountains, till she starved. Possibly the day might be endurable, but another night would drive her crazy. She sat on a ledge, planning and brooding, till she was startled by a call from Kells. Then slowly she retraced her steps.

"Don't you want to eat?" he asked.

"I'm not hungry," she replied.

"Well, eat anyhow—if it chokes you," he ordered.

Joan seated herself while he placed food and drink before her. She did not look at him and did not feel his gaze upon her. Far asunder as they had been yesterday the distance between them to-day was incalculably greater. She ate as much as she could swallow and pushed the rest away. Leaving the camp-fire, she began walking again, here and there, aimlessly, scarcely seeing what she looked at. There was a shadow over her, an impending portent of catastrophe, a moment standing dark and sharp out of the age-long hour. She leaned against the balsam and then she rested in the stone seat, and then she had to walk again. It might have been long, that time; she never knew how long or short. There came a strange flagging, sinking of her spirit, accompanied by vibrating, restless, uncontrollable muscular activity. Her nerves were on the verge of collapse.

It was then that a call from Kells, clear and ringing, thrilled all the weakness from her in a flash, and left her limp and cold. She saw him coming. His face looked amiable again, bright against what seemed a vague and veiled background. Like a mountaineer he strode. And she looked into his strange, gray glance to see unmasked the ruthless power, the leaping devil, the ungovernable passion she had sensed in him.

He grasped her arm and with a single pull swung her to him. "YOU'VE got to pay that ransom!"

He handled her as if he thought she resisted, but she was unresisting. She hung her head to hide her eyes. Then he placed an arm round her shoulders and half led, half dragged her toward the cabin.

Joan saw with startling distinctness the bits of balsam and pine at her feet and pale pink daisies in the grass, and then the dry withered boughs. She was in the cabin.

"Girl!... I'm hungry—for you!" he breathed, hoarsely. And turning her toward him, he embraced her, as if his nature was savage and he had to use a savage force.

If Joan struggled at all, it was only slightly, when she writhed and slipped, like a snake, to get her arm under his as it clasped her neck. Then she let herself go. He crushed her to him. He bent her backward—tilted her face with hard and eager hand. Like a madman, with hot working lips, he kissed her. She felt blinded—scorched. But her purpose was as swift and sure and wonderful as his passion was wild. The first reach of her groping hand found his gun-belt. Swift as light her hand slipped down. Her fingers touched the cold gun—grasped with thrill on thrill—slipped farther down, strong and sure to raise the hammer. Then with a leaping, strung intensity that matched his own she drew the gun. She raised it while her eyes were shut. She lay passive under his kisses—the devouring kisses of one whose manhood had been denied the sweetness, the glory, the fire, the life of woman's lips. It was a moment in which she met his primitive fury of possession with a woman's primitive fury of profanation. She pressed the gun against his side and pulled the trigger.

A thundering, muffled, hollow boom! The odor of burned powder stung her nostrils. Kells's hold on her tightened convulsively, loosened with strange, lessening power. She swayed back free of him, still with tight-shut eyes. A horrible cry escaped him—a cry of mortal agony. It wrenched her. And she looked to see him staggering amazed, stricken, at bay, like a wolf caught in cruel steel jaws. His hands came away from both sides, dripping with blood. They shook till the crimson drops spattered on the wall, on the boughs. Then he seemed to realize and he clutched at her with these bloody hands.

"God Almighty!" he panted. "You shot me!... You—you girl!... You she-cat... You knew—all the time... You she-cat!... Give me—that gun!"

"Kells, get back! I'll kill you!" she cried. The big gun, outstretched between them, began to waver.

Kells did not see the gun. In his madness he tried to move, to reach her, but he could not; he was sinking. His legs sagged under him, let him down to his knees, and but for the wall he would have fallen. Then a change transformed him. The black, turgid, convulsed face grew white and ghastly, with beads of clammy sweat and lines of torture. His strange eyes showed swiftly passing thought—wonder, fear, scorn—even admiration.

"Joan, you've done—for me!" he gasped. "You've broken my back!... It'll kill me! Oh the pain—the pain! And I can't stand pain! You—you girl! You innocent seventeen-year-old girl! You that couldn't hurt any creature! You so tender—so gentle!... Bah! you fooled me. The cunning of a woman! I ought—to know. A good woman's—more terrible than a—bad woman.... But I deserved this. Once I used—to be.... Only, the torture!... Why didn't you—kill me outright?... Joan—Randle—watch me—die! Since I had—to die—by rope or bullet—I'm glad you—you—did for me.... Man or beast—I believe—I loved you!"

Joan dropped the gun and sank beside him, helpless, horror-stricken, wringing her hands. She wanted to tell him she was sorry, that he drove her to it, that he must let her pray for him. But she could not speak. Her tongue clove to the roof of her mouth and she seemed strangling.

Another change, slower and more subtle, passed over Kells. He did not see Joan. He forgot her. The white shaded out of his face, leaving a gray like that of his somber eyes. Spirit, sense, life, were fading from him. The quivering of a racked body ceased. And all that seemed left was a lonely soul groping on the verge of the dim borderland between life and death. Presently his shoulders slipped along the wall and he fell, to lie limp and motionless before Joan. Then she fainted.

6

When Joan returned to consciousness she was lying half outside the opening of the cabin and above her was a drift of blue gun-smoke, slowly floating upward. Almost as swiftly as perception of that smoke came a shuddering memory. She lay still, listening. She did not hear a sound except the tinkle and babble and gentle rush of the brook. Kells was dead, then. And overmastering the horror of her act was a relief, a freedom, a lifting of her soul out of the dark dread, a something that whispered justification of the fatal deed.

She got up and, avoiding to look within the cabin, walked away. The sun was almost at the zenith. Where had the morning hours gone?

"I must get away," she said, suddenly. The thought quickened her. Down the canon the horses were grazing. She hurried along the trail, trying to decide whether to follow this dim old trail or endeavor to get out the way she had been brought in. She decided upon the latter. If she traveled slowly, and watched for familiar landmarks, things she had seen once, and hunted carefully for the tracks, she believed she might be successful. She had the courage to try. Then she caught her pony and led him back to camp.

"What shall I take?" she pondered. She decided upon very little—a blanket, a sack of bread and meat, and a canteen of water. She might need a weapon, also. There was only one, the gun with which she had killed Kells. It seemed utterly impossible to touch that hateful thing. But now that she had liberated herself, and at such cost, she must not yield to sentiment. Resolutely she started for the cabin, but when she reached it her steps were dragging. The long, dull-blue gun lay where she had dropped it. And out of the tail of averted eyes she saw a huddled shape along the wall. It was a sickening moment when she reached a shaking hand for the gun. And at that instant a low moan transfixed her.

She seemed frozen rigid. Was the place already haunted? Her heart swelled in her throat and a dimness came before her eyes. But another moan brought a swift realization—Kells was alive. And the cold, clamping sickness, the strangle in her throat, all the feelings of terror, changed and were lost in a flood of instinctive joy. He was not dead. She had not killed him. She did not have blood on her hands. She was not a murderer.

She whirled to look at him. There he lay, ghastly as a corpse. And all her woman's gladness fled. But there was compassion left to her, and, forgetting all else, she knelt beside him. He was as cold as stone. She felt no stir, no beat of pulse in temple or wrist. Then she placed her ear against his breast. His heart beat weakly.

"He's alive," she whispered. "But—he's dying.... What shall I do?"

Many thoughts flashed across her mind. She could not help him now; he would be dead soon; she did not need to wait there beside him; there was a risk of some of his comrades riding into that rendezvous. Suppose his back was not broken after all! Suppose she stopped the flow of blood, tended him, nursed him, saved his life? For if there were one chance of his living, which she doubted, it must be through her. Would he not be the same savage the hour he was well and strong again? What difference could she make in such a nature? The man was evil. He could not conquer evil. She had been witness to that. He had driven Roberts to draw and had killed him. No doubt he had deliberately and coldly murdered the two ruffians, Bill and Halloway, just so he could be free of their glances at her and be alone with her. He deserved to die there like a dog.

What Joan Randle did was surely a woman's choice. Carefully she rolled Kells over. The back of his vest and shirt was wet with blood. She got up to find a knife, towel, and water. As she returned to the cabin he moaned again.

Joan had dressed many a wound. She was not afraid of blood. The difference was that she had shed it. She felt sick, but her hands were firm as she cut open the vest and shirt, rolled them aside, and bathed his back. The big bullet had made a gaping wound, having apparently gone through the small of his back. The blood still flowed. She could not tell whether or not Kell's spine was broken, but she believed that the bullet had gone between bone and muscle, or had glanced. There was a blue welt just over his spine, in line with the course of the wound. She tore her scarf into strips and used it for compresses and bandages. Then she laid him back upon a saddle-blanket. She had done all that was possible for the present, and it gave her a strange sense of comfort. She even prayed for his life, and, if that must go, for his soul. Then she got up. He was unconscious, white, death-like. It seemed that his torture, his near approach to death, had robbed his face of ferocity, of ruthlessness, and of that strange amiable expression. But then, his eyes, those furnace-windows, were closed.

Joan waited for the end to come. The afternoon passed and she did not leave the cabin. It was possible that he might come to and want water. She had once administered to a miner who had been fatally crushed in an avalanche; and never could forget his husky call for water and the gratitude in his eyes.

Sunset, twilight, and night fell upon the canon. And she began to feel solitude as something tangible. Bringing saddle and blankets into the cabin, she made a bed just inside, and, facing the opening and the stars, she lay down to rest, if not to sleep. The darkness did not keep her from seeing the prostrate figure of Kells. He lay there as silent as if he were already dead. She was exhausted, weary for sleep, and unstrung. In the night her courage fled and she was frightened at shadows. The murmuring of insects seemed augmented into a roar; the mourn of wolf and scream of cougar made her start; the rising wind moaned like a lost spirit. Dark fancies beset her. Troop on troop of specters moved out of the black night, assembling there, waiting for Kells to join them. She thought she was riding homeward over the back trail, sure of her way, remembering every rod of that rough travel, until she got out of the mountains, only to be turned back by dead men. Then fancy and dream, and all the haunted gloom of canon and cabin, seemed slowly to merge into one immense blackness.

The sun, rimming the east wall, shining into Joan's face, awakened her. She had slept hours. She felt rested, stronger. Like the night, something dark had passed away from her. It did not seem strange to her that she should feel that Kells still lived. She knew it. And examination proved her right. In him there had been no change except that he had ceased to bleed. There was just a flickering of life in him, manifest only in his slow, faint heart-beats.

Joan spent most of that day in sitting beside Kells. The whole day seemed only an hour. Sometimes she would look down the canon trail, half expecting to see horsemen riding up. If any of Kells's comrades happened to come, what could she tell them? They would be as bad as he, without that one trait which had kept him human for a day. Joan pondered upon this. It would never do to let them suspect she had shot Kells. So, carefully cleaning the gun, she reloaded it. If any men came, she would tell them that Bill had done the shooting.

Kells lingered. Joan began to feel that he would live, though everything indicated the contrary. Her intelligence told her he would die, and her feeling said he would not. At times she lifted his head and got water into his mouth with a spoon. When she did this he would moan. That night, during the hours she lay awake, she gathered courage out of the very solitude and loneliness. She had nothing to fear, unless someone came to the canon. The next day in no wise differed from the preceding. And then there came the third day, with no change in Kells till near evening, when she thought he was returning to consciousness. But she must have been mistaken. For hours she watched patiently. He might return to consciousness just before the end, and want to speak, to send a message, to ask a prayer, to feel a human hand at the last.

That night the crescent moon hung over the canon. In the faint light Joan could see the blanched face of Kells, strange and sad, no longer seeming evil. The time came when his lips stirred. He tried to talk. She moistened his lips and gave him a drink. He murmured incoherently, sank again into a stupor, to rouse once more and babble tike a madman. Then he lay quietly for long—so long that sleep was claiming Joan. Suddenly he startled her by calling very faintly but distinctly: "Water! Water!"

Joan bent over him, lifting his head, helping him to drink. She could see his eyes, like dark holes in something white.

"Is—that—you—mother?" he whispered.

"Yes," replied Joan.

He sank immediately into another stupor or sleep, from which he did not rouse. That whisper of his—mother—touched Joan. Bad men had mothers just the same as any other kind of men. Even this Kells had a mother. He was still a young man. He had been youth, boy, child, baby. Some mother had loved him, cradled him, kissed his rosy baby hands, watched him grow with pride and glory, built castles in her dreams of his manhood, and perhaps prayed for him still, trusting he was strong and honored among men. And here he lay, a shattered wreck, dying for a wicked act, the last of many crimes. It was a tragedy. It made Joan think of the hard lot of mothers, and then of this unsettled Western wild, where men flocked in packs like wolves, and spilled blood like water, and held life nothing.

Joan sought her rest and soon slept. In the morning she did not at once go to Kells. Somehow she dreaded finding him conscious, almost as much as she dreaded the thought of finding him dead. When she did bend over him he was awake, and at sight of her he showed a faint amaze.

"Joan!" he whispered.

"Yes," she replied.

"Are you—with me still?"

"Of course, I couldn't leave you."

The pale eyes shadowed strangely, darkly. "I'm alive yet. And you stayed!... Was it yesterday—you threw my gun—on me?"

"No. Four days ago."

"Four! Is my back broken?"

"I don't know. I don't think so. It's a terrible wound. I—I did all I could."

"You tried to kill me—then tried to save me?"

She was silent to that.

"You're good—and you've been noble," he said. "But I wish—you'd only been bad. Then I'd curse you—and strangle you—presently."

"Perhaps you had best be quiet," replied Joan.

"No. I've been shot before. I'll get over this—if my back's not broken. How can we tell?"

"I've no idea."

"Lift me up."

"But you might open your wound," protested Joan.

"Lift me up!" The force of the man spoke even in his low whisper.

"But why—why?" asked Joan.

"I want to see—if I can sit up. If I can't—give me my gun."

"I won't let you have it," replied Joan. Then she slipped her arms under his and, carefully raising him to a sitting posture, released her hold.

"I'm—a—rank coward—about pain," he gasped, with thick drops standing out on his white face. "I can't—stand it."

But tortured or not, he sat up alone, and even had the will to bend his back. Then with a groan he fainted and fell into Joan's arms. She laid him down and worked over him for some time before she could bring him to. Then he was wan, suffering, speechless. But she believed he would live and told him so. He received that with a strange smile. Later, when she came to him with broth, he drank it gratefully.

"I'll beat this out," he said, weakly. "I'll recover. My back's not broken. I'll get well. Now you bring water and food in here—then go."

"Go?" she echoed.

"Yes. Don't go down the canon. You'd be worse off.... Take the back trail. You've got a chance to get out.... Go!"

"Leave you here? So weak you can't lift a cup! I won't."

"I'd rather you did."

"Why?"

"Because in a few days I'll begin to mend. Then I'll grow like—myself.... I think—I'm afraid I loved you.... It could only be hell for you. Go now, before it's too late!... If you stay—till I'm well—I'll never let you go!"

"Kells, I believe it would be cowardly for me to leave you here alone," she replied, earnestly. "You can't help yourself. You'd die."

"All the better. But I won't die. I'm hard to kill. Go, I tell you."

She shook her head. "This is bad for you—arguing. You're excited. Please be quiet."

"Joan Randle, if you stay—I'll halter you—keep you naked in a cave—curse you—beat you—murder you! Oh, it's in me!... Go, I tell you!"

"You're out of your head. Once for all—no!" she replied, firmly.

"You—you—" His voice failed in a terrible whisper....

In the succeeding days Kells did not often speak. His recovery was slow—a matter of doubt. Nothing was any plainer than the fact that if Joan had left him he would not have lived long. She knew it. And he knew it. When he was awake, and she came to him, a mournful and beautiful smile lit his eyes. The sight of her apparently hurt him and uplifted him. But he slept twenty hours out of every day, and while he slept he did not need Joan.

She came to know the meaning of solitude. There were days when she did not hear the sound of her own voice. A habit of silence, one of the significant forces of solitude, had grown upon her. Daily she thought less and felt more. For hours she did nothing. When she roused herself, compelled herself to think of these encompassing peaks of the lonely canon walls, the stately trees, all those eternally silent and changless features of her solitude, she hated them with a blind and unreasoning passion. She hated because she was losing her love for them, because they were becoming a part of her, because they were fixed and content and passionless. She liked to sit in the sun, feel its warmth, see its brightness; and sometimes she almost forgot to go back to her patient. She fought at times against an insidious change—a growing older—a going backward; at other times she drifted through hours that seemed quiet and golden, in which nothing happened. And by and by when she realized that the drifting hours were gradually swallowing up the restless and active hours, then strangely, she remembered Jim Cleve. Memory of him came to save her. She dreamed of him during the long, lonely, solemn days, and in the dark, silent climax of unbearable solitude—the night. She remembered his kisses, forgot her anger and shame, accepted the sweetness of their meaning, and so in the interminable hours of her solitude she dreamed herself into love for him.

Joan kept some record of days, until three weeks or thereabout passed, and then she lost track of time. It dragged along, yet looked at as the past, it seemed to have sped swiftly. The change in her, the growing old, the revelation and responsibility of serf, as a woman, made this experience appear to have extended over months.

Kells slowly became convalescent and then he had a relapse. Something happened, the nature of which Joan could not tell, and he almost died. There were days when his life hung in the balance, when he could not talk; and then came a perceptible turn for the better.

The store of provisions grew low, and Joan began to face another serious situation. Deer and rabbit were plentiful in the canon, but she could not kill one with a revolver. She thought she would be forced to sacrifice one of the horses. The fact that Kells suddenly showed a craving for meat brought this aspect of the situation to a climax. And that very morning while Joan was pondering the matter she saw a number of horsemen riding up the canon toward the cabin. At the moment she was relieved, and experienced nothing of the dread she had formerly felt while anticipating this very event.

"Kells," she said, quickly, "there are men riding up the trail."

"Good," he exclaimed, weakly, with a light on his drawn face. "They've been long in— getting here. How many?"

Joan counted them—five riders, and several pack-animals.

"Yes. It's Gulden."

"Gulden!" cried Joan, with a start.

Her exclamation and tone made Kells regard her attentively.

"You've heard of him? He's the toughest nut—on this border.... I never saw his like. You won't be safe. I'm so helpless.... What to say—to tell him!... Joan, if I should happen to croak— you want to get away quick... or shoot yourself."

How strange to hear this bandit warn her of peril the like of which she had encountered through him! Joan secured the gun and hid it in a niche between the logs. Then she looked out again.

The riders were close at hand now. The foremost one, a man of Herculean build, jumped his mount across the brook, and leaped off while he hauled the horse to a stop. The second rider came close behind him; the others approached leisurely, with the gait of the pack-animals.

"Ho, Kells!" called the big man. His voice had a loud, bold, sonorous kind of ring.

"Reckon he's here somewheres," said the other man, presently.

"Sure. I seen his hoss. Jack ain't goin' to be far from thet hoss."

Then both of them approached the cabin. Joan had never before seen two such striking, vicious-looking, awesome men. The one was huge—so wide and heavy and deep-set that he looked short—and he resembled a gorilla. The other was tall, slim, with a face as red as flame, and an expression of fierce keenness. He was stoop shouldered, yet he held his head erect in a manner that suggested a wolf scenting blood.

"Someone here, Pearce," boomed the big man.

"Why, Gul, if it ain't a girl!"

Joan moved out of the shadow of the wall of the cabin, and she pointed to the prostrate figure on the blankets.

"Howdy boys!" said Kells, wanly.

Gulden cursed in amaze while Pearce dropped to his knee with an exclamation of concern. Then both began to talk at once. Kells interrupted them by lifting a weak hand.

"No, I'm not going—to cash," he said. "I'm only starved—and in need of stimulants. Had my back half shot off."

"Who plugged you, Jack?"

"Gulden, it was your side-partner, Bill."

"Bill?" Gulden's voice held a queer, coarse constraint. Then he added, gruffly. "Thought you and him pulled together."

"Well, we didn't."

"And—where's Bill now?" This time Joan heard a slow, curious, cold note in the heavy voice, and she interpreted it as either doubt or deceit.

"Bill's dead and Halloway, too," replied Kells.

Gulden turned his massive, shaggy head in the direction of Joan. She had not the courage to meet the gaze upon her. The other man spoke:

"Split over the girl, Jack?"

"No," replied Kells, sharply. "They tried to get familiar with—MY WIFE—and I shot them both."

Joan felt a swift leap of hot blood all over her and then a coldness, a sickening, a hateful weakness.

"Wife!" ejaculated Gulden.

"Your real wife, Jack?" queried Pearce.

"Well, I guess, I'll introduce you... Joan, here are two of my friends—Sam Gulden and Red Pearce."

Gulden grunted something.

"Mrs. Kells, I'm glad to meet you," said Pearce.

Just then the other three men entered the cabin and Joan took advantage of the commotion they made to get out into the air. She felt sick, frightened, and yet terribly enraged. She staggered a little as she went out, and she knew she was as pale as death. These visitors thrust reality upon her with a cruel suddenness. There was something terrible in the mere presence of this Gulden. She had not yet dared to take a good look at him. But what she felt was overwhelming. She wanted to run. Yet escape now was infinitely more of a menace than before. If she slipped away it would be these new enemies who would pursue her, track her like hounds. She understood why Kells had introduced her as his wife. She hated the idea with a shameful and burning hate, but a moment's reflection taught her that Kells had answered once more to a good instinct. At the moment he had meant that to protect her. And further reflection persuaded Joan that she would be wise to act naturally and to carry out the deception as far as it was possible for her. It was her only hope. Her position had again grown perilous. She thought of the gun she had secreted, and it gave her strength to control her agitation and to return to the cabin outwardly calm.

The men had Kells half turned over with the flesh of his back exposed.

"Aw, Gul, it's whisky he needs," said one.

"If you let out any more blood he'll croak sure," protested another.

"Look how weak he is," said Red Pearce.

"It's a hell of a lot you know," roared Gulden. "I served my time—but that's none of your business.... Look here! See that blue spot!" Gulden pressed a huge finger down upon the blue welt on Kells's back. The bandit moaned. "That's lead—that's the bullet," declared Gulden.

"Wall, if you ain't correct!" exclaimed Pearce.

Kells turned his head. "When you punched that place—it made me numb all over. Gul, if you've located the bullet, cut it out."

Joan did not watch the operation. As she went away to the seat under the balsam she heard a sharp cry and then cheers. Evidently the grim Gulden had been both swift and successful.

Presently the men came out of the cabin and began to attend to their horses and the pack-train.

Pearce looked for Joan, and upon seeing her called out, "Kells wants you."

Joan found the bandit half propped up against a saddle with a damp and pallid face, but an altogether different look.

"Joan, that bullet was pressing on my spine," he said. "Now it's out, all that deadness is gone. I feel alive. I'll get well, soon.... Gulden was curious over the bullet. It's a forty-four caliber, and neither Bill Bailey nor Halloway used that caliber of gun. Gulden remembered. He's cunning. Bill was as near being a friend to this Gulden as any man I know of. I can't trust any of these men, particularly Gulden. You stay pretty close by me."

"Kells, you'll let me go soon—help me to get home?" implored Joan in a low voice.

"Girl, it'd never be safe now," he replied.

"Then later—soon—when it is safe?"

"We'll see.... But you're my wife now!"

With the latter words the man subtly changed. Something of the power she had felt in him before his illness began again to be manifested. Joan divined that these comrades had caused the difference in him.

"You won't dare—!" Joan was unable to conclude her meaning. A tight band compressed her breast and throat, and she trembled.

"Will you dare go out there and tell them you're NOT my wife?" he queried. His voice had grown stronger and his eyes were blending shadows of thought.

Joan knew that she dared not. She must choose the lesser of two evils. "No man—could be such a beast to a woman—after she'd saved his life," she whispered.

"I could be anything. You had your chance. I told you to go. I said if I ever got well I'd be as I was—before."

"But you'd have died."

"That would have been better for you..... Joan, I'll do this. Marry you honestly and leave the country. I've gold. I'm young. I love you. I intend to have you. And I'll begin life over again. What do you say?"

"Say? I'd die before—I'd marry you!" she panted.

"All right, Joan Randle," he replied, bitterly. "For a moment I saw a ghost. My old dead better self!... It's gone.... And you stay with me."

7

After dark Kells had his men build a fire before the open side of the cabin. He lay propped up on blankets and his saddle, while the others lounged or sat in a half-circle in the light, facing him.

Joan drew her blankets into a corner where the shadows were thick and she could see without being seen. She wondered how she would ever sleep near all these wild men—if she could ever sleep again. Yet she seemed more curious and wakeful than frightened. She had no way to explain it, but she felt the fact that her presence in the camp had a subtle influence, at once restraining and exciting. So she looked out upon the scene with wide-open eyes.

And she received more strongly than ever an impression of wildness. Even the camp-fire seemed to burn wildly; it did not glow and sputter and pale and brighten and sing like an honest camp-fire. It blazed in red, fierce, hurried flames, wild to consume the logs. It cast a baleful and sinister color upon the hard faces there. Then the blackness of the enveloping night was pitchy, without any bold outline of canon wall or companionship of stars. The coyotes were out in force and from all around came their wild sharp barks. The wind rose and mourned weirdly through the balsams.

But it was in the men that Joan felt mostly that element of wildness. Kells lay with his ghastly face clear in the play of the moving flare of light. It was an intelligent, keen, strong face, but evil. Evil power stood out in the lines, in the strange eyes, stranger then ever, now in shadow; and it seemed once more the face of an alert, listening, implacable man, with wild projects in mind, driving him to the doom he meant for others. Pearce's red face shone redder in that ruddy light. It was hard, lean, almost fleshless, a red mask stretched over a grinning skull. The one they called Frenchy was little, dark, small-featured, with piercing gimlet-like eyes, and a mouth ready to gush forth hate and violence. The next two were not particularly individualized by any striking aspect, merely looking border ruffians after the type of Bill and Halloway. But Gulden, who sat at the end of the half-circle, was an object that Joan could scarcely bring her gaze to study. Somehow her first glance at him put into her mind a strange idea—that she was a woman and therefore of all creatures or things in the world the farthest removed from him. She looked away, and found her gaze returning, fascinated, as if she were a bird and he a snake. The man was of huge frame, a giant whose every move suggested the acme of physical power. He was an animal—a gorilla with a shock of light instead of black hair, of pale instead of black skin. His features might have been hewn and hammered out with coarse, dull, broken chisels. And upon his face, in the lines and cords, in the huge caverns where his eyes hid, and in the huge gash that held strong, white fangs, had been stamped by nature and by life a terrible ferocity. Here was a man or a monster in whose presence Joan felt that she would rather be dead. He did not smoke; he did not indulge in the coarse, good-natured raillery, he sat there like a huge engine of destruction that needed no rest, but was forced to rest because of weaker attachments. On the other hand, he was not sullen or brooding. It was that he did not seem to think.

Kells had been rapidly gaining strength since the extraction of the bullet, and it was evident that his interest was growing proportionately. He asked questions and received most of his replies from Red Pearce. Joan did not listen attentively at first, but presently she regretted that she had not. She gathered that Kells's fame as the master bandit of the whole gold region of Idaho, Nevada, and northeastern California was a fame that he loved as much as the gold he stole. Joan sensed, through the replies of these men and their attitude toward Kells, that his power was supreme. He ruled the robbers and ruffians in his bands, and evidently they were scattered from Bannack to Lewiston and all along the border. He had power, likewise, over the border hawks not directly under his leadership. During the weeks of his enforced stay in the canon there had been a cessation of operations—the nature of which Joan merely guessed—and a gradual accumulation of idle wailing men in the main camp. Also she gathered, but vaguely, that though Kells had supreme power, the organization he desired was yet far from being consummated. He showed thoughtfulness and irritation by turns, and it was the subject of gold that drew his intensest interest.

"Reckon you figgered right, Jack," said Red Pearce, and paused as if before a long talk, while he refilled his pipe. "Sooner or later there'll be the biggest gold strike ever made in the West. Wagon-trains are met every day comin' across from Salt Lake. Prospectors are workin' in hordes down from Bannack. All the gulches an' valleys in the Bear Mountains have their camps. Surface gold everywhere an' easy to get where there's water. But there's diggin's all over. No big strike yet. It's bound to come sooner or later. An' then when the news hits the main-traveled roads an' reaches back into the mountains there's goin' to be a rush that'll make '49 an' '51 look sick. What do you say, Bate?"

"Shore will," replied a grizzled individual whom Kells had called Bate Wood. He was not so young as his companions, more sober, less wild, and slower of speech. "I saw both '49 and '51. Them was days! But I'm agreein' with Red. There shore will be hell on this Idaho border sooner or later. I've been a prospector, though I never hankered after the hard work of diggin' gold. Gold is hard to dig, easy to lose, an' easy to get from some other feller. I see the signs of a comin' strike somewhere in this region. Mebbe it's on now. There's thousands of prospectors in twos an' threes an' groups, out in the hills all over. They ain't a-goin' to tell when they do make a strike. But the gold must be brought out. An' gold is heavy. It ain't easy hid. Thet's how strikes are discovered. I shore reckon thet this year will beat '49 an' '51. An' fer two reasons. There's a steady stream of broken an' disappointed gold-seekers back-trailin' from California. There's a bigger stream of hopeful an' crazy fortune hunters travelin' in from the East. Then there's the wimmen an' gamblers an' such thet hang on. An' last the men thet the war is drivin' out here. Whenever an' wherever these streams meet, if there's a big gold strike, there'll be the hellishest time the world ever saw!"

"Boys," said Kells, with a ring in his weak voice, "it'll be a harvest for my Border Legion."

"Fer what?" queried Bate Wood, curiously.

All the others except Gulden turned inquiring and interested faces toward the bandit.

"The Border Legion," replied Kells.

"An' what's that?" asked Red Pearce, bluntly.

"Well, if the time's ripe for the great gold fever you say is coming, then it's ripe for the greatest band ever organized. I'll organize. I'll call it the Border Legion."

"Count me in as right-hand, pard," replied Red, with enthusiasm.

"An' shore me, boss," added Bate Wood.

The idea was received vociferously, at which demonstration the giant Gulden raised his massive head and asked, or rather growled, in a heavy voice what the fuss was about. His query, his roused presence, seemed to act upon the others, even Kells, with a strange, disquieting or halting force, as if here was a character or an obstacle to be considered. After a moment of silence Red Pearce explained the project.

"Huh! Nothing new in that," replied Gulden. "I belonged to one once. It was in Algiers. They called it the Royal Legion."

"Algiers. What's thet?" asked Bate Wood.

"Africa," replied Gulden.

"Say, Gul, you've been around some," said Red Pearce, admiringly. "What was the Royal Legion?"

"Nothing but a lot of devils from all over. The border there was the last place. Every criminal was safe from pursuit."

"What'd you do?"

"Fought among ourselves. Wasn't many in the Legion when I left."

"Shore thet ain't strange!" exclaimed Wood, significantly. But his inference was lost upon Gulden.

"I won't allow fighting in my Legion," said Kells, coolly. "I'll pick this band myself."

"Thet's the secret," rejoined Wood. "The right fellers. I've been in all kinds of bands. Why, I even was a vigilante in '51."

This elicited a laugh from his fellows, except the wooden-faced Gulden.

"How many do we want?" asked Red Pearce.

"The number doesn't matter. But they must be men I can trust and control. Then as lieutenants I'll need a few young fellows, like you, Red. Nervy, daring, cool, quick of wits."

Red Pearce enjoyed the praise bestowed upon him and gave his shoulders a swagger. "Speakin' of that, boss," he said, "reminds me of a chap who rode into Cabin Gulch a few weeks ago. Braced right into Beard's place, where we was all playin' faro, an' he asks for Jack Kells. Right off we all thought he was a guy who had a grievance, an' some of us was for pluggin' him. But I kinda liked him an' I cooled the gang down. Glad I did that. He wasn't wantin' to throw a gun. His intentions were friendly. Of course I didn't show curious about who or what he was. Reckoned he was a young feller who'd gone bad sudden-like an' was huntin' friends. An' I'm here to say, boss, that he was wild."

"What's his name?" asked Kells.

"Jim Cleve, he said," replied Pearce.

Joan Randle, hidden back in the shadows, forgotten or ignored by this bandit group, heard the name Jim Cleve with pain and fear, but not amaze. From the moment Pearce began his speech she had been prepared for the revelation of her runaway lover's name. She trembled, and grew a little sick. Jim had made no idle threat. What would she have given to live over again the moment that had alienated him?

"Jim Cleve," mused Kells. "Never heard of him. And I never forget a name or a face. What's he like?"

"Clean, rangy chap, big, but not too big," replied Pearce. "All muscle. Not more'n twenty three. Hard rider, hard fighter, hard gambler an' drinker—reckless as hell. If only you can steady him, boss! Ask Bate what he thinks."

"Well!" exclaimed Kells in surprise. "Strangers are everyday occurrences on this border. But I never knew one to impress you fellows as this Cleve.... Bate, what do you say? What's this Cleve done? You're an old head. Talk, sense, now."

"Done?" echoed Wood, scratching his grizzled head. "What in the hell ain't he done?... He rode in brazener than any feller thet ever stacked up against this outfit. An' straight-off he wins the outfit. I don't know how he done it. Mebbe it was because you seen he didn't care fer anythin' or anybody on earth. He stirred us up. He won all the money we had in camp—broke most of us—an' give it all back. He drank more'n the whole outfit, yet didn't get drunk. He threw his gun on Beady Jones fer cheatin' an' then on Beady's pard, Chick Williams. Didn't shoot to kill—jest winged 'em. But say, he's the quickest and smoothest hand to throw a gun thet ever hit this border. Don't overlook thet.... Kells, this Jim Cleve's a great youngster goin' bad quick. An' I'm here to add that he'll take some company along."

"Bate, you forgot to tell how he handled Luce," said Red Pearee. "You was there. I wasn't. Tell Kells that."

"Luce. I know the man. Go ahead, Bate," responded Kells.

"Mebbe it ain't any recommendation fer said Jim Cleve," replied Wood. "Though it did sorta warm me to him.... Boss, of course, you recollect thet little Brander girl over at Bear Lake village. She's old Brander's girl—worked in his store there. I've seen you talk sweet to her myself. Wal, it seems the old man an' some of his boys took to prospectin' an' fetched the girl along. Thet's how I understood it. Luce came bracin' in over at Cabin Gulch one day. As usual, we was drinkin' an' playin'. But young Cleve wasn't doin' neither. He had a strange, moody spell thet day, as I recollect. Luce sprung a job on us. We never worked with him or his outfit, but mebbe—you can't tell what'd come off if it hadn't been for Cleve. Luce had a job put up to ride down where ole Brander was washin' fer gold, take what he had—AN' the girl. Fact was the gold was only incidental. When somebody cornered Luce he couldn't swear there was gold worth goin' after. An' about then Jim Cleve woke up. He cussed Luce somethin' fearful. An' when Luce went for his gun, natural-like, why this Jim Cleve took it away from him. An' then he jumped Luce. He knocked an' threw him around an' he near beat him to death before we could interfere. Luce was shore near dead. All battered up—broken bones—an' what-all I can't say. We put him to bed an' he's there yet, an' he'll never be the same man he was."

A significant silence fell upon the group at the conclusion of Wood's narrative. Wood had liked the telling, and it made his listeners thoughtful. All at once the pale face of Kells turned slightly toward Gulden.

"Gulden, did you hear that?" asked Kells.

"Yes," replied the man.

"What do you think about this Jim Cleve—and the job he prevented?"

"Never saw Cleve. I'll look him up when we get back to camp. Then I'll go after the Brander girl."

How strangely his brutal assurance marked a line between him and his companions! There was something wrong, something perverse in this Gulden. Had Kells meant to bring that point out or to get an impression of Cleve?

Joan could not decide. She divined that there was antagonism between Gulden and all the others. And there was something else, vague and intangible, that might have been fear. Apparently Gulden was a criminal for the sake of crime. Joan regarded him with a growing terror—augmented the more because he alone kept eyes upon the corner where she was hidden—and she felt that compared with him the others, even Kells, of whose cold villainy she was assured, were but insignificant men of evil. She covered her head with a blanket to shut out sight of that shaggy, massive head and the great dark caves of eyes.

Thereupon Joan did not see or hear any more of the bandits. Evidently the conversation died down, or she, in the absorption of new thoughts, no longer heard. She relaxed, and suddenly seemed to quiver all over with the name she whispered to herself. "Jim! Jim! Oh, Jim!" And the last whisper was an inward sob. What he had done was terrible. It tortured her. She had not believed it in him. Yet, now she thought, how like him. All for her—in despair and spite—he had ruined himself. He would be killed out there in some drunken brawl, or, still worse, he would become a member of this bandit crew and drift into crime. That was a great blow to Joan—that the curse she had put upon him. How silly, false, and vain had been her coquetry, her indifference! She loved Jim Cleve. She had not known that when she started out to trail him, to fetch him back, but she knew it now. She ought to have known before.

The situation she had foreseen loomed dark and monstrous and terrible in prospect. Just to think of it made her body creep and shudder with cold terror. Yet there was that strange, inward, thrilling burn round her heart. Somewhere and soon she was coming face to face with this changed Jim Cleve—this boy who had become a reckless devil. What would he do? What could she do? Might he not despise her, scorn her, curse her, taking her at Kells's word, the wife of a bandit? But no! he would divine the truth in the flash of an eye. And then! She could not think what might happen, but it must mean blood-death. If he escaped Kells, how could he ever escape this Gulden—this huge vulture of prey?

Still, with the horror thick upon her, Joan could not wholly give up. The moment Jim Cleve's name and his ruin burst upon her ears, in the gossip of these bandits, she had become another girl—a girl wholly become a woman, and one with a driving passion to save if it cost her life. She lost her fear of Kells, of the others, of all except Gulden. He was not human, and instinctively she knew she could do nothing with him. She might influence the others, but never Gulden.

The torment in her brain eased then, and gradually she quieted down, with only a pang and a weight in her breast. The past seemed far away. The present was nothing. Only the future, that contained Jim Cleve, mattered to her. She would not have left the clutches of Kells, if at that moment she could have walked forth free and safe. She was going on to Cabin Gulch. And that thought was the last one in her weary mind as she dropped to sleep.

8

In three days—during which time Joan attended Kells as faithfully as if she were indeed his wife—he thought that he had gained sufficiently to undertake the journey to the main camp, Cabin Gulch. He was eager to get back there and imperious in his overruling of any opposition. The men could take turns at propping him in a saddle. So on the morning of the fourth day they packed for the ride.

During these few days Joan had verified her suspicion that Kells had two sides to his character; or it seemed, rather, that her presence developed a latent or a long-dead side. When she was with him, thereby distracting his attention, he was entirely different from what he was when his men surrounded him. Apparently he had no knowledge of this. He showed surprise and gratitude at Joan's kindness though never pity or compassion for her. That he had become infatuated with her Joan could no longer doubt. His strange eyes followed her; there was a dreamy light in them; he was mostly silent with her.

Before those few days had come to an end he had developed two things—a reluctance to let Joan leave his sight and an intolerance of the presence of the other men, particularly Gulden. Always Joan felt the eyes of these men upon her, mostly in unobtrusive glances, except Gulden's. The giant studied her with slow, cavernous stare, without curiosity or speculation or admiration. Evidently a woman was a new and strange creature to him and he was experiencing unfamiliar sensations. Whenever Joan accidentally met his gaze—for she avoided it as much as possible—she shuddered with sick memory of a story she had heard—how a huge and ferocious gorilla had stolen into an African village and run off with a white woman. She could not shake the memory. And it was this that made her kinder to Kells than otherwise would have been possible.

All Joan's faculties sharpened in this period. She felt her own development—the beginning of a bitter and hard education—an instinctive assimilation of all that nature taught its wild people and creatures, the first thing in elemental life—self-preservation. Parallel in her heart and mind ran a hopeless despair and a driving, unquenchable spirit. The former was fear, the latter love. She believed beyond a doubt that she had doomed herself along with Jim Cleve; she felt that she had the courage, the power, the love to save him, if not herself. And the reason that she did not falter and fail in this terrible situation was because her despair, great as it was, did not equal her love.

That morning, before being lifted upon his horse, Kells buckled on his gun-belt. The sheath and full round of shells and the gun made this belt a burden for a weak man. And so Red Pearce insisted. But Kells laughed in his face. The men, always excepting Gulden, were unfailing in kindness and care. Apparently they would have fought for Kells to the death. They were simple and direct in their rough feelings. But in Kells, Joan thought, was a character who was a product of this border wildness, yet one who could stand aloof from himself and see the possibilities, the unexpected, the meaning of that life. Kells knew that a man and yet another might show kindness and faithfulness one moment, but the very next, out of a manhood retrograded to the savage, out of the circumstance or chance, might respond to a primitive force far sundered from thought or reason, and rise to unbridled action. Joan divined that Kells buckled on his gun to be ready to protect her. But his men never dreamed his motive. Kells was a strong, bad man set among men like him, yet he was infinitely different because he had brains.

On the start of the journey Joan was instructed to ride before Kells and Pearce, who supported the leader in his saddle. The pack-drivers and Bate Wood and Frenchy rode ahead; Gulden held to the rear. And this order was preserved till noon, when the cavalcade halted for a rest in a shady, grassy, and well-watered nook. Kells was haggard, and his brow wet with clammy dew, and lined with pain. Yet he was cheerful and patient. Still he hurried the men through their tasks.

In an hour the afternoon travel was begun. The canon and its surroundings grew more rugged and of larger dimensions. Yet the trail appeared to get broader and better all the time. Joan noticed intersecting trails, running down from side canons and gulches. The descent was gradual, and scarcely evident in any way except in the running water and warmer air.

Kells, tired before the middle of the afternoon, and he would have fallen from his saddle but for the support of his fellows. One by one they held him up. And it was not easy work to ride alongside, holding him up. Joan observed that Gulden did not offer his services. He seemed a part of this gang, yet not of it. Joan never lost a feeling of his presence behind her, and from time to time, when he rode closer, the feeling grew stronger. Toward the close of that afternoon she became aware of Gulden's strange attention. And when a halt was made for camp she dreaded something nameless.

This halt occurred early, before sunset, and had been necessitated by the fact that Kells was fainting. They laid him out on blankets, with his head in his saddle. Joan tended him, and he recovered somewhat, though he lacked the usual keenness.

It was a busy hour with saddles, packs, horses, with wood to cut and fire to build and meal to cook. Kells drank thirstily, but refused food.

"Joan," he whispered, at an opportune moment, "I'm only tired—dead for sleep. You stay beside me. Wake me quick—if you want to!"

He closed his eyes wearily, without explaining, and soon slumbered. Joan did not choose to allow these men to see that she feared them or distrusted them or disliked them. She ate with them beside the fire. And this was their first opportunity to be close to her. The fact had an immediate and singular influence. Joan had no vanity, though she knew she was handsome. She forced herself to be pleasant, agreeable, even sweet. Their response was instant and growing. At first they were bold, then familiar and coarse. For years she had been used to rough men of the camps. These however, were different, and their jokes and suggestions had no effect because they were beyond her. And when this became manifest to them that aspect of their relation to her changed. She grasped the fact intuitively, and then she verified it by proof. Her heart beat strong and high. If she could hide her hate, her fear, her abhorrence, she could influence these wild men. But it all depended upon her charm, her strangeness, her femininity. Insensibly they had been influenced, and it proved that in the worst of men there yet survived some good. Gulden alone presented a contrast and a problem. He appeared aware of her presence while he sat there eating like a wolf, but it was as if she were only an object. The man watched as might have an animal.

Her experience at the camp-fire meal inclined her to the belief that, if there were such a possibility as her being safe at all, it would be owing to an unconscious and friendly attitude toward the companions she had been forced to accept. Those men were pleased, stirred at being in her vicinity. Joan came to a melancholy and fearful cognizance of her attraction. While at home she seldom had borne upon her a reality—that she was a woman. Her place, her person were merely natural. Here it was all different. To these wild men, developed by loneliness, fierce-blooded, with pulses like whips, a woman was something that thrilled, charmed, soothed, that incited a strange, insatiable, inexplicable hunger for the very sight of her. They did not realize it, but Joan did.

Presently Joan finished her supper and said: "I'll go hobble my horse. He strays sometimes."

"Shore I'll go, miss," said Bate Wood. He had never called her Mrs. Kells, but Joan believed he had not thought of the significance. Hardened old ruffian that he was. Joan regarded him as the best of a bad lot. He had lived long, and some of his life had not been bad.

"Let me go," added Pearce.

"No, thanks. I'll go myself," she replied.

She took the rope hobble off her saddle and boldly swung down the trail. Suddenly she heard two or more of the men speak at once, and then, low and clear: "Gulden, where'n hell are you goin'?" This was Red Pearce's voice.

Joan glanced back. Gulden had started down the trail after her. Her heart quaked, her knees shook, and she was ready to run back. Gulden halted, then turned away, growling. He acted as if caught in something surprising to himself.

"We're on to you, Gulden," continued Pearce, deliberately. "Be careful or we'll put Kells on."

A booming, angry curse was the response. The men grouped closer and a loud altercation followed. Joan almost ran down the trail and heard no more. If any one of them had started her way now she would have plunged into the thickets like a frightened deer. Evidently, however, they meant to let her alone. Joan found her horse, and before hobbling him she was assailed by a temptation to mount him and ride away. This she did not want to do and would not do under any circumstances; still, she could not prevent the natural instinctive impulse of a woman.

She crossed to the other side of the brook and returned toward camp under the spruce and balsam trees, She did not hurry. It was good to be alone, out of sight of those violent men, away from that constant wearing physical proof of catastrophe. Nevertheless, she did not feel free or safe for a moment; she peered fearfully into the shadows of the rocks and trees; and presently it was a relief to get back to the side of the sleeping Kells. He lay in a deep slumber of exhaustion. She arranged her own saddle and blankets near him, and prepared to meet the night as best she could. Instinctively she took a position where in one swift snatch she could get possession of Kells's gun.

It was about time of sunset, warm and still in the canon, with rosy lights fading upon the peaks. The men were all busy with one thing and another. Strange it was to see that Gulden, who Joan thought might be a shirker, did twice the work of any man, especially the heavy work. He seemed to enjoy carrying a log that would have overweighted two ordinary men. He was so huge, so active, so powerful that it was fascinating to watch him. They built the camp-fire for the night uncomfortably near Joan's position; however, remembering how cold the air would become later, she made no objection. Twilight set in and the men, through for the day, gathered near the fire.

Then Joan was not long in discovering that the situation had begun to impinge upon the feelings of each of these men. They looked at her differently. Some of them invented pretexts to approach her, to ask something, to offer service—anything to get near her. A personal and individual note had been injected into the attitude of each. Intuitively Joan guessed that Gulden's arising to follow her had turned their eyes inward. Gulden remained silent and inactive at the edge of the camp-fire circle of light, which flickered fitfully around him, making him seem a huge, gloomy ape of a man. So far as Joan could tell, Gulden never cast his eyes in her direction. That was a difference which left cause for reflection. Had that hulk of brawn and bone begun to think? Bate Wood's overtures to Joan were rough, but inexplicable to her because she dared not wholly trust him.

"An' shore, miss," he had concluded, in a hoarse whisper, "we-all know you ain't Kells's wife. Thet bandit wouldn't marry no woman. He's a woman-hater. He was famous fer thet over in California. He's run off with you—kidnapped you, thet's shore.... An' Gulden swears he shot his own men an' was in turn shot by you. Thet bullet-hole in his back was full of powder. There's liable to be a muss-up any time.... Shore, miss, you'd better sneak off with me tonight when they're all asleep. I'll git grub an' hosses, an' take you off to some prospector's camp. Then you can git home."

Joan only shook her head. Even if she could have felt trust in Wood—and she was of half a mind to believe him—it was too late. Whatever befell her mattered little if in suffering it she could save Jim Cleve from the ruin she had wrought.

Since this wild experience of Joan's had begun she had been sick so many times with raw and naked emotions hitherto unknown to her, that she believed she could not feel another new fear or torture. But these strange sensations grew by what they had been fed upon.

The man called Frenchy, was audacious, persistent, smiling, amorous-eyed, and rudely gallant. He cared no more for his companions than if they had not been there. He vied with Pearce in his attention, and the two of them discomfited the others. The situation might have been amusing had it not been so terrible. Always the portent was a shadow behind their interest and amiability and jealousy. Except for that one abrupt and sinister move of Gulden's—that of a natural man beyond deceit—there was no word, no look, no act at which Joan could have been offended. They were joking, sarcastic, ironical, and sullen in their relation to each other; but to Joan each one presented what was naturally or what he considered his kindest and most friendly front. A young and attractive woman had dropped into the camp of lonely wild men; and in their wild hearts was a rebirth of egotism, vanity, hunger for notice. They seemed as foolish as a lot of cock grouse preening themselves and parading before a single female. Surely in some heart was born real brotherhood for a helpless girl in peril. Inevitably in some of them would burst a flame of passion as it had in Kells.

Between this amiable contest for Joan's glances and replies, with its possibility of latent good to her, and the dark, lurking, unspoken meaning, such as lay in Gulden's brooding, Joan found another new and sickening torture.

"Say, Frenchy, you're no lady's man," declared Red Pearce, "an' you, Bate, you're too old. Move—pass by—sashay!" Pearce, good-naturedly, but deliberately, pushed the two men back.

"Shore she's Kells's lady, ain't she?" drawled Wood. "Ain't you all forgettin' thet?"

"Kells is asleep or dead," replied Pearce, and he succeeded in getting the field to himself.

"Where'd you meet Kells anyway?" he asked Joan, with his red face bending near hers.

Joan had her part to play. It was difficult, because she divined Pearce's curiosity held a trap to catch her in a falsehood. He knew—they all knew she was not Kells's wife. But if she were a prisoner she seemed a willing and contented one. The query that breathed in Pearce's presence was how was he to reconcile the fact of her submission with what he and his comrades had potently felt as her goodness?

"That doesn't concern anybody," replied Joan.

"Reckon not," said Pearce. Then he leaned nearer with intense face. "What I want to know— is Gulden right? Did you shoot Kells?"

In the dusk Joan reached back and clasped Kells hand.

For a man as weak and weary as he had been, it was remarkable how quickly a touch awakened him. He lifted his head.

"Hello! Who's that?" he called out, sharply.

Pearce rose guardedly, startled, but not confused. "It's only me, boss," he replied. "I was about to turn in, an' I wanted to know how you are—if I could do anythin'."

"I'm all right, Red," replied Kells, coolly. "Clear out and let me alone. All of you."

Pearce moved away with an amiable good-night and joined the others at the camp-fire. Presently they sought their blankets, leaving Gulden hunching there silent in the gloom.

"Joan, why did you wake me?" whispered Kells.

"Pearce asked me if I shot you," replied Joan. "I woke you instead of answering him."

"He did!" exclaimed Kells under his breath. Then he laughed. "Can't fool that gang. I guess it doesn't matter. Maybe it'd be well if they knew you shot me."

He appeared thoughtful, and lay there with the fading flare of the fire on his pale face. But he did not speak again. Presently he fell asleep.

Joan leaned back, within reach of him, with her head in her saddle, and pulling a blanket up over her, relaxed her limbs to rest. Sleep seemed the furthest thing from her. She wondered that she dared to think of it. The night had grown chilly; the wind was sweeping with low roar through the balsams; the fire burned dull and red. Joan watched the black, shapeless hulk that she knew to be Gulden. For a long time he remained motionless. By and by he moved, approached the fire, stood one moment in the dying ruddy glow, his great breadth and bulk magnified, with all about him vague and shadowy, but the more sinister for that. The cavernous eyes were only black spaces in that vast face, yet Joan saw them upon her. He lay down then among the other men and soon his deep and heavy breathing denoted the tranquil slumber of an ox.

For hours through changing shadows and starlight Joan lay awake, while a thousand thoughts besieged her, all centering round that vital and compelling one of Jim Cleve.

Only upon awakening, with the sun in her face, did Joan realize that she had actually slept.

The camp was bustling with activity. The horses were in, fresh and quarrelsome, with ears laid back. Kells was sitting upon a rock near the fire with a cup of coffee in his hand. He was looking better. When he greeted Joan his voice sounded stronger. She walked by Pearce and Frenchy and Gulden on her way to the brook, but they took no notice of her. Bate Wood, however, touched his sombrero and said: "Mornin', miss." Joan wondered if her memory of the preceding night were only a bad dream. There was a different atmosphere by daylight, and it was dominated by Kells. Presently she returned to camp refreshed and hungry. Gulden was throwing a pack, which action he performed with ease and dexterity. Pearce was cinching her saddle. Kells was talking, more like his old self than at any time since his injury.

Soon they were on the trail. For Joan time always passed swiftly on horseback. Movement and changing scene were pleasurable to her. The passing of time now held a strange expectancy, a mingled fear and hope and pain, for at the end of this trail was Jim Cleve. In other days she had flouted him, made fun of him, dominated him, everything except loved and feared him. And now she was assured of her love and almost convinced of her fear. The reputation these wild bandits gave Jim was astounding and inexplicable to Joan. She rode the miles thinking of Jim, dreading to meet him, longing to see him, and praying and planning for him.

About noon the cavalcade rode out of the mouth of a canon into a wide valley, surrounded by high, rounded foot-hills. Horses and cattle were grazing on the green levels. A wide, shallow, noisy stream split the valley. Joan could tell from the tracks at the crossing that this place, whatever and wherever it was, saw considerable travel; and she concluded the main rendezvous of the bandits was close at hand.

The pack drivers led across the stream and the valley to enter an intersecting ravine. It was narrow, rough-sided, and floored, but the trail was good. Presently it opened out into a beautiful V-shaped gulch, very different from the high-walled, shut-in canons. It had a level floor, through which a brook flowed, and clumps of spruce and pine, with here and there a giant balsam. Huge patches of wild flowers gave rosy color to the grassy slopes. At the upper end of this gulch Joan saw a number of widely separated cabins. This place, then, was Cabin Gulch.

Upon reaching the first cabin the cavalcade split up. There were men here who hallooed a welcome. Gulden halted with his pack-horse. Some of the others rode on. Wood drove other pack-animals off to the right, up the gentle slope. And Red Pearce, who was beside Kells, instructed Joan to follow them. They rode up to a bench of straggling spruce-trees, in the midst of which stood a large log cabin. It was new, as in fact all the structures in the Gulch appeared to be, and none of them had seen a winter. The chinks between the logs were yet open. This cabin was of the rudest make of notched logs one upon another, and roof of brush and earth. It was low and flat, but very long, and extending before the whole of it was a porch roof supported by posts. At one end was a corral. There were doors and windows with nothing in them. Upon the front wall, outside, hung saddles and bridles.

Joan had a swift, sharp gaze for the men who rose from their lounging to greet the travelers. Jim Cleve was not among them. Her heart left her throat then, and she breathed easier. How could she meet him?

Kells was in better shape than at noon of the preceding day. Still, he had to be lifted off his horse. Joan heard all the men talking at once. They crowded round Pearce, each lending a hand. However, Kells appeared able to walk into the cabin. It was Bate Wood who led Joan inside.

There was a long room, with stone fireplace, rude benches and a table, skins and blankets on the floor, and lanterns and weapons on the wall. At one end Joan saw a litter of cooking utensils and shelves of supplies.

Suddenly Kells's impatient voice silenced the clamor of questions. "I'm not hurt," he said. "I'm all right—only weak and tired. Fellows, this girl is my wife.... Joan, you'll find a room there—at the back of the cabin. Make yourself comfortable."

Joan was only too glad to act upon his suggestion. A door had been cut through the back wall. It was covered with a blanket. When she swept this aside she came upon several steep steps that led up to a smaller, lighter cabin of two rooms, separated by a partition of boughs. She dropped the blanket behind her and went up the steps. Then she saw that the new cabin had been built against an old one. It had no door or opening except the one by which she had entered. It was light because the chinks between the logs were open. The furnishings were a wide bench of boughs covered with blankets, a shelf with a blurred and cracked mirror hanging above it, a table made of boxes, and a lantern. This room was four feet higher than the floor of the other cabin. And at the bottom of the steps leaned a half-dozen slender trimmed poles. She gathered presently that these poles were intended to be slipped under crosspieces above and fastened by a bar below, which means effectually barricaded the opening. Joan could stand at the head of the steps and peep under an edge of the swinging blanket into the large room, but that was the only place she could see through, for the openings between the logs of each wall were not level. These quarters were comfortable, private, and could be shut off from intruders. Joan had not expected so much consideration from Kells and she was grateful.

She lay down to rest and think. It was really very pleasant here. There were birds nesting in the chinks; a ground squirrel ran along one of the logs and chirped at her; through an opening near her face she saw a wild rose-bush and the green slope of the gulch; a soft, warm, fragrant breeze blew in, stirring her hair. How strange that there could be beautiful and pleasant things here in this robber den; that time was the same here as elsewhere; that the sun shone and the sky gleamed blue. Presently she discovered that a lassitude weighted upon her and she could not keep her eyes open. She ceased trying, but intended to remain awake—to think, to listen, to wait. Nevertheless, she did fall asleep and did not awaken till disturbed by some noise. The color of the western sky told her that the afternoon was far spent. She had slept hours. Someone was knocking. She got up and drew aside the blanket. Bate Wood was standing near the door.

"Now, miss, I've supper ready," he said, "an' I was reckonin' you'd like me to fetch yours."

"Yes, thank you, I would," replied Joan.

In a few moments Wood returned carrying the top of a box upon which were steaming pans and cups. He handed this rude tray up to Joan.

"Shore I'm a first-rate cook, miss, when I've somethin' to cook," he said with a smile that changed his hard face.

She returned the smile with her thanks. Evidently Kells had a well-filled larder, and as Joan had fared on coarse and hard food for long, this supper was a luxury and exceedingly appetizing. While she was eating, the blanket curtain moved aside and Kells appeared. He dropped it behind him, but did not step up into the room. He was in his shirt-sleeves, had been clean shaven, and looked a different man.

"How do you like your—home?" he inquired, with a hint of his former mockery.

"I'm grateful for the privacy," she replied.

"You think you could be worse off, then?"

"I know it."

"Suppose Gulden kills me—and rules the gang—and takes you?... There's a story about him, the worst I've heard on this border. I'll tell you some day when I want to scare you bad."

"Gulden!" Joan shivered as she pronounced the name. "Are you and he enemies?"

"No man can have a friend on this border. We flock together like buzzards. There's safety in numbers, but we fight together, like buzzards over carrion."

"Kells, you hate this life?"

"I've always hated my life, everywhere. The only life I ever loved was adventure.... I'm willing to try a new one, if you'll go with me."

Joan shook her head.

"Why not? I'll marry you," he went on, speaking lower. "I've got gold; I'll get more."

"Where did you get the gold?" she asked

"I've relieved a good many overburdened travelers and prospectors," he replied.

"Kells, you're a—a villain!" exclaimed Joan, unable to contain her sudden heat. "You must be utterly mad—to ask me to marry you."

"No, I'm not mad," he rejoined, with a laugh. "Gulden's the mad one. He's crazy. He's got a twist in his brain. I'm no fool.... I've only lost my head over you. But compare marrying me, living and traveling among decent people and comfort, to camps like this. If I don't get drunk I'll be half decent to you. But I'll get shot sooner or later. Then you'll be left to Gulden."

"Why do you say HIM?" she queried, in a shudder of curiosity.

"Well, Gulden haunts me."

"He does me, too. He makes me lose my sense of proportion. Beside him you and the others seem good. But you ARE wicked."

"Then you won't marry me and go away somewhere?... Your choice is strange. Because I tell you the truth."

"Kells! I'm a woman. Something deep in me says you won't keep me here—you can't be so base. Not now, after I saved your life! It would be horrible—inhuman. I can't believe any man born of a woman could do it."

"But I want you—I love you!" he said, low and hard.

"Love! That's not love," she replied in scorn. "God only knows what it is."

"Call it what you like," he went on, bitterly. "You're a young, beautiful, sweet woman. It's wonderful to be near you. My life has been hell. I've had nothing. There's only hell to look forward to—and hell at the end. Why shouldn't I keep you here?"

"But, Kells, listen," she whispered, earnestly, "suppose I am young and beautiful and sweet— as you said. I'm utterly in your power. I'm compelled to seek your protection from even worse men. You're different from these others. You're educated. You must have had—a—a good mother. Now you're bitter, desperate, terrible. You hate life. You seem to think this charm you see in me will bring you something. Maybe a glimpse of joy! But how can it? You know better. How can it... unless I—I love you?"

Kells stared at her, the evil and hardness of his passion corded in his face. And the shadows of comprehending thought in his strange eyes showed the other side of the man. He was still staring at her while he reached to put aside the curtains; then he dropped his head and went out.

Joan sat motionless, watching the door where he had disappeared, listening to the mounting beats of her heart. She had only been frank and earnest with Kells. But he had taken a meaning from her last few words that she had not intended to convey. All that was woman in her—mounting, righting, hating—leaped to the power she sensed in herself. If she could be deceitful, cunning, shameless in holding out to Kells a possible return of his love, she could do anything with him. She knew it. She did not need to marry him or sacrifice herself. Joan was amazed that the idea remained an instant before her consciousness. But something had told her this was another kind of life than she had known, and all that was precious to her hung in the balance. Any falsity was justifiable, even righteous, under the circumstances. Could she formulate a plan that this keen bandit would not see through? The remotest possibility of her even caring for Kells—that was as much as she dared hint. But that, together with all the charm and seductiveness she could summon, might be enough. Dared she try it? If she tried and failed Kells would despise her, and then she was utterly lost. She was caught between doubt and hope. All that was natural and true in her shrank from such unwomanly deception; all that had been born of her wild experience inflamed her to play the game, to match Kells's villainy with a woman's unfathomable duplicity.

And while Joan was absorbed in thought the sun set, the light failed, twilight stole into the cabin, and then darkness. All this hour there had been a continual sound of men's voices in the large cabin, sometimes low and at other times loud. It was only when Joan distinctly heard the name Jim Cleve that she was startled out of her absorption, thrilling and flushing. In her eagerness she nearly fell as she stepped and gropped through the darkness to the door, and as she drew aside the blanket her hand shook.

The large room was lighted by a fire and half a dozen lanterns. Through a faint tinge of blue smoke Joan saw men standing and sitting and lounging around Kells, who had a seat where the light fell full upon him. Evidently a lull had intervened in the talk. The dark faces Joan could see were all turned toward the door expectantly.

"Bring him in, Bate, and let's look him over," said Kells.

Then Bate Wood appeared, elbowing his way in, and he had his hand on the arm of a tall, lithe fellow. When they got into the light Joan quivered as if she had been stabbed. That stranger with Wood was Jim Cleve—Jim Cleve in frame and feature, yet not the same she knew.

"Cleve, glad to meet you," greeted Kells, extending his hand.

"Thanks. Same to you," replied Cleve, and he met the proffered hand. His voice was cold and colorless, unfamiliar to Joan. Was this man really Jim Cleve?

The meeting of Kells and Cleve was significant because of Kells's interest and the silent attention of the men of his clan. It did not seem to mean anything to the white-faced, tragic-eyed Cleve. Joan gazed at him with utter amazement. She remembered a heavily built, florid Jim Cleve, an overgrown boy with a good-natured, lazy smile on his full face and sleepy eyes. She all but failed to recognize him in the man who stood there now, lithe and powerful, with muscles bulging in his coarse, white shirt. Joan's gaze swept over him, up and down, shivering at the two heavy guns he packed, till it was transfixed on his face. The old, or the other, Jim Cleve had been homely, with too much flesh on his face to show force or fire. This man seemed beautiful. But it was a beauty of tragedy. He was as white as Kells, but smoothly, purely white, without shadow or sunburn. His lips seemed to have set with a bitter, indifferent laugh. His eyes looked straight out, piercing, intent, haunted, and as dark as night. Great blue circles lay under them, lending still further depth and mystery. It was a sad, reckless face that wrung Joan's very heartstrings.

She had come too late to save his happiness, but she prayed that it was not too late to save his honor and his soul.

While she gazed there had been further exchange of speech between Kells and Cleve, and she had heard, though not distinguished, what was said. Kells was unmistakably friendly, as were the other men within range of Joan's sight. Cleve was surrounded; there were jesting and laughter; and then he was led to the long table where several men were already gambling.

Joan dropped the curtain, and in the darkness of her cabin she saw that white, haunting face, and when she covered her eyes she still saw it. The pain, the reckless violence, the hopeless indifference, the wreck and ruin in that face had been her doing. Why? How had Jim Cleve wronged her? He had loved her at her displeasure and had kissed her against her will. She had furiously upbraided him, and when he had finally turned upon her, threatening to prove he was no coward, she had scorned him with a girl's merciless injustice. All her strength and resolve left her, momentarily, after seeing Jim there. Like a woman, she weakened. She lay on the bed and writhed. Doubt, hopelessness, despair, again seized upon her, and some strange, yearning maddening emotion. What had she sacrificed? His happiness and her own—and both their lives!

The clamor in the other cabin grew so boisterous that suddenly when it stilled Joan was brought sharply to the significance of it. Again she drew aside the curtain and peered out.

Gulden, huge, stolid, gloomy, was entering the cabin. The man fell into the circle and faced Kell with the fire-light dancing in his cavernous eyes.

"Hello, Gulden!" said Kells, coolly. "What ails you?"

"Anybody tell you about Bill Bailey?" asked Gulden, heavily.

Kells did not show the least concern. "Tell me what?"

"That he died in a cabin, down in the valley?"

Kells gave a slight start and his eyes narrowed and shot steely glints. "No. It's news to me."

"Kells, you left Bailey for dead. But he lived. He was shot through, but he got there somehow—nobody knows. He was far gone when Beady Jones happened along. Before he died he sent word to me by Beady.... Are you curious to know what it was?"

"Not the least," replied Kells. "Bailey was—well, offensive to my wife. I shot him."

"He swore you drew on him in cold blood," thundered Gulden. "He swore it was for nothing—just so you could be alone with that girl!"

Kells rose in wonderful calmness, with only his pallor and a slight shaking of his hands to betray excitement. An uneasy stir and murmur ran through the room. Red Pearce, nearest at hand, stepped to Kells's side. All in a moment there was a deadly surcharged atmosphere there.

"Well, he swore right!... Now what's it to you?"

Apparently the fact and its confession were nothing particular to Gulden, or else he was deep where all considered him only dense and shallow.

"It's done. Bill's dead," continued Gulden. "But why do you double-cross the gang? What's the game? You never did it before.... That girl isn't your—"

"Shut up!" hissed Kells. Like a flash his hand flew out with his gun, and all about him was dark menace.

Gulden made no attempt to draw. He did not show surprise nor fear nor any emotion. He appeared plodding in mind. Red Pearce stepped between Kells and Gulden. There was a realization in the crowd, loud breaths, scraping of feet. Gulden turned away. Then Kells resumed his seat and his pipe as if nothing out of the ordinary had occurred.

9

Joan turned away from the door in a cold clamp of relief. The shadow of death hovered over these men. She must fortify herself to live under that shadow, to be prepared for any sudden violence, to stand a succession of shocks that inevitably would come. She listened. The men were talking and laughing now; there came a click of chips, the spat of a thrown card, the thump of a little sack of gold. Ahead of her lay the long hours of night in which these men would hold revel. Only a faint ray of light penetrated her cabin, but it was sufficient for her to distinguish objects. She set about putting the poles in place to barricade the opening. When she had finished she knew she was safe at least from intrusion. Who had constructed that rude door and for what purpose? Then she yielded to the temptation to peep once more under the edge of the curtain.

The room was cloudy and blue with smoke. She saw Jim Cleve at a table gambling with several ruffians. His back was turned, yet Joan felt the contrast of his attitude toward the game, compared with that of the others. They were tense, fierce, and intent upon every throw of a card. Cleve's very poise of head and movement of arm betrayed his indifference. One of the gamblers howled his disgust, slammed down his cards, and got up.

"He's cleaned out," said one, in devilish glee.

"Naw, he ain't," voiced another. "He's got two fruit-cans full of dust. I saw 'em.... He's just lay down—like a poisoned coyote."

"Shore I'm glad Cleve's got the luck, fer mebbe he'll give my gold back," spoke up another gamester, with a laugh.

"Wal, he certainlee is the chilvalus card sharp," rejoined the last player. "Jim, was you allus as lucky in love as in cards?"

"Lucky in love?... Sure!" answered Jim Cleve, with a mocking, reckless ring in his voice.

"Funny, ain't thet, boys? Now there's the boss. Kells can sure win the gurls, but he's a pore gambler." Kells heard this speech, and he laughed with the others. "Hey, you greaser, you never won any of my money," he said.

"Come an' set in, boss. Come an' see your gold fade away. You can't stop this Jim Cleve. Luck—bull luck straddles his neck. He'll win your gold—your hosses an' saddles an' spurs an' guns—an' your shirt, if you've nerve enough to bet it."

The speaker slapped his cards upon the table while he gazed at Cleve in grieved admiration. Kells walked over to the group and he put his hand on Cleve's shoulder.

"Say youngster," he said, genially, "you said you were just as lucky in love.... Now I had a hunch some BAD luck with a girl drove you out here to the border."

Kells spoke jestingly, in a way that could give no offense, even to the wildest of boys, yet there was curiosity, keenness, penetration, in his speech. It had not the slightest effect upon Jim Cleve.

"Bad luck and a girl?... To hell with both!" he said.

"Shore you're talkin' religion. Thet's where both luck an' gurls come from," replied the unlucky gamester. "Will one of you hawgs pass the whiskey?"

The increased interest with which Kells looked down upon Jim Cleve was not lost upon Joan. But she had seen enough, and, turning away, she stumbled to the bed and lay there with an ache in her heart.

"Oh," she whispered to herself, "he is ruined—ruined—ruined!... God forgive me!" She saw bright, cold stars shining between the logs. The night wind swept in cold and pure, with the dew of the mountain in it. She heard the mourn of wolves, the hoot of an owl, the distant cry of a panther, weird and wild. Yet outside there was a thick and lonely silence. In that other cabin, from which she was mercifully shut out, there were different sounds, hideous by contrast. By and by she covered her ears, and at length, weary from thought and sorrow, she drifted into slumber.

Next morning, long after she had awakened, the cabin remained quiet, with no one stirring. Morning had half gone before Wood knocked and gave her a bucket of water, a basin and towels. Later he came with her breakfast. After that she had nothing to do but pace the floor of her two rooms. One appeared to be only an empty shed, long in disuse. Her view from both rooms was restricted to the green slope of the gulch up to yellow crags and the sky. But she would rather have had this to watch than an outlook upon the cabins and the doings of these bandits.

About noon she heard the voice of Kells in low and earnest conversation with someone; she could not, however, understand what was said. That ceased, and then she heard Kells moving around. There came a clatter of hoofs as a horse galloped away from the cabin, after which a knock sounded on the wall.

"Joan," called Kells. Then the curtain was swept aside and Kells, appearing pale and troubled, stepped into her room.

"What's the matter?" asked Joan, hurriedly.

"Gulden shot two men this morning. One's dead. The other's in bad shape, so Red tells me. I haven't seen him."

"Who—who are they?" faltered Joan. She could not think of any man except Jim Cleve.

"Dan Small's the one's dead. The other they call Dick. Never heard his last name."

"Was it a fight?"

"Of course. And Gulden picked it. He's a quarrelsome man. Nobody can go against him. He's all the time like some men when they're drunk. I'm sorry I didn't bore him last night. I would have done it if it hadn't been for Red Pearce."

Kells seemed gloomy and concentrated on his situation and he talked naturally to Joan, as if she were one to sympathize. A bandit, then, in the details of his life, the schemes, troubles, friendships, relations, was no different from any other kind of a man. He was human, and things that might constitute black evil for observers were dear to him, a part of him. Joan feigned the sympathy she could not feel.

"I thought Gulden was your enemy."

Kells sat down on one of the box seats, and his heavy gun-sheath rested upon the floor. He looked at Joan now, forgetting she was a woman and his prisoner.

"I never thought of that till now," he said. "We always got along because I understood him. I managed him. The man hasn't changed in the least. He's always what he is. But there's a difference. I noticed that first over in Lost Canon. And Joan, I believe it's because Gulden saw you."

"Oh, no!" cried Joan, trembling.

"Maybe I'm wrong. Anyway something's wrong. Gulden never had a friend or a partner. I don't misunderstand his position regarding Bailey. What did he care for that soak? Gulden's cross-grained. He opposes anything or anybody. He's got a twist in his mind that makes him dangerous.... I wanted to get rid of him. I decided to—after last night. But now it seems that's no easy job."

"Why?" asked Joan, curiously.

"Pearce and Wood and Beard, all men I rely on, said it won't do. They hint Gulden is strong with my gang here, and all through the border. I was wild. I don't believe it. But as I'm not sure—what can I do?... They're all afraid of Gulden. That's it.... And I believe I am, too."

"You!" exclaimed Joan.

Kells actually looked ashamed. "I believe I am, Joan," he replied. "That Gulden is not a man. I never was afraid of a real man. He's—he's an animal."

"He made me think of a gorrilla," said Joan.

"There's only one man I know who's not afraid of Gulden. He's a new-comer here on the border. Jim Cleve he calls himself. A youngster I can't figure! But he'd slap the devil himself in the face. Cleve won't last long out here. Yet you can never tell. Men like him, who laugh at death, sometimes avert it for long. I was that way once.... Cleve heard me talking to Pearce about Gulden. And he said, 'Kells, I'll pick a fight with this Gulden and drive him out of the camp or kill him.'"

"What did you say?" queried Joan, trying to steady her voice as she averted her eyes.

"I said 'Jim, that wins me. But I don't want you killed.'... It certainly was nervy of the youngster. Said it just the same as—as he'd offer to cinch my saddle. Gulden can whip a roomful of men. He's done it. And as for a killer—I've heard of no man with his record."

"And that's why you fear him?"

"It's not," replied Kells, passionately, as if his manhood had been affronted. "It's because he's Gulden. There's something uncanny about him.... Gulden's a cannibal!"

Joan looked as if she had not heard aright.

"It's a cold fact. Known all over the border. Gulden's no braggart. But he's been known to talk. He was a sailor—a pirate. Once he was shipwrecked. Starvation forced him to be a cannibal. He told this in California, and in Nevada camps. But no one believed him. A few years ago he got snowed-up in the mountains back of Lewiston. He had two companions with him. They all began to starve. It was absolutely necessary to try to get out. They started out in the snow. Travel was desperately hard. Gulden told that his companions dropped. But he murdered them—and again saved his life by being a cannibal. After this became known his sailor yarns were no longer doubted.... There's another story about him. Once he got hold of a girl and took her into the mountains. After a winter he returned alone. He told that he'd kept her tied in a cave, without any clothes, and she froze to death."

"Oh, horrible!" moaned Joan.

"I don't know how true it is. But I believe it. Gulden is not a man. The worst of us have a conscience. We can tell right from wrong. But Gulden can't. He's beneath morals. He has no conception of manhood, such as I've seen in the lowest of outcasts. That cave story with the girl—that betrays him. He belongs back in the Stone Age. He's a thing.... And here on the border, if he wants, he can have all the more power because of what he is."

"Kells, don't let him see me!" entreated Joan.

The bandit appeared not to catch the fear in Joan's tone and look. She had been only a listener. Presently with preoccupied and gloomy mien, he left her alone.

Joan did not see him again, except for glimpses under the curtain, for three days. She kept the door barred and saw no one except Bate Wood, who brought her meals. She paced her cabin like a caged creature. During this period few men visited Kells's cabin, and these few did not remain long. Joan was aware that Kells was not always at home. Evidently he was able to go out. Upon the fourth day he called to her and knocked for admittance. Joan let him in, and saw that he was now almost well again, once more cool, easy, cheerful, with his strange, forceful air.

"Good day, Joan. You don't seem to be pining for your—negligent husband."

He laughed as if he mocked himself, but there was gladness in the very sight of her, and some indefinable tone in his voice that suggested respect.

"I didn't miss you," replied Joan. Yet it was a relief to see him.

"No, I imagine not," he said, dryly. "Well, I've been busy with men—with plans. Things are working out to my satisfaction. Red Pearce got around Gulden. There's been no split. Besides, Gulden rode off. Someone said he went after a little girl named Brander. I hope he gets shot.... Joan, we'll be leaving Cabin Gulch soon. I'm expecting news that'll change things. I won't leave you here. You'll have to ride the roughest trails. And your clothes are in tatters now. You've got to have something to wear."

"I should think so," replied Joan, fingering the thin, worn, ragged habit that had gone to pieces. "The first brush I ride through will tear this off."

"That's annoying," said Kells, with exasperation at himself. "Where on earth can I get you a dress? We're two hundred miles from everywhere. The wildest kind of country.... Say, did you ever wear a man's outfit?"

"Ye-es, when I went prospecting and hunting with my uncle," she replied, reluctantly.

Suddenly he had a daring and brilliant smile that changed his face completely. He rubbed his palms together. He laughed as if at a huge joke. He cast a measuring glance up and down her slender form.

"Just wait till I come back," he said.

He left her and she heard him rummaging around in the pile of trappings she had noted in a corner of the other cabin. Presently he returned carrying a bundle. This he unrolled on the bed and spread out the articles.

"Dandy Dale's outfit," he said, with animation. "Dandy was a would-be knight of the road. He dressed the part. But he tried to hold up a stage over here and an unappreciative passenger shot him. He wasn't killed outright. He crawled away and died. Some of my men found him and they fetched his clothes. That outfit cost a fortune. But not a man among us could get into it."

There was a black sombrero with heavy silver band; a dark-blue blouse and an embroidered buckskin vest; a belt full of cartridges and a pearl-handled gun; trousers of corduroy; high-top leather boots and gold mounted spurs, all of the finest material and workmanship.

"Joan, I'll make you a black mask out of the rim of a felt hat, and then you'll be grand." He spoke with the impulse and enthusiasm of a boy.

"Kells, you don't mean me to wear these?" asked Joan, incredulously.

"Certainly. Why not? Just the thing. A little fancy, but then you're a girl. We can't hide that. I don't want to hide it."

"I won't wear them," declared Joan.

"Excuse me—but you will," he replied, coolly and pleasantly.

"I won't!" cried Joan. She could not keep cool.

"Joan, you've got to take long rides with me. At night sometimes. Wild rides to elude pursuers sometimes. You'll go into camps with me. You'll have to wear strong, easy, free clothes. You'll have to be masked. Here the outfit is—as if made for you. Why, you're dead lucky. For this stuff is good and strong. It'll stand the wear, yet it's fit for a girl.... You put the outfit on, right now."

"I said I wouldn't!" Joan snapped.

"But what do you care if it belonged to a fellow who's dead?... There! See that hole in the shirt. That's a bullet-hole. Don't be squeamish. It'll only make your part harder."

"Mr. Kells, you seem to have forgotten entirely that I'm a—a girl."

He looked blank astonishment. "Maybe I have.... I'll remember. But you said you'd worn a man's things."

"I wore my brother's coat and overalls, and was lost in them," replied Joan.

His face began to work. Then he laughed uproariously. "I—under—stand. This'll fit—you—like a glove.... Fine! I'm dying to see you."

"You never will."

At that he grew sober and his eyes glinted. "You can't take a little fun. I'll leave you now for a while. When I come back you'll have that suit on!"

There was that in his voice then which she had heard when he ordered men.

Joan looked her defiance.

"If you don't have it on when I come I'll—I'll tear your rags off!... I can do that. You're a strong little devil, and maybe I'm not well enough yet to put this outfit on you. But I can get help.... If you anger me I might wait for—Gulden!"

Joan's legs grew weak under her, so that she had to sink on the bed. Kells would do absolutely and literally what he threatened. She understood now the changing secret in his eyes. One moment he was a certain kind of a man and the very next he was incalculably different. She instinctively recognized this latter personality as her enemy. She must use all the strength and wit and cunning and charm to keep his other personality in the ascendancy, else all was futile.

"Since you force me so—then I must," she said.

Kells left her without another word.

Joan removed her stained and torn dress and her worn-out boots; then hurriedly, for fear Kells might return, she put on the dead boy-bandit's outfit. Dandy Dale assuredly must have been her counterpart, for his things fitted her perfectly. Joan felt so strange that she scarcely had courage enough to look into the mirror. When she did look she gave a start that was of both amaze and shame. But for her face she never could have recognized herself. What had become of her height, her slenderness? She looked like an audacious girl in a dashing boy masquerade. Her shame was singular, inasmuch as it consisted of a burning hateful consciousness that she had not been able to repress a thrill of delight at her appearance, and that this costume strangely magnified every curve and swell of her body, betraying her feminity as nothing had ever done.

And just at that moment Kells knocked on the door and called, "Joan, are you dressed?"

"Yes," she replied. But the word seemed involuntary.

Then Kells came in.

It was an instinctive and frantic impulse that made Joan snatch up a blanket and half envelop herself in it. She stood with scarlet face and dilating eyes, trembling in every limb. Kells had entered with an expectant smile and that mocking light in his gaze. Both faded. He stared at the blanket—then at her face. Then he seemed to comprehend this ordeal. And he looked sorry for her.

"Why you—you little—fool!" he exclaimed, with emotion. And that emotion seemed to exasperate him. Turning away from her, he gazed out between the logs. Again, as so many times before, he appeared to be remembering something that was hard to recall, and vague.

Joan, agitated as she was, could not help but see the effect of her unexpected and unconscious girlishness. She comprehended that with the mind of the woman which had matured in her. Like Kells, she too, had different personalities.

"I'm trying to be decent to you," went on Kells, without turning. "I want to give you a chance to make the best of a bad situation. But you're a kid—a girl!... And I'm a bandit. A man lost to all good, who means to have you!"

"But you're NOT lost to all good," replied Joan, earnestly. "I can't understand what I do feel. But I know—if it had been Gulden instead of you—that I wouldn't have tried to hide my—myself behind this blanket. I'm no longer—AFRAID of you. That's why I acted—so—just like a girl caught.... Oh! can't you see!"

"No, I can't see," he replied. "I wish I hadn't fetched you here. I wish the thing hadn't happened. Now it's too late."

"It's never too late.... You—you haven't harmed me yet."

"But I love you," he burst out. "Not like I have. Oh! I see this—that I never really loved any woman before. Something's gripped me. It feels like that rope at my throat—when they were going to hang me."

Then Joan trembled in the realization that a tremendous passion had seized upon this strange, strong man. In the face of it she did not know how to answer him. Yet somehow she gathered courage in the knowledge.

Kells stood silent a long moment, looking out at the green slope. And then, as if speaking to himself, he said: "I stacked the deck and dealt myself a hand—a losing hand—and now I've got to play it!"

With that he turned to Joan. It was the piercing gaze he bent upon her that hastened her decision to resume the part she had to play. And she dropped the blanket. Kells's gloom and that iron hardness vanished. He smiled as she had never seen him smile. In that and his speechless delight she read his estimate of her appearance; and, notwithstanding the unwomanliness of her costume, and the fact of his notorious character, she knew she had never received so great a compliment. Finally he found his voice.

"Joan, if you're not the prettiest thing I ever saw in my life!"

"I can't get used to this outfit," said Joan. "I can't—I won't go away from this room in it."

"Sure you will. See here, this'll make a difference, maybe. You're so shy."

He held out a wide piece of black felt that evidently he had cut from a sombrero. This he measured over her forehead and eyes, and then taking his knife he cut it to a desired shape. Next he cut eyeholes in it and fastened to it a loop made of a short strip of buckskin.

"Try that.... Pull it down—even with your eyes. There!—take a look at yourself."

Joan faced the mirror and saw merely a masked stranger. She was no longer Joan Randle. Her identity had been absolutely lost.

"No one—who ever knew me—could recognize me now," she murmured, and the relieving thought centered round Jim Cleve.

"I hadn't figured on that," replied Kells. "But you're right.... Joan, if I don't miss my guess, it won't be long till you'll be the talk of mining-towns and camp-fires."

This remark of Kells's brought to Joan proof of his singular pride in the name he bore, and proof of many strange stories about bandits and wild women of the border. She had never believed any of these stories. They had seemed merely a part of the life of this unsettled wild country. A prospector would spend a night at a camp-fire and tell a weird story and pass on, never to be seen there again. Could there have been a stranger story than her life seemed destined to be? Her mind whirled with vague, circling thought—Kells and his gang, the wild trails, the camps, and towns, gold and stage-coaches, robbery, fights, murder, mad rides in the dark, and back to Jim Cleve and his ruin.

Suddenly Kells stepped to her from behind and put his arms around her. Joan grew stiff. She had been taken off her guard. She was in his arms and could not face him.

"Joan, kiss me," he whispered, with a softness, a richer, deeper note in his voice.

"No!" cried Joan, violently.

There was a moment of silence in which she felt his grasp slowly tighten—the heave of his breast.

"Then I'll make you," he said. So different was the voice now that another man might have spoken. Then he bent her backward, and, freeing one hand, brought it under her chin and tried to lift her face.

But Joan broke into fierce, violent resistance. She believed she was doomed, but that only made her the fiercer, the stronger. And with her head down, her arms straining, her body hard and rigidly unyielding she fought him all over the room, knocking over the table and seats, wrestling from wall to wall, till at last they fell across the bed and she broke his hold. Then she sprang up, panting, disheveled, and backed away from him. It had been a sharp, desperate struggle on her part and she was stronger than he. He was not a well man. He raised himself and put one hand to his breast. His face was haggard, wet, working with passion, gray with pain. In the struggle she had hurt him, perhaps reopened his wound.

"Did you—knife me—that it hurts so?" he panted, raising a hand that shook.

"I had—nothing.... I just—fought," cried Joan, breathlessly.

"You hurt me—again—damn you! I'm never free—from pain. But this's worse.... And I'm a coward.... And I'm a dog, too! Not half a man!—You slip of a girl—and I couldn't—hold you!"

His pain and shame were dreadful for Joan to see, because she felt sorry for him, and divined that behind them would rise the darker, grimmer force of the man. And she was right, for suddenly he changed. That which had seemed almost to make him abject gave way to a pale and bitter dignity. He took up Dandy Dale's belt, which Joan had left on the bed, and, drawing the gun from its sheath, he opened the cylinder to see if it was loaded, and then threw the gun at Joan's feet.

"There! Take it—and make a better job this time," he said.

The power in his voice seemed to force Joan to pick up the gun.

"What do—you mean?" she queried, haltingly.

"Shoot me again! Put me out of my pain—my misery.... I'm sick of it all. I'd be glad to have you kill me!"

"Kells!" exclaimed Joan, weakly.

"Take your chance—now—when I've no strength—to force you.... Throw the gun on me.... Kill me!"

He spoke with a terrible impelling earnestness, and the strength of his will almost hypnotized Joan into execution of his demand.

"You are mad," she said. "I don't want to kill you. I couldn't.... I just want you to—to be—decent to me."

"I have been—for me. I was only in fun this time—when I grabbed you. But the FEEL of you!... I can't be decent any more. I see things clear now.... Joan Randle, it's my life or your soul!"

He rose now, dark, shaken, stripped of all save the truth.

Joan dropped the gun from nerveless grasp.

"Is that your choice?" he asked hoarsely.

"I can't murder you!"

"Are you afraid of the other men—of Gulden? Is that why you can't kill me? You're afraid to be left—to try to get away?"

"I never thought of them."

"Then—my life or your soul!"

He stalked toward her, loomed over her, so that she put out trembling hands. After the struggle a reaction was coming to her. She was weakening. She had forgotten her plan.

"If you're merciless—then it must be—my soul," she whispered. "For I CAN'T murder you.... Could you take that gun now—and press it here—and murder ME?"

"No. For I love you."

"You don't love me. It's a blacker crime to murder the soul than the body."

Something in his strange eyes inspired Joan with a flashing, reviving divination. Back upon her flooded all that tide of woman's subtle incalculable power to allure, to charge, to hold. Swiftly she went close to Kells. She stretched out her hands. One was bleeding from rough contract with the log wall during the struggle. Her wrists were red, swollen, bruised from his fierce grasp.

"Look! See what you've done. You were a beast. You made me fight like a beast. My hands were claws—my whole body one hard knot of muscle. You couldn't hold me—you couldn't kiss me.... Suppose you ARE able to hold me—later. I'll only be the husk of a woman. I'll just be a cold shell, doubled-up, unrelaxed, a callous thing never to yield.... All that's ME, the girl, the woman you say you love—will be inside, shrinking, loathing, hating, sickened to death. You will only kiss—embrace—a thing you've degraded. The warmth, the sweetness, the quiver, the thrill, the response, the life—all that is the soul of a woman and makes her lovable will be murdered."

Then she drew still closer to Kells, and with all the wondrous subtlety of a woman in a supreme moment where a life and a soul hang in the balance, she made of herself an absolute contrast to the fierce, wild, unyielding creature who had fought him off.

"Let me show—you the difference," she whispered, leaning to him, glowing, soft, eager, terrible, with her woman's charm. "Something tells me—gives me strength.... What MIGHT be!... Only barely possible—if in my awful plight—you turned out to be a man, good instead of bad!... And—if it were possible—see the differences—in the woman.... I show you—to save my soul!"

She gave the fascinated Kells her hands, slipped into his arms, to press against his breast, and leaned against him an instant, all one quivering, surrendered body; and then lifting a white face, true in its radiance to her honest and supreme purpose to give him one fleeting glimpse of the beauty and tenderness and soul of love, she put warm and tremulous lips to his.

Then she fell away from him, shrinking and terrified. But he stood there as if something beyond belief had happened to him, and the evil of his face, the hard lines, the brute softened and vanished in a light of transformation.

"My God!" he breathed softly. Then he awakened as if from a trance, and, leaping down the steps, he violently swept aside the curtain and disappeared.

Joan threw herself upon the bed and spent the last of her strength in the relief of blinding tears. She had won. She believed she need never fear Kells again. In that one moment of abandon she had exalted him. But at what cost!

10

Next day, when Kells called Joan out into the other cabin, she verified her hope and belief, not so much in the almost indefinable aging and sadness of the man, as in the strong intuitive sense that her attraction had magnified for him and had uplifted him.

"You mustn't stay shut up in there any longer," he said. "You've lost weight and you're pale. Go out in the air and sun. You might as well get used to the gang. Bate Wood came to me this morning and said he thought you were the ghost of Dandy Dale. That name will stick to you. I don't care how you treat my men. But if you're friendly you'll fare better. Don't go far from the cabin. And if any man says or does a thing you don't like—flash your gun. Don't yell for me. You can bluff this gang to a standstill."

That was a trial for Joan, when she walked out into the light in Dandy Dale's clothes. She did not step very straight, and she could feel the cold prick of her face under the mask. It was not shame, but fear that gripped her. She would rather die than have Jim Cleve recognize her in that bold disguise. A line of dusty saddled horses stood heads and bridles down before the cabin, and a number of lounging men ceased talking when she appeared. It was a crowd that smelled of dust and horses and leather and whisky and tobacco. Joan did not recognize any one there, which fact aided her in a quick recovery of her composure. Then she found amusement in the absolute sensation she made upon these loungers. They stared, open-mouthed and motionless. One old fellow dropped his pipe from bearded lips and did not seem to note the loss. A dark young man, dissipated and wild-looking, with years of lawlessness stamped upon his face, was the first to move; and he, with awkward gallantry, but with amiable disposition. Joan wanted to run, yet she forced herself to stand there, apparently unconcerned before this battery of bold and curious eyes. That, once done, made the rest easier. She was grateful for the mask. And with her first low, almost incoherent, words in reply Joan entered upon the second phase of her experience with these bandits. Naturalness did not come soon, but it did come, and with it her wit and courage.

Used as she had become to the villainous countenances of the border ruffians, she yet upon closer study discovered wilder and more abandoned ones. Yet despite that, and a brazen, unconcealed admiration, there was not lacking kindliness and sympathy and good nature. Presently Joan sauntered away, and she went among the tired, shaggy horses and made friends with them. An occasional rider swung up the trail to dismount before Kells's cabin, and once two riders rode in, both staring—all eyes—at her. The meaning of her intent alertness dawned upon her then. Always, whatever she was doing or thinking or saying, behind it all hid the driving watchfulness for Jim Cleve. And the consciousness of this fixed her mind upon him. Where was he? What was he doing? Was he drunk or gambling or fighting or sleeping? Was he still honest? When she did meet him what would happen? How could she make herself and circumstances known to him before he killed somebody? A new fear had birth and grew—Cleve would recognize her in that disguise, mask and all.

She walked up and down for a while, absorbed with this new idea. Then an unusual commotion among the loungers drew her attention to a group of men on foot surrounding and evidently escorting several horsemen. Joan recognized Red Pearce and Frenchy, and then, with a start, Jim Cleve. They were riding up the trail. Joan's heart began to pound. She could not meet Jim; she dared not trust this disguise; all her plans were as if they had never been. She forgot Kells. She even forgot her fear of what Cleve might do. The meeting—the inevitable recognition—the pain Jim Cleve must suffer when the fact and apparent significance of her presence there burst upon him, these drove all else from Joan's mind. Mask or no mask, she could not face his piercing eyes, and like a little coward she turned to enter the cabin.

Before she got in, however, it was forced upon her that something unusual had roused the loungers. They had arisen and were interested in the approaching group. Loud talk dinned in Joan's ears. Then she went in the door as Kells stalked by, eyes agleam, without even noticing her. Once inside her cabin, with the curtain drawn, Joan's fear gave place to anxiety and curiosity.

There was no one in the large cabin. Through the outer door she caught sight of a part of the crowd, close together, heads up, all noisy. Then she heard Kells's authoritative voice, but she could understand nothing. The babel of hoarse voices grew louder. Kells appeared, entering the door with Pearce. Jim Cleve came next, and, once the three were inside, the crowd spilled itself after them like angry bees. Kells was talking, Pearce was talking, but their voices were lost. Suddenly Kells vented his temper.

"Shut up—the lot of you!" he yelled, and his power and position might have been measured by the menace he showed.

The gang became suddenly quiet.

"Now—what's up?" demanded Kells.

"Keep your shirt on, boss," replied Pearce, with good humor. "There ain't much wrong.... Cleve, here, throwed a gun on Gulden, that's all."

Kells gave a slight start, barely perceptible, but the intensity of it, and a fleeting tigerish gleam across his face, impressed Joan with the idea that he felt a fiendish joy. Her own heart clamped in a cold amaze.

"Gulden!" Kells's exclamation was likewise a passionate query.

"No, he ain't cashed," replied Pearce. "You can't kill that bull so easy. But he's shot up some. He's layin' over at Beard's. Reckon you'd better go over an' dress them shots."

"He can rot before I doctor him," replied Kells. "Where's Bate Wood?... Bate, you can take my kit and go fix Gulden up. And now, Red, what was all the roar about?"

"Reckon that was Gulden's particular pards tryin' to mix it with Cleve an' Cleve tryin' to mix it with them—an' ME in between!... I'm here to say, boss, that I had a time stavin' off a scrap."

During this rapid exchange between Kells and his lieutenant, Jim Cleve sat on the edge of the table, one dusty boot swinging so that his spur jangled, a wisp of a cigarette in his lips. His face was white except where there seemed to be bruises under his eyes. Joan had never seen him look like this. She guessed that he had been drunk—perhaps was still drunk. That utterly abandoned face Joan was so keen to read made her bite her tongue to keep from crying out. Yes, Jim was lost.

"What'd they fight about?" queried Kells.

"Ask Cleve," replied Pearce. "Reckon I'd just as lief not talk any more about him."

Then Kells turned to Cleve and stepped before him. Somehow these two men face to face thrilled Joan to her depths. They presented such contrasts. Kells was keen, imperious, vital, strong, and complex, with an unmistakable friendly regard for this young outcast. Cleve seemed aloof, detached, indifferent to everything, with a white, weary, reckless scorn. Both men were far above the gaping ruffians around them.

"Cleve, why'd you draw on Gulden?" asked Kells, sharply.

"That's my business," replied Cleve, slowly, and with his piercing eyes on Kells he blew a long, thin, blue stream of smoke upward.

"Sure.... But I remember what you asked me the other day—about Gulden. Was that why?"

"Nope," replied Cleve. "This was my affair."

"All right. But I'd like to know. Pearce says you're in bad with Gulden's friends. If I can't make peace between you I'll have to take sides."

"Kells, I don't need any one on my side," said Cleve, and he flung the cigarette away.

"Yes, you do," replied Kells, persuasively. "Every man on this border needs that. And he's lucky when he gets it."

"Well, I don't ask for it; I don't want it."

"That's your own business, too. I'm not insisting or advising."

Kells's force and ability to control men manifested itself in his speech and attitude. Nothing could have been easier than to rouse the antagonism of Jim Cleve, abnormally responding as he was to the wild conditions of this border environment.

"Then you're not calling my hand?" queried Cleve, with his dark, piercing glance on Kells.

"I pass, Jim," replied the bandit, easily.

Cleve began to roll another cigarette. Joan saw his strong, brown hands tremble, and she realized that this came from his nervous condition, not from agitation. Her heart ached for him. What a white, somber face, so terribly expressive of the overthrow of his soul! He had fled to the border in reckless fury at her—at himself. There in its wildness he had, perhaps, lost thought of himself and memory of her. He had plunged into the unrestrained border life. Its changing, raw, and fateful excitement might have made him forget, but behind all was the terrible seeking to destroy and be destroyed. Joan shuddered when she remembered how she had mocked this boy's wounded vanity—how scathingly she had said he did not possess manhood and nerve enough even to be bad.

"See here, Red," said Kells to Pearce, "tell me what happened—what you saw. Jim can't object to that."

"Sure," replied Pearce, thus admonished. "We was all over at Beard's an' several games was on. Gulden rode into camp last night. He's always sore, but last night it seemed more'n usual. But he didn't say much an' nothin' happened. We all reckoned his trip fell through. Today he was restless. He walked an' walked just like a cougar in a pen. You know how Gulden has to be on the move. Well, we let him alone, you can bet. But suddenlike he comes up to our table—me an' Cleve an' Beard an' Texas was playin' cards—an' he nearly kicks the table over. I grabbed the gold an' Cleve he saved the whisky. We'd been drinkin' an' Cleve most of all. Beard was white at the gills with rage an' Texas was soffocatin'. But we all was afraid of Gulden, except Cleve, as it turned out. But he didn't move or look mean. An' Gulden pounded on the table an' addressed himself to Cleve.

"'I've a job you'll like. Come on.'

"'Job? Say, man, you couldn't have a job I'd like,' replied Cleve, slow an' cool.

"You know how Gulden gets when them spells come over him. It's just plain cussedness. I've seen gunfighters lookin' for trouble—for someone to kill. But Gulden was worse than that. You all take my hunch—he's got a screw loose in his nut.

"'Cleve,' he said, 'I located the Brander gold-diggin's—an' the girl was there.'

"Some kind of a white flash went over Cleve. An' we all, rememberin' Luce, began to bend low, ready to duck. Gulden didn't look no different from usual. You can't see any change in him. But I for one felt all hell burnin' in him.

"'Oho! You have,' said Cleve, quick, like he was pleased. 'An' did you get her?'

"'Not yet. Just looked over the ground. I'm pickin' you to go with me. We'll split on the gold, an' I'll take the girl.'

"Cleve swung the whisky-bottle an' it smashed on Gulden's mug, knockin' him flat. Cleve was up, like a cat, gun burnin' red. The other fellers were dodgin' low. An' as I ducked I seen Gulden, flat on his back, draggin' at his gun. He stopped short an' his hand flopped. The side of his face went all bloody. I made sure he'd cashed, so I leaped up an' grabbed Cleve.

"It'd been all right if Gulden had only cashed. But he hadn't. He came to an' bellered fer his gun an' fer his pards. Why, you could have heard him for a mile.... Then, as I told you, I had trouble in holdin' back a general mix-up. An' while he was hollerin' about it I led them all over to you. Gulden is layin' back there with his ear shot off. An' that's all."

Kells, with thoughtful mien, turned from Pearce to the group of dark-faced men. "This fight settles one thing," he said to them. "We've got to have organization. If you're not all a lot of fools you'll see that. You need a head. Most of you swear by me, but some of you are for Gulden. Just because he's a bloody devil. These times are the wildest the West ever knew, and they're growing wilder. Gulden is a great machine for execution. He has no sense of fear. He's a giant. He loves to fight—to kill. But Gulden's all but crazy. This last deal proves that. I leave it to your common sense. He rides around hunting for some lone camp to rob. Or some girl to make off with. He does not plan with me or the men whose judgment I have confidence in. He's always without gold. And so are most of his followers. I don't know who they are. And I don't care. But here we split—unless they and Gulden take advice and orders from me. I'm not so much siding with Cleve. Any of you ought to admit that Gulden's kind of work will disorganize a gang. He's been with us for long. And he approaches Cleve with a job. Cleve is a stranger. He may belong here, but he's not yet one of us. Gulden oughtn't have approached him. It was no straight deal. We can't figure what Gulden meant exactly, but it isn't likely he wanted Cleve to go. It was a bluff. He got called.... You men think this over—whether you'll stick to Gulden or to me. Clear out now."

His strong, direct talk evidently impressed them, and in silence they crowded out of the cabin, leaving Pearce and Cleve behind.

"Jim, are you just hell-bent on fighting or do you mean to make yourself the champion of every poor girl in these wilds?"

Cleve puffed a cloud of smoke that enveloped his head "I don't pick quarrels," he replied.

"Then you get red-headed at the very mention of a girl."

A savage gesture of Cleve's suggested that Kells was right.

"Here, don't get red-headed at me," called Kells, with piercing sharpness. "I'll be your friend if you let me.... But declare yourself like a man—if you want me for a friend!"

"Kells, I'm much obliged," replied Cleve, with a semblance of earnestness. "I'm no good or I wouldn't be out here... But I can't stand for these—these deals with girls."

"You'll change," rejoined Kells, bitterly. "Wait till you live a few lonely years out here! You don't understand the border. You're young. I've seen the gold-fields of California and Nevada. Men go crazy with the gold fever. It's gold that makes men wild. If you don't get killed you'll change. If you live you'll see life on this border. War debases the moral force of a man, but nothing like what you'll experience here the next few years. Men with their wives and daughters are pouring into this range. They're all over. They're finding gold. They've tasted blood. Wait till the great gold strike comes! Then you'll see men and women go back ten thousand years... And then what'll one girl more or less matter?"

"Well, you see, Kells, I was loved so devotedly by one and made such a hero of—that I just can't bear to see any girl mistreated."

He almost drawled the words, and he was suave and cool, and his face was inscrutable, but a bitterness in his tone gave the lie to all he said and looked.

Pearce caught the broader inference and laughed as if at a great joke. Kells shook his head doubtfully, as if Cleve's transparent speech only added to the complexity. And Cleve turned away, as if in an instant he had forgotten his comrades.

Afterward, in the silence and darkness of night, Joan Randle lay upon her bed sleepless, haunted by Jim's white face, amazed at the magnificent madness of him, thrilled to her soul by the meaning of his attack on Gulden, and tortured by a love that had grown immeasurably full of the strength of these hours of suspense and the passion of this wild border.

Even in her dreams Joan seemed to be bending all her will toward that inevitable and fateful moment when she must stand before Jim Cleve. It had to be. Therefore she would absolutely compel herself to meet it, regardless of the tumult that must rise within her. When all had been said, her experience so far among the bandits, in spite of the shocks and suspense that had made her a different girl, had been infinitely more fortunate than might have been expected. She prayed for this luck to continue and forced herself into a belief that it would.

That night she had slept in Dandy Dale's clothes, except for the boots; and sometimes while turning in restless slumber she had been awakened by rolling on the heavy gun, which she had not removed from the belt. And at such moments, she had to ponder in the darkness, to realize that she, Joan Randle, lay a captive in a bandit's camp, dressed in a dead bandit's garb, and packing his gun—even while she slept. It was such an improbable, impossible thing. Yet the cold feel of the polished gun sent a thrill of certainty through her.

In the morning she at least did not have to suffer the shame of getting into Dandy Dale's clothes, for she was already in them. She found a grain of comfort even in that. When she had put on the mask and sombrero she studied the effect in her little mirror. And she again decided that no one, not even Jim Cleve, could recognize her in that disguise. Likewise she gathered courage from the fact that even her best girl friend would have found her figure unfamiliar and striking where once it had been merely tall and slender and strong, ordinarily dressed. Then how would Jim Cleve ever recognize her? She remembered her voice that had been called a contralto, low and deep; and how she used to sing the simple songs she knew. She could not disguise that voice. But she need not let Jim hear it. Then there was a return of the idea that he would instinctively recognize her—that no disguise could be proof to a lover who had ruined himself for her. Suddenly she realized how futile all her worry and shame. Sooner or later she must reveal her identity to Jim Cleve. Out of all this complexity of emotion Joan divined that what she yearned most for was to spare Cleve the shame consequent upon recognition of her and then the agony he must suffer at a false conception of her presence there. It was a weakness in her. When death menaced her lover and the most inconceivably horrible situation yawned for her, still she could only think of her passionate yearning to have him know, all in a flash, that she loved him, that she had followed him in remorse, that she was true to him and would die before being anything else.

And when she left her cabin she was in a mood to force an issue.

Kells was sitting at the table and being served by Bate Wood.

"Hello, Dandy!" he greeted her, in surprise and pleasure. "This's early for you."

Joan returned his greeting and said that she could not sleep all the time.

"You're coming round. I'll bet you hold up a stage before a month is out."

"Hold up a stage?" echoed Joan.

"Sure. It'll be great fun," replied Kells, with a laugh. "Here—sit down and eat with me.... Bate, come along lively with breakfast.... It's fine to see you there. That mask changes you, though. No one can see how pretty you are.... Joan, your admirer, Gulden, has been incapacitated for the present."

Then in evident satisfaction Kells repeated the story that Joan had heard Red Pearce tell the night before; and in the telling Kells enlarged somewhat upon Jim Cleve.

"I've taken a liking to Cleve," said Kells. "He's a strange youngster. But he's more man than boy. I think he's broken-hearted over some rotten girl who's been faithless or something. Most women are no good, Joan. A while ago I'd have said ALL women were that, but since I've known you I think—I know different. Still, one girl out of a million doesn't change a world."

"What will this J—jim C—cleve do—when he sees—me?" asked Joan, and she choked over the name.

"Don't eat so fast, girl," said Kells. "You're only seventeen years old and you've plenty of time.... Well, I've thought some about Cleve. He's not crazy like Gulden, but he's just as dangerous. He's dangerous because he doesn't know what he's doing—has absolutely no fear of death—and then he's swift with a gun. That's a bad combination. Cleve will kill a man presently. He's shot three already, and in Gulden's case he meant to kill. If once he kills a man—that'll make him a gun-fighter. I've worried a little about his seeing you. But I can manage him, I guess. He can't be scared or driven. But he may be led. I've had Red Pearce tell him you are my wife. I hope he believes it, for none of the other fellows believe it. Anyway, you'll meet this Cleve soon, maybe to-day, and I want you to be friendly. If I can steady him—stop his drinking—he'll be the best man for me on this border."

"I'm to help persuade him to join your band?" asked Joan, and she could not yet control her voice.

"Is that so black a thing?" queried Kells, evidently nettled, and he glared at her.

"I—I don't know," faltered Joan. "Is this—this boy a criminal yet?"

"No. He's only a fine, decent young chap gone wild—gone bad for some girl. I told you that. You don't seem to grasp the point. If I can control him he'll be of value to me—he'll be a bold and clever and dangerous man—he'll last out here. If I can't win him, why, he won't last a week longer. He'll be shot or knifed in a brawl. Without my control Cleve'll go straight to the hell he's headed for."

Joan pushed back her plate and, looking up, steadily eyed the bandit.

"Kells, I'd rather he ended his—his career quick—and went to—to—than live to be a bandit and murderer at your command."

Kells laughed mockingly, yet the savage action with which he threw his cup against the wall attested to the fact that Joan had strange power to hurt him.

"That's your sympathy, because I told you some girl drove him out here," said the bandit. "He's done for. You'll know that the moment you see him. I really think he or any man out here would be the better for my interest. Now, I want to know if you'll stand by me—put in a word to help influence this wild boy."

"I'll—I'll have to see him first," replied Joan.

"Well, you take it sort of hard," growled Kells. Then presently he brightened. "I seem always to forget that you're only a kid. Listen! Now you do as you like. But I want to warn you that you've got to get back the same kind of nerve"—here he lowered his voice and glanced at Bate Wood—"that you showed when you shot me. You're going to see some sights.... A great gold strike! Men grown gold-mad! Woman of no more account than a puff of cottonseed!... Hunger, toil, pain, disease, starvation, robbery, blood, murder, hanging, death—all nothing, nothing! There will be only gold. Sleepless nights—days of hell—rush and rush—all strangers with greedy eyes! The things that made life will be forgotten and life itself will be cheap. There will be only that yellow stuff—gold—over which men go mad and women sell their souls!"

After breakfast Kells had Joan's horse brought out of the corral and saddled.

"You must ride some every day. You must keep in condition," he said. "Pretty soon we may have a chase, and I don't want it to tear you to pieces."

"Where shall I ride?" asked Joan.

"Anywhere you like up and down the gulch."

"Are you going to have me watched?"

"Not if you say you won't run off."

"You trust me?"

"Yes."

"All right. I promise. And if I change my mind I'll tell you."

"Lord! don't do it, Joan. I—I—Well, you've come to mean a good deal to me. I don't know what I'd do if I lost you." As she mounted the horse Kells added, "Don't stand any raw talk from any of the gang."

Joan rode away, pondering in mind the strange fact that though she hated this bandit, yet she had softened toward him. His eyes lit when he saw her; his voice mellowed; his manner changed. He had meant to tell her again that he loved her, yet he controlled it. Was he ashamed? Had he seen into the depths of himself and despised what he had imagined love? There were antagonistic forces at war within him.

71

It was early morning and a rosy light tinged the fresh green. She let the eager horse break into a canter and then a gallop; and she rode up the gulch till the trail started into rough ground. Then turning, she went back, down under the pines and by the cabins, to where the gulch narrowed its outlet into the wide valley. Here she met several dusty horsemen driving a pack-train. One, a jovial ruffian, threw up his hands in mock surrender.

"Hands up, pards!" he exclaimed. "Reckon we've run agin' Dandy Dale come to life."

His companions made haste to comply and then the three regarded her with bold and roguish eyes. Joan had run square into them round a corner of slope and, as there was no room to pass, she had halted.

"Shore it's the Dandy Dale we heerd of," vouchsafed another.

"Thet's Dandy's outfit with a girl inside," added the third.

Joan wheeled her horse and rode back up the trail. The glances of these ruffians seemed to scorch her with the reality of her appearance. She wore a disguise, but her womanhood was more manifest in it than in her feminine garb. It attracted the bold glances of these men. If there were any possible decency among them, this outrageous bandit costume rendered it null. How could she ever continue to wear it? Would not something good and sacred within her be sullied by a constant exposure to the effect she had upon these vile border men? She did not think it could while she loved Jim Cleve; and with thought of him came a mighty throb of her heart to assure her that nothing mattered if only she could save him.

Upon the return trip up the gulch Joan found men in sight leading horses, chopping wood, stretching arms in cabin doors. Joan avoided riding near them, yet even at a distance she was aware of their gaze. One rowdy, half hidden by a window, curved hands round his mouth and called, softly, "Hullo, sweetheart!"

Joan was ashamed that she could feel insulted. She was amazed at the temper which seemed roused in her. This border had caused her feelings she had never dreamed possible to her. Avoiding the trail, she headed for the other side of the gulch. There were clumps of willows along the brook through which she threaded a way, looking for a good place to cross. The horse snorted for water. Apparently she was not going to find any better crossing, so she turned the horse into a narrow lane through the willows and, dismounting on a mossy bank, she slipped the bridle so the horse could drink.

Suddenly she became aware that she was not alone. But she saw no one in front of her or on the other side of her horse. Then she turned. Jim Cleve was in the act of rising from his knees. He had a towel in his hand. His face was wet. He stood no more than ten steps from her.

Joan could not have repressed a little cry to save her life. The surprise was tremendous. She could not move a finger. She expected to hear him call her name.

Cleve stared at her. His face, in the morning light, was as drawn and white as that of a corpse. Only his eyes seemed alive and they were flames. A lightning flash of scorn leaped to them. He only recognized in her a woman, and his scorn was for the creature that bandit garb proclaimed her to be. A sad and bitter smile crossed his face; and then it was followed by an expression that was a lash upon Joan's bleeding spirit. He looked at her shapely person with something of the brazen and evil glance that had been so revolting to her in the eyes of those ruffians. That was the unexpected—the impossible—in connection with Jim Cleve. How could she stand there under it—and live?

She jerked at the bridle, and, wading blindly across the brook, she mounted somehow, and rode with blurred sight back to the cabin. Kells appeared busy with men outside and did not accost her. She fled to her cabin and barricaded the door.

Then she hid her face on her bed, covered herself to shut out the light, and lay there, broken-hearted. What had been that other thing she had imagined was shame—that shrinking and burning she had suffered through Kells and his men? What was that compared to this awful thing? A brand of red-hot pitch, blacker and bitterer than death, had been struck brutally across her soul. By the man she loved—whom she would have died to save! Jim Cleve had seen in her only an abandoned creature of the camps. His sad and bitter smile had been for the thought that he could have loved anything of her sex. His scorn had been for the betrayed youth and womanhood suggested by her appearance. And then the thing that struck into Joan's heart was the fact that her grace and charm of person, revealed by this costume forced upon her, had aroused Jim Cleve's first response to the evil surrounding him, the first call to that baseness he must be assimilating from these border ruffians. That he could look at her so! The girl he had loved! Joan's agony lay not in the circumstance of his being as mistaken in her character as he had been in her identity, but that she, of all women, had to be the one who made him answer, like Kells and Gulden and all those ruffians, to the instincts of a beast.

"Oh, he'd been drunk—he was drunk!" whispered Joan. "He isn't to be blamed. He's not my old Jim. He's suffering—he's changed—he doesn't care. What could I expect—standing there like a hussy before him—in this—this indecent rig?... I must see him. I must tell him. If he recognized me now—and I had no chance to tell him why I'm here—why I look like this—that I love him—am still good—and true to him—if I couldn't tell him I'd—I'd shoot myself!"

Joan sobbed out the final words and then broke down. And when the spell had exercised its sway, leaving her limp and shaken and weak, she was the better for it. Slowly calmness returned so that she could look at her wild and furious rush from the spot where she had faced Jim Cleve, at the storm of shame ending in her collapse. She realized that if she had met Jim Cleve here in the dress in which she had left home there would have been the same shock of surprise and fear and love. She owed part of that breakdown to the suspense she had been under and then the suddenness of the meeting. Looking back at her agitation, she felt that it had been natural—that if she could only tell the truth to Jim Cleve the situation was not impossible. But the meeting, and all following it, bore tremendous revelation of how through all this wild experience she had learned to love Jim Cleve. But for his reckless flight and her blind pursuit, and then the anxiety, fear, pain, toil, and despair, she would never have known her woman's heart and its capacity for love.

11

Following that meeting, with all its power to change and strengthen Joan, there were uneventful days in which she rode the gulch trails and grew able to stand the jests and glances of the bandit's gang. She thought she saw and heard everything, yet insulated her true self in a callous and unreceptive aloofness from all that affronted her.

The days were uneventful because, while always looking for Jim Cleve, she never once saw him. Several times she heard his name mentioned. He was here and there—at Beard's off in the mountains. But he did not come to Kells's cabin, which fact, Joan gathered, had made Kells anxious. He did not want to lose Cleve. Joan peered from her covert in the evenings, and watched for Jim, and grew weary of the loud talk and laughter, the gambling and smoking and drinking. When there seemed no more chance of Cleve's coming, then Joan went to bed.

On these occasions Joan learned that Kells was passionately keen to gamble, that he was a weak hand at cards, an honest gambler, and, strangely enough, a poor loser. Moreover, when he lost he drank heavily, and under the influence of drink he was dangerous. There were quarrels when curses rang throughout the cabin, when guns were drawn, but whatever Kells's weaknesses might be, he was strong and implacable in the governing of these men.

That night when Gulden strode into the cabin was certainly not uneventful for Joan. Sight of him sent a chill to her marrow while a strange thrill of fire inflamed her. Was that great hulk of a gorilla prowling about to meet Jim Cleve? Joan thought that it might be the worse for him if he were. Then she shuddered a little to think that she had already been influenced by the wildness around her.

Gulden appeared well and strong, and but for the bandage on his head would have been as she remembered him. He manifested interest in the gambling of the players by surly grunts. Presently he said something to Kells.

"What?" queried the bandit, sharply, wheeling, the better to see Gulden.

The noise subsided. One gamester laughed knowingly.

"Lend me a sack of dust?" asked Gulden.

Kells's face showed amaze and then a sudden brightness.

"What! You want gold from me?"

"Yes. I'll pay it back."

"Gulden, I wasn't doubting that. But does your asking mean you've taken kindly to my proposition?"

"You can take it that way," growled Gulden. "I want gold." "I'm mighty glad, Gulden," replied Kells, and he looked as if he meant it. "I need you. We ought to get along.... Here."

He handed a small buckskin sack to Gulden. Someone made room for him on the other side of the table, and the game was resumed. It was interesting to watch them gamble. Red Pearce had a scale at his end of the table, and he was always measuring and weighing out gold-dust. The value of the gold appeared to be fifteen dollars to the ounce, but the real value of money did not actuate the gamblers. They spilled the dust on the table and ground as if it were as common as sand. Still there did not seem to be any great quantity of gold in sight. Evidently these were not profitable times for the bandits. More than once Joan heard them speak of a gold strike as honest people spoke of good fortune. And these robbers could only have meant that in case of a rich strike there would be gold to steal. Gulden gambled as he did everything else. At first he won and then he lost, and then he borrowed more from Kells, to win again. He paid back as he had borrowed and lost and won—without feeling. He had no excitement. Joan's intuition convinced her that if Gulden had any motive at all in gambling it was only an antagonism to men of his breed. Gambling was a contest, a kind of fight.

Most of the men except Gulden drank heavily that night. There had been fresh liquor come with the last pack-train. Many of them were drunk when the game broke up. Red Pearce and Wood remained behind with Kells after the others had gone, and Pearce was clever enough to cheat Kells before he left.

"Boss—thet there Red double—crossed you," said Bate Wood.

Kells had lost heavily, and he was under the influence of drink. He drove Wood out of the cabin, cursing him sullenly. Then he put in place the several bars that served as a door of his cabin. After that he walked unsteadily around, and all about his action and manner that was not aimless seemed to be dark and intermittent staring toward Joan's cabin. She felt sickened again with this new aspect of her situation, but she was not in the least afraid of Kells. She watched him till he approached her door and then she drew back a little. He paused before the blanket as if he had been impelled to halt from fear. He seemed to be groping in thought. Then he cautiously and gradually, by degrees, drew aside the blanket. He could not see Joan in the darkness, but she saw him plainly. He fumbled at the poles, and, finding that he could not budge them, he ceased trying. There was nothing forceful or strong about him, such as was manifest when he was sober. He stood there a moment, breathing heavily, in a kind of forlorn, undecided way, and then he turned back. Joan heard him snap the lanterns. The lights went out and all grew dark and silent.

Next morning at breakfast he was himself again, and if he had any knowledge whatever of his actions while he was drunk, he effectually concealed it from Joan.

Later, when Joan went outside to take her usual morning exercise, she was interested to see a rider tearing up the slope on a foam-flecked horse. Men shouted at him from the cabins and then followed without hats or coats. Bate Wood dropped Joan's saddle and called to Kells. The bandit came hurriedly out.

"Blicky!" he exclaimed, and then he swore under his breath in elation.

"Shore is Blicky!" said Wood, and his unusually mild eyes snapped with a glint unpleasant for Joan to see.

The arrival of this Blicky appeared to be occasion for excitement and Joan recalled the name as belonging to one of Kells's trusted men. He swung his leg and leaped from his saddle as the horse plunged to a halt. Blicky was a lean, bronzed young man, scarcely out of his teens, but there were years of hard life in his face. He slapped the dust in little puffs from his gloves. At sight of Kells he threw the gloves aloft and took no note of them when they fell. "STRIKE!" he called, piercingly.

"No!" ejaculated Kells, intensely.

Bate Wood let out a whoop which was answered by the men hurrying up the slope.

"Been on—for weeks!" panted Blicky. "It's big. Can't tell how big. Me an' Jesse Smith an' Handy Oliver hit a new road—over here fifty miles as a crow flies—a hundred by trail. We was plumb surprised. An' when we met pack-trains an' riders an' prairie-schooners an' a stage-coach we knew there was doin's over in the Bear Mountain range. When we came to the edge of the diggin's an' seen a whalin' big camp—like a beehive—Jesse an' Handy went on to get the lay of the land an' I hit the trail back to you. I've been a-comin' on an' off since before sundown yesterday.... Jesse gave one look an' then hollered. He said, 'Tell Jack it's big an' he wants to plan big. We'll be back there in a day or so with all details.'"

Joan watched Kells intently while he listened to this breathless narrative of a gold strike, and she was repelled by the singular flash of brightness—a radiance—that seemed to be in his eyes and on his face. He did not say a word, but his men shouted hoarsely around Blicky. He walked a few paces to and fro with hands strongly clenched, his lips slightly parted, showing teeth close-shut like those of a mastiff. He looked eager, passionate, cunning, hard as steel, and that strange brightness of elation slowly shaded to a dark, brooding menace. Suddenly he wheeled to silence the noisy men.

"Where're Pearce and Gulden? Do they know?" he demanded.

"Reckon no one knows but who's right here," replied Blicky.

"Red an' Gul are sleepin' off last night's luck," said Bate Wood.

"Have any of you seen young Cleve?" Kells went on. His voice rang quick and sharp.

No one spoke, and presently Kells cracked his fist into his open hand.

"Come on. Get the gang together at Beard's.... Boys, the time we've been gambling on has come. Jesse Smith saw '49 and '51. He wouldn't send me word like this—unless there was hell to pay.... Come on!"

He strode off down the slope with the men close around him, and they met other men on the way, all of whom crowded into the group, jostling, eager, gesticulating.

Joan was left alone. She felt considerably perturbed, especially at Kells's sharp inquiry for Jim Cleve. Kells might persuade him to join that bandit legion. These men made Joan think of wolves, with Kells the keen and savage leader. No one had given a thought to Blicky's horse and that neglect in border men was a sign of unusual preoccupation. The horse was in bad shape. Joan took off his saddle and bridle, and rubbed the dust-caked lather from his flanks, and led him into the corral. Then she fetched a bucket of water and let him drink sparingly, a little at a time.

Joan did not take her ride that morning. Anxious and curious, she waited for the return of Kells. But he did not come. All afternoon Joan waited and watched, and saw no sign of him or any of the other men. She knew Kells was forging with red-hot iron and blood that organization which she undesignedly had given a name—the Border Legion. It would be a terrible legion, of that she was assured. Kells was the evil genius to create an unparalleled scheme of crime; this wild and remote border, with its inaccessible fastness for hiding-places, was the place; all that was wanting was the time, which evidently had arrived. She remembered how her uncle had always claimed that the Bear Mountain range would see a gold strike which would disrupt the whole West and amaze the world. And Blicky had said a big strike had been on for weeks. Kells's prophecy of the wild life Joan would see had not been without warrant. She had already seen enough to whiten her hair, she thought, yet she divined her experience would shrink in comparison with what was to come. Always she lived in the future. She spent sleeping and waking hours in dreams, thoughts, actions, broodings, over all of which hung an ever-present shadow of suspense. When would she meet Jim Cleve again? When would he recognize her? What would he do? What could she do? Would Kells be a devil or a man at the end? Was there any justification of her haunting fear of Gulden—of her suspicion that she alone was the cause of his attitude toward Kells—of her horror at the unshakable presentiment and fancy that he was a gorilla and meant to make off with her? These, and a thousand other fears, some groundless, but many real and present, besieged Joan and left her little peace. What would happen next?

Toward sunset she grew tired of waiting, and hungry, besides, so she went into the cabin and prepared her own meal. About dark Kells strode in, and it took but a glance for Joan to see that matters had not gone to his liking. The man seemed to be burning inwardly. Sight of Joan absolutely surprised him. Evidently in the fever of this momentous hour he had forgotten his prisoner. Then, whatever his obsession, he looked like a man whose eyes were gladdened at sight of her and who was sorry to behold her there. He apologized that her supper had not been provided for her and explained that he had forgotten. The men had been crazy—hard to manage—the issue was not yet settled. He spoke gently. Suddenly he had that thoughtful mien which Joan had become used to associating with weakness in him.

"I wish I hadn't dragged you here," he said, taking her hands. "It's too late. I CAN'T lose you.... But the—OTHER WAY—isn't too late!"

"What way? What do you mean?" asked Joan.

"Girl, will you ride off with me to-night?" he whispered, hoarsely. "I swear I'll marry you—and become an honest man. To-morrow will be too late!... Will you?"

Joan shook her head. She was sorry for him. When he talked like this he was not Kells, the bandit. She could not resist a strange agitation at the intensity of his emotion. One moment he had entered—a bandit leader, planning blood, murder; the next, as his gaze found her, he seemed weakened, broken in the shaking grip of a hopeless love for her.

"Speak, Joan!" he said, with his hands tightening and his brow clouding.

"No, Kells," she replied.

"Why? Because I'm a red-handed bandit?"

"No. Because I—I don't love you."

"But wouldn't you rather be my wife—and have me honest—than become a slave here, eventually abandoned to—to Gulden and his cave and his rope?" Kells's voice rose as that other side of him gained dominance.

"Yes, I would.... But I KNOW you'll never harm me—or abandon me to—to that Gulden."

"HOW do you know?" he cried, with the blood thick at his temples.

"Because you're no beast any more.... And you—you do love me."

Kells thrust her from him so fiercely that she nearly fell.

"I'll get over it.... Then—look out!" he said, with dark bitterness.

With that he waved her back, apparently ordering her to her cabin, and turned to the door, through which the deep voices of men sounded nearer and nearer.

Joan stumbled in the darkness up the rude steps to her room, and, softly placing the poles in readiness to close her door, she composed herself to watch and wait. The keen edge of her nerves, almost amounting to pain, told her that this night of such moment for Kells would be one of singular strain and significance for her. But why she could not fathom. She felt herself caught by the changing tide of events—a tide that must sweep her on to flood. Kells had gone outside. The strong, deep voices' grew less distinct. Evidently the men were walking away. In her suspense Joan was disappointed. Presently, however, they returned; they had been walking to and fro. After a few moments Kells entered alone. The cabin was now so dark that Joan could barely distinguish the bandit. Then he lighted the lanterns. He hung up several on the wall and placed two upon the table. From somewhere among his effects he produced a small book and a pencil; these, with a heavy, gold-mounted gun, he laid on the table before the seat he manifestly meant to occupy. That done, he began a slow pacing up and down the room, his hands behind his back, his head bent in deep and absorbing thought. What a dark, sinister, plotting figure! Joan had seen many men in different attitudes of thought, but here was a man whose mind seemed to give forth intangible yet terrible manifestations of evil. The inside of that gloomy cabin took on another aspect; there was a meaning in the saddles and bridles and weapons on the wall; that book and pencil and gun seemed to contain the dark deeds of wild men; and all about the bandit hovered a power sinister in its menace to the unknown and distant toilers for gold.

Kells lifted his head, as if listening, and then the whole manner of the man changed. The burden that weighed upon him was thrown aside. Like a general about to inspect a line of soldiers Kells faced the door, keen, stern, commanding. The heavy tread of booted men, the clink of spurs, the low, muffled sound of voices, warned Joan that the gang had arrived. Would Jim Cleve be among them?

Joan wanted a better position in which to watch and listen. She thought a moment, and then carefully felt her way around to the other side of the steps, and here, sitting down with her feet hanging over the drop, she leaned against the wall and through a chink between the logs had a perfect view of the large cabin. The men were filing in silent and intense. Joan counted twenty-seven in all. They appeared to fall into two groups, and it was significant that the larger group lined up on the side nearest Kells, and the smaller back of Gulden. He had removed the bandage, and with a raw, red blotch where his right ear had been shot away, he was hideous. There was some kind of power emanating from him, but it was not that which, was so keenly vital and impelling in Kells. It was brute ferocity, dominating by sheer physical force. In any but muscular clash between Kells and Gulden the latter must lose. The men back of Gulden were a bearded, check-shirted, heavily armed group, the worst of that bad lot. All the younger, cleaner-cut men like Red Pearce and Frenchy and Beady Jones and Williams and the scout Blicky, were on the other side. There were two factions here, yet scarcely an antagonism, except possibly in the case of Kells. Joan felt that the atmosphere was supercharged with suspense and fatality and possibility—and anything might happen. To her great joy, Jim Cleve was not present.

"Where're Beard and Wood?" queried Kells.

"Workin' over Beard's sick hoss," replied Pearce. "They'll show up by an' by. Anythin' you say goes with them, you know."

"Did you find young Cleve?"

"No. He camps up in the timber somewheres. Reckon he'll be along, too."

Kells sat down at the head of the table, and, taking up the little book, he began to finger it while his pale eyes studied the men before him.

"We shuffled the deck pretty well over at Beard's," he said. "Now for the deal.... Who wants cards?... I've organized my Border Legion. I'll have absolute control, whether there're ten men or a hundred. Now, whose names go down in my book?"

Red Pearce stepped up and labored over the writing of his name. Blicky, Jones, Williams, and others followed suit. They did not speak, but each shook hands with the leader. Evidently Kells exacted no oath, but accepted each man's free action and his word of honor. There was that about the bandit which made such action as binding as ties of blood. He did not want men in his Legion who had not loyalty to him. He seemed the kind of leader to whom men would be true.

"Kells, say them conditions over again," requested one of the men, less eager to hurry with the matter.

At this juncture Joan was at once thrilled and frightened to see Jim Cleve enter the cabin. He appeared whiter of face, almost ghastly, and his piercing eyes swept the room, from Kells to Gulden, from men to men. Then he leaned against the wall, indistinct in the shadow. Kells gave no sign that he had noted the advent of Cleve.

"I'm the leader," replied Kells, deliberately. "I'll make the plans. I'll issue orders. No jobs without my knowledge. Equal shares in gold—man to man.... Your word to stand by me!"

A muttering of approval ran through the listening group.

"Reckon I'll join," said the man who had wished the conditions repeated. With that he advanced to the table and, apparently not being able to write, he made his mark in the book. Kells wrote the name below. The other men of this contingent one by one complied with Kells's requirements. This action left Gulden and his group to be dealt with.

"Gulden, are you still on the fence?" demanded Kells, coolly.

The giant strode stolidly forward to the table. As always before to Joan, he seemed to be a ponderous hulk, slow, heavy, plodding, with a mind to match.

"Kells, if we can agree I'll join," he said in his sonorous voice.

"You can bet you won't join unless we do agree," snapped Kells. "But—see here, Gulden. Let's be friendly. The border is big enough for both of us. I want you. I need you. Still, if we can't agree, let's not split and be enemies. How about it?"

Another muttering among the men attested to the good sense and good will of Kells's suggestion.

"Tell me what you're going to do—how you'll operate," replied Gulden.

Keils had difficulty in restraining his impatience and annoyance.

"What's that to you or any of you?" he queried. "You all know I'm the man to think of things. That's been proved. First it takes brains. I'll furnish them. Then it takes execution. You and Pearce and the gang will furnish that. What more do you need to know?"

"How're you going to operate?" persisted Gulden.

Kells threw up both hands as if it was useless to argue or reason with this desperado.

"All right, I'll tell you," he replied. "Listen.... I can't say what definite plans I'll make till Jesse Smith reports, and then when I get on the diggings. But here's a working basis. Now don't miss a word of this, Gulden—nor any of you men. We'll pack our outfits down to this gold strike. We'll build cabins on the outskirts of the town, and we won't hang together. The gang will be spread out. Most of you must make a bluff at digging gold. Be like other miners. Get in with cliques and clans. Dig, drink, gamble like the rest of them. Beard will start a gambling-place. Red Pearce will find some other kind of work. I'll buy up claims—employ miners to work them. I'll disguise myself and get in with the influential men and have a voice in matters. You'll all be scouts. You'll come to my cabin at night to report. We'll not tackle any little jobs. Miners going out with fifty or a hundred pounds of gold—the wagons—the stage-coach—these we'll have timed to rights, and whoever I detail on the job will hold them up. You must all keep sober, if that's possible. You must all absolutely trust to my judgment. You must all go masked while on a job. You must never speak a word that might direct suspicion to you. In this way we may work all summer without detection. The Border Legion will become mysterious and famous. It will appear to be a large number of men, operating all over. The more secretive we are the more powerful the effect on the diggings. In gold-camps, when there's a strike, all men are mad. They suspect each other. They can't organize. We shall have them helpless.... And in short, if it's as rich a strike as looks due here in these hills, before winter we can pack out all the gold our horses can carry."

Kells had begun under restraint, but the sound of his voice, the liberation of his great idea, roused him to a passion. The man radiated with passion. This, then, was his dream—the empire he aspired to.

He had a powerful effect upon his listeners, except Gulden; and it was evident to Joan that the keen bandit was conscious of his influence. Gulden, however, showed nothing that he had not already showed. He was always a strange, dominating figure. He contested the relations of things. Kells watched him—the men watched him—and Jim Cleve's piercing eyes glittered in the shadow, fixed upon that massive face. Manifestly Gulden meant to speak, but in his slowness there was no laboring, no pause from emotion. He had an idea and it moved like he moved.

"DEAD MEN TELL NO TALES!" The words boomed deep from his cavernous chest, a mutter that was a rumble, with something almost solemn in its note and certainly menacing, breathing murder. As Kells had propounded his ideas, revealing his power to devise a remarkable scheme and his passion for gold, so Gulden struck out with the driving inhuman blood-lust that must have been the twist, the knot, the clot in his brain. Kells craved notoriety and gold; Gulden craved to kill. In the silence that followed his speech these wild border ruffians judged him, measured him, understood him, and though some of them grew farther aloof from him, more of them sensed the safety that hid in his terrible implication.

But Kells rose against him.

"Gulden, you mean when we steal gold—to leave only dead men behind?" he queried, with a hiss in his voice.

The giant nodded grimly.

"But only fools kill—unless in self-defense," declared Kells, passionately.

"We'd last longer," replied Gulden, imperturbably.

"No—no. We'd never last so long. Killings rouse a mining-camp after a while—gold fever or no. That means a vigilante band."

"We can belong to the vigilantes, just as well as to your Legion," said Gulden.

The effect of this was to make Gulden appear less of a fool than Kells supposed him. The ruffians nodded to one another. They stirred restlessly. They were animated by a strange and provocative influence. Even Red Pearce and the others caught its subtlety. It was evil predominating in evil hearts. Blood and death loomed like a shadow here. The keen Kells saw the change working toward a transformation and he seemed craftily fighting something within him that opposed this cold ruthlessness of his men.

"Gulden, suppose I don't see it your way?" he asked.

"Then I won't join your Legion."

"What WILL you do?"

"I'll take the men who stand by me and go clean up that gold-camp."

From the fleeting expression on Kells's face Joan read that he knew Gulden's project would defeat his own and render both enterprises fatal.

"Gulden, I don't want to lose you," he said.

"You won't lose me if you see this thing right," replied Gulden. "You've got the brains to direct us. But, Kells, you're losing your nerve.... It's this girl you've got here!"

Gulden spoke without rancor or fear or feeling of any kind. He merely spoke the truth. And it shook Kells with an almost ungovernable fury.

Joan saw the green glare of his eyes—his gray working face—the flutter of his hand. She had an almost superhuman insight into the workings of his mind. She knew that then—he was fighting whether or not to kill Gulden on the spot. And she recognized that this was the time when Kells must kill Gulden or from that moment see a gradual diminishing of his power on the border. But Kells did not recognize that crucial height of his career. His struggle with his fury and hate showed that the thing uppermost in his mind was the need of conciliating Gulden and thus regaining a hold over the men.

"Gulden, suppose we waive the question till we're on the grounds?" he suggested.

"Waive nothing. It's one or the other with me," declared Gulden.

"Do you want to be leader of this Border Legion?" went on Kells, deliberately.

"No."

"Then what do you want?"

Gulden appeared at a loss for an instant reply. "I want plenty to do," he replied, presently. "I want to be in on everything. I want to be free to kill a man when I like."

"When you like!" retorted Kells, and added a curse. Then as if by magic his dark face cleared and there was infinite depth and craftiness in him. His opposition, and that hint of hate and loathing which detached him from Gulden, faded from his bearing. "Gulden, I'll split the difference between us. I'll leave you free to do as you like. But all the others—every man—must take orders from me."

Gulden reached out a huge hand. His instant acceptance evidently amazed Kells and the others.

"LET HER RIP!" Gulden exclaimed. He shook Kells's hand and then laboriously wrote his name in the little book.

In that moment Gulden stood out alone in the midst of wild abandoned men. What were Kells and this Legion to him? What was the stealing of more or less gold?

"Free to do as you like except fight my men," said Kells. "That's understood."

"If they don't pick a fight with me," added the giant, and he grinned.

One by one his followers went through with the simple observances that Kells's personality made a serious and binding compact.

"Anybody else?" called Kells, glancing round. The somberness was leaving his face.

"Here's Jim Cleve," said Pearce, pointing toward the wall.

"Hello, youngster! Come here. I'm wanting you bad," said Kells.

Cleve sauntered out of the shadow, and his glittering eyes were fixed on Gulden. There was an instant of waiting. Gulden looked at Cleve. Then Kells quickly strode between them.

"Say, I forgot you fellows had trouble," he said. He attended solely to Gulden. "You can't renew your quarrel now. Gulden, we've all fought together more or less, and then been good friends. I want Cleve to join us, but not against your ill will. How about it?"

"I've no ill will," replied the giant, and the strangeness of his remark lay in its evident truth. "But I won't stand to lose my other ear!"

Then the ruffians guffawed in hoarse mirth. Gulden, however, did not seem to see any humor in his remark. Kells laughed with the rest. Even Cleve's white face relaxed into a semblance of a smile.

"That's good. We're getting together," declared Kells. Then he faced Cleve, all about him expressive of elation, of assurance, of power. "Jim, will you draw cards in this deal?"

"What's the deal?" asked Cleve.

Then in swift, eloquent speech Kells launched the idea of his Border Legion, its advantages to any loose-footed, young outcast, and he ended his brief talk with much the same argument he had given Joan. Back there in her covert Joan listened and watched, mindful of the great need of controlling her emotions. The instant Jim Cleve had stalked into the light she had been seized by a spasm of trembling.

"Kells, I don't care two straws one way or another," replied Cleve.

The bandit appeared nonplussed. "You don't care whether you join my Legion or whether you don't?"

"Not a damn," was the indifferent answer.

"Then do me a favor," went on Kells. "Join to please me. We'll be good friends. You're in bad out here on the border. You might as well fall in with us."

"I'd rather go alone."

"But you won't last."

"It's a lot I care."

The bandit studied the reckless, white face. "See here, Cleve—haven't you got the nerve to be bad—thoroughly bad?"

Cleve gave a start as if he had been stung. Joan shut her eyes to blot out what she saw in his face. Kells had used part of the very speech with which she had driven Jim Cleve to his ruin. And those words galvanized him. The fatality of all this! Joan hated herself. Those very words of hers would drive this maddened and heartbroken boy to join Kells's band. She knew what to expect from Jim even before she opened her eyes; yet when she did open them it was to see him transformed and blazing.

Then Kells either gave way to leaping passion or simulated it in the interest of his cunning.

"Cleve, you're going down for a woman?" he queried, with that sharp, mocking ring in his voice.

"If you don't shut up you'll get there first," replied Cleve, menacingly.

"Bah!... Why do you want to throw a gun on me? I'm your friend: You're sick. You're like a poisoned pup. I say if you've got nerve you won't quit. You'll take a run for your money. You'll see life. You'll fight. You'll win some gold. There are other women. Once I thought I would quit for a woman. But I didn't. I never found the right one till I had gone to hell—out here on this border.... If you've got nerve, show me. Be a man instead of a crazy youngster. Spit out the poison.... Tell it before us all!... Some girl drove you to us?"

"Yes—a girl!" replied Cleve, hoarsely, as if goaded.

"It's too late to go back?"

"Too late!"

"There's nothing left but wild life that makes you forget?"

"Nothing.... Only I—can't forget!" he panted.

Cleve was in a torture of memory, of despair, of weakness. Joan saw how Kells worked upon Jim's feelings. He was only a hopeless, passionate boy in the hands of a strong, implacable man. He would be like wax to a sculptor's touch. Jim would bend to this bandit's will, and through his very tenacity of love and memory be driven farther on the road to drink, to gaming, and to crime.

Joan got to her feet, and with all her woman's soul uplifting and inflaming her she stood ready to meet the moment that portended.

Kells made a gesture of savage violence. "Show your nerve!... Join with me!... You'll make a name on this border that the West will never forget!"

That last hint of desperate fame was the crafty bandit's best trump. And it won. Cleve swept up a weak and nervous hand to brush the hair from his damp brow. The keenness, the fire, the aloofness had departed from him. He looked shaken as if by something that had been pointed out as his own cowardice.

"Sure, Kells," he said, recklessly. "Let me in the game.... And—by God—I'll play—the hand out!" He reached for the pencil and bent over the book.

"Wait!... Oh, WAIT!" cried Joan. The passion of that moment, the consciousness of its fateful portent and her situation, as desperate as Cleve's, gave her voice a singularly high and piercingly sweet intensity. She glided from behind the blanket—out of the shadow—into the glare of the lanterns—to face Kells and Cleve.

Kells gave one astounded glance at her, and then, divining her purpose, he laughed thrillingly and mockingly, as if the sight of her was a spur, as if her courage was a thing to admire, to permit, and to regret.

"Cleve, my wife, Dandy Dale," he said, suave and cool. "Let her persuade you—one way or another!"

The presence of a woman, however disguised, following her singular appeal, transformed Cleve. He stiffened erect and the flush died out of his face, leaving it whiter than ever, and the eyes that had grown dull quickened and began to burn. Joan felt her cheeks blanch. She all but fainted under that gaze. But he did not recognize her, though he was strangely affected.

"Wait!" she cried again, and she held to that high voice, so different from her natural tone. "I've been listening. I've heard all that's been said. Don't join this Border Legion.... You're young—and still, honest. For God's sake—don't go the way of these men! Kells will make you a bandit.... Go home—boy—go home!"

"Who are you—to speak to me of honesty—of home?" Cleve demanded.

"I'm only a—a woman.... But I can feel how wrong you are.... Go back to that girl—who—who drove you to the border.... She must repent. In a day you'll be too late.... Oh, boy, go home!

Girls never know their minds—their hearts. Maybe your girl—loved you!... Oh, maybe her heart is breaking now!"

A strong, muscular ripple went over Cleve, ending in a gesture of fierce protest. Was it pain her words caused, or disgust that such as she dared mention the girl he had loved? Joan could not tell. She only knew that Cleve was drawn by her presence, fascinated and repelled, subtly responding to the spirit of her, doubting what he heard and believing with his eyes.

"You beg me not to become a bandit?" he asked, slowly, as if revolving a strange idea.

"Oh, I implore you!"

"Why?"

"I told you. Because you're still good at heart. You've only been wild.... Because—"

"Are you the wife of Kells?" he flashed at her.

A reply seemed slowly wrenched from Joan's reluctant lips. "No!"

The denial left a silence behind it. The truth that all knew when spoken by her was a kind of shock. The ruffians gaped in breathless attention. Kells looked on with a sardonic grin, but he had grown pale. And upon the face of Cleve shone an immeasurable scorn.

"Not his wife!" exclaimed Cleve, softly.

His tone was unendurable to Joan. She began to shrink. A flame curled within her. How he must hate any creature of her sex!

"And you appeal to me!" he went on. Suddenly a weariness came over him. The complexity of women was beyond him. Almost he turned his back upon her. "I reckon such as you can't keep me from Kells—or blood—or hell!"

"Then you're a narrow-souled weakling—born to crime!" she burst out in magnificent wrath. "For however appearances are against me—I am a good woman!"

That stunned him, just as it drew Kells upright, white and watchful. Cleve seemed long in grasping its significance. His face was half averted. Then he turned slowly, all strung, and his hands clutched quiveringly at the air. No man of coolness and judgment would have addressed him or moved a step in that strained moment. All expected some such action as had marked his encounter with Luce and Gulden.

Then Cleve's gaze in unmistakable meaning swept over Joan's person. How could her appearance and her appeal be reconciled? One was a lie! And his burning eyes robbed Joan of spirit.

"He forced me to—to wear these," she faltered. "I'm his prisoner. I'm helpless."

With catlike agility Cleve leaped backward, so that he faced all the men, and when his hands swept to a level they held gleaming guns. His utter abandon of daring transfixed these bandits in surprise as much as fear. Kells appeared to take most to himself the menace.

"*I* CRAWL!" he said, huskily. "She speaks the God's truth.... But you can't help matters by killing me. Maybe she'd be worse off!"

He expected this wild boy to break loose, yet his wit directed him to speak the one thing calculated to check Cleve.

"Oh, don't shoot!" moaned Joan.

"You go outside," ordered Cleve. "Get on a horse and lead another near the door.... Go! I'll take you away from this."

Both temptation and terror assailed Joan. Surely that venture would mean only death to Jim and worse for her. She thrilled at the thought—at the possibility of escape—at the strange front of this erstwhile nerveless boy. But she had not the courage for what seemed only desperate folly.

"I'll stay," she whispered. "You go!"

"Hurry, woman!"

"No! No!"

"Do you want to stay with this bandit?"

"Oh, I must!"

"Then you love him?"

All the fire of Joan's heart flared up to deny the insult and all her woman's cunning fought to keep back words that inevitably must lead to revelation. She drooped, unable to hold up under her shame, yet strong to let him think vilely of her, for his sake. That way she had a barest chance.

"Get out of my sight!" he ejaculated, thickly. "I'd have fought for you."

Again that white, weary scorn radiated from him. Joan bit her tongue to keep from screaming. How could she live under this torment? It was she, Joan Randle, that had earned that scorn, whether he knew her or not. She shrank back, step by step, almost dazed, sick with a terrible inward, coldness, blinded by scalding tears. She found her door and stumbled in.

"Kells, I'm what you called me." She heard Cleve's voice, strangely far off. "There's no excuse... unless I'm not just right in my head about women.... Overlook my break or don't—as you like. But if you want me I'm ready for your Border Legion!"

85

12

Those bitter words of Cleve's, as if he mocked himself, were the last Joan heard, and they rang in her ears and seemed to reverberate through her dazed mind like a knell of doom. She lay there, all blackness about her, weighed upon by an insupportable burden; and she prayed that day might never dawn for her; a nightmare of oblivion ended at last with her eyes opening to the morning light.

She was cold and stiff. She had lain uncovered all the long hours of night. She had not moved a finger since she had fallen upon the bed, crushed by those bitter words with which Cleve had consented to join Kells's Legion. Since then Joan felt that she had lived years. She could not remember a single thought she might have had during those black hours; nevertheless, a decision had been formed in her mind, and it was that to-day she would reveal herself to Jim Cleve if it cost both their lives. Death was infinitely better than the suspense and fear and agony she had endured; and as for Jim, it would at least save him from crime.

Joan got up, a little dizzy and unsteady upon her feet. Her hands appeared clumsy and shaky. All the blood in her seemed to surge from heart to brain and it hurt her to breathe. Removing her mask, she bathed her face and combed her hair. At first she conceived an idea to go out without her face covered, but she thought better of it. Cleve's reckless defiance had communicated itself to her. She could not now be stopped.

Kells was gay and excited that morning. He paid her compliments. He said they would soon be out of this lonely gulch and she would see the sight of her life—a gold strike. She would see men wager a fortune on the turn of a card, lose, laugh, and go back to the digging. He said he would take her to Sacramento and 'Frisco and buy her everything any girl could desire. He was wild, voluble, unreasoning—obsessed by the anticipated fulfilment of his dream.

It was rather late in the morning and there were a dozen or more men in and around the cabin, all as excited as Kells. Preparations were already under way for the expected journey to the gold-field. Packs were being laid out, overhauled, and repacked; saddles and bridles and weapons were being worked over; clothes were being awkwardly mended. Horses were being shod, and the job was as hard and disagreeable for men as for horses. Whenever a rider swung up the slope, and one came every now and then, all the robbers would leave off their tasks and start eagerly for the newcomer. The name Jesse Smith was on everybody's lips. Any hour he might be expected to arrive and corroborate Blicky's alluring tale.

Joan saw or imagined she saw that the glances in the eyes of these men were yellow, like gold fire. She had seen miners and prospectors whose eyes shone with a strange glory of light that gold inspired, but never as those of Kells's bandit Legion. Presently Joan discovered that, despite the excitement, her effect upon them was more marked then ever, and by a difference that she was quick to feel. But she could not tell what this difference was—how their attitude had changed. Then she set herself the task of being useful. First she helped Bate Wood. He was roughly kind. She had not realized that there was sadness about her until he whispered: "Don't be downcast, miss. Mebbe it'll come out right yet!" That amazed Joan. Then his mysterious winks and glances, the sympathy she felt in him, all attested to some kind of a change. She grew keen to learn, but she did not know how. She felt the change in all the men. Then she went to Pearce and with all a woman's craft she exaggerated the silent sadness that had brought quick response from Wood. Red Pearce was even quicker. He did not seem to regard her proximity as that of a feminine thing which roused the devil in him. Pearce could not be other than coarse and vulgar, but there was pity in him. Joan sensed pity and some other quality still beyond her. This lieutenant of the bandit Kells was just as mysterious as Wood. Joan mended a great jagged rent in his buckskin shirt. Pearce appeared proud of her work; he tried to joke; he said amiable things. Then as she finished he glanced furtively round; he pressed her hand: "I had a sister once!" he whispered. And then with a dark and baleful hate: "Kells!—he'll get his over in the gold-camp!"

Joan turned away from Pearce still more amazed. Some strange, deep undercurrent was working here. There had been unmistakable hate for Kells in his dark look and a fierce implication in his portent of fatality. What had caused this sudden impersonal interest in her situation? What was the meaning of the subtle animosity toward the bandit leader? Was there no honor among evil men banded together for evil deeds? Were jealousy, ferocity, hate and faithlessness fostered by this wild and evil border life, ready at an instant's notice to break out? Joan divined the vain and futile and tragical nature of Kell's great enterprise. It could not succeed. It might bring a few days or weeks of fame, of blood-stained gold, of riotous gambling, but by its very nature it was doomed. It embraced failure and death.

Joan went from man to man, keener now on the track of this inexplicable change, sweetly and sadly friendly to each; and it was not till she encountered the little Frenchman that the secret was revealed. Frenchy was of a different race. Deep in the fiber of his being inculcated a sentiment, a feeling, long submerged in the darkness of a wicked life, and now that something came fleeting out of the depths—and it was respect for a woman. To Joan it was a flash of light. Yesterday these ruffians despised her; to-day they respected her. So they had believed what she had so desperately flung at Jim Cleve. They believed her good, they pitied her, they respected her, they responded to her effort to turn a boy back from a bad career. They were bandits, desperados, murderers, lost, but each remembered in her a mother or a sister. What each might have felt or done had he possessed her, as Kells possessed her, did not alter the case as it stood. A strange inconsistency of character made them hate Kells for what they might not have hated in themselves. Her appeal to Cleve, her outburst of truth, her youth and misfortune, had discovered to each a human quality. As in Kells something of nobility still lingered, a ghost among his ruined ideals, so in the others some goodness remained. Joan sustained an uplifting divination— no man was utterly bad. Then came the hideous image of the giant Gulden, the utter absence of soul in him, and she shuddered. Then came the thought of Jim Cleve, who had not believed her, who had bitterly made the fatal step, who might in the strange reversion of his character be beyond influence.

And it was at the precise moment when this thought rose to counteract the hope revived by the changed attitude of the men that Joan looked out to see Jim Cleve sauntering up, careless, untidy, a cigarette between his lips, blue blotches on his white face, upon him the stamp of abandonment. Joan suffered a contraction of heart that benumbed her breast. She stood a moment battling with herself. She was brave enough, desperate enough, to walk straight up to

Cleve, remove her mask and say, "I am Joan!" But that must be a last resource. She had no plan, yet she might force an opportunity to see Cleve alone.

A shout rose above the hubbub of voices. A tall man was pointing across the gulch where dust-clouds showed above the willows. Men crowded round him, all gazing in the direction of his hand, all talking at once.

"Jesse Smith's hoss, I swear!" shouted the tall man. "Kells, come out here!"

Kells appeared, dark and eager, at the door, and nimbly he leaped to the excited group. Pearce and Wood and others followed.

"What's up?" called the bandit. "Hello! Who's that riding bareback?"

"He's shore cuttin' the wind," said Wood.

"Blicky!" exclaimed the tall man. "Kells, there's news. I seen Jesse's hoss."

Kells let out a strange, exultant cry. The excited talk among the men gave place, to a subdued murmur, then subsided. Blicky was running a horse up the road, hanging low over him, like an Indian. He clattered to the bench, scattered the men in all directions. The fiery horse plunged and pounded. Blicky was gray of face and wild of aspect.

"Jesse's come!" he yelled, hoarsely, at Kells. "He jest fell off his hoss—all in! He wants you—an' all the gang! He's seen a million dollars in gold-dust!"

Absolute silence ensued after that last swift and startling speech. It broke to a commingling of yells and shouts. Blicky wheeled his horse and Kells started on a run. And there was a stampede and rush after him.

Joan grasped her opportunity. She had seen all this excitement, but she had not lost sight of Cleve. He got up from a log and started after the others. Joan flew to him, grasped him, startled him with the suddenness of her onslaught. But her tongue seemed cloven to the roof of her mouth, her lips weak and mute. Twice she strove to speak.

"Meet me—there!—among the pines—right away!" she whispered, with breathless earnestness. "It's life—or death—for me!"

As she released his arm he snatched at her mask. But she eluded him.

"Who ARE you?" he flashed.

Kells and his men were piling into the willows, leaping the brook, hurrying on. They had no thought but to get to Jesse Smith to hear of the gold strike. That news to them was as finding gold in the earth was to honest miners.

"Come!" cried Joan. She hurried away toward the corner of the cabin, then halted to see if he was following. He was, indeed. She ran round behind the cabin, out on the slope, halting at the first trees. Cleve came striding after her. She ran on, beginning to pant and stumble. The way he strode, the white grimness of him, frightened her. What would he, do? Again she went on, but not running now. There were straggling pines and spruces that soon hid the cabins. Beyond, a few rods, was a dense clump of pines, and she made for that. As she reached it she turned fearfully. Only Cleve was in sight. She uttered a sob of mingled relief, joy, and thankfulness. She and Cleve had not been observed. They would be out of sight in this little pine grove. At last! She could reveal herself, tell him why she was there, that she loved him, that she was as good as ever she had been. Why was she shaking like a leaf in the wind? She saw Cleve through a blur. He was almost running now. Involuntarily she fled into the grove. It was dark and cool; it smelled sweetly of pine; there were narrow aisles and little sunlit glades. She hurried on till a fallen tree blocked her passage. Here she turned—she would wait—the tree was good to lean against. There came Cleve, a dark, stalking shadow. She did not remember him like that. He entered the glade.

"Speak again!" he said, thickly. "Either I'm drunk or crazy!"

But Joan could not speak. She held out hands that shook—swept them to her face—tore at the mask. Then with a gasp she stood revealed.

If she had stabbed him straight through the heart he could not have been more ghastly. Joan saw him, in all the terrible transfiguration that came over him, but she had no conceptions, no thought of what constituted that change. After that check to her mind came a surge of joy.

"Jim!... Jim! It's Joan!" she breathed, with lips almost mute.

"JOAN!" he gasped, and the sound of his voice seemed to be the passing from horrible doubt to certainty.

Like a panther he leaped at her, fastened a powerful hand at the neck of her blouse, jerked her to her knees, and began to drag her. Joan fought his iron grasp. The twisting and tightening of her blouse choked her utterance. He did not look down upon her, but she could see him, the rigidity of his body set in violence, the awful shade upon his face, the upstanding hair on his head. He dragged her as if she had been an empty sack. Like a beast he was seeking a dark place—a hole to hide her. She was strangling; a distorted sight made objects dim; and now she struggled instinctively. Suddenly the clutch at her neck loosened; gaspingly came the intake of air to her lungs; the dark-red veil left her eyes. She was still upon her knees. Cleve stood before her, like a gray-faced demon, holding his gun level, ready to fire.

"Pray for your soul—and mine!"

"Jim! Oh Jim!... Will you kill yourself, too?"

"Yes! But pray, girl—quick!"

"Then I pray to God—not for my soul—but just for one more moment of life... TO TELL YOU, JIM!"

Cleve's face worked and the gun began to waver. Her reply had been a stroke of lightning into the dark abyss of his jealous agony.

Joan saw it, and she raised her quivering face, and she held up her arms to him. "To tell—you—Jim!" she entreated.

"What?" he rasped out.

"That I'm innocent—that I'm as good—a girl—as ever.. ever.... Let me tell you.... Oh, you're mistaken—terribly mistaken."

"Now, I know I'm drunk.... You, Joan Randle! You in that rig! You the companion of Jack Kells! Not even his wife! The jest of these foul-mouthed bandits! And you say you're innocent—good?... When you refused to leave him!"

"I was afraid to go—afraid you'd be killed," she moaned, beating her breast.

It must have seemed madness to him, a monstrous nightmare, a delirium of drink, that Joan Randle was there on her knees in a brazen male attire, lifting her arms to him, beseeching him, not to spare her life, but to believe in her innocence.

Joan burst into swift, broken utterance: "Only listen! I trailed you out—twenty miles from Hoadley. I met Roberts. He came with me. He lamed his horse—we had to camp. Kells rode down on us. He had two men. They camped there. Next morning he—killed Roberts—made off with me.... Then he killed his men—just to have me—alone to himself.... We crossed a range—camped in the canon. There he attacked me—and I—I shot him!... But I couldn't leave him—to die!" Joan hurried on with her narrative, gaining strength and eloquence as she saw the weakening of Cleve. "First he said I was his wife to fool that Gulden—and the others," she went on. "He meant to save me from them. But they guessed or found out.... Kells forced me into these bandit clothes. He's depraved, somehow. And I had to wear something. Kells hasn't harmed me—no one has. I've influence over him. He can't resist it. He's tried to force me to marry him. And he's tried to give up to his evil intentions. But he can't. There's good in him. I can make him feel it.... Oh, he loves me, and I'm not afraid of him any more.... It has been a terrible time for me, Jim, but I'm still—the same girl you knew—you used to—"

Cleve dropped the gun and he waved his hand before his eyes as if to dispel a blindness.

"But why—why?" he asked, incredulously. "Why did you leave Hoadley? That's forbidden. You knew the risk."

Joan gazed steadily up at him, to see the whiteness slowly fade out of his face. She had imagined it would be an overcoming of pride to betray her love, but she had been wrong. The moment was so full, so overpowering, that she seemed dumb. He had ruined himself for her, and out of that ruin had come the glory of her love. Perhaps it was all too late, but at least he would know that for love of him she had in turn sacrificed herself.

"Jim," she whispered, and with the first word of that betrayal a thrill, a tremble, a rush went over her, and all her blood seemed hot at her neck and face, "that night when you kissed me I was furious. But the moment you had gone I repented. I must have—cared for you then, but I didn't know.... Remorse seized me. And I set out on your trail to save you from yourself. And with the pain and fear and terror there was sometimes—the—the sweetness of your kisses. Then I knew I cared.... And with the added days of suspense and agony—all that told me of your throwing your life away—there came love.... Such love as otherwise I'd never have been big enough for! I meant to find you—to save you—to send you home!... I have found you, maybe too late to save your life, but not your soul, thank God!... That's why I've been strong enough to hold back Kells. I love you, Jim!... I love you! I couldn't tell you enough. My heart is bursting.... Say you believe me! Say you know I'm good—true to you—your Joan!... And kiss me—like you did that night when we were such blind fools. A boy and a girl who didn't know—and couldn't tell!—Oh, the sadness of it!.... Kiss me, Jim, before I—drop—at your feet!... If only you—believe—"

Joan was blinded by tears and whispering she knew not what when Cleve broke from his trance and caught her to his breast. She was fainting—hovering at the border of unconsciousness when his violence held her back from oblivion. She seemed wrapped to him and held so tightly there was no breath in her body, no motion, no stir of pulse. That vague, dreamy moment passed. She heard his husky, broken accents—she felt the pound of his heart against her breast. And he began to kiss her as she had begged him to. She quickened to thrilling, revivifying life. And she lifted her face, and clung round his neck, and kissed him, blindly, sweetly, passionately, with all her heart and soul in her lips, wanting only one thing in the world—to give that which she had denied him.

"Joan!... Joan!... Joan!" he murmured when their lips parted. "Am I dreaming—drunk—or crazy?"

"Oh, Jim, I'm real—you have me in your arms," she whispered. "Dear Jim—kiss me again—and say you believe me."

"Believe you?... I'm out of my mind with joy.... You loved me! You followed me!... And—that idea of mine—only an absurd, vile suspicion! I might have known—had I been sane!"

"There.... Oh, Jim!... Enough of madness. We've got to plan. Remember where we are. There's Kells, and this terrible situation to meet!"

He stared at her, slowly realizing, and then it was his turn to shake. "My God! I'd forgotten. I'll HAVE to kill you now!"

A reaction set in. If he had any self-control left he lost it, and like a boy whose fling into manhood had exhausted his courage he sank beside her and buried his face against her. And he cried in a low, tense, heartbroken way. For Joan it was terrible to hear him. She held his hand to her breast and implored him not to weaken now. But he was stricken with remorse—he had run off like a coward, he had brought her to this calamity—and he could not rise under it. Joan realized that he had long labored under stress of morbid emotion. Only a supreme effort could lift him out of it to strong and reasoning equilibrium, and that must come from her.

She pushed him away from her, and held him back where he must see her, and white-hot with passionate purpose, she kissed him. "Jim Cleve, if you've NERVE enough to be BAD you've nerve enough to save the girl who LOVES you—who BELONGS to you!"

He raised his face and it flashed from red to white. He caught the subtlety of her antithesis. With the very two words which had driven him away under the sting of cowardice she uplifted him; and with all that was tender and faithful and passionate in her meaning of surrender she settled at once and forever the doubt of his manhood. He arose trembling in every limb. Like a dog he shook himself. His breast heaved. The shades of scorn and bitterness and abandon might never have haunted his face. In that moment he had passed from the reckless and wild, sick rage of a weakling to the stern, realizing courage of a man. His suffering on this wild border had developed a different fiber of character; and at the great moment, the climax, when his moral force hung balanced between elevation and destruction, the woman had called to him, and her unquenchable spirit passed into him.

"There's only one thing—to get away," he said.

"Yes, but that's a terrible risk," she replied.

"We've a good chance now. I'll get horses. We can slip away while they're all excited."

"No—no. I daren't risk so much. Kells would find out at once. He'd be like a hound on our trail. But that's not all. I've a horror of Gulden. I can't explain. I FEEL it. He would know—he would take the trail. I'd never try to escape with Gulden in camp.... Jim, do you know what he's done?"

"He's a cannibal. I hate the sight of him. I tried to kill him. I wish I had killed him."

"I'm never safe while he's near."

"Then I will kill him."

"Hush! you'll not be desperate unless you have to be.... Listen. I'm safe with Kells for the present. And he's friendly to you. Let us wait. I'll keep trying to influence him. I have won the friendship of some of his men. We'll stay with him—travel with him. Surely we'd have a better chance to excape after we reach that gold-camp. You must play your part. But do it without drinking and fighting. I couldn't bear that. We'll see each other somehow. We'll plan. Then we'll take the first chance to get away."

"We might never have a better chance than we've got right now," he remonstrated.

"It may seem so to you. But I KNOW. I haven't watched these ruffians for nothing. I tell you Gulden has split with Kells because of me. I don't know how I know. And I think I'd die of terror out on the trail with two hundred miles to go—and that gorilla after me."

"But, Joan, if we once got away Gulden would never take you alive," said Jim, earnestly. "So you needn't fear that."

"I've uncanny horror of him. It's as if he were a gorilla—and would take me off even if I were dead!... No, Jim, let us wait. Let me select the time. I can do it. Trust me. Oh, Jim, now that I've saved you from being a bandit, I can do anything. I can fool Kells or Pearce or Wood—any of them, except Gulden."

"If Kells had to choose now between trailing you and rushing for the gold-camp, which would he do?"

"He'd trail me," she said.

"But Kells is crazy over gold. He has two passions. To steal gold, and to gamble with it."

"That may be. But he'd go after me first. So would Gulden. We can't ride these hills as they do. We don't know the trails—the water. We'd get lost. We'd be caught. And somehow I know that Gulden and his gang would find us first."

"You're probably right, Joan," replied Cleve. "But you condemn me to a living death.... To let you out of my sight with Kells or any of them! It'll be worse almost than my life was before."

"But, Jim, I'll be safe," she entreated. "It's the better choice of two evils. Our lives depend on reason, waiting, planning. And, Jim, I want to live for you."

"My brave darling, to hear you say that!" he exclaimed, with deep emotion. "When I never expected to see you again!... But the past is past. I begin over from this hour. I'll be what you want—do what you want."

Joan seemed irresistibly drawn to him again, and the supplication, as she lifted her blushing face, and the yielding, were perilously sweet.

"Jim, kiss me and hold me—the way—you did that night!"

And it was not Joan who first broke that embrace.

"Find my mask," she said.

Cleve picked up his gun and presently the piece of black felt. He held it as if it were a deadly thing.

"Put it on me."

He slipped the cord over her head and adjusted the mask so the holes came right for her eyes.

"Joan, it hides the—the GOODNESS of you," he cried. "No one can see your eyes now. No one will look at your face. That rig shows your—shows you off so! It's not decent.... But, O Lord! I'm bound to confess how pretty, how devilish, how seductive you are! And I hate it."

"Jim, I hate it, too. But we must stand it. Try not to shame me any more.... And now good-by. Keep watch for me—as I will for you—all the time."

Joan broke from him and glided out of the grove, away under the straggling pines, along the slope. She came upon her horse and she led him back to the corral. Many of the horses had strayed. There was no one at the cabin, but she saw men striding up the slope, Kells in the lead.

She had been fortunate. Her absence could hardly have been noted. She had just strength left to get to her room, where she fell upon the bed, weak and trembling and dizzy and unutterably grateful at her deliverance from the hateful, unbearable falsity of her situation.

13

It was afternoon before Joan could trust herself sufficiently to go out again, and when she did she saw that she attracted very little attention from the bandits.

Kells had a springy step, a bright eye, a lifted head, and he seemed to be listening. Perhaps he was—to the music of his sordid dreams. Joan watched him sometimes with wonder. Even a bandit—plotting gold robberies, with violence and blood merely means to an end—built castles in the air and lived with joy!

All that afternoon the bandits left camp in twos and threes, each party with pack burros and horses, packed as Joan had not seen them before on the border. Shovels and picks and old sieves and pans, these swinging or tied in prominent places, were evidence that the bandits meant to assume the characters of miners and prospectors. They whistled and sang. It was a lark. The excitement had subsided and the action begun. Only in Kells, under his radiance, could be felt the dark and sinister plot. He was the heart of the machine.

By sundown Kells, Pearce, Wood, Jim Cleve, and a robust, grizzled bandit, Jesse Smith, were left in camp. Smith was lame from his ride, and Joan gathered that Kells would have left camp but for the fact that Smith needed rest. He and Kells were together all the time, talking endlessly. Joan heard them argue a disputed point—would the men abide by Kells's plan and go by twos and threes into the gold-camp, and hide their relations as a larger band? Kells contended they would and Smith had his doubts.

"Jack, wait till you see Alder Creek!" ejaculated Smith, wagging his grizzled head. "Three thousand men, old an' young, of all kinds—gone gold—crazy! Alder Creek has got California's '49 and' '51 cinched to the last hole!" And the bandit leader rubbed his palms in great glee.

That evening they all had supper together in Kell's cabin. Bate Wood grumbled because he had packed most of his outfit. It so chanced that Joan sat directly opposite Jim Cleve, and while he ate he pressed her foot with his under the table. The touch thrilled Joan. Jim did not glance at her, but there was such a change in him that she feared it might rouse Kells's curiosity. This night, however, the bandit could not have seen anything except a gleam of yellow. He talked, he sat at table, but did not eat. After supper he sent Joan to her cabin, saying they would be on the trail at daylight. Joan watched them awhile from her covert. They had evidently talked themselves out, and Kells grew thoughtful. Smith and Pearce went outside, apparently to roll their beds on the ground under the porch roof. Wood, who said he was never a good sleeper, smoked his pipe. And Jim Cleve spread blankets along the wall in the shadow and and lay down. Joan could see his eyes shining toward the door. Of course he was thinking of her. But could he see her eyes? Watching her chance, she slipped a hand from behind the curtain, and she knew Cleve saw it. What a comfort that was! Joan's heart swelled. All might yet be well. Jim Cleve would be near her while she slept. She could sleep now without those dark dreams—without dreading to awaken to the light. Again she saw Kells pacing the room, silent, bent, absorbed, hands behind his back, weighted with his burden. It was impossible not to feel sorry for him. With all his intelligence and cunning power, his cause was hopeless. Joan knew that as she knew so many other things without understanding why. She had not yet sounded Jesse Smith, but not a man of all the others was true to Kells. They would be of his Border Legion, do his bidding, revel in their ill-gotten gains, and then, when he needed them most, be false to him.

When Joan was awakened her room was shrouded in gray gloom. A bustle sound from the big cabin, and outside horses stamped and men talked.

She sat alone at breakfast and ate by lantern-light. It was necessary to take a lantern back to her cabin, and she was so long in her preparations there that Kells called again. Somehow she did not want to leave this cabin. It seemed protective and private, and she feared she might not find such quarters again. Besides, upon the moment of leaving she discovered that she had grown attached to the place where she had suffered and thought and grown so much.

Kells had put out the lights. Joan hurried through the cabin and outside. The gray obscurity had given way to dawn. The air was cold, sweet, bracing with the touch of mountain purity in it. The men, except Kells, were all mounted, and the pack-train was in motion. Kells dragged the rude door into position, and then, mounting, he called to Joan to follow. She trotted her horse after him, down the slope, across the brook and through the wet willows, and out upon the wide trail. She glanced ahead, discerning that the third man from her was Jim Cleve; and that fact, in the start for Alder Creek, made all the difference in the world.

When they rode out of the narrow defile into the valley the sun was rising red and bright in a notch of the mountains. Clouds hung over distant peaks, and the patches of snow in the high canons shone blue and pink. Smith in the lead turned westward up the valley. Horses trooped after the cavalcade and had to be driven back. There were also cattle in the valley, and all these Kells left behind like an honest rancher who had no fear for his stock. Deer stood off with long ears pointed forward, watching the horses go by. There were flocks of quail, and whirring grouse, and bounding jack-rabbits, and occasionally a brace of sneaking coyotes. These and the wild flowers, and the waving meadow-grass, the yellow-stemmed willows, and the patches of alder, all were pleasurable to Joan's eyes and restful to her mind.

Smith soon led away from this valley up out of the head of a ravine, across a rough rock-strewn ridge, down again into a hollow that grew to be a canon. The trail was bad. Part of the time it was the bottom of a boulder-strewn brook where the horses slipped on the wet, round stones. Progress was slow and time passed. For Joan, however, it was a relief; and the slower they might travel the better she would like it. At the end of that journey there were Gulden and the others, and the gold-camp with its illimitable possibilities for such men.

At noon the party halted for a rest. The camp site was pleasant and the men were all agreeable. During the meal Kells found occasion to remark to Cleve:

"Say youngster, you've brightened up. Must be because of our prospects over here."

"Not that so much," replied Cleve. "I quit the whisky. To be honest, Kells, I was almost seeing snakes."

"I'm glad you quit. When you're drinking you're wild. I never yet saw the man who could drink hard and keep his head. I can't. But I don't drink much."

His last remark brought a response in laughter. Evidently his companions thought he was joking. He laughed himself and actually winked at Joan.

It happened to be Cleve whom Kells told to saddle Joan's horse, and as Joan tried the cinches, to see if they were too tight to suit her, Jim's hand came in contact with hers. That touch was like a message. Joan was thrilling all over as she looked at Jim, but he kept his face averted. Perhaps he did not trust his eyes.

Travel was resumed up the canon and continued steadily, though leisurely. But the trail was so rough, and so winding, that Joan believed the progress did not exceed three miles an hour. It was the kind of travel in which a horse could be helped and that entailed attention to the lay of the ground. Before Joan realized the hours were flying, the afternoon had waned. Smith kept on, however, until nearly dark before halting for camp.

The evening camp was a scene of activity, and all except Joan had work to do. She tried to lend a hand, but Wood told her to rest. This she was glad to do. When called to supper she had almost fallen asleep. After a long day's ride the business of eating precluded conversation. Later, however, the men began to talk between puffs on their pipes, and from the talk no one could have guessed that here was a band of robbers on their way to a gold camp. Jesse Smith had a sore foot and he was compared to a tenderfoot on his first ride. Smith retaliated in kind. Every consideration was shown Joan, and Wood particularly appeared assiduous in his desire for her comfort. All the men except Cleve paid her some kind attention; and he, of course, neglected her because he was afraid to go near her. Again she felt in Red Pearce a condemnation of the bandit leader who was dragging a girl over hard trails, making her sleep in the open, exposing her to danger and to men like himself and Gulden. In his own estimate Pearce, like every one of his kind, was not so slow as the others.

Joan watched and listened from her blankets, under a leafy tree, some few yards from the camp-fire. Once Kells turned to see how far distant she was, and then, lowering his voice, he told a story. The others laughed. Pearce followed with another, and he, too, took care that Joan could not hear. They grew closer for the mirth, and Smith, who evidently was a jolly fellow, set them to roaring. Jim Cleve laughed with them.

"Say, Jim, you're getting over it," remarked Kells.

"Over what?"

Kells paused, rather embarrassed for a reply, as evidently in the humor of the hour he had spoken a thought better left unsaid. But there was no more forbidding atmosphere about Cleve. He appeared to have rounded to good-fellowship after a moody and quarrelsome drinking spell.

"Why, over what drove you out here—and gave me a lucky chance at you," replied Kells, with a constrained laugh.

"Oh, you mean the girl?... Sure, I'm getting over that, except when I drink."

"Tell us, Jim," said Kells, curiously.

"Aw, you'll give me the laugh!" retorted Cleve.

"No, we won't unless your story's funny."

"You can gamble it wasn't funny," put in Red Pearce.

They all coaxed him, yet none of them, except Kells, was particularly curious; it was just that hour when men of their ilk were lazy and comfortable and full fed and good-humored round the warm, blazing camp-fire.

"All right," replied Cleve, and apparently, for all his complaisance, a call upon memory had its pain. "I'm from Montana. Range-rider in winter and in summer I prospected. Saved quite a little money, in spite of a fling now and then at faro and whisky.... Yes, there was a girl, I guess yes. She was pretty. I had a bad case over her. Not long ago I left all I had—money and gold and things—in her keeping, and I went prospecting again. We were to get married on my return. I stayed out six months, did well, and got robbed of all my dust."

Cleve was telling this fabrication in a matter-of-fact way, growing a little less frank as he proceeded, and he paused while he lifted sand and let it drift through his fingers, watching it curiously. All the men were interested and Kells hung on every word.

"When I got back," went on Cleve, "my girl had married another fellow. She'd given him all I left with her. Then I got drunk. While I was drunk they put up a job on me. It was her word that disgraced me and run me out of town.... So I struck west and drifted to the border."

"That's not all," said Kells, bluntly.

"Jim, I reckon you ain't tellin' what you did to thet lyin' girl an' the feller. How'd you leave them?" added Pearce.

But Cleve appeared to become gloomy and reticent.

"Wimmen can hand the double-cross to a man, hey, Kells?" queried Smith, with a broad grin.

"By gosh! I thought you'd been treated powerful mean!" exclaimed Bate Wood, and he was full of wrath.

"A treacherous woman!" exclaimed Kells, passionately. He had taken Cleve's story hard. The man must have been betrayed by women, and Cleve's story had irritated old wounds.

Directly Kells left the fire and repaired to his blankets, near where Joan lay. Probably he believed her asleep, for he neither looked nor spoke. Cleve sought his bed, and likewise Wood and Smith. Pearce was the last to leave, and as he stood up the light fell upon his red face, lean and bold like an Indian's. Then he passed Joan, looking down upon her and then upon the recumbent figure of Kells; and if his glance was not baleful and malignant, as it swept over the bandit, Joan believed her imagination must be vividly weird, and running away with her judgment.

The next morning began a day of toil. They had to climb over the mountain divide, a long, flat-topped range of broken rocks. Joan spared her horse to the limit of her own endurance. If there were a trail Smith alone knew it, for none was in evidence to the others. They climbed out of the notched head of the canon, and up a long slope of weathered shale that let the horses slide back a foot for every yard gained, and through a labyrinth of broken cliffs, and over bench and ridge to the height of the divide. From there Joan had a magnificent view. Foot-hills rolled round heads below, and miles away, in a curve of the range, glistened Bear Lake. The rest here at this height was counteracted by the fact that the altitude affected Joan. She was glad to be on the move again, and now the travel was downhill, so that she could ride. Still it was difficult, for horses were more easily lamed in a descent. It took two hours to descend the distance that had consumed all the morning to ascend. Smith led through valley after valley between foot-hills, and late in the afternoon halted by a spring in a timbered spot.

Joan ached in every muscle and she was too tired to care what happened round the camp-fire. Jim had been close to her all day and that had kept up her spirit. It was not yet dark when she lay down for the night.

"Sleep well, Dandy Dale," said Kells, cheerfully, yet not without pathos. "Alder Creek to-morrow!... Then you'll never sleep again!"

At times she seemed to feel that he regretted her presence, and always this fancy came to her with mocking or bantering suggestion that the costume and mask she wore made her a bandit's consort, and she could not escape the wildness of this gold-seeking life. The truth was that Kells saw the insuperable barrier between them, and in the bitterness of his love he lied to himself, and hated himself for the lie.

About the middle of the afternoon of the next day the tired cavalcade rode down out of the brush and rock into a new, broad, dusty road. It was so new that the stems of the cut brush along the borders were still white. But that road had been traveled by a multitude.

Out across the valley in the rear Joan saw a canvas-topped wagon, and she had not ridden far on the road when she saw a bobbing pack-burros to the fore. Kells had called Wood and Smith and Pearce and Cleve together, and now they went on in a bunch, all driving the pack-train. Excitement again claimed Kells; Pearce was alert and hawk-eyed; Smith looked like a hound on a scent; Cleve showed genuine feeling. Only Bate Wood remained proof to the meaning of that broad road.

All along, on either side, Joan saw wrecks of wagons, wheels, harness, boxes, old rags of tents blown into the brush, dead mules and burros. It seemed almost as if an army had passed that way. Presently the road crossed a wide, shallow brook of water, half clear and half muddy; and on the other side the road followed the course of the brook. Joan heard Smith call the stream Alder Creek, and he asked Kells if he knew what muddied water meant. The bandit's eyes flashed fire. Joan thrilled, for she, too, knew that up-stream there were miners washing earth for gold.

A couple of miles farther on creek and road entered the mouth of a wide spruce-timbered gulch. These trees hid any view of the slopes or floor of the gulch, and it was not till several more miles had been passed that the bandit rode out into what Joan first thought was a hideous slash in the forest made by fire. But it was only the devastation wrought by men. As far as she could see the timber was down, and everywhere began to be manifested signs that led her to expect habitations. No cabins showed, however, in the next mile. They passed out of the timbered part of the gulch into one of rugged, bare, and stony slopes, with bunches of sparse alder here and there. The gulch turned at right angles and a great gray slope shut out sight of what lay beyond. But, once round that obstruction, Kells halted his men with short, tense exclamation.

Joan saw that she stood high up on the slope, looking down upon the gold-camp. It was an interesting scene, but not beautiful. To Kells it must have been so, but to Joan it was even more hideous than the slash in the forest. Here and there, everywhere, were rude dugouts, little huts of brush, an occasional tent, and an occasional log cabin; and as she looked farther and farther these crude habitations of miners magnified in number and in dimensions till the white and black broken, mass of the town choked the narrow gulch.

"Wal, boss, what do you say to thet diggin's?" demanded Jesse Smith.

Kells drew a deep breath. "Old forty-niner, this beats all I ever saw!"

"Shore I've seen Sacramento look like thet!" added Bate Wood.

Pearce and Cleve gazed with fixed eyes, and, however different their emotions, they rivaled each other in attention.

"Jesse, what's the word?" queried Kells, with a sharp return to the business of the matter.

"I've picked a site on the other side of camp. Best fer us," he replied.

"Shall we keep to the road?"

"Certain-lee," he returned, with his grin.

Kells hesitated, and felt of his beard, probably conjecturing the possibilities of recognition.

"Whiskers make another man of you. Reckon you needn't expect to be known over here."

That decided Kells. He pulled his sombrero well down, shadowing his face. Then he remembered Joan and made a slight significant gesture at her mask.

"Kells, the people in this here camp wouldn't look at an army ridin' through," responded Smith. "It's every man fer hisself. An' wimmen, say! there's all kinds. I seen a dozen with veils, an' them's the same as masks." Nevertheless, Kells had Joan remove the mask and pull her sombrero down, and instructed her to ride in the midst of the group. Then they trotted on, soon catching up with the jogging pack-train.

What a strange ride that was for Joan! The slope resembled a magnified ant-hill with a horde of frantic ants in action. As she drew closer she saw these ants were men, digging for gold. Those near at hand could be plainly seen—rough, ragged, bearded men and smooth-faced boys. Farther on and up the slope, along the waterways and ravines, were miners so close they seemed almost to interfere with one another. The creek bottom was alive with busy, silent, violent men, bending over the water, washing and shaking and paddling, all desperately intent upon something. They had not time to look up. They were ragged, unkempt, barearmed and bare-legged, every last one of them with back bent. For a mile or more Kells's party trotted through this part of the diggings, and everywhere, on rocky bench and gravel bar and gray slope, were holes with men picking and shoveling in them. Some were deep and some were shallow; some long trenches and others mere pits. If all of these prospectors were finding gold, then gold was everywhere. And presently Joan did not need to have Kells tell her that all of these diggers were finding dust. How silent they were—how tense! They were not mechanical. It was a soul that drove them. Joan had seen many men dig for gold, and find a little now and then, but she had never seen men dig when they knew they were going to strike gold. That made the strange difference.

Joan calculated she must have seen a thousand miners in less than two miles of the gulch, and then she could not see up the draws and washes that intersected the slope, and she could not see beyond the camp.

But it was not a camp which she was entering; it was a tent-walled town, a city of squat log cabins, a long, motley, checkered jumble of structures thrown up and together in mad haste. The wide road split it in the middle and seemed a stream of color and life. Joan rode between two lines of horses, burros, oxen, mules, packs and loads and canvas-domed wagons and gaudy vehicles resembling gipsy caravans. The street was as busy as a beehive and as noisy as a bedlam. The sidewalks were rough-hewn planks and they rattled under the tread of booted men. There were tents on the ground and tents on floors and tents on log walls. And farther on began the lines of cabins-stores and shops and saloons—and then a great, square, flat structure with a flaring sign in crude gold letters, "Last Nugget," from which came the creak of iddles and scrape of boots, and hoarse mirth. Joan saw strange, wild-looking creatures—women that made her shrink; and several others of her sex, hurrying along, carrying sacks or buckets, worn and bewildered-looking women, the sight of whom gave her a pang. She saw lounging Indians and groups of lazy, bearded men, just like Kells's band, and gamblers in long, black coats, and frontiersmen in fringed buckskin, and Mexicans with swarthy faces under wide, peaked sombreros; and then in great majority, dominating that stream of life, the lean and stalwart miners, of all ages, in their check shirts and high boots, all packing guns, jostling along, dark-browed, somber, and intent. These last were the workers of this vast beehive; the others were the drones, the parasites.

Kell's party rode on through the town, and Smith halted them beyond the outskirts, near a grove of spruce-trees, where camp was to be made.

Joan pondered over her impression of Alder Creek. It was confused; she had seen too much. But out of what she had seen and heard loomed two contrasting features: a throng of toiling miners, slaves to their lust for gold and actuated by ambitions, hopes, and aims, honest, rugged, tireless workers, but frenzied in that strange pursuit; and a lesser crowd, like leeches, living for and off the gold they did not dig with blood of hand and sweat of brow.

Manifestly Jesse Smith had selected the spot for Kells's permanent location at Alder Creek with an eye for the bandit's peculiar needs. It was out of sight of town, yet within a hundred rods of the nearest huts, and closer than that to a sawmill. It could be approached by a shallow ravine that wound away toward the creek. It was backed up against a rugged bluff in which there was a narrow gorge, choked with pieces of weathered cliff; and no doubt the bandits could go and come in that direction. There was a spring near at hand and a grove of spruce-trees. The ground was rocky, and apparently unfit for the digging of gold.

While Bate Wood began preparations for supper, and Cleve built the fire, and Smith looked after the horses, Kells and Pearce stepped off the ground where the cabin was to be erected. They selected a level bench down upon which a huge cracked rock, as large as a house, had rolled. The cabin was to be backed up against this stone, and in the rear, under cover of it, a secret exit could be made and hidden. The bandit wanted two holes to his burrow.

When the group sat down to the meal the gulch was full of sunset colors. And, strangely, they were all some shade of gold. Beautiful golden veils, misty, ethereal, shone in rays across the gulch from the broken ramparts; and they seemed so brilliant, so rich, prophetic of the treasures of the hills. But that golden sunset changed. The sun went down red, leaving a sinister shadow over the gulch, growing darker and darker. Joan saw Cleve thoughtfully watching this transformation, and she wondered if he had caught the subtle mood of nature. For whatever had been the hope and brightness, the golden glory of this new Eldorado, this sudden uprising Alder Creek with its horde of brave and toiling miners, the truth was that Jack Kells and Gulden had ridden into the camp and the sun had gone down red. Joan knew that great mining-camps were always happy, rich, free, lucky, honest places till the fame of gold brought evil men. And she had not the slightest doubt that the sun of Alder Creek's brief and glad day had set forever.

Twilight was stealing down from the hills when Kells announced to his party: "Bate, you and Jesse keep camp. Pearce, you look out for any of the gang. But meet in the dark!... Cleve, you can go with me." Then he turned to Joan. "Do you want to go with us to see the sights or would you rather stay here?"

"I'd like to go, if only I didn't look so—so dreadful in this suit," she replied.

Kells laughed, and the camp-fire glare lighted the smiling faces of Pearce and Smith.

"Why, you'll not be seen. And you look far from dreadful."

"Can't you give me a—a longer coat?" faltered Joan.

Cleve heard, and without speaking he went to his saddle and unrolled his pack. Inside a slicker he had a gray coat. Joan had seen it many a time, and it brought a pang with memories of Hoadley. Had that been years ago? Cleve handed this coat to Joan.

"Thank you," she said.

Kells held the coat for her and she slipped into it. She seemed lost. It was long, coming way below her hips, and for the first time in days she felt she was Joan Randle again.

"Modesty is all very well in a woman, but it's not always becoming," remarked Kells. "Turn up your collar.... Pull down your hat—farther—There! If you won't go as a youngster now I'll eat Dandy Dale's outfit and get you silk dresses. Ha-ha!"

Joan was not deceived by his humor. He might like to look at her in that outrageous bandit costume; it might have pleased certain vain and notoriety-seeking proclivities of his, habits of his California road-agent days; but she felt that notwithstanding this, once she had donned the long coat he was relieved and glad in spite of himself. Joan had a little rush of feeling. Sometimes she almost liked this bandit. Once he must have been something very different.

They set out, Joan between Kells and Cleve. How strange for her! She had daring enough to feel for Jim's hand in the dark and to give it a squeeze. Then he nearly broke her fingers. She felt the fire in him. It was indeed a hard situation for him. The walking was rough, owing to the uneven road and the stones. Several times Joan stumbled and her spurs jangled. They passed ruddy camp-fires, where steam and smoke arose with savory odors, where red-faced men were eating; and they passed other camp-fires, burned out and smoldering. Some tents had dim lights, throwing shadows on the canvas, and others were dark. There were men on the road, all headed for town, gay, noisy and profane.

Then Joan saw uneven rows of lights, some dim and some bright, and crossing before them were moving dark figures. Again Kells bethought himself of his own disguise, and buried his chin in his scarf and pulled his wide-brimmed hat down so that hardly a glimpse of his face could be seen. Joan could not have recognized him at the distance of a yard.

They walked down the middle of the road, past the noisy saloons, past the big, flat structure with its sign "Last Nugget" and its open windows, where shafts of light shone forth, and all the way down to the end of town. Then Kells turned back. He scrutinized each group of men he met. He was looking for members of his Border Legion. Several times he left Cleve and Joan standing in the road while he peered into saloons. At these brief intervals Joan looked at Cleve with all her heart in her eyes. He never spoke. He seemed under a strain. Upon the return, when they reached the Last Nugget, Kells said:

"Jim, hang on to her like grim death! She's worth more than all the gold in Alder Creek!"

Then they started for the door.

Joan clung to Cleve on one side, and on the other, instinctively with a frightened girl's action, she let go Kells's arm and slipped her hand in his. He seemed startled. He bent to her ear, for the din made ordinary talk indistinguishable. That involuntary hand in his evidently had pleased and touched him, even hurt him, for his whisper was husky.

"It's all right—you're perfectly safe."

First Joan made out a glare of smoky lamps, a huge place full of smoke and men and sounds. Kells led the way slowly. He had his own reason for observance. There was a stench that sickened Joan—a blended odor of tobacco and rum and wet sawdust and smoking oil. There was a noise that appeared almost deafening—the loud talk and vacant laughter of drinking men, and a din of creaky fiddles and scraping boots and boisterous mirth. This last and dominating sound came from an adjoining room, which Joan could see through a wide opening. There was dancing, but Joan could not see the dancers because of the intervening crowd. Then her gaze came back to the features nearer at hand. Men and youths were lined up to a long bar nearly as high as her head. Then there were excited shouting groups round gambling games. There were men in clusters, sitting on upturned kegs, round a box for a table, and dirty bags of gold-dust were in evidence. The gamblers at the cards were silent, in strange contrast with the others; and in each group was at least one dark-garbed, hard-eyed gambler who was not a miner. Joan saw boys not yet of age, flushed and haggard, wild with the frenzy of winning and cast down in defeat. There were jovial, grizzled, old prospectors to whom this scene and company were pleasant reminders of bygone days. There were desperados whose glittering eyes showed they had no gold with which to gamble.

Joan suddenly felt Kells start and she believed she heard a low, hissing exclamation. And she looked for the cause. Then she saw familiar dark faces; they belonged to men of Kells's Legion. And with his broad back to her there sat the giant Gulden. Already he and his allies had gotten together in defiance of or indifference to Kells's orders. Some of them were already under the influence of drink, but, though they saw Kells, they gave no sign of recognition. Gulden did not see Joan, and for that she was thankful. And whether or not his presence caused it, the fact was that she suddenly felt as much of a captive as she had in Cabin Gulch, and feared that here escape would be harder because in a community like this Kells would watch her closely.

Kells led Joan and Cleve from one part of the smoky hall to another, and they looked on at the games and the strange raw life manifested there. The place was getting packed with men. Kells's party encountered Blicky and Beady Jones together. They passed by as strangers. Then Joan saw Beard and Chick Williams arm in arm, strolling about, like roystering miners. Williams telegraphed a keen, fleeting glance at Kells, then went on, to be lost in the crowd. Handy Oliver brushed by Kells, jostled him, apparently by accident, and he said, "Excuse me, mister!" There were other familiar faces. Kells's gang were all in Alder Creek and the dark machinations of the bandit leader had been put into operation. What struck Joan forcibly was that, though there were hilarity and comradeship, they were not manifested in any general way. These miners were strangers to one another; the groups were strangers; the gamblers were strangers; the newcomers were strangers; and over all hung an atmosphere of distrust. Good fellowship abided only in the many small companies of men who stuck together. The mining-camps that Joan had visited had been composed of an assortment of prospectors and hunters who made one big, jolly family. This was a gold strike, and the difference was obvious. The hunting for gold was one thing, in its relation to the searchers; after it had been found, in a rich field, the conditions of life and character changed. Gold had always seemed wonderful and beautiful to Joan; she absorbed here something that was the nucleus of hate. Why could not these miners, young and old, stay in their camps and keep their gold? That was the fatality. The pursuit was a dream—a glittering allurement; the possession incited a lust for more, and that was madness. Joan felt that in these reckless, honest miners there was a liberation of the same wild element which was the driving passion of Kells's Border Legion. Gold, then, was a terrible thing.

"Take me in there," said Joan, conscious of her own excitement, and she indicated the dance-hall.

Kells laughed as if at her audacity. But he appeared reluctant.

"Please take me—unless—" Joan did not know what to add, but she meant unless it was not right for her to see any more. A strange curiosity had stirred in her. After all, this place where she now stood was not greatly different from the picture imagination had conjured up. That dance-hall, however, was beyond any creation of Joan's mind.

"Let me have a look first," said Kells, and he left Joan with Cleve.

When he had gone Joan spoke without looking at Cleve, though she held fast to his arm.

"Jim, it could be dreadful here—all in a minute!" she whispered.

"You've struck it exactly," he replied. "All Alder Creek needed to make it hell was Kells and his gang."

"Thank Heaven I turned you back in time!... Jim, you'd have—have gone the pace here."

He nodded grimly. Then Kells returned and led them back through the room to another door where spectators were fewer. Joan saw perhaps a dozen couples of rough, whirling, jigging dancers in a half-circle of watching men. The hall was a wide platform of boards with posts holding a canvas roof. The sides, were open; the lights were situated at each end-huge, round, circus tent lamps. There were rude benches and tables where reeling men surrounded a woman. Joan saw a young miner in dusty boots and corduroys lying drunk or dead in the sawdust. Her eyes were drawn back to the dancers, and to the dance that bore some semblance to a waltz. In the din the music could scarcely be heard. As far as the men were concerned this dance was a bold and violent expression of excitement on the part of some, and for the rest a drunken, mad fling. Sight of the women gave Joan's curiosity a blunt check. She felt queer. She had not seen women like these, and their dancing, their actions, their looks, were beyond her understanding. Nevertheless, they shocked her, disgusted her, sickened her. And suddenly when it dawned upon her in unbelievable vivid suggestion that they were the wildest and most terrible element of this dark stream of humanity lured by gold, then she was appalled.

"Take me out of here!" she besought Kells, and he led her out instantly. They went through the gambling-hall and into the crowded street, back toward camp.

"You saw enough," said Kells, "but nothing to what will break out by and by. This camp is new. It's rich. Gold is the cheapest thing. It passes from hand to hand. Ten dollars an ounce. Buyers don't look at the scales. Only the gamblers are crooked. But all this will change."

Kells did not say what that change might be, but the click of his teeth was expressive. Joan did not, however, gather from it, and the dark meaning of his tone, that the Border Legion would cause this change. That was in the nature of events. A great strike of gold might enrich the world, but it was a catastrophe.

Long into the night Joan lay awake, and at times, stirring the silence, there was wafted to her on a breeze the low, strange murmur of the gold-camp's strife.

Joan slept late next morning, and was awakened by the unloading of lumber. Teams were drawing planks from the sawmill. Already a skeleton framework for Kells's cabin had been erected. Jim Cleve was working with the others, and they were sacrificing thoroughness to haste. Joan had to cook her own breakfast, which task was welcome, and after it had been finished she wished for something more to occupy her mind. But nothing offered. Finding a comfortable seat among some rocks where she would be inconspicuous, she looked on at the building of Kells's cabin. It seemed strange, and somehow comforting, to watch Jim Cleve work. He had never been a great worker. Would this experience on the border make a man of him? She felt assured of that.

If ever a cabin sprang up like a mushroom, that bandit rendezvous was the one. Kells worked himself, and appeared no mean hand. By noon the roof of clapboards was on, and the siding of the same material had been started. Evidently there was not to a be a fireplace inside.

Then a teamster drove up with a wagon-load of purchases Kells had ordered. Kells helped unload this and evidently was in search of articles. Presently he found them, and then approached Joan, to deposit before her an assortment of bundles little and big.

"There Miss Modestly," he said. "Make yourself some clothes. You can shake Dandy Dale's outfit, except when we're on the trail.... And, say, if you knew what I had to pay for this stuff you'd think there was a bigger robber in Alder Creek than Jack Kells.... And, come to think of it, my name's now Blight. You're my daughter, if any one asks." Joan was so grateful to him for the goods and the permission to get out of Dandy Dale's suit as soon as possible, that she could only smile her thanks. Kells stared at her, then turned abruptly away. Those little unconscious acts of hers seemed to affect him strangely. Joan remembered that he had intended to parade her in Dandy Dale's costume to gratify some vain abnormal side of his bandit's proclivities. He had weakened. Here was another subtle indication of the deterioration of the evil of him. How far would it go? Joan thought dreamily, and with a swelling heart, of her influence upon this hardened bandit, upon that wild boy, Jim Cleve.

All that afternoon, and part of the evening in the campfire light, and all of the next day Joan sewed, so busy that she scarcely lifted her eyes from her work. The following day she finished her dress, and with no little pride, for she had both taste and skill. Of the men, Bate Wood had been most interested in her task; and he would let things burn on the fire to watch her.

That day the rude cabin was completed. It contained one long room; and at the back a small compartment partitioned off from the rest, and built against and around a shallow cavern in the huge rock. This compartment was for Joan. There were a rude board door with padlock and key, a bench upon which blankets had been flung, a small square hole cut in the wall to serve as a window. What with her own few belongings and the articles of furniture that Kells bought for her, Joan soon had a comfortable room, even a luxury compared to what she had been used to for weeks. Certain it was that Kells meant to keep her a prisoner, or virtually so. Joan had no sooner spied the little window than she thought that it would be possible for Jim Cleve to talk to her there from the outside.

Kells verified Joan's suspicion by telling her that she was not to leave the cabin of her own accord, as she had been permitted to do back in Cabin Gulch; and Joan retorted that there she had made him a promise not to run away, which promise she now took back. That promise had worried her. She was glad to be honest with Kells. He gazed at her somberly.

"You'll be worse off it you do—and I'll be better off," he said. And then as an afterthought he added: "Gulden might not think you—a white elephant on his hands!... Remember his way, the cave and the rope!"

So, instinctively or cruelly he chose the right name to bring shuddering terror into Joan's soul.

14

Joan's opportunity for watching Kells and his men and overhearing their colloquies was as good as it had been back in Cabin Gulch. But it developed that where Kells had been open and frank he now became secret and cautious. She was aware that men, singly and in couples, visited him during the early hours of the night, and they had conferences in low, earnest tones. She could peer out of her little window and see dark, silent forms come up from the ravine at the back of the cabin, and leave the same way. None of them went round to the front door, where Bate Wood smoked and kept guard. Joan was able to hear only scraps of these earnest talks; and from part of one she gathered that for some reason or other Kells desired to bring himself into notice. Alder Creek must be made to know that a man of importance had arrived. It seemed to Joan that this was the very last thing which Kells ought to do. What magnificent daring the bandit had! Famous years before in California—with a price set upon his life in Nevada—and now the noted, if unknown, leader of border robbers in Idaho, he sought to make himself prominent, respected, and powerful. Joan found that in spite of her horror at the sinister and deadly nature of the bandit's enterprise she could not avoid an absorbing interest in his fortunes.

Next day Joan watched for an opportunity to tell Jim Cleve that he might come to her little window any time after dark to talk and plan with her. No chance presented itself. Joan wore the dress she had made, to the evident pleasure of Bate Wood and Pearce. They had conceived as strong an interest in her fortunes as she had in Kells's. Wood nodded his approval and Pearce said she was a lady once more. Strange it was to Joan that this villain Pearce, whom she could not have dared trust, grew open in his insinuating hints of Kells's blackguardism. Strange because Pearce was absolutely sincere!

When Jim Cleve did see Joan in her dress the first time he appeared so glad and relieved and grateful that she feared he might betray himself, so she got out of his sight.

Not long after that Kells called her from her room. He wore his somber and thoughtful cast of countenance. Red Pearce and Jesse Smith were standing at attention. Cleve was sitting on the threshold of the door and Wood leaned against the wall.

"Is there anything in the pack of stuff I bought you that you could use for a veil?" asked Kells of Joan.

"Yes," she replied.

"Get it," he ordered. "And your hat, too."

Joan went to her room and returned with the designated articles, the hat being that which she had worn when she left Hoadley.

"That'll do. Put it on—over your face—and let's see how you look."

Joan complied with this request, all the time wondering what Kells meant.

"I want it to disguise you, but not to hide your youth—your good looks," he said, and he arranged it differently about her face. "There!... You'd sure make any man curious to see you now.... Put on the hat."

Joan did so. Then Kells appeared to become more forcible.

"You're to go down into the town. Walk slow as far as the Last Nugget. Cross the road and come back. Look at every man you meet or see standing by. Don't be in the least frightened. Pearce and Smith will be right behind you. They'd get to you before anything could happen.... Do you understand?"

"Yes," replied Joan.

Red Pearce stirred uneasily. "Jack, I'm thinkin' some rough talk'll come her way," he said, darkly.

"Will you shut up!" replied Kells in quick passion. He resented some implication. "I've thought of that. She won't hear what's said to her.... Here," and he turned again to Joan, "take some cotton—or anything—and stuff up your ears. Make a good job of it."

Joan went back to her room and, looking about for something with which to execute Kells's last order, she stripped some soft, woolly bits from a fleece-lined piece of cloth. With these she essayed to deaden her hearing. Then she returned. Kells spoke to her, but, though she seemed dully to hear his voice, she could not distinguish what he said. She shook her head. With that Kells waved her out upon her strange errand.

Joan brushed against Cleve as she crossed the threshold. What would he think of this? She would not see his face. When she reached the first tents she could not resist the desire to look back. Pearce was within twenty yards of her and Smith about the same distance farther back. Joan was more curious than anything else. She divined that Kells wanted her to attract attention, but for what reason she was at a loss to say. It was significant that he did not intend to let her suffer any indignity while fulfilling this mysterious mission.

Not until Joan got well down the road toward the Last Nugget did any one pay any attention to her. A Mexican jabbered at her, showing his white teeth, flashing his sloe-black eyes. Young miners eyed her curiously, and some of them spoke. She met all kinds of men along the plank walk, most of whom passed by, apparently unobserving. She obeyed Kells to the letter. But for some reason she was unable to explain, when she got to the row of saloons, where lounging, evil-eyed rowdies accosted her, she found she had to disobey him, at least in one particular. She walked faster. Still that did not make her task much easier. It began to be an ordeal. The farther she got the bolder men grew. Could it have been that Kells wanted this sort of thing to happen to her? Joan had no idea what these men meant, but she believed that was because for the time being she was deaf. Assuredly their looks were not a compliment to any girl. Joan wanted to hurry now, and she had to force herself to walk at a reasonable gait. One persistent fellow walked beside her for several steps. Joan was not fool enough not to realize now that these wayfarers wanted to make her acquaintance. And she decided she would have something to say to Kells when she got back.

Below the Last Nugget she crossed the road and started upon the return trip. In front of this gambling-hell there were scattered groups of men, standing, and going in. A tall man in black detached himself and started out, as if to intercept her. He wore a long black coat, a black bow tie, and a black sombrero. He had little, hard, piercing eyes, as black as his dress. He wore gloves and looked immaculate, compared with the other men. He, too, spoke to Joan, turned to walk with her. She looked straight ahead now, frightened, and she wanted to run. He kept beside her, apparently talking. Joan heard only the low sound of his voice. Then he took her arm, gently, but with familiarity. Joan broke from him and quickened her pace.

"Say, there! Leave thet girl alone!"

This must have been yelled, for Joan certainly heard it. She recognized Red Pearce's voice. And she wheeled to look. Pearce had overhauled the gambler, and already men were approaching. Involuntarily Joan halted. What would happen? The gambler spoke to Pearce, made what appeared deprecating gestures, as if to explain. But Pearce looked angry.

"I'll tell her daddy!" he shouted.

Joan waited for no more. She almost ran. There would surely be a fight. Could that have been Kells's intention? Whatever it was, she had been subjected to a mortifying and embarrassing affront. She was angry, and she thought it might be just as well to pretend to be furious. Kells must not use her for his nefarious schemes. She hurried on, and, to her surprise, when she got within sight of the cabin both Pearce and Smith had almost caught up with her. Jim Cleve sat where she had last seen him. Also Kells was outside. The way he strode to and fro showed Joan his anxiety. There was more to this incident than she could fathom. She took the padding from her ears, to her intense relief, and, soon reaching the cabin, she tore off the veil and confronted Kells.

"Wasn't that a—a fine thing for you to do?" she demanded, furiously. And with the outburst she felt her face blazing. "If I'd any idea what you meant—you couldn't—have driven me!... I trusted you. And you sent me down there on some—shameful errand of yours. You're no gentleman!"

Joan realized that her speech, especially the latter part, was absurd. But it had a remarkable effect upon Kells. His face actually turned red. He stammered something and halted, seemingly at a loss for words. How singularly the slightest hint of any act or word of hers that approached a possible respect or tolerance worked upon this bandit! He started toward Joan appealingly, but she passed him in contempt and went to her room. She heard him cursing Pearce in a rage, evidently blaming his lieutenant for whatever had angered her.

"But you wanted her insulted!" protested Pearce, hotly.

"You mullet-head!" roared Kells. "I wanted some man—any man—to get just near enough to her so I could swear she'd been insulted. You let her go through that camp to meet real insult!... Why—! Pearce, I've a mind to shoot you!"

"Shoot!" retorted Pearce. "I obeyed orders as I saw them.... An' I want to say right here thet when it comes to anythin' concernin' this girl you're plumb off your nut. That's what. An' you can like it or lump it! I said before you'd split over this girl. An' I say it now!"

Through the door Joan had a glimpse of Cleve stepping between the angry men. This seemed unnecessary, however, for Pearce's stinging assertion had brought Kells to himself. There were a few more words, too low for Joan's ears, and then, accompanied by Smith, the three started off, evidently for the camp. Joan left her room and watched them from the cabin door. Bate Wood sat outside smoking.

"I'm declarin' my hand," he said to Joan, feelingly. "I'd never hev stood for thet scurvy trick. Now, miss, this's the toughest camp I ever seen. I mean tough as to wimmen! For it ain't begun to fan guns an' steal gold yet."

"Why did Kells want me insulted?" asked Joan.

"Wal, he's got to hev a reason for raisin' an orful fuss," replied Wood.

"Fuss?"

"Shore," replied Wood, dryly.

"What for?"

"Jest so he can walk out on the stage," rejoined Wood, evasively.

"It's mighty strange," said Joan.

"I reckon all about Mr. Kells is some strange these days. Red Pearce had it correct. Kells is a-goin' to split on you!"

"What do you mean by that?"

"Wal, he'll go one way an' the gang another."

"Why?" asked Joan, earnestly.

"Miss, there's some lot of reasons," said Wood, deliberately. "Fust, he did for Halloway an' Bailey, not because they wanted to treat you as he meant to, but just because he wanted to be alone. We're all wise thet you shot him—an' thet you wasn't his wife. An' since then we've seen him gradually lose his nerve. He organized his Legion an' makes his plan to run this Alder Creek red. He still hangs on to you. He'd kill any man thet batted an eye at you.... An' through all this, because he's not Jack Kells of old, he's lost his pull with the gang. Sooner or later he'll split."

"Have I any real friends among you?" asked Joan.

"Wal, I reckon."

"Are you my friend, Bate Wood?" she went on in sweet wistfulness.

The grizzled old bandit removed his pipe and looked at her with a glint in his bloodshot eyes,

"I shore am. I'll sneak you off now if you'll go. I'll stick a knife in Kells if you say so."

"Oh, no, I'm afraid to run off—and you needn't harm Kells. After all, he's good to me."

"Good to you!... When he keeps you captive like an Indian would? When he's given me orders to watch you—keep you locked up?"

Wood's snort of disgust and wrath was thoroughly genuine. Still Joan knew that she dared not trust him, any more than Pearce or the others. Their raw emotions would undergo a change if Kells's possession of her were transferred to them. It occurred to Joan, however, that she might use Wood's friendliness to some advantage.

"So I'm to be locked up?" she asked.

"You're supposed to be."

"Without any one to talk to?"

"Wal, you'll hev me, when you want. I reckon thet ain't much to look forward to. But I can tell you a heap of stories. An' when Kells ain't around, if you're careful not to get me ketched, you can do as you want."

"Thank you, Bate. I'm going to like you," replied Joan, sincerely, and then she went back to her room. There was sewing to do, and while she worked she thought, so that the hours sped. When the light got so poor that she could sew no longer she put the work aside and stood at her little window, watching the sunset. From the front of the cabin came the sound of subdued voices. Probably Kells and his men had returned, and she was sure of this when she heard the ring of Bate Wood's ax.

All at once an object darker than the stones arrested Joan's gaze. There was a man sitting on the far side of the little ravine. Instantly she recognized Jim Cleve. He was looking at the little window—at her. Joan believed he was there for just that purpose. Making sure that no one else was near to see, she put out her hand and waved it. Jim gave a guarded perceptible sign that he had observed her action, and almost directly got up and left. Joan needed no more than that to tell her how Jim's idea of communicating with her corresponded with her own. That night she would talk with him and she was thrilled through. The secrecy, the peril, somehow lent this prospect a sweetness, a zest, a delicious fear. Indeed, she was not only responding to love, but to daring, to defiance, to a wilder nameless element born of her environment and the needs of the hour.

Presently, Bate Wood called her in to supper. Pearce, Smith, and Cleve were finding seats at the table, but Kells looked rather sick. Joan observed him then more closely. His face was pale and damp, strangely shaded as if there were something dark under the pale skin. Joan had never seen him appear like this, and she shrank as from another and forbidding side of the man. Pearce and Smith acted naturally, ate with relish, and talked about the gold-diggings. Cleve, however, was not as usual; and Joan could not quite make out what constituted the dissimilarity. She hurried through her own supper and back to her room.

Already it was dark outside. Joan lay down to listen and wait. It seemed long, but probably was not long before she heard the men go outside, and the low thump of their footsteps as they went away. Then came the rattle and bang of Bate Wood's attack on the pans and pots. Bate liked to cook, but he hated to clean up afterward. By and by he settled down outside for his evening smoke and there was absolute quiet. Then Joan rose to stand at the window. She could see the dark mass of rock overhanging the cabin, the bluff beyond, and the stars. For the rest all was gloom.

She did not have to wait long. A soft step, almost indistinguishable, made her pulse beat quicker. She put her face out of the window, and on the instant a dark form seemed to loom up to meet her out of the shadow. She could not recognize that shape, yet she knew it belonged to Cleve.

"Joan," he whispered.

"Jim," she replied, just as low and gladly.

He moved closer, so that the hand she had gropingly put out touched him, then seemed naturally to slip along his shoulder, round his neck. And his face grew clearer in the shadow. His lips met hers, and Joan closed her eyes to that kiss. What hope, what strength for him and for her now in that meeting of lips!

"Oh, Jim! I'm so glad—to have you near—to touch you," she whispered.

"Do you love me still?" he whispered back, tensely.

"Still? More—more!"

"Say it, then."

"Jim, I love you!"

And their lips met again and clung, and it was he who drew back first.

"Dearest, why didn't you let me make a break to get away with you—before we came to this camp?"

"Oh, Jim, I told you. I was afraid. We'd have been caught. And Gulden—"

"We'll never have half the chance here. Kells means to keep you closely guarded. I heard the order. He's different now. He's grown crafty and hard. And the miners of this Alder Creek! Why, I'm more afraid to trust them than men like Wood or Pearce. They've gone clean crazy. Gold-mad! If you shouted for your life they wouldn't hear you. And if you could make them hear they wouldn't believe. This camp has sprung up in a night. It's not like any place I ever heard of. It's not human. It's so strange—so—Oh, I don't know what to say. I think I mean that men in a great gold strike become like coyotes at a carcass. You've seen that. No relation at all!"

"I'm frightened, too, Jim. I wish I'd had the courage to run when we were back in Cabin Gulch, But don't ever give up, not for a second! We can get away. We must plan and wait. Find out where we are—how far from Hoadley—what we must expect—whether it's safe to approach any one in this camp."

"Safe! I guess not, after to-day," he whispered, grimly.

"Why? What's happened?" she asked quickly.

"Joan, have you guessed yet why Kells sent you down into camp alone?"

"No."

"Listen.... I went with Kells and Smith and Pearce. They hurried straight to the Last Nugget. There was a crowd of men in front of the place. Pearce walked straight up to one—a gambler by his clothes. And he said in a loud voice. 'Here's the man!'... The gambler looked startled, turned pale, and went for his gun. But Kells shot him!... He fell dead, without a word. There was a big shout, then silence. Kells stood there with his smoking gun. I never saw the man so cool—so masterful. Then he addressed the crowd: 'This gambler insulted my daughter! My men here saw him. My name's Blight. I came here to buy up gold claims. And I want to say this: Your Alder Creek has got the gold. But it needs some of your best citizens to run it right, so a girl can be safe on the street.'"

"Joan, I tell you it was a magnificent bluff," went on Jim, excitedly. "And it worked. Kells walked away amid cheers. He meant to give an impression of character and importance. He succeeded. So far as I could tell, there wasn't a man present who did not show admiration for him. I saw that dead gambler kicked."

"Jim!" breathed Joan. "He killed him—just for that?"

"Just for that—the bloody devil!"

"But still—what for? Oh, it was cold-blooded murder."

"No, an even break. Kells made the gambler go for his gun. I'll have to say that for Kells."

"It doesn't change the thing. I'd forgotten what a monster he is."

"Joan, his motive is plain. This new gold-camp has not reached the blood-spilling stage yet. It hadn't, I should say. The news of this killing will fly. It'll focus minds on this claim-buyer, Blight. His deed rings true—like that of an honest man with a daughter to protect. He'll win sympathy. Then he talks as if he were prosperous. Soon he'll be represented in this changing, growing population as a man of importance. He'll play the card for all he's worth. Meanwhile, secretly he'll begin to rob the miners. It'll be hard to suspect him. His plot is just like the man— great!"

"Jim, oughtn't we tell?" whispered Joan, trembling.

"I've thought of that. Somehow I seem to feel guilty. But whom on earth could we tell? We wouldn't dare speak here.... Remember—you're a prisoner. I'm supposed to be a bandit—one of the Border Legion. How to get away from here and save our lives—that's what tortures me."

"Something tells me we'll escape, if only we can plan the right way. Jim, I'll have to be penned here, with nothing to do but wait. You must come every night!... Won't you?"

For an answer he kissed her again.

"Jim, what'll you do meanwhile?" she asked, anxiously.

"I'm going to work a claim. Dig for gold. I told Kells so to-day, and he was delighted. He said he was afraid his men wouldn't like the working part of his plan. It's hard to dig gold. Easy to steal it. But I'll dig a hole as big as a hill!... Wouldn't it be funny if I struck it rich?"

"Jim, you're getting the fever."

"Joan, if I did happen to run into a gold-pocket—there're lots of them found—would—you—marry me?"

The tenderness, the timidity, and the yearning in Cleve's voice told Joan as never before how he had hoped and feared and despaired. She patted his cheek with her hand, and in the darkness, with her heart swelling to make up for what she had done to him, she felt a boldness and a recklessness, sweet, tumultuous, irresistible.

"Jim, I'll marry you—whether you strike gold or not," she whispered.

And there was another blind, sweet moment. Then Cleve tore himself away, and Joan leaned at the window, watching the shadow, with tears in her eyes and an ache in her breast.

From that day Joan lived a life of seclusion in the small room. Kells wanted it so, and Joan thought best for the time being not to take advantage of Bate Wood's duplicity. Her meals were brought to her by Wood, who was supposed to unlock and lock her door. But Wood never turned the key in that padlock.

Prisoner though Joan was, the days and nights sped swiftly.

Kells was always up till late in the night and slept half of the next morning. It was his wont to see Joan every day about noon. He had a care for his appearance. When he came in he was dark, forbidding, weary, and cold. Manifestly he came to her to get rid of the imponderable burden of the present. He left it behind him. He never spoke a word of Alder Creek, of gold, of the Border Legion. Always he began by inquiring for her welfare, by asking what he could do for her, what he could bring her. Joan had an abhorrence of Keils in his absence that she never felt when he was with her; and the reason must have been that she thought of him, remembered him as the bandit, and saw him as another and growing character. Always mindful of her influence, she was as companionable, as sympathetic, as cheerful, and sweet as it was possible for her to be. Slowly he would warm and change under her charm, and the grim gloom, the dark strain, would pass from him. When that left he was indeed another person. Frankly he told Joan that the glimpse of real love she had simulated back there in Cabin Gulch was seldom out of his mind. No woman had ever kissed him like she had. That kiss had transfigured him. It haunted him. If he could not win kisses like that from Joan's lips, of her own free will, then he wanted none. No other woman's lips would ever touch his. And he begged Joan in the terrible earnestness of a stern and hungering outcast for her love. And Joan could only sadly shake her head and tell him she was sorry for him, that the more she really believed he loved her the surer she was that he would give her up. Then always he passionately refused. He must have her to keep, to look at as his treasure, to dream over, and hope against hope that she would love him some day. Women sometimes learned to love their captors, he said; and if she only learned, then he would take her away to Australia, to distant lands. But most of all he begged her to show him again what it meant to be loved by a good woman. And Joan, who knew that her power now lay in her unattainableness, feigned a wavering reluctance, when in truth any surrender was impossible. He left her with a spirit that her presence gave him, in a kind of trance, radiant, yet with mocking smile, as if he foresaw the overthrow of his soul through her, and in the light of that his waning power over his Legion was as nothing.

In the afternoon he went down into camp to strengthen the associations he had made, to buy claims, and to gamble. Upon his return Joan, peeping through a crack between the boards, could always tell whether he had been gambling, whether he had won or lost.

Most of the evenings he remained in his cabin, which after dark became a place of mysterious and stealthy action. The members of his Legion visited him, sometimes alone, never more than two together. Joan could hear them slipping in at the hidden aperture in the back of the cabin; she could hear the low voices, but seldom what was said; she could hear these night prowlers as they departed. Afterward Kells would have the lights lit, and then Joan could see into the cabin. Was that dark, haggard man Kells? She saw him take little buckskin sacks full of gold-dust and hide them under the floor. Then he would pace the room in his old familiar manner, like a caged tiger. Later his mood usually changed with the advent of Wood and Pearce and Smith and Cleve, who took turns at guard and going down into camp. Then Kells would join them in a friendly game for small stakes. Gambler though he was, he refused to allow any game there that might lead to heavy wagering. From the talk sometimes Joan learned that he played for exceedingly large stakes with gamblers and prosperous miners, usually with the same result—a loss. Sometimes he won, however, and then he would crow over Pearce and Smith, and delight in telling them how cunningly he had played.

Jim Cleve had his bed up under the bulge of bluff, in a sheltered nook. Kells had appeared to like this idea, for some reason relative to his scout system, which he did not explain. And Cleve was happy about it because this arrangement left him absolutely free to have his nightly rendezvous with Joan at her window, sometime between dark and midnight. Her bed was right under the window: if awake she could rest on her knees and look out; and if she was asleep he could thrust a slender stick between the boards to awaken her. But the fact was that Joan lived for these stolen meetings, and unless he could not come until very late she waited wide-eyed and listening for him. Then, besides, as long as Kells was stirring in the cabin she spent her time spying upon him.

Jim Cleve had gone to an unfrequented part of the gulch, for no particular reason, and here he had located his claim. The very first day he struck gold. And Kells, more for advertisement than for any other motive, had his men stake out a number of claims near Cleve's, and bought them. Then they had a little field of their own. All found the rich pay-dirt, but it was Cleve to whom the goddess of fortune turned her bright face. As he had been lucky at cards, so he was lucky at digging. His claim paid big returns. Kells spread the news, and that part of the gulch saw a rush of miners.

Every night Joan had her whispered hour with Cleve, and each succeeding one was the sweeter. Jim had become a victim of the gold fever. But, having Joan to steady him, he did not lose his head. If he gambled it was to help out with his part. He was generous to his comrades. He pretended to drink, but did not drink at all. Jim seemed to regard his good fortune as Joan's also. He believed if he struck it rich he could buy his sweetheart's freedom. He claimed that Kells was drunk for gold to gamble away. Joan let Jim talk, but she coaxed him and persuaded him to follow a certain line of behavior, she planned for him, she thought for him, she influenced him to hide the greater part of his gold-dust, and let it be known that he wore no gold-belt. She had a growing fear that Jim's success was likely to develop a temper in him inimical to the cool, waiting, tolerant policy needed to outwit Kells in the end. It seemed the more gold Jim acquired the more passionate he became, the more he importuned Joan, the more he hated Kells. Gold had gotten into his blood, and it was Joan's task to keep him sane. Naturally she gained more by yielding herself to Jim's caresses than by any direct advice or admonishment. It was her love that held Jim in check.

One night, the instant their hands met Joan knew that Jim was greatly excited or perturbed.

"Joan," he whispered, thrillingly, with his lips at her ear, "I've made myself solid with Kells! Oh, the luck of it!"

"Tell me!" whispered Joan, and she leaned against those lips.

"It was early to-night at the Nugget. I dropped in as usual. Kells was playing faro again with that gambler they call Flash. He's won a lot of Kells's gold—a crooked gambler. I looked on. And some of the gang were there—Pearce, Blicky, Handy Oliver, and of course Gulden, but all separated. Kells was losing and sore. But he was game. All at once he caught Flash in a crooked trick, and he yelled in a rage. He sure had the gang and everybody else looking. I expected—and so did all the gang—to see Kells pull his gun. But strange how gambling affects him! He only cursed Flash—called him right. You know that's about as bad as death to a professional gambler in a place like Alder Creek. Flash threw a derringer on Kells. He had it up his sleeve. He meant to kill Kells, and Kells had no chance. But Flash, having the drop, took time to talk, to make his bluff go strong with the crowd. And that's where he made a mistake. I jumped and knocked the gun out of his hand. It went off—burned my wrist. Then I slugged Mr. Flash good—he didn't get up.... Kells called the crowd around and, showing the cards as they lay, coolly proved that Flash was what everybody suspected. Then Kells said to me—I'll never forget how he looked: 'Youngster, he meant to do for me. I never thought of my gun. You see!... I'll kill him the next time we meet.... I've owed my life to men more than once. I never forget. You stood pat with me before. And now you're ace high!'"

"Was it fair of you?" asked Joan.

"Yes. Flash is a crooked gambler. I'd rather be a bandit.... Besides, all's fair in love! And I was thinking of you when I saved Kells!"

"Flash will be looking for you," said Joan, fearfully.

"Likely. And if he finds me he wants to be quick. But Kells will drive him out of camp or kill him. I tell you, Kells is the biggest man in Alder Creek. There's talk of office—a mayor and all that—and if the miners can forget gold long enough they'll elect Kells. But the riffraff, these bloodsuckers who live off the miners, they'd rather not have any office in Alder Creek."

And upon another night Cleve in serious and somber mood talked about the Border Legion and its mysterious workings. The name had found prominence, no one knew how, and Alder Creek knew no more peaceful sleep. This Legion was supposed to consist of a strange, secret band of unknown bandits and road-agents, drawing its members from all that wild and trackless region called the border. Rumor gave it a leader of cunning and ruthless nature. It operated all over the country at the same time, and must have been composed of numerous smaller bands, impossible to detect. Because its victims never lived to tell how or by whom they had been robbed! This Legion worked slowly and in the dark. It did not bother to rob for little gain. It had strange and unerring information of large quantities of gold-dust. Two prospectors going out on the Bannack road, packing fifty pounds of gold, were found shot to pieces. A miner named Black, who would not trust his gold to the stage-express, and who left Adler Creek against advice, was never seen or heard of again. Four other miners of the camp, known to carry considerable gold, were robbed and killed at night on their way to their cabins. And another was found dead in his bed. Robbers had crept to his tent, slashed the canvas, murdered him while he slept, and made off with his belt of gold.

An evil day of blood had fallen upon Alder Creek. There were terrible and implacable men in the midst of the miners, by day at honest toil, learning who had gold, and murdering by night. The camp had never been united, but this dread fact disrupted any possible unity. Every man, or every little group of men, distrusted the other, watched and spied and lay awake at night. But the robberies continued, one every few days, and each one left no trace. For dead men could not talk.

Thus was ushered in at Alder Creek a regime of wildness that had no parallel in the earlier days of '49 and '51. Men frenzied by the possession of gold or greed for it responded to the wildness of that time and took their cue from this deadly and mysterious Border Legion. The gold-lust created its own blood-lust. Daily the population of Alder Creek grew in the new gold-seekers and its dark records kept pace. With distrust came suspicion and with suspicion came fear, and with fear came hate—and these, in already distorted minds, inflamed a hell. So that the most primitive passions of mankind found outlet and held sway. The operations of the Border Legion were lost in deeds done in the gambling dens, in the saloons, and on the street, in broad day. Men fought for no other reason than that the incentive was in the charged air. Men were shot at gaming-tables—and the game went on. Men were killed in the dance-halls, dragged out, marking a line of blood on the rude floor—and the dance went on. Still the pursuit of gold went on, more frenzied than ever, and still the greater and richer claims were struck. The price of gold soared and the commodities of life were almost beyond the dreams of avarice. It was a tune in which the worst of men's natures stalked forth, hydra-headed and deaf, roaring for gold, spitting fire, and shedding blood. It was a time when gold and fire and blood were one. It was a tune when a horde of men from every class and nation, of all ages and characters, met on a field were motives and ambitions and faiths and traits merged into one mad instinct of gain. It was worse than the time of the medieval crimes of religion; it made war seem a brave and honorable thing; it robbed manhood of that splendid and noble trait, always seen in shipwrecked men or those hopelessly lost in the barren north, the divine will not to retrograde to the savage. It was a time, for all it enriched the world with yellow treasure, when might was right, when men were hopeless, when death stalked rampant. The sun rose gold and it set red. It was the hour of Gold!

One afternoon late, while Joan was half dreaming, half dozing the hours away, she was thoroughly aroused by the tramp of boots and loud voices of excited men. Joan slipped to the peephole in the partition. Bate Wood had raised a warning hand to Kells, who stood up, facing the door. Red Pearce came bursting in, wild-eyed and violent. Joan imagined he was about to cry out that Kells had been betrayed.

"Kells, have you—heard?" he panted.

"Not so loud, you—!" replied Kells, coolly. "My name's Blight.... Who's with you?"

"Only Jesse an' some of the gang. I couldn't steer them away. But there's nothin' to fear."

"What's happened? What haven't I heard?"

"The camp's gone plumb ravin' crazy.... Jim Cleve found the biggest nugget ever dug in Idaho!... THIRTY POUNDS!"

Kells seemed suddenly to inflame, to blaze with white passion. "Good for Jim!" he yelled, ringingly. He could scarcely have been more elated if he had made the strike himself.

Jesse Smith came stamping in, with a crowd elbowing their way behind him. Joan had a start of the old panic at sight of Gulden. For once the giant was not slow nor indifferent. His big eyes glared. He brought back to Joan the sickening sense of the brute strength of his massive presence. Some of his cronies were with him. For the rest, there were Blicky and Handy Oliver and Chick Williams. The whole group bore resemblance to a pack of wolves about to leap upon its prey. Yet, in each man, excepting Gulden, there was that striking aspect of exultation.

"Where's Jim?" demanded Kells.

"He's comin' along," replied Pearce. "He's sure been runnin' a gantlet. His strike stopped work in the diggin's. What do you think of that, Kells? The news spread like smoke before wind. Every last miner in camp has jest got to see thet lump of gold."

"Maybe I don't want to see it!" exclaimed Kells. "A thirty-pounder! I heard of one once, sixty pounds, but I never saw it. You can't believe till you see."

"Jim's comin' up the road now," said one of the men near the door. "Thet crowd hangs on.... But I reckon he's shakin' them."

"What'll Cleve do with this nugget?"

Gulden's big voice, so powerful, yet feelingless, caused a momentary silence. The expression of many faces changed. Kells looked startled, then annoyed.

"Why, Gulden, that's not my affair—nor yours," replied Kells. "Cleve dug it and it belongs to him."

"Dug or stole—it's all the same," responded Gulden.

Kell's threw up his hands as if it were useless and impossible to reason with this man.

Then the crowd surged round the door with shuffling boots and hoarse, mingled greetings to Cleve, who presently came plunging in out of the melee.

His face wore a flush of radiance; his eyes were like diamonds. Joan thrilled and thrilled at sight of him. He was beautiful. Yet there was about him a more striking wildness. He carried a gun in one hand and in the other an object wrapped in his scarf. He flung this upon the table in front of Kells. It made a heavy, solid thump. The ends of the scarf flew aside, and there lay a magnificent nugget of gold, black and rusty in parts, but with a dull, yellow glitter in others.

"Boss, what'll you bet against that?" cried Cleve, with exulting laugh. He was like a boy.

Kells reached for the nugget as if it were not an actual object, and when his hands closed on it he fondled it and weighed it and dug his nails into it and tasted it.

"My God!" he ejaculated, in wondering ecstasy. Then this, and the excitement, and the obsession all changed into sincere gladness. "Jim, you're born lucky. You, the youngster born unlucky in love! Why, you could buy any woman with this!"

"Could I? Find me one," responded Cleve, with swift boldness.

Kells laughed. "I don't know any worth so much."

"What'll I do with it?" queried Cleve.

"Why, you fool youngster! Has it turned your head, too? What'd you do with the rest of your dust? You've certainly been striking it rich."

"I spent it—lost it—lent it—gave some away and—saved a little."

"Probably you'll do the same with this. You're a good fellow, Jim."

"But this nugget means a lot of money. Between six and seven thousand dollars."

"You won't need advice how to spend it, even if it was a million.... Tell me, Jim, how'd you strike it?"

"Funny about that," replied Cleve. "Things were poor for several days. Dug off branches into my claim. One grew to be a deep hole in gravel, hard to dig. My claim was once the bed of a stream, full of rocks that the water had rolled down once. This hole sort of haunted me. I'd leave it when my back got so sore I couldn't bend, but always I'd return. I'd say there wasn't a darned grain of gold in that gravel; then like a fool I'd go back and dig for all I was worth. No chance of finding blue dirt down there! But I kept on. And to-day when my pick hit what felt like a soft rock—I looked and saw the gleam of gold!... You ought to have seen me claw out that nugget! I whooped and brought everybody around. The rest was a parade.... Now I'm embarrassed by riches. What to do with it?"

"Wal, go back to Montana an' make thet fool girl sick," suggested one of the men who had heard Jim's fictitious story of himself.

"Dug or stole is all the same!" boomed the imperturbable Gulden.

Kells turned white with rage, and Cleve swept a swift and shrewd glance at the giant.

"Sure, that's my idea," declared Cleve. "I'll divide as—as we planned."

"You'll do nothing of the kind," retorted Kells. "You dug for that gold and it's yours."

"Well, boss, then say a quarter share to you and the same to me—and divide the rest among the gang."

"No!" exclaimed Kells, violently.

Joan imagined he was actuated as much by justice to Cleve as opposition to Gulden.

"Jim Cleve, you're a square pard if I ever seen one," declared Pearce, admiringly. "An' I'm here to say thet I wouldn't hev a share of your nugget."

"Nor me," spoke up Jesse Smith.

"I pass, too," said Chick Williams.

"Jim, if I was dyin' fer a drink I wouldn't stand fer thet deal," added Blicky, with a fine scorn.

These men, and others who spoke or signified their refusal, attested to the living truth that there was honor even among robbers. But there was not the slightest suggestion of change in Gulden's attitude or of those back of him.

"Share and share alike for me!" he muttered, grimly, with those great eyes upon the nugget.

Kells, with an agile bound, reached the table and pounded it with his fist, confronting the giant.

"So you say!" he hissed in dark passion. "You've gone too far, Gulden. Here's where I call you!... You don't get a gram of that gold nugget. Jim's worked like a dog. If he digs up a million I'll see he gets it all. Maybe you loafers haven't a hunch what Jim's done for you. He's helped our big deal more than you or I. His honest work has made it easy for me to look honest. He's supposed to be engaged to marry my daughter. That more than anything was a blind. It made my stand, and I tell you that stand is high in this camp. Go down there and swear Blight is Jack Kells! See what you get!... That's all.... I'm dealing the cards in this game!"

Kells did not cow Gulden—for it was likely the giant lacked the feeling of fear—but he overruled him by sheer strength of spirit.

Gulden backed away stolidly, apparently dazed by his own movements; then he plunged out the door, and the ruffians who had given silent but sure expression of their loyalty tramped after him.

"Reckon thet starts the split!" declared Red Pearce.

"Suppose you'd been in Jim's place!" flashed Kells.

"Jack, I ain't sayin' a word. You was square. I'd want you to do the same by me.... But fetchin' the girl into the deal—"

Kells's passionate and menacing gesture shut Pearce's lips. He lifted a hand, resignedly, and went out.

"Jim," said Kells, earnestly, "take my hunch. Hide your nugget. Don't send it out with the stage to Bannack. It'd never get there.... And change the place where you sleep!"

"Thanks," replied Cleve, brightly. "I'll hide my nugget all right. And I'll take care of myself."

Later that night Joan waited at her window for Jim. It was so quiet that she could hear the faint murmur of the shallow creek. The sky was dusky blue; the stars were white, the night breeze sweet and cool. Her first flush of elation for Jim having passed, she experienced a sinking of courage. Were they not in peril enough without Jim's finding a fortune? How dark and significant had been Kells's hint! There was something splendid in the bandit. Never had Joan felt so grateful to him. He was a villain, yet he was a man. What hatred he showed for Gulden! These rivals would surely meet in a terrible conflict—for power—for gold. And for her!—she added, involuntarily, with a deep, inward shudder. Once the thought had flashed through her mind, it seemed like a word of revelation.

Then she started as a dark form rose out of the shadow under her and a hand clasped hers. Jim! and she lifted her face.

"Joan! Joan! I'm rich! rich!" he babbled, wildly.

"Ssssh!" whispered Joan, softly, in his ear. "Be careful. You're wild to-night.... I saw you come in with the nugget. I heard you.... Oh, you lucky Jim! I'll tell you what to do with it!"

"Darling! It's all yours. You'll marry me now?"

"Sir! Do you take me for a fortune-hunter? I marry you for your gold? Never!"

"Joan!"

"I've promised," she said.

"I won't go away now. I'll work my claim," he began, excitedly. And he went on so rapidly that Joan could not keep track of his words. He was not so cautious as formerly. She remonstrated with him, all to no purpose. Not only was he carried away by possession of gold and assurance of more, but he had become masterful, obstinate, and illogical. He was indeed hopeless to-night—the gold had gotten into his blood. Joan grew afraid he would betray their secret and realized there had come still greater need for a woman's wit. So she resorted to a never-failing means of silencing him, of controlling him—her lips on his.

15

For several nights these stolen interviews were apparently the safer because of Joan's tender blinding of her lover. But it seemed that in Jim's condition of mind this yielding of her lips and her whispers of love had really been a mistake. Not only had she made the situation perilously sweet for herself, but in Jim's case she had added the spark to the powder. She realized her blunder when it was too late. And the fact that she did not regret it very much, and seemed to have lost herself in a defiant, reckless spell, warned her again that she, too, was answering to the wildness of the time and place. Joan's intelligence had broadened wonderfully in this period of her life, just as all her feelings had quickened. If gold had developed and intensified and liberated the worst passions of men, so the spirit of that atmosphere had its baneful effect upon her. Joan deplored this, yet she had the keenness to understand that it was nature fitting her to survive.

Back upon her fell that weight of suspense—what would happen next? Here in Alder Creek there did not at present appear to be the same peril which had menaced her before, but she would suffer through fatality to Cleve or Kells. And these two slept at night under a shadow that held death, and by day they walked on a thin crust over a volcano. Joan grew more and more fearful of the disclosures made when Kells met his men nightly in the cabin. She feared to hear, but she must hear, and even if she had not felt it necessary to keep informed of events, the fascination of the game would have impelled her to listen. And gradually the suspense she suffered augmented into a magnified, though vague, assurance of catastrophe, of impending doom. She could not shake off the gloomy presentiment. Something terrible was going to happen. An experience begun as tragically as hers could only end in a final and annihilating stroke. Yet hope was unquenchable, and with her fear kept pace a driving and relentless spirit.

One night at the end of a week of these interviews, when Joan attempted to resist Jim, to plead with him, lest in his growing boldness he betray them, she found him a madman.

"I'll pull you right out of this window," he said, roughly, and then with his hot face pressed against hers tried to accomplish the thing he threatened.

"Go on—pull me to pieces!" replied Joan, in despair and pain. "I'd be better off dead! And—you—hurt me—so!"

"Hurt you!" he whispered, hoarsely, as if he had never dreamed of such possibility. And then suddenly he was remorseful. He begged her to forgive him. His voice was broken, husky, pleading. His remorse, like every feeling of his these days, was exaggerated, wild, with that raw tinge of gold-blood in it. He made so much noise that Joan, more fearful than ever of discovery, quieted him with difficulty.

"Does Kells see you often—these days?" asked Jim, suddenly.

Joan had dreaded this question, which she had known would inevitably come. She wanted to lie; she knew she ought to lie; but it was impossible.

"Every day," she whispered. "Please—Jim—never mind that. Kells is good—he's all right to me.... And you and I have so little time together."

"Good!" exclaimed Cleve. Joan felt the leap of his body under her touch. "Why, if I'd tell you what he sends that gang to do—you'd—you'd kill him in his sleep."

"Tell me," replied Joan. She had a morbid, irresistible desire to learn.

"No.... And WHAT does Kells do—when he sees you every day?"

"He talks."

"What about?"

"Oh, everything except about what holds him here. He talks to me to forget himself."

"Does he make love to you?"

Joan maintained silence. What would she do with this changed and hopeless Jim Cleve?

"Tell me!" Jim's hands gripped her with a force that made her wince. And now she grew as afraid of him as she had been for him. But she had spirit enough to grow angry, also.

"Certainly he does."

Jim Cleve echoed her first word, and then through grinding teeth he cursed. "I'm going to—stop it!" he panted, and his eyes looked big and dark and wild in the starlight.

"You can't. I belong to Kells. You at least ought to have sense enough to see that."

"Belong to him!... For God's sake! By what right?"

"By the right of possession. Might is right here on the border. Haven't you told me that a hundred times? Don't you hold your claim—your gold—by the right of your strength? It's the law of this border. To be sure Kells stole me. But just now I belong to him. And lately I see his consideration—his kindness in the light of what he could do if he held to that border law.... And of all the men I've met out here Kells is the least wild with this gold fever. He sends his men out to do murder for gold; he'd sell his soul to gamble for gold; but just the same, he's more of a man than—"

"Joan!" he interrupted, piercingly. "You love this bandit!"

"You're a fool!" burst out Joan.

"I guess—I—am," he replied in terrible, slow earnestness. He raised himself and appeared to loom over her and released his hold.

But Joan fearfully retained her clasp on his arm, and when he surged to get away she was hard put to it to hold him.

"Jim! Where are you going?"

He stood there a moment, a dark form against the night shadow, like an outline of a man cut from black stone.

"I'll just step around—there."

"Oh, what for?" whispered Joan.

"I'm going to kill Kells."

Joan got both arms round his neck and with her head against him she held him tightly, trying, praying to think how to meet this long-dreaded moment. After all, what was the use to try? This was the hour of Gold! Sacrifice, hope, courage, nobility, fidelity—these had no place here now. Men were the embodiment of passion—ferocity. They breathed only possession, and the thing in the balance was death. Women were creatures to hunger and fight for, but womanhood was nothing. Joan knew all this with a desperate hardening certainty, and almost she gave in. Strangely, thought of Gulden flashed up to make her again strong! Then she raised her face and began the old pleading with Jim, but different this time, when it seemed that absolutely all was at stake. She begged him, she importuned him, to listen to reason, to be guided by her, to fight the wildness that had obsessed him, to make sure that she would not be left alone. All in vain! He swore he would kill Kells and any other bandit who stood in the way of his leading her free out of that cabin. He was wild to fight. He might never have felt fear of these robbers. He would not listen to any possibility of defeat for himself, or the possibility that in the event of Kells's death she would be worse off. He laughed at her strange, morbid fears of Gulden. He was immovable.

"Jim!... Jim! You'll break my heart!" she whispered, wailingly. "Oh! WHAT can I do?"

Then Joan released her clasp and gave up to utter defeat. Cleve was silent. He did not seem to hear the shuddering little sobs that shook her. Suddenly he bent close to her.

"There's one thing you can do. If you'll do it I won't kill Kells. I'll obey your every word."

"What is it? Tell me!"

"Marry me!" he whispered, and his voice trembled.

"MARRY YOU!" exclaimed Joan. She was confounded. She began to fear Jim was out of his head.

"I mean it. Marry me. Oh, Joan, will you—will you? It'll make the difference. That'll steady me. Don't you want to?"

"Jim, I'd be the happiest girl in the world if—if I only COULD marry you!" she breathed, passionately.

"But will you—will you? Say yes! Say yes!"

"YES!" replied Joan in her desperation. "I hope that pleases you. But what on earth is the use to talk about it now?"

Cleve seemed to expand, to grow taller, to thrill under her nervous hands. And then he kissed her differently. She sensed a shyness, a happiness, a something hitherto foreign to his attitude. It was spiritual, and somehow she received an uplift of hope.

"Listen," he whispered. "There's a preacher down in camp. I've seen him—talked with him. He's trying to do good in that hell down there. I know I can trust him. I'll confide in him—enough. I'll fetch him up here tomorrow night—about this time. Oh, I'll be careful—very careful. And he can marry us right here by the window. Joan, will you do it?... Somehow, whatever threatens you or me—that'll be my salvation!... I've suffered so. It's been burned in my heart that YOU would never marry me. Yet you say you love me!... Prove it!... MY WIFE!... Now, girl, a word will make a man of me!"

"Yes!" And with the word she put her lips to his with all her heart in them. She felt him tremble. Yet almost instantly he put her from him.

"Look for me to-morrow about this time," he whispered. "Keep your nerve.... Good night."

That night Joan dreamed strange, weird, unremembered dreams. The next day passed like a slow, unreal age. She ate little of what was brought to her. For the first time she denied Kells admittance and she only vaguely sensed his solicitations. She had no ear for the murmur of voices in Kells's room. Even the loud and angry notes of a quarrel between Kells and his men did not distract her.

At sunset she leaned out of the little window, and only then, with the gold fading on the peaks and the shadow gathering under the bluff, did she awaken to reality. A broken mass of white cloud caught the glory of the sinking sun. She had never seen a golden radiance like that. It faded and dulled. But a warm glow remained. At twilight and then at dusk this glow lingered.

Then night fell. Joan was exceedingly sensitive to the sensations of light and shadow, of sound and silence, of dread and hope, of sadness and joy.

That pale, ruddy glow lingered over the bold heave of the range in the west. It was like a fire that would not go out, that would live to-morrow, and burn golden. The sky shone with deep, rich blue color fired with a thousand stars, radiant, speaking, hopeful. And there was a white track across the heavens. The mountains flung down their shadows, impenetrable, like the gloomy minds of men; and everywhere under the bluffs and slopes, in the hollows and ravines, lay an enveloping blackness, hiding its depth and secret and mystery.

Joan listened. Was there sound or silence? A faint and indescribably low roar, so low that it might have been real or false, came on the soft night breeze. It was the roar of the camp down there—the strife, the agony, the wild life in ceaseless action—the strange voice of gold, roaring greed and battle and death over the souls of men. But above that, presently, rose the murmur of the creek, a hushed and dreamy flow of water over stones. It was hurrying to get by this horde of wild men, for it must bear the taint of gold and blood. Would it purge itself and clarify in the valleys below, on its way to the sea? There was in its murmur an imperishable and deathless note of nature, of time; and this was only a fleeting day of men and gold.

Only by straining her ears could Joan hear these sounds, and when she ceased that, then she seemed to be weighed upon and claimed by silence. It was not a silence like that of Lost Canon, but a silence of solitude where her soul stood alone. She was there on earth, yet no one could hear her mortal cry. The thunder of avalanches or the boom of the sea might have lessened her sense of utter loneliness.

And that silence fitted the darkness, and both were apostles of dread. They spoke to her. She breathed dread on that silent air and it filled her breast. There was nothing stable in the night shadows. The ravine seemed to send forth stealthy, noiseless shapes, specter and human, man and phantom, each on the other's trail.

If Jim would only come and let her see that he was safe for the hour! A hundred times she imagined she saw him looming darker than the shadows. She had only to see him now, to feel his hand, and dread might be lost. Love was something beyond the grasp of mind. Love had confounded Jim Cleve; it had brought up kindness and honor from the black depths of a bandit's heart; it had transformed her from a girl into a woman. Surely with all its greatness it could not be lost; surely in the end it must triumph over evil.

Joan found that hope was fluctuating, but eternal. It took no stock of intelligence. It was a matter of feeling. And when she gave rein to it for a moment, suddenly it plunged her into sadness. To hope was to think! Poor Jim! It was his fool's paradise. Just to let her be his wife! That was the apex of his dream. Joan divined that he might yield to her wisdom, he might become a man, but his agony would be greater. Still, he had been so intense, so strange, so different that she could not but feel joy in his joy.

Then at a soft footfall, a rustle, and a moving shadow Joan's mingled emotions merged into a poignant sense of the pain and suspense and tenderness of the actual moment.

"Joan—Joan," came the soft whisper.

She answered, and there was a catch in her breath.

The moving shadow split into two shadows that stole closer, loomed before her. She could not tell which belonged to Jim till he touched her. His touch was potent. It seemed to electrify her.

"Dearest, we're here—this is the parson," said Jim, like a happy boy. "I—"

"Ssssh!" whispered Joan. "Not so loud.... Listen!"

Kells was holding a rendezvous with members of his Legion. Joan even recognized his hard and somber tone, and the sharp voice of Red Pearce, and the drawl of Handy Oliver.

"All right. I'll be quiet," responded Cleve, cautiously. "Joan, you're to answer a few questions."

Then a soft hand touched Joan, and a voice differently keyed from any she had heard on the border addressed her.

"What is your name?" asked the preacher.

Joan told him.

"Can you tell anything about yourself? This young man is—is almost violent. I'm not sure. Still I want to—"

"I can't tell much," replied Joan, hurriedly. "I'm an honest girl. I'm free to—to marry him. I—I love him!... Oh, I want to help him. We—we are in trouble here. I daren't say how."

"Are you over eighteen?" "Yes, sir."

"Do your parents object to this young man?"

"I have no parents. And my uncle, with whom I lived before I was brought to this awful place, he loves Jim. He always wanted me to marry him."

"Take his hand, then."

Joan felt the strong clasp of Jim's fingers, and that was all which seemed real at the moment. It seemed so dark and shadowy round these two black forms in front of her window. She heard a mournful wail of a lone wolf and it intensified the weird dream that bound her. She heard her shaking, whispered voice repeating the preacher's words. She caught a phrase of a low-murmured prayer. Then one dark form moved silently away. She was alone with Jim.

"Dearest Joan!" he whispered. "It's over! It's done!... Kiss me!"

She lifted her lips and Jim seemed to kiss her more sweetly, with less violence.

"Oh, Joan, that you'd really have me! I can't believe it.... Your HUSBAND."

That word dispelled the dream and the pain which had held Joan, leaving only the tenderness, magnified now a hundredfold.

And that instant when she was locked in Cleve's arms, when the silence was so beautiful and full, she heard the heavy pound of a gun-butt upon the table in Kells's room.

"Where is Cleve?" That was the voice of Kells, stern, demanding.

Joan felt a start, a tremor run over Jim. Then he stiffened.

"I can't locate him," replied Red Pearce. "It was the same last night an' the one before. Cleve jest disappears these nights—about this time.... Some woman's got him!"

"He goes to bed. Can't you find where he sleeps?"

"No."

"This job's got to go through and he's got to do it."

"Bah!" taunted Pearce. "Gulden swears you can't make Cleve do a job. And so do I!"

"Go out and yell for Cleve!... Damn you all! I'll show you!"

Then Joan heard the tramp of heavy boots, then a softer tramp on the ground outside the cabin. Joan waited, holding her breath. She felt Jim's heart beating. He stood like a post. He, like Joan, was listening, as if for a trumpet of doom.

"HALLO, JIM!" rang out Pearce's stentorian call. It murdered the silence. It boomed under the bluff, and clapped in echo, and wound away, mockingly. It seemed to have shrieked to the whole wild borderland the breaking-point of the bandit's power.

So momentous was the call that Jim Cleve seemed to forget Joan, and she let him go without a word. Indeed, he was gone before she realized it, and his dark form dissolved in the shadows. Joan waited, listening with abated breathing. On this side of the cabin there was absolute silence. She believed that Jim would slip around under cover of night and return by the road from camp. Then what would he do? The question seemed to puzzle her.

Joan leaned there at her window for moments greatly differing from those vaguely happy ones just passed. She had sustained a shock that had left her benumbed with a dull pain. What a rude, raw break the voice of Kells had made in her brief forgetfulness! She was returning now to reality. Presently she would peer through the crevice between the boards into the other room, and she shrank from the ordeal. Kells, and whoever was with him, maintained silence. Occasionally she heard the shuffle of a boot and a creak of the loose floor boards. She waited till anxiety and fear compelled her to look.

The lamps were burning; the door was wide open. Apparently Kells's rule of secrecy had been abandoned. One glance at Kells was enough to show Joan that he was sick and desperate. Handy Oliver did not wear his usual lazy good humor. Red Pearce sat silent and sullen, a smoking, unheeded pipe in his hand. Jesse Smith was gloomy. The only other present was Bate Wood, and whatever had happened had in no wise affected him. These bandits were all waiting. Presently quick footsteps on the path outside caused them all to look toward the door. That tread was familiar to Joan, and suddenly her mouth was dry, her tongue stiff. What was Jim Cleve coming to meet? How sharp and decided his walk! Then his dark form crossed the bar of light outside the door, and he entered, bold and cool, and with a weariness that must have been simulated.

"Howdy boys!" he said.

Only Kells greeted him in response. The bandit eyed him curiously. The others added suspicion to their glances.

"Did you hear Red's yell?" queried Kells, presently.

"I'd have heard that roar if I'd been dead," replied Cleve, bluntly. "And I didn't like it!... I was coming up the road and I heard Pearce yell. I'll bet every man in camp heard it."

"How'd you know Pearce yelled for you?"

"I recognized his voice."

Cleve's manner recalled to Joan her first sight of him over in Cabin Gulch. He was not so white or haggard, but his eyes were piercing, and what had once been recklessness now seemed to be boldness. He deliberately studied Pearce. Joan trembled, for she divined what none of these robbers knew, and it was that Pearce was perilously near death. It was there for Joan to read in Jim's dark glance.

"Where've you been all these nights?" queried the bandit leader.

"Is that any of your business—when you haven't had need of me?" returned Cleve.

"Yes, it's my business. And I've sent for you. You couldn't be found."

"I've been here for supper every night."

"I don't talk to any men in daylight. You know my hours for meeting. And you've not come."

"You should have told me. How was I to know?"

"I guess you're right. But where've you been?"

"Down in camp. Faro, most of the time. Bad luck, too."

Red Pearce's coarse face twisted into a scornful sneer. It must have been a lash to Kells.

"Pearce says you're chasing a woman," retorted the bandit leader.

"Pearce lies!" flashed Cleve. His action was as swift. And there he stood with a gun thrust hard against Pearce's side.

"JIM! Don't kill him!" yelled Kells, rising.

Pearce's red face turned white. He stood still as a stone, with his gaze fixed in fascinated fear upon Cleve's gun.

A paralyzing surprise appeared to hold the group.

"Can you prove what you said?" asked Cleve, low and hard.

Joan knew that if Pearce did have the proof which would implicate her he would never live to tell it.

"Cleve—I don't—know nothin'," choked out Pearce. "I jest figgered—it was a woman!"

Cleve slowly lowered the gun and stepped back. Evidently that satisfied him. But Joan had an intuitive feeling that Pearce lied.

"You want to be careful how you talk about me," said Cleve.

Kells purled out a suspended breath and he flung the sweat from his brow. There was about him, perhaps more than the others, a dark realization of how close the call had been for Pearce.

"Jim, you're not drunk?"

"No."

"But you're sore?"

"Sure I'm sore. Pearce put me in bad with you, didn't he?"

"No. You misunderstood me. Red hasn't a thing against you. And neither he nor anybody else could put you in bad with me."

"All right. Maybe I was hasty. But I'm not wasting time these days," replied Cleve. "I've no hard feelings.... Pearce, do you want to shake hands—or hold that against me?"

"He'll shake, of course," said Kells.

Pearce extended his hand, but with a bad grace. He was dominated. This affront of Cleve's would rankle in him.

"Kells, what do you want with me?" demanded Cleve.

A change passed over Kells, and Joan could not tell just what it was, but somehow it seemed to suggest a weaker man.

"Jim, you've been a great card for me," began Kells, impressively. "You've helped my game—and twice you saved my life. I think a lot of you.... If you stand by me now I swear I'll return the trick some day.... Will you stand by me?"

"Yes," replied Cleve, steadily, but he grew pale. "What's the trouble?"

"By—, it's bad enough!" exclaimed Kells, and as he spoke the shade deepened in his haggard face. "Gulden has split my Legion. He has drawn away more than half my men. They have been drunk and crazy ever since. They've taken things into their own hands. You see the result as well as I. That camp down there is fire and brimstone. Some one of that drunken gang has talked. We're none of us safe any more. I see suspicion everywhere. I've urged getting a big stake and then hitting the trail for the border. But not a man sticks to me in that. They all want the free, easy, wild life of this gold-camp. So we're anchored till—till... But maybe it's not too late. Pearce, Oliver, Smith—all the best of my Legion—profess loyalty to me. If we all pull together maybe we can win yet. But they've threatened to split, too. And it's all on your account!"

"Mine?" ejaculated Cleve.

"Yes. Now it's nothing to make you flash your gun. Remember you said you'd stand by me.... Jim, the fact is—all the gang to a man believe you're double-crossing me!"

"In what way?" queried Cleve, blanching.

"They think you're the one who has talked. They blame you for the suspicion that's growing."

"Well, they're absolutely wrong," declared Cleve, in a ringing voice.

"I know they are. Mind you I'm not hinting I distrust you. I don't. I swear by you. But Pearce—"

"So it's Pearce," interrupted Cleve, darkly. "I thought you said he hadn't tried to put me in bad with you."

"He hasn't. He simply spoke his convictions. He has a right to them. So have all the men. And, to come to the point, they all think you're crooked because you're honest!"

"I don't understand," replied Cleve, slowly.

"Jim, you rode into Cabin Gulch, and you raised some trouble. But you were no bandit. You joined my Legion, but you've never become a bandit. Here you've been an honest miner. That suited my plan and it helped. But it's got so it doesn't suit my men. You work every day hard. You've struck it rich. You're well thought of in Alder Creek. You've never done a dishonest thing. Why, you wouldn't turn a crooked trick in a card game for a sack full of gold. This has hurt you with my men. They can't see as I see, that you're as square as you are game. They see you're an honest miner. They believe you've got into a clique—that you've given us away. I don't blame Pearce or any of my men. This is a time when men's intelligence, if they have any, doesn't operate. Their brains are on fire. They see gold and whisky and blood, and they feel gold and whisky and blood. That's all. I'm glad that the gang gives you the benefit of a doubt and a chance to stand by me."

"A chance!"

"Yes. They've worked out a job for you alone. Will you undertake it?"

"I'll have to," replied Cleve.

"You certainly will if you want the gang to justify my faith in you. Once you pull off a crooked deal, they'll switch and swear by you. Then we'll get together, all of us, and plan what to do about Gulden and his outfit. They'll run our heads, along with their own, right into the noose."

"What is this—this job?" labored Cleve. He was sweating now and his hair hung damp over his brow. He lost that look which had made him a bold man and seemed a boy again, weak, driven, bewildered.

Kells averted his gaze before speaking again. He hated to force this task upon Cleve. Joan felt, in the throbbing pain of the moment, that if she never had another reason to like this bandit, she would like him for the pity he showed.

"Do you know a miner named Creede?" asked Kells, rapidly.

"A husky chap, short, broad, something like Gulden for shape, only not so big—fellow with a fierce red beard?" asked Cleve.

"I never saw him," replied Kells. "But Pearce has. How does Cleve's description fit Creede?"

"He's got his man spotted," answered Pearce.

"All right, that's settled," went on Kells, warming to his subject. "This fellow Creede wears a heavy belt of gold. Blicky never makes a mistake. Creede's partner left on yesterday's stage for Bannack. He'll be gone a few days. Creede is a hard worker-one of the hardest. Sometimes he goes to sleep at his supper. He's not the drinking kind. He's slow, thick-headed. The best time for this job will be early in the evening—just as soon as his lights are out. Locate the tent. It stands at the head of a little wash and there's a bleached pine-tree right by the tent. To-morrow night as soon as it gets dark crawl up this wash—be careful—wait till the right time—then finish the job quick!"

"How—finish—it?" asked Cleve, hoarsely.

Kells was scintillating now, steely, cold, radiant. He had forgotten the man before him in the prospect of the gold.

"Creede's cot is on the side of the tent opposite the tree. You won't have to go inside. Slit the canvas. It's a rotten old tent. Kill Creede with your knife.... Get his belt.... Be bold, cautious, swift! That's your job. Now what do you say?"

"All right," responded Cleve, somberly, and with a heavy tread he left the room.

After Jim had gone Joan still watched and listened. She was in distress over his unfortunate situation, but she had no fear that he meant to carry out Kells's plan. This was a critical time for Jim, and therefore for her. She had no idea what Jim could do; all she thought was what he would not do.

Kells gazed triumphantly at Pearce. "I told you the youngster would stand by me. I never put him on a job before."

"Reckon I figgered wrong, boss," replied Pearce.

"He looked sick to me, but game," said Handy Oliver. "Kells is right, Red, an' you've been sore-headed over nothin'!"

"Mebbe. But ain't it good figgerin' to make Cleve do some kind of a job, even if he is on the square?"

They all acquiesced to this, even Kells slowly nodding his head.

"Jack, I've thought of another an' better job for young Cleve," spoke up Jesse Smith, with his characteristic grin.

"You'll all be setting him jobs now," replied Kells. "What's yours?"

"You spoke of plannin' to get together once more—what's left of us. An' there's thet bull-head Gulden."

"You're sure right," returned the leader, grimly, and he looked at Smith as if he would welcome any suggestion.

"I never was afraid to speak my mind," went on Smith. Here he lost his grin and his coarse mouth grew hard. "Gulden will have to be killed if we're goin' to last!"

"Wood, what do you say?" queried Kells, with narrowing eyes.

Bate Wood nodded as approvingly as if he had been asked about his bread.

126

"Oliver, what do you say?"

"Wal, I'd love to wait an' see Gul hang, but if you press me, I'll agree to stand pat with the cards Jesse's dealt," replied Handy Oliver.

Then Kells turned with a bright gleam upon his face. "And you—Pearce?"

"I'd say yes in a minute if I'd not have to take a hand in thet job," replied Pearce, with a hard laugh. "Gulden won't be so easy to kill. He'll pack a gunful of lead. I'll gamble if the gang of us cornered him in this cabin he'd do for most of us before we killed him."

"Gul sleep alone, no one knows where," said Handy Oliver. "An' he can't be surprised. Red's correct. How're we goin' to kill him?"

"If you gents will listen you'll find out," rejoined Jesse Smith. "Thet's the job for young Cleve. He can do it. Sure Gulden never was afraid of any man. But somethin' about Cleve bluffed him. I don't know what. Send Cleve out after Gulden. He'll call him face to face, anywhere, an' beat him to a gun!... Take my word for it."

"Jesse, that's the grandest idea you ever had," said Kells, softly. His eyes shone. The old power came back to his face. "I split on Gulden. With him once out of the way—!"

"Boss, are you goin' to make thet Jim Cleve's second job?" inquired Pearce, curiously.

"I am," replied Kells, with his jaw corded and stiff. "If he pulls thet off you'll never hear a yap from me so long as I live. An' I'll eat out of Cleve's hand."

Joan could bear to hear no more. She staggered to her bed and fell there, all cramped as if in a cold vise. However Jim might meet the situation planned for murdering Creede, she knew he would not shirk facing Gulden with deadly intent. He hated Gulden because she had a horror of him. Would these hours of suspense never end? Must she pass from one torture to another until—?

Sleep did not come for a long time. And when it did she suffered with nightmares from which it seemed she could never awaken.

The day, when at last it arrived, was no better than the night. It wore on endlessly, and she who listened so intently found it one of the silent days. Only Bate Wood remained at the cabin. He appeared kinder than usual, but Joan did not want to talk. She ate her meals, and passed the hours watching from the window and lying on the bed. Dusk brought Kells and Pearce and Smith, but not Jim Cleve. Handy Oliver and Blicky arrived at supper-time.

"Reckon Jim's appetite is pore," remarked Bate Wood, reflectively. "He ain't been in to-day."

Some of the bandits laughed, but Kells had a twinge, if Joan ever saw a man have one. The dark, formidable, stern look was on his face. He alone of the men ate sparingly, and after the meal he took to his bent posture and thoughtful pacing. Joan saw the added burden of another crime upon his shoulders. Conversation, which had been desultory, and such as any miners or campers might have indulged in, gradually diminished to a word here and there, and finally ceased. Kells always at this hour had a dampening effect upon his followers. More and more he drew aloof from them, yet he never realized that. He might have been alone. But often he glanced out of the door, and appeared to listen. Of course he expected Jim Cleve to return, but what did he expect of him? Joan had a blind faith that Jim would be cunning enough to fool Kells and Pearce. So much depended upon it!

Some of the bandits uttered an exclamation. Then silently, like a shadow, Jim Cleve entered.

Joan's heart leaped and seemed to stand still. Jim could not have locked more terrible if he were really a murderer. He opened his coat. Then he flung a black object upon the table and it fell with a soft, heavy, sodden thud. It was a leather belt packed with gold.

When Kells saw that he looked no more at the pale Cleve. His clawlike hand swept out for the belt, lifted and weighed it. Likewise the other bandits, with gold in sight, surged round Kells, forgetting Cleve.

"Twenty pounds!" exclaimed Kells, with a strange rapture in his voice.

"Let me heft it?" asked Pearce, thrillingly.

Joan saw and heard so much, then through a kind of dimness, that she could not wipe away, her eyes beheld Jim. What was the awful thing that she interpreted from his face, his mien? Was this a part he was playing to deceive Kells? The slow-gathering might of her horror came with the meaning of that gold-belt. Jim had brought back the gold-belt of the miner Creede. He had, in his passion to remain near her, to save her in the end, kept his word to Kells and done the ghastly deed.

Joan reeled and sank back upon the bed, blindly, with darkening sight and mind.

16

Joan returned to consciousness with a sense of vague and unlocalized pain which she thought was that old, familiar pang of grief. But once fully awakened, as if by a sharp twinge, she became aware that the pain was some kind of muscular throb in her shoulder. The instant she was fully sure of this the strange feeling ceased. Then she lay wide-eyed in the darkness, waiting and wondering.

Suddenly the slight sharp twing was repeated. It seemed to come from outside her flesh. She shivered a little, thinking it might be a centipede. When she reached for her shoulder her hand came in contact with a slender stick that had been thrust through a crack between the boards. Jim was trying to rouse her. This had been his method on several occasions when she had fallen asleep after waiting long for him.

Joan got up to the window, dizzy and sick with the resurging memory of Jim's return to Kells with that gold-belt.

Jim rose out of the shadow and felt for her, clasped her close. Joan had none of the old thrill; her hands slid loosely round his; and every second the weight inwardly grew heavier.

"Joan! I had a time waking you," whispered Jim, and then he kissed her. "Why, you're as cold as ice."

"Jim—I—I must have fainted," she replied.

"What for?" "I was peeping into Kells's cabin, when you—you—"

"Poor kid!" he interrupted, tenderly. "You've had so much to bear!... Joan, I fooled Kells. Oh, I was slick!... He ordered me out on a job—to kill a miner! Fancy that! And what do you think? I know Creede well. He's a good fellow. I traded my big nugget for his gold-belt!"

"You TRADED—you—didn't—kill him!" faltered Joan.

"Hear the child talk!" exclaimed Cleve, with a low laugh.

Joan suddenly clung to him with all her might, quivering in a silent joy. It had not occurred to Jim what she might have thought.

"Listen," he went on. "I traded my nugget. It was worth a great deal more than Creede's gold-belt. He knew this. He didn't want to trade. But I coaxed him. I persuaded him to leave camp—to walk out on the road to Bannack. To meet the stage somewhere and go on to Bannack, and stay a few days. He sure was curious. But I kept my secret.... Then I came back here, gave the belt to Kells, told him I had followed Creede in the dark, had killed him and slid him into a deep hole in the creek.... Kells and Pearce—none of them paid any attention to my story. I had the gold-belt. That was enough. Gold talks—fills the ears of these bandits.... I have my share of Creede's gold-dust in my pocket. Isn't that funny? Alas for my—YOUR big nugget! But we've got to play the game. Besides, I've sacks and cans of gold hidden away. Joan, what'll we do with it all? You're my wife now. And, oh! If we can only get away with it you'll be rich!"

Joan could not share his happiness any more than she could understand his spirit. She remembered.

"Jim—dear—did Kells tell you what your—next job was to be?" she whispered, haltingly.

Cleve swore under his breath, but loud enough to make Joan swiftly put her hand over his lips and caution him.

"Joan, did you hear that about Gulden?" he asked.

"Oh yes."

"I'm sorry. I didn't mean to tell you. Yes, I've got my second job. And this one I can't shirk or twist around."

Joan held to him convulsively. She could scarcely speak.

"Girl, don't lose your nerve!" he said, sternly. "When you married me you made me a man. I'll play my end of the game. Don't fear for me. You plan when we can risk escape. I'll obey you to the word."

"But Jim—oh, Jim!" she moaned. "You're as wild as these bandits. You can't see your danger.... That terrible Gulden!... You don't mean to meet him—fight him?... Say you won't!"

"Joan, I'll meet him—and I'll KILL him," whispered Jim, with a piercing intensity. "You never knew I was swift with a gun. Well, I didn't, either, till I struck the border. I know now. Kells is the only man I've seen who can throw a gun quicker than I. Gulden is a big bull. He's slow. I'll get into a card-game with him—I'll quarrel over gold—I'll smash him as I did once before—and this time I won't shoot off his ear. I've my nerve now. Kells swore he'd do anything for me if I stand by him now. I will. You never can tell. Kells is losing his grip. And my standing by him may save you."

Joan drew a deep breath. Jim Cleve had indeed come into manhood. She crushed down her womanish fears and rose dauntless to the occasion. She would never weaken him by a lack of confidence.

"Jim, Kells's plot draws on to a fatal close," she said, earnestly. "I feel it. He's doomed. He doesn't realize that yet. He hopes and plots on. When he falls, then he'll be great—terrible. We must get away before that comes. What you said about Creede has given me an idea. Suppose we plan to slip out some night soon, and stop the stage next day on its way to Bannack?"

"I've thought of that. But we must have horses."

"Let's go afoot. We'd be safer. There'd not be so much to plan."

"But if we go on foot we must pack guns and grub—and there's my gold-dust. Fifty pounds or more! It's yours, Joan.... You'll need it all. You love pretty clothes and things. And now I'll get them for you or—or die."

"Hush! That's foolish talk, with our very lives at stake. Let me plan some more. Oh, I think so hard!... And, Jim, there's another thing. Red Pearce was more than suspicious about your absence from the cabin at certain hours. What he hinted to Kells about a woman in the case! I'm afraid he suspects or knows."

"He had me cold, too," replied Cleve, thoughtfully. "But he swore he knew nothing."

"Jim, trust a woman's instinct. Pearce lied. That gun at his side made him a liar. He knew you'd kill him if he betrayed himself by a word. Oh, look out for him!"

Cleve did not reply. It struck Joan that he was not listening, at least to her. His head was turned, rigid and alert. He had his ear to the soft wind. Suddenly Joan heard a faint rustle-then another. They appeared to come from the corner of the cabin. Silently Cleve sank down into the shadow and vanished. Low, stealthy footsteps followed, but Joan was not sure whether or not Cleve made them. They did not seem to come from the direction he usually took. Besides, when he was careful he never made the slightest noise. Joan strained her ears, only to catch the faint sounds of the night. She lay back upon her bed, worried and anxious again, and soon the dread returned. There were to be no waking or sleeping hours free from this portent of calamity.

Next morning Joan awaited Kells, as was her custom, but he did not appear. This was the third time in a week that he had forgotten or avoided her or had been prevented from seeing her. Joan was glad, yet the fact was not reassuring. The issue for Kells was growing from trouble to disaster.

Early in the afternoon she heard Kells returning from camp. He had men with him. They conversed in low, earnest tones. Joan was about to spy up on them when Kells's step approached her door. He rapped and spoke:

"Put on Dandy Dale's suit and mask, and come out here," he said.

The tone of his voice as much as the content of his words startled Joan so that she did not at once reply.

"Do you hear?" he called, sharply.

"Yes," replied Joan.

Then he went back to his men, and the low, earnest conversation was renewed.

Reluctantly Joan took down Dandy Dale's things from the pegs, and with a recurring shame she divested herself of part of her clothes and donned the suit and boots and mask and gun. Her spirit rose, however, at the thought that this would be a disguise calculated to aid her in the escape with Cleve. But why had Kells ordered the change? Was he in danger and did he mean to flee from Alder Creek? Joan found the speculation a relief from that haunting, persistent thought of Jim Cleve and Gulden. She was eager to learn, still she hesitated at the door. It was just as hard as ever to face those men.

But it must be, so with a wrench she stepped out boldly.

Kells looked worn and gray. He had not slept. But his face did not wear the shade she had come to associate with his gambling and drinking. Six other men were present, and Joan noted coats and gloves and weapons and spurs. Kells turned to address her. His face lighted fleetingly.

"I want you to be ready to ride any minute," he said.

"Why?" asked Joan.

"We may HAVE to, that's all," he replied.

His men, usually so keen when they had a chance to ogle Joan, now scarcely gave her a glance. They were a dark, grim group, with hard eyes and tight lips. Handy Oliver was speaking.

"I tell you, Gulden swore he seen Creede—on the road—in the lamplight—last night AFTER Jim Cleve got here."

"Gulden must have been mistaken," declared Kells, impatiently.

"He ain't the kind to make mistakes," replied Oliver.

"Gul's seen Creede's ghost, thet's what," suggested Blicky, uneasily. "I've seen a few in my time."

Some of the bandits nodded gloomily.

"Aw!" burst out Red Pearce. "Gulden never seen a ghost in his life. If he seen Creede he's seen him ALIVE!"

"Shore you're right, Red," agreed Jesse Smith.

"But, men—Cleve brought in Creede's belt—and we've divided the gold," said Kells. "You all know Creede would have to be dead before that belt could be unbuckled from him. There's a mistake."

"Boss, it's my idee thet Gul is only makin' more trouble," put in Bate Wood. "I seen him less than an hour ago. I was the first one Gul talked to. An' he knew Jim Cleve did for Creede. How'd he know? Thet was supposed to be a secret. What's more, Gul told me Cleve was on the job to kill him. How'd he ever find thet out?... Sure as God made little apples Cleve never told him!"

Kells's face grew livid and his whole body vibrated. "Maybe one of Gulden's gang was outside, listening when we planned Cleve's job," he suggested. But his look belied his hope.

"Naw! There's a nigger in the wood-pile, you can gamble on thet," blurted out the sixth bandit, a lean faced, bold-eye, blond-mustached fellow whose name Joan had never heard.

"I won't believe it," replied Kells, doggedly. "And you, Budd, you're accusing somebody present of treachery—or else Cleve. He's the only one not here who knew."

"Wal, I always said thet youngster was slick," replied Budd.

"Will you accuse him to his face?"

"I shore will. Glad of the chance."

"Then you're drunk or just a fool."

"Thet so?"

"Yes, that's so," flashed Kells. "You don't know Cleve. He'll kill you. He's lightning with a gun. Do you suppose I'd set him on Gulden's trail if I wasn't sure? Why I wouldn't care to—"

"Here comes Cleve," interrupted Pearce, sharply.

Rapid footsteps sounded without. Then Joan saw Jim Cleve darken the doorway. He looked keen and bold. Upon sight of Joan in her changed attire he gave a slight start.

"Budd, here's Cleve," called out Red Pearce, mockingly. "Now, say it to his face!"

In the silence that ensued Pearce's spirit dominated the moment with its cunning, hate, and violence. But Kells savagely leaped in front of the men, still master of the situation.

"Red, what's got into you?" he hissed. "You're cross-grained lately. You're sore. Any more of this and I'll swear you're a disorganizer.... Now, Budd, you keep your mouth shut. And you, Cleve, you pay no heed to Budd if he does gab.... We're in bad and all the men have chips on their shoulders. We've got to stop fighting among ourselves."

"Wal, boss, there's a power of sense in a good example," dryly remarked Bate Wood. His remark calmed Kells and eased the situation.

"Jim, did you meet Gulden?" queried Kells, eagerly.

"Can't find him anywhere," replied Cleve. "I've loafed in the saloons and gambling-hells where he hangs out. But he didn't show up. He's in camp. I know that for a fact. He's laying low for some reason."

"Gulden's been tipped off, Jim," said Kells, earnestly. "He told Bate Wood you were out to kill him."

"I'm glad. It wasn't a fair hand you were going to deal him," responded Cleve. "But who gave my job away? Someone in this gang wants me done for—more than Gulden."

Cleve's flashing gaze swept over the motionless men and fixed hardest upon Red Pearce. Pearce gave back hard look for hard look.

"Gulden told Oliver more," continued Kells, and he pulled Cleve around to face him. "Gulden swore he saw Creede alive last night.... LATE LAST NIGHT!"

"That's funny," replied Cleve, without the flicker of an eyelash.

"It's not funny. But it's queer. Gulden hasn't the moral sense to lie. Bate says he wants to make trouble between you and me. I doubt that. I don't believe Gulden could see a ghost, either. He's simply mistaken some miner for Creede."

"He sure has, unless Creede came back to life. I'm not sitting on his chest now, holding him down."

Kells drew back, manifestly convinced and relieved. This action seemed to be a magnet for Pearce. He detached himself from the group, and, approaching Kells, tapped him significantly on the shoulder; and whether by design or accident the fact was that he took a position where Kells was between him and Cleve.

"Jack, you're being double-crossed here—an' by more 'n one," he said, deliberately. "But if you want me to talk you've got to guarantee no gun-play."

"Speak up, Red," replied Kells, with a glinting eye. "I swear there won't be a gun pulled."

The other men shifted from one foot to another and there were deep-drawn breaths. Jim Cleve alone seemed quiet and cool. But his eyes were ablaze.

"Fust off an' for instance here's one who's double-crossin' you," said Pearce, in slow, tantalizing speech, as if he wore out this suspense to torture Kells. And without ever glancing at Joan he jerked a thumb, in significant gesture, at her.

Joan leaned back against the wall, trembling and cold all over. She read Pearce's mind. He knew her secret and meant to betray her and Jim. He hated Kells and wanted to torture him. If only she could think quickly and speak! But she seemed dumb and powerless.

"Pearce, what do you mean?" demanded Kells.

"The girl's double-crossin' you," replied Pearce. With the uttered words he grew pale and agitated.

Suddenly Kells appeared to become aware of Joan's presence and that the implication was directed toward her. Then, many and remarkable as had been the changes Joan had seen come over him, now occurred one wholly greater. It had all his old amiability, his cool, easy manner, veiling a deep and hidden ruthlessness, terrible in contrast.

"Red, I thought our talk concerned men and gold and—things," he said, with a cool, slow softness that had a sting, "but since you've nerve enough or are crazy enough to speak of—her— why, explain your meaning."

Pearce's jaw worked so that he could scarcely talk. He had gone too far—realized it too late.

"She meets a man—back there—at her window," he panted. "They whisper in the dark for hours. I've watched an' heard them. An' I'd told you before, but I wanted to make sure who he was.... I know him now!... An' remember I seen him climb in an' out—"

Kells's whole frame leaped. His gun was a flash of blue and red and white all together. Pearce swayed upright, like a tree chopped at the roots, and then fell, face up, eyes set—dead. The bandit leader stood over him with the smoking gun.

"My Gawd, Jack!" gasped Handy Oliver. "You swore no one would pull a gun—an' here you've killed him yourself!... YOU'VE DOUBLE-CROSSED YOURSELF! An' if I die for it I've got to tell you Red wasn't lyin' then!"

Kells's radiance fled, leaving him ghastly. He stared at Oliver.

"You've double-crossed yourself an' your pards," went on Oliver, pathetically. "What's your word amount to? Do you expect the gang to stand for this?... There lays Red Pearce dead. An' for what? Jest once—relyin' on your oath—he speaks out what might have showed you. An' you kill him!... If I knowed what he knowed I'd tell you now with thet gun in your hand! But I don't know. Only I know he wasn't lyin'.... Ask the girl!... An' as for me, I reckon I'm through with you an' your Legion. You're done, Kells—your head's gone—you've broke over thet slip of a woman!"

Oliver spoke with a rude and impressive dignity. When he ended he strode out into the sunlight.

Kells was shaken by this forceful speech, yet he was not in any sense a broken man. "Joan—you heard Pearce," said he, passionately. "He lied about you. I had to kill him. He hinted—Oh, the low-lived dog! He could not know a good woman. He lied—and there he is—dead! I wouldn't fetch him back for a hundred Legions!"

"But it—it wasn't—all—a lie," said Joan, and her words came haltingly because a force stronger than her cunning made her speak. She had reached a point where she could not deceive Kells to save her life.

"WHAT!" he thundered.

"Pearce told the truth—except that no one ever climbed in my window. That's false. No one could climb in. It's too small.... But I did whisper—to someone."

Kells had to moisten his lips to speak. "Who?"

"I'll never tell you."

"Who?... I'll kill him!"

"No—no. I won't tell. I won't let you kill another man on my account."

"I'll choke it out of you."

"You can't. There's no use to threaten me, or hurt me, either."

Kells seemed dazed. "Whisper! For hours! In the dark!... But, Joan, what for? Why such a risk?"

Joan shook her head.

"Were you just unhappy—lonesome? Did some young miner happen to see you there in daylight—then come at night? Wasn't it only accident? Tell me."

"I won't—and I won't because I don't want you to spill more blood."

"For my sake," he queried, with the old, mocking tone. Then he grew dark with blood in his face, fierce with action of hands and body as he bent nearer her. "Maybe you like him too well to see him shot?... Did you—whisper often to this stranger?"

Joan felt herself weakening. Kells was so powerful in spirit and passion that she seemed unable to fight him. She strove to withhold her reply, but it burst forth, involuntarily.

"Yes—often."

That roused more than anger and passion. Jealousy flamed from him and it transformed him into a devil.

"You held hands out of that window—and kissed—in the dark?" he cried, with working lips.

Joan had thought of this so fearfully and intensely—she had battled so to fortify herself to keep it secret—that he had divined it, had read her mind. She could not control herself. The murder of Pearce had almost overwhelmed her. She had not the strength to bite her tongue. Suggestion alone would have drawn her then—and Kells's passionate force was hypnotic.

"Yes," she whispered.

He appeared to control a developing paroxysm of rage.

"That settles you," he declared darkly. "But I'll do one more decent thing by you. I'll marry you." Then he wheeled to his men. "Blicky, there's a parson down in camp. Go on the run. Fetch him back if you have to push him with a gun."

Blicky darted through the door and his footsteps thudded out of hearing.

"You can't force me to marry you," said Joan. "I—I won't open my lips."

"That's your affair. I've no mind to coax you," he replied, bitterly. "But if you don't I'll try Gulden's way with a woman.... You remember. Gulden's way! A cave and a rope!"

Joan's legs gave out under her and she sank upon a pile of blankets. Then beyond Kells she saw Jim Cleve. With all that was left of her spirit she flashed him a warning—a meaning—a prayer not to do the deed she divined was his deadly intent. He caught it and obeyed. And he flashed back a glance which meant that, desperate as her case was, it could never be what Kells threatened.

"Men, see me through this," said Kells to the silent group. "Then any deal you want—I'm on. Stay here or—sack the camp! Hold up the stage express with gold for Bannack! Anything for a big stake! Then the trail and the border."

He began pacing the floor. Budd and Smith strolled outside. Bate Wood fumbled in his pockets for pipe and tobacco. Cleve sat down at the table and leaned on his hands. No one took notice of the dead Pearce. Here was somber and terrible sign of the wildness of the border clan— that Kells could send out for a parson to marry him to a woman he hopelessly loved, there in the presence of murder and death, with Pearce's distorted face upturned in stark and ghastly significance.

It might have been a quarter of an hour, though to Joan it seemed an endless time, until footsteps and voices outside announced the return of Blicky.

He held by the arm a slight man whom he was urging along with no gentle force. This stranger's face presented as great a contrast to Blicky's as could have been imagined. His apparel proclaimed his calling. There were consternation and bewilderment in his expression, but very little fear.

"He was preachin' down there in a tent," said Blicky, "an I jest waltzed him up without explainin'."

"Sir, I want to be married at once," declared Kells, peremptorily.

"Certainly. I'm at your service," replied the preacher. "But I deplore the—the manner in which I've been approached."

"You'll excuse haste," rejoined the bandit. "I'll pay you well." Kells threw a small buckskin sack of gold-dust upon the table, and then he turned to Joan. "Come, Joan," he said, in the tone that brooked neither resistance nor delay.

It was at that moment that the preacher first noticed Joan. Was her costume accountable for his start? Joan had remembered his voice and she wondered if he would remember hers. Certainly Jim had called her Joan more than once on the night of the marriage. The preacher's eyes grew keener. He glanced from Joan to Kells, and then at the other men, who had come in.

Jim Cleve stood behind Jesse Smith's broad person, and evidently the preacher did not see him. That curious gaze, however, next discovered the dead man on the floor. Then to the curiosity and anxiety upon the preacher's face was added horror.

"A minister of God is needed here, but not in the capacity you name," he said. "I'll perform no marriage ceremony in the presence of—murder."

"Mr. Preacher, you'll marry me quick or you'll go along with him," replied Kells, deliberately.

"I cannot be forced." The preacher still maintained some dignity, but he had grown pale.

"*I* can force you. Get ready now!... Joan, come here!"

Kells spoke sternly, yet something of the old, self-mocking spirit was in his tone. His intelligence was deriding the flesh and blood of him, the beast, the fool. It spoke that he would have his way and that the choice was fatal for him.

Joan shook her head. In one stride Kells reached her and swung her spinning before him. The physical violence acted strangely upon Joan—roused her rage.

"I wouldn't marry you to save my life—even if I could!" she burst out.

At her declaration the preacher gave a start that must have been suspicion or confirmation, or both. He bent low to peer into the face of the dead Pearce. When he arose he was shaking his head. Evidently he had decided that Pearce was not the man to whom he had married Joan.

"Please remove your mask," he said to Joan.

She did so, swiftly, without a tremor. The preacher peered into her face again, as he had upon the night he had married her to Jim. He faced Kells again.

"I am beyond your threats," he said, now with calmness. "I can't marry you to a woman who already has a husband.... But I don't see that husband here."

"You don't see that husband here!" echoed the bewildered Kells. He stared with open mouth. "Say, have you got a screw loose?"

The preacher, in his swift glance, had apparently not observed the half-hidden Cleve. Certainly it appeared now that he would have no attention for any other than Kells. The bandit was a study. His astonishment was terrific and held him like a chain. Suddenly he lurched.

"What did you say?" he roared, his face flaming.

"I can't marry you to a woman who already has a husband."

Swift as light the red flashed out of Kells's face. "Did you ever see her before?" he asked.

"Yes," replied the preacher.

"Where and when?"

"Here—at the back of this cabin—a few nights ago."

It hurt Joan to look at Kells now, yet he seemed wonderful to behold. She felt as guilty as if she had really been false to him. Her heart labored high in her breast. This was the climax—the moment of catastrophe. Another word and Jim Cleve would be facing Kells. The blood pressure in Joan's throat almost strangled her.

"At the back of this cabin!... At her window?"

"Yes."

"What were you there for?"

"In my capacity as minister. I was summoned to marry her."

"To marry her?" gasped Kells.

"Yes. She is Joan Randle, from Hoadley, Idaho. She is over eighteen. I understood she was detained here against her will. She loved an honest young miner of the camp. He brought me up here one night. And I married them."

"YOU—MARRIED—THEM!"

"Yes."

Kells was slow in assimilating the truth and his action corresponded with his mind. Slowly his hand moved toward his gun. He drew it, threw it aloft. And then all the terrible evil in the man flamed forth. But as he deliberately drew down on the preacher Blicky leaped forward and knocked up the gun. Flash and report followed; the discharge went into the roof. Blicky grasped Kells's arm and threw his weight upon it to keep it down.

"I fetched thet parson here," he yelled, "an you ain't a-goin' to kill him!... Help, Jesse!... He's crazy! He'll do it!"

Jesse Smith ran to Blicky's aid and tore the gun out of Kells's hand. Jim Cleve grasped the preacher by the shoulders and, whirling him around, sent him flying out of the door.

"Run for your life!" he shouted.

Blicky and Jesse Smith were trying to hold the lunging Kells.

"Jim, you block the door," called Jesse. "Bate, you grab any loose guns an' knives.... Now, boss, rant an' be damned!"

They released Kells and backed away, leaving him the room. Joan's limbs seemed unable to execute her will.

"Joan! It's true," he exclaimed, with whistling breath.

"Yes."

"WHO?" he bellowed.

"I'll never tell."

He reached for her with hands like claws, as if he meant to tear her, rend her. Joan was helpless, weak, terrified. Those shaking, clutching hands reached for her throat and yet never closed round it. Kells wanted to kill her, but he could not. He loomed over her, dark, speechless, locked in his paroxysm of rage. Perhaps then came a realization of ruin through her. He hated her because he loved her. He wanted to kill her because of that hate, yet he could not harm her, even hurt her. And his soul seemed in conflict with two giants—the evil in him that was hate, and the love that was good. Suddenly he flung her aside. She stumbled over Pearce's body, almost falling, and staggered back to the wall. Kells had the center of the room to himself. Like a mad steer in a corral he gazed about, stupidly seeking some way to escape. But the escape Kells longed for was from himself. Then either he let himself go or was unable longer to control his rage. He began to plunge around. His actions were violent, random, half insane. He seemed to want to destroy himself and everything. But the weapons were guarded by his men and the room contained little he could smash. There was something magnificent in his fury, yet childish and absurd. Even under its influence and his abandonment he showed a consciousness of its futility. In a few moments the inside of the cabin was in disorder and Kells seemed a disheveled, sweating, panting wretch. The rapidity and violence of his action, coupled with his fury, soon exhausted him. He fell from plunging here and there to pacing the floor. And even the dignity of passion passed from him. He looked a hopeless, beaten, stricken man, conscious of defeat.

Jesse Smith approached the bandit leader. "Jack, here's your gun," he said. "I only took it because you was out of your head.... An' listen, boss. There's a few of us left."

That was Smith's expression of fidelity, and Kells received it with a pallid, grateful smile.

"Bate, you an' Jim clean up this mess," went on Smith. "An', Blicky, come here an' help me with Pearce. We'll have to plant him."

The stir begun by the men was broken by a sharp exclamation from Cleve.

"Kells, here comes Gulden—Beady Jones, Williams, Beard!"

The bandit raised his head and paced back to where he could look out.

Bate Wood made a violent and significant gesture. "Somethin' wrong," he said, hurriedly. "An' it's more'n to do with Gul!... Look down the road. See thet gang. All excited an' wavin' hands an' runnin'. But they're goin' down into camp."

Jesse Smith turned a gray face toward Kells. "Boss, there's hell to pay! I've seen THET kind of excitement before."

Kells thrust the men aside and looked out. He seemed to draw upon a reserve strength, for he grew composed even while he gazed. "Jim, get in the other room," he ordered, sharply. "Joan— you go, too. Keep still."

Joan hurried to comply. Jim entered after her and closed the door. Instinctively they clasped hands, drew close together.

"Jim, what does it mean?" she whispered, fearfully. "Gulden!"

"He must be looking for me," replied Jim. "But there's more doing. Did you see that crowd down the road?"

"No. I couldn't see out."

"Listen."

Heavy tramp boots sounded without. Silently Joan led Jim to the crack between the boards through which she had spied upon the bandits. Jim peeped through, and Joan saw his hand go to his gun. Then she looked.

Gulden was being crowded into the cabin by fierce, bulging-jawed men who meant some kind of dark business. The strangest thing about that entrance was its silence. In a moment they were inside, confronting Kells with his little group. Beard, Jones, Williams, former faithful allies of Kells, showed a malignant opposition. And the huge Gulden resembled an enraged gorilla. For an instant his great, pale, cavernous eyes glared. He had one hand under his coat and his position had a sinister suggestion. But Kells stood cool and sure. When Gulden moved Kells's gun was leaping forth. But he withheld his fire, for Gulden had only a heavy round object wrapped in a handkerchief.

"Look there!" he boomed, and he threw the object on the table.

The dull, heavy, sodden thump had a familiar ring. Joan heard Jim gasp and his hand tightened spasmodically upon hers.

Slowly the ends of the red scarf slid down to reveal an irregularly round, glinting lump. When Joan recognized it her heart seemed to burst.

"Jim Cleve's nugget!" ejaculated Kells. "Where'd you get that?"

Gulden leaned across the table, his massive jaw working. "I found it on the miner Creede," replied the giant, stridently.

Then came a nervous shuffling of boots on the creaky boards. In the silence a low, dull murmur of distant voices could be heard, strangely menacing. Kells stood transfixed, white as a sheet.

"On Creede!"

"Yes."

"Where was his—his body?"

"I left it out on the Bannack trail."

The bandit leader appeared mute.

"Kells, I followed Creede out of camp last night," fiercely declared Gulden.... "I killed him!... I found this nugget on him!"

17

Apparently to Kells that nugget did not accuse Jim Cleve of treachery. Not only did this possibility seem lost upon the bandit leader, but also the sinister intent of Gulden and his associates.

"Then Jim didn't kill Creede!" cried Kells.

A strange light flashed across his face. It fitted the note of gladness in his exclamation. How strange that in his amaze there should be relief instead of suspicion! Joan thought she understood Kells. He was glad that he had not yet made a murderer out of Cleve.

Gulden appeared slow in rejoining. "I told you I got Creede," he said. "And we want to know if this says to you what it says to us."

His huge, hairy hand tapped the nugget. Then Kells caught the implication.

"What does it say to you?" he queried, coolly, and he eyed Gulden and then the grim men behind him.

"Somebody in the gang is crooked. Somebody's giving you the double-cross. We've known that for long. Jim Cleve goes out to kill Creede. He comes in with Creede's gold-belt—and a lie!... We think Cleve is the crooked one."

"No! You're way off, Gulden," replied Kells, earnestly. "That boy is absolutely square. He's lied to me about Creede. But I can excuse that. He lost his nerve. He's only a youngster. To knife a man in his sleep—that was too much for Jim!... And I'm glad! I see it all now. Jim's swapped his big nugget for Creede's belt. And in the bargain he exacted that Creede hit the trail out of camp. You happened to see Creede and went after him yourself.... Well, I don't see where you've any kick coming. For you've ten times the money in Cleve's nugget that there was in a share of Creede's gold."

"That's not my kick," declared Gulden. "What you say about Cleve may be true. But I don't believe it. And the gang is sore. Things have leaked out. We're watched. We're not welcome in the gambling-places any more. Last night I was not allowed to sit in the game at Belcher's."

"You think Cleve has squealed?" queried Kells.

"Yes."

"I'll bet you every ounce of dust I've got that you're wrong," declared Kells. "A straight, square bet against anything you want to put up!"

Kells's ringing voice was nothing if not convincing.

"Appearances are against Cleve," growled Gulden, dubiously. Always he had been swayed by the stronger mind of the leader.

"Sure they are," agreed Kells.

"Then what do you base your confidence on?"

"Just my knowledge of men. Jim Cleve wouldn't squeal.... Gulden, did anybody tell you that?"

"Yes," replied Gulden, slowly. "Red Pearce."

"Pearce was a liar," said Kells, bitterly. "I shot him for lying to me."

Gulden stared. His men muttered and gazed at one another and around the cabin.

"Pearce told me you set Cleve to kill me," suddenly spoke up the giant.

If he expected to surprise Kells he utterly failed.

"That's another and bigger lie," replied the bandit leader, disgustedly. "Gulden, do you think my mind's gone?"

"Not quite," replied Gulden, and he seemed as near a laugh as was possible for him.

"Well, I've enough mind left not to set a boy to kill such a man as you."

Gulden might have been susceptible to flattery. He turned to his men. They, too, had felt Kells's subtle influence. They were ready to veer round like weather-vanes.

"Red Pearce has cashed, an' he can't talk for himself," said Beady Jones, as if answering to the unspoken thought of all.

"Men, between you and me, I had more queer notions about Pearce than Cleve," announced Gulden, gruffly. "But I never said so because I had no proof."

"Red shore was sore an' strange lately," added Chick Williams. "Me an' him were pretty thick once—but not lately."

The giant Gulden scratched his head and swore. Probably he had no sense of justice and was merely puzzled.

"We're wastin' a lot of time," put in Beard, anxiously. "Don't fergit there's somethin' comin' off down in camp, an' we ain't sure what."

"Bah! Haven't we heard whispers of vigilantes for a week?" queried Gulden.

Then some one of the men looked out of the door and suddenly whistled.

"Who's thet on a hoss?"

Gulden's gang crowded to the door.

"Thet's Handy Oliver."

"No!"

"Shore is. I know him. But it ain't his hoss.... Say, he's hurryin'."

Low exclamations of surprise and curiosity followed. Kells and his men looked attentively, but no one spoke. The clatter of hoofs on the stony road told of a horse swiftly approaching— pounding to a halt before the cabin.

"Handy!... Air you chased?... What's wrong?... You shore look pale round the gills." These and other remarks were flung out the door.

"Where's Kells? Let me in," replied Oliver, hoarsely.

The crowd jostled and split to admit the long, lean Oliver. He stalked straight toward Kells, till the table alone stood between them. He was gray of face, breathing hard, resolute and stern.

"Kells, I throwed—you—down!" he said, with outstretched hand. It was a gesture of self-condemnation and remorse.

"What of that?" demanded Kells, with his head leaping like the strike of an eagle.

"I'm takin' it back!"

Kells met the outstretched hand with his own and wrung it. "Handy, I never knew you to right—about—face. But I'm glad.... What's changed you so quickly?"

"VIGILANTES!"

Kells's animation and eagerness suddenly froze. "VIGILANTES!" he ground out.

"No rumor, Kells, this time. I've sure some news.... Come close, all you fellows. You, Gulden, come an' listen. Here's where we git together closer'n ever."

Gulden surged forward with his group. Handy Oliver was surrounded by pale, tight faces, dark-browed and hardeyed.

He gazed at them, preparing them for a startling revelation. "Men, of all the white-livered traitors as ever was Red Pearce was the worst!" he declared, hoarsely.

No one moved or spoke.

"AN' HE WAS A VIGILANTE!"

A low, strange sound, almost a roar, breathed through the group.

"Listen now an' don't interrupt. We ain't got a lot of time.... So never mind how I happened to find out about Pearce. It was all accident, an' jest because I put two an' two together.... Pearce was approached by one of this secret vigilante band, an' he planned to sell the Border Legion outright. There was to be a big stake in it for him. He held off day after day, only tippin' off some of the gang. There's Dartt an' Singleton an' Frenchy an' Texas all caught red-handed at jobs. Pearce put the vigilantes to watchin' them jest to prove his claim.... Aw! I've got the proofs! Jest wait. Listen to me!... You all never in your lives seen a snake like Red Pearce. An' the job he had put up on us was grand. To-day he was to squeal on the whole gang. You know how he began on Kells—an' how with his oily tongue he asked a guarantee of no gun-play. But he figgered Kells wrong for once. He accused Kells's girl an' got killed for his pains. Mebbe it was part of his plan to git the girl himself. Anyway, he had agreed to betray the Border Legion to-day. An' if he hadn't been killed by this time we'd all be tied up, ready for the noose!... Mebbe thet wasn't a lucky shot of the boss's. Men, I was the first to declare myself against Kells, an' I'm here now to say thet I was a fool. So you've all been fools who've bucked against him. If this ain't provin' it, what can!

"But I must hustle with my story.... They was havin' a trial down at the big hall, an' thet place was sure packed. No diggin' gold to-day!... Think of what thet means for Alder Creek. I got inside where I could stand on a barrel an' see. Dartt an' Singleton an' Frenchy an' Texas was bein' tried by a masked court. A man near me said two of them had been proved guilty. It didn't take long to make out a case against Texas an' Frenchy. Miners there recognized them an' identified them. They was convicted an' sentenced to be hung!.. Then the offer was made to let them go free out of the border if they'd turn state's evidence an' give away the leader an' men of the Border Legion. Thet was put up to each prisoner. Dartt he never answered at all. An' Singleton told them to go to hell. An' Texas he swore he was only a common an' honest road-agent, an' never heard of the Legion. But the Frenchman showed a yellow streak. He might have taken the offer. But Texas cussed him tumble, an' made him ashamed to talk. But if they git Frenchy away from Texas they'll make him blab. He's like a greaser. Then there was a delay. The big crowd of miners yelled for ropes. But the vigilantes are waitin', an' it's my hunch they're waitin' for Pearce."

"So! And where do we stand?" cried Kells, clear and cold.

"We're not spotted yet, thet's certain," replied Oliver, "else them masked vigilantes would have been on the job before now. But it's not sense to figger we can risk another day.... I reckon it's hit the trail back to Cabin Gulch."

"Gulden, what do you say?" queried Kells, sharply.

"I'll go or stay—whatever you want," replied the giant. In this crisis he seemed to be glad to have Kells decide the issue. And his followers resembled sheep ready to plunge after the leader.

But though Kells, by a strange stroke, had been made wholly master of the Legion, he did not show the old elation or radiance. Perhaps he saw more clearly than ever before. Still he was quick, decisive, strong, equal to the occasion.

"Listen—all of you," he said. "Our horses and outfits are hidden in a gulch several miles below camp. We've got to go that way. We can't pack any grub or stuff from here. We'll risk going through camp. Now leave here two or three at a time, and wait down there on the edge of the crowd for me. When I come we'll stick together. Then all do as I do."

Gulden put the nugget under his coat and strode out, accompanied by Budd and Jones. They hurried away. The others went in couples. Soon only Bate Wood and Handy Oliver were left with Kells.

"Now you fellows go," said Kells. "Be sure to round up the gang down there and wait for me."

When they had gone he called for Jim and Joan to come out.

All this time Joan's hand had been gripped in Jim's, and Joan had been so absorbed that she had forgotten the fact. He released her and faced her, silent, pale. Then he went out. Joan swiftly followed.

Kells was buckling on his spurs. "You heard?" he said, the moment he saw Jim's face.

"Yes," replied Jim.

"So much the better. We've got to rustle.... Joan, put on that long coat of Cleve's. Take off your mask.... Jim, get what gold you have, and hurry. If we're gone when you come back hurry down the road. I want you with me."

Cleve stalked out, and Joan ran into her room and put on the long coat. She had little time to choose what possessions she could take; and that choice fell upon the little saddle-bag, into which she hurriedly stuffed comb and brush and soap—all it would hold. Then she returned to the larger room.

Kells had lifted a plank of the floor, and was now in the act of putting small buckskin sacks of gold into his pockets. They made his coat bulge at the sides.

"Joan, stick some meat and biscuits in your pockets," he said. "I'd never get hungry with my pockets full of gold. But you might."

Joan rummaged around in Bate Wood's rude cupboard.

"These biscuits are as heavy as gold—and harder," she said.

Kells flashed a glance at her that held pride, admiration, and sadness. "You are the gamest girl I ever knew! I wish I'd—But that's too late!... Joan, if anything happens to me stick close to Cleve. I believe you can trust him. Come on now."

Then he strode out of the cabin. Joan had almost to run to keep up with him. There were no other men now in sight. She knew that Jim would follow soon, because his gold-dust was hidden in the cavern back of her room, and he would not need much time to get it. Nevertheless, she anxiously looked back. She and Kells had gone perhaps a couple of hundred yards before Jim appeared, and then he came on the run. At a point about opposite the first tents he joined Kells.

"Jim, how about guns?" asked the bandit.

"I've got two," replied Cleve.

"Good! There's no telling—Jim, I'm afraid of the gang. They're crazy. What do you think?"

"I don't know. It's a hard proposition."

"We'll get away, all right. Don't worry about that. But the gang will never come together again." This singular man spoke with melancholy. "Slow up a little now," he added. "We don't want to attract attention.... But where is there any one to see us?... Jim, did I have you figured right about the Creede job?"

"You sure did. I just lost my nerve."

"Well, no matter."

Then Kells appeared to forget that. He stalked on with keen glances searching everywhere, until suddenly, when he saw round a bend of the road, he halted with grating teeth. That road was empty all the way to the other end of camp, but there surged a dark mob of men. Kells stalked forward again. The Last Nugget appeared like an empty barn. How vacant and significant the whole center of camp! Kells did not speak another word.

Joan hurried on between Kells and Cleve. She was trying to fortify herself to meet what lay at the end of the road. A strange, hoarse roar of men and an upflinging of arms made her shudder. She kept her eyes lowered and clung to the arms of her companions.

Finally they halted. She felt the crowd before she saw it. A motley assemblage with what seemed craned necks and intent backs! They were all looking forward and upward. But she forced her glance down.

Kells stood still. Jim's grip was hard upon her arm. Presently men grouped round Kells. She heard whispers. They began to walk slowly, and she was pushed and led along. More men joined the group. Soon she and Kells and Jim were hemmed in a circle. Then she saw the huge form of Gulden, the towering Oliver, and Smith and Blicky, Beard, Jones, Williams, Budd, and others. The circle they formed appeared to be only one of many groups, all moving, whispering, facing from her. Suddenly a sound like the roar of a wave agitated that mass of men. It was harsh, piercing, unnatural, yet it had a note of wild exultation. Then came the stamp and surge, and then the upflinging of arms, and then the abrupt strange silence, broken only by a hiss or an escaping breath, like a sob. Beyond all Joan's power to resist was a deep, primitive desire to look.

There over the heads of the mob—from the bench of the slope—rose grotesque structures of new-hewn lumber. On a platform stood black, motionless men in awful contrast with a dangling object that doubled up and curled upon itself in terrible convulsions. It lengthened while it swayed; it slowed its action while it stretched. It took on the form of a man. He swung by a rope round his neck. His head hung back. His hands beat. A long tremor shook the body; then it was still, and swayed to and fro, a dark, limp thing.

Joan's gaze was riveted in horror. A dim, red haze made her vision imperfect. There was a sickening riot within her.

There were masked men all around the platform—a solid phalanx of them on the slope above. They were heavily armed. Other masked men stood on the platform. They seemed rigid figures—stiff, jerky when they moved. How different from the two forms swaying below!

The structure was a rude scaffold and the vigilantes had already hanged two bandits.

Two others with hands bound behind their backs stood farther along the platform under guard. Before each dangled a noose.

Joan recognized Texas and Frenchy. And on the instant the great crowd let out a hard breath that ended in silence.

The masked leader of the vigilantes was addressing Texas: "We'll spare your life if you confess. Who's the head of this Border Legion?"

"Shore it's Red Pearce!... Haw! Haw! Haw!"

"We'll give you one more chance," came the curt reply.

Texas appeared to become serious and somber. "I swear to God it's Pearce!" he declared.

"A lie won't save you. Come, the truth! We think we know, but we want proof! Hurry!"

"You can go where it's hot!" responded Texas.

The leader moved his hand and two other masked men stepped forward.

"Have you any message to send any one—anything to say?" he asked.

"Nope."

"Have you any request to make?"

"Hang that Frenchman before me! I want to see him kick."

Nothing more was said. The two men adjusted the noose round the doomed man's neck. Texas refused the black cap. And he did not wait for the drop to be sprung. He walked off the platform into space as Joan closed her eyes.

Again that strange, full, angry, and unnatural roar waved through the throng of watchers. It was terrible to hear. Joan felt the violent action of that crowd, although the men close round her were immovable as stones. She imagined she could never open her eyes to see Texas hanging there. Yet she did—and something about his form told her that he had died instantly. He had been brave and loyal even in dishonor. He had more than once spoken a kind word to her. Who could tell what had made him an outcast? She breathed a prayer for his soul.

The vigilantes were bolstering up the craven Frenchy. He could not stand alone. They put the rope round his neck and lifted him off the platform—then let him down. He screamed in his terror. They cut short his cries by lifting him again. This time they held him up several seconds. His face turned black. His eyes bulged. His breast heaved. His legs worked with the regularity of a jumping-jack. They let him down and loosened the noose. They were merely torturing him to wring a confession from him. He had been choked severely and needed a moment to recover. When he did it was to shrink back in abject terror from that loop of rope dangling before his eyes.

The vigilante leader shook the noose in his face and pointed to the swaying forms of the dead bandits.

Frenchy frothed at the mouth as he shrieked out words in his native tongue, but any miner there could have translated their meaning.

The crowd heaved forward, as if with one step, then stood in a strained silence.

"Talk English!" ordered the vigilante.

"I'll tell! I'll tell!"

Joan became aware of a singular tremor in Kells's arm, which she still clasped. Suddenly it jerked. She caught a gleam of blue. Then the bellow of a gun almost split her ears. Powder burned her cheek. She saw Frenchy double up and collapse on the platform.

For an instant there was a silence in which every man seemed petrified. Then burst forth a hoarse uproar and the stamp of many boots. All in another instant pandemonium broke out. The huge crowd split in every direction. Joan felt Cleve's strong arm around her—felt herself borne on a resistless tide of yelling, stamping, wrestling men. She had a glimpse of Kells's dark face drawing away from her; another of Gulden's giant form in Herculean action, tossing men aside like ninepins; another of weapons aloft. Savage, wild-eyed men fought to get into the circle whence that shot had come. They broke into it, but did not know then whom to attack or what to do. And the rushing of the frenzied miners all around soon disintegrated Kells's band and bore its several groups in every direction. There was not another shot fired.

Joan was dragged and crushed in the melee. Not for rods did her feet touch the ground. But in the clouds of dust and confusion of struggling forms she knew Jim still held her, and she clasped him with all her strength. Presently her feet touched the earth; she was not jostled and pressed; then she felt free to walk; and with Jim urging her they climbed a rock-strewn slope till a cabin impeded further progress. But they had escaped the stream.

Below was a strange sight. A scaffold shrouded in dust-clouds; a band of bewildered vigilantes with weapons drawn, waiting for they knew not what; three swinging, ghastly forms and a dead man on the platform; and all below, a horde of men trying to escape from one another. That shot of Kells's had precipitated a rush. No miner knew who the vigilantes were nor the members of the Border Legion. Every man there expected a bloody battle—distrusted the man next to him—and had given way to panic. The vigilantes had tried to crowd together for defense and all the others had tried to escape. It was a wild scene, born of wild justice and blood at fever-heat, the climax of a disordered time where gold and violence reigned supreme. It could only happen once, but it was terrible while it lasted. It showed the craven in men; it proved the baneful influence of gold; it brought, in its fruition, the destiny of Alder Creek Camp. For it must have been that the really brave and honest men in vast majority retraced their steps while the vicious kept running. So it seemed to Joan.

She huddled against Jim there in the shadow of the cabin wall, and not for long did either speak. They watched and listened. The streams of miners turned back toward the space around the scaffold where the vigilantes stood grouped, and there rose a subdued roar of excited voices. Many small groups of men conversed together, until the vigilante leader brought all to attention by addressing the populace in general. Joan could not hear what he said and had no wish to hear.

"Joan, it all happened so quickly, didn't it?" whispered Jim, shaking his head as if he was not convinced of reality.

"Wasn't he—terrible!" whispered Joan in reply.

"He! Who?"

"Kells." In her mind the bandit leader dominated all that wild scene.

"Terrible, if you like. But I'd say great!... The nerve of him! In the face of a hundred vigilantes and thousands of miners! But he knew what that shot would do!"

"Never! He never thought of that," declared Joan, earnestly. "I felt him tremble. I had a glimpse of his face.... Oh!... First in his mind was his downfall, and, second, the treachery of Frenchy. I think that shot showed Kells as utterly desperate, but weak. He couldn't have helped it—if that had been the last bullet in his gun."

Jim Cleve looked strangely at Joan, as if her eloquence was both persuasive and incomprehensible.

"Well, that was a lucky shot for us—and him, too."

"Do you think he got away?" she asked, eagerly.

"Sure. They all got away. Wasn't that about the maddest crowd you ever saw?"

"No wonder. In a second every man there feared the man next to him would shoot. That showed the power of Kells's Border Legion. If his men had been faithful and obedient he never would have fallen."

"Joan! You speak as if you regret it!"

"Oh, I am ashamed," replied Joan. "I don't mean that. I don't know what I do mean. But still I'm sorry for Kells. I suffered so much.... Those long, long hours of suspense.... And his fortunes seemed my fortunes—my very life—and yours, too, Jim."

"I think I understand, dear," said Jim, soberly.

"Jim, what'll we do now? Isn't it strange to feel free?"

"I feel as queer as you. Let me think," replied Jim.

They huddled there in comparative seclusion for a long time after that. Joan tried to think of plans, but her mind seemed, unproductive. She felt half dazed. Jim, too, appeared to be laboring under the same kind of burden. Moreover, responsibility had been added to his.

The afternoon waned till the sun tipped the high range in the west. The excitement of the mining populace gradually wore away, and toward sunset strings of men filed up the road and across the open. The masked vigilantes disappeared, and presently only a quiet and curious crowd was left round the grim scaffold and its dark swinging forms. Joan's one glance showed that the vigilantes had swung Frenchy's dead body in the noose he would have escaped by treachery. They had hanged him dead. What a horrible proof of the temper of these newborn vigilantes! They had left the bandits swinging. What sight was so appalling as these limp, dark, swaying forms? Dead men on the ground had a dignity—at least the dignity of death. And death sometimes had a majesty. But here both life and death had been robbed and there was only horror. Joan felt that all her life she would be haunted.

"Joan, we've got to leave Alder Creek," declared Cleve, finally. He rose to his feet. The words seemed to have given him decision. "At first I thought every bandit in the gang would run as far as he could from here. But—you can't tell what these wild men will do. Gulden, for instance! Common sense ought to make them hide for a spell. Still, no matter what's what, we must leave.... Now, how to go?"

"Let's walk. If we buy horses or wait for the stage we'll have to see men here—and I'm afraid—"

"But, Joan, there'll be bandits along the road sure. And the trails, wherever they are, would be less safe."

"Let's travel by night and rest by day."

"That won't do, with so far to go and no pack."

"Then part of the way."

"No. We'd better take the stage for Bannack. If it starts at all it'll be under armed guard. The only thing is—will it leave soon?... Come, Joan, we'll go down into camp."

Dusk had fallen and lights had begun to accentuate the shadows. Joan kept close beside Jim, down the slope, and into the road. She felt like a guilty thing and every passing man or low-conversing group frightened her. Still she could not help but see that no one noticed her or Jim, and she began to gather courage. Jim also acquired confidence. The growing darkness seemed a protection. The farther up the street they passed, the more men they met. Again the saloons were in full blast. Alder Creek had returned to the free, careless tenor of its way. A few doors this side of the Last Nugget was the office of the stage and express company. It was a wide tent with the front canvas cut out and a shelf-counter across the opening. There was a dim, yellow lamplight. Half a dozen men lounged in front, and inside were several more, two of whom appeared to be armed guards. Jim addressed no one in particular.

"When does the next stage leave for Bannack?"

A man looked up sharply from the papers that littered a table before him. "It leaves when we start it," he replied, curtly.

"Well, when will that be?"

"What's that to you?" he replied, with a question still more curt.

"I want to buy seats for two."

"That's different. Come in and let's look you over.... Hello! it's young Cleve. I didn't recognize you. Excuse me. We're a little particular these days."

The man's face lighted. Evidently he knew Jim and thought well of him. This reassured Joan and stilled the furious beating of her heart. She saw Jim hand over a sack of gold, from which the agent took the amount due for the passage. Then he returned the sack and whispered something in Jim's ear. Jim rejoined her and led her away, pressing her arm close to his side.

"It's all right," he whispered, excitedly. "Stage leaves just before daylight. It used to leave in the middle of the fore-noon. But they want a good start to-morrow."

"They think it might be held up?"

"He didn't say so. But there's every reason to suspect that.... Joan, I sure hope it won't. Me with all this gold. Why, I feel as if I weighed a thousand pounds."

"What'll we do now?" she inquired.

Jim halted in the middle of the road. It was quite dark now. The lights of the camp were flaring; men were passing to and fro; the loose boards on the walks rattled to their tread; the saloons had begun to hum; and there was a discordant blast from the Last Nugget.

"That's it—what'll we do?" he asked in perplexity.

Joan had no idea to advance, but with the lessening of her fear and the gradual clearing of her mind she felt that she would not much longer be witless.

"We've got to eat and get some rest," said Jim, sensibly.

"I'll try to eat—but I don't think I'll be able to sleep tonight," replied Joan.

Jim took her to a place kept by a Mexican. It appeared to consist of two tents, with opening in front and door between. The table was a plank resting upon two barrels, and another plank, resting upon kegs, served as a seat. There was a smoking lamp that flickered. The Mexican's tableware was of a crudeness befitting his house, but it was clean and he could cook—two facts that Joan appreciated after her long experience of Bate Wood. She and Jim were the only customers of the Mexican, who spoke English rather well and was friendly. Evidently it pleased him to see the meal enjoyed. Both the food and the friendliness had good effect upon Jim Cleve. He ceased to listen all the time and to glance furtively out at every footstep.

"Joan, I guess it'll turn out all right," he said, clasping her hand as it rested upon the table. Suddenly he looked bright-eyed and shy. He leaned toward her. "Do you remember—we are married?" he whispered.

Joan was startled. "Of course," she replied hastily. But had she forgotten?

"You're my wife."

Joan looked at him and felt her nerves begin to tingle. A soft, warm wave stole over her.

Like a boy he laughed. "This was our first meal together—on our honeymoon!"

"Jim!" The blood burned in Joan's face.

"There you sit—you beautiful... But you're not a girl now. You're Dandy Dale."

"Don't call me that!" exclaimed Joan.

"But I shall—always. We'll keep that bandit suit always. You can dress up sometimes to show off—to make me remember—to scare the—the kids—"

"Jim Cleve!"

"Oh, Joan, I'm afraid to be happy. But I can't help it. We're going to get away. You belong to me. And I've sacks and sacks of gold-dust. Lord! I've no idea how much! But you can never spend all the money. Isn't it just like a dream?"

Joan smiled through tears, and failed trying to look severe.

"Get me and the gold away—safe—before you crow," she said.

That sobered him. He led her out again into the dark street with its dark forms crossing to and fro before the lights.

"It's a long time before morning. Where can I take you—so you can sleep a little?" he muttered.

"Find a place where we can sit down and wait," she suggested.

"No." He pondered a moment. "I guess there's no risk."

Then he led her up the street and through that end of camp out upon the rough, open slope. They began to climb. The stars were bright, but even so Joan stumbled often over the stones. She wondered how Jim could get along so well in the dark and she clung to his arm. They did not speak often, and then only in whispers. Jim halted occasionally to listen or to look up at the bold, black bluff for his bearings. Presently he led her among broken fragments of cliff, and half carried her over rougher ground, into a kind of shadowy pocket or niche.

"Here's where I slept," he whispered.

He wrapped a blanket round her, and then they sat down against the rock, and she leaned upon his shoulder.

"I have your coat and the blanket, too," she said. "Won't you be cold?"

He laughed. "Now don't talk any more. You're white and fagged-out. You need to rest—to sleep."

"Sleep? How impossible!" she murmured.

"Why, your eyes are half shut now.... Anyway, I'll not talk to you. I want to think."

"Jim!... kiss me—good night," she whispered.

He bent over rather violently, she imagined. His head blotted out the light of the stars. He held her tightly for a moment. She felt him shake. Then he kissed her on the cheek and abruptly drew away. How strange he seemed!

For that matter, everything was strange. She had never seen the stars so bright, so full of power, so close. All about her the shadows gathered protectingly, to hide her and Jim. The silence spoke. She saw Jim's face in the starlight and it seemed so keen, so listening, so thoughtful, so beautiful. He would sit there all night, wide-eyed and alert, guarding her, waiting for the gray of dawn. How he had changed! And she was his wife! But that seemed only a dream. It needed daylight and sight of her ring to make that real.

A warmth and languor stole over her; she relaxed comfortably; after all, she would sleep. But why did that intangible dread hang on to her soul? The night was so still and clear and perfect—a radiant white night of stars—and Jim was there, holding her—and to-morrow they would ride away. That might be, but dark, dangling shapes haunted her, back in her mind, and there, too, loomed Kells. Where was he now? Gone—gone on his bloody trail with his broken fortunes and his desperate bitterness! He had lost her. The lunge of that wild mob had parted them. A throb of pain and shame went through her, for she was sorry. She could not understand why, unless it was because she had possessed some strange power to instil or bring up good in him. No woman could have been proof against that. It was monstrous to know that she had power to turn him from an evil life, yet she could not do it. It was more than monstrous to realize that he had gone on spilling blood and would continue to go on when she could have prevented it—could have saved many poor miners who perhaps had wives or sweethearts somewhere. Yet there was no help for it. She loved Jim Cleve. She might have sacrificed herself, but she would not sacrifice him for all the bandits and miners on the border.

Joan felt that she would always be haunted and would always suffer that pang for Kells. She would never lie down in the peace and quiet of her home, wherever that might be, without picturing Kells, dark and forbidding and burdened, pacing some lonely cabin or riding a lonely trail or lying with his brooding face upturned to the lonely stars. Sooner or later he would meet his doom. It was inevitable. She pictured over that sinister scene of the dangling forms; but no—Kells would never end that way. Terrible as he was, he had not been born to be hanged. He might be murdered in his sleep, by one of that band of traitors who were traitors because in the nature of evil they had to be. But more likely some gambling-hell, with gold and life at stake, would see his last fight. These bandits stole gold and gambled among themselves and fought. And that fight which finished Kells must necessarily be a terrible one. She seemed to see into a lonely cabin where a log fire burned low and lamps flickered and blue smoke floated in veils and men lay prone on the floor—Kells, stark and bloody, and the giant Gulden, dead at last and more terrible in death, and on the rude table bags of gold and dull, shining heaps of gold, and scattered on the floor, like streams of sand and useless as sand, dust of gold—the Destroyer.

18

All Joan's fancies and dreams faded into obscurity, and when she was aroused it seemed she had scarcely closed her eyes. But there was the gray gloom of dawn. Jim was shaking her gently.

"No, you weren't sleepy—it's just a mistake," he said, helping her to arise. "Now we'll get out of here."

They threaded a careful way out of the rocks, then hurried down the slope. In the grayness Joan saw the dark shape of a cabin and it resembled the one Kells had built. It disappeared. Presently when Jim led her into a road she felt sure that this cabin had been the one where she had been a prisoner for so long. They hurried down the road and entered the camp. There were no lights. The tents and cabins looked strange and gloomy. The road was empty. Not a sound broke the stillness. At the bend Joan saw a stage-coach and horses looming up in what seemed gray distance. Jim hurried her on.

They reached the stage. The horses were restive. The driver was on the seat, whip and reins in hand. Two men sat beside him with rifles across their knees. The door of the coach hung open. There were men inside, one of whom had his head out of the window. The barrel of a rifle protruded near him. He was talking in a low voice to a man apparently busy at the traces.

"Hello, Cleve! You're late," said another man, evidently the agent. "Climb aboard. When'll you be back?"

"I hardly know," replied Cleve, with hesitation.

"All right. Good luck to you." He closed the coach door after Joan and Jim. "Let 'em go, Bill."

The stage started with a jerk. To Joan what an unearthly creak and rumble it made, disturbing the silent dawn! Jim squeezed her hand with joy. They were on the way!

Joan and Jim had a seat to themselves. Opposite sat three men—the guard with his head half out of the window, a bearded miner who appeared stolid or drowsy, and a young man who did not look rough and robust enough for a prospector. None of the three paid any particular attention to Joan and Jim.

The road had a decided slope down-hill, and Bill, the driver, had the four horses on a trot. The rickety old stage appeared to be rattling to pieces. It lurched and swayed, and sometimes jolted over rocks and roots. Joan was hard put to it to keep from being bumped off the seat. She held to a brace on one side and to Jim on the other. And when the stage rolled down into the creek and thumped over boulders Joan made sure that every bone in her body would be broken. This crossing marked the mouth of the gulch, and on the other side the road was smooth.

"We're going the way we came," whispered Jim in her ear.

This was surprising, for Joan had been sure that Bannack lay in the opposite direction. Certainly this fact was not reassuring to her. Perhaps the road turned soon.

Meanwhile the light brightened, the day broke, and the sun reddened the valley. Then it was as light inside the coach as outside. Joan might have spared herself concern as to her fellow-passengers. The only one who noticed her was the young man, and he, after a stare and a half-smile, lapsed into abstraction. He looked troubled, and there was about him no evidence of prosperity. Jim held her hand under a fold of the long coat, and occasionally he spoke of something or other outside that caught his eye. And the stage rolled on rapidly, seemingly in pursuit of the steady roar of hoofs.

Joan imagined she recognized the brushy ravine out of which Jesse Smith had led that day when Kells's party came upon the new road. She believed Jim thought so, too, for he gripped her hand unusually hard. Beyond that point Joan began to breathe more easily. There seemed no valid reason now why every mile should not separate them farther from the bandits, and she experienced relief.

Then the time did not drag so. She wanted to talk to Jim, yet did not, because of the other passengers. Jim himself appeared influenced by their absorption in themselves. Besides, the keen, ceaseless vigilance of the guard was not without its quieting effect. Danger lurked ahead in the bends of that road. Joan remembered hearing Kells say that the Bannack stage had never been properly held up by road-agents, but that when he got ready for the job it would be done right. Riding grew to be monotonous and tiresome. With the warmth of the sun came the dust and flies, and all these bothered Joan. She did not have her usual calmness, and as the miles steadily passed her nervousness increased.

The road left the valley and climbed between foot-hills and wound into rockier country. Every dark gulch brought to Joan a trembling, breathless spell. What places for ambush! But the stage bowled on.

At last her apprehensions wore out and she permitted herself the luxury of relaxing, of leaning back and closing her eyes. She was tired, drowsy, hot. There did not seem to be a breath of air.

Suddenly Joan's ears burst to an infernal crash of guns. She felt the whip and sting of splinters sent flying by bullets. Harsh yells followed, then the scream of a horse in agony, the stage lurching and slipping to a halt, and thunder of heavy guns overhead.

Jim yelled at her—threw her down on the seat. She felt the body of the guard sink against her knees. Then she seemed to feel, to hear through an icy, sickening terror.

A scattering volley silenced the guns above. Then came the pound of hoofs, the snort of frightened horses.

"Jesse Smith! Stop!" called Jim, piercingly.

"Hold on thar, Beady!" replied a hoarse voice. "Damn if it ain't Jim Cleve!"

"Ho, Gul!" yelled another voice, and Joan recognized it as Blicky's.

Then Jim lifted her head, drew her up. He was white with fear.

"Dear—are—you—hurt?"

"No. I'm only—scared," she replied.

Joan looked out to see bandits on foot, guns in hand, and others mounted, all gathering near the coach. Jim opened the door, and, stepping out, bade her follow. Joan had to climb over the dead guard. The miner and the young man huddled down on their seat.

"If it ain't Jim an' Kells's girl—Dandy Dale!" ejaculated Smith. "Fellers, this means somethin'.... Say, youngster, hope you ain't hurt—or the girl?"

"No. But that's not your fault," replied Cleve. "Why did you want to plug the coach full of lead?"

"This beats me," said Smith. "Kells sent you out in the stage! But when he gave us the job of holdin' it up he didn't tell us you'd be in there.... When an' where'd you leave him?"

"Sometime last night—in camp—near our cabin," replied Jim, quick as a flash. Manifestly he saw his opportunity "He left Dandy Dale with me. Told us to take the stage this morning. I expected him to be in it or to meet us."

"Didn't you have no orders?"

"None, except to take care of the girl till he came. But he did tell me he'd have more to say."

Smith gazed blankly from Cleve to Blicky, and then at Gulden, who came slowly forward, his hair ruffed, his gun held low. Joan followed the glance of his great gray eyes, and she saw the stage-driver hanging dead over his seat, and the guards lying back of him. The off-side horse of the leaders lay dead in his traces, with his mate nosing at him.

"Who's in there?" boomed Gulden, and he thrust hand and gun in at the stage door. "Come out!"

The young man stumbled out, hands above his head, pallid and shaking, so weak he could scarcely stand.

Gulden prodded the bearded miner. "Come out here, you!"

The man appeared to be hunched forward in a heap.

"Guess he's plugged," said Smith. "But he ain't cashed. Hear him breathe?... Heaves like a sick hoss."

Gulden reached with brawny arm and with one pull he dragged the miner off the seat and out into the road, where he flopped with a groan. There was blood on his neck and hands. Gulden bent over him, tore at his clothes, tore harder at something, and then, with a swing, he held aloft a broad, black belt, sagging heavy with gold.

"Hah!" he boomed. It was just an exclamation, horrible to hear, but it did not express satisfaction or exultation. He handed the gold-belt to the grinning Budd, and turned to the young man.

"Got any gold?"

"No. I—I wasn't a miner," replied the youth huskily.

Gulden felt for a gold-belt, then slapped at his pockets. "Turn round!" ordered the giant.

"Aw, Gul let him go!" remonstrated Jesse Smith.

Blicky laid a restraining hand upon Gulden's broad shoulder.

"Turn round!" repeated Gulden, without the slightest sign of noticing his colleagues.

But the youth understood and he turned a ghastly livid hue.

"For God's sake—don't murder me!" he gasped. "I had—nothing—no gold—no gun!"

Gulden spun him round like a top and pushed him forward. They went half a dozen paces, then the youth staggered, and turning, he fell on his knees.

"Don't—kill—me!" he entreated.

Joan, seeing Jim Cleve stiffen and crouch, thought of him even in that horrible moment; and she gripped his arm with all her might. They must endure.

The other bandits muttered, but none moved a hand.

Gulden thrust out the big gun. His hair bristled on his head, and his huge frame seemed instinct with strange vibration, like some object of tremendous weight about to plunge into resistless momentum.

Even the stricken youth saw his doom. "Let—me—pray!" he begged.

Joan did not fault, but a merciful unclamping of muscle-bound rigidity closed her eyes.

"Gul!" yelled Blicky, with passion. "I ain't a-goin' to let you kill this kid! There's no sense in it. We're spotted back in Alder Creek.... Run, kid! Run!"

Then Joan opened her eyes to see the surly Gulden's arm held by Blicky, and the youth running blindly down the road. Joan's relief and joy were tremendous. But still she answered to the realizing shock of what Gulden had meant to do. She leaned against Cleve, all within and without a whirling darkness of fire. The border wildness claimed her then. She had the spirit, though not the strength, to fight. She needed the sight and sound of other things to restore her equilibrium. She would have welcomed another shock, an injury. And then she was looking down upon the gasping miner. He was dying. Hurriedly Joan knelt beside him to lift his head. At her call Cleve brought a canteen. But the miner could not drink and he died with some word unspoken.

Dizzily Joan arose, and with Cleve half supporting her she backed off the road to a seat on the bank. She saw the bandits now at business-like action. Blicky and Smith were cutting the horses out of their harness: Beady Jones, like a ghoul, searched the dead men; the three bandits whom Joan knew only by sight were making up a pack; Budd was standing beside the stage with his, expectant grin; and Gulden, with the agility of the gorilla he resembled, was clambering over the top of the stage. Suddenly from under the driver's seat he hauled a buckskin sack. It was small, but heavy. He threw it down to Budd, almost knocking over that bandit. Budd hugged the sack and yelled like an Indian. The other men whooped and ran toward him. Gulden hauled out another sack. Hands to the number of a dozen stretched clutchingly. When he threw the sack there was a mad scramble. They fought, but it was only play. They were gleeful. Blicky secured the prize and he held it aloft in triumph. Assuredly he would have waved it had it not been so heavy. Gulden drew out several small sacks, which he provokingly placed on the seat in front of him. The bandits below howled in protest. Then the giant, with his arm under the seat, his huge frame bowed, heaved powerfully upon something, and his face turned red. He halted in his tugging to glare at his bandit comrades below. If his great cavernous eyes expressed any feeling it was analogous to the reluctance manifest in his posture—he regretted the presence of his gang. He would rather have been alone. Then with deep-muttered curse and mighty heave he lifted out a huge buckskin sack, tied and placarded and marked.

"ONE HUNDRED POUNDS!" he boomed.

It seemed to Joan then that a band of devils surrounded the stage, all roaring at the huge, bristling demon above, who glared and bellowed down at them.

Finally Gulden stilled the tumult, which, after all, was one of frenzied joy.

"Share and share alike!" he thundered, now black in the face. "Do you fools want to waste time here on the road, dividing up this gold?"

"What you say goes," shouted Budd.

There was no dissenting voice.

"What a stake!" ejaculated Blicky. "Gul, the boss had it figgered. Strange, though, he hasn't showed up!"

"Where'll we go?" queried Gulden. "Speak up, you men."

The unanimous selection was Cabin Gulch. Plainly Gulden did not like this, but he was just.

"All right. Cabin Gulch it is. But nobody outside of Kells and us gets a share in this stake."

Many willing hands made short work of preparation. Gulden insisted on packing all the gold upon his saddle, and had his will. He seemed obsessed; he never glanced at Joan. It was Jesse Smith who gave the directions and orders. One of the stage-horses was packed. Another, with a blanket for a saddle, was given Cleve to ride. Blicky gallantly gave his horse to Joan, shortened his stirrups to fit her, and then whistled at the ridgy back of the stage-horse he elected to ride. Gulden was in a hurry, and twice he edged off, to be halted by impatient calls. Finally the cavalcade was ready; Jesse Smith gazed around upon the scene with the air of a general overlooking a vanquished enemy.

"Whoever fust runs acrost this job will have blind staggers, don't you forgit thet!"

"What's Kells goin' to figger?" asked Blicky, sharply.

"Nothin' fer Kells! He wasn't in at the finish!" declared Budd.

Blicky gazed darkly at him, but made no comment.

"I tell you Blick, I can't git this all right in my head," said Smith.

"Say, ask Jim again. Mebbe, now the job's done, he can talk," suggested Blicky.

Jim Cleve heard and appeared ready for that question.

"I don't know much more than I told you. But I can guess. Kells had this big shipment of gold spotted. He must have sent us in the stage for some reason. He said he'd tell me what to expect and do. But he didn't come back. Sure he knew you'd do the job. And just as sure he expected to be on hand. He'll turn up soon."

This ruse of Jim's did not sound in the least logical or plausible to Joan, but it was readily accepted by the bandits. Apparently what they knew of Kells's movements and plans since the break-up at Alder Creek fitted well with Cleve's suggestions.

"Come on!" boomed Gulden, from the fore. "Do you want to rot here?"

Then without so much as a backward glance at the ruin they left behind the bandits fell into line. Jesse Smith led straight off the road into a shallow brook and evidently meant to keep in it. Gulden followed; next came Beady Jones; then the three bandits with the pack-horse and the other horses; Cleve and Joan, close together, filed in here; and last came Budd and Blicky. It was rough, slippery traveling and the riders spread out. Cleve, however, rode beside Joan. Once, at an opportune moment, he leaned toward her.

"We'd better run for it at the first chance," he said, somberly.

"No!... GULDEN!" Joan had to moisten her lips to speak the monster's name.

"He'll never think of you while he has all that gold."

Joan's intelligence grasped this, but her morbid dread, terribly augmented now, amounted almost to a spell. Still, despite the darkness of her mind, she had a flash of inspiration and of spirit.

"Kells is my only hope!... If he doesn't join us soon—then we'll run!... And if we can't escape that"—Joan made a sickening gesture toward the fore—"you must kill me before—before—"

Her voice trailed off, failing.

"I will!" he promised through locked teeth.

And then they rode on, with dark, faces bent over the muddy water and treacherous stones.

When Jesse Smith led out of that brook it was to ride upon bare rock. He was not leaving any trail. Horses and riders were of no consideration. And he was a genius for picking hard ground and covering it. He never slackened his gait, and it seemed next to impossible to keep him in sight.

For Joan the ride became toil and the toil became pain. But there was no rest. Smith kept mercilessly onward. Sunset and twilight and night found the cavalcade still moving. Then it halted just as Joan was about to succumb. Jim lifted her off her horse and laid her upon the grass. She begged for water, and she drank and drank. But she wanted no food. There was a heavy, dull beating in her ears, a band tight round her forehead. She was aware of the gloom, of the crackling of fires, of leaping shadows, of the passing of men to and fro near her, and, most of all, rendering her capable of a saving shred of self-control, she was aware of Jim's constant companionship and watchfulness. Then sounds grew far off and night became a blur.

Morning when it came seemed an age removed from that hideous night. Her head had cleared, and but for the soreness of body and limb she would have begun the day strong. There appeared little to eat and no time to prepare it. Gulden was rampant for action. Like a miser he guarded the saddle packed with gold. This tune his comrades were as eager as he to be on the move. All were obsessed by the presence of gold. Only one hour loomed in their consciousness—that of the hour of division. How fatal and pitiful and terrible! Of what possible use or good was gold to them?

The ride began before sunrise. It started and kept on at a steady trot. Smith led down out of the rocky slopes and fastnesses into green valleys. Jim Cleve, riding bareback on a lame horse, had his difficulties. Still he kept close beside or behind Joan all the way. They seldom spoke, and then only a word relative to this stern business of traveling in the trail of a hard-riding bandit. Joan bore up better this day, as far as her mind was concerned. Physically she had all she could do to stay in the saddle. She learned of what steel she was actually made—what her slender frame could endure. That day's ride seemed a thousand miles long, and never to end. Yet the implacable Smith did finally halt, and that before dark.

Camp was made near water. The bandits were a jovial lot, despite a lack of food. They talked of the morrow. All—the world—lay beyond the next sunrise. Some renounced their pipes and sought their rest just to hurry on the day. But Gulden, tireless, sleepless, eternally vigilant, guarded the saddle of gold and brooded over it, and seemed a somber giant carved out of the night. And Blicky, nursing some deep and late-developed scheme, perhaps in Kells's interest or his own, kept watch over Gulden and all.

Jim cautioned Joan to rest, and importuned her and promised to watch while she slept.

Joan saw the stars through her shut eyelids. All the night seemed to press down and softly darken.

The sun was shining red when the cavalcade rode up Cabin Gulch. The grazing cattle stopped to watch and the horses pranced and whistled. There were flowers and flitting birds, and glistening dew on leaves, and a shining swift flow of water—the brightness of morning and nature smiled in Cabin Gulch.

Well indeed Joan remembered the trail she had ridden so often. How that clump of willow where first she had confronted Jim thrilled her now! The pines seemed welcoming her. The gulch had a sense of home in it for her, yet it was fearful. How much had happened there! What might yet happen!

Then a clear, ringing call stirred her pulse. She glanced up the slope. Tall and straight and dark, there on the bench, with hand aloft, stood the bandit Kells.

19

The weary, dusty cavalcade halted on the level bench before the bandit's cabin. Gulden boomed a salute to Kells. The other men shouted greeting. In the wild exultation of triumph they still held him as chief. But Kells was not deceived. He even passed by that heavily laden, gold-weighted saddle. He had eyes only for Joan.

"Girl, I never was so glad to see any one!" he exclaimed in husky amaze. "How did it happen? I never—"

Jim Cleve leaned over to interrupt Kells. "It was great, Kells—that idea of yours putting us in the stagecoach you meant to hold up," said Cleve, with a swift, meaning glance. "But it nearly was the end of us. You didn't catch up. The gang didn't know we were inside, and they shot the old stage full of holes."

"Aha! So that's it," replied Kells, slowly. "But the main point is—you brought her through. Jim, I can't ever square that."

"Oh, maybe you can," laughed Cleve, as he dismounted.

Suddenly Kells became aware of Joan's exhaustion and distress. "Joan, you're not hurt?" he asked in swift anxiety.

"No, only played out."

"You look it. Come." He lifted her out of the saddle and, half carrying, half leading her, took her into the cabin, and through the big room to her old apartment. How familiar it seemed to Joan! A ground-squirrel frisked along a chink between the logs, chattering welcome. The place was exactly as Joan had left it.

Kells held Joan a second, as if he meant to embrace her, but he did not. "Lord, it's good to see you! I never expected to again.... But you can tell me all about yourself after you rest.... I was just having breakfast. I'll fetch you some."

"Were you alone here?" asked Joan.

"Yes. I was with Bate and Handy—"

"Hey, Kells!" roared the gang, from the outer room.

Kells held aside the blanket curtain so that Joan was able to see through the door. The men were drawn up in a half-circle round the table, upon which were the bags of gold.

Kells whistled low. "Joan, there'll be trouble now," he said, "but don't you fear. I'll not forget you."

Despite his undoubted sincerity Joan felt a subtle change in him, and that, coupled with the significance of his words, brought a return of the strange dread. Kells went out and dropped the curtain behind him. Joan listened.

"Share and share alike!" boomed the giant Gulden.

"Say!" called Kells, gaily, "aren't you fellows going to eat first?"

Shouts of derision greeted his sally.

"I'll eat gold-dust," added Budd.

"Have it your own way, men," responded Kells. "Blicky, get the scales down off of that shelf.... Say, I'll bet anybody I'll have the most dust by sundown."

More shouts of derision were flung at him.

"Who wants to gamble now?"

"Boss, I'll take thet bet."

"Haw! Haw! You won't look so bright by sundown."

Then followed a moment's silence, presently broken by a clink of metal on the table.

"Boss, how'd you ever git wind of this big shipment of gold?" asked Jesse Smith.

"I've had it spotted. But Handy Oliver was the scout."

"We'll shore drink to Handy!" exclaimed one of the bandits.

"An' who was sendin' out this shipment?" queried the curious Smith. "Them bags are marked all the same."

"It was a one-man shipment," replied Kells. "Sent out by the boss miner of Alder Creek. They call him Overland something."

That name brought Joan to her feet with a thrilling fire. Her uncle, old Bill Hoadley, was called "Overland." Was it possible that the bandits meant him? It could hardly be; that name was a common one in the mountains.

"Shore, I seen Overland lots of times," said Budd. "An' he got wise to my watchin' him."

"Somebody tipped it off that the Legion was after his gold," went on Kells. "I suppose we have Pearce to thank for that. But it worked out well for us. The hell we raised there at the lynching must have thrown a scare into Overland. He had nerve enough to try to send his dust to Bannack on the very next stage. He nearly got away with it, too. For it was only lucky accident that Handy heard the news."

The name Overland drew Joan like a magnet and she arose to take her old position, where she could peep in upon the bandits. One glance at Jim Cleve told her that he, too, had been excited by the name. Then it occurred to Joan that her uncle could hardly have been at Alder Creek without Jim knowing it. Still, among thousands of men, all wild and toiling and self-sufficient, hiding their identities, anything might be possible. After a few moments, however, Joan leaned to the improbability of the man being her uncle.

Kells sat down before the table and Blicky stood beside him with the gold-scales. The other bandits lined up opposite. Jim Cleve stood to one side, watching, brooding.

"You can't weigh it all on these scales," said Blicky.

"That's sure," replied Kells. "We'll divide the small bags first.... Ten shares—ten equal parts!... Spill out the bags. Blick. And hurry. Look how hungry Gulden looks!... Somebody cook your breakfast while we divide the gold."

"Haw! Haw!"

"Ho! Ho!"

"Who wants to eat?"

The bandits were gay, derisive, scornful, eager, like a group of boys, half surly, half playful, at a game.

"Wal, I shore want to see my share weighted," drawled Budd.

Kells moved—his gun flashed—he slammed it hard upon the table.

"Budd, do you question my honesty?" he asked, quick and hard.

"No offense, boss. I was just talkin'."

That quick change of Kells's marked a subtle difference in the spirit of the bandits and the occasion. Gaiety and good humor and badinage ended. There were no more broad grins or friendly leers or coarse laughs. Gulden and his groups clustered closer to the table, quiet, intense, watchful, suspicious.

It did not take Kells and his assistant long to divide the smaller quantity of the gold.

"Here, Gulden," he said, and handed the giant a bag. Jesse.... Bossert.... Pike.... Beady.... Braverman... "Blicky."

"Here, Jim Cleve, get in the game," he added, throwing a bag at Jim. It was heavy. It hit Jim with a thud and dropped to the ground. He stooped to reach it.

"That leaves one for Handy and one for me," went on Kells. "Blicky, spill out the big bag."

Presently Joan saw a huge mound of dull, gleaming yellow. The color of it leaped to the glinting eyes of the bandits. And it seemed to her that a shadow hovered over them. The movements of Kells grew tense and hurried. Beads of sweat stood out upon his brow. His hands were not steady.

Soon larger bags were distributed to the bandits. That broke the waiting, the watchfulness, but not the tense eagerness. The bandits were now like leashed hounds. Blicky leaned before Kells and hit the table with his fist.

"Boss, I've a kick comin'," he said.

"Come on with it," replied the leader.

"Ain't Gulden a-goin' to divide up thet big nugget?"

"He is if he's square."

A chorus of affirmatives from the bandits strengthened Kells's statement. Gulden moved heavily and ponderously, and he pushed some of his comrades aside to get nearer to Kells.

"Wasn't it my right to do a job by myself—when I wanted?" he demanded.

"No. I agreed to let you fight when you wanted. To kill a man when you liked!... That was the agreement."

"What'd I kill a man for?"

No one answered that in words, but the answer was there, in dark faces.

"I know what I meant," continued Gulden. "And I'm going to keep this nugget."

There was a moment's silence. It boded ill to the giant.

"So—he declares himself," said Blicky, hotly. "Boss, what you say goes."

"Let him keep it," declared Kells, scornfully. "I'll win it from him and divide it with the gang."

That was received with hoarse acclaims by all except Gulden. He glared sullenly. Kells stood up and shook a long finger in the giant's face.

"I'll win your nugget," he shouted. "I'll beat you at any game.... I call your hand.... Now if you've got any nerve!"

"Come on!" boomed the giant, and he threw his gold down upon the table with a crash.

The bandits closed in around the table with sudden, hard violence, all crowding for seats.

"I'm a-goin' to set in the game!" yelled Blicky.

"We'll all set in," declared Jesse Smith.

"Come on!" was Gulden's acquiescence.

"But we all can't play at once," protested Kells. "Let's make up two games."

"Naw!"

"Some of you eat, then, while the others get cleaned out."

"Thet's it—cleaned out!" ejaculated Budd, meanly. "You seem to be sure, Kells. An' I guess I'll keep shady of thet game."

"That's twice for you, Budd," flashed the bandit leader. "Beware of the third time!"

"Hyar, fellers, cut the cards fer who sets in an' who sets out," called Blicky, and he slapped a deck of cards upon the table.

With grim eagerness, as if drawing lots against fate, the bandits bent over and drew cards. Budd, Braverman, and Beady Jones were the ones excluded from the game.

"Beady, you fellows unpack those horses and turn them loose. And bring the stuff inside," said Kells.

Budd showed a surly disregard, but the other two bandits got up willingly and went out.

Then the game began, with only Cleve standing, looking on. The bandits were mostly silent; they moved their hands, and occasionally bent forward. It was every man against his neighbor. Gulden seemed implacably indifferent and played like a machine. Blicky sat eager and excited, under a spell. Jesse Smith was a slow, cool, shrewed gambler. Bossert and Pike, two ruffians almost unknown to Joan, appeared carried away by their opportunity. And Kells began to wear that strange, rapt, weak expression that gambling gave him.

Presently Beady Jones and Braverman bustled in, carrying the packs. Then Budd jumped up and ran to them. He returned to the table, carrying a demijohn, which he banged upon the table.

"Whisky!" exclaimed Kells. "Take that away. We can't drink and gamble."

"Watch me!" replied Blicky.

"Let them drink, Kells," declared Gulden. "We'll get their dust quicker. Then we can have our game."

Kells made no more comment. The game went on and the aspect of it changed. When Kells himself began to drink, seemingly unconscious of the fact, Joan's dread increased greatly, and, leaving the peep-hole, she lay back upon the bed. Always a sword had hung over her head. Time after time by some fortunate circumstance or by courage or wit or by an act of Providence she had escaped what strangely menaced. Would she escape it again? For she felt the catastrophe coming. Did Jim recognize that fact? Remembering the look on his face, she was assured that he did. Then he would be quick to seize upon any possible chance to get her away; and always he would be between her and those bandits. At most, then, she had only death to fear—death that he would mercifully deal to her if the worst came. And as she lay there listening to the slow-rising murmur of the gamblers, with her thought growing clearer, she realized it was love of Jim and fear for him—fear that he would lose her—that caused her cold dread and the laboring breath and the weighted heart. She had cost Jim this terrible experience and she wanted to make up to him for it, to give him herself and all her life.

Joan lay there a long time, thinking and suffering, while the strange, morbid desire to watch Kells and Gulden grew stronger and stronger, until it was irresistible. Her fate, her life, lay in the balance between these two men. She divined that.

She returned to her vantage-point, and as she glanced through she vibrated to a shock. The change that had begun subtly, intangibly, was now a terrible and glaring difference. That great quantity of gold, the equal chance of every gambler, the marvelous possibilities presented to evil minds, and the hell that hid in that black bottle—these had made playthings of every bandit except Gulden. He was exactly the same as ever. But to see the others sent a chill of ice along Joan's veins. Kells was white and rapt. Plain to see—he had won! Blicky was wild with rage. Jesse Smith sat darker, grimmer, but no longer cool. There was hate in the glance he fastened upon Kells as he bet. Beady Jones and Braverman showed an inflamed and impotent eagerness to take their turn. Budd sat in the game now, and his face wore a terrible look. Joan could not tell what passion drove him, but she knew he was a loser. Pike and Bossert likewise were losers, and stood apart, sullen, watching with sick, jealous rage. Jim Cleve had reacted to the strain, and he was white, with nervous, clutching hands and piercing glances. And the game went on with violent slap of card or pound of fist upon the table, with the slide of a bag of gold or the little, sodden thump of its weight, with savage curses at loss and strange, raw exultation at gain, with hurry and violence—more than all, with the wildness of the hour and the wildness of these men, drawing closer and closer to the dread climax that from the beginning had been foreshadowed.

Suddenly Budd rose and bent over the table, his cards clutched in a shaking hand, his face distorted and malignant, his eyes burning at Kells. Passionately he threw the cards down.

"There!" he yelled, hoarsely, and he stilled the noise.

"No good!" replied Kells, tauntingly. "Is there any other game you play?"

Budd bent low to see the cards in Kells's hand, and then, straightening his form, he gazed with haggard fury at the winner. "You've done me!... I'm cleaned—I'm busted!" he raved.

"You were easy. Get out of the game," replied Kells, with an exultant contempt. It was not the passion of play that now obsessed him, but the passion of success.

"I said you done me," burst out Budd, insanely. "You're slick with the cards!"

The accusation acted like magic to silence the bandits, to check movement, to clamp the situation. Kells was white and radiant; he seemed careless and nonchalant.

"All right, Budd," he replied, but his tone did not suit his strange look. "That's three times for you!"

Swift as a flash he shot. Budd fell over Gulden, and the giant with one sweep of his arm threw the stricken bandit off. Budd fell heavily, and neither moved nor spoke.

"Pass me the bottle," went on Kells, a little hoarse shakiness in his voice. "And go on with the game!"

"Can I set in now?" asked Beady Jones, eagerly.

"You and Jack wait. This's getting to be all between Kells an' me," said Gulden.

"We've sure got Blicky done!" exclaimed Kells. There was something taunting about the leader's words. He did not care for the gold. It was the fight to win. It was his egotism.

"Make this game faster an' bigger, will you?" retorted Blicky, who seemed inflamed.

"Boss, a little luck makes you lofty," interposed Jesse Smith in dark disdain. "Pretty soon you'll show yellow clear to your gizzard!"

The gold lay there on the table. It was only a means to an end. It signified nothing. The evil, the terrible greed, the brutal lust, were in the hearts of the men. And hate, liberated, rampant, stalked out unconcealed, ready for blood.

"Gulden, change the game to suit these gents," taunted Kells.

"Double stakes. Cut the cards!" boomed the giant, instantly.

Blicky lasted only a few more deals of the cards, then he rose, loser of all his share, a passionate and venomous bandit, ready for murder. But he kept his mouth shut and looked wary.

"Boss, can't we set in now?" demanded Beady Jones.

"Say, Beady, you're in a hurry to lose your gold," replied Kells. "Wait till I beat Gulden and Smith."

Luck turned against Jesse Smith. He lost first to Gulden, then to Kells, and presently he rose, a beaten, but game man. He reached for the whisky.

"Fellers, I reckon I can enjoy Kells's yellow streak more when I ain't playin'," he said.

The bandit leader eyed Smith with awakening rancor, as if a persistent hint of inevitable weakness had its effect. He frowned, and the radiance left his face for the forbidding cast.

"Stand around, you men, and see some real gambling," he said.

At this moment in the contest Kells had twice as much gold as Gulden, there being a huge mound of little buckskin sacks in front of him.

They began staking a bag at a time and cutting the cards, the higher card winning. Kells won the first four cuts. How strangely that radiance returned to his face! Then he lost and won, and won and lost. The other bandits grouped around, only Jones and Braverman now manifesting any eagerness. All were silent. There were suspense, strain, mystery in the air. Gulden began to win consistently and Kells began to change. It was a sad and strange sight to see this strong man's nerve and force gradually deteriorate under a fickle fortune. The time came when half the amount he had collected was in front of Gulden. The giant was imperturbable. He might have been a huge animal, or destiny, or something inhuman that knew the run of luck would be his. As he had taken losses so he greeted gains—with absolute indifference. While Kells's hands shook the giant's were steady and slow and sure. It must have been hateful to Kells—this faculty of Gulden's to meet victory identically as he met defeat. The test of a great gambler's nerve was not in sustaining loss, but in remaining cool with victory. The fact grew manifest that Gulden was a great gambler and Kells was not. The giant had no emotion, no imagination. And Kells seemed all fire and whirling hope and despair and rage. His vanity began to bleed to death. This game was the deciding contest. The scornful and exultant looks of his men proved how that game was going. Again and again Kells's unsteady hand reached for one of the whisky bottles. Once with a low curse he threw an empty bottle through the door.

"Hey, boss, ain't it about time—" began Jesse Smith. But whatever he had intended to say, he thought better of, withholding it. Kells's sudden look and movement were unmistakable.

The goddess of chance, as false as the bandit's vanity, played with him. He brightened under a streak of winning. But just as his face began to lose its haggard shade, to glow, the tide again turned against him. He lost and lost, and with each bag of gold-dust went something of his spirit. And when he was reduced to his original share he indeed showed that yellow streak which Jesse Smith had attributed to him. The bandit's effort to pull himself together, to be a man before that scornful gang, was pitiful and futile. He might have been magnificent, confronted by other issues, of peril or circumstance, but there he was craven. He was a man who should never have gambled.

One after the other, in quick succession, he lost the two bags of gold, his original share. He had lost utterly. Gulden had the great heap of dirty little buckskin sacks, so significant of the hidden power within.

Joan was amazed and sick at sight of Kells then, and if it had been possible she would have withdrawn her gaze. But she was chained there. The catastrophe was imminent.

Kells stared down at the gold. His jaw worked convulsively. He had the eyes of a trapped wolf. Yet he seemed not wholly to comprehend what had happened to him.

Gulden rose, slow, heavy, ponderous, to tower over his heap of gold. Then this giant, who had never shown an emotion, suddenly, terribly blazed.

"One more bet—a cut of the cards—my whole stake of gold!" he boomed.

The bandits took a stride forward as one man, then stood breathless.

"One bet!" echoed Kells, aghast. "Against what?"

"AGAINST THE GIRL!"

Joan sank against the wall, a piercing torture in her breast. She clutched the logs to keep from falling. So that was the impending horror. She could not unrivet her eyes from the paralyzed Kells, yet she seemed to see Jim Cleve leap straight up, and then stand, equally motionless, with Kells.

"One cut of the cards—my gold against the girl!" boomed the giant.

Kells made a movement as if to go for his gun. But it failed. His hand was a shaking leaf.

"You always bragged on your nerve!" went on Gulden, mercilessly. "You're the gambler of the border!... Come on."

Kells stood there, his doom upon him. Plain to all was his torture, his weakness, his defeat. It seemed that with all his soul he combated something, only to fail.

"ONE CUT—MY GOLD AGAINST YOUR GIRL!"

The gang burst into one concerted taunt. Like snarling, bristling wolves they craned their necks at Kells.

"No, damn—you! No!" cried Kells, in hoarse, broken fury. With both hands before him he seemed to push back the sight of that gold, of Gulden, of the malignant men, of a horrible temptation.

"Reckon, boss, thet yellow streak is operatin'!" sang out Jesse Smith.

But neither gold, nor Gulden, nor men, nor taunts ruined Kells at this perhaps most critical crisis of his life. It was the mad, clutching, terrible opportunity presented. It was the strange and terrible nature of the wager. What vision might have flitted through the gambler's mind! But neither vision of loss nor gain moved him. There, licking like a flame at his soul, consuming the good in him at a blast, overpowering his love, was the strange and magnificent gamble. He could not resist it.

Speechless, with a motion of his hand, he signified his willingness.

"Blicky, shuffle the cards," boomed Gulden.

Blicky did so and dropped the deck with a slap in the middle of the table.

"Cut!" called Gulden.

Kells's shaking hand crept toward the deck.

Jim Cleve suddenly appeared to regain power of speech and motion. "Don't, Kells, don't!" he cried, piercingly, as he leaped forward.

But neither Kells nor the others heard him, or even saw his movement.

Kells cut the deck. He held up his card. It was the king of hearts. What a transformation! His face might have been that of a corpse suddenly revivified with glorious, leaping life.

"Only an ace can beat thet!" muttered Jesse Smith into the silence.

Gulden reached for the deck as if he knew every card left was an ace. His cavernous eyes gloated over Kells. He cut, and before he looked himself he let Kells see the card.

"You can't beat my streak!" he boomed.

Then he threw the card upon the table. It was the ace of spades.

Kells seemed to shrivel, to totter, to sink. Jim Cleve went quickly to him, held to him.

"Kells, go say good—by to your girl!" boomed Gulden. "I'll want her pretty soon.... Come on, you Beady and Braverman. Here's your chance to get even."

Gulden resumed his seat, and the two bandits invited to play were eager to comply, while the others pressed close once more.

Jim Cleve led the dazed Kells toward the door into Joan's cabin. For Joan just then all seemed to be dark.

When she recovered she was lying on the bed and Jim was bending over her. He looked frantic with grief and desperation and fear.

"Jim! Jim!" she moaned, grasping his hands. He helped her to sit up. Then she saw Kells standing there. He looked abject, stupid, drunk. Yet evidently he had begun to comprehend the meaning of his deed.

"Kells," began Cleve, in low, hoarse tones, as he stepped forward with a gun. "I'm going to kill you—and Joan—and myself!"

Kells stared at Cleve. "Go ahead. Kill me. And kill the girl, too. That'll be better for her now. But why kill yourself?"

"I love her. She's my wife!"

The deadness about Kells suddenly changed. Joan flung herself before him.

"Kells—listen," she whispered in swift, broken passion. "Jim Cleve was—my sweetheart—back in Hoadley. We quarreled. I taunted him. I said he hadn't nerve enough—even to be bad. He left me—bitterly enraged. Next day I trailed him. I wanted to fetch him back.... You remember—how you met me with Robert—how you killed Roberts? And all the rest?... When Jim and I met out here—I was afraid to tell you. I tried to influence him. I succeeded—till we got to Alder Creek. There he went wild. I married him—hoping to steady him.... Then the day of the lynching—we were separated from you in the crowd. That night we hid—and next morning took the stage. Gulden and his gang held up the stage. They thought you had put us there. We fooled them, but we had to come on—here to Cabin Gulch—hoping to tell—that you'd let us go.... And now—now—"

Joan had not strength to go on. The thought of Gulden made her faint.

"It's true, Kells," added Cleve, passionately, as he faced the incredulous bandit. "I swear it. Why, you ought to see now!"

"My God, boy, I DO see!" gasped Kells. That dark, sodden thickness of comprehension and feeling, indicative of the hold of drink, passed away swiftly. The shock had sobered him.

Instantly Joan saw it—saw in him the return of the other and better Kells, how stricken with remorse. She slipped to her knees and clasped her arms around him. He tried to break her hold, but she held on.

"Get up!" he ordered, violently. "Jim, pull her away!... Girl, don't do that in front of me... I've just gambled away—"

"Her life, Kells, only that, I swear," cried Cleve.

"Kells, listen," began Joan, pleadingly. "You will not let that—that CANNIBAL have me?"

"No, by God!" replied Kells, thickly. "I was drunk—crazy.... Forgive me, girl! You see—how did I know—what was coming?... Oh, the whole thing is hellish!"

"You loved me once," whispered Joan, softly. "Do you love me still?... Kells, can't you see? It's not too late to save my life—and YOUR soul!... Can't you see? You have been bad. But if you save me now—from Gulden—save me for this boy I've almost ruined—you—you.... God will forgive you!... Take us away—go with us—and never come back to the border."

"Maybe I can save you," he muttered, as if to himself. He appeared to want to think, but to be bothered by the clinging arms around him. Joan felt a ripple go over his body and he seemed to heighten, and the touch of his hands thrilled.

Then, white and appealing, Cleve added his importunity.

"Kells, I saved your life once. You said you'd remember it some day. Now—now!... For God's sake don't make me shoot her!"

Joan rose from her knees, but she still clasped Kells. She seemed to feel the mounting of his spirit, to understand how in this moment he was rising out of the depths. How strangely glad she was for him!

"Joan, once you showed me what the love of a good woman really was. I've never seen the same since then. I've grown better in one way—worse in all others.... I let down. I was no man for the border. Always that haunted me. Believe me, won't you—despite all?"

Joan felt the yearning in him for what he dared not ask. She read his mind. She knew he meant, somehow, to atone for his wrong.

"I'll show you again," she whispered. "I'll tell you more. If I'd never loved Jim Cleve—if I'd met you, I'd have loved you.... And, bandit or not, I'd have gone with you to the end of the world!"

"Joan!" The name was almost a sob of joy and pain. Sight of his face then blinded Joan with her tears. But when he caught her to him, in a violence that was a terrible renunciation, she gave her embrace, her arms, her lips without the vestige of a lie, with all of womanliness and sweetness and love and passion. He let her go and turned away, and in that instant Joan had a final divination that this strange man could rise once to heights as supreme as the depths of his soul were dark. She dashed away her tears and wiped the dimness from her eyes. Hope resurged. Something strong and sweet gave her strength.

When Kells wheeled he was the Kells of her earlier experience—cool, easy, deadly, with the smile almost amiable, and the strange, pale eyes. Only the white radiance of him was different. He did not look at her.

"Jim, will you do exactly what I tell you?"

"Yes, I promise," replied Jim.

"How many guns have you?"

"Two."

"Give me one of them."

Cleve held out the gun that all the while he had kept in his hand. Kells took it and put it in his pocket.

"Pull your other gun—be ready," said he, swiftly. "But don't you shoot once till I go down!... Then do your best.... Save the last bullet for Joan—in case—"

"I promise," replied Cleve, steadily.

Then Kells drew a knife from a sheath at his belt. It had a long, bright blade. Joan had seen him use it many a time round the camp-fire. He slipped the blade up his sleeve, retaining the haft of the knife in his hand. He did not speak another word. Nor did he glance at Joan again. She had felt his gaze while she had embraced him, as she raised her lips. That look had been his last. Then he went out. Jim knelt beside the door, peering between post and curtain.

Joan staggered to the chink between the logs. She would see that fight if it froze her blood—the very marrow of her bones.

The gamblers were intent upon their game. Not a dark face looked up as Kells sauntered toward the table. Gulden sat with his back to the door. There was a shaft of sunlight streaming in, and Kells blocked it, sending a shadow over the bent heads of the gamesters. How significant that shadow—a blackness barring gold! Still no one paid any attention to Kells.

He stepped closer. Suddenly he leaped into swift and terrible violence. Then with a lunge he drove the knife into Gulden's burly neck.

Up heaved the giant, his mighty force overturning table and benches and men. An awful boom, strangely distorted and split, burst from him.

Then Kells blocked the door with a gun in each hand, but only the one in his right hand spurted white and red. Instantly there followed a mad scramble—hoarse yells, over which that awful roar of Gulden's predominated—and the bang of guns. Clouds of white smoke veiled the scene, and with every shot the veil grew denser. Red flashes burst from the ground where men were down, and from each side of Kells. His form seemed less instinct with force; it had shortened; he was sagging. But at intervals the red spurt and report of his gun showed he was fighting. Then a volley from one side made him stagger against the door. The clear spang of a Winchester spoke above the heavy boom of the guns.

Joan's eyesight recovered from its blur or else the haze of smoke drifted, for she saw better. Gulden's actions fascinated her, horrified her. He had evidently gone crazy. He groped about the room, through the smoke, to and fro before the fighting, yelling bandits, grasping with huge hands for something. His sense of direction, his equilibrium, had become affected. His awful roar still sounded above the din, but it was weakening. His giant's strength was weakening. His legs bent and buckled under him. All at once he whipped out his two big guns and began to fire as he staggered—at random. He killed the wounded Blicky. In the melee he ran against Jesse Smith and thrust both guns at him. Jesse saw the peril and with a shriek he fired point-blank at Gulden. Then as Gulden pulled triggers both men fell. But Gulden rose, bloody-browed, bawling, still a terrible engine of destruction. He seemed to glare in one direction and shoot in another. He pointed the guns and apparently pulled the triggers long after the shots had all been fired.

Kells was on his knees now with only one gun. This wavered and fell, wavered and fell. His left arm hung broken. But his face flashed white through the thin, drifting clouds of smoke.

Besides Gulden the bandit Pike was the only one not down, and he was hard hit. When he shot his last he threw the gun away, and, drawing a knife, he made at Kells. Kells shot once more, and hit Pike, but did not stop him. Silence, after the shots and yells, seemed weird, and the groping giant, trying to follow Pike, resembled a huge phantom. With one wrench he tore off a leg of the overturned table and brandished that. He swayed now, and there was a whistle where before there had been a roar.

Pike fell over the body of Blicky and got up again. The bandit leader staggered to his feet, flung the useless gun in Pike's face, and closed with him in weak but final combat. They lurched and careened to and fro, with the giant Gulden swaying after them. Thus they struggled until Pike moved under Gulden's swinging club. The impetus of the blow carried Gulden off his balance. Kells seized the haft of the knife still protruding from the giant's neck, and he pulled upon it with all his might. Gulden heaved up again, and the movement enabled Kells to pull out the knife. A bursting gush of blood, thick and heavy, went flooding before the giant as he fell.

Kells dropped the knife, and, tottering, surveyed the scene before him—the gasping Gulden, and all the quiet forms. Then he made a few halting steps, and dropped near the door.

Joan tried to rush out, but what with the unsteadiness of her limbs and Jim holding her as he went out, too, she seemed long in getting to Kells.

She knelt beside him, lifted his head. His face was white—his eyes were open. But they were only the windows of a retreating soul. He did not know her. Consciousness was gone. Then swiftly life fled.

20

Cleve steadied Joan in her saddle, and stood a moment beside her, holding her hands. The darkness seemed clearing before her eyes and the sick pain within her seemed numbing out.

"Brace up! Hang—to your saddle!" Jim was saying, earnestly. "Any moment some of the other bandits might come.... You lead the way. I'll follow and drive the pack-horse."

"But, Jim, I'll never be able to find the back-trail," said Joan.

"I think you will. You'll remember every yard of the trail on which you were brought in here. You won't realize that till you see."

Joan started and did not look back. Cabin Gulch was like a place in a dream. It was a relief when she rode out into the broad valley. The grazing horses lifted their heads to whistle. Joan saw the clumps of bushes and the flowers, the waving grass, but never as she had seen them before. How strange that she knew exactly which way to turn, to head, to cross! She trotted her horse so fast that Jim called to say he could not drive a pack-animal and keep to her gait. Every rod of the trail lessened a burden. Behind was something hideous and incomprehensible and terrible; before beckoned something beginning to seem bright. And it was not the ruddy, calm sunset, flooding the hills with color. That something called from beyond the hills.

She led straight to a camp-site she remembered long before she came to it; and the charred logs of the fire, the rocks, the tree under which she had lain—all brought back the emotions she had felt there. She grew afraid of the twilight, and when night settled down there were phantoms stalking in the shadows. When Cleve, in his hurried camp duties, went out of her sight, she wanted to cry out to him, but had not the voice; and when he was close still she trembled and was cold. He wrapped blankets round her and held her in his arms, yet the numb chill and the dark clamp of mind remained with her. Long she lay awake. The stars were pitiless. When she shut her eyes the blackness seemed unendurable. She slept, to wake out of nightmare, and she dared sleep no more. At last the day came.

For Joan that faint trail seemed a broad road, blazoned through the wild canons and up the rocky fastness and through the thick brakes. She led on and on and up and down, never at fault, with familiar landmarks near and far. Cleve hung close to her, and now his call to her or to the pack-horse took on a keener note. Every rough and wild mile behind them meant so much. They did not halt at the noon hour. They did not halt at the next camp-site, still more darkly memorable to Joan. And sunset found them miles farther on, down on the divide, at the head of Lost Canon.

Here Joan ate and drank, and slept the deep sleep of exhaustion. Sunrise found them moving, and through the winding, wild canon they made fast travel. Both time and miles passed swiftly. At noon they reached the little open cabin, and they dismounted for a rest and a drink at the spring. Joan did not speak a word here. That she could look into the cabin where she had almost killed a bandit, and then, through silent, lonely weeks, had nursed him back to life, was a proof that the long ride and distance were helping her, sloughing away the dark deadlock to hope and brightness. They left the place exactly as they had found it, except that Cleve plucked the card from the bark of the balsam-tree—Gulden's ace—of—hearts target with its bullet—holes.

Then they rode on, out of that canon, over the rocky ridge, down into another canon, on and on, past an old camp-site, along a babbling brook for miles, and so at last out into the foot—hills.

Toward noon of the next day, when approaching a clump of low trees in a flat valley, Joan pointed ahead.

"Jim—it was in there—where Roberts and I camped—and—"

"You ride around. I'll catch up with you," replied Cleve.

She made a wide detour, to come back again to her own trail, so different here. Presently Cleve joined her. His face was pale and sweaty, and he looked sick. They rode on silently, and that night they camped without water on her own trail, made months before. The single tracks were there, sharp and clear in the earth, as if imprinted but a day.

Next morning Joan found that as the wild border lay behind her so did the dark and hateful shadow of gloom. Only the pain remained, and it had softened. She could think now.

Jim Cleve cheered up. Perhaps it was her brightening to which he responded. They began to talk and speech liberated feeling. Miles of that back-trail they rode side by side, holding hands, driving the pack-horse ahead, and beginning to talk of old associations. Again it was sunset when they rode down the hill toward the little village of Hoadley. Joan's heart was full, but Jim was gay.

"Won't I have it on your old fellows!" he teased. But he was grim, too.

"Jim! You—won't tell—just yet!" she faltered.

"I'll introduce you as my wife! They'll all think we eloped."

"No. They'll say I ran after you!... Please, Jim! Keep it secret a little. It'll be hard for me. Aunt Jane will never understand."

"Well, I'll keep it secret till you want to tell—for two things," he said.

"What?"

"Meet me to—night, under the spruces where we had that quarrel. Meet just like we did then, but differently. Will you?"

"I'll be—so glad."

"And put on your mask now!... You know, Joan, sooner or later your story will be on everybody's tongue. You'll be Dandy Dale as long as you live near this border. Wear the mask, just for fun. Imagine your Aunt Jane—and everybody!"

"Jim! I'd forgotten how I look!" exclaimed Joan in dismay. "I didn't bring your long coat. Oh, I can't face them in this suit!"

"You'll have to. Besides, you look great. It's going to tickle me—the sensation you make. Don't you see, they'll never recognize you till you take the mask off.... Please, Joan."

She yielded, and donned the black mask, not without a twinge. And thus they rode across the log bridge over the creek into the village. The few men and women they met stared in wonder, and, recognizing Cleve, they grew excited. They followed, and others joined them.

"Joan, won't it be strange if Uncle Bill really is the Overland of Alder Creek? We've packed out every pound of Overland's gold. Oh! I hope—I believe he's your uncle.... Wouldn't it be great, Joan?"

But Joan could not answer. The word gold was a stab. Besides, she saw Aunt Jane and two neighbors standing before a log cabin, beginning to show signs of interest in the approaching procession.

Joan fell back a little, trying to screen herself behind Jim. Then Jim halted with a cheery salute.

"For the land's sake!" ejaculated a sweet-faced, gray-haired woman.

"If it isn't Jim Cleve!" cried another.

Jim jumped off and hugged the first speaker. She seemed overjoyed to see him and then overcome. Her face began to work.

"Jim! We always hoped you'd—you'd fetch Joan back!"

"Sure!" shouted Jim, who had no heart now for even an instant's deception. "There she is!"

"Who?... What?"

Joan slipped out of her saddle and, tearing off the mask, she leaped forward with a little sob.

"Auntie! Auntie!... It's Joan—alive—well!... Oh, so glad to be home!... Don't look at my clothes—look at me!"

Aunt Jane evidently sustained a shock of recognition, joy, amaze, consternation, and shame, of which all were subservient to the joy. She cried over Joan and murmured over her. Then, suddenly alive to the curious crowd, she put Joan from her.

"You—you wild thing! You desperado! I always told Bill you'd run wild some day!... March in the house and get out of that indecent rig!"

That night under the spruces, with the starlight piercing the lacy shadows, Joan waited for Jim Cleve. It was one of the white, silent, mountain nights. The brook murmured over the stones and the wind rustled the branches.

The wonder of Joan's home-coming was in learning that Uncle Bill Hoadley was indeed Overland, the discoverer of Alder Creek. Years and years of profitless toil had at last been rewarded in this rich gold strike.

Joan hated to think of gold. She had wanted to leave the gold back in Cabin Gulch, and she would have done so had Jim permitted it. And to think that all that gold which was not Jim Cleve's belonged to her uncle! She could not believe it.

Fatal and terrible forever to Joan would be the significance of gold. Did any woman in the world or any man know the meaning of gold as well as she knew it? How strange and enlightening and terrible had been her experience! She had grown now not to blame any man, honest miner or bloody bandit. She blamed only gold. She doubted its value. She could not see it a blessing. She absolutely knew its driving power to change the souls of men. Could she ever forget that vast ant-hill of toiling diggers and washers, blind and deaf and dumb to all save gold?

Always limned in figures of fire against the black memory would be the forms of those wild and violent bandits! Gulden, the monster, the gorilla, the cannibal! Horrible as was the memory of him, there was no horror in thought of his terrible death. That seemed to be the one memory that did not hurt.

But Kells was indestructible—he lived in her mind. Safe out of the border now and at home, she could look back clearly. Still all was not clear and never would be. She saw Kells the ruthless bandit, the organizer, the planner, and the blood-spiller. He ought have no place in a good woman's memory. Yet he had. She never condoned one of his deeds or even his intentions.

She knew her intelligence was not broad enough to grasp the vastness of his guilt. She believed he must have been the worst and most terrible character on that wild border. That border had developed him. It had produced the time and the place and the man. And therein lay the mystery. For over against this bandit's weakness and evil she could contrast strength and nobility. She alone had known the real man in all the strange phases of his nature, and the darkness of his crime faded out of her mind. She suffered remorse—almost regret. Yet what could she have done? There had been no help for that impossible situation as, there was now no help for her in a right and just placing of Kells among men. He had stolen her—wantonly murdering for the sake of lonely, fruitless hours with her; he had loved her—and he had changed; he had gambled away her soul and life—a last and terrible proof of the evil power of gold; and in the end he had saved her—he had gone from her white, radiant, cool, with strange, pale eyes and his amiable, mocking smile, and all the ruthless force of his life had expended itself in one last magnificent stand. If only he had known her at the end—when she lifted his head! But no—there had been only the fading light—the strange, weird look of a retreating soul, already alone forever.

A rustling of leaves, a step thrilled Joan out of her meditation.

Suddenly she was seized from behind, and Jim Cleve showed that though he might be a joyous and grateful lover, he certainly would never be an actor. For if he desired to live over again that fatal meeting and quarrel which had sent them out to the border, he failed utterly in his part. There was possession in the gentle grasp of his arms and bliss in the trembling of his lips.

"Jim, you never did it that way!" laughed Joan. "If you had—do you think I could ever have been furious?"

Jim in turn laughed happily. "Joan, that's exactly the way I stole upon you and mauled you!".

"You think so! Well, I happen to remember. Now you sit here and make believe you are Joan. And let me be Jim Cleve!... I'll show you!"

Joan stole away in the darkness, and noiselessly as a shadow she stole back—to enact that violent scene as it lived in her memory.

Jim was breathless, speechless, choked.

"That's how you treated me," she said.

"I—I don't believe I could have—been such a—a bear!" panted Jim.

"But you were. And consider—I've not half your strength."

"Then all I say is—you did right to drive me off.... Only you should never have trailed me out to the border."

"Ah!... But, Jim, in my fury I discovered my love!"

THE CALL OF THE CANYON

CHAPTER I

What subtle strange message had come to her out of the West? Carley Burch laid the letter in her lap and gazed dreamily through the window.

It was a day typical of early April in New York, rather cold and gray, with steely sunlight. Spring breathed in the air, but the women passing along Fifty-seventh Street wore furs and wraps. She heard the distant clatter of an L train and then the hum of a motor car. A hurdy-gurdy jarred into the interval of quiet.

"Glenn has been gone over a year," she mused, "three months over a year—and of all his strange letters this seems the strangest yet."

She lived again, for the thousandth time, the last moments she had spent with him. It had been on New-Year's Eve, 1918. They had called upon friends who were staying at the McAlpin, in a suite on the twenty-first floor overlooking Broadway. And when the last quarter hour of that eventful and tragic year began slowly to pass with the low swell of whistles and bells, Carley's friends had discreetly left her alone with her lover, at the open window, to watch and hear the old year out, the new year in. Glenn Kilbourne had returned from France early that fall, shell-shocked and gassed, and otherwise incapacitated for service in the army—a wreck of his former sterling self and in many unaccountable ways a stranger to her. Cold, silent, haunted by something, he had made her miserable with his aloofness. But as the bells began to ring out the year that had been his ruin Glenn had drawn her close, tenderly, passionately, and yet strangely, too.

"Carley, look and listen!" he had whispered.

Under them stretched the great long white flare of Broadway, with its snow-covered length glittering under a myriad of electric lights. Sixth Avenue swerved away to the right, a less brilliant lane of blanched snow. The L trains crept along like huge fire-eyed serpents. The hum of the ceaseless moving line of motor cars drifted upward faintly, almost drowned in the rising clamor of the street. Broadway's gay and thoughtless crowds surged to and fro, from that height merely a thick stream of black figures, like contending columns of ants on the march. And everywhere the monstrous electric signs flared up vivid in white and red and green; and dimmed and paled, only to flash up again.

Ring out the Old! Ring in the New! Carley had poignantly felt the sadness of the one, the promise of the other. As one by one the siren factory whistles opened up with deep, hoarse bellow, the clamor of the street and the ringing of the bells were lost in a volume of continuous sound that swelled on high into a magnificent roar. It was the voice of a city—of a nation. It was the voice of a people crying out the strife and the agony of the year—pealing forth a prayer for the future.

Glenn had put his lips to her ear: "It's like the voice in my soul!" Never would she forget the shock of that. And how she had stood spellbound, enveloped in the mighty volume of sound no longer discordant, but full of great, pregnant melody, until the white ball burst upon the tower of the Times Building, showing the bright figures 1919.

The new year had not been many minutes old when Glenn Kilbourne had told her he was going West to try to recover his health.

Carley roused out of her memories to take up the letter that had so perplexed her. It bore the postmark, Flagstaff, Arizona. She reread it with slow pondering thoughtfulness.

WEST FORK,

March 25.

DEAR CARLEY:

It does seem my neglect in writing you is unpardonable. I used to be a pretty fair correspondent, but in that as in other things I have changed.

One reason I have not answered sooner is because your letter was so sweet and loving that it made me feel an ungrateful and unappreciative wretch. Another is that this life I now lead does not induce writing. I am outdoors all day, and when I get back to this cabin at night I am too tired for anything but bed.

Your imperious questions I must answer—and that must, of course, is a third reason why I have delayed my reply. First, you ask, "Don't you love me any more as you used to?"... Frankly, I do not. I am sure my old love for you, before I went to France, was selfish, thoughtless, sentimental, and boyish. I am a man now. And my love for you is different. Let me assure you that it has been about all left to me of what is noble and beautiful. Whatever the changes in me for the worse, my love for you, at least, has grown better, finer, purer.

And now for your second question, "Are you coming home as soon as you are well again?"... Carley, I am well. I have delayed telling you this because I knew you would expect me to rush back East with the telling. But—the fact is, Carley, I am not coming—just yet. I wish it were possible for me to make you understand. For a long time I seem to have been frozen within. You know when I came back from France I couldn't talk. It's almost as bad as that now. Yet all that I was then seems to have changed again. It is only fair to you to tell you that, as I feel now, I hate the city, I hate people, and particularly I hate that dancing, drinking, lounging set you chase with. I don't want to come East until I am over that, you know... Suppose I never get over it? Well, Carley, you can free yourself from me by one word that I could never utter. I could never break our engagement. During the hell I went through in the war my attachment to you saved me from moral ruin, if it did not from perfect honor and fidelity. This is another thing I despair of making you understand. And in the chaos I've wandered through since the war my love for you was my only anchor. You never guessed, did you, that I lived on your letters until I got well. And now the fact that I might get along without them is no discredit to their charm or to you.

It is all so hard to put in words, Carley. To lie down with death and get up with death was nothing. To face one's degradation was nothing. But to come home an incomprehensibly changed man—and to see my old life as strange as if it were the new life of another planet—to try to slip into the old groove—well, no words of mine can tell you how utterly impossible it was.

My old job was not open to me, even if I had been able to work. The government that I fought for left me to starve, or to die of my maladies like a dog, for all it cared.

I could not live on your money, Carley. My people are poor, as you know. So there was nothing for me to do but to borrow a little money from my friends and to come West. I'm glad I had the courage to come. What this West is I'll never try to tell you, because, loving the luxury and excitement and glitter of the city as you do, you'd think I was crazy.

Getting on here, in my condition, was as hard as trench life. But now, Carley—something has come to me out of the West. That, too, I am unable to put into words. Maybe I can give you an inkling of it. I'm strong enough to chop wood all day. No man or woman passes my cabin in a month. But I am never lonely. I love these vast red canyon walls towering above me. And the silence is so sweet. Think of the hellish din that filled my ears. Even now—sometimes, the brook here changes its babbling murmur to the roar of war. I never understood anything of the meaning of nature until I lived under these looming stone walls and whispering pines.

So, Carley, try to understand me, or at least be kind. You know they came very near writing, "Gone west!" after my name, and considering that, this "Out West" signifies for me a very fortunate difference. A tremendous difference! For the present I'll let well enough alone.

Adios. Write soon. Love from

GLEN

Carley's second reaction to the letter was a sudden upflashing desire to see her lover—to go out West and find him. Impulses with her were rather rare and inhibited, but this one made her tremble. If Glenn was well again he must have vastly changed from the moody, stone-faced, and haunted-eyed man who had so worried and distressed her. He had embarrassed her, too, for sometimes, in her home, meeting young men there who had not gone into the service, he had seemed to retreat into himself, singularly aloof, as if his world was not theirs.

Again, with eager eyes and quivering lips, she read the letter. It contained words that lifted her heart. Her starved love greedily absorbed them. In them she had excuse for any resolve that might bring Glenn closer to her. And she pondered over this longing to go to him.

Carley had the means to come and go and live as she liked. She did not remember her father, who had died when she was a child. Her mother had left her in the care of a sister, and before the war they had divided their time between New York and Europe, the Adirondacks and Florida, Carley had gone in for Red Cross and relief work with more of sincerity than most of her set. But she was really not used to making any decision as definite and important as that of going out West alone. She had never been farther west than Jersey City; and her conception of the West was a hazy one of vast plains and rough mountains, squalid towns, cattle herds, and uncouth ill-clad men.

So she carried the letter to her aunt, a rather slight woman with a kindly face and shrewd eyes, and who appeared somewhat given to old-fashioned garments.

"Aunt Mary, here's a letter from Glenn," said Carley. "It's more of a stumper than usual. Please read it."

"Dear me! You look upset," replied the aunt, mildly, and, adjusting her spectacles, she took the letter.

Carley waited impatiently for the perusal, conscious of inward forces coming more and more to the aid of her impulse to go West. Her aunt paused once to murmur how glad she was that Glenn had gotten well. Then she read on to the close.

"Carley, that's a fine letter," she said, fervently. "Do you see through it?"

"No, I don't," replied Carley. "That's why I asked you to read it."

"Do you still love Glenn as you used to before—"

"Why, Aunt Mary!" exclaimed Carley, in surprise.

"Excuse me, Carley, if I'm blunt. But the fact is young women of modern times are very different from my kind when I was a girl. You haven't acted as though you pined for Glenn. You gad around almost the same as ever."

"What's a girl to do?" protested Carley.

"You are twenty-six years old, Carley," retorted Aunt Mary.

"Suppose I am. I'm as young—as I ever was."

"Well, let's not argue about modern girls and modern times. We never get anywhere," returned her aunt, kindly. "But I can tell you something of what Glenn Kilbourne means in that letter—if you want to hear it."

"I do—indeed."

"The war did something horrible to Glenn aside from wrecking his health. Shell-shock, they said! I don't understand that. Out of his mind, they said! But that never was true. Glenn was as sane as I am, and, my dear, that's pretty sane, I'll have you remember. But he must have suffered some terrible blight to his spirit—some blunting of his soul. For months after he returned he walked as one in a trance. Then came a change. He grew restless. Perhaps that change was for the better. At least it showed he'd roused. Glenn saw you and your friends and the life you lead, and all the present, with eyes from which the scales had dropped. He saw what was wrong. He never said so to me, but I knew it. It wasn't only to get well that he went West. It was to get away.... And, Carley Burch, if your happiness depends on him you had better be up and doing—or you'll lose him!"

"Aunt Mary!" gasped Carley.

"I mean it. That letter shows how near he came to the Valley of the Shadow—and how he has become a man.... If I were you I'd go out West. Surely there must be a place where it would be all right for you to stay."

"Oh, yes," replied Carley, eagerly. "Glenn wrote me there was a lodge where people went in nice weather—right down in the canyon not far from his place. Then, of course, the town—Flagstaff—isn't far.... Aunt Mary, I think I'll go."

"I would. You're certainly wasting your time here."

"But I could only go for a visit," rejoined Carley, thoughtfully. "A month, perhaps six weeks, if I could stand it."

"Seems to me if you can stand New York you could stand that place," said Aunt Mary, dryly.

"The idea of staying away from New York any length of time—why, I couldn't do it I... But I can stay out there long enough to bring Glenn back with me."

"That may take you longer than you think," replied her aunt, with a gleam in her shrewd eyes. "If you want my advice you will surprise Glenn. Don't write him—don't give him a chance to—well to suggest courteously that you'd better not come just yet. I don't like his words 'just yet.'"

"Auntie, you're—rather—more than blunt," said Carley, divided between resentment and amaze. "Glenn would be simply wild to have me come."

"Maybe he would. Has he ever asked you?"

"No-o—come to think of it, he hasn't," replied Carley, reluctantly. "Aunt Mary, you hurt my feelings."

"Well, child, I'm glad to learn your feelings are hurt," returned the aunt. "I'm sure, Carley, that underneath all this—this blase ultra something you've acquired, there's a real heart. Only you must hurry and listen to it—or—"

"Or what?" queried Carley.

Aunt Mary shook her gray head sagely. "Never mind what. Carley, I'd like your idea of the most significant thing in Glenn's letter."

"Why, his love for me, of course!" replied Carley.

"Naturally you think that. But I don't. What struck me most were his words, 'out of the West.' Carley, you'd do well to ponder over them."

"I will," rejoined Carley, positively. "I'll do more. I'll go out to his wonderful West and see what he meant by them."

Carley Burch possessed in full degree the prevailing modern craze for speed. She loved a motor-car ride at sixty miles an hour along a smooth, straight road, or, better, on the level seashore of Ormond, where on moonlight nights the white blanched sand seemed to flash toward her. Therefore quite to her taste was the Twentieth Century Limited which was hurtling her on the way to Chicago. The unceasingly smooth and even rush of the train satisfied something in her. An old lady sitting in an adjoining seat with a companion amused Carley by the remark: "I wish we didn't go so fast. People nowadays haven't time to draw a comfortable breath. Suppose we should run off the track!"

Carley had no fear of express trains, or motor cars, or transatlantic liners; in fact, she prided herself in not being afraid of anything. But she wondered if this was not the false courage of association with a crowd. Before this enterprise at hand she could not remember anything she had undertaken alone. Her thrills seemed to be in abeyance to the end of her journey. That night her sleep was permeated with the steady low whirring of the wheels. Once, roused by a jerk, she lay awake in the darkness while the thought came to her that she and all her fellow passengers were really at the mercy of the engineer. Who was he, and did he stand at his throttle keen and vigilant, thinking of the lives intrusted to him? Such thoughts vaguely annoyed Carley, and she dismissed them.

A long half-day wait in Chicago was a tedious preliminary to the second part of her journey. But at last she found herself aboard the California Limited, and went to bed with a relief quite a stranger to her. The glare of the sun under the curtain awakened her. Propped up on her pillows, she looked out at apparently endless green fields or pastures, dotted now and then with little farmhouses and tree-skirted villages. This country, she thought, must be the prairie land she remembered lay west of the Mississippi.

Later, in the dining car, the steward smilingly answered her question: "This is Kansas, and those green fields out there are the wheat that feeds the nation."

Carley was not impressed. The color of the short wheat appeared soft and rich, and the boundless fields stretched away monotonously. She had not known there was so much flat land in the world, and she imagined it might be a fine country for automobile roads. When she got back to her seat she drew the blinds down and read her magazines. Then tiring of that, she went back to the observation car. Carley was accustomed to attracting attention, and did not resent it, unless she was annoyed. The train evidently had a full complement of passengers, who, as far as Carley could see, were people not of her station in life. The glare from the many windows, and the rather crass interest of several men, drove her back to her own section. There she discovered that some one had drawn up her window shades. Carley promptly pulled them down and settled herself comfortably. Then she heard a woman speak, not particularly low: "I thought people traveled west to see the country." And a man replied, rather dryly. "Wal, not always." His companion went on: "If that girl was mine I'd let down her skirt." The man laughed and replied: "Martha, you're shore behind the times. Look at the pictures in the magazines."

Such remarks amused Carley, and later she took advantage of an opportunity to notice her neighbors. They appeared a rather quaint old couple, reminding her of the natives of country towns in the Adirondacks. She was not amused, however, when another of her woman neighbors, speaking low, referred to her as a "lunger." Carley appreciated the fact that she was pale, but she assured herself that there ended any possible resemblance she might have to a consumptive. And she was somewhat pleased to hear this woman's male companion forcibly voice her own convictions. In fact, he was nothing if not admiring.

Kansas was interminably long to Carley, and she went to sleep before riding out of it. Next morning she found herself looking out at the rough gray and black land of New Mexico. She searched the horizon for mountains, but there did not appear to be any. She received a vague, slow-dawning impression that was hard to define. She did not like the country, though that was not the impression which eluded her. Bare gray flats, low scrub-fringed hills, bleak cliffs, jumble after jumble of rocks, and occasionally a long vista down a valley, somehow compelling—these passed before her gaze until she tired of them. Where was the West Glenn had written about? One thing seemed sure, and it was that every mile of this crude country brought her nearer to him. This recurring thought gave Carley all the pleasure she had felt so far in this endless ride. It struck her that England or France could be dropped down into New Mexico and scarcely noticed.

By and by the sun grew hot, the train wound slowly and creakingly upgrade, the car became full of dust, all of which was disagreeable to Carley. She dozed on her pillow for hours, until she was stirred by a passenger crying out, delightedly: "Look! Indians!"

Carley looked, not without interest. As a child she had read about Indians, and memory returned images both colorful and romantic. From the car window she espied dusty flat barrens, low squat mud houses, and queer-looking little people, children naked or extremely ragged and dirty, women in loose garments with flares of red, and men in white man's garb, slovenly and motley. All these strange individuals stared apathetically as the train slowly passed.

"Indians," muttered Carley, incredulously. "Well, if they are the noble red people, my illusions are dispelled." She did not look out of the window again, not even when the brakeman called out the remarkable name of Albuquerque.

Next day Carley's languid attention quickened to the name of Arizona, and to the frowning red walls of rock, and to the vast rolling stretches of cedar-dotted land. Nevertheless, it affronted her. This was no country for people to live in, and so far as she could see it was indeed uninhabited. Her sensations were not, however, limited to sight. She became aware of unfamiliar disturbing little shocks or vibrations in her ear drums, and after that a disagreeable bleeding of the nose. The porter told her this was owing to the altitude. Thus, one thing and another kept Carley most of the time away from the window, so that she really saw very little of the country. From what she had seen she drew the conviction that she had not missed much. At sunset she deliberately gazed out to discover what an Arizona sunset was like just a pale yellow flare! She had seen better than that above the Palisades. Not until reaching Winslow did she realize how near she was to her journey's end and that she would arrive at Flagstaff after dark. She grew conscious of nervousness. Suppose Flagstaff were like these other queer little towns!

Not only once, but several times before the train slowed down for her destination did Carley wish she had sent Glenn word to meet her. And when, presently, she found herself standing out in the dark, cold, windy night before a dim-lit railroad station she more than regretted her decision to surprise Glenn. But that was too late and she must make the best of her poor judgment.

Men were passing to and fro on the platform, some of whom appeared to be very dark of skin and eye, and were probably Mexicans. At length an expressman approached Carley, soliciting patronage. He took her bags and, depositing them in a wagon, he pointed up the wide street: "One block up an' turn. Hotel Wetherford." Then he drove off. Carley followed, carrying her small satchel. A cold wind, driving the dust, stung her face as she crossed the street to a high sidewalk that extended along the block. There were lights in the stores and on the corners, yet she seemed impressed by a dark, cold, windy bigness. Many people, mostly men, were passing up and down, and there were motor cars everywhere. No one paid any attention to her. Gaining the corner of the block, she turned, and was relieved to see the hotel sign. As she entered the lobby a clicking of pool balls and the discordant rasp of a phonograph assailed her ears. The expressman set down her bags and left Carley standing there. The clerk or proprietor was talking from behind his desk to several men, and there were loungers in the lobby. The air was thick with tobacco smoke. No one paid any attention to Carley until at length she stepped up to the desk and interrupted the conversation there.

"Is this a hotel?" she queried, brusquely.

The shirt-sleeved individual leisurely turned and replied, "Yes, ma'am."

And Carley said: "No one would recognize it by the courtesy shown. I have been standing here waiting to register."

With the same leisurely case and a cool, laconic stare the clerk turned the book toward her. "Reckon people round here ask for what they want."

Carley made no further comment. She assuredly recognized that what she had been accustomed to could not be expected out here. What she most wished to do at the moment was to get close to the big open grate where a cheery red-and-gold fire cracked. It was necessary, however, to follow the clerk. He assigned her to a small drab room which contained a bed, a bureau, and a stationary washstand with one spigot. There was also a chair. While Carley removed her coat and hat the clerk went downstairs for the rest of her luggage. Upon his return Carley learned that a stage left the hotel for Oak Creek Canyon at nine o'clock next morning. And this cheered her so much that she faced the strange sense of loneliness and discomfort with something of fortitude. There was no heat in the room, and no hot water. When Carley squeezed the spigot handle there burst forth a torrent of water that spouted up out of the washbasin to deluge her. It was colder than any ice water she had ever felt. It was piercingly cold. Hard upon the surprise and shock Carley suffered a flash of temper. But then the humor of it struck her and she had to laugh.

"Serves you right—you spoiled doll of luxury!" she mocked. "This is out West. Shiver and wait on yourself!"

Never before had she undressed so swiftly nor felt grateful for thick woollen blankets on a hard bed. Gradually she grew warm. The blackness, too, seemed rather comforting.

"I'm only twenty miles from Glenn," she whispered. "How strange! I wonder will he be glad." She felt a sweet, glowing assurance of that. Sleep did not come readily. Excitement had laid hold of her nerves, and for a long time she lay awake. After a while the chug of motor cars, the click of pool balls, the murmur of low voices all ceased. Then she heard a sound of wind outside, an intermittent, low moaning, new to her ears, and somehow pleasant. Another sound greeted her— the musical clanging of a clock that struck the quarters of the hour. Some time late sleep claimed her.

Upon awakening she found she had overslept, necessitating haste upon her part. As to that, the temperature of the room did not admit of leisurely dressing. She had no adequate name for the feeling of the water. And her fingers grew so numb that she made what she considered a disgraceful matter of her attire.

Downstairs in the lobby another cheerful red fire burned in the grate. How perfectly satisfying was an open fireplace! She thrust her numb hands almost into the blaze, and simply shook with the tingling pain that slowly warmed out of them. The lobby was deserted. A sign directed her to a dining room in the basement, where of the ham and eggs and strong coffee she managed to partake a little. Then she went upstairs into the lobby and out into the street.

A cold, piercing air seemed to blow right through her. Walking to the near corner, she paused to look around. Down the main street flowed a leisurely stream of pedestrians, horses, cars, extending between two blocks of low buildings. Across from where she stood lay a vacant lot, beyond which began a line of neat, oddly constructed houses, evidently residences of the town. And then lifting her gaze, instinctively drawn by something obstructing the sky line, she was suddenly struck with surprise and delight.

"Oh! how perfectly splendid!" she burst out.

Two magnificent mountains loomed right over her, sloping up with majestic sweep of green and black timber, to a ragged tree-fringed snow area that swept up cleaner and whiter, at last to lift pure glistening peaks, noble and sharp, and sunrise-flushed against the blue.

Carley had climbed Mont Blanc and she had seen the Matterhorn, but they had never struck such amaze and admiration from her as these twin peaks of her native land.

"What mountains are those?" she asked a passer-by.

"San Francisco Peaks, ma'am," replied the man.

"Why, they can't be over a mile away!" she said.

"Eighteen miles, ma'am," he returned, with a grin. "Shore this Arizonie air is deceivin'."

"How strange," murmured Carley. "It's not that way in the Adirondacks."

She was still gazing upward when a man approached her and said the stage for Oak Creek Canyon would soon be ready to start, and he wanted to know if her baggage was ready. Carley hurried back to her room to pack.

She had expected the stage would be a motor bus, or at least a large touring car, but it turned out to be a two-seated vehicle drawn by a team of ragged horses. The driver was a little wizen-faced man of doubtful years, and he did not appear obviously susceptible to the importance of his passenger. There was considerable freight to be hauled, besides Carley's luggage, but evidently she was the only passenger.

"Reckon it's goin' to be a bad day," said the driver. "These April days high up on the desert are windy an' cold. Mebbe it'll snow, too. Them clouds hangin' around the peaks ain't very promisin'. Now, miss, haven't you a heavier coat or somethin'?"

"No, I have not," replied Carley. "I'll have to stand it. Did you say this was desert?"

"I shore did. Wal, there's a hoss blanket under the seat, an' you can have that," he replied, and, climbing to the seat in front of Carley, he took up the reins and started the horses off at a trot.

At the first turning Carley became specifically acquainted with the driver's meaning of a bad day. A gust of wind, raw and penetrating, laden with dust and stinging sand, swept full in her face. It came so suddenly that she was scarcely quick enough to close her eyes. It took considerable clumsy effort on her part with a handkerchief, aided by relieving tears, to clear her sight again. Thus uncomfortably Carley found herself launched on the last lap of her journey.

All before her and alongside lay the squalid environs of the town. Looked back at, with the peaks rising behind, it was not unpicturesque. But the hard road with its sheets of flying dust, the bleak railroad yards, the round pens she took for cattle corrals, and the sordid debris littering the approach to a huge sawmill,—these were offensive in Carley's sight. From a tall dome-like stack rose a yellowish smoke that spread overhead, adding to the lowering aspect of the sky. Beyond the sawmill extended the open country sloping somewhat roughly, and evidently once a forest, but now a hideous bare slash, with ghastly burned stems of trees still standing, and myriads of stumps attesting to denudation.

The bleak road wound away to the southwest, and from this direction came the gusty wind. It did not blow regularly so that Carley could be on her guard. It lulled now and then, permitting her to look about, and then suddenly again whipping dust into her face. The smell of the dust was as unpleasant as the sting. It made her nostrils smart. It was penetrating, and a little more of it would have been suffocating. And as a leaden gray bank of broken clouds rolled up the wind grew stronger and the air colder. Chilled before, Carley now became thoroughly cold.

There appeared to be no end to the devastated forest land, and the farther she rode the more barren and sordid grew the landscape. Carley forgot about the impressive mountains behind her. And as the ride wore into hours, such was her discomfort and disillusion that she forgot about Glenn Kilbourne. She did not reach the point of regretting her adventure, but she grew mightily unhappy. Now and then she espied dilapidated log cabins and surroundings even more squalid than the ruined forest. What wretched abodes! Could it be possible that people had lived in them? She imagined men had but hardly women and children. Somewhere she had forgotten an idea that women and children were extremely scarce in the West.

Straggling bits of forest—yellow pines, the driver called the trees—began to encroach upon the burned-over and arid barren land. To Carley these groves, by reason of contrast and proof of what once was, only rendered the landscape more forlorn and dreary. Why had these miles and miles of forest been cut? By money grubbers, she supposed, the same as were devastating the Adirondacks. Presently, when the driver had to halt to repair or adjust something wrong with the harness, Carley was grateful for a respite from cold inaction. She got out and walked. Sleet began to fall, and when she resumed her seat in the vehicle she asked the driver for the blanket to cover her. The smell of this horse blanket was less endurable than the cold. Carley huddled down into a state of apathetic misery. Already she had enough of the West.

But the sleet storm passed, the clouds broke, the sun shone through, greatly mitigating her discomfort. By and by the road led into a section of real forest, unspoiled in any degree. Carley saw large gray squirrels with tufted ears and white bushy tails. Presently the driver pointed out a flock of huge birds, which Carley, on second glance, recognized as turkeys, only these were sleek and glossy, with flecks of bronze and black and white, quite different from turkeys back East. "There must be a farm near," said Carley, gazing about.

"No, ma'am. Them's wild turkeys," replied the driver, "an' shore the best eatin' you ever had in your life."

A little while afterwards, as they were emerging from the woodland into more denuded country, he pointed out to Carley a herd of gray white-rumped animals that she took to be sheep.

"An' them's antelope," he said. "Once this desert was overrun by antelope. Then they nearly disappeared. An' now they're increasin' again."

More barren country, more bad weather, and especially an exceedingly rough road reduced Carley to her former state of dejection. The jolting over roots and rocks and ruts was worse than uncomfortable. She had to hold on to the seat to keep from being thrown out. The horses did not appreciably change their gait for rough sections of the road. Then a more severe jolt brought Carley's knee in violent contact with an iron bolt on the forward seat, and it hurt her so acutely that she had to bite her lips to keep from screaming. A smoother stretch of road did not come any too soon for her.

It led into forest again. And Carley soon became aware that they had at last left the cut and burned-over district of timberland behind. A cold wind moaned through the treetops and set the drops of water pattering down upon her. It lashed her wet face. Carley closed her eyes and sagged in her seat, mostly oblivious to the passing scenery. "The girls will never believe this of me," she soliloquized. And indeed she was amazed at herself. Then thought of Glenn strengthened her. It did not really matter what she suffered on the way to him. Only she was disgusted at her lack of stamina, and her appalling sensitiveness to discomfort.

"Wal, hyar's Oak Creek Canyon," called the driver.

Carley, rousing out of her weary preoccupation, opened her eyes to see that the driver had halted at a turn of the road, where apparently it descended a fearful declivity.

The very forest-fringed earth seemed to have opened into a deep abyss, ribbed by red rock walls and choked by steep mats of green timber. The chasm was a V-shaped split and so deep that looking downward sent at once a chill and a shudder over Carley. At that point it appeared narrow and ended in a box. In the other direction, it widened and deepened, and stretched farther on between tremendous walls of red, and split its winding floor of green with glimpses of a gleaming creek, bowlder-strewn and ridged by white rapids. A low mellow roar of rushing waters floated up to Carley's ears. What a wild, lonely, terrible place! Could Glenn possibly live down there in that ragged rent in the earth? It frightened her—the sheer sudden plunge of it from the heights. Far down the gorge a purple light shone on the forested floor. And on the moment the sun burst through the clouds and sent a golden blaze down into the depths, transforming them incalculably. The great cliffs turned gold, the creek changed to glancing silver, the green of trees vividly freshened, and in the clefts rays of sunlight burned into the blue shadows. Carley had never gazed upon a scene like this. Hostile and prejudiced, she yet felt wrung from her an acknowledgment of beauty and grandeur. But wild, violent, savage! Not livable! This insulated rift in the crust of the earth was a gigantic burrow for beasts, perhaps for outlawed men—not for a civilized person—not for Glenn Kilbourne.

"Don't be scart, ma'am," spoke up the driver. "It's safe if you're careful. An' I've druv this manys the time."

Carley's heartbeats thumped at her side, rather denying her taunted assurance of fearlessness. Then the rickety vehicle started down at an angle that forced her to cling to her seat.

CHAPTER II

Carley, clutching her support, with abated breath and prickling skin, gazed in fascinated suspense over the rim of the gorge. Sometimes the wheels on that side of the vehicle passed within a few inches of the edge. The brakes squeaked, the wheels slid; and she could hear the scrape of the iron-shod hoofs of the horses as they held back stiff legged, obedient to the wary call of the driver.

The first hundred yards of that steep road cut out of the cliff appeared to be the worst. It began to widen, with descents less precipitous. Tips of trees rose level with her gaze, obstructing sight of the blue depths. Then brush appeared on each side of the road. Gradually Carley's strain relaxed, and also the muscular contraction by which she had braced herself in the seat. The horses began to trot again. The wheels rattled. The road wound around abrupt corners, and soon the green and red wall of the opposite side of the canyon loomed close. Low roar of running water rose to Carley's ears. When at length she looked out instead of down she could see nothing but a mass of green foliage crossed by tree trunks and branches of brown and gray. Then the vehicle bowled under dark cool shade, into a tunnel with mossy wet cliff on one side, and close-standing trees on the other.

"Reckon we're all right now, unless we meet somebody comin' up," declared the driver.

Carley relaxed. She drew a deep breath of relief. She had her first faint intimation that perhaps her extensive experience of motor cars, express trains, transatlantic liners, and even a little of airplanes, did not range over the whole of adventurous life. She was likely to meet something, entirely new and striking out here in the West.

The murmur of falling water sounded closer. Presently Carley saw that the road turned at the notch in the canyon, and crossed a clear swift stream. Here were huge mossy boulders, and red walls covered by lichens, and the air appeared dim and moist, and full of mellow, hollow roar. Beyond this crossing the road descended the west side of the canyon, drawing away and higher from the creek. Huge trees, the like of which Carley had never seen, began to stand majestically up out of the gorge, dwarfing the maples and white-spotted sycamores. The driver called these great trees yellow pines.

At last the road led down from the steep slope to the floor of the canyon. What from far above had appeared only a green timber-choked cleft proved from close relation to be a wide winding valley, tip and down, densely forested for the most part, yet having open glades and bisected from wall to wall by the creek. Every quarter of a mile or so the road crossed the stream; and at these fords Carley again held on desperately and gazed out dubiously, for the creek was deep, swift, and full of bowlders. Neither driver nor horses appeared to mind obstacles. Carley was splashed and jolted not inconsiderably. They passed through groves of oak trees, from which the creek manifestly derived its name; and under gleaming walls, cold, wet, gloomy, and silent; and between lines of solemn wide-spreading pines. Carley saw deep, still green pools eddying under huge massed jumble of cliffs, and stretches of white water, and then, high above the treetops, a wild line of canyon rim, cold against the sky. She felt shut in from the world, lost in an unscalable rut of the earth. Again the sunlight had failed, and the gray gloom of the canyon oppressed her. It struck Carley as singular that she could not help being affected by mere weather, mere heights and depths, mere rock walls and pine trees, and rushing water. For really, what had these to do with her? These were only physical things that she was passing. Nevertheless, although she resisted sensation, she was more and more shot through and through with the wildness and savageness of this canyon.

A sharp turn of the road to the right disclosed a slope down the creek, across which showed orchards and fields, and a cottage nestling at the base of the wall. The ford at this crossing gave Carley more concern than any that had been passed, for there was greater volume and depth of water. One of the horses slipped on the rocks, plunged up and on with great splash. They crossed, however, without more mishap to Carley than further acquaintance with this iciest of waters. From this point the driver turned back along the creek, passed between orchards and fields, and drove along the base of the red wall to come suddenly upon a large rustic house that had been hidden from Carley's sight. It sat almost against the stone cliff, from which poured a white foamy sheet of water. The house was built of slabs with the bark on, and it had a lower and upper porch running all around, at least as far as the cliff. Green growths from the rock wall overhung the upper porch. A column of blue smoke curled lazily upward from a stone chimney. On one of the porch posts hung a sign with rude lettering: "Lolomi Lodge."

"Hey, Josh, did you fetch the flour?" called a woman's voice from inside.

"Hullo I Reckon I didn't forgit nothin'," replied the man, as he got down. "An' say, Mrs. Hutter, hyar's a young lady from Noo Yorrk."

That latter speech of the driver's brought Mrs. Hutter out on the porch. "Flo, come here," she called to some one evidently near at hand. And then she smilingly greeted Carley.

"Get down an' come in, miss," she said. "I'm sure glad to see you."

Carley, being stiff and cold, did not very gracefully disengage herself from the high muddy wheel and step. When she mounted to the porch she saw that Mrs. Hutter was a woman of middle age, rather stout, with strong face full of fine wavy lines, and kind dark eyes.

"I'm Miss Burch," said Carley.

"You're the girl whose picture Glenn Kilbourne has over his fireplace," declared the woman, heartily. "I'm sure glad to meet you, an' my daughter Flo will be, too."

That about her picture pleased and warmed Carley. "Yes, I'm Glenn Kilbourne's fiancee. I've come West to surprise him. Is he here.... Is—is he well?"

"Fine. I saw him yesterday. He's changed a great deal from what he was at first. Most all the last few months. I reckon you won't know him.... But you're wet an' cold an' you look fagged. Come right in to the fire."

"Thank you; I'm all right," returned Carley.

At the doorway they encountered a girl of lithe and robust figure, quick in her movements. Carley was swift to see the youth and grace of her; and then a face that struck Carley as neither pretty nor beautiful, but still wonderfully attractive.

"Flo, here's Miss Burch," burst out Mrs. Hutter, with cheerful importance. "Glenn Kilbourne's girl come all the way from New York to surprise him!"

"Oh, Carley, I'm shore happy to meet you!" said the girl, in a voice of slow drawling richness. "I know you. Glenn has told me all about you."

If this greeting, sweet and warm as it seemed, was a shock to Carley, she gave no sign. But as she murmured something in reply she looked with all a woman's keenness into the face before her. Flo Hutter had a fair skin generously freckled; a mouth and chin too firmly cut to suggest a softer feminine beauty; and eyes of clear light hazel, penetrating, frank, fearless. Her hair was very abundant, almost silver-gold in color, and it was either rebellious or showed lack of care. Carley liked the girl's looks and liked the sincerity of her greeting; but instinctively she reacted antagonistically because of the frank suggestion of intimacy with Glenn.

But for that she would have been spontaneous and friendly rather than restrained.

They ushered Carley into a big living room and up to a fire of blazing logs, where they helped divest her of the wet wraps. And all the time they talked in the solicitous way natural to women who were kind and unused to many visitors. Then Mrs. Hutter bustled off to make a cup of hot coffee while Flo talked.

"We'll shore give you the nicest room—with a sleeping porch right under the cliff where the water falls. It'll sing you to sleep. Of course you needn't use the bed outdoors until it's warmer. Spring is late here, you know, and we'll have nasty weather yet. You really happened on Oak Creek at its least attractive season. But then it's always—well, just Oak Creek. You'll come to know."

"I dare say I'll remember my first sight of it and the ride down that cliff road," said Carley, with a wan smile.

"Oh, that's nothing to what you'll see and do," returned Flo, knowingly. "We've had Eastern tenderfeet here before. And never was there a one of them who didn't come to love Arizona."

"Tenderfoot! It hadn't occurred to me. But of course—" murmured Carley.

Then Mrs. Hutter returned, carrying a tray, which she set upon a chair, and drew to Carley's side. "Eat an' drink," she said, as if these actions were the cardinally important ones of life. "Flo, you carry her bags up to that west room we always give to some particular person we want to love Lolomi." Next she threw sticks of wood upon the fire, making it crackle and blaze, then seated herself near Carley and beamed upon her.

"You'll not mind if we call you Carley?" she asked, eagerly.

"Oh, indeed no! I—I'd like it," returned Carley, made to feel friendly and at home in spite of herself.

"You see it's not as if you were just a stranger," went on Mrs. Hutter. "Tom—that's Flo's father—took a likin' to Glenn Kilbourne when he first came to Oak Creek over a year ago. I wonder if you all know how sick that soldier boy was.... Well, he lay on his back for two solid weeks—in the room we're givin' you. An' I for one didn't think he'd ever get up. But he did. An' he got better. An' after a while he went to work for Tom. Then six months an' more ago he invested in the sheep business with Tom. He lived with us until he built his cabin up West Fork. He an' Flo have run together a good deal, an' naturally he told her about you. So you see you're not a stranger. An' we want you to feel you're with friends."

"I thank you, Mrs. Hutter," replied Carley, feelingly. "I never could thank you enough for being good to Glenn. I did not know he was so—so sick. At first he wrote but seldom."

"Reckon he never wrote you or told you what he did in the war," declared Mrs. Hutter.

"Indeed he never did!"

"Well, I'll tell you some day. For Tom found out all about him. Got some of it from a soldier who came to Flagstaff for lung trouble. He'd been in the same company with Glenn. We didn't know this boy's name while he was in Flagstaff. But later Tom found out. John Henderson. He was only twenty-two, a fine lad. An' he died in Phoenix. We tried to get him out here. But the boy wouldn't live on charity. He was always expectin' money—a war bonus, whatever that was. It didn't come. He was a clerk at the El Tovar for a while. Then he came to Flagstaff. But it was too cold an' he stayed there too long."

"Too bad," rejoined Carley, thoughtfully. This information as to the suffering of American soldiers had augmented during the last few months, and seemed to possess strange, poignant power to depress Carley. Always she had turned away from the unpleasant. And the misery of unfortunates was as disturbing almost as direct contact with disease and squalor. But it had begun to dawn upon Carley that there might occur circumstances of life, in every way affronting her comfort and happiness, which it would be impossible to turn her back upon.

At this juncture Flo returned to the room, and again Carley was struck with the girl's singular freedom of movement and the sense of sure poise and joy that seemed to emanate from her presence.

"I've made a fire in your little stove," she said. "There's water heating. Now won't you come up and change those traveling clothes. You'll want to fix up for Glenn, won't you?"

Carley had to smile at that. This girl indeed was frank and unsophisticated, and somehow refreshing. Carley rose.

"You are both very good to receive me as a friend," she said. "I hope I shall not disappoint you.... Yes, I do want to improve my appearance before Glenn sees me.... Is there any way I can send word to him—by someone who has not seen me?"

"There shore is. I'll send Charley, one of our hired boys."

"Thank you. Then tell him to say there is a lady here from New York to see him, and it is very important."

Flo Hutter clapped her hands and laughed with glee. Her gladness gave Carley a little twinge of conscience. Jealously was an unjust and stifling thing.

Carley was conducted up a broad stairway and along a boarded hallway to a room that opened out on the porch. A steady low murmur of falling water assailed her ears. Through the open door she saw across the porch to a white tumbling lacy veil of water falling, leaping, changing, so close that it seemed to touch the heavy pole railing of the porch.

This room resembled a tent. The sides were of canvas. It had no ceiling. But the rough-hewn shingles of the roof of the house sloped down closely. The furniture was home made. An Indian rug covered the floor. The bed with its woolly clean blankets and the white pillows looked inviting.

"Is this where Glenn lay—when he was sick?" queried Carley.

"Yes," replied Flo, gravely, and a shadow darkened her eyes. "I ought to tell you all about it. I will some day. But you must not be made unhappy now.... Glenn nearly died here. Mother or I never left his side—for a while there—when life was so bad."

She showed Carley how to open the little stove and put the short billets of wood inside and work the damper; and cautioning her to keep an eye on it so that it would not get too hot, she left Carley to herself.

Carley found herself in an unfamiliar mood. There came a leap of her heart every time she thought of the meeting with Glenn, so soon now to be, but it was not that which was unfamiliar. She seemed to have a difficult approach to undefined and unusual thoughts. All this was so different from her regular life. Besides she was tired. But these explanations did not suffice. There was a pang in her breast which must owe its origin to the fact that Glenn Kilbourne had been ill in this little room and some other girl than Carley Burch had nursed him. "Am I jealous?" she whispered. "No!" But she knew in her heart that she lied. A woman could no more help being jealous, under such circumstances, than she could help the beat and throb of her blood. Nevertheless, Carley was glad Flo Hutter had been there, and always she would be grateful to her for that kindness.

Carley disrobed and, donning her dressing gown, she unpacked her bags and hung her things upon pegs under the curtained shelves. Then she lay down to rest, with no intention of slumber. But there was a strange magic in the fragrance of the room, like the piny tang outdoors, and in the feel of the bed, and especially in the low, dreamy hum and murmur of the waterfall. She fell asleep. When she awakened it was five o'clock. The fire in the stove was out, but the water was still warm. She bathed and dressed, not without care, yet as swiftly as was her habit at home; and she wore white because Glenn had always liked her best in white. But it was assuredly not a gown to wear in a country house where draughts of cold air filled the unheated rooms and halls. So she threw round her a warm sweater-shawl, with colorful bars becoming to her dark eyes and hair.

All the time that she dressed and thought, her very being seemed to be permeated by that soft murmuring sound of falling water. No moment of waking life there at Lolomi Lodge, or perhaps of slumber hours, could be wholly free of that sound. It vaguely tormented Carley, yet was not uncomfortable. She went out upon the porch. The small alcove space held a bed and a rustic chair. Above her the peeled poles of the roof descended to within a few feet of her head. She had to lean over the rail of the porch to look up. The green and red rock wall sheered ponderously near. The waterfall showed first at the notch of a fissure, where the cliff split; and down over smooth places the water gleamed, to narrow in a crack with little drops, and suddenly to leap into a thin white sheet.

Out from the porch the view was restricted to glimpses between the pines, and beyond to the opposite wall of the canyon. How shut-in, how walled in this home!

"In summer it might be good to spend a couple of weeks here," soliloquized Carley. "But to live here? Heavens! A person might as well be buried."

Heavy footsteps upon the porch below accompanied by a man's voice quickened Carley's pulse. Did they belong to Glenn? After a strained second she decided not. Nevertheless, the acceleration of her blood and an unwonted glow of excitement, long a stranger to her, persisted as she left the porch and entered the boarded hall. How gray and barn-like this upper part of the house! From the head of the stairway, however, the big living room presented a cheerful contrast. There were warm colors, some comfortable rockers, a lamp that shed a bright light, and an open fire which alone would have dispelled the raw gloom of the day.

A large man in corduroys and top boots advanced to meet Carley. He had a clean-shaven face that might have been hard and stern but for his smile, and one look into his eyes revealed their resemblance to Flo's.

"I'm Tom Hutter, an' I'm shore glad to welcome you to Lolomi, Miss Carley," he said. His voice was deep and slow. There were ease and force in his presence, and the grip he gave Carley's hand was that of a man who made no distinction in hand-shaking. Carley, quick in her perceptions, instantly liked him and sensed in him a strong personality. She greeted him in turn and expressed her thanks for his goodness to Glenn. Naturally Carley expected him to say something about her fiance, but he did not.

"Well, Miss Carley, if you don't mind, I'll say you're prettier than your picture," said Hutter. "An' that is shore sayin' a lot. All the sheep herders in the country have taken a peep at your picture. Without permission, you understand."

"I'm greatly flattered," laughed Carley.

"We're glad you've come," replied Hutter, simply. "I just got back from the East myself. Chicago an' Kansas City. I came to Arizona from Illinois over thirty years ago. An' this was my first trip since. Reckon I've not got back my breath yet. Times have changed, Miss Carley. Times an' people!"

Mrs. Hutter bustled in from the kitchen, where manifestly she had been importantly engaged. "For the land's sakes!" she exclaimed, fervently, as she threw up her hands at sight of Carley. Her expression was indeed a compliment, but there was a suggestion of shock in it. Then Flo came in. She wore a simple gray gown that reached the top of her high shoes.

"Carley, don't mind mother," said Flo. "She means your dress is lovely. Which is my say, too.... But, listen. I just saw Glenn comin' up the road."

Carley ran to the open door with more haste than dignity. She saw a tall man striding along. Something about him appeared familiar. It was his walk—an erect swift carriage, with a swing of the march still visible. She recognized Glenn. And all within her seemed to become unstable. She watched him cross the road, face the house. How changed! No—this was not Glenn Kilbourne. This was a bronzed man, wide of shoulder, roughly garbed, heavy limbed, quite different from the Glenn she remembered. He mounted the porch steps. And Carley, still unseen herself, saw his face. Yes—Glenn! Hot blood seemed to be tingling liberated in her veins. Wheeling away, she backed against the wall behind the door and held up a warning finger to Flo, who stood nearest. Strange and disturbing then, to see something in Flo Hutter's eyes that could be read by a woman in only one way!

A tall form darkened the doorway. It strode in and halted.

"Flo!—who—where?" he began, breathlessly.

His voice, so well remembered, yet deeper, huskier, fell upon Carley's ears as something unconsciously longed for. His frame had so filled out that she did not recognize it. His face, too, had unbelievably changed—not in the regularity of feature that had been its chief charm, but in contour of cheek and vanishing of pallid hue and tragic line. Carley's heart swelled with joy. Beyond all else she had hoped to see the sad fixed hopelessness, the havoc, gone from his face. Therefore the restraint and nonchalance upon which Carley prided herself sustained eclipse.

"Glenn! Look—who's—here!" she called, in voice she could not have steadied to save her life. This meeting was more than she had anticipated.

Glenn whirled with an inarticulate cry. He saw Carley. Then—no matter how unreasonable or exacting had been Carley's longings, they were satisfied.

"You!" he cried, and leaped at her with radiant face.

Carley not only did not care about the spectators of this meeting, but forgot them utterly. More than the joy of seeing Glenn, more than the all-satisfying assurance to her woman's heart that she was still beloved, welled up a deep, strange, profound something that shook her to her depths. It was beyond selfishness. It was gratitude to God and to the West that had restored him.

"Carley! I couldn't believe it was you," he declared, releasing her from his close embrace, yet still holding her.

"Yes, Glenn—it's I—all you've left of me," she replied, tremulously, and she sought with unsteady hands to put up her dishevelled hair. "You—you big sheep herder! You Goliath!"

"I never was so knocked off my pins," he said. "A lady to see me—from New York!... Of course it had to be you. But I couldn't believe. Carley, you were good to come."

Somehow the soft, warm look of his dark eyes hurt her. New and strange indeed it was to her, as were other things about him. Why had she not come West sooner? She disengaged herself from his hold and moved away, striving for the composure habitual with her. Flo Hutter was standing before the fire, looking down. Mrs. Hutter beamed upon Carley.

"Now let's have supper," she said.

"Reckon Miss Carley can't eat now, after that hug Glenn gave her," drawled Tom Hutter. "I was some worried. You see Glenn has gained seventy pounds in six months. An' he doesn't know his strength."

"Seventy pounds!" exclaimed Carley, gayly. "I thought it was more."

"Carley, you must excuse my violence," said Glenn. "I've been hugging sheep. That is, when I shear a sheep I have to hold him."

They all laughed, and so the moment of readjustment passed. Presently Carley found herself sitting at table, directly across from Flo. A pearly whiteness was slowly warming out of the girl's face. Her frank clear eyes met Carley's and they had nothing to hide. Carley's first requisite for character in a woman was that she be a thoroughbred. She lacked it often enough herself to admire it greatly in another woman. And that moment saw a birth of respect and sincere liking in her for this Western girl. If Flo Hutter ever was a rival she would be an honest one.

Not long after supper Tom Hutter winked at Carley and said he "reckoned on general principles it was his hunch to go to bed." Mrs. Hutter suddenly discovered tasks to perform elsewhere. And Flo said in her cool sweet drawl, somehow audacious and tantalizing, "Shore you two will want to spoon."

"Now, Flo, Eastern girls are no longer old-fashioned enough for that," declared Glenn.

"Too bad! Reckon I can't see how love could ever be old-fashioned. Good night, Glenn. Good night, Carley."

Flo stood an instant at the foot of the dark stairway where the light from the lamp fell upon her face. It seemed sweet and earnest to Carley. It expressed unconscious longing, but no envy. Then she ran up the stairs to disappear.

"Glenn, is that girl in love with you?" asked Carley, bluntly.

To her amaze, Glenn laughed. When had she heard him laugh? It thrilled her, yet nettled her a little.

"If that isn't like you!" he ejaculated. "Your very first words after we are left alone! It brings back the East, Carley."

"Probably recall to memory will be good for you," returned Carley. "But tell me. Is she in love with you?"

"Why, no, certainly not!" replied Glenn. "Anyway, how could I answer such a question? It just made me laugh, that's all."

"Humph! I can remember when you were not above making love to a pretty girl. You certainly had me worn to a frazzle—before we became engaged," said Carley.

"Old times! How long ago they seem!... Carley, it's sure wonderful to see you."

"How do you like my gown?" asked Carley, pirouetting for his benefit.

"Well, what little there is of it is beautiful," he replied, with a slow smile. "I always liked you best in white. Did you remember?"

"Yes. I got the gown for you. And I'll never wear it except for you."

"Same old coquette—same old eternal feminine," he said, half sadly. "You know when you look stunning.... But, Carley, the cut of that—or rather the abbreviation of it—inclines me to think that style for women's clothes has not changed for the better. In fact, it's worse than two years ago in Paris and later in New York. Where will you women draw the line?"

"Women are slaves to the prevailing mode," rejoined Carley. "I don't imagine women who dress would ever draw a line, if fashion went on dictating."

"But would they care so much—if they had to work—plenty of work—and children?" inquired Glenn, wistfully.

"Glenn! Work and children for modern women? Why, you are dreaming!" said Carley, with a laugh.

She saw him gaze thoughtfully into the glowing embers of the fire, and as she watched him her quick intuition grasped a subtle change in his mood. It brought a sternness to his face. She could hardly realize she was looking at the Glenn Kilbourne of old.

"Come close to the fire," he said, and pulled up a chair for her. Then he threw more wood upon the red coals. "You must be careful not to catch cold out here. The altitude makes a cold dangerous. And that gown is no protection."

"Glenn, one chair used to be enough for us," she said, archly, standing beside him.

But he did not respond to her hint, and, a little affronted, she accepted the proffered chair. Then he began to ask questions rapidly. He was eager for news from home—from his people—from old friends. However he did not inquire of Carley about her friends. She talked unremittingly for an hour, before she satisfied his hunger. But when her turn came to ask questions she found him reticent.

He had fallen upon rather hard days at first out here in the West; then his health had begun to improve; and as soon as he was able to work his condition rapidly changed for the better; and now he was getting along pretty well. Carley felt hurt at his apparent disinclination to confide in her. The strong cast of his face, as if it had been chiseled in bronze; the stern set of his lips and the jaw that protruded lean and square cut; the quiet masked light of his eyes; the coarse roughness of his brown hands, mute evidence of strenuous labors—these all gave a different impression from his brief remarks about himself. Lastly there was a little gray in the light-brown hair over his temples. Glenn was only twenty-seven, yet he looked ten years older. Studying him so, with the memory of earlier years in her mind, she was forced to admit that she liked him infinitely more as he was now. He seemed proven. Something had made him a man. Had it been his love for her, or the army service, or the war in France, or the struggle for life and health afterwards? Or had it been this rugged, uncouth West? Carley felt insidious jealousy of this last possibility. She feared this West. She was going to hate it. She had womanly intuition enough to see in Flo Hutter a girl somehow to be reckoned with. Still, Carley would not acknowledge to herself that his simple, unsophisticated Western girl could possibly be a rival. Carley did not need to consider the fact that she had been spoiled by the attention of men. It was not her vanity that precluded Flo Hutter as a rival.

Gradually the conversation drew to a lapse, and it suited Carley to let it be so. She watched Glenn as he gazed thoughtfully into the amber depths of the fire. What was going on in his mind? Carley's old perplexity suddenly had rebirth. And with it came an unfamiliar fear which she could not smother. Every moment that she sat there beside Glenn she was realizing more and more a yearning, passionate love for him. The unmistakable manifestation of his joy at sight of her, the strong, almost rude expression of his love, had called to some responsive, but hitherto unplumbed deeps of her. If it had not been for these undeniable facts Carley would have been panic-stricken. They reassured her, yet only made her state of mind more dissatisfied.

"Carley, do you still go in for dancing?" Glenn asked, presently, with his thoughtful eyes turning to her.

"Of course. I like dancing, and it's about all the exercise I get," she replied.

"Have the dances changed—again?"

"It's the music, perhaps, that changes the dancing. Jazz is becoming popular. And about all the crowd dances now is an infinite variation of fox-trot."

"No waltzing?"

"I don't believe I waltzed once this winter."

"Jazz? That's a sort of tinpanning, jiggly stuff, isn't it?"

"Glenn, it's the fever of the public pulse," replied Carley. "The graceful waltz, like the stately minuet, flourished back in the days when people rested rather than raced."

"More's the pity," said Glenn. Then after a moment, in which his gaze returned to the fire, he inquired rather too casually, "Does Morrison still chase after you?"

"Glenn, I'm neither old—nor married," she replied, laughing.

"No, that's true. But if you were married it wouldn't make any difference to Morrison."

Carley could not detect bitterness or jealousy in his voice. She would not have been averse to hearing either. She gathered from his remark, however, that he was going to be harder than ever to understand. What had she said or done to make him retreat within himself, aloof, impersonal, unfamiliar? He did not impress her as loverlike. What irony of fate was this that held her there yearning for his kisses and caresses as never before, while he watched the fire, and talked as to a mere acquaintance, and seemed sad and far away? Or did she merely imagine that? Only one thing could she be sure of at that moment, and it was that pride would never be her ally.

"Glenn, look here," she said, sliding her chair close to his and holding out her left hand, slim and white, with its glittering diamond on the third finger.

He took her hand in his and pressed it, and smiled at her. "Yes, Carley, it's a beautiful, soft little hand. But I think I'd like it better if it were strong and brown, and coarse on the inside—from useful work."

"Like Flo Hutter's?" queried Carley.

"Yes."

Carley looked proudly into his eyes. "People are born in different stations. I respect your little Western friend, Glenn, but could I wash and sweep, milk cows and chop wood, and all that sort of thing?"

"I suppose you couldn't," he admitted, with a blunt little laugh.

"Would you want me to?" she asked.

"Well, that's hard to say," he replied, knitting his brows. "I hardly know. I think it depends on you.... But if you did do such work wouldn't you be happier?"

"Happier! Why Glenn, I'd be miserable!... But listen. It wasn't my beautiful and useless hand I wanted you to see. It was my engagement ring."

"Oh!—Well?" he went on, slowly.

"I've never had it off since you left New York," she said, softly. "You gave it to me four years ago. Do you remember? It was on my twenty-second birthday. You said it would take two months' salary to pay the bill."

"It sure did," he retorted, with a hint of humor.

"Glenn, during the war it was not so—so very hard to wear this ring as an engagement ring should be worn," said Carley, growing more earnest. "But after the war—especially after your departure West it was terribly hard to be true to the significance of this betrothal ring. There was a let-down in all women. Oh, no one need tell me! There was. And men were affected by that and the chaotic condition of the times. New York was wild during the year of your absence. Prohibition was a joke.—Well, I gadded, danced, dressed, drank, smoked, motored, just the same as the other women in our crowd. Something drove me to. I never rested. Excitement seemed to be happiness—Glenn, I am not making any plea to excuse all that. But I want you to know—how under trying circumstances—I was absolutely true to you. Understand me. I mean true as regards love. Through it all I loved you just the same. And now I'm with you, it seems, oh, so much more!... Your last letter hurt me. I don't know just how. But I came West to see you—to tell you this—and to ask you.... Do you want this ring back?"

"Certainly not," he replied, forcibly, with a dark flush spreading over his face.

"Then—you love me?" she whispered.

"Yes—I love you," he returned, deliberately. "And in spite of all you say—very probably more than you love me.... But you, like all women, make love and its expression the sole object of life. Carley, I have been concerned with keeping my body from the grave and my soul from hell."

"But—dear—you're well now?" she returned, with trembling lips.

"Yes, I've almost pulled out."

"Then what is wrong?"

"Wrong?—With me or you," he queried, with keen, enigmatical glance upon her.

"What is wrong between us? There is something."

"Carley, a man who has been on the verge—as I have been—seldom or never comes back to happiness. But perhaps—"

"You frighten me," cried Carley, and, rising, she sat upon the arm of his chair and encircled his neck with her arms. "How can I help if I do not understand? Am I so miserably little?...

Glenn, must I tell you? No woman can live without love. I need to be loved. That's all that's wrong with me."

"Carley, you are still an imperious, mushy girl," replied Glenn, taking her into his arms. "I need to be loved, too. But that's not what is wrong with me. You'll have to find it out yourself."

"You're a dear old Sphinx," she retorted.

"Listen, Carley," he said, earnestly. "About this love-making stuff. Please don't misunderstand me. I love you. I'm starved for your kisses. But—is it right to ask them?"

"Right! Aren't we engaged? And don't I want to give them?"

"If I were only sure we'd be married!" he said, in low, tense voice, as if speaking more to himself.

"Married!" cried Carley, convulsively clasping him. "Of course we'll be married. Glenn, you wouldn't jilt me?"

"Carley, what I mean is that you might never really marry me," he answered, seriously.

"Oh, if that's all you need be sure of, Glenn Kilbourne, you may begin to make love to me now."

It was late when Carley went up to her room. And she was in such a softened mood, so happy and excited and yet disturbed in mind, that the coldness and the darkness did not matter in the least. She undressed in pitchy blackness, stumbling over chair and bed, feeling for what she needed. And in her mood this unusual proceeding was fun. When ready for bed she opened the door to take a peep out. Through the dense blackness the waterfall showed dimly opaque. Carley felt a soft mist wet her face. The low roar of the falling water seemed to envelop her. Under the cliff wall brooded impenetrable gloom. But out above the treetops shone great stars, wonderfully white and radiant and cold, with a piercing contrast to the deep clear blue of sky. The waterfall hummed into an absolutely dead silence. It emphasized the silence. Not only cold was it that made Carley shudder. How lonely, how lost, how hidden this canyon!

Then she hurried to bed, grateful for the warm woolly blankets. Relaxation and thought brought consciousness of the heat of her blood, the beat and throb and swell of her heart, of the tumult within her. In the lonely darkness of her room she might have faced the truth of her strangely renewed and augmented love for Glenn Kilbourne. But she was more concerned with her happiness. She had won him back. Her presence, her love had overcome his restraint. She thrilled in the sweet consciousness of her woman's conquest. How splendid he was! To hold back physical tenderness, the simple expressions of love, because he had feared they might unduly influence her! He had grown in many ways. She must be careful to reach up to his ideals. That about Flo Hutter's toil-hardened hands! Was that significance somehow connected with the rift in the lute? For Carley admitted to herself that there was something amiss, something incomprehensible, something intangible that obtruded its menace into her dream of future happiness. Still, what had she to fear, so long as she could be with Glenn?

And yet there were forced upon her, insistent and perplexing, the questions—was her love selfish? was she considering him? was she blind to something he could see? Tomorrow and next day and the days to come held promise of joyous companionship with Glenn, yet likewise they seemed full of a portent of trouble for her, or fight and ordeal, of lessons that would make life significant for her.

CHAPTER III

Carley was awakened by rattling sounds in her room. The raising of sleepy eyelids disclosed Flo on her knees before the little stove, in the act of lighting a fire.

"Mawnin', Carley," she drawled. "It's shore cold. Reckon it'll snow today, worse luck, just because you're here. Take my hunch and stay in bed till the fire burns up."

"I shall do no such thing," declared Carley, heroically.

"We're afraid you'll take cold," said Flo. "This is desert country with high altitude. Spring is here when the sun shines. But it's only shinin' in streaks these days. That means winter, really. Please be good."

"Well, it doesn't require much self-denial to stay here awhile longer," replied Carley, lazily.

Flo left with a parting admonition not to let the stove get red-hot. And Carley lay snuggled in the warm blankets, dreading the ordeal of getting out into that cold bare room. Her nose was cold. When her nose grew cold, it being a faithful barometer as to temperature, Carley knew there was frost in the air. She preferred summer. Steam-heated rooms with hothouse flowers lending their perfume had certainly not trained Carley for primitive conditions. She had a spirit, however, that was waxing a little rebellious to all this intimation as to her susceptibility to colds and her probable weakness under privation. Carley got up. Her bare feet landed upon the board floor instead of the Navajo rug, and she thought she had encountered cold stone. Stove and hot water notwithstanding, by the time she was half dressed she was also half frozen. "Some actor fellow once said w-when you w-went West you were c-camping out," chattered Carley. "Believe me, he said something."

The fact was Carley had never camped out. Her set played golf, rode horseback, motored and house-boated, but they had never gone in for uncomfortable trips. The camps and hotels in the Adirondacks were as warm and luxurious as Carley's own home. Carley now missed many things. And assuredly her flesh was weak. It cost her effort of will and real pain to finish lacing her boots. As she had made an engagement with Glenn to visit his cabin, she had donned an outdoor suit. She wondered if the cold had anything to do with the perceptible diminishing of the sound of the waterfall. Perhaps some of the water had frozen, like her fingers.

Carley went downstairs to the living room, and made no effort to resist a rush to the open fire. Flo and her mother were amused at Carley's impetuosity. "You'll like that stingin' of the air after you get used to it," said Mrs. Hutter. Carley had her doubts. When she was thoroughly thawed out she discovered an appetite quite unusual for her, and she enjoyed her breakfast. Then it was time to sally forth to meet Glenn.

"It's pretty sharp this mawnin'," said Flo. "You'll need gloves and sweater."

Having fortified herself with these, Carley asked how to find West Fork Canyon.

"It's down the road a little way," replied Flo. "A great narrow canyon opening on the right side. You can't miss it."

Flo accompanied her as far as the porch steps. A queer-looking individual was slouching along with ax over his shoulder.

"There's Charley," said Flo. "He'll show you." Then she whispered: "He's sort of dotty sometimes. A horse kicked him once. But mostly he's sensible."

At Flo's call the fellow halted with a grin. He was long, lean, loose jointed, dressed in blue overalls stuck into the tops of muddy boots, and his face was clear olive without beard or line. His brow bulged a little, and from under it peered out a pair of wistful brown eyes that reminded Carley of those of a dog she had once owned.

"Wal, it ain't a-goin' to be a nice day," remarked Charley, as he tried to accommodate his strides to Carley's steps.

"How can you tell?" asked Carley. "It looks clear and bright."

"Naw, this is a dark mawnin'. Thet's a cloudy sun. We'll hev snow on an' off."

"Do you mind bad weather?"

"Me? All the same to me. Reckon, though, I like it cold so I can loaf round a big fire at night."

"I like a big fire, too."

"Ever camped out?" he asked.

"Not what you'd call the real thing," replied Carley.

"Wal, thet's too bad. Reckon it'll be tough fer you," he went on, kindly. "There was a gurl tenderfoot heah two years ago an' she had a hell of a time. They all joked her, 'cept me, an' played tricks on her. An' on her side she was always puttin' her foot in it. I was shore sorry fer her."

"You were very kind to be an exception," murmured Carley.

"You look out fer Tom Hutter, an' I reckon Flo ain't so darn above layin' traps fer you. 'Specially as she's sweet on your beau. I seen them together a lot."

"Yes?" interrogated Carley, encouragingly.

"Kilbourne is the best fellar thet ever happened along Oak Creek. I helped him build his cabin. We've hunted some together. Did you ever hunt?"

"No."

"Wal, you've shore missed a lot of fun," he said. "Turkey huntin'. Thet's what fetches the gurls. I reckon because turkeys are so good to eat. The old gobblers hev begun to gobble now. I'll take you gobbler huntin' if you'd like to go."

"I'm sure I would."

"There's good trout fishin' along heah a little later," he said, pointing to the stream. "Crick's too high now. I like West Fork best. I've ketched some lammin' big ones up there."

Carley was amused and interested. She could not say that Charley had shown any indication of his mental peculiarity to her. It took considerable restraint not to lead him to talk more about Flo and Glenn. Presently they reached the turn in the road, opposite the cottage Carley had noticed yesterday, and here her loquacious escort halted.

"You take the trail heah," he said, pointing it out, "an' foller it into West Fork. So long, an' don't forget we're goin' huntin' turkeys."

Carley smiled her thanks, and, taking to the trail, she stepped out briskly, now giving attention to her surroundings. The canyon had widened, and the creek with its deep thicket of green and white had sheered to the left. On her right the canyon wall appeared to be lifting higher—and higher. She could not see it well, owing to intervening treetops. The trail led her through a grove of maples and sycamores, out into an open park-like bench that turned to the right toward the cliff. Suddenly Carley saw a break in the red wall. It was the intersecting canyon, West Fork. What a narrow red-walled gateway! Huge pine trees spread wide gnarled branches over her head. The wind made soft rush in their tops, sending the brown needles lightly on the air. Carley turned the bulging corner, to be halted by a magnificent spectacle. It seemed a mountain wall loomed over her. It was the western side of this canyon, so lofty that Carley had to tip back her head to see the top. She swept her astonished gaze down the face of this tremendous red mountain wall and then slowly swept it upward again. This phenomenon of a cliff seemed beyond the comprehension of her sight. It looked a mile high. The few trees along its bold rampart resembled short spear-pointed bushes outlined against the steel gray of sky. Ledges, caves, seams, cracks, fissures, beetling red brows, yellow crumbling crags, benches of green growths and niches choked with brush, and bold points where single lonely pine trees grew perilously, and blank walls a thousand feet across their shadowed faces—these features gradually took shape in Carley's confused sight, until the colossal mountain front stood up before her in all its strange, wild, magnificent ruggedness and beauty.

"Arizona! Perhaps this is what he meant," murmured Carley. "I never dreamed of anything like this.... But, oh! it overshadows me—bears me down! I could never have a moment's peace under it."

It fascinated her. There were inaccessible ledges that haunted her with their remote fastnesses. How wonderful would it be to get there, rest there, if that were possible! But only eagles could reach them. There were places, then, that the desecrating hands of man could not touch. The dark caves were mystically potent in their vacant staring out at the world beneath them. The crumbling crags, the toppling ledges, the leaning rocks all threatened to come thundering down at the breath of wind. How deep and soft the red color in contrast with the green! How splendid the sheer bold uplift of gigantic steps! Carley found herself marveling at the forces that had so rudely, violently, and grandly left this monument to nature.

"Well, old Fifth Avenue gadder!" called a gay voice. "If the back wall of my yard so halts you—what will you ever do when you see the Painted Desert, or climb Sunset Peak, or look down into the Grand Canyon?"

"Oh, Glenn, where are you?" cried Carley, gazing everywhere near at hand. But he was farther away. The clearness of his voice had deceived her. Presently she espied him a little distance away, across a creek she had not before noticed.

"Come on," he called. "I want to see you cross the stepping stones."

Carley ran ahead, down a little slope of clean red rock, to the shore of the green water. It was clear, swift, deep in some places and shallow in others, with white wreathes or ripples around the rocks evidently placed there as a means to cross. Carley drew back aghast.

"Glenn, I could never make it," she called.

"Come on, my Alpine climber," he taunted. "Will you let Arizona daunt you?"

"Do you want me to fall in and catch cold?" she cried, desperately.

"Carley, big women might even cross the bad places of modern life on stepping stones of their dead selves!" he went on, with something of mockery. "Surely a few physical steps are not beyond you."

"Say, are you mangling Tennyson or just kidding me?" she demanded slangily.

"My love, Flo could cross here with her eyes shut."

That thrust spurred Carley to action. His words were jest, yet they held a hint of earnest. With her heart at her throat Carley stepped on the first rock, and, poising, she calculated on a running leap from stone to stone. Once launched, she felt she was falling downhill. She swayed, she splashed, she slipped; and clearing the longest leap from the last stone to shore she lost her balance and fell into Glenn's arms. His kisses drove away both her panic and her resentment.

"By Jove! I didn't think you'd even attempt it!" he declared, manifestly pleased. "I made sure I'd have to pack you over—in fact, rather liked the idea."

"I wouldn't advise you to employ any such means again—to dare me," she retorted.

"That's a nifty outdoor suit you've on," he said, admiringly. "I was wondering what you'd wear. I like short outing skirts for women, rather than trousers. The service sort of made the fair sex dippy about pants."

"It made them dippy about more than that," she replied. "You and I will never live to see the day that women recover their balance."

"I agree with you," replied Glenn.

Carley locked her arm in his. "Honey, I want to have a good time today. Cut out all the other women stuff.... Take me to see your little gray home in the West. Or is it gray?"

He laughed. "Why, yes, it's gray, just about. The logs have bleached some."

Glenn led her away up a trail that climbed between bowlders, and meandered on over piny mats of needles under great, silent, spreading pines; and closer to the impondering mountain wall, where at the base of the red rock the creek murmured strangely with hollow gurgle, where the sun had no chance to affect the cold damp gloom; and on through sweet-smelling woods, out into the sunlight again, and across a wider breadth of stream; and up a slow slope covered with stately pines, to a little cabin that faced the west.

"Here we are, sweetheart," said Glenn. "Now we shall see what you are made of."

Carley was non-committal as to that. Her intense interest precluded any humor at this moment. Not until she actually saw the log cabin Glenn had erected with his own hands had she been conscious of any great interest. But sight of it awoke something unaccustomed in Carley. As she stepped into the cabin her heart was not acting normally for a young woman who had no illusions about love in a cottage.

Glenn's cabin contained one room about fifteen feet wide by twenty long. Between the peeled logs were lines of red mud, hard dried. There was a small window opposite the door. In one corner was a couch of poles, with green tips of pine boughs peeping from under the blankets. The floor consisted of flat rocks laid irregularly, with many spaces of earth showing between. The open fireplace appeared too large for the room, but the very bigness of it, as well as the blazing sticks and glowing embers, appealed strongly to Carley. A rough-hewn log formed the mantel, and on it Carley's picture held the place of honor. Above this a rifle lay across deer antlers. Carley paused here in her survey long enough to kiss Glenn and point to her photograph.

"You couldn't have pleased me more."

To the left of the fireplace was a rude cupboard of shelves, packed with boxes, cans, bags, and utensils. Below the cupboard, hung upon pegs, were blackened pots and pans, a long-handled skillet, and a bucket. Glenn's table was a masterpiece. There was no danger of knocking it over. It consisted of four poles driven into the ground, upon which had been nailed two wide slabs. This table showed considerable evidence of having been scrubbed scrupulously clean. There were two low stools, made out of boughs, and the seats had been covered with woolly sheep hide. In the right-hand corner stood a neat pile of firewood, cut with an ax, and beyond this hung saddle and saddle blanket, bridle and spurs. An old sombrero was hooked upon the pommel of the saddle. Upon the wall, higher up, hung a lantern, resting in a coil of rope that Carley took to be a lasso. Under a shelf upon which lay a suitcase hung some rough wearing apparel.

Carley noted that her picture and the suit case were absolutely the only physical evidences of Glenn's connection with his Eastern life. That had an unaccountable effect upon Carley. What had she expected? Then, after another survey of the room, she began to pester Glenn with questions. He had to show her the spring outside and the little bench with basin and soap. Sight of his soiled towel made her throw up her hands. She sat on the stools. She lay on the couch. She rummaged into the contents of the cupboard. She threw wood on the fire. Then, finally, having exhausted her search and inquiry, she flopped down on one of the stools to gaze at Glenn in awe and admiration and incredulity.

"Glenn—you've actually lived here!" she ejaculated.

"Since last fall before the snow came," he said, smiling.

"Snow! Did it snow?" she inquired.

"Well, I guess. I was snowed in for a week."

"Why did you choose this lonely place—way off from the Lodge?" she asked, slowly.

"I wanted to be by myself," he replied, briefly.

"You mean this is a sort of camp-out place?"

"Carley, I call it my home," he replied, and there was a low, strong sweetness in his voice she had never heard before.

That silenced her for a while. She went to the door and gazed up at the towering wall, more wonderful than ever, and more fearful, too, in her sight. Presently tears dimmed her eyes. She did not understand her feeling; she was ashamed of it; she hid it from Glenn. Indeed, there was something terribly wrong between her and Glenn, and it was not in him. This cabin he called home gave her a shock which would take time to analyze. At length she turned to him with gay utterance upon her lips. She tried to put out of her mind a dawning sense that this close-to-the-earth habitation, this primitive dwelling, held strange inscrutable power over a self she had never divined she possessed. The very stones in the hearth seemed to call out from some remote past, and the strong sweet smell of burnt wood thrilled to the marrow of her bones. How little she knew of herself! But she had intelligence enough to understand that there was a woman in her, the female of the species; and through that the sensations from logs and stones and earth and fire had strange power to call up the emotions handed down to her from the ages. The thrill, the queer heartbeat, the vague, haunting memory of something, as of a dim childhood adventure, the strange prickling sense of dread—these abided with her and augmented while she tried to show Glenn her pride in him and also how funny his cabin seemed to her.

Once or twice he hesitatingly, and somewhat appealingly, she imagined, tried to broach the subject of his work there in the West. But Carley wanted a little while with him free of disagreeable argument. It was a foregone conclusion that she would not like his work. Her intention at first had been to begin at once to use all persuasion in her power toward having him go back East with her, or at the latest some time this year. But the rude log cabin had checked her impulse. She felt that haste would be unwise.

"Glenn Kilbourne, I told you why I came West to see you," she said, spiritedly. "Well, since you still swear allegiance to your girl from the East, you might entertain her a little bit before getting down to business talk."

"All right, Carley," he replied, laughing. "What do you want to do? The day is at your disposal. I wish it were June. Then if you didn't fall in love with West Fork you'd be no good."

"Glenn, I love people, not places," she returned.

"So I remember. And that's one thing I don't like. But let's not quarrel. What'll we do?"

"Suppose you tramp with me all around, until I'm good and hungry. Then we'll come back here—and you can cook dinner for me."

"Fine! Oh, I know you're just bursting with curiosity to see how I'll do it. Well, you may be surprised, miss."

"Let's go," she urged.

"Shall I take my gun or fishing rod?"

"You shall take nothing but me," retorted Carley. "What chance has a girl with a man, if he can hunt or fish?"

So they went out hand in hand. Half of the belt of sky above was obscured by swiftly moving gray clouds. The other half was blue and was being slowly encroached upon by the dark storm-like pall. How cold the air! Carley had already learned that when the sun was hidden the atmosphere was cold. Glenn led her down a trail to the brook, where he calmly picked her up in his arms, quite easily, it appeared, and leisurely packed her across, kissing her half a dozen times before he deposited her on her feet.

"Glenn, you do this sort of thing so well that it makes me imagine you have practice now and then," she said.

"No. But you are pretty and sweet, and like the girl you were four years ago. That takes me back to those days."

"I thank you. That's dear of you. I think I am something of a cat.... I'll be glad if this walk leads us often to the creek."

Spring might have been fresh and keen in the air, but it had not yet brought much green to the brown earth or to the trees. The cotton-woods showed a light feathery verdure. The long grass was a bleached white, and low down close to the sod fresh tiny green blades showed. The great fern leaves were sear and ragged, and they rustled in the breeze. Small gray sheath-barked trees with clumpy foliage and snags of dead branches, Glenn called cedars; and, grotesque as these were, Carley rather liked them. They were approachable, not majestic and lofty like the pines, and they smelled sweetly wild, and best of all they afforded some protection from the bitter wind. Carley rested better than she walked. The huge sections of red rock that had tumbled from above also interested Carley, especially when the sun happened to come out for a few moments and brought out their color. She enjoyed walking on the fallen pines, with Glenn below, keeping pace with her and holding her hand. Carley looked in vain for flowers and birds. The only living things she saw were rainbow trout that Glenn pointed out to her in the beautiful clear pools. The way the great gray bowlders trooped down to the brook as if they were cattle going to drink; the dark caverns under the shelving cliffs, where the water murmured with such hollow mockery;

the low spear-pointed gray plants, resembling century plants, and which Glenn called mescal cactus, each with its single straight dead stalk standing on high with fluted head; the narrow gorges, perpendicularly walled in red, where the constricted brook plunged in amber and white cascades over fall after fall, tumbling, rushing, singing its water melody—these all held singular appeal for Carley as aspects of the wild land, fascinating for the moment, symbolic of the lonely red man and his forbears, and by their raw contrast making more necessary and desirable and elevating the comforts and conventions of civilization. The cave man theory interested Carley only as mythology.

Lonelier, wilder, grander grew Glenn's canyon. Carley was finally forced to shift her attention from the intimate objects of the canyon floor to the aloof and unattainable heights. Singular to feel the difference! That which she could see close at hand, touch if she willed, seemed to, become part of her knowledge, could be observed and so possessed and passed by. But the gold-red ramparts against the sky, the crannied cliffs, the crags of the eagles, the lofty, distant blank walls, where the winds of the gods had written their wars—these haunted because they could never be possessed. Carley had often gazed at the Alps as at celebrated pictures. She admired, she appreciated—then she forgot. But the canyon heights did not affect her that way. They vaguely dissatisfied, and as she could not be sure of what they dissatisfied, she had to conclude that it was in herself. To see, to watch, to dream, to seek, to strive, to endure, to find! Was that what they meant? They might make her thoughtful of the vast earth, and its endless age, and its staggering mystery. But what more!

The storm that had threatened blackened the sky, and gray scudding clouds buried the canyon rims, and long veils of rain and sleet began to descend. The wind roared through the pines, drowning the roar of the brook. Quite suddenly the air grew piercingly cold. Carley had forgotten her gloves, and her pockets had not been constructed to protect hands. Glenn drew her into a sheltered nook where a rock jutted out from overhead and a thicket of young pines helped break the onslaught of the wind. There Carley sat on a cold rock, huddled up close to Glenn, and wearing to a state she knew would be misery. Glenn not only seemed content; he was happy. "This is great," he said. His coat was open, his hands uncovered, and he watched the storm and listened with manifest delight. Carley hated to betray what a weakling she was, so she resigned herself to her fate, and imagined she felt her fingers numbing into ice, and her sensitive nose slowly and painfully freezing.

The storm passed, however, before Carley sank into abject and open wretchedness. She managed to keep pace with Glenn until exercise warmed her blood. At every little ascent in the trail she found herself laboring to get her breath. There was assuredly evidence of abundance of air in this canyon, but somehow she could not get enough of it. Glenn detected this and said it was owing to the altitude. When they reached the cabin Carley was wet, stiff, cold, exhausted. How welcome the shelter, the open fireplace! Seeing the cabin in new light, Carley had the grace to acknowledge to herself that, after all, it was not so bad.

"Now for a good fire and then dinner," announced Glenn, with the air of one who knew his ground.

"Can I help?" queried Carley.

"Not today. I do not want you to spring any domestic science on me now." Carley was not averse to withholding her ignorance. She watched Glenn with surpassing curiosity and interest. First he threw a quantity of wood upon the smoldering fire.

"I have ham and mutton of my own raising," announced Glenn, with importance. "Which would you prefer?"

"Of your own raising. What do you mean?" queried Carley.

"My dear, you've been so steeped in the fog of the crowd that you are blind to the homely and necessary things of living. I mean I have here meat of both sheep and hog that I raised myself. That is to say, mutton and ham. Which do you like?"

"Ham!" cried Carley, incredulously.

Without more ado Glenn settled to brisk action, every move of which Carley watched with keen eyes. The usurping of a woman's province by a man was always an amusing thing. But for Glenn Kilbourne—what more would it be? He evidently knew what he wanted, for every movement was quick, decisive. One after another he placed bags, cans, sacks, pans, utensils on the table. Then he kicked at the roaring fire, settling some of the sticks. He strode outside to return with a bucket of water, a basin, towel, and soap. Then he took down two queer little iron pots with heavy lids. To each pot was attached a wire handle. He removed the lids, then set both the pots right on the fire or in it. Pouring water into the basin, he proceeded to wash his hands. Next he took a large pail, and from a sack he filled it half full of flour. To this he added baking powder and salt. It was instructive for Carley to see him run his skillful fingers all through that flour, as if searching for lumps. After this he knelt before the fire and, lifting off one of the iron pots with a forked stick, he proceeded to wipe out the inside of the pot and grease it with a piece of fat. His next move was to rake out a pile of the red coals, a feat he performed with the stick, and upon these he placed the pot. Also he removed the other pot from the fire, leaving it, however, quite close.

"Well, all eyes?" he bantered, suddenly staring at her. "Didn't I say I'd surprise you?"

"Don't mind me. This is about the happiest and most bewildered moment—of my life," replied Carley.

Returning to the table, Glenn dug at something in a large red can. He paused a moment to eye Carley.

"Girl, do you know how to make biscuits?" he queried.

"I might have known in my school days, but I've forgotten," she replied.

"Can you make apple pie?" he demanded, imperiously.

"No," rejoined Carley.

"How do you expect to please your husband?"

"Why—by marrying him, I suppose," answered Carley, as if weighing a problem.

"That has been the universal feminine point of view for a good many years," replied Glenn, flourishing a flour-whitened hand. "But it never served the women of the Revolution or the pioneers. And they were the builders of the nation. It will never serve the wives of the future, if we are to survive."

"Glenn, you rave!" ejaculated Carley, not knowing whether to laugh or be grave. "You were talking of humble housewifely things."

"Precisely. The humble things that were the foundation of the great nation of Americans. I meant work and children."

Carley could only stare at him. The look he flashed at her, the sudden intensity and passion of his ringing words, were as if he gave her a glimpse into the very depths of him. He might have begun in fun, but he had finished otherwise. She felt that she really did not know this man. Had he arraigned her in judgment? A flush, seemingly hot and cold, passed over her. Then it relieved her to see that he had returned to his task.

He mixed the shortening with the flour, and, adding water, he began a thorough kneading. When the consistency of the mixture appeared to satisfy him he took a handful of it, rolled it into a ball, patted and flattened it into a biscuit, and dropped it into the oven he had set aside on the hot coals. Swiftly he shaped eight or ten other biscuits and dropped them as the first. Then he put the heavy iron lid on the pot, and with a rude shovel, improvised from a flattened tin can, he shoveled red coals out of the fire, and covered the lid with them. His next move was to pare and slice potatoes, placing these aside in a pan. A small black coffee-pot half full of water, was set on a glowing part of the fire. Then he brought into use a huge, heavy knife, a murderous-looking implement it appeared to Carley, with which he cut slices of ham. These he dropped into the second pot, which he left uncovered. Next he removed the flour sack and other inpedimenta from the table, and proceeded to set places for two—blue-enamel plate and cup, with plain, substantial-looking knives, forks, and spoons. He went outside, to return presently carrying a small crock of butter. Evidently he had kept the butter in or near the spring. It looked dewy and cold and hard. After that he peeped under the lid of the pot which contained the biscuits. The other pot was sizzling and smoking, giving forth a delicious savory odor that affected Carley most agreeably. The coffee-pot had begun to steam. With a long fork Glenn turned the slices of ham and stood a moment watching them. Next he placed cans of three sizes upon the table; and these Carley conjectured contained sugar, salt, and pepper. Carley might not have been present, for all the attention he paid to her. Again he peeped at the biscuits. At the edge of the hot embers he placed a tin plate, upon which he carefully deposited the slices of ham. Carley had not needed sight of them to know she was hungry; they made her simply ravenous. That done, he poured the pan of sliced potatoes into the pot. Carley judged the heat of that pot to be extreme. Next he removed the lid from the other pot, exposing biscuits slightly browned; and evidently satisfied with these, he removed them from the coals. He stirred the slices of potatoes round and round; he emptied two heaping tablespoonfuls of coffee into the coffee-pot.

"Carley," he said, at last turning to her with a warm smile, "out here in the West the cook usually yells, 'Come and get it.' Draw up your stool."

And presently Carley found herself seated across the crude table from Glenn, with the background of chinked logs in her sight, and the smart of wood smoke in her eyes. In years past she had sat with him in the soft, subdued, gold-green shadows of the Astor, or in the sumptuous atmosphere of the St. Regis. But this event was so different, so striking, that she felt it would have limitless significance. For one thing, the look of Glenn! When had he ever seemed like this, wonderfully happy to have her there, consciously proud of this dinner he had prepared in half an hour, strangely studying her as one on trial? This might have had its effect upon Carley's reaction to the situation, making it sweet, trenchant with meaning, but she was hungry enough and the dinner was good enough to make this hour memorable on that score alone. She ate until she was actually ashamed of herself. She laughed heartily, she talked, she made love to Glenn. Then suddenly an idea flashed into her quick mind.

"Glenn, did this girl Flo teach you to cook?" she queried, sharply.

"No. I always was handy in camp. Then out here I had the luck to fall in with an old fellow who was a wonderful cook. He lived with me for a while. ... Why, what difference would it have made—had Flo taught me?"

Carley felt the heat of blood in her face. "I don't know that it would have made a difference. Only—I'm glad she didn't teach you. I'd rather no girl could teach you what I couldn't."

"You think I'm a pretty good cook, then?" he asked.

"I've enjoyed this dinner more than any I've ever eaten."

"Thanks, Carley. That'll help a lot," he said, gayly, but his eyes shone with earnest, glad light. "I hoped I'd surprise you. I've found out here that I want to do things well. The West stirs something in a man. It must be an unwritten law. You stand or fall by your own hands. Back East you know meals are just occasions—to hurry through—to dress for—to meet somebody— to eat because you have to eat. But out here they are different. I don't know how. In the city, producers, merchants, waiters serve you for money. The meal is a transaction. It has no significance. It is money that keeps you from starvation. But in the West money doesn't mean much. You must work to live."

Carley leaned her elbows on the table and gazed at him curiously and admiringly. "Old fellow, you're a wonder. I can't tell you how proud I am of you. That you could come West weak and sick, and fight your way to health, and learn to be self-sufficient! It is a splendid achievement. It amazes me. I don't grasp it. I want to think. Nevertheless I—"

"What?" he queried, as she hesitated.

"Oh, never mind now," she replied, hastily, averting her eyes.

The day was far spent when Carley returned to the Lodge—and in spite of the discomfort of cold and sleet, and the bitter wind that beat in her face as she struggled up the trail—it was a day never to be forgotten. Nothing had been wanting in Glenn's attention or affection. He had been comrade, lover, all she craved for. And but for his few singular words about work and children there had been no serious talk. Only a play day in his canyon and his cabin! Yet had she appeared at her best? Something vague and perplexing knocked at the gate of her consciousness.

CHAPTER IV

Two warm sunny days in early May inclined Mr. Hutter to the opinion that pleasant spring weather was at hand and that it would be a propitious time to climb up on the desert to look after his sheep interests. Glenn, of course, would accompany him.

"Carley and I will go too," asserted Flo.

"Reckon that'll be good," said Hutter, with approving nod.

His wife also agreed that it would be fine for Carley to see the beautiful desert country round Sunset Peak. But Glenn looked dubious.

"Carley, it'll be rather hard," he said. "You're soft, and riding and lying out will stove you up. You ought to break in gradually."

"I rode ten miles today," rejoined Carley. "And didn't mind it—much." This was a little deviation from stern veracity.

"Shore Carley's well and strong," protested Flo. "She'll get sore, but that won't kill her."

Glenn eyed Flo with rather penetrating glance. "I might drive Carley round about in the car," he said.

"But you can't drive over those lava flats, or go round, either. We'd have to send horses in some cases miles to meet you. It's horseback if you go at all."

"Shore we'll go horseback," spoke up Flo. "Carley has got it all over that Spencer girl who was here last summer."

"I think so, too. I am sure I hope so. Because you remember what the ride to Long Valley did to Miss Spencer," rejoined Glenn.

"What?" inquired Carley.

"Bad cold, peeled nose, skinned shin, saddle sores. She was in bed two days. She didn't show much pep the rest of her stay here, and she never got on another horse."

"Oh, is that all, Glenn?" returned Carley, in feigned surprise. "Why, I imagined from your tone that Miss Spencer's ride must have occasioned her discomfort.... See here, Glenn. I may be a tenderfoot, but I'm no mollycoddle."

"My dear, I surrender," replied Glenn, with a laugh. "Really, I'm delighted. But if anything happens—don't you blame me. I'm quite sure that a long horseback ride, in spring, on the desert, will show you a good many things about yourself."

That was how Carley came to find herself, the afternoon of the next day, astride a self-willed and unmanageable little mustang, riding in the rear of her friends, on the way through a cedar forest toward a place called Deep Lake.

Carley had not been able yet, during the several hours of their journey, to take any pleasure in the scenery or in her mount. For in the first place there was nothing to see but scrubby little gnarled cedars and drab-looking rocks; and in the second this Indian pony she rode had discovered she was not an adept horsewoman and had proceeded to take advantage of the fact. It did not help Carley's predicament to remember that Glenn had decidedly advised her against riding this particular mustang. To be sure, Flo had approved of Carley's choice, and Mr. Hutter, with a hearty laugh, had fallen in line: "Shore. Let her ride one of the broncs, if she wants." So this animal she bestrode must have been a bronc, for it did not take him long to elicit from Carley a muttered, "I don't know what bronc means, but it sounds like this pony acts."

Carley had inquired the animal's name from the young herder who had saddled him for her.

"Wal, I reckon he ain't got much of a name," replied the lad, with a grin, as he scratched his head. "For us boys always called him Spillbeans."

"Humph! What a beautiful cognomen!" ejaculated Carley, "But according to Shakespeare any name will serve. I'll ride him or—or—"

So far there had not really been any necessity for the completion of that sentence. But five miles of riding up into the cedar forest had convinced Carley that she might not have much farther to go. Spillbeans had ambled along well enough until he reached level ground where a long bleached grass waved in the wind. Here he manifested hunger, then a contrary nature, next insubordination, and finally direct hostility. Carley had urged, pulled, and commanded in vain. Then when she gave Spillbeans a kick in the flank he jumped stiff legged, propelling her up out of the saddle, and while she was descending he made the queer jump again, coming up to meet her. The jolt she got seemed to dislocate every bone in her body. Likewise it hurt. Moreover, along with her idea of what a spectacle she must have presented, it quickly decided Carley that Spillbeans was a horse that was not to be opposed. Whenever he wanted a mouthful of grass he stopped to get it. Therefore Carley was always in the rear, a fact which in itself did not displease her. Despite his contrariness, however, Spillbeans had apparently no intention of allowing the other horses to get completely out of sight.

Several times Flo waited for Carley to catch up. "He's loafing on you, Carley. You ought to have on a spur. Break off a switch and beat him some." Then she whipped the mustang across the flank with her bridle rein, which punishment caused Spillbeans meekly to trot on with alacrity. Carley had a positive belief that he would not do it for her. And after Flo's repeated efforts, assisted by chastisement from Glenn, had kept Spillbeans in a trot for a couple of miles Carley began to discover that the trotting of a horse was the most uncomfortable motion possible to imagine. It grew worse. It became painful. It gradually got unendurable. But pride made Carley endure it until suddenly she thought she had been stabbed in the side. This strange piercing pain must be what Glenn had called a "stitch" in the side, something common to novices on horseback. Carley could have screamed. She pulled the mustang to a walk and sagged in her saddle until the pain subsided. What a blessed relief! Carley had keen sense of the difference between riding in Central Park and in Arizona. She regretted her choice of horses. Spillbeans was attractive to look at, but the pleasure of riding him was a delusion. Flo had said his gait resembled the motion of a rocking chair. This Western girl, according to Charley, the sheep herder, was not above playing Arizona jokes. Be that as it might, Spillbeans now manifested a desire to remain with the other horses, and he broke out of a walk into a trot. Carley could not keep him from trotting. Hence her state soon wore into acute distress.

Her left ankle seemed broken. The stirrup was heavy, and as soon as she was tired she could no longer keep its weight from drawing her foot in. The inside of her right knee was as sore as a boil. Besides, she had other pains, just as severe, and she stood momentarily in mortal dread of that terrible stitch in her side. If it returned she knew she would fall off. But, fortunately, just when she was growing weak and dizzy, the horses ahead slowed to a walk on a descent. The road wound down into a wide deep canyon. Carley had a respite from her severest pains. Never before had she known what it meant to be so grateful for relief from anything.

The afternoon grew far advanced and the sunset was hazily shrouded in gray. Hutter did not like the looks of those clouds. "Reckon we're in for weather," he said. Carley did not care what happened. Weather or anything else that might make it possible to get off her horse! Glenn rode beside her, inquiring solicitously as to her pleasure. "Ride of my life!" she lied heroically. And it helped some to see that she both fooled and pleased him.

Beyond the canyon the cedared desert heaved higher and changed its aspect. The trees grew larger, bushier, greener, and closer together, with patches of bleached grass between, and russet-lichened rocks everywhere. Small cactus plants bristled sparsely in open places; and here and there bright red flowers—Indian paintbrush, Flo called them—added a touch of color to the gray. Glenn pointed to where dark banks of cloud had massed around the mountain peaks. The scene to the west was somber and compelling.

At last the men and the pack-horses ahead came to a halt in a level green forestland with no high trees. Far ahead a chain of soft gray round hills led up to the dark heaved mass of mountains. Carley saw the gleam of water through the trees. Probably her mustang saw or scented it, because he started to trot. Carley had reached a limit of strength, endurance, and patience. She hauled him up short. When Spillbeans evinced a stubborn intention to go on Carley gave him a kick. Then it happened.

She felt the reins jerked out of her hands and the saddle propel her upward. When she descended it was to meet that before-experienced jolt.

"Look!" cried Flo. "That bronc is going to pitch."

"Hold on, Carley!" yelled Glenn.

Desperately Carley essayed to do just that. But Spillbeans jolted her out of the saddle. She came down on his rump and began to slide back and down. Frightened and furious, Carley tried to hang to the saddle with her hands and to squeeze the mustang with her knees. But another jolt broke her hold, and then, helpless and bewildered, with her heart in her throat and a terrible sensation of weakness, she slid back at each upheave of the muscular rump until she slid off and to the ground in a heap. Whereupon Spillbeans trotted off toward the water.

Carley sat up before Glenn and Flo reached her. Manifestly they were concerned about her, but both were ready to burst with laughter. Carley knew she was not hurt and she was so glad to be off the mustang that, on the moment, she could almost have laughed herself.

"That beast is well named," she said. "He spilled me, all right. And I presume I resembled a sack of beans."

"Carley—you're—not hurt?" asked Glenn, choking, as he helped her up.

"Not physically. But my feelings are."

Then Glenn let out a hearty howl of mirth, which was seconded by a loud guffaw from Hutter. Flo, however, appeared to be able to restrain whatever she felt. To Carley she looked queer.

"Pitch! You called it that," said Carley.

"Oh, he didn't really pitch. He just humped up a few times," replied Flo, and then when she saw how Carley was going to take it she burst into a merry peal of laughter. Charley, the sheep herder was grinning, and some of the other men turned away with shaking shoulders.

"Laugh, you wild and woolly Westerners!" ejaculated Carley. "It must have been funny. I hope I can be a good sport.... But I bet you I ride him tomorrow."

"Shore you will," replied Flo.

Evidently the little incident drew the party closer together. Carley felt a warmth of good nature that overcame her first feeling of humiliation. They expected such things from her, and she should expect them, too, and take them, if not fearlessly or painlessly, at least without resentment.

Carley walked about to ease her swollen and sore joints, and while doing so she took stock of the camp ground and what was going on. At second glance the place had a certain attraction difficult for her to define. She could see far, and the view north toward those strange gray-colored symmetrical hills was one that fascinated while it repelled her. Near at hand the ground sloped down to a large rock-bound lake, perhaps a mile in circumference. In the distance, along the shore she saw a white conical tent, and blue smoke, and moving gray objects she took for sheep.

The men unpacked and unsaddled the horses, and, hobbling their forefeet together, turned them loose. Twilight had fallen and each man appeared to be briskly set upon his own task. Glenn was cutting around the foot of a thickly branched cedar where, he told Carley, he would make a bed for her and Flo. All that Carley could see that could be used for such purpose was a canvas-covered roll. Presently Glenn untied a rope from round this, unrolled it, and dragged it under the cedar. Then he spread down the outer layer of canvas, disclosing a considerable thickness of blankets. From under the top of these he pulled out two flat little pillows. These he placed in position, and turned back some of the blankets.

"Carley, you crawl in here, pile the blankets up, and the tarp over them," directed Glenn. "If it rains pull the tarp up over your head—and let it rain."

This direction sounded in Glenn's cheery voice a good deal more pleasurable than the possibilities suggested. Surely that cedar tree could not keep off rain or snow.

"Glenn, how about—about animals—and crawling things, you know?" queried Carley.

"Oh, there are a few tarantulas and centipedes, and sometimes a scorpion. But these don't crawl around much at night. The only thing to worry about are the hydrophobia skunks."

"What on earth are they?" asked Carley, quite aghast.

"Skunks are polecats, you know," replied Glenn, cheerfully. "Sometimes one gets bitten by a coyote that has rabies, and then he's a dangerous customer. He has no fear and he may run across you and bite you in the face. Queer how they generally bite your nose. Two men have been bitten since I've been here. One of them died, and the other had to go to the Pasteur Institute with a well-developed case of hydrophobia."

"Good heavens!" cried Carley, horrified.

"You needn't be afraid," said Glenn. "I'll tie one of the dogs near your bed."

Carley wondered whether Glenn's casual, easy tone had been adopted for her benefit or was merely an assimilation from this Western life. Not improbably Glenn himself might be capable of playing a trick on her. Carley endeavored to fortify herself against disaster, so that when it befell she might not be wholly ludicrous.

With the coming of twilight a cold, keen wind moaned through the cedars. Carley would have hovered close to the fire even if she had not been too tired to exert herself. Despite her aches, she did justice to the supper. It amazed her that appetite consumed her to the extent of overcoming a distaste for this strong, coarse cooking. Before the meal ended darkness had fallen, a windy raw darkness that enveloped heavily like a blanket. Presently Carley edged closer to the fire, and there she stayed, alternately turning back and front to the welcome heat. She seemingly roasted hands, face, and knees while her back froze. The wind blew the smoke in all directions. When she groped around with blurred, smarting eyes to escape the hot smoke, it followed her. The other members of the party sat comfortably on sacks or rocks, without much notice of the smoke that so exasperated Carley. Twice Glenn insisted that she take a seat he had fixed for her, but she preferred to stand and move around a little.

By and by the camp tasks of the men appeared to be ended, and all gathered near the fire to lounge and smoke and talk. Glenn and Hutter engaged in interested conversation with two Mexicans, evidently sheep herders. If the wind and cold had not made Carley so uncomfortable she might have found the scene picturesque. How black the night! She could scarcely distinguish the sky at all. The cedar branches swished in the wind, and from the gloom came a low sound of waves lapping a rocky shore. Presently Glenn held up a hand.

"Listen, Carley!" he said.

Then she heard strange wild yelps, staccato, piercing, somehow infinitely lonely. They made her shudder.

"Coyotes," said Glenn. "You'll come to love that chorus. Hear the dogs bark back."

Carley listened with interest, but she was inclined to doubt that she would ever become enamoured of such wild cries.

"Do coyotes come near camp?" she queried.

"Shore. Sometimes they pull your pillow out from under your head," replied Flo, laconically.

Carley did not ask any more questions. Natural history was not her favorite study and she was sure she could dispense with any first-hand knowledge of desert beasts. She thought, however, she heard one of the men say, "Big varmint prowlin' round the sheep." To which Hutter replied, "Reckon it was a bear." And Glenn said, "I saw his fresh track by the lake. Some bear!"

The heat from the fire made Carley so drowsy that she could scarcely hold up her head. She longed for bed even if it was out there in the open. Presently Flo called her: "Come. Let's walk a little before turning in."

So Carley permitted herself to be led to and fro down an open aisle between some cedars. The far end of that aisle, dark, gloomy, with the bushy secretive cedars all around, caused Carley apprehension she was ashamed to admit. Flo talked eloquently about the joys of camp life, and how the harder any outdoor task was and the more endurance and pain it required, the more pride and pleasure one had in remembering it. Carley was weighing the import of these words when suddenly Flo clutched her arm. "What's that?" she whispered, tensely.

Carley stood stockstill. They had reached the furthermost end of that aisle, but had turned to go back. The flare of the camp fire threw a wan light into the shadows before them. There came a rustling in the brush, a snapping of twigs. Cold tremors chased up and down Carley's back.

"Shore it's a varmint, all right. Let's hurry," whispered Flo.

Carley needed no urging. It appeared that Flo was not going to run. She walked fast, peering back over her shoulder, and, hanging to Carley's arm, she rounded a large cedar that had obstructed some of the firelight. The gloom was not so thick here. And on the instant Carley espied a low, moving object, somehow furry, and gray in color. She gasped. She could not speak. Her heart gave a mighty throb and seemed to stop.

"What—do you see?" cried Flo, sharply, peering ahead. "Oh!... Come, Carley. Run!"

Flo's cry showed she must nearly be strangled with terror. But Carley was frozen in her tracks. Her eyes were riveted upon the gray furry object. It stopped. Then it came faster. It magnified. It was a huge beast. Carley had no control over mind, heart, voice, or muscle. Her legs gave way. She was sinking. A terrible panic, icy, sickening, rending, possessed her whole body.

The huge gray thing came at her. Into the rushing of her ears broke thudding sounds. The thing leaped up. A horrible petrifaction suddenly made stone of Carley. Then she saw a gray mantlelike object cast aside to disclose the dark form of a man. Glenn!

"Carley, dog-gone it! You don't scare worth a cent," he laughingly complained.

She collapsed into his arms. The liberating shock was as great as had been her terror. She began to tremble violently. Her hands got back a sense of strength to clutch. Heart and blood seemed released from that ice-banded vise.

"Say, I believe you were scared," went on Glenn, bending over her.

"Scar-ed!" she gasped. "Oh—there's no word—to tell—what I was!"

Flo came running back, giggling with joy. "Glenn, she shore took you for a bear. Why, I felt her go stiff as a post!... Ha! Ha! Ha! Carley, now how do you like the wild and woolly?"

"Oh! You put up a trick on me!" ejaculated Carley. "Glenn, how could you? ... Such a terrible trick! I wouldn't have minded something reasonable. But that! Oh, I'll never forgive you!"

Glenn showed remorse, and kissed her before Flo in a way that made some little amends. "Maybe I overdid it," he said. "But I thought you'd have a momentary start, you know, enough to make you yell, and then you'd see through it. I only had a sheepskin over my shoulders as I crawled on hands and knees."

"Glenn, for me you were a prehistoric monster—a dinosaur, or something," replied Carley.

It developed, upon their return to the campfire circle, that everybody had been in the joke; and they all derived hearty enjoyment from it.

"Reckon that makes you one of us," said Hutter, genially. "We've all had our scares."

Carley wondered if she were not so constituted that such trickery alienated her. Deep in her heart she resented being made to show her cowardice. But then she realized that no one had really seen any evidence of her state. It was fun to them.

Soon after this incident Hutter sounded what he called the roll-call for bed. Following Flo's instructions, Carley sat on their bed, pulled off her boots, folded coat and sweater at her head, and slid down under the blankets. How strange and hard a bed! Yet Carley had the most delicious sense of relief and rest she had ever experienced. She straightened out on her back with a feeling that she had never before appreciated the luxury of lying down.

Flo cuddled up to her in quite sisterly fashion, saying: "Now don't cover your head. If it rains I'll wake and pull up the tarp. Good night, Carley." And almost immediately she seemed to fall asleep.

For Carley, however, sleep did not soon come. She had too many aches; the aftermath of her shock of fright abided with her; and the blackness of night, the cold whip of wind over her face, and the unprotected helplessness she felt in this novel bed, were too entirely new and disturbing to be overcome at once. So she lay wide eyed, staring at the dense gray shadow, at the flickering lights upon the cedar. At length her mind formed a conclusion that this sort of thing might be worth the hardship once in a lifetime, anyway. What a concession to Glenn's West! In the secret seclusion of her mind she had to confess that if her vanity had not been so assaulted and humiliated she might have enjoyed herself more. It seemed impossible, however, to have thrills and pleasures and exaltations in the face of discomfort, privation, and an uneasy half-acknowledged fear. No woman could have either a good or a profitable time when she was at her worst. Carley thought she would not be averse to getting Flo Hutter to New York, into an atmosphere wholly strange and difficult, and see how she met situation after situation unfamiliar to her. And so Carley's mind drifted on until at last she succumbed to drowsiness.

A voice pierced her dreams of home, of warmth and comfort. Something sharp, cold, and fragrant was scratching her eyes. She opened them. Glenn stood over her, pushing a sprig of cedar into her face.

"Carley, the day is far spent," he said, gayly. "We want to roll up your bedding. Will you get out of it?"

"Hello, Glenn! What time is it?" she replied.

"It's nearly six."

"What!... Do you expect me to get up at that ungodly hour?"

"We're all up. Flo's eating breakfast. It's going to be a bad day, I'm afraid. And we want to get packed and moving before it starts to rain."

"Why do girls leave home?" she asked, tragically.

"To make poor devils happy, of course," he replied, smiling down upon her.

That smile made up to Carley for all the clamoring sensations of stiff, sore muscles. It made her ashamed that she could not fling herself into this adventure with all her heart. Carley essayed to sit up. "Oh, I'm afraid my anatomy has become disconnected!... Glenn, do I look a sight?" She never would have asked him that if she had not known she could bear inspection at such an inopportune moment.

"You look great," he asserted, heartily. "You've got color. And as for your hair—I like to see it mussed that way. You were always one to have it dressed—just so.... Come, Carley, rustle now."

Thus adjured, Carley did her best under adverse circumstances. And she was gritting her teeth and complimenting herself when she arrived at the task of pulling on her boots. They were damp and her feet appeared to have swollen. Moreover, her ankles were sore. But she accomplished getting into them at the expense of much pain and sundry utterances more forcible than elegant. Glenn brought her warm water, a mitigating circumstance. The morning was cold and thought of that biting desert water had been trying.

"Shore you're doing fine," was Flo's greeting. "Come and get it before we throw it out."

Carley made haste to comply with the Western mandate, and was once again confronted with the singular fact that appetite did not wait upon the troubles of a tenderfoot. Glenn remarked that at least she would not starve to death on the trip.

"Come, climb the ridge with me," he invited. "I want you to take a look to the north and east."

He led her off through the cedars, up a slow red-earth slope, away from the lake. A green moundlike eminence topped with flat red rock appeared near at hand and not at all a hard climb.

Nevertheless, her eyes deceived her, as she found to the cost of her breath. It was both far away and high.

"I like this location," said Glenn. "If I had the money I'd buy this section of land—six hundred and forty acres—and make a ranch of it. Just under this bluff is a fine open flat bench for a cabin. You could see away across the desert clear to Sunset Peak. There's a good spring of granite water. I'd run water from the lake down into the lower flats, and I'd sure raise some stock."

"What do you call this place?" asked Carley, curiously.

"Deep Lake. It's only a watering place for sheep and cattle. But there's fine grazing, and it's a wonder to me no one has ever settled here."

Looking down, Carley appreciated his wish to own the place; and immediately there followed in her a desire to get possession of this tract of land before anyone else discovered its advantages, and to hold it for Glenn. But this would surely conflict with her intention of persuading Glenn to go back East. As quickly as her impulse had been born it died.

Suddenly the scene gripped Carley. She looked from near to far, trying to grasp the illusive something. Wild lonely Arizona land! She saw ragged dumpy cedars of gray and green, lines of red earth, and a round space of water, gleaming pale under the lowering clouds; and in the distance isolated hills, strangely curved, wandering away to a black uplift of earth obscured in the sky.

These appeared to be mere steps leading her sight farther and higher to the cloud-navigated sky, where rosy and golden effulgence betokened the sun and the east. Carley held her breath. A transformation was going on before her eyes.

"Carley, it's a stormy sunrise," said Glenn.

His words explained, but they did not convince. Was this sudden-bursting glory only the sun rising behind storm clouds? She could see the clouds moving while they were being colored. The universal gray surrendered under some magic paint brush. The rifts widened, and the gloom of the pale-gray world seemed to vanish. Beyond the billowy, rolling, creamy edges of clouds, white and pink, shone the soft exquisite fresh blue sky. And a blaze of fire, a burst of molten gold, sheered up from behind the rim of cloud and suddenly poured a sea of sunlight from east to west. It transfigured the round foothills. They seemed bathed in ethereal light, and the silver mists that overhung them faded while Carley gazed, and a rosy flush crowned the symmetrical domes. Southward along the horizon line, down-dropping veils of rain, just touched with the sunrise tint, streamed in drifting slow movement from cloud to earth. To the north the range of foothills lifted toward the majestic dome of Sunset Peak, a volcanic upheaval of red and purple cinders, bare as rock, round as the lower hills, and wonderful in its color. Full in the blaze of the rising sun it flaunted an unchangeable front. Carley understood now what had been told her about this peak. Volcanic fires had thrown up a colossal mound of cinders burned forever to the hues of the setting sun. In every light and shade of day it held true to its name. Farther north rose the bold bulk of the San Francisco Peaks, that, half lost in the clouds, still dominated the desert scene. Then as Carley gazed the rifts began to close. Another transformation began, the reverse of what she watched. The golden radiance of sunrise vanished, and under a gray, lowering, coalescing pall of cloud the round hills returned to their bleak somberness, and the green desert took again its cold sheen.

"Wasn't it fine, Carley?" asked Glenn. "But nothing to what you will experience. I hope you stay till the weather gets warm. I want you to see a summer dawn on the Painted Desert, and a noon with the great white clouds rolling up from the horizon, and a sunset of massed purple and gold. If they do not get you then I'll give up."

Carley murmured something of her appreciation of what she had just seen. Part of his remark hung on her ear, thought-provoking and disturbing. He hoped she would stay until summer! That was kind of him. But her visit must be short and she now intended it to end with his return East with her. If she did not persuade him to go he might not want to go for a while, as he had written—"just yet." Carley grew troubled in mind. Such mental disturbance, however, lasted no longer than her return with Glenn to camp, where the mustang Spillbeans stood ready for her to mount. He appeared to put one ear up, the other down, and to look at her with mild surprise, as if to say: "What—hello—tenderfoot! Are you going to ride me again?"

Carley recalled that she had avowed she would ride him. There was no alternative, and her misgivings only made matters worse. Nevertheless, once in the saddle, she imagined she had the hallucination that to ride off so, with the long open miles ahead, was really thrilling. This remarkable state of mind lasted until Spillbeans began to trot, and then another day of misery beckoned to Carley with gray stretches of distance.

She was to learn that misery, as well as bliss, can swallow up the hours. She saw the monotony of cedar trees, but with blurred eyes; she saw the ground clearly enough, for she was always looking down, hoping for sandy places or rocky places where her mustang could not trot.

At noon the cavalcade ahead halted near a cabin and corral, which turned out to be a sheep ranch belonging to Hutter. Here Glenn was so busy that he had no time to devote to Carley. And Flo, who was more at home on a horse than on the ground, rode around everywhere with the men. Most assuredly Carley could not pass by the chance to get off Spillbeans and to walk a little. She found, however, that what she wanted most was to rest. The cabin was deserted, a dark, damp place with a rank odor. She did not stay long inside.

Rain and snow began to fall, adding to what Carley felt to be a disagreeable prospect. The immediate present, however, was cheered by a cup of hot soup and some bread and butter which the herder Charley brought her. By and by Glenn and Hutter returned with Flo, and all partook of some lunch.

All too soon Carley found herself astride the mustang again. Glenn helped her don the slicker, an abominable sticky rubber coat that bundled her up and tangled her feet round the stirrups. She was glad to find, though, that it served well indeed to protect her from raw wind and rain.

"Where do we go from here?" Carley inquired, ironically.

Glenn laughed in a way which proved to Carley that he knew perfectly well how she felt. Again his smile caused her self-reproach. Plain indeed was it that he had really expected more of her in the way of complaint and less of fortitude. Carley bit her lips.

Thus began the afternoon ride. As it advanced the sky grew more threatening, the wind rawer, the cold keener, and the rain cut like little bits of sharp ice. It blew in Carley's face. Enough snow fell to whiten the open patches of ground. In an hour Carley realized that she had the hardest task of her life to ride to the end of the day's journey. No one could have guessed her plight. Glenn complimented her upon her adaptation to such unpleasant conditions. Flo evidently was on the lookout for the tenderfoot's troubles. But as Spillbeans, had taken to lagging at a walk, Carley was enabled to conceal all outward sign of her woes. It rained, hailed, sleeted, snowed, and grew colder all the time. Carley's feet became lumps of ice. Every step the mustang took sent acute pains ramifying from bruised and raw places all over her body.

Once, finding herself behind the others and out of sight in the cedars, she got off to walk awhile, leading the mustang. This would not do, however, because she fell too far in the rear. Mounting again, she rode on, beginning to feel that nothing mattered, that this trip would be the end of Carley Burch. How she hated that dreary, cold, flat land the road bisected without end. It felt as if she rode hours to cover a mile. In open stretches she saw the whole party straggling along, separated from one another, and each for himself. They certainly could not be enjoying themselves. Carley shut her eyes, clutched the pommel of the saddle, trying to support her weight. How could she endure another mile? Alas! there might be many miles. Suddenly a terrible shock seemed to rack her. But it was only that Spillbeans had once again taken to a trot. Frantically she pulled on the bridle. He was not to be thwarted. Opening her eyes, she saw a cabin far ahead which probably was the destination for the night. Carley knew she would never reach it, yet she clung on desperately. What she dreaded was the return of that stablike pain in her side. It came, and life seemed something abject and monstrous. She rode stiff legged, with her hands propping her stiffly above the pommel, but the stabbing pain went right on, and in deeper. When the mustang halted his trot beside the other horses Carley was in the last extremity. Yet as Glenn came to her, offering a hand, she still hid her agony. Then Flo called out gayly: "Carley, you've done twenty-five miles on as rotten a day as I remember. Shore we all hand it to you. And I'm confessing I didn't think you'd ever stay the ride out. Spillbeans is the meanest nag we've got and he has the hardest gait."

CHAPTER V

Later Carley leaned back in a comfortable seat, before a blazing fire that happily sent its acrid smoke up the chimney, pondering ideas in her mind.

There could be a relation to familiar things that was astounding in its revelation. To get off a horse that had tortured her, to discover an almost insatiable appetite, to rest weary, aching body before the genial warmth of a beautiful fire—these were experiences which Carley found to have been hitherto unknown delights. It struck her suddenly and strangely that to know the real truth about anything in life might require infinite experience and understanding. How could one feel immense gratitude and relief, or the delight of satisfying acute hunger, or the sweet comfort of rest, unless there had been circumstances of extreme contrast? She had been compelled to suffer cruelly on horseback in order to make her appreciate how good it was to get down on the ground. Otherwise she never would have known. She wondered, then, how true that principle might be in all experience. It gave strong food for thought. There were things in the world never before dreamed of in her philosophy.

Carley was wondering if she were narrow and dense to circumstances of life differing from her own when a remark of Flo's gave pause to her reflections.

"Shore the worst is yet to come." Flo had drawled.

Carley wondered if this distressing statement had to do in some way with the rest of the trip. She stifled her curiosity. Painful knowledge of that sort would come quickly enough.

"Flo, are you girls going to sleep here in the cabin?" inquired Glenn.

"Shore. It's cold and wet outside," replied Flo.

"Well, Felix, the Mexican herder, told me some Navajos had been bunking here."

"Navajos? You mean Indians?" interposed Carley, with interest.

"Shore do," said Flo. "I knew that. But don't mind Glenn. He's full of tricks, Carley. He'd give us a hunch to lie out in the wet."

Hutter burst into his hearty laugh. "Wal, I'd rather get some things any day than a bad cold."

"Shore I've had both," replied Flo, in her easy drawl, "and I'd prefer the cold. But for Carley's sake—"

"Pray don't consider me," said Carley. The rather crude drift of the conversation affronted her.

"Well, my dear," put in Glenn, "it's a bad night outside. We'll all make our beds here."

"Glenn, you shore are a nervy fellow," drawled Flo.

Long after everybody was in bed Carley lay awake in the blackness of the cabin, sensitively fidgeting and quivering over imaginative contact with creeping things. The fire had died out. A cold air passed through the room. On the roof pattered gusts of rain. Carley heard a rustling of mice. It did not seem possible that she could keep awake, yet she strove to do so. But her pangs of body, her extreme fatigue soon yielded to the quiet and rest of her bed, engendering a drowsiness that proved irresistible.

Morning brought fair weather and sunshine, which helped to sustain Carley in her effort to brave out her pains and woes. Another disagreeable day would have forced her to humiliating defeat. Fortunately for her, the business of the men was concerned with the immediate neighborhood, in which they expected to stay all morning.

"Flo, after a while persuade Carley to ride with you to the top of this first foothill," said Glenn. "It's not far, and it's worth a good deal to see the Painted Desert from there. The day is clear and the air free from dust."

"Shore. Leave it to me. I want to get out of camp, anyhow. That conceited hombre, Lee Stanton, will be riding in here," answered Flo, laconically.

The slight knowing smile on Glenn's face and the grinning disbelief on Mr. Hutter's were facts not lost upon Carley. And when Charley, the herder, deliberately winked at Carley, she conceived the idea that Flo, like many women, only ran off to be pursued. In some manner Carley did not seek to analyze, the purported advent of this Lee Stanton pleased her. But she did admit to her consciousness that women, herself included, were both as deep and mysterious as the sea, yet as transparent as an inch of crystal water.

It happened that the expected newcomer rode into camp before anyone left. Before he dismounted he made a good impression on Carley, and as he stepped down in lazy, graceful action, a tall lithe figure, she thought him singularly handsome. He wore black sombrero, flannel shirt, blue jeans stuffed into high boots, and long, big-roweled spurs.

"How are you-all?" was his greeting.

From the talk that ensued between him and the men, Carley concluded that he must be overseer of the sheep hands. Carley knew that Hutter and Glenn were not interested in cattle raising. And in fact they were, especially Hutter, somewhat inimical to the dominance of the range land by cattle barons of Flagstaff.

"When's Ryan goin' to dip?" asked Hutter.

"Today or tomorrow," replied Stanton.

"Reckon we ought to ride over," went on Hutter. "Say, Glenn, do you reckon Miss Carley could stand a sheep-dip?"

This was spoken in a low tone, scarcely intended for Carley, but she had keen ears and heard distinctly. Not improbably this sheep-dip was what Flo meant as the worst to come. Carley adopted a listless posture to hide her keen desire to hear what Glenn would reply to Hutter.

"I should say not!" whispered Glenn, fiercely.

"Cut out that talk. She'll hear you and want to go."

Whereupon Carley felt mount in her breast an intense and rebellious determination to see a sheep-dip. She would astonish Glenn. What did he want, anyway? Had she not withstood the torturing trot of the hardest-gaited horse on the range? Carley realized she was going to place considerable store upon that feat. It grew on her.

When the consultation of the men ended, Lee Stanton turned to Flo. And Carley did not need to see the young man look twice to divine what ailed him. He was caught in the toils of love. But seeing through Flo Hutter was entirely another matter.

"Howdy, Lee!" she said, coolly, with her clear eyes on him. A tiny frown knitted her brow. She did not, at the moment, entirely approve of him.

"Shore am glad to see you, Flo," he said, with rather a heavy expulsion of breath. He wore a cheerful grin that in no wise deceived Flo, or Carley either. The young man had a furtive expression of eye.

"Ahuh!" returned Flo.

"I was shore sorry about—about that—" he floundered, in low voice.

"About what?"

"Aw, you know, Flo."

Carley strolled out of hearing, sure of two things—that she felt rather sorry for Stanton, and that his course of love did not augur well for smooth running. What queer creatures were women! Carley had seen several million coquettes, she believed; and assuredly Flo Hutter belonged to the species.

Upon Carley's return to the cabin she found Stanton and Flo waiting for her to accompany them on a ride up the foothill. She was so stiff and sore that she could hardly mount into the saddle; and the first mile of riding was something like a nightmare. She lagged behind Flo and Stanton, who apparently forgot her in their quarrel.

The riders soon struck the base of a long incline of rocky ground that led up to the slope of the foothill. Here rocks and gravel gave place to black cinders out of which grew a scant bleached grass. This desert verdure was what lent the soft gray shade to the foothill when seen from a distance. The slope was gentle, so that the ascent did not entail any hardship. Carley was amazed at the length of the slope, and also to see how high over the desert she was getting. She felt lifted out of a monotonous level. A green-gray league-long cedar forest extended down toward Oak Creek. Behind her the magnificent bulk of the mountains reached up into the stormy clouds, showing white slopes of snow under the gray pall.

The hoofs of the horses sank in the cinders. A fine choking dust assailed Carley's nostrils. Presently, when there appeared at least a third of the ascent still to be accomplished and Flo dismounted to walk, leading their horses. Carley had no choice but to do likewise. At first walking was a relief. Soon, however, the soft yielding cinders began to drag at her feet. At every step she slipped back a few inches, a very annoying feature of climbing. When her legs seemed to grow dead Carley paused for a little rest. The last of the ascent, over a few hundred yards of looser cinders, taxed her remaining strength to the limit. She grew hot and wet and out of breath. Her heart labored. An unreasonable antipathy seemed to attend her efforts. Only her ridiculous vanity held her to this task. She wanted to please Glenn, but not so earnestly that she would have kept on plodding up this ghastly bare mound of cinders. Carley did not mind being a tenderfoot, but she hated the thought of these Westerners considering her a weakling. So she bore the pain of raw blisters and the miserable sensation of staggering on under a leaden weight.

Several times she noted that Flo and Stanton halted to face each other in rather heated argument. At least Stanton's red face and forceful gestures attested to heat on his part. Flo evidently was weary of argument, and in answer to a sharp reproach she retorted, "Shore I was different after he came." To which Stanton responded by a quick passionate shrinking as if he had been stung.

Carley had her own reaction to this speech she could not help hearing; and inwardly, at least, her feeling must have been similar to Stanton's. She forgot the object of this climb and looked off to her right at the green level without really seeing it. A vague sadness weighed upon her soul. Was there to be a tangle of fates here, a conflict of wills, a crossing of loves? Flo's terse confession could not be taken lightly. Did she mean that she loved Glenn? Carley began to fear it. Only another reason why she must persuade Glenn to go back East! But the closer Carley came to what she divined must be an ordeal the more she dreaded it. This raw, crude West might have confronted her with a situation beyond her control. And as she dragged her weighted feet through the cinders, kicking, up little puffs of black dust, she felt what she admitted to be an unreasonable resentment toward these Westerners and their barren, isolated, and boundless world.

"Carley," called Flo, "come—looksee, as the Indians say. Here is Glenn's Painted Desert, and I reckon it's shore worth seeing."

To Carley's surprise, she found herself upon the knob of the foothill. And when she looked out across a suddenly distinguishable void she seemed struck by the immensity of something she was unable to grasp. She dropped her bridle; she gazed slowly, as if drawn, hearing Flo's voice.

"That thin green line of cottonwoods down there is the Little Colorado River," Flo was saying. "Reckon it's sixty miles, all down hill. The Painted Desert begins there and also the Navajo Reservation. You see the white strips, the red veins, the yellow bars, the black lines. They are all desert steps leading up and up for miles. That sharp black peak is called Wildcat. It's about a hundred miles. You see the desert stretching away to the right, growing dim—lost in distance? We don't know that country. But that north country we know as landmarks, anyway. Look at that saw-tooth range. The Indians call it Echo Cliffs. At the far end it drops off into the Colorado River. Lee's Ferry is there—about one hundred and sixty miles. That ragged black rent is the Grand Canyon. Looks like a thread, doesn't it? But Carley, it's some hole, believe me. Away to the left you see the tremendous wall rising and turning to come this way. That's the north wall of the Canyon. It ends at the great bluff—Greenland Point. See the black fringe above the bar of gold. That's a belt of pine trees. It's about eighty miles across this ragged old stone washboard of a desert. ... Now turn and look straight and strain your sight over Wildcat. See the rim purple dome. You must look hard. I'm glad it's clear and the sun is shining. We don't often get this view.... That purple dome is Navajo Mountain, two hundred miles and more away!"

Carley yielded to some strange drawing power and slowly walked forward until she stood at the extreme edge of the summit.

What was it that confounded her sight? Desert slope—down and down—color—distance—space! The wind that blew in her face seemed to have the openness of the whole world back of it. Cold, sweet, dry, exhilarating, it breathed of untainted vastness. Carley's memory pictures of the Adirondacks faded into pastorals; her vaunted images of European scenery changed to operetta settings. She had nothing with which to compare this illimitable space.

"Oh!—America!" was her unconscious tribute.

Stanton and Flo had come on to places beside her. The young man laughed. "Wal, now Miss Carley, you couldn't say more. When I was in camp trainin' for service overseas I used to remember how this looked. An' it seemed one of the things I was goin' to fight for. Reckon I didn't the idea of the Germans havin' my Painted Desert. I didn't get across to fight for it, but I shore was willin'."

"You see, Carley, this is our America," said Flo, softly.

Carley had never understood the meaning of the word. The immensity of the West seemed flung at her. What her vision beheld, so far-reaching and boundless, was only a dot on the map.

"Does any one live—out there?" she asked, with slow sweep of hand.

"A few white traders and some Indian tribes," replied Stanton. "But you can ride all day an' next day an' never see a livin' soul."

What was the meaning of the gratification in his voice? Did Westerners court loneliness? Carley wrenched her gaze from the desert void to look at her companions. Stanton's eyes were narrowed; his expression had changed; lean and hard and still, his face resembled bronze. The careless humor was gone, as was the heated flush of his quarrel with Flo. The girl, too, had subtly changed, had responded to an influence that had subdued and softened her. She was mute; her eyes held a light, comprehensive and all-embracing; she was beautiful then. For Carley, quick to read emotion, caught a glimpse of a strong, steadfast soul that spiritualized the brown freckled face.

Carley wheeled to gaze out and down into this incomprehensible abyss, and on to the far up-flung heights, white and red and yellow, and so on to the wonderful mystic haze of distance. The significance of Flo's designation of miles could not be grasped by Carley. She could not estimate distance. But she did not need that to realize her perceptions were swallowed up by magnitude. Hitherto the power of her eyes had been unknown. How splendid to see afar! She could see— yes—but what did she see? Space first, annihilating space, dwarfing her preconceived images, and then wondrous colors! What had she known of color? No wonder artists failed adequately and truly to paint mountains, let alone the desert space. The toiling millions of the crowded cities were ignorant of this terrible beauty and sublimity. Would it have helped them to see? But just to breathe that untainted air, just to see once the boundless open of colored sand and rock—to realize what the freedom of eagles meant would not that have helped anyone?

And with the thought there came to Carley's quickened and struggling mind a conception of freedom. She had not yet watched eagles, but she now gazed out into their domain. What then must be the effect of such environment on people whom it encompassed? The idea stunned Carley. Would such people grow in proportion to the nature with which they were in conflict? Hereditary influence could not be comparable to such environment in the shaping of character.

"Shore I could stand here all day," said Flo. "But it's beginning to cloud over and this high wind is cold. So we'd better go, Carley."

"I don't know what I am, but it's not cold," replied Carley.

"Wal, Miss Carley, I reckon you'll have to come again an' again before you get a comfortable feelin' here," said Stanton.

It surprised Carley to see that this young Westerner had hit upon the truth. He understood her. Indeed she was uncomfortable. She was oppressed, vaguely unhappy. But why? The thing there—the infinitude of open sand and rock—was beautiful, wonderful, even glorious. She looked again.

Steep black-cindered slope, with its soft gray patches of grass, sheered down and down, and out in rolling slope to merge upon a cedar-dotted level. Nothing moved below, but a red-tailed hawk sailed across her vision. How still—how gray the desert floor as it reached away, losing its black dots, and gaining bronze spots of stone! By plain and prairie it fell away, each inch of gray in her sight magnifying into its league-long roll. On and on, and down across dark lines that were steppes, and at last blocked and changed by the meandering green thread which was the verdure of a desert river. Beyond stretched the white sand, where whirlwinds of dust sent aloft their funnel-shaped spouts; and it led up to the horizon-wide ribs and ridges of red and walls of yellow and mountains of black, to the dim mound of purple so ethereal and mystic against the deep-blue cloud-curtained band of sky.

And on the moment the sun was obscured and that world of colorful flame went out, as if a blaze had died.

Deprived of its fire, the desert seemed to retreat, to fade coldly and gloomily, to lose its great landmarks in dim obscurity. Closer, around to the north, the canyon country yawned with innumerable gray jaws, ragged and hard, and the riven earth took on a different character. It had no shadows. It grew flat and, like the sea, seemed to mirror the vast gray cloud expanse. The sublime vanished, but the desolate remained. No warmth—no movement—no life! Dead stone it was, cut into a million ruts by ruthless ages. Carley felt that she was gazing down into chaos.

At this moment, as before, a hawk had crossed her vision, so now a raven sailed by, black as coal, uttering a hoarse croak.

"Quoth the raven—" murmured Carley, with a half-bitter laugh, as she turned away shuddering in spite of an effort of self-control. "Maybe he meant this wonderful and terrible West is never for such as I.... Come, let us go."

Carley rode all that afternoon in the rear of the caravan, gradually succumbing to the cold raw wind and the aches and pains to which she had subjected her flesh. Nevertheless, she finished the day's journey, and, sorely as she needed Glenn's kindly hand, she got off her horse without aid.

Camp was made at the edge of the devastated timber zone that Carley had found so dispiriting. A few melancholy pines were standing, and everywhere, as far as she could see southward, were blackened fallen trees and stumps. It was a dreary scene. The few cattle grazing on the bleached grass appeared as melancholy as the pines. The sun shone fitfully at sunset, and then sank, leaving the land to twilight and shadows.

Once in a comfortable seat beside the camp fire, Carley had no further desire to move. She was so far exhausted and weary that she could no longer appreciate the blessing of rest. Appetite, too, failed her this meal time. Darkness soon settled down. The wind moaned through the pines. She was indeed glad to crawl into bed, and not even the thought of skunks could keep her awake.

Morning disclosed the fact that gray clouds had been blown away. The sun shone bright upon a white-frosted land. The air was still. Carley labored at her task of rising, and brushing her hair, and pulling on her boots; and it appeared her former sufferings were as naught compared with the pangs of this morning. How she hated the cold, the bleak, denuded forest land, the emptiness, the roughness, the crudeness! If this sort of feeling grew any worse she thought she would hate Glenn. Yet she was nonetheless set upon going on, and seeing the sheep-dip, and riding that fiendish mustang until the trip was ended.

Getting in the saddle and on the way this morning was an ordeal that made Carley actually sick. Glenn and Flo both saw how it was with her, and they left her to herself. Carley was grateful for this understanding. It seemed to proclaim their respect. She found further matter for satisfaction in the astonishing circumstance that after the first dreadful quarter of an hour in the saddle she began to feel easier. And at the end of several hours of riding she was not suffering any particular pain, though she was weaker.

At length the cut-over land ended in a forest of straggling pines, through which the road wound southward, and eventually down into a wide shallow canyon. Through the trees Carley saw a stream of water, open fields of green, log fences and cabins, and blue smoke. She heard the chug of a gasoline engine and the baa-baa of sheep. Glenn waited for her to catch up with him, and he said: "Carley, this is one of Hutter's sheep camps. It's not a—a very pleasant place. You won't care to see the sheep-dip. So I'm suggesting you wait here—"

"Nothing doing, Glenn," she interrupted. "I'm going to see what there is to see."

"But, dear—the men—the way they handle sheep—they'll—really it's no sight for you," he floundered.

"Why not?" she inquired, eying him.

"Because, Carley—you know how you hate the—the seamy side of things. And the stench—why, it'll make you sick!"

"Glenn, be on the level," she said. "Suppose it does. Wouldn't you think more of me if I could stand it?"

"Why, yes," he replied, reluctantly, smiling at her, "I would. But I wanted to spare you. This trip has been hard. I'm sure proud of you. And, Carley—you can overdo it. Spunk is not everything. You simply couldn't stand this."

"Glenn, how little you know a woman!" she exclaimed. "Come along and show me your old sheep-dip."

They rode out of the woods into an open valley that might have been picturesque if it had not been despoiled by the work of man. A log fence ran along the edge of open ground and a mud dam held back a pool of stagnant water, slimy and green. As Carley rode on the baa-baa of sheep became so loud that she could scarcely hear Glenn talking.

Several log cabins, rough hewn and gray with age, stood down inside the inclosure; and beyond there were large corrals. From the other side of these corrals came sounds of rough voices of men, a trampling of hoofs, heavy splashes, the beat of an engine, and the incessant baaing of the sheep.

At this point the members of Hutter's party dismounted and tied their horses to the top log of the fence. When Carley essayed to get off Glenn tried to stop her, saying she could see well enough from there. But Carley got down and followed Flo. She heard Hutter call to Glenn: "Say, Ryan is short of men. We'll lend a hand for a couple of hours."

Presently Carley reached Flo's side and the first corral that contained sheep. They formed a compact woolly mass, rather white in color, with a tinge of pink. When Flo climbed up on the fence the flock plunged as one animal and with a trampling roar ran to the far side of the corral. Several old rams with wide curling horns faced around; and some of the ewes climbed up on the densely packed mass. Carley rather enjoyed watching them. She surely could not see anything amiss in this sight.

The next corral held a like number of sheep, and also several Mexicans who were evidently driving them into a narrow lane that led farther down. Carley saw the heads of men above other corral fences, and there was also a thick yellowish smoke rising from somewhere.

"Carley, are you game to see the dip?" asked Flo, with good nature that yet had a touch of taunt in it.

"That's my middle name," retorted Carley, flippantly.

Both Glenn and this girl seemed to be bent upon bringing out Carley's worst side, and they were succeeding. Flo laughed. The ready slang pleased her.

She led Carley along that log fence, through a huge open gate, and across a wide pen to another fence, which she scaled. Carley followed her, not particularly overanxious to look ahead. Some thick odor had begun to reach Carley's delicate nostrils. Flo led down a short lane and climbed another fence, and sat astride the top log. Carley hurried along to clamber up to her side, but stood erect with her feet on the second log of the fence.

Then a horrible stench struck Carley almost like a blow in the face, and before her confused sight there appeared to be drifting smoke and active men and running sheep, all against a background of mud. But at first it was the odor that caused Carley to close her eyes and press her knees hard against the upper log to keep from reeling. Never in her life had such a sickening nausea assailed her. It appeared to attack her whole body. The forerunning qualm of seasickness was as nothing to this. Carley gave a gasp, pinched her nose between her fingers so she could not smell, and opened her eyes.

Directly beneath her was a small pen open at one end into which sheep were being driven from the larger corral. The drivers were yelling. The sheep in the rear plunged into those ahead of them, forcing them on. Two men worked in this small pen. One was a brawny giant in undershirt and overalls that appeared filthy. He held a cloth in his hand and strode toward the nearest sheep. Folding the cloth round the neck of the sheep, he dragged it forward, with an ease which showed great strength, and threw it into a pit that yawned at the side. Souse went the sheep into a murky, muddy pool and disappeared. But suddenly its head came up and then its shoulders. And it began half to walk and half swim down what appeared to be a narrow boxlike ditch that contained other floundering sheep. Then Carley saw men on each side of this ditch bending over with poles that had crooks at the end, and their work was to press and pull the sheep along to the end of the ditch, and drive them up a boarded incline into another corral where many other sheep huddled, now a dirty muddy color like the liquid into which they had been emersed. Souse! Splash! In went sheep after sheep. Occasionally one did not go under. And then a man would press it under with the crook and quickly lift its head. The work went on with precision and speed, in spite of the yells and trampling and baa-baas, and the incessant action that gave an effect of confusion.

Carley saw a pipe leading from a huge boiler to the ditch. The dark fluid was running out of it. From a rusty old engine with big smokestack poured the strangling smoke. A man broke open a sack of yellow powder and dumped it into the ditch. Then he poured an acid-like liquid after it.

"Sulphur and nicotine," yelled Flo up at Carley. "The dip's poison. If a sheep opens his mouth he's usually a goner. But sometimes they save one."

Carley wanted to tear herself away from this disgusting spectacle. But it held her by some fascination. She saw Glenn and Hutter fall in line with the other men, and work like beavers. These two pacemakers in the small pen kept the sheep coming so fast that every worker below had a task cut out for him. Suddenly Flo squealed and pointed.

"There! that sheep didn't come up," she cried. "Shore he opened his mouth."

Then Carley saw Glenn energetically plunge his hooked pole in and out and around until he had located the submerged sheep. He lifted its head above the dip. The sheep showed no sign of life. Down on his knees dropped Glenn, to reach the sheep with strong brown hands, and to haul it up on the ground, where it flopped inert. Glenn pummeled it and pressed it, and worked on it much as Carley had seen a life-guard work over a half-drowned man. But the sheep did not respond to Glenn's active administrations.

"No use, Glenn," yelled Hutter, hoarsely. "That one's a goner."

Carley did not fail to note the state of Glenn's hands and arms and overalls when he returned to the ditch work. Then back and forth Carley's gaze went from one end to the other of that scene. And suddenly it was arrested and held by the huge fellow who handled the sheep so brutally. Every time he dragged one and threw it into the pit he yelled: "Ho! Ho!" Carley was impelled to look at his face, and she was amazed to meet the rawest and boldest stare from evil eyes that had ever been her misfortune to incite. She felt herself stiffen with a shock that was unfamiliar. This man was scarcely many years older than Glenn, yet he had grizzled hair, a seamed and scarred visage, coarse, thick lips, and beetling brows, from under which peered gleaming light eyes. At every turn he flashed them upon Carley's face, her neck, the swell of her bosom. It was instinct that caused her hastily to close her riding coat. She felt as if her flesh had been burned. Like a snake he fascinated her. The intelligence in his bold gaze made the beastliness of it all the harder to endure, all the stronger to arouse.

"Come, Carley, let's rustle out of this stinkin' mess," cried Flo.

Indeed, Carley needed Flo's assistance in clambering down out of the choking smoke and horrid odor.

"Adios, pretty eyes," called the big man from the pen.

"Well," ejaculated Flo, when they got out, "I'll bet I call Glenn good and hard for letting you go down there."

"It was—my—fault," panted Carley. "I said I'd stand it."

"Oh, you're game, all right. I didn't mean the dip.... That sheep-slinger is Haze Ruff, the toughest hombre on this range. Shore, now, wouldn't I like to take a shot at him?... I'm going to tell dad and Glenn."

"Please don't," returned Carley, appealingly.

"I shore am. Dad needs hands these days. That's why he's lenient. But Glenn will cowhide Ruff and I want to see him do it."

In Flo Hutter then Carley saw another and a different spirit of the West, a violence unrestrained and fierce that showed in the girl's even voice and in the piercing light of her eyes.

They went back to the horses, got their lunches from the saddlebags, and, finding comfortable seats in a sunny, protected place, they ate and talked. Carley had to force herself to swallow. It seemed that the horrid odor of dip and sheep had permeated everything. Glenn had known her better than she had known herself, and he had wished to spare her an unnecessary and disgusting experience. Yet so stubborn was Carley that she did not regret going through with it.

"Carley, I don't mind telling you that you've stuck it out better than any tenderfoot we ever had here," said Flo.

"Thank you. That from a Western girl is a compliment I'll not soon forget," replied Carley.

"I shore mean it. We've had rotten weather. And to end the little trip at this sheep-dip hole! Why, Glenn certainly wanted you to stack up against the real thing!"

"Flo, he did not want me to come on the trip, and especially here," protested Carley.

"Shore I know. But he let you."

"Neither Glenn nor any other man could prevent me from doing what I wanted to do."

"Well, if you'll excuse me," drawled Flo, "I'll differ with you. I reckon Glenn Kilbourne is not the man you knew before the war."

"No, he is not. But that does not alter the case."

"Carley, we're not well acquainted," went on Flo, more carefully feeling her way, "and I'm not your kind. I don't know your Eastern ways. But I know what the West does to a man. The war ruined your friend—both his body and mind.... How sorry mother and I were for Glenn, those days when it looked he'd sure 'go west,' for good!... Did you know he'd been gassed and that he had five hemorrhages?"

"Oh! I knew his lungs had been weakened by gas. But he never told me about having hemorrhages."

"Well, he shore had them. The last one I'll never forget. Every time he'd cough it would fetch the blood. I could tell!... Oh, it was awful. I begged him not to cough. He smiled—like a ghost smiling—and he whispered, 'I'll quit.'... And he did. The doctor came from Flagstaff and packed him in ice. Glenn sat propped up all night and never moved a muscle. Never coughed again! And the bleeding stopped. After that we put him out on the porch where he could breathe fresh air all the time. There's something wonderfully healing in Arizona air. It's from the dry desert and here it's full of cedar and pine. Anyway Glenn got well. And I think the West has cured his mind, too."

"Of what?" queried Carley, in an intense curiosity she could scarcely hide.

"Oh, God only knows!" exclaimed Flo, throwing up her gloved hands. "I never could understand. But I hated what the war did to him."

Carley leaned back against the log, quite spent. Flo was unwittingly torturing her. Carley wanted passionately to give in to jealousy of this Western girl, but she could not do it. Flo Hutter deserved better than that. And Carley's baser nature seemed in conflict with all that was noble in her. The victory did not yet go to either side. This was a bad hour for Carley. Her strength had about played out, and her spirit was at low ebb.

"Carley, you're all in," declared Flo. "You needn't deny it. I'm shore you've made good with me as a tenderfoot who stayed the limit. But there's no sense in your killing yourself, nor in me letting you. So I'm going to tell dad we want to go home."

She left Carley there. The word home had struck strangely into Carley's mind and remained there. Suddenly she realized what it was to be homesick. The comfort, the ease, the luxury, the rest, the sweetness, the pleasure, the cleanliness, the gratification to eye and ear—to all the senses—how these thoughts came to haunt her! All of Carley's will power had been needed to sustain her on this trip to keep her from miserably failing. She had not failed. But contact with the West had affronted, disgusted, shocked, and alienated her. In that moment she could not be fair minded; she knew it; she did not care.

Carley gazed around her. Only one of the cabins was in sight from this position. Evidently it was a home for some of these men. On one side the peaked rough roof had been built out beyond the wall, evidently to serve as a kind of porch. On that wall hung the motliest assortment of things Carley had ever seen—utensils, sheep and cow hides, saddles, harness, leather clothes, ropes, old sombreros, shovels, stove pipe, and many other articles for which she could find no name. The most striking characteristic manifest in this collection was that of service. How they had been used! They had enabled people to live under primitive conditions. Somehow this fact inhibited Carley's sense of repulsion at their rude and uncouth appearance. Had any of her forefathers ever been pioneers? Carley did not know, but the thought was disturbing. It was thought-provoking. Many times at home, when she was dressing for dinner, she had gazed into the mirror at the graceful lines of her throat and arms, at the proud poise of her head, at the alabaster whiteness of her skin, and wonderingly she had asked of her image: "Can it be possible that I am a descendant of cavemen?" She had never been able to realize it, yet she knew it was true. Perhaps somewhere not far back along her line there had been a great-great-grandmother who had lived some kind of a primitive life, using such implements and necessaries as hung on this cabin wall, and thereby helped some man to conquer the wilderness, to live in it, and reproduce his kind. Like flashes Glenn's words came back to Carley—"Work and children!"

Some interpretation of his meaning and how it related to this hour held aloof from Carley. If she would ever be big enough to understand it and broad enough to accept it the time was far distant. Just now she was sore and sick physically, and therefore certainly not in a receptive state of mind. Yet how could she have keener impressions than these she was receiving? It was all a problem. She grew tired of thinking. But even then her mind pondered on, a stream of consciousness over which she had no control. This dreary woods was deserted. No birds, no squirrels, no creatures such as fancy anticipated! In another direction, across the canyon, she saw cattle, gaunt, ragged, lumbering, and stolid. And on the moment the scent of sheep came on the breeze. Time seemed to stand still here, and what Carley wanted most was for the hours and days to fly, so that she would be home again.

At last Flo returned with the men. One quick glance at Glenn convinced Carley that Flo had not yet told him about the sheep dipper, Haze Ruff.

"Carley, you're a real sport," declared Glenn, with the rare smile she loved. "It's a dreadful mess. And to think you stood it!... Why, old Fifth Avenue, if you needed to make another hit with me you've done it!"

His warmth amazed and pleased Carley. She could not quite understand why it would have made any difference to him whether she had stood the ordeal or not. But then every day she seemed to drift a little farther from a real understanding of her lover. His praise gladdened her, and fortified her to face the rest of this ride back to Oak Creek.

Four hours later, in a twilight so shadowy that no one saw her distress, Carley half slipped and half fell from her horse and managed somehow to mount the steps and enter the bright living room. A cheerful red fire blazed on the hearth; Glenn's hound, Moze, trembled eagerly at sight of her and looked up with humble dark eyes; the white-clothed dinner table steamed with savory dishes. Flo stood before the blaze, warming her hands. Lee Stanton leaned against the mantel, with eyes on her, and every line of his lean, hard face expressed his devotion to her. Hutter was taking his seat at the head of the table. "Come an' get it—you-all," he called, heartily. Mrs. Hutter's face beamed with the spirit of that home. And lastly, Carley saw Glenn waiting for her, watching her come, true in this very moment to his stern hope for her and pride in her, as she dragged her weary, spent body toward him and the bright fire.

By these signs, or the effect of them, Carley vaguely realized that she was incalculably changing, that this Carley Burch had become a vastly bigger person in the sight of her friends, and strangely in her own a lesser creature.

CHAPTER VI

If spring came at all to Oak Creek Canyon it warmed into summer before Carley had time to languish with the fever characteristic of early June in the East.

As if by magic it seemed the green grass sprang up, the green buds opened into leaves, the bluebells and primroses bloomed, the apple and peach blossoms burst exquisitely white and pink against the blue sky. Oak Creek fell to a transparent, beautiful brook, leisurely eddying in the stone walled nooks, hurrying with murmur and babble over the little falls. The mornings broke clear and fragrantly cool, the noon hours seemed to lag under a hot sun, the nights fell like dark mantles from the melancholy star-sown sky.

Carley had stubbornly kept on riding and climbing until she killed her secret doubt that she was really a thoroughbred, until she satisfied her own insistent vanity that she could train to a point where this outdoor life was not too much for her strength. She lost flesh despite increase of appetite; she lost her pallor for a complexion of gold-brown she knew her Eastern friends would admire; she wore out the blisters and aches and pains; she found herself growing firmer of muscle, lither of line, deeper of chest. And in addition to these physical manifestations there were subtle intimations of a delight in a freedom of body she had never before known, of an exhilaration in action that made her hot and made her breathe, of a sloughing off of numberless petty and fussy and luxurious little superficialities which she had supposed were necessary to her happiness. What she had undertaken in vain conquest of Glenn's pride and Flo Hutter's Western tolerance she had found to be a boomerang. She had won Glenn's admiration; she had won the Western girl's recognition. But her passionate, stubborn desire had been ignoble, and was proved so by the rebound of her achievement, coming home to her with a sweetness she had not the courage to accept. She forced it from her. This West with its rawness, its ruggedness, she hated.

Nevertheless, the June days passed, growing dreamily swift, growing more incomprehensibly full; and still she had not broached to Glenn the main object of her visit—to take him back East. Yet a little while longer! She hated his work and had not talked of that. Yet an honest consciousness told her that as time flew by she feared more and more to tell him that he was wasting his life there and that she could not bear it. Still was he wasting it? Once in a while a timid and unfamiliar Carley Burch voiced a pregnant query. Perhaps what held Carley back most was the happiness she achieved in her walks and rides with Glenn. She lingered because of them. Every day she loved him more, and yet—there was something. Was it in her or in him? She had a woman's assurance of his love and sometimes she caught her breath—so sweet and strong was the tumultuous emotion it stirred. She preferred to enjoy while she could, to dream instead of think. But it was not possible to hold a blank, dreamy, lulled consciousness all the time. Thought would return. And not always could she drive away a feeling that Glenn would never be her slave. She divined something in his mind that kept him gentle and kindly, restrained always, sometimes melancholy and aloof, as if he were an impassive destiny waiting for the iron consequences he knew inevitably must fall. What was this that he knew which she did not know? The idea haunted her. Perhaps it was that which compelled her to use all her woman's wiles and

226

charms on Glenn. Still, though it thrilled her to see she made him love her more as the days passed, she could not blind herself to the truth that no softness or allurement of hers changed this strange restraint in him. How that baffled her! Was it resistance or knowledge or nobility or doubt?

Flo Hutter's twentieth birthday came along the middle of June, and all the neighbors and range hands for miles around were invited to celebrate it.

For the second time during her visit Carley put on the white gown that had made Flo gasp with delight, and had stunned Mrs. Hutter, and had brought a reluctant compliment from Glenn. Carley liked to create a sensation. What were exquisite and expensive gowns for, if not that?

It was twilight on this particular June night when she was ready to go downstairs, and she tarried a while on the long porch. The evening star, so lonely and radiant, so cold and passionless in the dusky blue, had become an object she waited for and watched, the same as she had come to love the dreaming, murmuring melody of the waterfall. She lingered there. What had the sights and sounds and smells of this wild canyon come to mean to her? She could not say. But they had changed her immeasurably.

Her soft slippers made no sound on the porch, and as she turned the corner of the house, where shadows hovered thick, she heard Lee Stanton's voice:

"But, Flo, you loved me before Kilbourne came."

The content, the pathos, of his voice chained Carley to the spot. Some situations, like fate, were beyond resisting.

"Shore I did," replied Flo, dreamily. This was the voice of a girl who was being confronted by happy and sad thoughts on her birthday.

"Don't you—love me—still?" he asked, huskily.

"Why, of course, Lee! I don't change," she said.

"But then, why—" There for the moment his utterance or courage failed.

"Lee, do you want the honest to God's truth?"

"I reckon—I do."

"Well, I love you just as I always did," replied Flo, earnestly. "But, Lee, I love him more than you or anybody."

"My Heaven! Flo—you'll ruin us all!" he exclaimed, hoarsely.

"No, I won't either. You can't say I'm not level headed. I hated to tell you this, Lee, but you made me."

"Flo, you love me an' him—two men?" queried Stanton, incredulously.

"I shore do," she drawled, with a soft laugh. "And it's no fun."

"Reckon I don't cut much of a figure alongside Kilbourne," said Stanton, disconsolately.

"Lee, you could stand alongside any man," replied Flo, eloquently. "You're Western, and you're steady and loyal, and you'll—well, some day you'll be like dad. Could I say more?... But, Lee, this man is different. He is wonderful. I can't explain it, but I feel it. He has been through hell's fire. Oh! will I ever forget his ravings when he lay so ill? He means more to me than just one man. He's American. You're American, too, Lee, and you trained to be a soldier, and you would have made a grand one—if I know old Arizona. But you were not called to France.... Glenn Kilbourne went. God only knows what that means. But he went. And there's the difference. I saw the wreck of him. I did a little to save his life and his mind. I wouldn't be an American girl if I didn't love him.... Oh, Lee, can't you understand?"

"I reckon so. I'm not begrudging Glenn what—what you care. I'm only afraid I'll lose you."

"I never promised to marry you, did I?"

"Not in words. But kisses ought to—?"

"Yes, kisses mean a lot," she replied. "And so far I stand committed. I suppose I'll marry you some day and be blamed lucky. I'll be happy, too—don't you overlook that hunch.... You needn't worry. Glenn is in love with Carley. She's beautiful, rich—and of his class. How could he ever see me?"

"Flo, you can never tell," replied Stanton, thoughtfully. "I didn't like her at first. But I'm comin' round. The thing is, Flo, does she love him as you love him?"

"Oh, I think so—I hope so," answered Flo, as if in distress.

"I'm not so shore. But then I can't savvy her. Lord knows I hope so, too. If she doesn't—if she goes back East an' leaves him here—I reckon my case—"

"Hush! I know she's out here to take him back. Let's go downstairs now."

"Aw, wait—Flo," he begged. "What's your hurry?... Come-give me—"

"There! That's all you get, birthday or no birthday," replied Flo, gayly.

Carley heard the soft kiss and Stanton's deep breath, and then footsteps as they walked away in the gloom toward the stairway. Carley leaned against the log wall. She felt the rough wood—smelled the rusty pine rosin. Her other hand pressed her bosom where her heart beat with unwonted vigor. Footsteps and voices sounded beneath her. Twilight had deepened into night. The low murmur of the waterfall and the babble of the brook floated to her strained ears.

Listeners never heard good of themselves. But Stanton's subtle doubt of any depth to her, though it hurt, was not so conflicting as the ringing truth of Flo Hutter's love for Glenn. This unsought knowledge powerfully affected Carley. She was forewarned and forearmed now. It saddened her, yet did not lessen her confidence in her hold on Glenn. But it stirred to perplexing pitch her curiosity in regard to the mystery that seemed to cling round Glenn's transformation of character. This Western girl really knew more about Glenn than his fiancee knew. Carley suffered a humiliating shock when she realized that she had been thinking of herself, of her love, her life, her needs, her wants instead of Glenn's. It took no keen intelligence or insight into human nature to see that Glenn needed her more than she needed him.

Thus unwontedly stirred and upset and flung back upon pride of herself, Carley went downstairs to meet the assembled company. And never had she shown to greater contrast, never had circumstance and state of mind contrived to make her so radiant and gay and unbending. She heard many remarks not intended for her far-reaching ears. An old grizzled Westerner remarked to Hutter: "Wall, she's shore an unbroke filly." Another of the company—a woman—remarked: "Sweet an' pretty as a columbine. But I'd like her better if she was dressed decent." And a gaunt range rider, who stood with others at the porch door, looking on, asked a comrade: "Do you reckon that's style back East?" To which the other replied: "Mebbe, but I'd gamble they're short on silk back East an' likewise sheriffs."

Carley received some meed of gratification out of the sensation she created, but she did not carry her craving for it to the point of overshadowing Flo. On the contrary, she contrived to have Flo share the attention she received. She taught Flo to dance the fox-trot and got Glenn to dance with her. Then she taught it to Lee Stanton. And when Lee danced with Flo, to the infinite wonder and delight of the onlookers, Carley experienced her first sincere enjoyment of the evening.

Her moment came when she danced with Glenn. It reminded her of days long past and which she wanted to return again. Despite war tramping and Western labors Glenn retained something of his old grace and lightness. But just to dance with him was enough to swell her heart, and for once she grew oblivious to the spectators.

"Glenn, would you like to go to the Plaza with me again, and dance between dinner courses, as we used to?" she whispered up to him.

"Sure I would—unless Morrison knew you were to be there," he replied.

"Glenn!... I would not even see him."

"Any old time you wouldn't see Morrison!" he exclaimed, half mockingly.

His doubt, his tone grated upon her. Pressing closer to him, she said, "Come back and I'll prove it."

But he laughed and had no answer for her. At her own daring words Carley's heart had leaped to her lips. If he had responded, even teasingly, she could have burst out with her longing to take him back. But silence inhibited her, and the moment passed.

At the end of that dance Hutter claimed Glenn in the interest of neighboring sheep men. And Carley, crossing the big living room alone, passed close to one of the porch doors. Some one, indistinct in the shadow, spoke to her in low voice: "Hello, pretty eyes!"

Carley felt a little cold shock go tingling through her. But she gave no sign that she had heard. She recognized the voice and also the epithet. Passing to the other side of the room and joining the company there, Carley presently took a casual glance at the door. Several men were lounging there. One of them was the sheep dipper, Haze Ruff. His bold eyes were on her now, and his coarse face wore a slight, meaning smile, as if he understood something about her that was a secret to others. Carley dropped her eyes. But she could not shake off the feeling that wherever she moved this man's gaze followed her. The unpleasantness of this incident would have been nothing to Carley had she at once forgotten it. Most unaccountably, however, she could not make herself unaware of this ruffian's attention. It did no good for her to argue that she was merely the cynosure of all eyes. This Ruff's tone and look possessed something heretofore unknown to Carley. Once she was tempted to tell Glenn. But that would only cause a fight, so she kept her counsel. She danced again, and helped Flo entertain her guests, and passed that door often; and once stood before it, deliberately, with all the strange and contrary impulse so inscrutable in a woman, and never for a moment wholly lost the sense of the man's boldness. It dawned upon her, at length, that the singular thing about this boldness was its difference from any, which had ever before affronted her. The fool's smile meant that he thought she saw his attention, and, understanding it perfectly, had secret delight in it. Many and various had been the masculine egotisms which had come under her observation. But quite beyond Carley was this brawny sheep dipper, Haze Ruff. Once the party broke up and the guests had departed, she instantly forgot both man and incident.

Next day, late in the afternoon, when Carley came out on the porch, she was hailed by Flo, who had just ridden in from down the canyon.

"Hey Carley, come down. I shore have something to tell you," she called.

Carley did not use any time pattering down that rude porch stairway. Flo was dusty and hot, and her chaps carried the unmistakable scent of sheep-dip.

"Been over to Ryan's camp an' shore rode hard to beat Glenn home," drawled Flo.

"Why?" queried Carley, eagerly.

"Reckon I wanted to tell you something Glenn swore he wouldn't let me tell. ... He makes me tired. He thinks you can't stand things."

"Oh! Has he been—hurt?"

"He's skinned an' bruised up some, but I reckon he's not hurt."

"Flo—what happened?" demanded Carley, anxiously.

"Carley, do you know Glenn can fight like the devil?" asked Flo.

"No, I don't. But I remember he used to be athletic. Flo, you make me nervous. Did Glenn fight?"

"I reckon he did," drawled Flo.

"With whom?"

"Nobody else but that big hombre, Haze Ruff."

"Oh!" gasped Carley, with a violent start. "That—that ruffian! Flo, did you see—were you there?"

"I shore was, an' next to a horse race I like a fight," replied the Western girl. "Carley, why didn't you tell me Haze Ruff insulted you last night?"

"Why, Flo—he only said, 'Hello, pretty eyes,' and I let it pass!" said Carley, lamely.

"You never want to let anything pass, out West. Because next time you'll get worse. This turn your other cheek doesn't go in Arizona. But we shore thought Ruff said worse than that. Though from him that's aplenty."

"How did you know?"

"Well, Charley told it. He was standing out here by the door last night an' he heard Ruff speak to you. Charley thinks a heap of you an' I reckon he hates Ruff. Besides, Charley stretches things. He shore riled Glenn, an' I want to say, my dear, you missed the best thing that's happened since you got here."

"Hurry—tell me," begged Carley, feeling the blood come to her face.

"I rode over to Ryan's place for dad, an' when I got there I knew nothing about what Ruff said to you," began Flo, and she took hold of Carley's hand. "Neither did dad. You see, Glenn hadn't got there yet. Well, just as the men had finished dipping a bunch of sheep Glenn came riding down, lickety cut."

"'Now what the hell's wrong with Glenn?' said dad, getting up from where we sat.

"Shore I knew Glenn was mad, though I never before saw him that way. He looked sort of grim an' black.... Well, he rode right down on us an' piled off. Dad yelled at him an' so did I. But Glenn made for the sheep pen. You know where we watched Haze Ruff an' Lorenzo slinging the sheep into the dip. Ruff was just about to climb out over the fence when Glenn leaped up on it."

"'Say, Ruff,' he said, sort of hard, 'Charley an' Ben tell me they heard you speak disrespectfully to Miss Burch last night.'"

"Dad an' I ran to the fence, but before we could catch hold of Glenn he'd jumped down into the pen."

"'I'm not carin' much for what them herders say,' replied Ruff."

"'Do you deny it?' demanded Glenn.

"'I ain't denyin' nothin', Kilbourne,' growled Ruff. 'I might argue against me bein' disrespectful. That's a matter of opinion.'

"'You'll apologize for speaking to Miss Burch or I'll beat you up an' have Hutter fire you.'

"'Wal, Kilbourne, I never eat my words,' replied Ruff.

"Then Glenn knocked him flat. You ought to have heard that crack. Sounded like Charley hitting a steer with a club. Dad yelled: 'Look out, Glenn. He packs a gun!'—Ruff got up mad clear through I reckon. Then they mixed it. Ruff got in some swings, but he couldn't reach Glenn's face. An' Glenn batted him right an' left, every time in his ugly mug. Ruff got all bloody an' he cussed something awful. Glenn beat him against the fence an' then we all saw Ruff reach for a gun or knife. All the men yelled. An' shore I screamed. But Glenn saw as much as we saw. He got fiercer. He beat Ruff down to his knees an' swung on him hard. Deliberately knocked Ruff into the dip ditch. What a splash! It wet all of us. Ruff went out of sight. Then he rolled up like a huge hog. We were all scared now. That dip's rank poison, you know. Reckon Ruff knew that. He floundered along an' crawled up at the end. Anyone could see that he had mouth an' eyes tight shut. He began to grope an' feel around, trying to find the way to the pond. One of the men led him out. It was great to see him wade in the water an' wallow an' souse his head under. When he came out the men got in front of him any stopped him. He shore looked bad.... An' Glenn called to him, 'Ruff, that sheep-dip won't go through your tough hide, but a bullet will!'"

Not long after this incident Carley started out on her usual afternoon ride, having arranged with Glenn to meet her on his return from work.

Toward the end of June Carley had advanced in her horsemanship to a point where Flo lent her one of her own mustangs. This change might not have had all to do with a wonderful difference in riding, but it seemed so to Carley. There was as much difference in horses as in people. This mustang she had ridden of late was of Navajo stock, but he had been born and raised and broken at Oak Creek. Carley had not yet discovered any objection on his part to do as she wanted him to. He liked what she liked, and most of all he liked to go. His color resembled a pattern of calico, and in accordance with Western ways his name was therefore Calico. Left to choose his own gait, Calico always dropped into a gentle pace which was so easy and comfortable and swinging that Carley never tired of it. Moreover, he did not shy at things lying in the road or rabbits darting from bushes or at the upwhirring of birds. Carley had grown attached to Calico before she realized she was drifting into it; and for Carley to care for anything or anybody was a serious matter, because it did not happen often and it lasted. She was exceedingly tenacious of affection.

June had almost passed and summer lay upon the lonely land. Such perfect and wonderful weather had never before been Carley's experience. The dawns broke cool, fresh, fragrant, sweet, and rosy, with a breeze that seemed of heaven rather than earth, and the air seemed tremulously full of the murmur of falling water and the melody of mocking birds. At the solemn noontides the great white sun glared down hot—so hot that it burned the skin, yet strangely was a pleasant burn. The waning afternoons were Carley's especial torment, when it seemed the sounds and winds of the day were tiring, and all things were seeking repose, and life must soften to an unthinking happiness. These hours troubled Carley because she wanted them to last, and because she knew for her this changing and transforming time could not last. So long as she did not think she was satisfied.

Maples and sycamores and oaks were in full foliage, and their bright greens contrasted softly with the dark shine of the pines. Through the spaces between brown tree trunks and the white-spotted holes of the sycamores gleamed the amber water of the creek. Always there was murmur of little rills and the musical dash of little rapids. On the surface of still, shady pools trout broke to make ever-widening ripples. Indian paintbrush, so brightly carmine in color, lent touch of fire to the green banks, and under the oaks, in cool dark nooks where mossy bowlders lined the stream, there were stately nodding yellow columbines. And high on the rock ledges shot up the wonderful mescal stalks, beginning to blossom, some with tints of gold and others with tones of red.

Riding along down the canyon, under its looming walls, Carley wondered that if unawares to her these physical aspects of Arizona could have become more significant than she realized. The thought had confronted her before. Here, as always, she fought it and denied it by the simple defense of elimination. Yet refusing to think of a thing when it seemed ever present was not going to do forever. Insensibly and subtly it might get a hold on her, never to be broken. Yet it was infinitely easier to dream than to think.

But the thought encroached upon her that it was not a dreamful habit of mind she had fallen into of late. When she dreamed or mused she lived vaguely and sweetly over past happy hours or dwelt in enchanted fancy upon a possible future. Carley had been told by a Columbia professor that she was a type of the present age—a modern young woman of materialistic mind. Be that as it might, she knew many things seemed loosening from the narrowness and tightness of her character, sloughing away like scales, exposing a new and strange and susceptible softness of fiber. And this blank habit of mind, when she did not think, and now realized that she was not dreaming, seemed to be the body of Carley Burch, and her heart and soul stripped of a shell. Nerve and emotion and spirit received something from her surroundings. She absorbed her environment. She felt. It was a delightful state. But when her own consciousness caused it to elude her, then she both resented and regretted. Anything that approached permanent attachment to this crude and untenanted West Carley would not tolerate for a moment. Reluctantly she admitted it had bettered her health, quickened her blood, and quite relegated Florida and the Adirondacks, to little consideration.

"Well, as I told Glenn," soliloquized Carley, "every time I'm almost won over a little to Arizona she gives me a hard jolt. I'm getting near being mushy today. Now let's see what I'll get. I suppose that's my pessimism or materialism. Funny how Glenn keeps saying its the jolts, the hard knocks, the fights that are best to remember afterward. I don't get that at all."

Five miles below West Fork a road branched off and climbed the left side of the canyon. It was a rather steep road, long and zigzaging, and full of rocks and ruts. Carley did not enjoy ascending it, but she preferred the going up to coming down. It took half an hour to climb.

Once up on the flat cedar-dotted desert she was met, full in the face, by a hot dusty wind coming from the south. Carley searched her pockets for her goggles, only to ascertain that she had forgotten them. Nothing, except a freezing sleety wind, annoyed and punished Carley so much as a hard puffy wind, full of sand and dust. Somewhere along the first few miles of this road she was to meet Glenn. If she turned back for any cause he would be worried, and, what concerned her more vitally, he would think she had not the courage to face a little dust. So Carley rode on.

The wind appeared to be gusty. It would blow hard awhile, then lull for a few moments. On the whole, however, it increased in volume and persistence until she was riding against a gale. She had now come to a bare, flat, gravelly region, scant of cedars and brush, and far ahead she could see a dull yellow pall rising high into the sky. It was a duststorm and it was sweeping down on the wings of that gale. Carley remembered that somewhere along this flat there was a log cabin which had before provided shelter for her and Flo when they were caught in a rainstorm. It seemed unlikely that she had passed by this cabin.

Resolutely she faced the gale and knew she had a task to find that refuge. If there had been a big rock or bushy cedar to offer shelter she would have welcomed it. But there was nothing. When the hard dusty gusts hit her, she found it absolutely necessary to shut her eyes. At intervals less windy she opened them, and rode on, peering through the yellow gloom for the cabin. Thus she got her eyes full of dust—an alkali dust that made them sting and smart. The fiercer puffs of wind carried pebbles large enough to hurt severely. Then the dust clogged her nose and sand got between her teeth. Added to these annoyances was a heat like a blast from a furnace. Carley perspired freely and that caked the dust on her face. She rode on, gradually growing more uncomfortable and miserable. Yet even then she did not utterly lose a sort of thrilling zest in being thrown upon her own responsibility. She could hate an obstacle, yet feel something of pride in holding her own against it.

Another mile of buffeting this increasing gale so exhausted Carley and wrought upon her nerves that she became nearly panic-stricken. It grew harder and harder not to turn back. At last she was about to give up when right at hand through the flying dust she espied the cabin. Riding behind it, she dismounted and tied the mustang to a post. Then she ran around to the door and entered.

What a welcome refuge! She was all right now, and when Glenn came along she would have added to her already considerable list another feat for which he would commend her. With aid of her handkerchief, and the tears that flowed so copiously, Carley presently freed her eyes of the blinding dust. But when she essayed to remove it from her face she discovered she would need a towel and soap and hot water.

The cabin appeared to be enveloped in a soft, swishing, hollow sound. It seeped and rustled. Then the sound lulled, only to rise again. Carley went to the door, relieved and glad to see that the duststorm was blowing by. The great sky-high pall of yellow had moved on to the north. Puffs of dust were whipping along the road, but no longer in one continuous cloud. In the west, low down the sun was sinking, a dull magenta in hue, quite weird and remarkable.

"I knew I'd get the jolt all right," soliloquized Carley, wearily, as she walked to a rude couch of poles and sat down upon it. She had begun to cool off. And there, feeling dirty and tired, and slowly wearing to the old depression, she composed herself to wait.

Suddenly she heard the clip-clop of hoofs. "There! that's Glenn," she cried, gladly, and rising, she ran to the door.

She saw a big bay horse bearing a burly rider. He discovered her at the same instant, and pulled his horse.

"Ho! Ho! if it ain't Pretty Eyes!" he called out, in gay, coarse voice.

Carley recognized the voice, and then the epithet, before her sight established the man as Haze Ruff. A singular stultifying shock passed over her.

"Wal, by all thet's lucky!" he said, dismounting. "I knowed we'd meet some day. I can't say I just laid fer you, but I kept my eyes open."

Manifestly he knew she was alone, for he did not glance into the cabin.

"I'm waiting for—Glenn," she said, with lips she tried to make stiff.

"Shore I reckoned thet," he replied, genially. "But he won't be along yet awhile."

He spoke with a cheerful inflection of tone, as if the fact designated was one that would please her; and his swarthy, seamy face expanded into a good-humored, meaning smile. Then without any particular rudeness he pushed her back from the door, into the cabin, and stepped across the threshold.

"How dare—you!" cried Carley. A hot anger that stirred in her seemed to be beaten down and smothered by a cold shaking internal commotion, threatening collapse. This man loomed over her, huge, somehow monstrous in his brawny uncouth presence. And his knowing smile, and the hard, glinting twinkle of his light eyes, devilishly intelligent and keen, in no wise lessened the sheer brutal force of him physically. Sight of his bulk was enough to terrorize Carley.

"Me! Aw, I'm a darin' hombre an' a devil with the wimmin," he said, with a guffaw.

Carley could not collect her wits. The instant of his pushing her back into the cabin and following her had shocked her and almost paralyzed her will. If she saw him now any the less fearful she could not so quickly rally her reason to any advantage.

"Let me out of here," she demanded.

"Nope. I'm a-goin' to make a little love to you," he said, and he reached for her with great hairy hands.

Carley saw in them the strength that had so easily swung the sheep. She saw, too, that they were dirty, greasy hands. And they made her flesh creep.

"Glenn will kill—you," she panted.

"What fer?" he queried, in real or pretended surprise. "Aw, I know wimmin. You'll never tell him."

"Yes, I will."

"Wal, mebbe. I reckon you're lyin', Pretty Eyes," he replied, with a grin. "Anyhow, I'll take a chance."

"I tell you—he'll kill you," repeated Carley, backing away until her weak knees came against the couch.

"What fer, I ask you?" he demanded.

"For this—this insult."

"Huh! I'd like to know who's insulted you. Can't a man take an invitation to kiss an' hug a girl—without insultin' her?"

"Invitation!... Are you crazy?" queried Carley, bewildered.

"Nope, I'm not crazy, an' I shore said invitation.... I meant thet white shimmy dress you wore the night of Flo's party. Thet's my invitation to get a little fresh with you, Pretty Eyes!"

Carley could only stare at him. His words seemed to have some peculiar, unanswerable power.

"Wal, if it wasn't an invitation, what was it?" he asked, with another step that brought him within reach of her. He waited for her answer, which was not forthcoming.

"Wal, you're gettin' kinda pale around the gills," he went on, derisively. "I reckoned you was a real sport.... Come here."

He fastened one of his great hands in the front of her coat and gave her a pull. So powerful was it that Carley came hard against him, almost knocking her breathless. There he held her a moment and then put his other arm round her. It seemed to crush both breath and sense out of her. Suddenly limp, she sank strengthless. She seemed reeling in darkness. Then she felt herself thrust away from him with violence. She sank on the couch and her head and shoulders struck the wall.

"Say, if you're a-goin' to keel over like thet I pass," declared Ruff, in disgust. "Can't you Eastern wimmin stand nothin?"

Carley's eyes opened and beheld this man in an attitude of supremely derisive protest.

"You look like a sick kitten," he added. "When I get me a sweetheart or wife I want her to be a wild cat."

His scorn and repudiation of her gave Carley intense relief. She sat up and endeavored to collect her shattered nerves. Ruff gazed down at her with great disapproval and even disappointment.

"Say, did you have some fool idee I was a-goin' to kill you?" he queried, gruffly.

"I'm afraid—I did," faltered Carley. Her relief was a release; it was so strange that it was gratefulness.

"Wal, I reckon I wouldn't have hurt you. None of these flop-over Janes for me!... An' I'll give you a hunch, Pretty Eyes. You might have run acrost a fellar thet was no gentleman!"

Of all the amazing statements that had ever been made to Carley, this one seemed the most remarkable.

"What'd you wear thet onnatural white dress fer?" he demanded, as if he had a right to be her judge.

"Unnatural?" echoed Carley.

"Shore. Thet's what I said. Any woman's dress without top or bottom is onnatural. It's not right. Why, you looked like—like"—here he floundered for adequate expression—"like one of the devil's angels. An' I want to hear why you wore it."

"For the same reason I'd wear any dress," she felt forced to reply.

"Pretty Eyes, thet's a lie. An' you know it's a lie. You wore thet white dress to knock the daylights out of men. Only you ain't honest enough to say so.... Even me or my kind! Even us, who're dirt under your little feet. But all the same we're men, an' mebbe better men than you think. If you had to put that dress on, why didn't you stay in your room? Naw, you had to come down an' strut around an' show off your beauty. An' I ask you—if you're a nice girl like Flo Hutter—what'd you wear it fer?"

Carley not only was mute; she felt rise and burn in her a singular shame and surprise.

"I'm only a sheep dipper," went on Ruff, "but I ain't no fool. A fellar doesn't have to live East an' wear swell clothes to have sense. Mebbe you'll learn thet the West is bigger'n you think. A man's a man East or West. But if your Eastern men stand for such dresses as thet white one they'd do well to come out West awhile, like your lover, Glenn Kilbourne. I've been rustlin' round here ten years, an' I never before seen a dress like yours—an' I never heerd of a girl bein' insulted, either. Mebbe you think I insulted you. Wal, I didn't. Fer I reckon nothin' could insult you in thet dress.... An' my last hunch is this, Pretty Eyes. You're not what a hombre like me calls either square or game. Adios."

His bulky figure darkened the doorway, passed out, and the light of the sky streamed into the cabin again. Carley sat staring. She heard Ruff's spurs tinkle, then the ring of steel on stirrup, a sodden leathery sound as he mounted, and after that a rapid pound of hoofs, quickly dying away.

He was gone. She had escaped something raw and violent. Dazedly she realized it, with unutterable relief. And she sat there slowly gathering the nervous force that had been shattered. Every word that he had uttered was stamped in startling characters upon her consciousness. But she was still under the deadening influence of shock. This raw experience was the worst the West had yet dealt her. It brought back former states of revulsion and formed them in one whole irrefutable and damning judgment that seemed to blot out the vaguely dawning and growing happy susceptibilities. It was, perhaps, just as well to have her mind reverted to realistic fact. The presence of Haze Ruff, the astounding truth of the contact with his huge sheep-defiled hands, had been profanation and degradation under which she sickened with fear and shame. Yet hovering back of her shame and rising anger seemed to be a pale, monstrous, and indefinable thought, insistent and accusing, with which she must sooner or later reckon. It might have been the voice of the new side of her nature, but at that moment of outraged womanhood, and of revolt against the West, she would not listen. It might, too, have been the still small voice of conscience. But decision of mind and energy coming to her then, she threw off the burden of emotion and perplexity, and forced herself into composure before the arrival of Glenn.

The dust had ceased to blow, although the wind had by no means died away. Sunset marked the west in old rose and gold, a vast flare. Carley espied a horseman far down the road, and presently recognized both rider and steed. He was coming fast. She went out and, mounting her mustang, she rode out to meet Glenn. It did not appeal to her to wait for him at the cabin; besides hoof tracks other than those made by her mustang might have been noticed by Glenn. Presently he came up to her and pulled his loping horse.

"Hello! I sure was worried," was his greeting, as his gloved hand went out to her. "Did you run into that sandstorm?"

"It ran into me, Glenn, and buried me," she laughed.

His fine eyes lingered on her face with glad and warm glance, and the keen, apprehensive penetration of a lover.

"Well, under all that dust you look scared," he said.

"Scared! I was worse than that. When I first ran into the flying dirt I was only afraid I'd lose my way—and my complexion. But when the worst of the storm hit me—then I feared I'd lose my breath."

"Did you face that sand and ride through it all?" he queried.

"No, not all. But enough. I went through the worst of it before I reached the cabin," she replied.

"Wasn't it great?"

"Yes—great bother and annoyance," she said, laconically.

Whereupon he reached with long, arm and wrapped it round her as they rocked side by side. Demonstrations of this nature were infrequent with Glenn. Despite losing one foot out of a stirrup and her seat in the saddle Carley rather encouraged it. He kissed her dusty face, and then set her back.

"By George! Carley, sometimes I think you've changed since you've been here," he said, with warmth. "To go through that sandstorm without one kick—one knock at my West!"

"Glenn, I always think of what Flo says—the worst is yet to come," replied Carley, trying to hide her unreasonable and tumultuous pleasure at words of praise from him.

"Carley Burch, you don't know yourself," he declared, enigmatically.

"What woman knows herself? But do you know me?"

"Not I. Yet sometimes I see depths in you—wonderful possibilities—submerged under your poise—under your fixed, complacent idle attitude toward life."

This seemed for Carley to be dangerously skating near thin ice, but she could not resist a retort:

"Depths in me? Why I am a shallow, transparent stream like your West Fork! ... And as for possibilities—may I ask what of them you imagine you see?"

"As a girl, before you were claimed by the world, you were earnest at heart. You had big hopes and dreams. And you had intellect, too. But you have wasted your talents, Carley. Having money, and spending it, living for pleasure, you have not realized your powers.... Now, don't look hurt. I'm not censuring you. It's just the way of modern life. And most of your friends have been more careless, thoughtless, useless than you. The aim of their existence is to be comfortable, free from work, worry, pain. They want pleasure, luxury. And what a pity it is! The best of you girls regard marriage as an escape, instead of responsibility. You don't marry to get your shoulders square against the old wheel of American progress—to help some man make good—to bring a troop of healthy American kids into the world. You bare your shoulders to the gaze of the multitude and like it best if you are strung with pearls."

"Glenn, you distress me when you talk like this," replied Carley, soberly. "You did not use to talk so. It seems to me you are bitter against women."

"Oh no, Carley! I am only sad," he said. "I only see where once I was blind. American women are the finest on earth, but as a race, if they don't change, they're doomed to extinction."

"How can you say such things?" demanded Carley, with spirit.

"I say them because they are true. Carley, on the level now, tell me how many of your immediate friends have children."

Put to a test, Carley rapidly went over in mind her circle of friends, with the result that she was somewhat shocked and amazed to realize how few of them were even married, and how the babies of her acquaintance were limited to three. It was not easy to admit this to Glenn.

"My dear," replied he, "if that does not show you the handwriting on the wall, nothing ever will."

"A girl has to find a husband, doesn't she?" asked Carley, roused to defense of her sex. "And if she's anybody she has to find one in her set. Well, husbands are not plentiful. Marriage certainly is not the end of existence these days. We have to get along somehow. The high cost of living is no inconsiderable factor today. Do you know that most of the better-class apartment houses in New York will not take children? Women are not all to blame. Take the speed mania.

Men must have automobiles. I know one girl who wanted a baby, but her husband wanted a car. They couldn't afford both."

"Carley, I'm not blaming women more than men," returned Glenn. "I don't know that I blame them as a class. But in my own mind I have worked it all out. Every man or woman who is genuinely American should read the signs of the times, realize the crisis, and meet it in an American way. Otherwise we are done as a race. Money is God in the older countries. But it should never become God in America. If it does we will make the fall of Rome pale into insignificance."

"Glenn, let's put off the argument," appealed Carley. "I'm not—just up to fighting you today. Oh—you needn't smile. I'm not showing a yellow streak, as Flo puts it. I'll fight you some other time."

"You're right, Carley," he assented. "Here we are loafing six or seven miles from home. Let's rustle along."

Riding fast with Glenn was something Carley had only of late added to her achievements. She had greatest pride in it. So she urged her mustang to keep pace with Glenn's horse and gave herself up to the thrill of the motion and feel of wind and sense of flying along. At a good swinging lope Calico covered ground swiftly and did not tire. Carley rode the two miles to the rim of the canyon, keeping alongside of Glenn all the way. Indeed, for one long level stretch she and Glenn held hands. When they arrived at the descent, which necessitated slow and careful riding, she was hot and tingling and breathless, worked by the action into an exuberance of pleasure. Glenn complimented her riding as well as her rosy cheeks. There was indeed a sweetness in working at a task as she had worked to learn to ride in Western fashion. Every turn of her mind seemed to confront her with sobering antitheses of thought. Why had she come to love to ride down a lonely desert road, through ragged cedars where the wind whipped her face with fragrant wild breath, if at the same time she hated the West? Could she hate a country, however barren and rough, if it had saved the health and happiness of her future husband? Verily there were problems for Carley to solve.

Early twilight purple lay low in the hollows and clefts of the canyon. Over the western rim a pale ghost of the evening star seemed to smile at Carley, to bid her look and look. Like a strain of distant music, the dreamy hum of falling water, the murmur and melody of the stream, came again to Carley's sensitive ear.

"Do you love this?" asked Glenn, when they reached the green-forested canyon floor, with the yellow road winding away into the purple shadows.

"Yes, both the ride—and you," flashed Carley, contrarily. She knew he had meant the deep-walled canyon with its brooding solitude.

"But I want you to love Arizona," he said.

"Glenn, I'm a faithful creature. You should be glad of that. I love New York."

"Very well, then. Arizona to New York," he said, lightly brushing her cheek with his lips. And swerving back into his saddle, he spurred his horse and called back over his shoulder: "That mustang and Flo have beaten me many a time. Come on."

It was not so much his words as his tone and look that roused Carley. Had he resented her loyalty to the city of her nativity? Always there was a little rift in the lute. Had his tone and look meant that Flo might catch him if Carley could not? Absurd as the idea was, it spurred her to recklessness. Her mustang did not need any more than to know she wanted him to run. The road was of soft yellow earth flanked with green foliage and overspread by pines. In a moment she was racing at a speed she had never before half attained on a horse. Down the winding road Glenn's big steed sped, his head low, his stride tremendous, his action beautiful. But Carley saw the distance between them diminishing. Calico was overtaking the bay. She cried out in the thrilling excitement of the moment. Glenn saw her gaining and pressed his mount to greater speed. Still he could not draw away from Calico. Slowly the little mustang gained. It seemed to Carley that riding him required no effort at all. And at such fast pace, with the wind roaring in her ears, the walls of green vague and continuous in her sight, the sting of pine tips on cheek and neck, the yellow road streaming toward her, under her, there rose out of the depths of her, out of the tumult of her breast, a sense of glorious exultation. She closed in on Glenn. From the flying hoofs of his horse shot up showers of damp sand and gravel that covered Carley's riding habit and spattered in her face. She had to hold up a hand before her eyes. Perhaps this caused her to lose something of her confidence, or her swing in the saddle, for suddenly she realized she was not riding well. The pace was too fast for her inexperience. But nothing could have stopped her then. No fear or awkwardness of hers should be allowed to hamper that thoroughbred mustang. Carley felt that Calico understood the situation; or at least he knew he could catch and pass this big bay horse, and he intended to do it. Carley was hard put to it to hang on and keep the flying sand from blinding her.

When Calico drew alongside the bay horse and brought Carley breast to breast with Glenn, and then inch by inch forged ahead of him, Carley pealed out an exultant cry. Either it frightened Calico or inspired him, for he shot right ahead of Glenn's horse. Then he lost the smooth, wonderful action. He seemed hurtling through space at the expense of tremendous muscular action. Carley could feel it. She lost her equilibrium. She seemed rushing through a blurred green and black aisle of the forest with a gale in her face. Then, with a sharp jolt, a break, Calico plunged to the sand. Carley felt herself propelled forward out of the saddle into the air, and down to strike with a sliding, stunning force that ended in sudden dark oblivion.

Upon recovering consciousness she first felt a sensation of oppression in her chest and a dull numbness of her whole body. When she opened her eyes she saw Glenn bending over her, holding her head on his knee. A wet, cold, reviving sensation evidently came from the handkerchief with which he was mopping her face.

"Carley, you can't be hurt—really!" he was ejaculating, in eager hope. "It was some spill. But you lit on the sand and slid. You can't be hurt."

The look of his eyes, the tone of his voice, the feel of his hands were such that Carley chose for a moment to pretend to be very badly hurt indeed. It was worth taking a header to get so much from Glenn Kilbourne. But she believed she had suffered no more than a severe bruising and scraping.

"Glenn—dear," she whispered, very low and very eloquently. "I think—my back—is broken.... You'll be free—soon."

Glenn gave a terrible start and his face turned a deathly white. He burst out with quavering, inarticulate speech.

Carley gazed up at him and then closed her eyes. She could not look at him while carrying on such deceit. Yet the sight of him and the feel of him then were inexpressibly blissful to her. What she needed most was assurance of his love. She had it. Beyond doubt, beyond morbid fancy, the truth had proclaimed itself, filling her heart with joy.

Suddenly she flung her arms up around his neck. "Oh—Glenn! It was too good a chance to miss!... I'm not hurt a bit."

CHAPTER VII

The day came when Carley asked Mrs. Hutter: "Will you please put up a nice lunch for Glenn and me? I'm going to walk down to his farm where he's working, and surprise him."

"That's a downright fine idea," declared Mrs. Hutter, and forthwith bustled away to comply with Carley's request.

So presently Carley found herself carrying a bountiful basket on her arm, faring forth on an adventure that both thrilled and depressed her. Long before this hour something about Glenn's work had quickened her pulse and given rise to an inexplicable admiration. That he was big and strong enough to do such labor made her proud; that he might want to go on doing it made her ponder and brood.

The morning resembled one of the rare Eastern days in June, when the air appeared flooded by rich thick amber light. Only the sun here was hotter and the shade cooler.

Carley took to the trail below where West Fork emptied its golden-green waters into Oak Creek. The red walls seemed to dream and wait under the blaze of the sun; the heat lay like a blanket over the still foliage; the birds were quiet; only the murmuring stream broke the silence of the canyon. Never had Carley felt more the isolation and solitude of Oak Creek Canyon. Far indeed from the madding crowd! Only Carley's stubbornness kept her from acknowledging the sense of peace that enveloped her—that and the consciousness of her own discontent. What would it be like to come to this canyon—to give up to its enchantments? That, like many another disturbing thought, had to go unanswered, to be driven into the closed chambers of Carley's mind, there to germinate subconsciously, and stalk forth some day to overwhelm her.

The trail led along the creek, threading a maze of bowlders, passing into the shade of cottonwoods, and crossing sun-flecked patches of sand. Carley's every step seemed to become slower. Regrets were assailing her. Long indeed had she overstayed her visit to the West. She must not linger there indefinitely. And mingled with misgiving was a surprise that she had not tired of Oak Creek. In spite of all, and of the dislike she vaunted to herself, the truth stared at her—she was not tired.

The long-delayed visit to see Glenn working on his own farm must result in her talking to him about his work; and in a way not quite clear she regretted the necessity for it. To disapprove of Glenn! She received faint intimations of wavering, of uncertainty, of vague doubt. But these were cried down by the dominant and habitable voice of her personality.

Presently through the shaded and shadowed breadth of the belt of forest she saw gleams of a sunlit clearing. And crossing this space to the border of trees she peered forth, hoping to espy Glenn at his labors. She saw an old shack, and irregular lines of rude fence built of poles of all sizes and shapes, and several plots of bare yellow ground, leading up toward the west side of the canyon wall. Could this clearing be Glenn's farm? Surely she had missed it or had not gone far enough. This was not a farm, but a slash in the forested level of the canyon floor, bare and somehow hideous. Dead trees were standing in the lots. They had been ringed deeply at the base by an ax, to kill them, and so prevent their foliage from shading the soil. Carley saw a long pile of rocks that evidently had been carried from the plowed ground. There was no neatness, no regularity, although there was abundant evidence of toil. To clear that rugged space, to fence it, and plow it, appeared at once to Carley an extremely strenuous and useless task. Carley persuaded herself that this must be the plot of ground belonging to the herder Charley, and she was about to turn on down the creek when far up under the bluff she espied a man. He was stalking along and bending down, stalking along and bending down. She recognized Glenn. He was planting something in the yellow soil.

Curiously Carley watched him, and did not allow her mind to become concerned with a somewhat painful swell of her heart. What a stride he had! How vigorous he looked, and earnest! He was as intent upon this job as if he had been a rustic. He might have been failing to do it well, but he most certainly was doing it conscientiously. Once he had said to her that a man should never be judged by the result of his labors, but by the nature of his effort. A man might strive with all his heart and strength, yet fail. Carley watched him striding along and bending down, absorbed in his task, unmindful of the glaring hot sun, and somehow to her singularly detached from the life wherein he had once moved and to which she yearned to take him back. Suddenly an unaccountable flashing query assailed her conscience: How dare she want to take him back? She seemed as shocked as if some stranger had accosted her. What was this dimming of her eye, this inward tremulousness; this dammed tide beating at an unknown and riveted gate of her intelligence? She felt more then than she dared to face. She struggled against something in herself. The old habit of mind instinctively resisted the new, the strange. But she did not come off wholly victorious. The Carley Burch whom she recognized as of old, passionately hated this life and work of Glenn Kilbourne's, but the rebel self, an unaccountable and defiant Carley, loved him all the better for them.

Carley drew a long deep breath before she called Glenn. This meeting would be momentous and she felt no absolute surety of herself.

Manifestly he was surprised to hear her call, and, dropping his sack and implement, he hurried across the tilled ground, sending up puffs of dust. He vaulted the rude fence of poles, and upon sight of her called out lustily. How big and virile he looked! Yet he was gaunt and strained. It struck Carley that he had not looked so upon her arrival at Oak Creek. Had she worried him? The query gave her a pang.

"Sir Tiller of the Fields," said Carley, gayly, "see, your dinner! I brought it and I am going to share it."

"You old darling!" he replied, and gave her an embrace that left her cheek moist with the sweat of his. He smelled of dust and earth and his body was hot. "I wish to God it could be true for always!"

His loving, bearish onslaught and his words quite silenced Carley. How at critical moments he always said the thing that hurt her or inhibited her! She essayed a smile as she drew back from him.

"It's sure good of you," he said, taking the basket. "I was thinking I'd be through work sooner today, and was sorry I had not made a date with you. Come, we'll find a place to sit."

Whereupon he led her back under the trees to a half-sunny, half-shady bench of rock overhanging the stream. Great pines overshadowed a still, eddying pool. A number of brown butterflies hovered over the water, and small trout floated like spotted feathers just under the surface. Drowsy summer enfolded the sylvan scene.

Glenn knelt at the edge of the brook, and, plunging his hands in, he splashed like a huge dog and bathed his hot face and head, and then turned to Carley with gay words and laughter, while he wiped himself dry with a large red scarf. Carley was not proof against the virility of him then, and at the moment, no matter what it was that had made him the man he looked, she loved it.

"I'll sit in the sun," he said, designating a place. "When you're hot you mustn't rest in the shade, unless you've coat or sweater. But you sit here in the shade."

"Glenn, that'll put us too far apart," complained Carley. "I'll sit in the sun with you."

The delightful simplicity and happiness of the ensuing hour was something Carley believed she would never forget.

"There! we've licked the platter clean," she said. "What starved bears we were!.... I wonder if I shall enjoy eating—when I get home. I used to be so finnicky and picky."

"Carley, don't talk about home," said Glenn, appealingly.

"You dear old farmer, I'd love to stay here and just dream—forever," replied Carley, earnestly. "But I came on purpose to talk seriously."

"Oh, you did! About what?" he returned, with some quick, indefinable change of tone and expression.

"Well, first about your work. I know I hurt your feelings when I wouldn't listen. But I wasn't ready. I wanted to—to just be gay with you for a while. Don't think I wasn't interested. I was. And now, I'm ready to hear all about it—and everything."

She smiled at him bravely, and she knew that unless some unforeseen shock upset her composure, she would be able to conceal from him anything which might hurt his feelings.

"You do look serious," he said, with keen eyes on her.

"Just what are your business relations with Hutter?" she inquired.

"I'm simply working for him," replied Glenn. "My aim is to get an interest in his sheep, and I expect to, some day. We have some plans. And one of them is the development of that Deep Lake section. You remember—you were with us. The day Spillbeans spilled you?"

"Yes, I remember. It was a pretty place," she replied.

Carley did not tell him that for a month past she had owned the Deep Lake section of six hundred and forty acres. She had, in fact, instructed Hutter to purchase it, and to keep the transaction a secret for the present. Carley had never been able to understand the impulse that prompted her to do it. But as Hutter had assured her it was a remarkably good investment on very little capital, she had tried to persuade herself of its advantages. Back of it all had been an irresistible desire to be able some day to present to Glenn this ranch site he loved. She had concluded he would never wholly dissociate himself from this West; and as he would visit it now and then, she had already begun forming plans of her own. She could stand a month in Arizona at long intervals.

"Hutter and I will go into cattle raising some day," went on Glenn. "And that Deep Lake place is what I want for myself."

"What work are you doing for Hutter?" asked Carley.

"Anything from building fence to cutting timber," laughed Glenn. "I've not yet the experience to be a foreman like Lee Stanton. Besides, I have a little business all my own. I put all my money in that."

"You mean here—this—this farm?"

"Yes. And the stock I'm raisin'. You see I have to feed corn. And believe me, Carley, those cornfields represent some job."

"I can well believe that," replied Carley. "You—you looked it."

"Oh, the hard work is over. All I have to do now it to plant and keep the weeds out."

"Glenn, do sheep eat corn?"

"I plant corn to feed my hogs."

"Hogs?" she echoed, vaguely.

"Yes, hogs," he said, with quiet gravity. "The first day you visited my cabin I told you I raised hogs, and I fried my own ham for your dinner."

"Is that what you—put your money in?"

"Yes. And Hutter says I've done well."

"Hogs!" ejaculated Carley, aghast.

"My dear, are you growin' dull of comprehension?" retorted Glenn. "H-o-g-s." He spelled the word out. "I'm in the hog-raising business, and pretty blamed well pleased over my success so far."

Carley caught herself in time to quell outwardly a shock of amaze and revulsion. She laughed, and exclaimed against her stupidity. The look of Glenn was no less astounding than the content of his words. He was actually proud of his work. Moreover, he showed not the least sign that he had any idea such information might be startlingly obnoxious to his fiancee.

"Glenn! It's so—so queer," she ejaculated. "That you—Glenn Kilbourne-should ever go in for—for hogs!... It's unbelievable. How'd you ever—ever happen to do it?"

"By Heaven! you're hard on me!" he burst out, in sudden dark, fierce passion. "How'd I ever happen to do it?... What was there left for me? I gave my soul and heart and body to the government—to fight for my country. I came home a wreck. What did my government do for me? What did my employers do for me? What did the people I fought for do for me?... Nothing—so help me God—nothing!... I got a ribbon and a bouquet—a little applause for an hour—and then the sight of me sickened my countrymen. I was broken and used. I was absolutely forgotten.... But my body, my life, my soul meant all to me. My future was ruined, but I wanted to live. I had killed men who never harmed me—I was not fit to die.... I tried to live. So I fought out my battle alone. Alone!... No one understood. No one cared. I came West to keep from dying of consumption in sight of the indifferent mob for whom I had sacrificed myself. I chose to die on my feet away off alone somewhere.... But I got well. And what made me well— and saved my soul—was the first work that offered. Raising and tending hogs!"

The dead whiteness of Glenn's face, the lightning scorn of his eyes, the grim, stark strangeness of him then had for Carley a terrible harmony with this passionate denunciation of her, of her kind, of the America for whom he had lost all.

"Oh, Glenn!—forgive—me!" she faltered. "I was only—talking. What do I know? Oh, I am blind—blind and little!"

She could not bear to face him for a moment, and she hung her head. Her intelligence seemed concentrating swift, wild thoughts round the shock to her consciousness. By that terrible expression of his face, by those thundering words of scorn, would she come to realize the mighty truth of his descent into the abyss and his rise to the heights. Vaguely she began to see. An awful sense of her deadness, of her soul-blighting selfishness, began to dawn upon her as something monstrous out of dim, gray obscurity. She trembled under the reality of thoughts that were not new. How she had babbled about Glenn and the crippled soldiers! How she had imagined she sympathized! But she had only been a vain, worldly, complacent, effusive little fool. She had here the shock of her life, and she sensed a greater one, impossible to grasp.

"Carley, that was coming to you," said Glenn, presently, with deep, heavy expulsion of breath.

"I only know I love you—more—more," she cried, wildly, looking up and wanting desperately to throw herself in his arms.

"I guess you do—a little," he replied. "Sometimes I feel you are a kid. Then again you represent the world—your world with its age-old custom—its unalterable.... But, Carley, let's get back to my work."

"Yes—yes," exclaimed Carley, gladly. "I'm ready to—to go pet your hogs—anything."

"By George! I'll take you up," he declared. "I'll bet you won't go near one of my hogpens."

"Lead me to it!" she replied, with a hilarity that was only a nervous reversion of her state.

"Well, maybe I'd better hedge on the bet," he said, laughing again. "You have more in you than I suspect. You sure fooled me when you stood for the sheep-dip. But, come on, I'll take you anyway."

So that was how Carley found herself walking arm in arm with Glenn down the canyon trail. A few moments of action gave her at least an appearance of outward composure. And the state of her emotion was so strained and intense that her slightest show of interest must deceive Glenn into thinking her eager, responsive, enthusiastic. It certainly appeared to loosen his tongue. But Carley knew she was farther from normal than ever before in her life, and that the subtle, inscrutable woman's intuition of her presaged another shock. Just as she had seemed to change, so had the aspects of the canyon undergone some illusive transformation. The beauty of green foliage and amber stream and brown tree trunks and gray rocks and red walls was there; and the summer drowsiness and languor lay as deep; and the loneliness and solitude brooded with its same eternal significance. But some nameless enchantment, perhaps of hope, seemed no longer to encompass her. A blow had fallen upon her, the nature of which only time could divulge.

Glenn led her around the clearing and up to the base of the west wall, where against a shelving portion of the cliff had been constructed a rude fence of poles. It formed three sides of a pen, and the fourth side was solid rock. A bushy cedar tree stood in the center. Water flowed from under the cliff, which accounted for the boggy condition of the red earth. This pen was occupied by a huge sow and a litter of pigs.

Carley climbed on the fence and sat there while Glenn leaned over the top pole and began to wax eloquent on a subject evidently dear to his heart. Today of all days Carley made an inspiring listener. Even the shiny, muddy, suspicious old sow in no wise daunted her fictitious courage. That filthy pen of mud a foot deep, and of odor rancid, had no terrors for her. With an arm round Glenn's shoulder she watched the rooting and squealing little pigs, and was amused and interested, as if they were far removed from the vital issue of the hour. But all the time as she looked and laughed, and encouraged Glenn to talk, there seemed to be a strange, solemn, oppressive knocking at her heart. Was it only the beat-beat-beat of blood?

"There were twelve pigs in that litter," Glenn was saying, "and now you see there are only nine. I've lost three. Mountain lions, bears, coyotes, wild cats are all likely to steal a pig. And at first I was sure one of these varmints had been robbing me. But as I could not find any tracks, I knew I had to lay the blame on something else. So I kept watch pretty closely in daytime, and at night I shut the pigs up in the corner there, where you see I've built a pen. Yesterday I heard squealing—and, by George! I saw an eagle flying off with one of my pigs. Say, I was mad. A great old bald-headed eagle—the regal bird you see with America's stars and stripes had degraded himself to the level of a coyote. I ran for my rifle, and I took some quick shots at him as he flew up. Tried to hit him, too, but I failed. And the old rascal hung on to my pig. I watched him carry it to that sharp crag way up there on the rim."

"Poor little piggy!" exclaimed Carley. "To think of our American emblem—our stately bird of noble warlike mien—our symbol of lonely grandeur and freedom of the heights—think of him being a robber of pigpens!—Glenn, I begin to appreciate the many-sidedness of things. Even my hide-bound narrowness is susceptible to change. It's never too late to learn. This should apply to the Society for the Preservation of the American Eagle."

Glenn led her along the base of the wall to three other pens, in each of which was a fat old sow with a litter. And at the last enclosure, that owing to dry soil was not so dirty, Glenn picked up a little pig and held it squealing out to Carley as she leaned over the fence. It was fairly white and clean, a little pink and fuzzy, and certainly cute with its curled tall.

"Carley Burch, take it in your hands," commanded Glenn.

The feat seemed monstrous and impossible of accomplishment for Carley. Yet such was her temper at the moment that she would have undertaken anything.

"Why, shore I will, as Flo says," replied Carley, extending her ungloved hands. "Come here, piggy. I christen you Pinky." And hiding an almost insupportable squeamishness from Glenn, she took the pig in her hands and fondled it.

"By George!" exclaimed Glenn, in huge delight. "I wouldn't have believed it. Carley, I hope you tell your fastidious and immaculate Morrison that you held one of my pigs in your beautiful hands."

"Wouldn't it please you more to tell him yourself?" asked Carley.

"Yes, it would," declared Glenn, grimly.

This incident inspired Glenn to a Homeric narration of his hog-raising experience. In spite of herself the content of his talk interested her. And as for the effect upon her of his singular enthusiasm, it was deep and compelling. The little-boned Berkshire razorback hogs grew so large and fat and heavy that their bones broke under their weight. The Duroc jerseys were the best breed in that latitude, owing to their larger and stronger bones, that enabled them to stand up under the greatest accumulation of fat.

Glenn told of his droves of pigs running wild in the canyon below. In summertime they fed upon vegetation, and at other seasons on acorns, roots, bugs, and grubs. Acorns, particularly, were good and fattening feed. They ate cedar and juniper berries, and pinyon nuts. And therefore they lived off the land, at little or no expense to the owner. The only loss was from beasts and birds of prey. Glenn showed Carley how a profitable business could soon be established. He meant to fence off side canyons and to segregate droves of his hogs, and to raise abundance of corn for winter feed. At that time there was a splendid market for hogs, a condition Hutter claimed would continue indefinitely in a growing country. In conclusion Glenn eloquently told how in his necessity he had accepted gratefully the humblest of labors, to find in the hard pursuit of it a rejuvenation of body and mind, and a promise of independence and prosperity.

When he had finished, and excused himself to go repair a weak place in the corral fence, Carley sat silent, wrapped in strange meditation.

Whither had faded the vulgarity and ignominy she had attached to Glenn's raising of hogs? Gone—like other miasmas of her narrow mind! Partly she understood him now. She shirked consideration of his sacrifice to his country. That must wait. But she thought of his work, and the more she thought the less she wondered.

First he had labored with his hands. What infinite meaning lay unfolding to her vision! Somewhere out of it all came the conception that man was intended to earn his bread by the sweat of his brow. But there was more to it than that. By that toil and sweat, by the friction of horny palms, by the expansion and contraction of muscle, by the acceleration of blood, something great and enduring, something physical and spiritual, came to a man. She understood then why she would have wanted to surrender herself to a man made manly by toil; she understood how a woman instinctively leaned toward the protection of a man who had used his hands—who had strength and red blood and virility who could fight like the progenitors of the race. Any toil was splendid that served this end for any man. It all went back to the survival of the fittest. And suddenly Carley thought of Morrison. He could dance and dangle attendance upon her, and amuse her—but how would he have acquitted himself in a moment of peril? She had her doubts. Most assuredly he could not have beaten down for her a ruffian like Haze Ruff. What then should be the significance of a man for a woman?

Carley's querying and answering mind reverted to Glenn. He had found a secret in this seeking for something through the labor of hands. All development of body must come through exercise of muscles. The virility of cell in tissue and bone depended upon that. Thus he had found in toil the pleasure and reward athletes had in their desultory training. But when a man learned this secret the need of work must become permanent. Did this explain the law of the Persians that every man was required to sweat every day?

Carley tried to picture to herself Glenn's attitude of mind when he had first gone to work here in the West. Resolutely she now denied her shrinking, cowardly sensitiveness. She would go to the root of this matter, if she had intelligence enough. Crippled, ruined in health, wrecked and broken by an inexplicable war, soul-blighted by the heartless, callous neglect of government and public, on the verge of madness at the insupportable facts, he had yet been wonderful enough, true enough to himself and God, to fight for life with the instinct of a man, to fight for his mind with a noble and unquenchable faith. Alone indeed he had been alone! And by some miracle beyond the power of understanding he had found day by day in his painful efforts some hope and strength to go on. He could not have had any illusions. For Glenn Kilbourne the health and happiness and success most men held so dear must have seemed impossible. His slow, daily, tragic, and terrible task must have been something he owed himself. Not for Carley Burch! She like all the others had failed him. How Carley shuddered in confession of that! Not for the country which had used him and cast him off! Carley divined now, as if by a flash of lightning, the meaning of Glenn's strange, cold, scornful, and aloof manner when he had encountered young men of his station, as capable and as strong as he, who had escaped the service of the army. For him these men did not exist. They were less than nothing. They had waxed fat on lucrative jobs; they had basked in the presence of girls whose brothers and lovers were in the trenches or on the turbulent sea, exposed to the ceaseless dread and almost ceaseless toil of war. If Glenn's spirit had lifted him to endurance of war for the sake of others, how then could it fail him in a precious duty of fidelity to himself? Carley could see him day by day toiling in his lonely canyon—plodding to his lonely cabin. He had been playing the game—fighting it out alone as surely he knew his brothers of like misfortune were fighting.

So Glenn Kilbourne loomed heroically in Carley's transfigured sight. He was one of Carley's battle-scarred warriors. Out of his travail he had climbed on stepping-stones of his dead self. Resurgam! That had been his unquenchable cry. Who had heard it? Only the solitude of his lonely canyon, only the waiting, dreaming, watching walls, only the silent midnight shadows, only the white, blinking, passionless stars, only the wild creatures of his haunts, only the moaning wind in the pines—only these had been with him in his agony. How near were these things to God?

Carley's heart seemed full to bursting. Not another single moment could her mounting love abide in a heart that held a double purpose. How bitter the assurance that she had not come West to help him! It was self, self, all self that had actuated her. Unworthy indeed was she of the love of this man. Only a lifetime of devotion to him could acquit her in the eyes of her better self. Sweetly and madly raced the thrill and tumult of her blood. There must be only one outcome to her romance. Yet the next instant there came a dull throbbing—an oppression which was pain— an impondering vague thought of catastrophe. Only the fearfulness of love perhaps!

She saw him complete his task and wipe his brown moist face and stride toward her, coming nearer, tall and erect with something added to his soldierly bearing, with a light in his eyes she could no longer bear.

The moment for which she had waited more than two months had come at last.

"Glenn—when will you go back East?" she asked, tensely and low.

The instant the words were spent upon her lips she realized that he had always been waiting and prepared for this question that had been so terrible for her to ask.

"Carley," he replied gently, though his voice rang, "I am never going back East."

An inward quivering hindered her articulation.

"Never?" she whispered.

"Never to live, or stay any while," he went on. "I might go some time for a little visit.... But never to live."

"Oh—Glenn!" she gasped, and her hands fluttered out to him. The shock was driving home. No amaze, no incredulity succeeded her reception of the fact. It was a slow stab. Carley felt the cold blanch of her skin. "Then—this is it—the something I felt strange between us?"

"Yes, I knew—and you never asked me," he replied.

"That was it? All the time you knew," she whispered, huskily. "You knew. ... I'd never— marry you—never live out here?"

"Yes, Carley, I knew you'd never be woman enough—American enough—to help me reconstruct my broken life out here in the West," he replied, with a sad and bitter smile.

That flayed her. An insupportable shame and wounded vanity and clamoring love contended for dominance of her emotions. Love beat down all else.

"Dearest—I beg of you—don't break my heart," she implored.

"I love you, Carley," he answered, steadily, with piercing eyes on hers.

"Then come back—home—home with me."

"No. If you love me you will be my wife."

"Love you! Glenn, I worship you," she broke out, passionately. "But I could not live here—I could not."

"Carley, did you ever read of the woman who said, 'Whither thou goest, there will I go'..."

"Oh, don't be ruthless! Don't judge me.... I never dreamed of this. I came West to take you back."

"My dear, it was a mistake," he said, gently, softening to her distress. "I'm sorry I did not write you more plainly. But, Carley, I could not ask you to share this—this wilderness home with me. I don't ask it now. I always knew you couldn't do it. Yet you've changed so—that I hoped against hope. Love makes us blind even to what we see."

"Don't try to spare me. I'm slight and miserable. I stand abased in my own eyes. I thought I loved you. But I must love best the crowd—people—luxury—fashion—the damned round of things I was born to."

"Carley, you will realize their insufficiency too late," he replied, earnestly. "The things you were born to are love, work, children, happiness."

"Don't! don't!... they are hollow mockery for me," she cried, passionately. "Glenn, it is the end. It must come—quickly.... You are free."

"I do not ask to be free. Wait. Go home and look at it again with different eyes. Think things over. Remember what came to me out of the West. I will always love you—and I will be here—hoping—"

"I—I cannot listen," she returned, brokenly, and she clenched her hands tightly to keep from wringing them. "I—I cannot face you.... Here is—your ring.... You—are—free.... Don't stop me—don't come.... Oh, Glenn, good-by!"

With breaking heart she whirled away from him and hurried down the slope toward the trail. The shade of the forest enveloped her. Peering back through the trees, she saw Glenn standing where she had left him, as if already stricken by the loneliness that must be his lot. A sob broke from Carley's throat. She hated herself. She was in a terrible state of conflict. Decision had been wrenched from her, but she sensed unending strife. She dared not look back again. Stumbling and breathless, she hurried on. How changed the atmosphere and sunlight and shadow of the canyon! The looming walls had pitiless eyes for her flight. When she crossed the mouth of West Fork an almost irresistible force breathed to her from under the stately pines.

An hour later she had bidden farewell to the weeping Mrs. Hutter, and to the white-faced Flo, and Lolomi Lodge, and the murmuring waterfall, and the haunting loneliness of Oak Creek Canyon.

CHAPTER VIII

At Flagstaff, where Carley arrived a few minutes before train time, she was too busily engaged with tickets and baggage to think of herself or of the significance of leaving Arizona. But as she walked into the Pullman she overheard a passenger remark, "Regular old Arizona sunset," and that shook her heart. Suddenly she realized she had come to love the colorful sunsets, to watch and wait for them. And bitterly she thought how that was her way to learn the value of something when it was gone.

The jerk and start of the train affected her with singular depressing shock. She had burned her last bridge behind her. Had she unconsciously hoped for some incredible reversion of Glenn's mind or of her own? A sense of irreparable loss flooded over her—the first check to shame and humiliation.

From her window she looked out to the southwest. Somewhere across the cedar and pine-greened uplands lay Oak Creek Canyon, going to sleep in its purple and gold shadows of sunset. Banks of broken clouds hung to the horizon, like continents and islands and reefs set in a turquoise sea. Shafts of sunlight streaked down through creamy-edged and purple-centered clouds. Vast flare of gold dominated the sunset background.

When the train rounded a curve Carley's strained vision became filled with the upheaved bulk of the San Francisco Mountains. Ragged gray grass slopes and green forests on end, and black fringed sky lines, all pointed to the sharp clear peaks spearing the sky. And as she watched, the peaks slowly flushed with sunset hues, and the sky flared golden, and the strength of the eternal mountains stood out in sculptured sublimity. Every day for two months and more Carley had watched these peaks, at all hours, in every mood; and they had unconsciously become a part of her thought. The train was relentlessly whirling her eastward. Soon they must become a memory. Tears blurred her sight. Poignant regret seemed added to the anguish she was suffering. Why had she not learned sooner to see the glory of the mountains, to appreciate the beauty and solitude? Why had she not understood herself?

The next day through New Mexico she followed magnificent ranges and valleys—so different from the country she had seen coming West—so supremely beautiful that she wondered if she had only acquired the harvest of a seeing eye.

But it was at sunset of the following day, when the train was speeding down the continental slope of prairie land beyond the Rockies, that the West took its ruthless revenge.

Masses of strange cloud and singular light upon the green prairie, and a luminosity in the sky, drew Carley to the platform of her car, which was the last of the train. There she stood, gripping the iron gate, feeling the wind whip her hair and the iron-tracked ground speed from under her, spellbound and stricken at the sheer wonder and glory of the firmament, and the mountain range that it canopied so exquisitely.

A rich and mellow light, singularly clear, seemed to flood out of some unknown source. For the sun was hidden. The clouds just above Carley hung low, and they were like thick, heavy smoke, mushrooming, coalescing, forming and massing, of strange yellow cast of nature. It shaded westward into heliotrope and this into a purple so royal, so matchless and rare that Carley understood why the purple of the heavens could never be reproduced in paint. Here the cloud mass thinned and paled, and a tint of rose began to flush the billowy, flowery, creamy white. Then came the surpassing splendor of this cloud pageant—a vast canopy of shell pink, a sun-fired surface like an opal sea, rippled and webbed, with the exquisite texture of an Oriental fabric, pure, delicate, lovely—as no work of human hands could be. It mirrored all the warm, pearly tints of the inside whorl of the tropic nautilus. And it ended abruptly, a rounded depth of bank, on a broad stream of clear sky, intensely blue, transparently blue, as if through the lambent depths shone the infinite firmament. The lower edge of this stream took the golden lightning of the sunset and was notched for all its horizon-long length by the wondrous white glistening-peaked range of the Rockies. Far to the north, standing aloof from the range, loomed up the grand black bulk and noble white dome of Pikes Peak.

Carley watched the sunset transfiguration of cloud and sky and mountain until all were cold and gray. And then she returned to her seat, thoughtful and sad, feeling that the West had mockingly flung at her one of its transient moments of loveliness.

Nor had the West wholly finished with her. Next day the mellow gold of the Kansas wheat fields, endless and boundless as a sunny sea, rich, waving in the wind, stretched away before her aching eyes for hours and hours. Here was the promise fulfilled, the bountiful harvest of the land, the strength of the West. The great middle state had a heart of gold.

East of Chicago Carley began to feel that the long days and nights of riding, the ceaseless turning of the wheels, the constant and wearing stress of emotion, had removed her an immeasurable distance of miles and time and feeling from the scene of her catastrophe. Many days seemed to have passed. Many had been the hours of her bitter regret and anguish.

Indiana and Ohio, with their green pastoral farms, and numberless villages, and thriving cities, denoted a country far removed and different from the West, and an approach to the populous East. Carley felt like a wanderer coming home. She was restlessly and impatiently glad. But her weariness of body and mind, and the close atmosphere of the car, rendered her extreme discomfort. Summer had laid its hot hand on the low country east of the Mississippi.

Carley had wired her aunt and two of her intimate friends to meet her at the Grand Central Station. This reunion soon to come affected Carley in recurrent emotions of relief, gladness, and shame. She did not sleep well, and arose early, and when the train reached Albany she felt that she could hardly endure the tedious hours. The majestic Hudson and the palatial mansions on the wooded bluffs proclaimed to Carley that she was back in the East. How long a time seemed to have passed! Either she was not the same or the aspect of everything had changed. But she believed that as soon as she got over the ordeal of meeting her friends, and was home again, she would soon see things rationally.

At last the train sheered away from the broad Hudson and entered the environs of New York. Carley sat perfectly still, to all outward appearances a calm, superbly-poised New York woman returning home, but inwardly raging with contending tides. In her own sight she was a disgraceful failure, a prodigal sneaking back to the ease and protection of loyal friends who did not know her truly. Every familiar landmark in the approach to the city gave her a thrill, yet a vague unsatisfied something lingered after each sensation.

Then the train with rush and roar crossed the Harlem River to enter New York City. As one waking from a dream Carley saw the blocks and squares of gray apartment houses and red buildings, the miles of roofs and chimneys, the long hot glaring streets full of playing children and cars. Then above the roar of the train sounded the high notes of a hurdy-gurdy. Indeed she was home. Next to startle her was the dark tunnel, and then the slowing of the train to a stop. As she walked behind a porter up the long incline toward the station gate her legs seemed to be dead.

In the circle of expectant faces beyond the gate she saw her aunt's, eager and agitated, then the handsome pale face of Eleanor Harmon, and beside her the sweet thin one of Beatrice Lovell. As they saw her how quick the change from expectancy to joy! It seemed they all rushed upon her, and embraced her, and exclaimed over her together. Carley never recalled what she said. But her heart was full.

"Oh, how perfectly stunning you look!" cried Eleanor, backing away from Carley and gazing with glad, surprised eyes.

"Carley!" gasped Beatrice. "You wonderful golden-skinned goddess!... You're young again, like you were in our school days."

It was before Aunt Mary's shrewd, penetrating, loving gaze that Carley quailed.

"Yes, Carley, you look well—better than I ever saw you, but—but—"

"But I don't look happy," interrupted Carley. "I am happy to get home—to see you all... But—my—my heart is broken!"

A little shocked silence ensued, then Carley found herself being led across the lower level and up the wide stairway. As she mounted to the vast-domed cathedral-like chamber of the station a strange sensation pierced her with a pang. Not the old thrill of leaving New York or returning! Nor was it the welcome sight of the hurrying, well-dressed throng of travelers and commuters, nor the stately beauty of the station. Carley shut her eyes, and then she knew. The dim light of vast space above, the looming gray walls, shadowy with tracery of figures, the lofty dome like the blue sky, brought back to her the walls of Oak Creek Canyon and the great caverns under the ramparts. As suddenly as she had shut her eyes Carley opened them to face her friends.

"Let me get it over—quickly," she burst out, with hot blood surging to her face. "I—I hated the West. It was so raw—so violent—so big. I think I hate it more—now.... But it changed me—made me over physically—and did something to my soul—God knows what.... And it has saved Glenn. Oh! he is wonderful! You would never know him.... For long I had not the courage to tell him I came to bring him back East. I kept putting it off. And I rode, I climbed, I camped, I lived outdoors. At first it nearly killed me. Then it grew bearable, and easier, until I forgot. I wouldn't be honest if I didn't admit now that somehow I had a wonderful time, in spite of all.... Glenn's business is raising hogs. He has a hog ranch. Doesn't it sound sordid? But things are not always what they sound—or seem. Glenn is absorbed in his work. I hated it—I expected to ridicule it. But I ended by infinitely respecting him. I learned through his hog-raising the real nobility of work.... Well, at last I found courage to ask him when he was coming back to New York. He said 'never!'... I realized then my blindness, my selfishness. I could not be his wife and live there. I could not. I was too small, too miserable, too comfort-loving—too spoiled. And all the time he knew this—knew I'd never be big enough to marry him.... That broke my heart. I left him free—

and here I am.... I beg you—don't ask me any more—and never to mention it to me—so I can forget."

The tender unspoken sympathy of women who loved her proved comforting in that trying hour. With the confession ruthlessly made the hard compression in Carley's breast subsided, and her eyes cleared of a hateful dimness. When they reached the taxi stand outside the station Carley felt a rush of hot devitalized air from the street. She seemed not to be able to get air into her lungs.

"Isn't it dreadfully hot?" she asked.

"This is a cool spell to what we had last week," replied Eleanor.

"Cool!" exclaimed Carley, as she wiped her moist face. "I wonder if you Easterners know the real significance of words."

Then they entered a taxi, to be whisked away apparently through a labyrinthine maze of cars and streets, where pedestrians had to run and jump for their lives. A congestion of traffic at Fifth Avenue and Forty-second Street halted their taxi for a few moments, and here in the thick of it Carley had full assurance that she was back in the metropolis. Her sore heart eased somewhat at sight of the streams of people passing to and fro. How they rushed! Where were they going? What was their story? And all the while her aunt held her hand, and Beatrice and Eleanor talked as fast as their tongues could wag. Then the taxi clattered on up the Avenue, to turn down a side street and presently stop at Carley's home. It was a modest three-story brown-stone house. Carley had been so benumbed by sensations that she did not imagine she could experience a new one. But peering out of the taxi, she gazed dubiously at the brownish-red stone steps and front of her home.

"I'm going to have it painted," she muttered, as if to herself.

Her aunt and her friends laughed, glad and relieved to hear such a practical remark from Carley. How were they to divine that this brownish-red stone was the color of desert rocks and canyon walls?

In a few more moments Carley was inside the house, feeling a sense of protection in the familiar rooms that had been her home for seventeen years. Once in the sanctity of her room, which was exactly as she had left it, her first action was to look in the mirror at her weary, dusty, heated face. Neither the brownness of it nor the shadow appeared to harmonize with the image of her that haunted the mirror.

"Now!" she whispered low. "It's done. I'm home. The old life—or a new life? How to meet either. Now!"

Thus she challenged her spirit. And her intelligence rang at her the imperative necessity for action, for excitement, for effort that left no time for rest or memory or wakefulness. She accepted the issue. She was glad of the stern fight ahead of her. She set her will and steeled her heart with all the pride and vanity and fury of a woman who had been defeated but who scorned defeat. She was what birth and breeding and circumstance had made her. She would seek what the old life held.

What with unpacking and chatting and telephoning and lunching, the day soon passed. Carley went to dinner with friends and later to a roof garden. The color and light, the gayety and music, the news of acquaintances, the humor of the actors—all, in fact, except the unaccustomed heat and noise, were most welcome and diverting. That night she slept the sleep of weariness.

Awakening early, she inaugurated a habit of getting up at once, instead of lolling in bed, and breakfasting there, and reading her mail, as had been her wont before going West. Then she went over business matters with her aunt, called on her lawyer and banker, took lunch with Rose Maynard, and spent the afternoon shopping. Strong as she was, the unaccustomed heat and the hard pavements and the jostle of shoppers and the continual rush of sensations wore her out so completely that she did not want any dinner. She talked to her aunt a while, then went to bed.

Next day Carley motored through Central Park, and out of town into Westchester County, finding some relief from the stiffing heat. But she seemed to look at the dusty trees and the worn greens without really seeing them. In the afternoon she called on friends, and had dinner at home with her aunt, and then went to a theatre. The musical comedy was good, but the almost unbearable heat and the vitiated air spoiled her enjoyment. That night upon arriving home at midnight she stepped out of the taxi, and involuntarily, without thought, looked up to see the stars. But there were no stars. A murky yellow-tinged blackness hung low over the city. Carley recollected that stars, and sunrises and sunsets, and untainted air, and silence were not for city dwellers. She checked any continuation of the thought.

A few days sufficed to swing her into the old life. Many of Carley's friends had neither the leisure nor the means to go away from the city during the summer. Some there were who might have afforded that if they had seen fit to live in less showy apartments, or to dispense with cars. Other of her best friends were on their summer outings in the Adirondacks. Carley decided to go with her aunt to Lake Placid about the first of August. Meanwhile she would keep going and doing.

She had been a week in town before Morrison telephoned her and added his welcome. Despite the gay gladness of his voice, it irritated her. Really, she scarcely wanted to see him. But a meeting was inevitable, and besides, going out with him was in accordance with the plan she had adopted. So she made an engagement to meet him at the Plaza for dinner. When with slow and pondering action she hung up the receiver it occurred to her that she resented the idea of going to the Plaza. She did not dwell on the reason why.

When Carley went into the reception room of the Plaza that night Morrison was waiting for her—the same slim, fastidious, elegant, sallow-faced Morrison whose image she had in mind, yet somehow different. He had what Carley called the New York masculine face, blase and lined, with eyes that gleamed, yet had no fire. But at sight of her his face lighted up.

"By Jove! but you've come back a peach!" he exclaimed, clasping her extended hand. "Eleanor told me you looked great. It's worth missing you to see you like this."

"Thanks, Larry," she replied. "I must look pretty well to win that compliment from you. And how are you feeling? You don't seem robust for a golfer and horseman. But then I'm used to husky Westerners."

"Oh, I'm fagged with the daily grind," he said. "I'll be glad to get up in the mountains next month. Let's go down to dinner."

They descended the spiral stairway to the grillroom, where an orchestra was playing jazz, and dancers gyrated on a polished floor, and diners in evening dress looked on over their cigarettes.

"Well, Carley, are you still finicky about the eats?" he queried, consulting the menu.

"No. But I prefer plain food," she replied.

"Have a cigarette," he said, holding out his silver monogrammed case.

"Thanks, Larry. I—I guess I'll not take up smoking again. You see, while I was West I got out of the habit."

"Yes, they told me you had changed," he returned. "How about drinking?"

"Why, I thought New York had gone dry!" she said, forcing a laugh.

"Only on the surface. Underneath it's wetter than ever."

"Well, I'll obey the law."

He ordered a rather elaborate dinner, and then turning his attention to Carley, gave her closer scrutiny. Carley knew then that he had become acquainted with the fact of her broken engagement. It was a relief not to need to tell him.

"How's that big stiff, Kilbourne?" asked Morrison, suddenly. "Is it true he got well?"

"Oh—yes! He's fine," replied Carley with eyes cast down. A hot knot seemed to form deep within her and threatened to break and steal along her veins. "But if you please—I do not care to talk of him."

"Naturally. But I must tell you that one man's loss is another's gain."

Carley had rather expected renewed courtship from Morrison. She had not, however, been prepared for the beat of her pulse, the quiver of her nerves, the uprising of hot resentment at the mere mention of Kilbourne. It was only natural that Glenn's former rivals should speak of him, and perhaps disparagingly. But from this man Carley could not bear even a casual reference. Morrison had escaped the army service. He had been given a high-salaried post at the ship-yards—the duties of which, if there had been any, he performed wherever he happened to be. Morrison's father had made a fortune in leather during the war. And Carley remembered Glenn telling her he had seen two whole blocks in Paris piled twenty feet deep with leather army goods that were never used and probably had never been intended to be used. Morrison represented the not inconsiderable number of young men in New York who had gained at the expense of the valiant legion who had lost. But what had Morrison gained? Carley raised her eyes to gaze steadily at him. He looked well-fed, indolent, rich, effete, and supremely self-satisfied. She could not see that he had gained anything. She would rather have been a crippled ruined soldier.

"Larry, I fear gain and loss are mere words," she said. "The thing that counts with me is what you are."

He stared in well-bred surprise, and presently talked of a new dance which had lately come into vogue. And from that he passed on to gossip of the theatres. Once between courses of the dinner he asked Carley to dance, and she complied. The music would have stimulated an Egyptian mummy, Carley thought, and the subdued rose lights, the murmur of gay voices, the glide and grace and distortion of the dancers, were exciting and pleasurable. Morrison had the suppleness and skill of a dancing-master. But he held Carley too tightly, and so she told him, and added, "I imbibed some fresh pure air while I was out West—something you haven't here—and I don't want it all squeezed out of me."

The latter days of July Carley made busy—so busy that she lost her tan and appetite, and something of her splendid resistance to the dragging heat and late hours. Seldom was she without some of her friends. She accepted almost any kind of an invitation, and went even to Coney Island, to baseball games, to the motion pictures, which were three forms of amusement not customary with her. At Coney Island, which she visited with two of her younger girl friends, she had the best time since her arrival home. What had put her in accord with ordinary people? The baseball games, likewise pleased her. The running of the players and the screaming of the spectators amused and excited her. But she hated the motion pictures with their salacious and absurd misrepresentations of life, in some cases capably acted by skillful actors, and in others a silly series of scenes featuring some doll-faced girl.

But she refused to go horseback riding in Central Park. She refused to go to the Plaza. And these refusals she made deliberately, without asking herself why.

On August 1st she accompanied her aunt and several friends to Lake Placid, where they established themselves at a hotel. How welcome to Carley's strained eyes were the green of mountains, the soft gleam of amber water! How sweet and refreshing a breath of cool pure air! The change from New York's glare and heat and dirt, and iron-red insulating walls, and thronging millions of people, and ceaseless roar and rush, was tremendously relieving to Carley. She had burned the candle at both ends. But the beauty of the hills and vales, the quiet of the forest, the sight of the stars, made it harder to forget. She had to rest. And when she rested she could not always converse, or read, or write.

For the most part her days held variety and pleasure. The place was beautiful, the weather pleasant, the people congenial. She motored over the forest roads, she canoed along the margin of the lake, she played golf and tennis. She wore exquisite gowns to dinner and danced during the evenings. But she seldom walked anywhere on the trails and, never alone, and she never climbed the mountains and never rode a horse.

Morrison arrived and added his attentions to those of other men. Carley neither accepted nor repelled them. She favored the association with married couples and older people, and rather shunned the pairing off peculiar to vacationists at summer hotels. She had always loved to play and romp with children, but here she found herself growing to avoid them, somehow hurt by sound of pattering feet and joyous laughter. She filled the days as best she could, and usually earned quick slumber at night. She staked all on present occupation and the truth of flying time.

CHAPTER IX

The latter part of September Carley returned to New York.

Soon after her arrival she received by letter a formal proposal of marriage from Elbert Harrington, who had been quietly attentive to her during her sojourn at Lake Placid. He was a lawyer of distinction, somewhat older than most of her friends, and a man of means and fine family. Carley was quite surprised. Harrington was really one of the few of her acquaintances whom she regarded as somewhat behind the times, and liked him the better for that. But she could not marry him, and replied to his letter in as kindly a manner as possible. Then he called personally.

"Carley, I've come to ask you to reconsider," he said, with a smile in his gray eyes. He was not a tall or handsome man, but he had what women called a nice strong face.

"Elbert, you embarrass me," she replied, trying to laugh it out. "Indeed I feel honored, and I thank you. But I can't marry you."

"Why not?" he asked, quietly.

"Because I don't love you," she replied.

"I did not expect you to," he said. "I hoped in time you might come to care. I've known you a good many years, Carley. Forgive me if I tell you I see you are breaking—wearing yourself down. Maybe it is not a husband you need so much now, but you do need a home and children. You are wasting your life."

"All you say may be true, my friend," replied Carley, with a helpless little upflinging of hands. "Yet it does not alter my feelings."

"But you will marry sooner or later?" he queried, persistently.

This straightforward question struck Carley as singularly as if it was one she might never have encountered. It forced her to think of things she had buried.

"I don't believe I ever will," she answered, thoughtfully.

"That is nonsense, Carley," he went on. "You'll have to marry. What else can you do? With all due respect to your feelings—that affair with Kilbourne is ended—and you're not the wishy-washy heartbreak kind of a girl."

"You can never tell what a woman will do," she said, somewhat coldly.

"Certainly not. That's why I refuse to take no. Carley, be reasonable. You like me—respect me, do you not?"

"Why, of course I do!"

"I'm only thirty-five, and I could give you all any sensible woman wants," he said. "Let's make a real American home. Have you thought at all about that, Carley? Something is wrong today. Men are not marrying. Wives are not having children. Of all the friends I have, not one has a real American home. Why, it is a terrible fact! But, Carley, you are not a sentimentalist, or a melancholiac. Nor are you a waster. You have fine qualities. You need something to do, some one to care for."

"Pray do not think me ungrateful, Elbert," she replied, "nor insensible to the truth of what you say. But my answer is no!"

When Harrington had gone Carley went to her room, and precisely as upon her return from Arizona she faced her mirror skeptically and relentlessly. "I am such a liar that I'll do well to look at myself," she meditated. "Here I am again. Now! The world expects me to marry. But what do I expect?"

There was a raw unheated wound in Carley's heart. Seldom had she permitted herself to think about it, let alone to probe it with hard materialistic queries. But custom to her was as inexorable as life. If she chose to live in the world she must conform to its customs. For a woman marriage was the aim and the end and the all of existence. Nevertheless, for Carley it could not be without love. Before she had gone West she might have had many of the conventional modern ideas about women and marriage. But because out there in the wilds her love and perception had broadened, now her arraignment of herself and her sex was bigger, sterner, more exacting. The months she had been home seemed fuller than all the months of her life. She had tried to forget and enjoy; she had not succeeded; but she had looked with far-seeing eyes at her world. Glenn Kilbourne's tragic fate had opened her eyes.

Either the world was all wrong or the people in it were. But if that were an extravagant and erroneous supposition, there certainly was proof positive that her own small individual world was wrong. The women did not do any real work; they did not bear children; they lived on excitement and luxury. They had no ideals. How greatly were men to blame? Carley doubted her judgment here. But as men could not live without the smiles and comradeship and love of women, it was only natural that they should give the women what they wanted. Indeed, they had no choice. It was give or go without. How much of real love entered into the marriages among her acquaintances? Before marriage Carley wanted a girl to be sweet, proud, aloof, with a heart of golden fire. Not attainable except through love! It would be better that no children be born at all unless born of such beautiful love. Perhaps that was why so few children were born. Nature's balance and revenge! In Arizona Carley had learned something of the ruthlessness and inevitableness of nature. She was finding out she had learned this with many other staggering facts.

"I love Glenn still," she whispered, passionately, with trembling lips, as she faced the tragic-eyed image of herself in the mirror. "I love him more—more. Oh, my God! If I were honest I'd cry out the truth! It is terrible. ... I will always love him. How then could I marry any other man? I would be a lie, a cheat. If I could only forget him—only kill that love. Then I might love another man—and if I did love him—no matter what I had felt or done before, I would be worthy. I could feel worthy. I could give him just as much. But without such love I'd give only a husk—a body without soul."

Love, then, was the sacred and holy flame of life that sanctioned the begetting of children. Marriage might be a necessity of modern time, but it was not the vital issue. Carley's anguish revealed strange and hidden truths. In some inexplicable way Nature struck a terrible balance—revenged herself upon a people who had no children, or who brought into the world children not created by the divinity of love, unyearned for, and therefore somehow doomed to carry on the blunders and burdens of life.

Carley realized how right and true it might be for her to throw herself away upon an inferior man, even a fool or a knave, if she loved him with that great and natural love of woman; likewise it dawned upon her how false and wrong and sinful it would be to marry the greatest or the richest or the noblest man unless she had that supreme love to give him, and knew it was reciprocated.

"What am I going to do with my life?" she asked, bitterly and aghast. "I have been—I am a waster. I've lived for nothing but pleasurable sensation. I'm utterly useless. I do absolutely no good on earth."

Thus she saw how Harrington's words rang true—how they had precipitated a crisis for which her unconscious brooding had long made preparation.

"Why not give up ideals and be like the rest of my kind?" she soliloquized.

That was one of the things which seemed wrong with modern life. She thrust the thought from her with passionate scorn. If poor, broken, ruined Glenn Kilbourne could cling to an ideal and fight for it, could not she, who had all the world esteemed worth while, be woman enough to do the same? The direction of her thought seemed to have changed. She had been ready for rebellion. Three months of the old life had shown her that for her it was empty, vain, farcical, without one redeeming feature. The naked truth was brutal, but it cut clean to wholesome consciousness. Such so-called social life as she had plunged into deliberately to forget her unhappiness had failed her utterly. If she had been shallow and frivolous it might have done otherwise. Stripped of all guise, her actions must have been construed by a penetrating and impartial judge as a mere parading of her decorated person before a number of males with the purpose of ultimate selection.

"I've got to find some work," she muttered, soberly.

At the moment she heard the postman's whistle outside; and a little later the servant brought up her mail. The first letter, large, soiled, thick, bore the postmark Flagstaff, and her address in Glenn Kilbourne's writing.

Carley stared at it. Her heart gave a great leap. Her hand shook. She sat down suddenly as if the strength of her legs was inadequate to uphold her.

"Glenn has—written me!" she whispered, in slow, halting realization. "For what? Oh, why?"

The other letters fell off her lap, to lie unnoticed. This big thick envelope fascinated her. It was one of the stamped envelopes she had seen in his cabin. It contained a letter that had been written on his rude table, before the open fire, in the light of the doorway, in that little log-cabin under the spreading pines of West Ford Canyon. Dared she read it? The shock to her heart passed; and with mounting swell, seemingly too full for her breast, it began to beat and throb a wild gladness through all her being. She tore the envelope apart and read:

DEAR CARLEY:

I'm surely glad for a good excuse to write you.

Once in a blue moon I get a letter, and today Hutter brought me one from a soldier pard of mine who was with me in the Argonne. His name is Virgil Rust—queer name, don't you think?—and he's from Wisconsin. Just a rough-diamond sort of chap, but fairly well educated. He and I were in some pretty hot places, and it was he who pulled me out of a shell crater. I'd "gone west" sure then if it hadn't been for Rust.

Well, he did all sorts of big things during the war. Was down several times with wounds. He liked to fight and he was a holy terror. We all thought he'd get medals and promotion. But he didn't get either. These much-desired things did not always go where they were best deserved.

Rust is now lying in a hospital in Bedford Park. His letter is pretty blue. All he says about why he's there is that he's knocked out. But he wrote a heap about his girl. It seems he was in love with a girl in his home town—a pretty, big-eyed lass whose picture I've seen—and while he was overseas she married one of the chaps who got out of fighting. Evidently Rust is deeply hurt. He wrote: "I'd not care so... if she'd thrown me down to marry an old man or a boy who couldn't have gone to war." You see, Carley, service men feel queer about that sort of thing. It's something we got over there, and none of us will ever outlive it. Now, the point of this is that I am asking you to go see Rust, and cheer him up, and do what you can for the poor devil. It's a good deal to ask of you, I know, especially as Rust saw your picture many a time and knows you were my girl. But you needn't tell him that you—we couldn't make a go of it.

And, as I am writing this to you, I see no reason why I shouldn't go on in behalf of myself.

The fact is, Carley, I miss writing to you more than I miss anything of my old life. I'll bet you have a trunkful of letters from me—unless you've destroyed them. I'm not going to say how I miss your letters. But I will say you wrote the most charming and fascinating letters of anyone I ever knew, quite aside from any sentiment. You knew, of course, that I had no other girl correspondent. Well, I got along fairly well before you came West, but I'd be an awful liar if I denied I didn't get lonely for you and your letters. It's different now that you've been to Oak Creek. I'm alone most of the time and I dream a lot, and I'm afraid I see you here in my cabin, and along the brook, and under the pines, and riding Calico—which you came to do well—and on my hogpen fence—and, oh, everywhere! I don't want you to think I'm down in the mouth, for I'm not. I'll take my medicine. But, Carley, you spoiled me, and I miss hearing from you, and I don't see why it wouldn't be all right for you to send me a friendly letter occasionally.

It is autumn now. I wish you could see Arizona canyons in their gorgeous colors. We have had frost right along and the mornings are great. There's a broad zigzag belt of gold halfway up the San Francisco peaks, and that is the aspen thickets taking on their fall coat. Here in the canyon you'd think there was blazing fire everywhere. The vines and the maples are red, scarlet, carmine, cerise, magenta, all the hues of flame. The oak leaves are turning russet gold, and the sycamores are yellow green. Up on the desert the other day I rode across a patch of asters, lilac and lavender, almost purple. I had to get off and pluck a handful. And then what do you think? I dug up the whole bunch, roots and all, and planted them on the sunny side of my cabin. I rather guess your love of flowers engendered this remarkable susceptibility in me.

I'm home early most every afternoon now, and I like the couple of hours loafing around. Guess it's bad for me, though. You know I seldom hunt, and the trout in the pool here are so tame now they'll almost eat out of my hand. I haven't the heart to fish for them. The squirrels, too, have grown tame and friendly. There's a red squirrel that climbs up on my table. And there's a chipmunk who lives in my cabin and runs over my bed. I've a new pet—the little pig you christened Pinky. After he had the wonderful good fortune to be caressed and named by you I couldn't think of letting him grow up in an ordinary piglike manner. So I fetched him home. My dog, Moze, was jealous at first and did not like this intrusion, but now they are good friends and sleep together. Flo has a kitten she's going to give me, and then, as Hutter says, I'll be "Jake."

My occupation during these leisure hours perhaps would strike my old friends East as idle, silly, mawkish. But I believe you will understand me.

I have the pleasure of doing nothing, and of catching now and then a glimpse of supreme joy in the strange state of thinking nothing. Tennyson came close to this in his "Lotus Eaters." Only to see—only to feel is enough!

Sprawled on the warm sweet pine needles, I breathe through them the breath of the earth and am somehow no longer lonely. I cannot, of course, see the sunset, but I watch for its coming on the eastern wall of the canyon. I see the shadow slowly creep up, driving the gold before it, until at last the canyon rim and pines are turned to golden fire. I watch the sailing eagles as they streak across the gold, and swoop up into the blue, and pass out of sight. I watch the golden flush fade to gray, and then, the canyon slowly fills with purple shadows. This hour of twilight is the silent and melancholy one. Seldom is there any sound save the soft rush of the water over the stones, and that seems to die away. For a moment, perhaps, I am Hiawatha alone in his forest home, or a more primitive savage, feeling the great, silent pulse of nature, happy in unconsciousness, like a beast of the wild. But only for an instant do I ever catch this fleeting state. Next I am Glenn Kilbourne of West Fork, doomed and haunted by memories of the past. The great looming walls then become no longer blank. They are vast pages of the history of my life, with its past and present, and, alas! its future. Everything time does is written on the stones. And my stream seems to murmur the sad and ceaseless flow of human life, with its music and its misery.

Then, descending from the sublime to the humdrum and necessary, I heave a sigh, and pull myself together, and go in to make biscuits and fry ham. But I should not forget to tell you that before I do go in, very often my looming, wonderful walls and crags weave in strange shadowy characters the beautiful and unforgettable face of Carley Burch!

I append what little news Oak Creek affords.

That blamed old bald eagle stole another of my pigs.

I am doing so well with my hog-raising that Hutter wants to come in with me, giving me an interest in his sheep.

It is rumored some one has bought the Deep Lake section I wanted for a ranch. I don't know who. Hutter was rather noncommittal.

Charley, the herder, had one of his queer spells the other day, and swore to me he had a letter from you. He told the blamed lie with a sincere and placid eye, and even a smile of pride. Queer guy, that Charley!

Flo and Lee Stanton had another quarrel—the worst yet, Lee tells me. Flo asked a girl friend out from Flag and threw her in Lee's way, so to speak, and when Lee retaliated by making love to the girl Flo got mad. Funny creatures, you girls! Flo rode with me from High Falls to West Fork, and never showed the slightest sign of trouble. In fact she was delightfully gay. She rode Calico, and beat me bad in a race.

Adios, Carley. Won't you write me?

GLENN.

No sooner had Carley read the letter through to the end than she began it all over again, and on this second perusal she lingered over passages—only to reread them. That suggestion of her face sculptured by shadows on the canyon walls seemed to thrill her very soul.

She leaped up from the reading to cry out something that was unutterable. All the intervening weeks of shame and anguish and fury and strife and pathos, and the endless striving to forget, were as if by the magic of a letter made nothing but vain oblations.

"He loves me still!" she whispered, and pressed her breast with clenching hands, and laughed in wild exultance, and paced her room like a caged lioness. It was as if she had just awakened to the assurance she was beloved. That was the shibboleth—the cry by which she sounded the closed depths of her love and called to the stricken life of a woman's insatiate vanity.

Then she snatched up the letter, to scan it again, and, suddenly grasping the import of Glenn's request, she hurried to the telephone to find the number of the hospital in Bedford Park. A nurse informed her that visitors were received at certain hours and that any attention to disabled soldiers was most welcome.

Carley motored out there to find the hospital merely a long one-story frame structure, a barracks hastily thrown up for the care of invalided men of the service. The chauffeur informed her that it had been used for that purpose during the training period of the army, and later when injured soldiers began to arrive from France.

A nurse admitted Carley into a small bare anteroom. Carley made known her errand.

"I'm glad it's Rust you want to see," replied the nurse. "Some of these boys are going to die. And some will be worse off if they live. But Rust may get well if he'll only behave. You are a relative—or friend?"

"I don't know him," answered Carley. "But I have a friend who was with him in France."

The nurse led Carley into a long narrow room with a line of single beds down each side, a stove at each end, and a few chairs. Each bed appeared to have an occupant and those nearest Carley lay singularly quiet. At the far end of the room were soldiers on crutches, wearing bandages on their beads, carrying their arms in slings. Their merry voices contrasted discordantly with their sad appearance.

Presently Carley stood beside a bed and looked down upon a gaunt, haggard young man who lay propped up on pillows.

"Rust—a lady to see you," announced the nurse.

Carley had difficulty in introducing herself. Had Glenn ever looked like this? What a face! It's healed scar only emphasized the pallor and furrows of pain that assuredly came from present wounds. He had unnaturally bright dark eyes, and a flush of fever in his hollow cheeks.

"How do!" he said, with a wan smile. "Who're you?"

"I'm Glenn Kilbourne's fiancee," she replied, holding out her hand.

"Say, I ought to've known you," he said, eagerly, and a warmth of light changed the gray shade of his face. "You're the girl Carley! You're almost like my—my own girl. By golly! You're some looker! It was good of you to come. Tell me about Glenn."

Carley took the chair brought by the nurse, and pulling it close to the bed, she smiled down upon him and said: "I'll be glad to tell you all I know—presently. But first you tell me about yourself. Are you in pain? What is your trouble? You must let me do everything I can for you, and these other men."

Carley spent a poignant and depth-stirring hour at the bedside of Glenn's comrade. At last she learned from loyal lips the nature of Glenn Kilbourne's service to his country. How Carley clasped to her sore heart the praise of the man she loved—the simple proofs of his noble disregard of self! Rust said little about his own service to country or to comrade. But Carley saw enough in his face. He had been like Glenn. By these two Carley grasped the compelling truth of the spirit and sacrifice of the legion of boys who had upheld American traditions. Their children and their children's children, as the years rolled by into the future, would hold their heads higher and prouder. Some things could never die in the hearts and the blood of a race. These boys, and the girls who had the supreme glory of being loved by them, must be the ones to revive the Americanism of their forefathers. Nature and God would take care of the slackers, the cowards who cloaked their shame with bland excuses of home service, of disability, and of dependence.

Carley saw two forces in life—the destructive and constructive. On the one side greed, selfishness, materialism: on the other generosity, sacrifice, and idealism. Which of them builded for the future? She saw men as wolves, sharks, snakes, vermin, and opposed to them men as lions and eagles. She saw women who did not inspire men to fare forth to seek, to imagine, to dream, to hope, to work, to fight. She began to have a glimmering of what a woman might be.

That night she wrote swiftly and feverishly, page after page, to Glenn, only to destroy what she had written. She could not keep her heart out of her words, nor a hint of what was becoming a sleepless and eternal regret. She wrote until a late hour, and at last composed a letter she knew did not ring true, so stilted and restrained was it in all passages save those concerning news of Glenn's comrade and of her own friends. "I'll never—never write him again," she averred with stiff lips, and next moment could have laughed in mockery at the bitter truth. If she had ever had any courage, Glenn's letter had destroyed it. But had it not been a kind of selfish, false courage, roused to hide her hurt, to save her own future? Courage should have a thought of others. Yet shamed one moment at the consciousness she would write Glenn again and again, and exultant the next with the clamouring love, she seemed to have climbed beyond the self that had striven to forget. She would remember and think though she died of longing.

Carley, like a drowning woman, caught at straws. What a relief and joy to give up that endless nagging at her mind! For months she had kept ceaselessly active, by associations which were of no help to her and which did not make her happy, in her determination to forget. Suddenly then she gave up to remembrance. She would cease trying to get over her love for Glenn, and think of him and dream about him as much as memory dictated. This must constitute the only happiness she could have.

The change from strife to surrender was so novel and sweet that for days she felt renewed. It was augmented by her visits to the hospital in Bedford Park. Through her bountiful presence Virgil Rust and his comrades had many dull hours of pain and weariness alleviated and brightened. Interesting herself in the condition of the seriously disabled soldiers and possibility of their future took time and work Carley gave willingly and gladly. At first she endeavored to get acquaintances with means and leisure to help the boys, but these overtures met with such little success that she quit wasting valuable time she could herself devote to their interests.

Thus several weeks swiftly passed by. Several soldiers who had been more seriously injured than Rust improved to the extent that they were discharged. But Rust gained little or nothing. The nurse and doctor both informed Carley that Rust brightened for her, but when she was gone he lapsed into somber indifference. He did not care whether he ate or not, or whether he got well or died.

"If I do pull out, where'll I go and what'll I do?" he once asked the nurse.

Carley knew that Rust's hurt was more than loss of a leg, and she decided to talk earnestly to him and try to win him to hope and effort. He had come to have a sort of reverence for her. So, biding her time, she at length found opportunity to approach his bed while his comrades were asleep or out of hearing. He endeavored to laugh her off, and then tried subterfuge, and lastly he cast off his mask and let her see his naked soul.

"Carley, I don't want your money or that of your kind friends—whoever they are—you say will help me to get into business," he said. "God knows I thank you and it warms me inside to find some one who appreciates what I've given. But I don't want charity.... And I guess I'm pretty sick of the game. I'm sorry the Boches didn't do the job right."

"Rust, that is morbid talk," replied Carley. "You're ill and you just can't see any hope. You must cheer up—fight yourself; and look at the brighter side. It's a horrible pity you must be a cripple, but Rust, indeed life can be worth living if you make it so."

"How could there be a brighter side when a man's only half a man—" he queried, bitterly.

"You can be just as much a man as ever," persisted Carley, trying to smile when she wanted to cry.

"Could you care for a man with only one leg?" he asked, deliberately.

"What a question! Why, of course I could!"

"Well, maybe you are different. Glenn always swore even if he was killed no slacker or no rich guy left at home could ever get you. Maybe you haven't any idea how much it means to us fellows to know there are true and faithful girls. But I'll tell you, Carley, we fellows who went across got to see things strange when we came home. The good old U. S. needs a lot of faithful girls just now, believe me."

"Indeed that's true," replied Carley. "It's a hard time for everybody, and particularly you boys who have lost so—so much."

"I lost all, except my life—and I wish to God I'd lost that," he replied, gloomily.

"Oh, don't talk so!" implored Carley in distress. "Forgive me, Rust, if I hurt you. But I must tell you—that—that Glenn wrote me—you'd lost your girl. Oh, I'm sorry! It is dreadful for you now. But if you got well—and went to work—and took up life where you left it—why soon your pain would grow easier. And you'd find some happiness yet."

"Never for me in this world."

"But why, Rust, why? You're no—no—Oh! I mean you have intelligence and courage. Why isn't there anything left for you?"

"Because something here's been killed," he replied, and put his hand to his heart.

"Your faith? Your love of—of everything? Did the war kill it?"

"I'd gotten over that, maybe," he said, drearily, with his somber eyes on space that seemed lettered for him. "But she half murdered it—and they did the rest."

"They? Whom do you mean, Rust?"

"Why, Carley, I mean the people I lost my leg for!" he replied, with terrible softness.

"The British? The French?" she queried, in bewilderment.

"No!" he cried, and turned his face to the wall.

Carley dared not ask him more. She was shocked. How helplessly impotent all her earnest sympathy! No longer could she feel an impersonal, however kindly, interest in this man. His last ringing word had linked her also to his misfortune and his suffering. Suddenly he turned away from the wall. She saw him swallow laboriously. How tragic that thin, shadowed face of agony! Carley saw it differently. But for the beautiful softness of light in his eyes, she would have been unable to endure gazing longer.

"Carley, I'm bitter," he said, "but I'm not rancorous and callous, like some of the boys. I know if you'd been my girl you'd have stuck to me."

"Yes," Carley whispered.

"That makes a difference," he went on, with a sad smile. "You see, we soldiers all had feelings. And in one thing we all felt alike. That was we were going to fight for our homes and our women. I should say women first. No matter what we read or heard about standing by our allies, fighting for liberty or civilization, the truth was we all felt the same, even if we never breathed it.... Glenn fought for you. I fought for Nell.... We were not going to let the Huns treat you as they treated French and Belgian girls.... And think! Nell was engaged to me—she loved me—and, by God! She married a slacker when I lay half dead on the battlefield!"

"She was not worth loving or fighting for," said Carley, with agitation.

"Ah! now you've said something," he declared. "If I can only hold to that truth! What does one girl amount to? I do not count. It is the sum that counts. We love America—our homes—our women!... Carley, I've had comfort and strength come to me through you. Glenn will have his reward in your love. Somehow I seem to share it, a little. Poor Glenn! He got his, too. Why, Carley, that guy wouldn't let you do what he could do for you. He was cut to pieces—"

"Please—Rust—don't say any more. I am unstrung," she pleaded.

"Why not? It's due you to know how splendid Glenn was.... I tell you, Carley, all the boys here love you for the way you've stuck to Glenn. Some of them knew him, and I've told the rest. We thought he'd never pull through. But he has, and we know how you helped. Going West to see him! He didn't write it to me, but I know.... I'm wise. I'm happy for him—the lucky dog. Next time you go West—"

"Hush!" cried Carley. She could endure no more. She could no longer be a lie.

"You're white—you're shaking," exclaimed Rust, in concern. "Oh, I—what did I say? Forgive me—"

"Rust, I am no more worth loving and fighting for than your Nell."

"What!" he ejaculated.

"I have not told you the truth," she said, swiftly. "I have let you believe a lie.... I shall never marry Glenn. I broke my engagement to him."

Slowly Rust sank back upon the pillow, his large luminous eyes piercingly fixed upon her, as if he would read her soul.

"I went West—yes—" continued Carley. "But it was selfishly. I wanted Glenn to come back here.... He had suffered as you have. He nearly died. But he fought—he fought—Oh! he went through hell! And after a long, slow, horrible struggle he began to mend. He worked. He went to raising hogs. He lived alone. He worked harder and harder.... The West and his work saved him, body and soul.... He had learned to love both the West and his work. I did not blame him. But I could not live out there. He needed me. But I was too little—too selfish. I could not marry him. I gave him up. ... I left—him—alone!"

Carley shrank under the scorn in Rust's eyes.

"And there's another man," he said, "a clean, straight, unscarred fellow who wouldn't fight!"

"Oh, no—I—I swear there's not," whispered Carley.

"You, too," he replied, thickly. Then slowly he turned that worn dark face to the wall. His frail breast heaved. And his lean hand made her a slight gesture of dismissal, significant and imperious.

Carley fled. She could scarcely see to find the car. All her internal being seemed convulsed, and a deadly faintness made her sick and cold.

CHAPTER X

Carley's edifice of hopes, dreams, aspirations, and struggles fell in ruins about her. It had been built upon false sands. It had no ideal for foundation. It had to fall.

Something inevitable had forced her confession to Rust. Dissimulation had been a habit of her mind; it was more a habit of her class than sincerity. But she had reached a point in her mental strife where she could not stand before Rust and let him believe she was noble and faithful when she knew she was neither. Would not the next step in this painful metamorphosis of her character be a fierce and passionate repudiation of herself and all she represented?

She went home and locked herself in her room, deaf to telephone and servants. There she gave up to her shame. Scorned—despised—dismissed by that poor crippled flame-spirited Virgil Rust! He had reverenced her, and the truth had earned his hate. Would she ever forget his look—incredulous—shocked—bitter—and blazing with unutterable contempt? Carley Burch was only another Nell—a jilt—a mocker of the manhood of soldiers! Would she ever cease to shudder at memory of Rust's slight movement of hand? Go! Get out of my sight! Leave me to my agony as you left Glenn Kilbourne alone to fight his! Men such as I am do not want the smile of your face, the touch of your hand! We gave for womanhood! Pass on to lesser men who loved the fleshpots and who would buy your charms! So Carley interpreted that slight gesture, and writhed in her abasement.

Rust threw a white, illuminating light upon her desertion of Glenn. She had betrayed him. She had left him alone. Dwarfed and stunted was her narrow soul! To a man who had given all for her she had returned nothing. Stone for bread! Betrayal for love! Cowardice for courage!

The hours of contending passions gave birth to vague, slow-forming revolt.

She became haunted by memory pictures and sounds and smells of Oak Creek Canyon. As from afar she saw the great sculptured rent in the earth, green and red and brown, with its shining, flashing ribbons of waterfalls and streams. The mighty pines stood up magnificent and stately. The walls loomed high, shadowed under the shelves, gleaming in the sunlight, and they seemed dreaming, waiting, watching. For what? For her return to their serene fastnesses—to the little gray log cabin. The thought stormed Carley's soul.

Vivid and intense shone the images before her shut eyes. She saw the winding forest floor, green with grass and fern, colorful with flower and rock. A thousand aisles, glades, nooks, and caverns called her to come. Nature was every woman's mother. The populated city was a delusion. Disease and death and corruption stalked in the shadows of the streets. But her canyon promised hard work, playful hours, dreaming idleness, beauty, health, fragrance, loneliness, peace, wisdom, love, children, and long life. In the hateful shut-in isolation of her room Carley stretched forth her arms as if to embrace the vision. Pale close walls, gleaming placid stretches of brook, churning amber and white rapids, mossy banks and pine-matted ledges, the towers and turrets and ramparts where the eagles wheeled—she saw them all as beloved images lost to her save in anguished memory.

She heard the murmur of flowing water, soft, low, now loud, and again lulling, hollow and eager, tinkling over rocks, bellowing into the deep pools, washing with silky seep of wind-swept waves the hanging willows. Shrill and piercing and far-aloft pealed the scream of the eagle. And she seemed to listen to a mocking bird while he mocked her with his melody of many birds. The bees hummed, the wind moaned, the leaves rustled, the waterfall murmured. Then came the sharp rare note of a canyon swift, most mysterious of birds, significant of the heights.

A breath of fragrance seemed to blow with her shifting senses. The dry, sweet, tangy canyon smells returned to her—of fresh-cut timber, of wood smoke, of the cabin fire with its steaming pots, of flowers and earth, and of the wet stones, of the redolent pines and the pungent cedars.

And suddenly, clearly, amazingly, Carley beheld in her mind's sight the hard features, the bold eyes, the slight smile, the coarse face of Haze Ruff. She had forgotten him. But he now returned. And with memory of him flashed a revelation as to his meaning in her life. He had appeared merely a clout, a ruffian, an animal with man's shape and intelligence. But he was the embodiment of the raw, crude violence of the West. He was the eyes of the natural primitive man, believing what he saw. He had seen in Carley Burch the paraded charm, the unashamed and serene front, the woman seeking man. Haze Ruff had been neither vile nor base nor unnatural. It had been her subjection to the decadence of feminine dress that had been unnatural. But Ruff had found her a lie. She invited what she did not want. And his scorn had been commensurate with the falsehood of her. So might any man have been justified in his insult to her, in his rejection of her. Haze Ruff had found her unfit for his idea of dalliance. Virgil Rust had found her false to the ideals of womanhood for which he had sacrificed all but life itself. What then had Glenn Kilbourne found her? He possessed the greatness of noble love. He had loved her before the dark and changeful tide of war had come between them. How had he judged her? That last sight of him standing alone, leaning with head bowed, a solitary figure trenchant with suggestion of tragic resignation and strength, returned to flay Carley. He had loved, trusted, and hoped. She saw now what his hope had been—that she would have instilled into her blood the subtle, red, and revivifying essence of calling life in the open, the strength of the wives of earlier years, an emanation from canyon, desert, mountain, forest, of health, of spirit, of forward-gazing natural love, of the mysterious saving instinct he had gotten out of the West. And she had been too little too steeped in the indulgence of luxurious life too slight-natured and pale-blooded! And suddenly there pierced into the black storm of Carley's mind a blazing, white-streaked thought—she had left Glenn to the Western girl, Flo Hutter. Humiliated, and abased in her own sight, Carley fell prey to a fury of jealousy.

She went back to the old life. But it was in a bitter, restless, critical spirit, conscious of the fact that she could derive neither forgetfulness nor pleasure from it, nor see any release from the habit of years.

One afternoon, late in the fall, she motored out to a Long Island club where the last of the season's golf was being enjoyed by some of her most intimate friends. Carley did not play. Aimlessly she walked around the grounds, finding the autumn colors subdued and drab, like her mind. The air held a promise of early winter. She thought that she would go South before the cold came. Always trying to escape anything rigorous, hard, painful, or disagreeable! Later she returned to the clubhouse to find her party assembled on an inclosed porch, chatting and partaking of refreshment. Morrison was there. He had not taken kindly to her late habit of denying herself to him.

During a lull in the idle conversation Morrison addressed Carley pointedly. "Well, Carley, how's your Arizona hog-raiser?" he queried, with a little gleam in his usually lusterless eyes.

"I have not heard lately," she replied, coldly.

The assembled company suddenly quieted with a portent inimical to their leisurely content of the moment. Carley felt them all looking at her, and underneath the exterior she preserved with extreme difficulty, there burned so fierce an anger that she seemed to have swelling veins of fire.

"Queer how Kilbourne went into raising hogs," observed Morrison. "Such a low-down sort of work, you know."

"He had no choice," replied Carley. "Glenn didn't have a father who made tainted millions out of the war. He had to work. And I must differ with you about its being low-down. No honest work is that. It is idleness that is low down."

"But so foolish of Glenn when he might have married money," rejoined Morrison, sarcastcally.

"The honor of soldiers is beyond your ken, Mr. Morrison."

He flushed darkly and bit his lip.

"You women make a man sick with this rot about soldiers," he said, the gleam in his eye growing ugly. "A uniform goes to a woman's head no matter what's inside it. I don't see where your vaunted honor of soldiers comes in considering how they accepted the let-down of women during and after the war."

"How could you see when you stayed comfortably at home?" retorted Carley.

"All I could see was women falling into soldiers' arms," he said, sullenly.

"Certainly. Could an American girl desire any greater happiness—or opportunity to prove her gratitude?" flashed Carley, with proud uplift of head.

"It didn't look like gratitude to me," returned Morrison.

"Well, it was gratitude," declared Carley, ringingly. "If women of America did throw themselves at soldiers it was not owing to the moral lapse of the day. It was woman's instinct to save the race! Always, in every war, women have sacrificed themselves to the future. Not vile, but noble!... You insult both soldiers and women, Mr. Morrison. I wonder—did any American girls throw themselves at you?"

Morrison turned a dead white, and his mouth twisted to a distorted checking of speech, disagreeable to see.

"No, you were a slacker," went on Carley, with scathing scorn. "You let the other men go fight for American girls. Do you imagine one of them will ever marry you?... All your life, Mr. Morrison, you will be a marked man—outside the pale of friendship with real American men and the respect of real American girls."

Morrison leaped up, almost knocking the table over, and he glared at Carley as he gathered up his hat and cane. She turned her back upon him. From that moment he ceased to exist for Carley. She never spoke to him again.

Next day Carley called upon her dearest friend, whom she had not seen for some time.

"Carley dear, you don't look so very well," said Eleanor, after greetings had been exchanged.

"Oh, what does it matter how I look?" queried Carley, impatiently.

"You were so wonderful when you got home from Arizona."

"If I was wonderful and am now commonplace you can thank your old New York for it."

"Carley, don't you care for New York any more?" asked Eleanor.

"Oh, New York is all right, I suppose. It's I who am wrong."

"My dear, you puzzle me these days. You've changed. I'm sorry. I'm afraid you're unhappy."

"Me? Oh, impossible! I'm in a seventh heaven," replied Carley, with a hard little laugh. "What 're you doing this afternoon? Let's go out—riding—or somewhere."

"I'm expecting the dressmaker."

"Where are you going to-night?"

"Dinner and theater. It's a party, or I'd ask you."

"What did you do yesterday and the day before, and the days before that?"

Eleanor laughed indulgently, and acquainted Carley with a record of her social wanderings during the last few days.

"The same old things—over and over again! Eleanor don't you get sick of it?" queried Carley.

"Oh yes, to tell the truth," returned Eleanor, thoughtfully. "But there's nothing else to do."

"Eleanor, I'm no better than you," said Carley, with disdain. "I'm as useless and idle. But I'm beginning to see myself—and you—and all this rotten crowd of ours. We're no good. But you're married, Eleanor. You're settled in life. You ought to do something. I'm single and at loose ends. Oh, I'm in revolt!... Think, Eleanor, just think. Your husband works hard to keep you in this expensive apartment. You have a car. He dresses you in silks and satins. You wear diamonds. You eat your breakfast in bed. You loll around in a pink dressing gown all morning. You dress for lunch or tea. You ride or golf or worse than waste your time on some lounge lizard, dancing till time to come home to dress for dinner. You let other men make love to you. Oh, don't get sore. You do.... And so goes the round of your life. What good on earth are you, anyhow? You're just a—a gratification to the senses of your husband. And at that you don't see much of him."

"Carley, how you rave!" exclaimed her friend. "What has gotten into you lately? Why, everybody tells me you're—you're queer! The way you insulted Morrison—how unlike you, Carley!"

"I'm glad I found the nerve to do it. What do you think, Eleanor?"

"Oh, I despise him. But you can't say the things you feel."

"You'd be bigger and truer if you did. Some day I'll break out and flay you and your friends alive."

"But, Carley, you're my friend and you're just exactly like we are. Or you were, quite recently."

"Of course, I'm your friend. I've always loved you, Eleanor," went on Carley, earnestly. "I'm as deep in this—this damned stagnant muck as you, or anyone. But I'm no longer blind. There's something terribly wrong with us women, and it's not what Morrison hinted."

"Carley, the only thing wrong with you is that you jilted poor Glenn—and are breaking your heart over him still."

"Don't—don't!" cried Carley, shrinking. "God knows that is true. But there's more wrong with me than a blighted love affair."

"Yes, you mean the modern feminine unrest?"

"Eleanor, I positively hate that phrase 'modern feminine unrest!' It smacks of ultra—ultra— Oh! I don't know what. That phrase ought to be translated by a Western acquaintance of mine— one Haze Ruff. I'd not like to hurt your sensitive feelings with what he'd say. But this unrest means speed-mad, excitement-mad, fad-mad, dress-mad, or I should say undress-mad, culture-mad, and Heaven only knows what else. The women of our set are idle, luxurious, selfish, pleasure-craving, lazy, useless, work-and-children shirking, absolutely no good."

"Well, if we are, who's to blame?" rejoined Eleanor, spiritedly. "Now, Carley Burch, you listen to me. I think the twentieth-century girl in America is the most wonderful female creation of all the ages of the universe. I admit it. That is why we are a prey to the evils attending greatness. Listen. Here is a crying sin—an infernal paradox. Take this twentieth-century girl, this American girl who is the finest creation of the ages. A young and healthy girl, the most perfect type of culture possible to the freest and greatest city on earth—New York! She holds absolutely an unreal, untrue position in the scheme of existence. Surrounded by parents, relatives, friends, suitors, and instructive schools of every kind, colleges, institutions, is she really happy, is she really living?"

"Eleanor," interrupted Carley, earnestly, "she is not.... And I've been trying to tell you why."

"My dear, let me get a word in, will you," complained Eleanor. "You don't know it all. There are as many different points of view as there are people.... Well, if this girl happened to have a new frock, and a new beau to show it to, she'd say, 'I'm the happiest girl in the world.' But she is nothing of the kind. Only she doesn't know that. She approaches marriage, or, for that matter, a more matured life, having had too much, having been too well taken care of, knowing too much. Her masculine satellites—father, brothers, uncles, friends, lovers—all utterly spoil her. Mind you, I mean, girls like us, of the middle class—which is to say the largest and best class of Americans. We are spoiled.... This girl marries. And life goes on smoothly, as if its aim was to exclude friction and effort. Her husband makes it too easy for her. She is an ornament, or a toy, to be kept in a luxurious cage. To soil her pretty hands would be disgraceful! Even if she can't afford a maid, the modern devices of science make the care of her four-room apartment a farce. Electric dish-washer, clothes-washer, vacuum-cleaner, and the near-by delicatessen and the caterer simply rob a young wife of her housewifely heritage. If she has a baby—which happens occasionally, Carley, in spite of your assertion—it very soon goes to the kindergarten. Then what does she find to do with hours and hours? If she is not married, what on earth can she find to do?"

"She can work," replied Carley, bluntly.

"Oh yes, she can, but she doesn't," went on Eleanor. "You don't work. I never did. We both hated the idea. You're calling spades spades, Carley, but you seem to be riding a morbid, impractical thesis. Well, our young American girl or bride goes in for being rushed or she goes in for fads, the ultra stuff you mentioned. New York City gets all the great artists, lecturers, and surely the great fakirs. The New York women support them. The men laugh, but they furnish the money. They take the women to the theaters, but they cut out the reception to a Polish princess, a lecture by an Indian magician and mystic, or a benefit luncheon for a Home for Friendless Cats. The truth is most of our young girls or brides have a wonderful enthusiasm worthy of a better cause. What is to become of their surplus energy, the bottled-lightning spirit so characteristic of modern girls? Where is the outlet for intense feelings? What use can they make of education or of gifts? They just can't, that's all. I'm not taking into consideration the new-woman species, the faddist or the reformer. I mean normal girls like you and me. Just think, Carley. A girl's every wish, every need, is almost instantly satisfied without the slightest effort on her part to obtain it. No struggle, let alone work! If women crave to achieve something outside of the arts, you know, something universal and helpful which will make men acknowledge her worth, if not the equality, where is the opportunity?"

"Opportunities should be made," replied Carley.

"There are a million sides to this question of the modern young woman—the fin-de-siecle girl. I'm for her!"

"How about the extreme of style in dress for this remarkably-to-be-pitied American girl you champion so eloquently?" queried Carley, sarcastically.

"Immoral!" exclaimed Eleanor with frank disgust.

"You admit it?"

"To my shame, I do."

"Why do women wear extreme clothes? Why do you and I wear open-work silk stockings, skirts to our knees, gowns without sleeves or bodices?"

"We're slaves to fashion," replied Eleanor, "That's the popular excuse."

"Bah!" exclaimed Carley.

Eleanor laughed in spite of being half nettled. "Are you going to stop wearing what all the other women wear—and be looked at askance? Are you going to be dowdy and frumpy and old-fashioned?"

"No. But I'll never wear anything again that can be called immoral. I want to be able to say why I wear a dress. You haven't answered my question yet. Why do you wear what you frankly admit is disgusting?"

"I don't know, Carley," replied Eleanor, helplessly. "How you harp on things! We must dress to make other women jealous and to attract men. To be a sensation! Perhaps the word 'immoral' is not what I mean. A woman will be shocking in her obsession to attract, but hardly more than that, if she knows it."

"Ah! So few women realize how they actually do look. Haze Ruff could tell them."

"Haze Ruff. Who in the world is he or she?" asked Eleanor.

"Haze Ruff is a he, all right," replied Carley, grimly.

"Well, who is he?"

"A sheep-dipper in Arizona," answered Carley, dreamily.

"Humph! And what can Mr. Ruff tell us?"

"He told me I looked like one of the devil's angels—and that I dressed to knock the daylights out of men."

"Well, Carley Burch, if that isn't rich!" exclaimed Eleanor, with a peal of laughter. "I dare say you appreciate that as an original compliment."

"No.... I wonder what Ruff would say about jazz—I just wonder," murmured Carley.

"Well, I wouldn't care what he said, and I don't care what you say," returned Eleanor. "The preachers and reformers and bishops and rabbis make me sick. They rave about jazz. Jazz—the discordant note of our decadence! Jazz—the harmonious expression of our musicless, mindless, soulless materialism!—The idiots! If they could be women for a while they would realize the error of their ways. But they will never, never abolish jazz—never, for it is the grandest, the most wonderful, the most absolutely necessary thing for women in this terrible age of smotheration."

"All right, Eleanor, we understand each other, even if we do not agree," said Carley. "You leave the future of women to chance, to life, to materialism, not to their own conscious efforts. I want to leave it to free will and idealism."

"Carley, you are getting a little beyond me," declared Eleanor, dubiously.

"What are you going to do? It all comes home to each individual woman. Her attitude toward life."

"I'll drift along with the current, Carley, and be a good sport," replied Eleanor, smiling.

"You don't care about the women and children of the future? You'll not deny yourself now, and think and work, and suffer a little, in the interest of future humanity?"

"How you put things, Carley!" exclaimed Eleanor, wearily. "Of course I care—when you make me think of such things. But what have I to do with the lives of people in the years to come?"

"Everything. America for Americans! While you dawdle, the life blood is being sucked out of our great nation. It is a man's job to fight; it is a woman's to save.... I think you've made your choice, though you don't realize it. I'm praying to God that I'll rise to mine."

Carley had a visitor one morning earlier than the usual or conventional time for calls.

"He wouldn't give no name," said the maid. "He wears soldier clothes, ma'am, and he's pale, and walks with a cane."

"Tell him I'll be right down," replied Carley.

Her hands trembled while she hurriedly dressed. Could this caller be Virgil Rust? She hoped so, but she doubted.

As she entered the parlor a tall young man in worn khaki rose to meet her. At first glance she could not name him, though she recognized the pale face and light-blue eyes, direct and steady.

"Good morning, Miss Burch," he said. "I hope you'll excuse so early a call. You remember me, don't you? I'm George Burton, who had the bunk next to Rust's."

"Surely I remember you, Mr. Burton, and I'm glad to see you," replied Carley, shaking hands with him. "Please sit down. Your being here must mean you're discharged from the hospital."

"Yes, I was discharged, all right," he said.

"Which means you're well again. That is fine. I'm very glad."

"I was put out to make room for a fellow in bad shape. I'm still shaky and weak," he replied. "But I'm glad to go. I've pulled through pretty good, and it'll not be long until I'm strong again. It was the 'flu' that kept me down."

"You must be careful. May I ask where you're going and what you expect to do?"

"Yes, that's what I came to tell you," he replied, frankly. "I want you to help me a little. I'm from Illinois and my people aren't so badly off. But I don't want to go back to my home town down and out, you know. Besides, the winters are cold there. The doctor advises me to go to a little milder climate. You see, I was gassed, and got the 'flu' afterward. But I know I'll be all right if I'm careful.... Well, I've always had a leaning toward agriculture, and I want to go to Kansas. Southern Kansas. I want to travel around till I find a place I like, and there I'll get a job. Not too hard a job at first—that's why I'll need a little money. I know what to do. I want to lose myself in the wheat country and forget the—the war. I'll not be afraid of work, presently.... Now, Miss Burch, you've been so kind—I'm going to ask you to lend me a little money. I'll pay it back. I can't promise just when. But some day. Will you?"

"Assuredly I will," she replied, heartily. "I'm happy to have the opportunity to help you. How much will you need for immediate use? Five hundred dollars?"

"Oh no, not so much as that," he replied. "Just railroad fare home, and then to Kansas, and to pay board while I get well, you know, and look around."

"We'll make it five hundred, anyway," she replied, and, rising, she went toward the library. "Excuse me a moment." She wrote the check and, returning, gave it to him.

"You're very good," he said, rather low.

"Not at all," replied Carley. "You have no idea how much it means to me to be permitted to help you. Before I forget, I must ask you, can you cash that check here in New York?"

"Not unless you identify me," he said, ruefully, "I don't know anyone I could ask."

"Well, when you leave here go at once to my bank—it's on Thirty-fourth Street—and I'll telephone the cashier. So you'll not have any difficulty. Will you leave New York at once?"

"I surely will. It's an awful place. Two years ago when I came here with my company I thought it was grand. But I guess I lost something over there. ... I want to be where it's quiet. Where I won't see many people."

"I think I understand," returned Carley. "Then I suppose you're in a hurry to get home? Of course you have a girl you're just dying to see?"

"No, I'm sorry to say I haven't," he replied, simply. "I was glad I didn't have to leave a sweetheart behind, when I went to France. But it wouldn't be so bad to have one to go back to now."

"Don't you worry!" exclaimed Carley. "You can take your choice presently. You have the open sesame to every real American girl's heart."

"And what is that?" he asked, with a blush.

"Your service to your country," she said, gravely.

"Well," he said, with a singular bluntness, "considering I didn't get any medals or bonuses, I'd like to draw a nice girl."

"You will," replied Carley, and made haste to change the subject. "By the way, did you meet Glenn Kilbourne in France?"

"Not that I remember," rejoined Burton, as he got up, rising rather stiffly by aid of his cane. "I must go, Miss Burch. Really I can't thank you enough. And I'll never forget it."

"Will you write me how you are getting along?" asked Carley, offering her hand.

"Yes."

Carley moved with him out into the hall and to the door. There was a question she wanted to ask, but found it strangely difficult of utterance. At the door Burton fixed a rather penetrating gaze upon her.

"You didn't ask me about Rust," he said.

"No, I—I didn't think of him—until now, in fact," Carley lied.

"Of course then you couldn't have heard about him. I was wondering."

"I have heard nothing."

"It was Rust who told me to come to you," said Burton. "We were talking one day, and he—well, he thought you were true blue. He said he knew you'd trust me and lend me money. I couldn't have asked you but for him."

"True blue! He believed that. I'm glad.... Has he spoken of me to you since I was last at the hospital?"

"Hardly," replied Burton, with the straight, strange glance on her again.

Carley met this glance and suddenly a coldness seemed to envelop her. It did not seem to come from within though her heart stopped beating. Burton had not changed—the warmth, the gratitude still lingered about him. But the light of his eyes! Carley had seen it in Glenn's, in Rust's—a strange, questioning, far-off light, infinitely aloof and unutterably sad. Then there came a lift of her heart that released a pang. She whispered with dread, with a tremor, with an instinct of calamity.

"How about—Rust?"

"He's dead."

The winter came, with its bleak sea winds and cold rains and blizzards of snow. Carley did not go South. She read and brooded, and gradually avoided all save those true friends who tolerated her.

She went to the theater a good deal, showing preference for the drama of strife, and she did not go anywhere for amusement. Distraction and amusement seemed to be dead issues for her. But she could become absorbed in any argument on the good or evil of the present day. Socialism reached into her mind, to be rejected. She had never understood it clearly, but it seemed to her a state of mind where dissatisfied men and women wanted to share what harder working or more gifted people possessed. There were a few who had too much of the world's goods and many who had too little. A readjustment of such inequality and injustice must come, but Carley did not see the remedy in Socialism.

She devoured books on the war with a morbid curiosity and hope that she would find some illuminating truth as to the uselessness of sacrificing young men in the glory and prime of their lives. To her war appeared a matter of human nature rather than politics. Hate really was an effect of war. In her judgment future wars could be avoided only in two ways—by men becoming honest and just or by women refusing to have children to be sacrificed. As there seemed no indication whatever of the former, she wondered how soon all women of all races would meet on a common height, with the mounting spirit that consumed her own heart. Such time must come. She granted every argument for war and flung against it one ringing passionate truth—agony of mangled soldiers and agony of women and children. There was no justification for offensive war. It was monstrous and hideous. If nature and evolution proved the absolute need of strife, war, blood, and death in the progress of animal and man toward perfection, then it would be better to abandon this Christless code and let the race of man die out.

All through these weeks she longed for a letter from Glenn. But it did not come. Had he finally roused to the sweetness and worth and love of the western girl, Flo Hutter? Carley knew absolutely, through both intelligence and intuition, that Glenn Kilbourne would never love Flo. Yet such was her intensity and stress at times, especially in the darkness of waking hours, that jealousy overcame her and insidiously worked its havoc. Peace and a strange kind of joy came to her in dreams of her walks and rides and climbs in Arizona, of the lonely canyon where it always seemed afternoon, of the tremendous colored vastness of that Painted Desert. But she resisted these dreams now because when she awoke from them she suffered such a yearning that it became unbearable. Then she knew the feeling of the loneliness and solitude of the hills. Then she knew the sweetness of the murmur of falling water, the wind in the pines, the song of birds, the white radiance of the stars, the break of day and its gold-flushed close. But she had not yet divined their meaning. It was not all love for Glenn Kilbourne. Had city life palled upon her solely because of the absence of her lover? So Carley plodded on, like one groping in the night, fighting shadows.

One day she received a card from an old schoolmate, a girl who had married out of Carley's set, and had been ostracized. She was living down on Long Island, at a little country place named Wading River. Her husband was an electrician—something of an inventor. He worked hard. A baby boy had just come to them. Would not Carley run down on the train to see the youngster?

That was a strong and trenchant call. Carley went. She found indeed a country village, and on the outskirts of it a little cottage that must have been pretty in summer, when the green was on vines and trees. Her old schoolmate was rosy, plump, bright-eyed, and happy. She saw in Carley no change—a fact that somehow rebounded sweetly on Carley's consciousness. Elsie prattled of herself and her husband and how they had worked to earn this little home, and then the baby.

When Carley saw the adorable dark-eyed, pink-toed, curly-fisted baby she understood Elsie's happiness and reveled in it. When she felt the soft, warm, living little body in her arms, against her breast, then she absorbed some incalculable and mysterious strength. What were the trivial, sordid, and selfish feelings that kept her in tumult compared to this welling emotion? Had she the secret in her arms? Babies and Carley had never become closely acquainted in those infrequent meetings that were usually the result of chance. But Elsie's baby nestled to her breast and cooed to her and clung to her finger. When at length the youngster was laid in his crib it seemed to Carley that the fragrance and the soul of him remained with her.

"A real American boy!" she murmured.

"You can just bet he is," replied Elsie. "Carley, you ought to see his dad."

"I'd like to meet him," said Carley, thoughtfully. "Elsie, was he in the service?"

"Yes. He was on one of the navy transports that took munitions to France. Think of me, carrying this baby, with my husband on a boat full of explosives and with German submarines roaming the ocean! Oh, it was horrible!"

"But he came back, and now all's well with you," said Carley, with a smile of earnestness. "I'm very glad, Elsie."

"Yes—but I shudder when I think of a possible war in the future. I'm going to raise boys, and girls, too, I hope—and the thought of war is torturing."

Carley found her return train somewhat late, and she took advantage of the delay to walk out to the wooded headlands above the Sound.

It was a raw March day, with a steely sun going down in a pale-gray sky. Patches of snow lingered in sheltered brushy places. This bit of woodland had a floor of soft sand that dragged at Carley's feet. There were sere and brown leaves still fluttering on the scrub-oaks. At length Carley came out on the edge of the bluff with the gray expanse of sea beneath her, and a long wandering shore line, ragged with wreckage or driftwood. The surge of water rolled in—a long, low, white, creeping line that softly roared on the beach and dragged the pebbles gratingly back. There was neither boat nor living creature in sight.

Carley felt the scene ease a clutching hand within her breast. Here was loneliness and solitude vastly different from that of Oak Creek Canyon, yet it held the same intangible power to soothe. The swish of the surf, the moan of the wind in the evergreens, were voices that called to her. How many more miles of lonely land than peopled cities! Then the sea—how vast! And over that the illimitable and infinite sky, and beyond, the endless realms of space. It helped her somehow to see and hear and feel the eternal presence of nature. In communion with nature the significance of life might be realized. She remembered Glenn quoting: "The world is too much with us. ... Getting and spending, we lay waste our powers." What were our powers? What did God intend men to do with hands and bodies and gifts and souls? She gazed back over the bleak land and then out across the broad sea. Only a millionth part of the surface of the unsubmerged earth knew the populous abodes of man. And the lonely sea, inhospitable to stable homes of men, was thrice the area of the land. Were men intended, then, to congregate in few places, to squabble and to bicker and breed the discontents that led to injustice, hatred, and war? What a mystery it all was! But Nature was neither false nor little, however cruel she might be.

Once again Carley fell under the fury of her ordeal. Wavering now, restless and sleepless, given to violent starts and slow spells of apathy, she was wearing to defeat.

That spring day, one year from the day she had left New York for Arizona, she wished to spend alone. But her thoughts grew unbearable. She summed up the endless year. Could she live another like it? Something must break within her.

She went out. The air was warm and balmy, carrying that subtle current which caused the mild madness of spring fever. In the Park the greening of the grass, the opening of buds, the singing of birds, the gladness of children, the light on the water, the warm sun—all seemed to reproach her. Carley fled from the Park to the home of Beatrice Lovell; and there, unhappily, she encountered those of her acquaintance with whom she had least patience. They forced her to think too keenly of herself. They appeared carefree while she was miserable.

Over teacups there were waging gossip and argument and criticism. When Carley entered with Beatrice there was a sudden hush and then a murmur.

"Hello, Carley! Now say it to our faces," called out Geralda Conners, a fair, handsome young woman of thirty, exquisitely gowned in the latest mode, and whose brilliantly tinted complexion was not the natural one of health.

"Say what, Geralda?" asked Carley. "I certainly would not say anything behind your backs that I wouldn't repeat here."

"Eleanor has been telling us how you simply burned us up."

"We did have an argument. And I'm not sure I said all I wanted to."

"Say the rest here," drawled a lazy, mellow voice. "For Heaven's sake, stir us up. If I could get a kick out of anything I'd bless it."

"Carley, go on the stage," advised another. "You've got Elsie Ferguson tied to the mast for looks. And lately you're surely tragic enough."

"I wish you'd go somewhere far off!" observed a third. "My husband is dippy about you."

"Girls, do you know that you actually have not one sensible idea in your heads?" retorted Carley.

"Sensible? I should hope not. Who wants to be sensible?"

Geralda battered her teacup on a saucer. "Listen," she called. "I wasn't kidding Carley. I am good and sore. She goes around knocking everybody and saying New York backs Sodom off the boards. I want her to come out with it right here."

"I dare say I've talked too much," returned Carley. "It's been a rather hard winter on me. Perhaps, indeed, I've tried the patience of my friends."

"See here, Carley," said Geralda, deliberately, "just because you've had life turn to bitter ashes in your mouth you've no right to poison it for us. We all find it pretty sweet. You're an unsatisfied woman and if you don't marry somebody you'll end by being a reformer or fanatic."

"I'd rather end that way than rot in a shell," retorted Carley.

"I declare, you make me see red, Carley," flashed Geralda, angrily. "No wonder Morrison roasts you to everybody. He says Glenn Kilbourne threw you down for some Western girl. If that's true it's pretty small of you to vent your spleen on us."

Carley felt the gathering of a mighty resistless force, But Geralda Conners was nothing to her except the target for a thunderbolt.

"I have no spleen," she replied, with a dignity of passion. "I have only pity. I was as blind as you. If heartbreak tore the scales from my eyes, perhaps that is well for me. For I see something terribly wrong in myself, in you, in all of us, in the life of today."

"You keep your pity to yourself. You need it," answered Geralda, with heat. "There's nothing wrong with me or my friends or life in good old New York."

"Nothing wrong!" cried Carley. "Listen. Nothing wrong in you or life today—nothing for you women to make right? You are blind as bats—as dead to living truth as if you were buried. Nothing wrong when thousands of crippled soldiers have no homes—no money—no friends—no work—in many cases no food or bed?... Splendid young men who went away in their prime to fight for you and came back ruined, suffering! Nothing wrong when sane women with the vote might rid politics of partisanship, greed, crookedness? Nothing wrong when prohibition is mocked by women—when the greatest boon ever granted this country is derided and beaten down and cheated? Nothing wrong when there are half a million defective children in this city? Nothing wrong when there are not enough schools and teachers to educate our boys and girls, when those teachers are shamefully underpaid? Nothing wrong when the mothers of this great country let their youngsters go to the dark motion picture halls and night after night in thousands of towns over all this broad land see pictures that the juvenile court and the educators and keepers of reform schools say make burglars, crooks, and murderers of our boys and vampires of our girls? Nothing wrong when these young adolescent girls ape you and wear stockings rolled under their knees below their skirts and use a lip stick and paint their faces and darken their eyes and pluck their eyebrows and absolutely do not know what shame is? Nothing wrong when you may find in any city women standing at street corners distributing booklets on birth control? Nothing wrong when great magazines print no page or picture without its sex appeal? Nothing wrong when the automobile, so convenient for the innocent little run out of town, presents the greatest evil that ever menaced American girls! Nothing wrong when money is god—when luxury, pleasure, excitement, speed are the striven for? Nothing wrong when some of your husbands spend more of their time with other women than with you? Nothing wrong with jazz—where the lights go out in the dance hall and the dancers jiggle and toddle and wiggle in a frenzy? Nothing wrong in a country where the greatest college cannot report birth of one child to each graduate in ten years? Nothing wrong with race suicide and the incoming horde of foreigners?... Nothing wrong with you women who cannot or will not stand childbirth? Nothing wrong with most of you, when if you did have a child, you could not nurse it?... Oh, my God, there's nothing wrong with America except that she staggers under a Titanic burden that only mothers of sons can remove!... You doll women, you parasites, you toys of men, you silken-wrapped geisha girls, you painted, idle, purring cats, you parody of the females of your species—find brains enough if you can to see the doom hanging over you and revolt before it is too late!"

CHAPTER XI

Carley burst in upon her aunt.

"Look at me, Aunt Mary!" she cried, radiant and exultant. "I'm going back out West to marry Glenn and live his life!"

The keen old eyes of her aunt softened and dimmed. "Dear Carley, I've known that for a long time. You've found yourself at last."

Then Carley breathlessly babbled her hastily formed plans, every word of which seemed to rush her onward.

"You're going to surprise Glenn again?" queried Aunt Mary.

"Oh, I must! I want to see his face when I tell him."

"Well, I hope he won't surprise you," declared the old lady. "When did you hear from him last?"

"In January. It seems ages—but—Aunt Mary, you don't imagine Glenn—"

"I imagine nothing," interposed her aunt. "It will turn out happily and I'll have some peace in my old age. But, Carley, what's to become of me?"

"Oh, I never thought!" replied Carley, blankly. "It will be lonely for you. Auntie, I'll come back in the fall for a few weeks. Glenn will let me."

"Let you? Ye gods! So you've come to that? Imperious Carley Burch!... Thank Heaven, you'll now be satisfied to be let do things."

"I'd—I'd crawl for him," breathed Carley.

"Well, child, as you can't be practical, I'll have to be," replied Aunt Mary, seriously. "Fortunately for you I am a woman of quick decision. Listen. I'll go West with you. I want to see the Grand Canyon. Then I'll go on to California, where I have old friends I've not seen for years. When you get your new home all fixed up I'll spend awhile with you. And if I want to come back to New York now and then I'll go to a hotel. It is settled. I think the change will benefit me."

"Auntie, you make me very happy. I could ask no more," said Carley.

Swiftly as endless tasks could make them the days passed. But those on the train dragged interminably.

Carley sent her aunt through to the Canyon while she stopped off at Flagstaff to store innumerable trunks and bags. The first news she heard of Glenn and the Hutters was that they had gone to the Tonto Basin to buy hogs and would be absent at least a month. This gave birth to a new plan in Carley's mind. She would doubly surprise Glenn. Wherefore she took council with some Flagstaff business men and engaged them to set a force of men at work on the Deep Lake property, making the improvements she desired, and hauling lumber, cement, bricks, machinery, supplies—all the necessaries for building construction. Also she instructed them to throw up a tent house for her to live in during the work, and to engage a reliable Mexican man with his wife for servants. When she left for the Canyon she was happier than ever before in her life.

It was near the coming of sunset when Carley first looked down into the Grand Canyon. She had forgotten Glenn's tribute to this place. In her rapturous excitement of preparation and travel the Canyon had been merely a name. But now she saw it and she was stunned.

What a stupendous chasm, gorgeous in sunset color on the heights, purpling into mystic shadows in the depths! There was a wonderful brightness of all the millions of red and yellow and gray surfaces still exposed to the sun. Carley did not feel a thrill, because feeling seemed inhibited. She looked and looked, yet was reluctant to keep on looking. She possessed no image in mind with which to compare this grand and mystic spectacle. A transformation of color and shade appeared to be going on swiftly, as if gods were changing the scenes of a Titanic stage. As she gazed the dark fringed line of the north rim turned to burnished gold, and she watched that with fascinated eyes. It turned rose, it lost its fire, it faded to quiet cold gray. The sun had set.

Then the wind blew cool through the pinyons on the rim. There was a sweet tang of cedar and sage on the air and that indefinable fragrance peculiar to the canyon country of Arizona. How it brought back to Carley remembrance of Oak Creek! In the west, across the purple notches of the abyss, a dull gold flare showed where the sun had gone down.

In the morning at eight o'clock there were great irregular black shadows under the domes and peaks and escarpments. Bright Angel Canyon was all dark, showing dimly its ragged lines. At noon there were no shadows and all the colossal gorge lay glaring under the sun. In the evening Carley watched the Canyon as again the sun was setting.

Deep dark-blue shadows, like purple sails of immense ships, in wonderful contrast with the bright sunlit slopes, grew and rose toward the east, down the canyons and up the walls that faced the west. For a long while there was no red color, and the first indication of it was a dull bronze. Carley looked down into the void, at the sailing birds, at the precipitous slopes, and the dwarf spruces and the weathered old yellow cliffs. When she looked up again the shadows out there were no longer dark. They were clear. The slopes and depths and ribs of rock could be seen through them. Then the tips of the highest peaks and domes turned bright red. Far to the east she discerned a strange shadow, slowly turning purple. One instant it grew vivid, then began to fade. Soon after that all the colors darkened and slowly the pale gray stole over all.

At night Carley gazed over and into the black void. But for the awful sense of depth she would not have known the Canyon to be there. A soundless movement of wind passed under her. The chasm seemed a grave of silence. It was as mysterious as the stars and as aloof and as inevitable. It had held her senses of beauty and proportion in abeyance.

At another sunrise the crown of the rim, a broad belt of bare rock, turned pale gold under its fringed dark line of pines. The tips of the peak gleamed opal. There was no sunrise red, no fire. The light in the east was a pale gold under a steely green-blue sky. All the abyss of the Canyon was soft, gray, transparent, and the belt of gold broadened downward, making shadows on the west slopes of the mesas and escarpments. Far down in the shadows she discerned the river, yellow, turgid, palely gleaming. By straining her ears Carley heard a low dull roar as of distant storm. She stood fearfully at the extreme edge of a stupendous cliff, where it sheered dark and forbidding, down and down, into what seemed red and boundless depths of Hades. She saw gold spots of sunlight on the dark shadows, proving that somewhere, impossible to discover, the sun was shining through wind-worn holes in the sharp ridges. Every instant Carley grasped a different effect. Her studied gaze absorbed an endless changing. And at last she realized that sun and light and stars and moon and night and shade, all working incessantly and mutably over shapes and lines and angles and surfaces too numerous and too great for the sight of man to hold, made an ever-changing spectacle of supreme beauty and colorful grandeur.

She talked very little while at the Canyon. It silenced her. She had come to see it at the critical time of her life and in the right mood. The superficialities of the world shrunk to their proper insignificance. Once she asked her aunt: "Why did not Glenn bring me here?" As if this Canyon proved the nature of all things!

But in the end Carley found that the rending strife of the transformation of her attitude toward life had insensibly ceased. It had ceased during the long watching of this cataclysm of nature, this canyon of gold-banded black-fringed ramparts, and red-walled mountains which sloped down to be lost in purple depths. That was final proof of the strength of nature to soothe, to clarify, to stabilize the tried and weary and upward-gazing soul. Stronger than the recorded deeds of saints, stronger than the eloquence of the gifted uplifters of men, stronger than any words ever written, was the grand, brooding, sculptured aspect of nature. And it must have been so because thousands of years before the age of saints or preachers—before the fret and symbol and figure were cut in stone—man must have watched with thought-developing sight the wonders of the earth, the monuments of time, the glooming of the dark-blue sea, the handiwork of God.

In May, Carley returned to Flagstaff to take up with earnest inspiration the labors of homebuilding in a primitive land.

It required two trucks to transport her baggage and purchases out to Deep Lake. The road was good for eighteen miles of the distance, until it branched off to reach her land, and from there it was desert rock and sand. But eventually they made it; and Carley found herself and belongings dumped out into the windy and sunny open. The moment was singularly thrilling and full of transport. She was free. She had shaken off the shackles. She faced lonely, wild, barren desert that must be made habitable by the genius of her direction and the labor of her hands. Always a thought of Glenn hovered tenderly, dreamily in the back of her consciousness, but she welcomed the opportunity to have a few weeks of work and activity and solitude before taking up her life with him. She wanted to adapt herself to the metamorphosis that had been wrought in her.

To her amazement and delight, a very considerable progress had been made with her plans. Under a sheltered red cliff among the cedars had been erected the tents where she expected to live until the house was completed. These tents were large, with broad floors high off the ground, and there were four of them. Her living tent had a porch under a wide canvas awning. The bed was a boxlike affair, raised off the floor two feet, and it contained a great, fragrant mass of cedar boughs upon which the blankets were to be spread. At one end was a dresser with large mirror, and a chiffonier. There were table and lamp, a low rocking chair, a shelf for books, a row of hooks upon which to hang things, a washstand with its necessary accessories, a little stove and a neat stack of cedar chips and sticks. Navajo rugs on the floor lent brightness and comfort.

Carley heard the rustling of cedar branches over her head, and saw where they brushed against the tent roof. It appeared warm and fragrant inside, and protected from the wind, and a subdued white light filtered through the canvas. Almost she felt like reproving herself for the comfort surrounding her. For she had come West to welcome the hard knocks of primitive life.

It took less than an hour to have her trunks stored in one of the spare tents, and to unpack clothes and necessaries for immediate use. Carley donned the comfortable and somewhat shabby outdoor garb she had worn at Oak Creek the year before; and it seemed to be the last thing needed to make her fully realize the glorious truth of the present.

"I'm here," she said to her pale, yet happy face in the mirror. "The impossible has happened. I have accepted Glenn's life. I have answered that strange call out of the West."

She wanted to throw herself on the sunlit woolly blankets of her bed and hug them, to think and think of the bewildering present happiness, to dream of the future, but she could not lie or sit still, nor keep her mind from grasping at actualities and possibilities of this place, nor her hands from itching to do things.

It developed, presently, that she could not have idled away the time even if she had wanted to, for the Mexican woman came for her, with smiling gesticulation and jabber that manifestly meant dinner. Carley could not understand many Mexican words, and herein she saw another task. This swarthy woman and her sloe-eyed husband favorably impressed Carley.

Next to claim her was Hoyle, the superintendent. "Miss Burch," he said, "in the early days we could run up a log cabin in a jiffy. Axes, horses, strong arms, and a few pegs—that was all we needed. But this house you've planned is different. It's good you've come to take the responsibility."

Carley had chosen the site for her home on top of the knoll where Glenn had taken her to show her the magnificent view of mountains and desert. Carley climbed it now with beating heart and mingled emotions. A thousand times already that day, it seemed, she had turned to gaze up at the noble white-clad peaks. They were closer now, apparently looming over her, and she felt a great sense of peace and protection in the thought that they would always be there. But she had not yet seen the desert that had haunted her for a year. When she reached the summit of the knoll and gazed out across the open space it seemed that she must stand spellbound. How green the cedared foreground—how gray and barren the downward slope—how wonderful the painted steppes! The vision that had lived in her memory shrank to nothingness. The reality was immense, more than beautiful, appalling in its isolation, beyond comprehension with its lure and strength to uplift.

But the superintendent drew her attention to the business at hand.

Carley had planned an L-shaped house of one story. Some of her ideas appeared to be impractical, and these she abandoned. The framework was up and half a dozen carpenters were lustily at work with saw and hammer.

"We'd made better progress if this house was in an ordinary place," explained Hoyle. "But you see the wind blows here, so the framework had to be made as solid and strong as possible. In fact, it's bolted to the sills."

Both living room and sleeping room were arranged so that the Painted Desert could be seen from one window, and on the other side the whole of the San Francisco Mountains. Both rooms were to have open fireplaces. Carley's idea was for service and durability. She thought of comfort in the severe winters of that high latitude, but elegance and luxury had no more significance in her life.

Hoyle made his suggestions as to changes and adaptations, and, receiving her approval, he went on to show her what had been already accomplished. Back on higher ground a reservoir of concrete was being constructed near an ever-flowing spring of snow water from the peaks. This water was being piped by gravity to the house, and was a matter of greatest satisfaction to Hoyle, for he claimed that it would never freeze in winter, and would be cold and abundant during the hottest and driest of summers. This assurance solved the most difficult and serious problem of ranch life in the desert.

Next Hoyle led Carley down off the knoll to the wide cedar valley adjacent to the lake. He was enthusiastic over its possibilities. Two small corrals and a large one had been erected, the latter having a low flat barn connected with it. Ground was already being cleared along the lake where alfalfa and hay were to be raised. Carley saw the blue and yellow smoke from burning brush, and the fragrant odor thrilled her. Mexicans were chopping the cleared cedars into firewood for winter use.

The day was spent before she realized it. At sunset the carpenters and mechanics left in two old Ford cars for town. The Mexicans had a camp in the cedars, and the Hoyles had theirs at the spring under the knoll where Carley had camped with Glenn and the Hutters. Carley watched the golden rosy sunset, and as the day ended she breathed deeply as if in unutterable relief. Supper found her with appetite she had long since lost. Twilight brought cold wind, the staccato bark of coyotes, the flicker of camp fires through the cedars. She tried to embrace all her sensations, but they were so rapid and many that she failed.

The cold, clear, silent night brought back the charm of the desert. How flaming white the stars! The great spire-pointed peaks lifted cold pale-gray outlines up into the deep star-studded sky. Carley walked a little to and fro, loath to go to her tent, though tired. She wanted calm. But instead of achieving calmness she grew more and more towards a strange state of exultation.

Westward, only a matter of twenty or thirty miles, lay the deep rent in the level desert—Oak Creek Canyon. If Glenn had been there this night would have been perfect, yet almost unendurable. She was again grateful for his absence. What a surprise she had in store for him! And she imagined his face in its change of expression when she met him. If only he never learned of her presence in Arizona until she made it known in person! That she most longed for. Chances were against it, but then her luck had changed. She looked to the eastward where a pale luminosity of afterglow shone in the heavens. Far distant seemed the home of her childhood, the friends she had scorned and forsaken, the city of complaining and striving millions. If only some miracle might illumine the minds of her friends, as she felt that hers was to be illumined here in the solitude. But she well realized that not all problems could be solved by a call out of the West. Any open and lonely land that might have saved Glenn Kilbourne would have sufficed for her. It was the spirit of the thing and not the letter. It was work of any kind and not only that of ranch life. Not only the raising of hogs!

Carley directed stumbling steps toward the light of her tent. Her eyes had not been used to such black shadow along the ground. She had, too, squeamish feminine fears of hydrophobia skunks, and nameless animals or reptiles that were imagined denizens of the darkness. She gained her tent and entered. The Mexican, Gino, as he called himself, had lighted her lamp and fire. Carley was chilled through, and the tent felt so warm and cozy that she could scarcely believe it. She fastened the screen door, laced the flaps across it, except at the top, and then gave herself up to the lulling and comforting heat.

There were plans to perfect; innumerable things to remember; a car and accessories, horses, saddles, outfits to buy. Carley knew she should sit down at her table and write and figure, but she could not do it then.

For a long time she sat over the little stove, toasting her knees and hands, adding some chips now and then to the red coals. And her mind seemed a kaleidoscope of changing visions, thoughts, feelings. At last she undressed and blew out the lamp and went to bed.

Instantly a thick blackness seemed to enfold her and silence as of a dead world settled down upon her. Drowsy as she was, she could not close her eyes nor refrain from listening. Darkness and silence were tangible things. She felt them. And they seemed suddenly potent with magic charm to still the tumult of her, to soothe and rest, to create thoughts she had never thought before. Rest was more than selfish indulgence. Loneliness was necessary to gain consciousness of the soul. Already far back in the past seemed Carley's other life.

By and by the dead stillness awoke to faint sounds not before perceptible to her—a low, mournful sough of the wind in the cedars, then the faint far-distant note of a coyote, sad as the night and infinitely wild.

Days passed. Carley worked in the mornings with her hands and her brains. In the afternoons she rode and walked and climbed with a double object, to work herself into fit physical condition and to explore every nook and corner of her six hundred and forty acres.

Then what she had expected and deliberately induced by her efforts quickly came to pass. Just as the year before she had suffered excruciating pain from aching muscles, and saddle blisters, and walking blisters, and a very rending of her bones, so now she fell victim to them again. In sunshine and rain she faced the desert. Sunburn and sting of sleet were equally to be endured. And that abomination, the hateful blinding sandstorm, did not daunt her. But the weary hours of abnegation to this physical torture at least held one consoling recompense as compared with her experience of last year, and it was that there was no one interested to watch for her weaknesses and failures and blunders. She could fight it out alone.

Three weeks of this self-imposed strenuous training wore by before Carley was free enough from weariness and pain to experience other sensations. Her general health, evidently, had not been so good as when she had first visited Arizona. She caught cold and suffered other ills attendant upon an abrupt change of climate and condition. But doggedly she kept at her task. She rode when she should have been in bed; she walked when she should have ridden; she climbed when she should have kept to level ground. And finally by degrees so gradual as not to be noticed except in the sum of them she began to mend.

Meanwhile the construction of her house went on with uninterrupted rapidity. When the low, slanting, wide-eaved roof was completed Carley lost further concern about rainstorms. Let them come. When the plumbing was all in and Carley saw verification of Hoyle's assurance that it would mean a gravity supply of water ample and continual, she lost her last concern as to the practicability of the work. That, and the earning of her endurance, seemed to bring closer a wonderful reward, still nameless and spiritual, that had been unattainable, but now breathed to her on the fragrant desert wind and in the brooding silence.

The time came when each afternoon's ride or climb called to Carley with increasing delight. But the fact that she must soon reveal to Glenn her presence and transformation did not seem to be all the cause. She could ride without pain, walk without losing her breath, work without blistering her hands; and in this there was compensation. The building of the house that was to become a home, the development of water resources and land that meant the making of a ranch—these did not altogether constitute the anticipation of content. To be active, to accomplish things, to recall to mind her knowledge of manual training, of domestic science, of designing and painting, to learn to cook—these were indeed measures full of reward, but they were not all. In her wondering, pondering meditation she arrived at the point where she tried to assign to her love the growing fullness of her life. This, too, splendid and all-pervading as it was, she had to reject. Some exceedingly illusive and vital significance of life had insidiously come to Carley.

One afternoon, with the sky full of white and black rolling clouds and a cold wind sweeping through the cedars, she halted to rest and escape the chilling gale for a while. In a sunny place, under the lee of a gravel bank, she sought refuge. It was warm here because of the reflected sunlight and the absence of wind. The sand at the bottom of the bank held a heat that felt good to her cold hands. All about her and over her swept the keen wind, rustling the sage, seeping the sand, swishing the cedars, but she was out of it, protected and insulated. The sky above showed blue between the threatening clouds. There were no birds or living creatures in sight. Certainly the place had little of color or beauty or grace, nor could she see beyond a few rods. Lying there, without any particular reason that she was conscious of, she suddenly felt shot through and through with exhilaration.

Another day, the warmest of the spring so far, she rode a Navajo mustang she had recently bought from a passing trader; and at the farthest end of her section, in rough wooded and ridged ground she had not explored, she found a canyon with red walls and pine trees and gleaming streamlet and glades of grass and jumbles of rock. It was a miniature canyon, to be sure, only a quarter of a mile long, and as deep as the height of a lofty pine, and so narrow that it seemed only the width of a lane, but it had all the features of Oak Creek Canyon, and so sufficed for the exultant joy of possession. She explored it. The willow brakes and oak thickets harbored rabbits and birds. She saw the white flags of deer running away down the open. Up at the head where the canyon boxed she flushed a flock of wild turkeys. They ran like ostriches and flew like great brown chickens. In a cavern Carley found the den of a bear, and in another place the bleached bones of a steer.

She lingered here in the shaded depths with a feeling as if she were indeed lost to the world. These big brown and seamy-barked pines with their spreading gnarled arms and webs of green needles belonged to her, as also the tiny brook, the blue bells smiling out of the ferns, the single stalk of mescal on a rocky ledge.

Never had sun and earth, tree and rock, seemed a part of her being until then. She would become a sun-worshiper and a lover of the earth. That canyon had opened there to sky and light for millions of years; and doubtless it had harbored sheep herders, Indians, cliff dwellers, barbarians. She was a woman with white skin and a cultivated mind, but the affinity for them existed in her. She felt it, and that an understanding of it would be good for body and soul.

Another day she found a little grove of jack pines growing on a flat mesa-like bluff, the highest point on her land. The trees were small and close together, mingling their green needles overhead and their discarded brown ones on the ground. From here Carley could see afar to all points of the compass—the slow green descent to the south and the climb to the black-timbered distance; the ridged and canyoned country to the west, red vents choked with green and rimmed with gray; to the north the grand upflung mountain kingdom crowned with snow; and to the east the vastness of illimitable space, the openness and wildness, the chased and beaten mosaic of colored sands and rocks.

Again and again she visited this lookout and came to love its isolation, its command of wondrous prospects, its power of suggestion to her thoughts. She became a creative being, in harmony with the live things around her. The great life-dispensing sun poured its rays down upon her, as if to ripen her; and the earth seemed warm, motherly, immense with its all-embracing arms. She no longer plucked the bluebells to press to her face, but leaned to them. Every blade of gramma grass, with its shining bronze-tufted seed head, had significance for her. The scents of the desert began to have meaning for her. She sensed within her the working of a great leveling process through which supreme happiness would come.

June! The rich, thick, amber light, like a transparent reflection from some intense golden medium, seemed to float in the warm air. The sky became an azure blue. In the still noontides, when the bees hummed drowsily and the flies buzzed, vast creamy-white columnar clouds rolled up from the horizon, like colossal ships with bulging sails. And summer with its rush of growing things was at hand.

Carley rode afar, seeking in strange places the secret that eluded her. Only a few days now until she would ride down to Oak Creek Canyon! There was a low, singing melody of wind in the cedars. The earth became too beautiful in her magnified sight. A great truth was dawning upon her—that the sacrifice of what she had held as necessary to the enjoyment of life—that the strain of conflict, the labor of hands, the forcing of weary body, the enduring of pain, the contact with the earth—had served somehow to rejuvenate her blood, quicken her pulse, intensify her sensorial faculties, thrill her very soul, lead her into the realm of enchantment.

One afternoon a dull, lead-black-colored cinder knoll tempted her to explore its bare heights. She rode up until her mustang sank to his knees and could climb no farther. From there she essayed the ascent on foot. It took labor. But at last she gained the summit, burning, sweating, panting.

The cinder hill was an extinct crater of a volcano. In the center of it lay a deep bowl, wondrously symmetrical, and of a dark lusterless hue. Not a blade of grass was there, nor a plant. Carley conceived a desire to go to the bottom of this pit. She tried the cinders of the edge of the slope. They had the same consistency as those of the ascent she had overcome. But here there was a steeper incline. A tingling rush of daring seemed to drive her over the rounded rim, and, once started down, it was as if she wore seven-league boots. Fear left her. Only an exhilarating emotion consumed her. If there were danger, it mattered not. She strode down with giant steps, she plunged, she started avalanches to ride them until they stopped, she leaped, and lastly she fell, to roll over the soft cinders to the pit.

There she lay. It seemed a comfortable resting place. The pit was scarcely six feet across. She gazed upward and was astounded. How steep was the rounded slope on all sides! There were no sides; it was a circle. She looked up at a round lake of deep translucent sky. Such depth of blue, such exquisite rare color! Carley imagined she could gaze through it to the infinite beyond.

She closed her eyes and rested. Soon the laboring of heart and breath calmed to normal, so that she could not hear them. Then she lay perfectly motionless. With eyes shut she seemed still to look, and what she saw was the sunlight through the blood and flesh of her eyelids. It was red, as rare a hue as the blue of sky. So piercing did it grow that she had to shade her eyes with her arm.

Again the strange, rapt glow suffused her body. Never in all her life had she been so absolutely alone. She might as well have been in her grave. She might have been dead to all earthy things and reveling in spirit in the glory of the physical that had escaped her in life. And she abandoned herself to this influence.

She loved these dry, dusty cinders; she loved the crater here hidden from all save birds; she loved the desert, the earth—above all, the sun. She was a product of the earth—a creation of the sun. She had been an infinitesimal atom of inert something that had quickened to life under the blazing magic of the sun. Soon her spirit would abandon her body and go on, while her flesh and bone returned to dust. This frame of hers, that carried the divine spark, belonged to the earth. She had only been ignorant, mindless, feelingless, absorbed in the seeking of gain, blind to the truth. She had to give. She had been created a woman; she belonged to nature; she was nothing save a mother of the future. She had loved neither Glenn Kilbourne nor life itself. False education, false standards, false environment had developed her into a woman who imagined she must feed her body on the milk and honey of indulgence.

She was abased now—woman as animal, though saved and uplifted by her power of immortality. Transcendental was her female power to link life with the future. The power of the plant seed, the power of the earth, the heat of the sun, the inscrutable creation-spirit of nature, almost the divinity of God—these were all hers because she was a woman. That was the great secret, aloof so long. That was what had been wrong with life—the woman blind to her meaning, her power, her mastery.

So she abandoned herself to the woman within her. She held out her arms to the blue abyss of heaven as if to embrace the universe. She was Nature. She kissed the dusty cinders and pressed her breast against the warm slope. Her heart swelled to bursting with a glorious and unutterable happiness.

That afternoon as the sun was setting under a gold-white scroll of cloud Carley got back to Deep Lake.

A familiar lounging figure crossed her sight. It approached to where she had dismounted. Charley, the sheep herder of Oak Creek!

"Howdy!" he drawled, with his queer smile. "So it was you-all who had this Deep Lake section?"

"Yes. And how are you, Charley?" she replied, shaking hands with him.

"Me? Aw, I'm tip-top. I'm shore glad you got this ranch. Reckon I'll hit you for a job."

"I'd give it to you. But aren't you working for the Hutters?"

"Nope. Not any more. Me an' Stanton had a row with them."

How droll and dry he was! His lean, olive-brown face, with its guileless clear eyes and his lanky figure in blue jeans vividly recalled Oak Creek to Carley.

"Oh, I'm sorry," returned she haltingly, somehow checked in her warm rush of thought. "Stanton?... Did he quit too?"

"Yep. He sure did."

"What was the trouble?"

"Reckon because Flo made up to Kilbourne," replied Charley, with a grin.

"Ah! I—I see," murmured Carley. A blankness seemed to wave over her. It extended to the air without, to the sense of the golden sunset. It passed. What should she ask—what out of a thousand sudden flashing queries? "Are—are the Hutters back?"

"Sure. Been back several days. I reckoned Hoyle told you. Mebbe he didn't know, though. For nobody's been to town."

"How is—how are they all?" faltered Carley. There was a strange wall here between her thought and her utterance.

"Everybody satisfied, I reckon," replied Charley.

"Flo—how is she?" burst out Carley.

"Aw, Flo's loony over her husband," drawled Charley, his clear eyes on Carley's.

"Husband!" she gasped.

"Sure. Flo's gone an' went an' done what I swore on."

"Who?" whispered Carley, and the query was a terrible blade piercing her heart.

"Now who'd you reckon on?" asked Charley, with his slow grin.

Carley's lips were mute.

"Wal, it was your old beau thet you wouldn't have," returned Charley, as he gathered up his long frame, evidently to leave. "Kilbourne! He an' Flo came back from the Tonto all hitched up."

CHAPTER XII

Vague sense of movement, of darkness, and of cold attended Carley's consciousness for what seemed endless time.

A fall over rocks and a severe thrust from a sharp branch brought an acute appreciation of her position, if not of her mental state. Night had fallen. The stars were out. She had stumbled over a low ledge. Evidently she had wandered around, dazedly and aimlessly, until brought to her senses by pain. But for a gleam of campfires through the cedars she would have been lost. It did not matter. She was lost, anyhow. What was it that had happened?

Charley, the sheep herder! Then the thunderbolt of his words burst upon her, and she collapsed to the cold stones. She lay quivering from head to toe. She dug her fingers into the moss and lichen. "Oh, God, to think—after all—it happened!" she moaned. There had been a rending within her breast, as of physical violence, from which she now suffered anguish. There were a thousand stinging nerves. There was a mortal sickness of horror, of insupportable heartbreaking loss. She could not endure it. She could not live under it.

She lay there until energy supplanted shock. Then she rose to rush into the darkest shadows of the cedars, to grope here and there, hanging her head, wringing her hands, beating her breast. "It can't be true," she cried. "Not after my struggle—my victory—not now!" But there had been no victory. And now it was too late. She was betrayed, ruined, lost. That wonderful love had wrought transformation in her—and now havoc. Once she fell against the branches of a thick cedar that upheld her. The fragrance which had been sweet was now bitter. Life that had been bliss was now hateful! She could not keep still for a single moment.

Black night, cedars, brush, rocks, washes, seemed not to obstruct her. In a frenzy she rushed on, tearing her dress, her hands, her hair. Violence of some kind was imperative. All at once a pale gleaming open space, shimmering under the stars, lay before her. It was water. Deep Lake! And instantly a hideous terrible longing to destroy herself obsessed her. She had no fear. She could have welcomed the cold, slimy depths that meant oblivion. But could they really bring oblivion? A year ago she would have believed so, and would no longer have endured such agony. She had changed. A cursed strength had come to her, and it was this strength that now augmented her torture. She flung wide her arms to the pitiless white stars and looked up at them. "My hope, my faith, my love have failed me," she whispered. "They have been a lie. I went through hell for them. And now I've nothing to live for.... Oh, let me end it all!"

If she prayed to the stars for mercy, it was denied her. Passionlessly they blazed on. But she could not kill herself. In that hour death would have been the only relief and peace left to her. Stricken by the cruelty of her fate, she fell back against the stones and gave up to grief. Nothing was left but fierce pain. The youth and vitality and intensity of her then locked arms with anguish and torment and a cheated, unsatisfied love. Strength of mind and body involuntarily resisted the ravages of this catastrophe. Will power seemed nothing, but the flesh of her, that medium of exquisite sensation, so full of life, so prone to joy, refused to surrender. The part of her that felt fought terribly for its heritage.

All night long Carley lay there. The crescent moon went down, the stars moved on their course, the coyotes ceased to wail, the wind died away, the lapping of the waves along the lake shore wore to gentle splash, the whispering of the insects stopped as the cold of dawn approached. The darkest hour fell—hour of silence, solitude, and melancholy, when the desert lay tranced, cold, waiting, mournful without light of moon or stars or sun.

In the gray dawn Carley dragged her bruised and aching body back to her tent, and, fastening the door, she threw off wet clothes and boots and fell upon her bed. Slumber of exhaustion came to her.

When she awoke the tent was light and the moving shadows of cedar boughs on the white canvas told that the sun was straight above. Carley ached as never before. A deep pang seemed invested in every bone. Her heart felt swollen out of proportion to its space in her breast. Her breathing came slow and it hurt. Her blood was sluggish. Suddenly she shut her eyes. She loathed the light of day. What was it that had happened?

Then the brutal truth flashed over her again, in aspect new, with all the old bitterness. For an instant she experienced a suffocating sensation as if the canvas had sagged under the burden of heavy air and was crushing her breast and heart. Then wave after wave of emotion swept over her. The storm winds of grief and passion were loosened again. And she writhed in her misery.

Some one knocked on her door. The Mexican woman called anxiously. Carley awoke to the fact that her presence was not solitary on the physical earth, even if her soul seemed stricken to eternal loneliness. Even in the desert there was a world to consider. Vanity that had bled to death, pride that had been crushed, availed her not here. But something else came to her support. The lesson of the West had been to endure, not to shirk—to face an issue, not to hide. Carley got up, bathed, dressed, brushed and arranged her dishevelled hair. The face she saw in the mirror excited her amaze and pity. Then she went out in answer to the call for dinner. But she could not eat. The ordinary functions of life appeared to be deadened.

The day happened to be Sunday, and therefore the workmen were absent. Carley had the place to herself. How the half-completed house mocked her! She could not bear to look at it. What use could she make of it now? Flo Hutter had become the working comrade of Glenn Kilbourne, the mistress of his cabin. She was his wife and she would be the mother of his children.

That thought gave birth to the darkest hour of Carley Burch's life. She became possessed as by a thousand devils. She became merely a female robbed of her mate. Reason was not in her, nor charity, nor justice. All that was abnormal in human nature seemed coalesced in her, dominant, passionate, savage, terrible. She hated with an incredible and insane ferocity. In the seclusion of her tent, crouched on her bed, silent, locked, motionless, she yet was the embodiment of all terrible strife and storm in nature. Her heart was a maelstrom and would have whirled and sucked down to hell all the beings that were men. Her soul was a bottomless gulf, filled with the gales and the fires of jealousy, superhuman to destroy.

That fury consumed all her remaining strength, and from the relapse she sank to sleep.

Morning brought the inevitable reaction. However long her other struggles, this monumental and final one would be brief. She realized that, yet was unable to understand how it could be possible, unless shock or death or mental aberration ended the fight. An eternity of emotion lay back between this awakening of intelligence and the hour of her fall into the clutches of primitive passion.

That morning she faced herself in the mirror and asked, "Now—what do I owe you?" It was not her voice that answered. It was beyond her. But it said: "Go on! You are cut adrift. You are alone. You owe none but yourself!... Go on! Not backward—not to the depths—but up—upward!"

She shuddered at such a decree. How impossible for her! All animal, all woman, all emotion, how could she live on the cold, pure heights? Yet she owed something intangible and inscrutable to herself. Was it the thing that woman lacked physically, yet contained hidden in her soul? An element of eternal spirit to rise! Because of heartbreak and ruin and irreparable loss must she fall? Was loss of love and husband and children only a test? The present hour would be swallowed in the sum of life's trials. She could not go back. She would not go down. There was wrenched from her tried and sore heart an unalterable and unquenchable decision—to make her own soul prove the evolution of woman. Vessel of blood and flesh she might be, doomed by nature to the reproduction of her kind, but she had in her the supreme spirit and power to carry on the progress of the ages—the climb of woman out of the darkness.

Carley went out to the workmen. The house should be completed and she would live in it. Always there was the stretching and illimitable desert to look at, and the grand heave upward of the mountains. Hoyle was full of zest for the practical details of the building. He saw nothing of the havoc wrought in her. Nor did the other workmen glance more than casually at her. In this Carley lost something of a shirking fear that her loss and grief were patent to all eyes.

That afternoon she mounted the most spirited of the mustangs she had purchased from the Indians. To govern him and stick on him required all her energy. And she rode him hard and far, out across the desert, across mile after mile of cedar forest, clear to the foothills. She rested there, absorbed in gazing desertward, and upon turning back again, she ran him over the level stretches. Wind and branch threshed her seemingly to ribbons. Violence seemed good for her. A fall had no fear for her now. She reached camp at dusk, hot as fire, breathless and strengthless. But she had earned something. Such action required constant use of muscle and mind. If need be she could drive both to the very furthermost limit. She could ride and ride—until the future, like the immensity of the desert there, might swallow her. She changed her clothes and rested a while. The call to supper found her hungry. In this fact she discovered mockery of her grief. Love was not the food of life. Exhausted nature's need of rest and sleep was no respecter of a woman's emotion.

Next day Carley rode northward, wildly and fearlessly, as if this conscious activity was the initiative of an endless number of rides that were to save her. As before the foothills called her, and she went on until she came to a very high one.

Carley dismounted from her panting horse, answering the familiar impulse to attain heights by her own effort.

"Am I only a weakling?" she asked herself. "Only a creature mined by the fever of the soul!... Thrown from one emotion to another? Never the same. Yearning, suffering, sacrificing, hoping, and changing—forever the same! What is it that drives me? A great city with all its attractions has failed to help me realize my life. So have friends failed. So has the world. What can solitude and grandeur do?... All this obsession of mine—all this strange feeling for simple elemental earthly things likewise will fail me. Yet I am driven. They would call me a mad woman."

It took Carley a full hour of slow body-bending labor to climb to the summit of that hill. High, steep, and rugged, it resisted ascension. But at last she surmounted it and sat alone on the heights, with naked eyes, and an unconscious prayer on her lips.

What was it that had happened? Could there be here a different answer from that which always mocked her?

She had been a girl, not accountable for loss of mother, for choice of home and education. She had belonged to a class. She had grown to womanhood in it. She had loved, and in loving had escaped the evil of her day, if not its taint. She had lived only for herself. Conscience had awakened—but, alas! too late. She had overthrown the sordid, self-seeking habit of life; she had awakened to real womanhood; she had fought the insidious spell of modernity and she had defeated it; she had learned the thrill of taking root in new soil, the pain and joy of labor, the bliss of solitude, the promise of home and love and motherhood. But she had gathered all these marvelous things to her soul too late for happiness.

"Now it is answered," she declared aloud. "That is what has happened?... And all that is past.... Is there anything left? If so what?"

She flung her query out to the winds of the desert. But the desert seemed too gray, too vast, too remote, too aloof, too measureless. It was not concerned with her little life. Then she turned to the mountain kingdom.

It seemed overpoweringly near at hand. It loomed above her to pierce the fleecy clouds. It was only a stupendous upheaval of earth-crust, grown over at the base by leagues and leagues of pine forest, belted along the middle by vast slanting zigzag slopes of aspen, rent and riven toward the heights into canyon and gorge, bared above to cliffs and corners of craggy rock, whitened at the sky-piercing peaks by snow. Its beauty and sublimity were lost upon Carley now; she was concerned with its travail, its age, its endurance, its strength. And she studied it with magnified sight.

What incomprehensible subterranean force had swelled those immense slopes and lifted the huge bulk aloft to the clouds? Cataclysm of nature—the expanding or shrinking of the earth—vast volcanic action under the surface! Whatever it had been, it had left its expression of the travail of the universe. This mountain mass had been hot gas when flung from the parent sun, and now it was solid granite. What had it endured in the making? What indeed had been its dimensions before the millions of years of its struggle?

Eruption, earthquake, avalanche, the attrition of glacier, the erosion of water, the cracking of frost, the weathering of rain and wind and snow—these it had eternally fought and resisted in vain, yet still it stood magnificent, frowning, battle-scarred and undefeated. Its sky-piercing peaks were as cries for mercy to the Infinite. This old mountain realized its doom. It had to go, perhaps to make room for a newer and better kingdom. But it endured because of the spirit of nature. The great notched circular line of rock below and between the peaks, in the body of the mountains, showed where in ages past the heart of living granite had blown out, to let loose on all the near surrounding desert the streams of black lava and the hills of black cinders. Despite its fringe of green it was hoary with age. Every looming gray-faced wall, massive and sublime, seemed a monument of its mastery over time. Every deep-cut canyon, showing the skeleton ribs, the caverns and caves, its avalanche-carved slides, its long, fan-shaped, spreading taluses, carried conviction to the spectator that it was but a frail bit of rock, that its life was little and brief, that upon it had been laid the merciless curse of nature. Change! Change must unknit the very knots of the center of the earth. So its strength lay in the sublimity of its defiance. It meant to endure to the last rolling grain of sand. It was a dead mountain of rock, without spirit, yet it taught a grand lesson to the seeing eye.

Life was only a part, perhaps an infinitely small part of nature's plan. Death and decay were just as important to her inscrutable design. The universe had not been created for life, ease, pleasure, and happiness of a man creature developed from lower organisms. If nature's secret was the developing of a spirit through all time, Carley divined that she had it within her. So the present meant little.

"I have no right to be unhappy," concluded Carley. "I had no right to Glenn Kilbourne. I failed him. In that I failed myself. Neither life nor nature failed me—nor love. It is no longer a mystery. Unhappiness is only a change. Happiness itself is only change. So what does it matter? The great thing is to see life—to understand—to feel—to work—to fight—to endure. It is not my fault I am here. But it is my fault if I leave this strange old earth the poorer for my failure.... I will no longer be little. I will find strength. I will endure.... I still have eyes, ears, nose, taste. I can feel the sun, the wind, the nip of frost. Must I slink like a craven because I've lost the love of one man? Must I hate Flo Hutter because she will make Glenn happy? Never!... All of this seems better so, because through it I am changed. I might have lived on, a selfish clod!"

Carley turned from the mountain kingdom and faced her future with the profound and sad and far-seeing look that had come with her lesson. She knew what to give. Sometime and somewhere there would be recompense. She would hide her wound in the faith that time would heal it. And the ordeal she set herself, to prove her sincerity and strength, was to ride down to Oak Creek Canyon.

Carley did not wait many days. Strange how the old vanity held her back until something of the havoc in her face should be gone!

One morning she set out early, riding her best horse, and she took a sheep trail across country. The distance by road was much farther. The June morning was cool, sparkling, fragrant. Mocking birds sang from the topmost twig of cedars; doves cooed in the pines; sparrow hawks sailed low over the open grassy patches. Desert primroses showed their rounded pink clusters in sunny places, and here and there burned the carmine of Indian paintbrush. Jack rabbits and cotton-tails bounded and scampered away through the sage. The desert had life and color and movement this June day. And as always there was the dry fragrance on the air.

Her mustang had been inured to long and consistent travel over the desert. Her weight was nothing to him and he kept to the swinging lope for miles. As she approached Oak Creek Canyon, however, she drew him to a trot, and then a walk. Sight of the deep red-walled and green-floored canyon was a shock to her.

The trail came out on the road that led to Ryan's sheep camp, at a point several miles west of the cabin where Carley had encountered Haze Ruff. She remembered the curves and stretches, and especially the steep jump-off where the road led down off the rim into the canyon. Here she dismounted and walked. From the foot of this descent she knew every rod of the way would be familiar to her, and, womanlike, she wanted to turn away and fly from them. But she kept on and mounted again at level ground.

The murmur of the creek suddenly assailed her ears—sweet, sad, memorable, strangely powerful to hurt. Yet the sound seemed of long ago. Down here summer had advanced. Rich thick foliage overspread the winding road of sand. Then out of the shade she passed into the sunnier regions of isolated pines. Along here she had raced Calico with Glenn's bay; and here she had caught him, and there was the place she had fallen. She halted a moment under the pine tree where Glenn had held her in his arms. Tears dimmed her eyes. If only she had known then the truth, the reality! But regrets were useless.

By and by a craggy red wall loomed above the trees, and its pipe-organ conformation was familiar to Carley. She left the road and turned to go down to the creek. Sycamores and maples and great bowlders, and mossy ledges overhanging the water, and a huge sentinel pine marked the spot where she and Glenn had eaten their lunch that last day. Her mustang splashed into the clear water and halted to drink. Beyond, through the trees, Carley saw the sunny red-earthed clearing that was Glenn's farm. She looked, and fought herself, and bit her quivering lip until she tasted blood. Then she rode out into the open.

The whole west side of the canyon had been cleared and cultivated and plowed. But she gazed no farther. She did not want to see the spot where she had given Glenn his ring and had parted from him. She rode on. If she could pass West Fork she believed her courage would rise to the completion of this ordeal. Places were what she feared. Places that she had loved while blindly believing she hated! There the narrow gap of green and blue split the looming red wall. She was looking into West Fork. Up there stood the cabin. How fierce a pang rent her breast! She faltered at the crossing of the branch stream, and almost surrendered. The water murmured, the leaves rustled, the bees hummed, the birds sang—all with some sad sweetness that seemed of the past.

Then the trail leading up West Fork was like a barrier. She saw horse tracks in it. Next she descried boot tracks the shape of which was so well-remembered that it shook her heart. There were fresh tracks in the sand, pointing in the direction of the Lodge. Ah! that was where Glenn lived now. Carley strained at her will to keep it fighting her memory. The glory and the dream were gone!

A touch of spur urged her mustang into a gallop. The splashing ford of the creek—the still, eddying pool beyond—the green orchards—the white lacy waterfall—and Lolomi Lodge!

Nothing had altered. But Carley seemed returning after many years. Slowly she dismounted—slowly she climbed the porch steps. Was there no one at home? Yet the vacant doorway, the silence—something attested to the knowledge of Carley's presence. Then suddenly Mrs. Hutter fluttered out with Flo behind her.

"You dear girl—I'm so glad!" cried Mrs. Hutter, her voice trembling.

"I'm glad to see you, too," said Carley, bending to receive Mrs. Hutter's embrace. Carley saw dim eyes—the stress of agitation, but no surprise.

"Oh, Carley!" burst out the Western girl, with voice rich and full, yet tremulous.

"Flo, I've come to wish you happiness," replied Carley, very low.

Was it the same Flo? This seemed more of a woman—strange now—white and strained—beautiful, eager, questioning. A cry of gladness burst from her. Carley felt herself enveloped in strong close clasp—and then a warm, quick kiss of joy. It shocked her, yet somehow thrilled. Sure was the welcome here. Sure was the strained situation, also, but the voice rang too glad a note for Carley. It touched her deeply, yet she could not understand. She had not measured the depth of Western friendship.

"Have you—seen Glenn?" queried Flo, breathlessly.

"Oh no, indeed not," replied Carley, slowly gaining composure. The nervous agitation of these women had stilled her own. "I just rode up the trail. Where is he?"

"He was here—a moment ago," panted Flo. "Oh, Carley, we sure are locoed. ... Why, we only heard an hour ago—that you were at Deep Lake.... Charley rode in. He told us.... I thought my heart would break. Poor Glenn! When he heard it.... But never mind me. Jump your horse and run to West Fork!"

The spirit of her was like the strength of her arms as she hurried Carley across the porch and shoved her down the steps.

"Climb on and run, Carley," cried Flo. "If you only knew how glad he'll be that you came!"

Carley leaped into the saddle and wheeled the mustang. But she had no answer for the girl's singular, almost wild exultance. Then like a shot the spirited mustang was off down the lane. Carley wondered with swelling heart. Was her coming such a wondrous surprise—so unexpected and big in generosity—something that would make Kilbourne as glad as it had seemed to make Flo? Carley thrilled to this assurance.

Down the lane she flew. The red walls blurred and the sweet wind whipped her face. At the trail she swerved the mustang, but did not check his gait. Under the great pines he sped and round the bulging wall. At the rocky incline leading to the creek she pulled the fiery animal to a trot. How low and clear the water! As Carley forded it fresh cool drops splashed into her face. Again she spurred her mount and again trees and walls rushed by. Up and down the yellow bits of trail—on over the brown mats of pine needles—until there in the sunlight shone the little gray log cabin with a tall form standing in the door. One instant the canyon tilted on end for Carley and she was riding into the blue sky. Then some magic of soul sustained her, so that she saw clearly. Reaching the cabin she reined in her mustang.

"Hello, Glenn! Look who's here!" she cried, not wholly failing of gayety.

He threw up his sombrero.

"Whoopee!" he yelled, in stentorian voice that rolled across the canyon and bellowed in hollow echo and then clapped from wall to wall. The unexpected Western yell, so strange from Glenn, disconcerted Carley. Had he only answered her spirit of greeting? Had hers rung false?

But he was coming to her. She had seen the bronze of his face turn to white. How gaunt and worn he looked. Older he appeared, with deeper lines and whiter hair. His jaw quivered.

"Carley Burch, so it was you?" he queried, hoarsely.

"Glenn, I reckon it was," she replied. "I bought your Deep Lake ranch site. I came back too late.... But it is never too late for some things.... I've come to wish you and Flo all the happiness in the world—and to say we must be friends."

The way he looked at her made her tremble. He strode up beside the mustang, and he was so tall that his shoulder came abreast of her. He placed a big warm hand on hers, as it rested, ungloved, on the pommel of the saddle.

"Have you seen Flo?" he asked.

"I just left her. It was funny—the way she rushed me off after you. As if there weren't two—"

Was it Glenn's eyes or the movement of his hand that checked her utterance? His gaze pierced her soul. His hand slid along her arm to her waist—around it. Her heart seemed to burst.

"Kick your feet out of the stirrups," he ordered.

Instinctively she obeyed. Then with a strong pull he hauled her half out of the saddle, pellmell into his arms. Carley had no resistance. She sank limp, in an agony of amaze. Was this a dream? Swift and hard his lips met hers—and again—and again....

"Oh, my God!—Glenn, are—you—mad?" she whispered, almost swooning.

"Sure—I reckon I am," he replied, huskily, and pulled her all the way out of the saddle.

Carley would have fallen but for his support. She could not think. She was all instinct. Only the amaze—the sudden horror—drifted—faded as before fires of her heart!

"Kiss me!" he commanded.

She would have kissed him if death were the penalty. How his face blurred in her dimmed sight! Was that a strange smile? Then he held her back from him.

"Carley—you came to wish Flo and me happiness?" he asked.

"Oh, yes—yes.... Pity me, Glenn—let me go. I meant well.... I should—never have come."

"Do you love me?" he went on, with passionate, shaking clasp.

"God help me—I do—I do!... And now it will kill me!"

"What did that damned fool Charley tell you?"

The strange content of his query, the trenchant force of it, brought her upright, with sight suddenly cleared. Was this giant the tragic Glenn who had strode to her from the cabin door?

"Charley told me—you and Flo—were married," she whispered.

"You didn't believe him!" returned Glenn.

She could no longer speak. She could only see her lover, as if transfigured, limned dark against the looming red wall.

"That was one of Charley's queer jokes. I told you to beware of him. Flo is married, yes—and very happy.... I'm unutterably happy, too—but I'm not married. Lee Stanton was the lucky bridegroom.... Carley, the moment I saw you I knew you had come back to me."

DESERT GOLD

PROLOGUE

I

A FACE haunted Cameron—a woman's face. It was there in the white heart of the dying campfire; it hung in the shadows that hovered over the flickering light; it drifted in the darkness beyond.

This hour, when the day had closed and the lonely desert night set in with its dead silence, was one in which Cameron's mind was thronged with memories of a time long past—of a home back in Peoria, of a woman he had wronged and lost, and loved too late. He was a prospector for gold, a hunter of solitude, a lover of the drear, rock-ribbed infinitude, because he wanted to be alone to remember.

A sound disturbed Cameron's reflections. He bent his head listening. A soft wind fanned the paling embers, blew sparks and white ashes and thin smoke away into the enshrouding circle of blackness. His burro did not appear to be moving about. The quiet split to the cry of a coyote. It rose strange, wild, mournful—not the howl of a prowling upland beast baying the campfire or barking at a lonely prospector, but the wail of a wolf, full-voiced, crying out the meaning of the desert and the night. Hunger throbbed in it—hunger for a mate, for offspring, for life. When it ceased, the terrible desert silence smote Cameron, and the cry echoed in his soul. He and that wandering wolf were brothers.

Then a sharp clink of metal on stone and soft pads of hoofs in sand prompted Cameron to reach for his gun, and to move out of the light of the waning campfire. He was somewhere along the wild border line between Sonora and Arizona; and the prospector who dared the heat and barrenness of that region risked other dangers sometimes as menacing.

Figures darker than the gloom approached and took shape, and in the light turned out to be those of a white man and a heavily packed burro.

"Hello there," the man called, as he came to a halt and gazed about him. "I saw your fire. May I make camp here?"

Cameron came forth out of the shadow and greeted his visitor, whom he took for a prospector like himself. Cameron resented the breaking of his lonely campfire vigil, but he respected the law of the desert.

The stranger thanked him, and then slipped the pack from his burro. Then he rolled out his pack and began preparations for a meal. His movements were slow and methodical.

Cameron watched him, still with resentment, yet with a curious and growing interest. The campfire burst into a bright blaze, and by its light Cameron saw a man whose gray hair somehow did not seem to make him old, and whose stooped shoulders did not detract from an impression of rugged strength.

"Find any mineral?" asked Cameron, presently.

His visitor looked up quickly, as if startled by the sound of a human voice. He replied, and then the two men talked a little. But the stranger evidently preferred silence. Cameron understood that. He laughed grimly and bent a keener gaze upon the furrowed, shadowy face. Another of those strange desert prospectors in whom there was some relentless driving power besides the lust for gold! Cameron felt that between this man and himself there was a subtle affinity, vague and undefined, perhaps born of the divination that here was a desert wanderer like himself, perhaps born of a deeper, an unintelligible relation having its roots back in the past. A long-forgotten sensation stirred in Cameron's breast, one so long forgotten that he could not recognize it. But it was akin to pain.

II

When he awakened he found, to his surprise, that his companion had departed. A trail in the sand led off to the north. There was no water in that direction. Cameron shrugged his shoulders; it was not his affair; he had his own problems. And straightway he forgot his strange visitor.

Cameron began his day, grateful for the solitude that was now unbroken, for the canyon-furrowed and cactus-spired scene that now showed no sign of life. He traveled southwest, never straying far from the dry stream bed; and in a desultory way, without eagerness, he hunted for signs of gold.

The work was toilsome, yet the periods of rest in which he indulged were not taken because of fatigue. He rested to look, to listen, to feel. What the vast silent world meant to him had always been a mystical thing, which he felt in all its incalculable power, but never understood.

That day, while it was yet light, and he was digging in a moist white-bordered wash for water, he was brought sharply up by hearing the crack of hard hoofs on stone. There down the canyon came a man and a burro. Cameron recognized them.

"Hello, friend," called the man, halting. "Our trails crossed again. That's good."

"Hello," replied Cameron, slowly. "Any mineral sign to-day?"

"No."

They made camp together, ate their frugal meal, smoked a pipe, and rolled in their blankets without exchanging many words. In the morning the same reticence, the same aloofness characterized the manner of both. But Cameron's companion, when he had packed his burro and was ready to start, faced about and said: "We might stay together, if it's all right with you."

"I never take a partner," replied Cameron.

"You're alone; I'm alone," said the other, mildly. "It's a big place. If we find gold there'll be enough for two."

"I don't go down into the desert for gold alone," rejoined Cameron, with a chill note in his swift reply.

His companion's deep-set, luminous eyes emitted a singular flash. It moved Cameron to say that in the years of his wandering he had met no man who could endure equally with him the blasting heat, the blinding dust storms, the wilderness of sand and rock and lava and cactus, the terrible silence and desolation of the desert. Cameron waved a hand toward the wide, shimmering, shadowy descent of plain and range. "I may strike through the Sonora Desert. I may head for Pinacate or north for the Colorado Basin. You are an old man."

"I don't know the country, but to me one place is the same as another," replied his companion. For moments he seemed to forget himself, and swept his far-reaching gaze out over the colored gulf of stone and sand. Then with gentle slaps he drove his burro in behind Cameron. "Yes, I'm old. I'm lonely, too. It's come to me just lately. But, friend, I can still travel, and for a few days my company won't hurt you."

"Have it your way," said Cameron.

They began a slow march down into the desert. At sunset they camped under the lee of a low mesa. Cameron was glad his comrade had the Indian habit of silence. Another day's travel found the prospectors deep in the wilderness. Then there came a breaking of reserve, noticeable in the elder man, almost imperceptibly gradual in Cameron. Beside the meager mesquite campfire this gray-faced, thoughtful old prospector would remove his black pipe from his mouth to talk a little; and Cameron would listen, and sometimes unlock his lips to speak a word. And so, as Cameron began to respond to the influence of a desert less lonely than habitual, he began to take keener note of his comrade, and found him different from any other he had ever encountered in the wilderness. This man never grumbled at the heat, the glare, the driving sand, the sour water, the scant fare. During the daylight hours he was seldom idle. At night he sat dreaming before the fire or paced to and fro in the gloom. He slept but little, and that long after Cameron had had his own rest. He was tireless, patient, brooding.

Cameron's awakened interest brought home to him the realization that for years he had shunned companionship. In those years only three men had wandered into the desert with him, and these had left their bones to bleach in the shifting sands. Cameron had not cared to know their secrets. But the more he studied this latest comrade the more he began to suspect that he might have missed something in the others. In his own driving passion to take his secret into the limitless abode of silence and desolation, where he could be alone with it, he had forgotten that life dealt shocks to other men. Somehow this silent comrade reminded him.

One afternoon late, after they had toiled up a white, winding wash of sand and gravel, they came upon a dry waterhole. Cameron dug deep into the sand, but without avail. He was turning to retrace weary steps back to the last water when his comrade asked him to wait. Cameron watched him search in his pack and bring forth what appeared to be a small, forked branch of a peach tree. He grasped the prongs of the fork and held them before him with the end standing straight out, and then he began to walk along the stream bed. Cameron, at first amused, then amazed, then pitying, and at last curious, kept pace with the prospector. He saw a strong tension of his comrade's wrists, as if he was holding hard against a considerable force. The end of the peach branch began to quiver and turn. Cameron reached out a hand to touch it, and was astounded at feeling a powerful vibrant force pulling the branch downward. He felt it as a magnetic shock. The branch kept turning, and at length pointed to the ground.

"Dig here," said the prospector.

"What!" ejaculated Cameron. Had the man lost his mind?

Then Cameron stood by while his comrade dug in the sand. Three feet he dug—four—five, and the sand grew dark, then moist. At six feet water began to seep through.

"Get the little basket in my pack," he said.

Cameron complied, and saw his comrade drop the basket into the deep hole, where it kept the sides from caving in and allowed the water to seep through. While Cameron watched, the basket filled. Of all the strange incidents of his desert career this was the strangest. Curiously he picked up the peach branch and held it as he had seen it held. The thing, however, was dead in his hands.

"I see you haven't got it," remarked his comrade. "Few men have."

"Got what?" demanded Cameron.

"A power to find water that way. Back in Illinois an old German used to do that to locate wells. He showed me I had the same power. I can't explain. But you needn't look so dumfounded. There's nothing supernatural about it."

"You mean it's a simple fact—that some men have a magnetism, a force or power to find water as you did?"

"Yes. It's not unusual on the farms back in Illinois, Ohio, Pennsylvania. The old German I spoke of made money traveling round with his peach fork."

"What a gift for a man in the desert!"

Cameron's comrade smiled—the second time in all those days.

They entered a region where mineral abounded, and their march became slower. Generally they took the course of a wash, one on each side, and let the burros travel leisurely along nipping at the bleached blades of scant grass, or at sage or cactus, while they searched in the canyons and under the ledges for signs of gold. When they found any rock that hinted of gold they picked off a piece and gave it a chemical test. The search was fascinating. They interspersed the work with long, restful moments when they looked afar down the vast reaches and smoky shingles to the line of dim mountains. Some impelling desire, not all the lure of gold, took them to the top of mesas and escarpments; and here, when they had dug and picked, they rested and gazed out at the wide prospect. Then, as the sun lost its heat and sank lowering to dent its red disk behind far-distant spurs, they halted in a shady canyon or likely spot in a dry wash and tried for water. When they found it they unpacked, gave drink to the tired burros, and turned them loose. Dead mesquite served for the campfire. While the strange twilight deepened into weird night they sat propped against stones, with eyes on the dying embers of the fire, and soon they lay on the sand with the light of white stars on their dark faces.

Each succeeding day and night Cameron felt himself more and more drawn to this strange man. He found that after hours of burning toil he had insensibly grown nearer to his comrade. He reflected that after a few weeks in the desert he had always become a different man. In civilization, in the rough mining camps, he had been a prey to unrest and gloom. But once down on the great billowing sweep of this lonely world, he could look into his unquiet soul without bitterness. Did not the desert magnify men? Cameron believed that wild men in wild places, fighting cold, heat, starvation, thirst, barrenness, facing the elements in all their ferocity, usually retrograded, descended to the savage, lost all heart and soul and became mere brutes. Likewise he believed that men wandering or lost in the wilderness often reversed that brutal order of life and became noble, wonderful, super-human. So now he did not marvel at a slow stir stealing warmer along his veins, and at the premonition that perhaps he and this man, alone on the desert, driven there by life's mysterious and remorseless motive, were to see each other through God's eyes.

His companion was one who thought of himself last. It humiliated Cameron that in spite of growing keenness he could not hinder him from doing more than an equal share of the day's work. The man was mild, gentle, quiet, mostly silent, yet under all his softness he seemed to be made of the fiber of steel. Cameron could not thwart him. Moreover, he appeared to want to find gold for Cameron, not for himself. Cameron's hands always trembled at the turning of rock that promised gold; he had enough of the prospector's passion for fortune to thrill at the chance of a strike. But the other never showed the least trace of excitement.

One night they were encamped at the head of a canyon. The day had been exceedingly hot, and long after sundown the radiation of heat from the rocks persisted. A desert bird whistled a wild, melancholy note from a dark cliff, and a distant coyote wailed mournfully. The stars shone white until the huge moon rose to burn out all their whiteness. And on this night Cameron watched his comrade, and yielded to interest he had not heretofore voiced.

"Pardner, what drives you into the desert?"

"Do I seem to be a driven man?"

"No. But I feel it. Do you come to forget?"

"Yes."

"Ah!" softly exclaimed Cameron. Always he seemed to have known that. He said no more. He watched the old man rise and begin his nightly pace to and fro, up and down. With slow, soft tread, forward and back, tirelessly and ceaselessly, he paced that beat. He did not look up at the stars or follow the radiant track of the moon along the canyon ramparts. He hung his head. He was lost in another world. It was a world which the lonely desert made real. He looked a dark, sad, plodding figure, and somehow impressed Cameron with the helplessness of men.

Cameron grew acutely conscious of the pang in his own breast, of the fire in his heart, the strife and torment of his passion-driven soul. He had come into the desert to remember a woman. She appeared to him then as she had looked when first she entered his life—a golden-haired girl, blue-eyed, white-skinned, red-lipped, tall and slender and beautiful. He had never forgotten, and an old, sickening remorse knocked at his heart. He rose and climbed out of the canyon and to the top of a mesa, where he paced to and fro and looked down into the weird and mystic shadows, like the darkness of his passion, and farther on down the moon track and the glittering stretches that vanished in the cold, blue horizon. The moon soared radiant and calm, the white stars shone serene. The vault of heaven seemed illimitable and divine. The desert surrounded him, silver-streaked and black-mantled, a chaos of rock and sand, silent, austere, ancient, always waiting. It spoke to Cameron. It was a naked corpse, but it had a soul. In that wild solitude the white stars looked down upon him pitilessly and pityingly. They had shone upon a desert that might once have been alive and was now dead, and might again throb with life, only to die. It was a terrible ordeal for him to stand alone and realize that he was only a man facing eternity. But that was what gave him strength to endure. Somehow he was a part of it all, some atom in that vastness, somehow necessary to an inscrutable purpose, something indestructible in that desolate world of ruin and death and decay, something perishable and changeable and growing under all the fixity of heaven. In that endless, silent hall of desert there was a spirit; and Cameron felt hovering near him what he imagined to be phantoms of peace.

He returned to camp and sought his comrade.

"I reckon we're two of a kind," he said. "It was a woman who drove me into the desert. But I come to remember. The desert's the only place I can do that."

"Was she your wife?" asked the elder man.

"No."

A long silence ensued. A cool wind blew up the canyon, sifting the sand through the dry sage, driving away the last of the lingering heat. The campfire wore down to a ruddy ashen heap.

"I had a daughter," said Cameron's comrade. "She lost her mother at birth. And I—I didn't know how to bring up a girl. She was pretty and gay. It was the—the old story."

His words were peculiarly significant to Cameron. They distressed him. He had been wrapped up in his remorse. If ever in the past he had thought of any one connected with the girl he had wronged he had long forgotten. But the consequences of such wrong were far-reaching. They struck at the roots of a home. Here in the desert he was confronted by the spectacle of a splendid man, a father, wasting his life because he could not forget—because there was nothing left to live for. Cameron understood better now why his comrade was drawn by the desert.

"Well, tell me more?" asked Cameron, earnestly.

"It was the old, old story. My girl was pretty and free. The young bucks ran after her. I guess she did not run away from them. And I was away a good deal—working in another town. She was in love with a wild fellow. I knew nothing of it till too late. He was engaged to marry her. But he didn't come back. And when the disgrace became plain to all, my girl left home. She went West. After a while I heard from her. She was well—working—living for her baby. A long time passed. I had no ties. I drifted West. Her lover had also gone West. In those days everybody went West. I trailed him, intending to kill him. But I lost his trail. Neither could I find any trace of her. She had moved on, driven, no doubt, by the hound of her past. Since then I have taken to the wilds, hunting gold on the desert."

"Yes, it's the old, old story, only sadder, I think," said Cameron; and his voice was strained and unnatural. "Pardner, what Illinois town was it you hailed from?"

"Peoria."

"And your—your name?" went on Cameron huskily.

"Warren—Jonas Warren."

That name might as well have been a bullet. Cameron stood erect, motionless, as men sometimes stand momentarily when shot straight through the heart. In an instant, when thoughts resurged like blinding flashes of lightning through his mind, he was a swaying, quivering, terror-stricken man. He mumbled something hoarsely and backed into the shadow. But he need not have feared discovery, however surely his agitation might have betrayed him. Warren sat brooding over the campfire, oblivious of his comrade, absorbed in the past.

Cameron swiftly walked away in the gloom, with the blood thrumming thick in his ears, whispering over and over:

"Merciful God! Nell was his daughter!"

III

As thought and feeling multiplied, Cameron was overwhelmed. Beyond belief, indeed, was it that out of the millions of men in the world two who had never seen each other could have been driven into the desert by memory of the same woman. It brought the past so close. It showed Cameron how inevitably all his spiritual life was governed by what had happened long ago. That which made life significant to him was a wandering in silent places where no eye could see him with his secret. Some fateful chance had thrown him with the father of the girl he had wrecked. It was incomprehensible; it was terrible. It was the one thing of all possible happenings in the world of chance that both father and lover would have found unendurable.

Cameron's pain reached to despair when he felt this relation between Warren and himself. Something within him cried out to him to reveal his identity. Warren would kill him; but it was not fear of death that put Cameron on the rack. He had faced death too often to be afraid. It was the thought of adding torture to this long-suffering man. All at once Cameron swore that he would not augment Warren's trouble, or let him stain his hands with blood. He would tell the truth of Nell's sad story and his own, and make what amends he could.

Then Cameron's thought shifted from father to daughter. She was somewhere beyond the dim horizon line. In those past lonely hours by the campfire his fancy had tortured him with pictures of Nell. But his remorseful and cruel fancy had lied to him. Nell had struggled upward out of menacing depths. She had reconstructed a broken life. And now she was fighting for the name and happiness of her child. Little Nell! Cameron experienced a shuddering ripple in all his being—the physical rack of an emotion born of a new and strange consciousness.

As Cameron gazed out over the blood-red, darkening desert suddenly the strife in his soul ceased. The moment was one of incalculable change, in which his eyes seemed to pierce the vastness of cloud and range, and mystery of gloom and shadow—to see with strong vision the illimitable space before him. He felt the grandeur of the desert, its simplicity, its truth. He had learned at last the lesson it taught. No longer strange was his meeting and wandering with Warren. Each had marched in the steps of destiny; and as the lines of their fates had been inextricably tangled in the years that were gone, so now their steps had crossed and turned them toward one common goal. For years they had been two men marching alone, answering to an inward driving search, and the desert had brought them together. For years they had wandered alone in silence and solitude, where the sun burned white all day and the stars burned white all night, blindly following the whisper of a spirit. But now Cameron knew that he was no longer blind, and in this flash of revelation he felt that it had been given him to help Warren with his burden.

He returned to camp trying to evolve a plan. As always at that long hour when the afterglow of sunset lingered in the west, Warren plodded to and fro in the gloom. All night Cameron lay awake thinking.

In the morning, when Warren brought the burros to camp and began preparations for the usual packing, Cameron broke silence.

"Pardner, your story last night made me think. I want to tell you something about myself. It's hard enough to be driven by sorrow for one you've loved, as you've been driven; but to suffer sleepless and eternal remorse for the ruin of one you've loved as I have suffered—that is hell.... Listen. In my younger days—it seems long now, yet it's not so many years—I was wild. I wronged the sweetest and loveliest girl I ever knew. I went away not dreaming that any disgrace might come to her. Along about that time I fell into terrible moods—I changed—I learned I really loved her. Then came a letter I should have gotten months before. It told of her trouble— importuned me to hurry to save her. Half frantic with shame and fear, I got a marriage certificate and rushed back to her town. She was gone—had been gone for weeks, and her disgrace was known. Friends warned me to keep out of reach of her father. I trailed her—found her. I married her. But too late!... She would not live with me. She left me—I followed her west, but never found her."

Warren leaned forward a little and looked into Cameron's eyes, as if searching there for the repentance that might make him less deserving of a man's scorn.

Cameron met the gaze unflinchingly, and again began to speak:

"You know, of course, how men out here somehow lose old names, old identities. It won't surprise you much to learn my name really isn't Cameron, as I once told you."

Warren stiffened upright. It seemed that there might have been a blank, a suspension, between his grave interest and some strange mood to come.

Cameron felt his heart bulge and contract in his breast; all his body grew cold; and it took tremendous effort for him to make his lips form words.

"Warren, I'm the man you're hunting. I'm Burton. I was Nell's lover!"

The old man rose and towered over Cameron, and then plunged down upon him, and clutched at his throat with terrible stifling hands. The harsh contact, the pain awakened Cameron to his peril before it was too late. Desperate fighting saved him from being hurled to the ground and stamped and crushed. Warren seemed a maddened giant. There was a reeling, swaying, wrestling struggle before the elder man began to weaken. The Cameron, buffeted, bloody, half-stunned, panted for speech.

"Warren—hold on! Give me—a minute. I married Nell. Didn't you know that?... I saved the child!"

Cameron felt the shock that vibrated through Warren. He repeated the words again and again. As if compelled by some resistless power, Warren released Cameron, and, staggering back, stood with uplifted, shaking hands. In his face was a horrible darkness.

"Warren! Wait—listen!" panted Cameron. "I've got that marriage certificate—I've had it by me all these years. I kept it—to prove to myself I did right."

The old man uttered a broken cry.

Cameron stole off among the rocks. How long he absented himself or what he did he had no idea. When he returned Warren was sitting before the campfire, and once more he appeared composed. He spoke, and his voice had a deeper note; but otherwise he seemed as usual.

They packed the burros and faced the north together.

Cameron experienced a singular exaltation. He had lightened his comrade's burden. Wonderfully it came to him that he had also lightened his own. From that hour it was not torment to think of Nell. Walking with his comrade through the silent places, lying beside him under the serene luminous light of the stars, Cameron began to feel the haunting presence of invisible things that were real to him—phantoms whispering peace. In the moan of the cool wind, in the silken seep of sifting sand, in the distant rumble of a slipping ledge, in the faint rush of a shooting star he heard these phantoms of peace coming with whispers of the long pain of men at the last made endurable. Even in the white noonday, under the burning sun, these phantoms came to be real to him. In the dead silence of the midnight hours he heard them breathing nearer on the desert wind—nature's voices of motherhood, whispers of God, peace in the solitude.

IV

There came a morning when the sun shone angry and red through a dull, smoky haze.

"We're in for sandstorms," said Cameron.

They had scarcely covered a mile when a desert-wide, moaning, yellow wall of flying sand swooped down upon them. Seeking shelter in the lee of a rock, they waited, hoping the storm was only a squall, such as frequently whipped across the open places. The moan increased to a roar, and the dull red slowly dimmed, to disappear in the yellow pall, and the air grew thick and dark. Warren slipped the packs from the burros. Cameron feared the sandstorms had arrived some weeks ahead of their usual season.

The men covered their heads and patiently waited. The long hours dragged, and the storm increased in fury. Cameron and Warren wet scarfs with water from their canteens, and bound them round their faces, and then covered their heads. The steady, hollow bellow of flying sand went on. It flew so thickly that enough sifted down under the shelving rock to weight the blankets and almost bury the men. They were frequently compelled to shake off the sand to keep from being borne to the ground. And it was necessary to keep digging out the packs. The floor of their shelter gradually rose higher and higher. They tried to eat, and seemed to be grinding only sand between their teeth. They lost the count of time. They dared not sleep, for that would have meant being buried alive. The could only crouch close to the leaning rock, shake off the sand, blindly dig out their packs, and every moment gasp and cough and choke to fight suffocation.

The storm finally blew itself out. It left the prospectors heavy and stupid for want of sleep. Their burros had wandered away, or had been buried in the sand. Far as eye could reach the desert had marvelously changed; it was now a rippling sea of sand dunes. Away to the north rose the peak that was their only guiding mark. They headed toward it, carrying a shovel and part of their packs.

At noon the peak vanished in the shimmering glare of the desert. The prospectors pushed on, guided by the sun. In every wash they tried for water. With the forked peach branch in his hands Warren always succeeded in locating water. They dug, but it lay too deep. At length, spent and sore, they fell and slept through that night and part of the next day. Then they succeeded in getting water, and quenched their thirst, and filled the canteens, and cooked a meal.

The burning day found them in an interminably wide plain, where there was no shelter from the fierce sun. The men were exceedingly careful with their water, though there was absolute necessity of drinking a little every hour. Late in the afternoon they came to a canyon that they believed was the lower end of the one in which they had last found water. For hours they traveled toward its head, and, long after night had set, found what they sought. Yielding to exhaustion, they slept, and next day were loath to leave the waterhole. Cool night spurred them on with canteens full and renewed strength.

Morning told Cameron that they had turned back miles into the desert, and it was desert new to him. The red sun, the increasing heat, and especially the variety and large size of the cactus plants warned Cameron that he had descended to a lower level. Mountain peaks loomed on all sides, some near, others distant; and one, a blue spur, splitting the glaring sky far to the north, Cameron thought he recognized as a landmark. The ascent toward it was heartbreaking, not in steepness, but in its league-and-league-long monotonous rise. Cameron knew there was only one hope—to make the water hold out and never stop to rest. Warren began to weaken. Often he had to halt. The burning white day passed, and likewise the night, with its white stars shining so pitilessly cold and bright.

Cameron measured the water in his canteen by its weight. Evaporation by heat consumed as much as he drank. During one of the rests, when he had wetted his parched mouth and throat, he found opportunity to pour a little water from his canteen into Warren's.

At first Cameron had curbed his restless activity to accommodate the pace of his elder comrade. But now he felt that he was losing something of his instinctive and passionate zeal to get out of the desert. The thought of water came to occupy his mind. He began to imagine that his last little store of water did not appreciably diminish. He knew he was not quite right in his mind regarding water; nevertheless, he felt this to be more of fact than fancy, and he began to ponder.

When next they rested he pretended to be in a kind of stupor; but he covertly watched Warren. The man appeared far gone, yet he had cunning. He cautiously took up Cameron's canteen and poured water into it from his own.

This troubled Cameron. The old irritation at not being able to thwart Warren returned to him. Cameron reflected, and concluded that he had been unwise not to expect this very thing. Then, as his comrade dropped into weary rest, he lifted both canteens. If there were any water in Warren's, it was only very little. Both men had been enduring the terrible desert thirst, concealing it, each giving his water to the other, and the sacrifice had been useless.

Instead of ministering to the parched throats of one or both, the water had evaporated. When Cameron made sure of this, he took one more drink, the last, and poured the little water left into Warren's canteen. He threw his own away.

Soon afterward Warren discovered the loss.

"Where's your canteen?" he asked.

"The heat was getting my water, so I drank what was left."

"My son!" said Warren.

The day opened for them in a red and green hell of rock and cactus. Like a flame the sun scorched and peeled their faces. Warren went blind from the glare, and Cameron had to lead him. At last Warren plunged down, exhausted, in the shade of a ledge.

Cameron rested and waited, hopeless, with hot, weary eyes gazing down from the height where he sat. The ledge was the top step of a ragged gigantic stairway. Below stretched a sad, austere, and lonely valley. A dim, wide streak, lighter than the bordering gray, wound down the valley floor. Once a river had flowed there, leaving only a forlorn trace down the winding floor of this forlorn valley.

Movement on the part of Warren attracted Cameron's attention. Evidently the old prospector had recovered his sight and some of his strength, for he had arisen, and now began to walk along the arroyo bed with his forked peach branch held before him. He had clung to the precious bit of wood. Cameron considered the prospect for water hopeless, because he saw that the arroyo had once been a canyon, and had been filled with sands by desert winds. Warren, however, stopped in a deep pit, and, cutting his canteen in half, began to use one side of it as a scoop. He scooped out a wide hollow, so wide that Cameron was certain he had gone crazy. Cameron gently urged him to stop, and then forcibly tried to make him. But these efforts were futile. Warren worked with slow, ceaseless, methodical movement. He toiled for what seemed hours. Cameron, seeing the darkening, dampening sand, realized a wonderful possibility of water, and he plunged into the pit with the other half of the canteen. Then both men toiled, round and round the wide hole, down deeper and deeper. The sand grew moist, then wet. At the bottom of the deep pit the sand coarsened, gave place to gravel. Finally water welled in, a stronger volume than Cameron ever remembered finding on the desert. It would soon fill the hole and run over. He marveled at the circumstance. The time was near the end of the dry season. Perhaps an underground stream flowed from the range behind down to the valley floor, and at this point came near to the surface. Cameron had heard of such desert miracles.

The finding of water revived Cameron's flagging hopes. But they were short-lived. Warren had spend himself utterly.

"I'm done. Don't linger," he whispered. "My son, go—go!"

Then he fell. Cameron dragged him out of the sand pit to a sheltered place under the ledge. While sitting beside the failing man Cameron discovered painted images on the wall. Often in the desert he had found these evidences of a prehistoric people. Then, from long habit, he picked up a piece of rock and examined it. Its weight made him closely scrutinize it. The color was a peculiar black. He scraped through the black rust to find a piece of gold. Around him lay scattered heaps of black pebbles and bits of black, weathered rock and pieces of broken ledge, and they showed gold.

"Warren! Look! See it! Feel it! Gold!"

But Warren had never cared, and now he was too blind to see.

"Go—go!" he whispered.

Cameron gazed down the gray reaches of the forlorn valley, and something within him that was neither intelligence nor emotion—something inscrutably strange—impelled him to promise.

Then Cameron built up stone monuments to mark his gold strike. That done, he tarried beside the unconscious Warren. Moments passed—grew into hours. Cameron still had strength left to make an effort to get out of the desert. But that same inscrutable something which had ordered his strange involuntary promise to Warren held him beside his fallen comrade. He watched the white sun turn to gold, and then to red and sink behind mountains in the west. Twilight stole into the arroyo. It lingered, slowly turning to gloom. The vault of blue black lightened to the blinking of stars. Then fell the serene, silent, luminous desert night.

Cameron kept his vigil. As the long hours wore on he felt creep over him the comforting sense that he need not forever fight sleep. A wan glow flared behind the dark, uneven horizon, and a melancholy misshapen moon rose to make the white night one of shadows. Absolute silence claimed the desert. It was mute. Then that inscrutable something breathed to him, telling him when he was alone. He need not have looked at the dark, still face beside him.

Another face haunted Cameron's—a woman's face. It was there in the white moonlit shadows; it drifted in the darkness beyond; it softened, changed to that of a young girl, sweet, with the same dark, haunting eyes of her mother. Cameron prayed to that nameless thing within him, the spirit of something deep and mystical as life. He prayed to that nameless thing outside, of which the rocks and the sand, the spiked cactus and the ragged lava, the endless waste, with its vast star-fired mantle, were but atoms. He prayed for mercy to a woman—for happiness to her child. Both mother and daughter were close to him then. Time and distance were annihilated. He had faith—he saw into the future. The fateful threads of the past, so inextricably woven with his error, wound out their tragic length here in this forlorn desert.

Cameron then took a little tin box from his pocket, and, opening it, removed a folded certificate. He had kept a pen, and now he wrote something upon the paper, and in lieu of ink he wrote with blood. The moon afforded him enough light to see; and, having replaced the paper, he laid the little box upon a shelf of rock. It would remain there unaffected by dust, moisture, heat, time. How long had those painted images been there clear and sharp on the dry stone walls? There were no trails in that desert, and always there were incalculable changes. Cameron saw this mutable mood of nature—the sands would fly and seep and carve and bury; the floods would dig and cut; the ledges would weather in the heat and rain; the avalanches would slide; the cactus seeds would roll in the wind to catch in a niche and split the soil with thirsty roots. Years would pass. Cameron seemed to see them, too; and likewise destiny leading a child down into this forlorn waste, where she would find love and fortune, and the grave of her father.

Cameron covered the dark, still face of his comrade from the light of the waning moon.

That action was the severing of his hold on realities. They fell away from him in final separation. Vaguely, dreamily he seemed to behold his soul. Night merged into gray day; and night came again, weird and dark. Then up out of the vast void of the desert, from the silence and illimitableness, trooped his phantoms of peace. Majestically they formed around him, marshalling and mustering in ceremonious state, and moved to lay upon him their passionless serenity.

I

OLD FRIENDS

RICHARD GALE reflected that his sojourn in the West had been what his disgusted father had predicted—idling here and there, with no objective point or purpose.

It was reflection such as this, only more serious and perhaps somewhat desperate, that had brought Gale down to the border. For some time the newspapers had been printing news of Mexican revolution, guerrilla warfare, United States cavalry patrolling the international line, American cowboys fighting with the rebels, and wild stories of bold raiders and bandits. But as opportunity, and adventure, too, had apparently given him a wide berth in Montana, Wyoming, Colorado, he had struck southwest for the Arizona border, where he hoped to see some stirring life. He did not care very much what happened. Months of futile wandering in the hope of finding a place where he fitted had inclined Richard to his father's opinion.

It was after dark one evening in early October when Richard arrived in Casita. He was surprised to find that it was evidently a town of importance. There was a jostling, jabbering, sombreroed crowd of Mexicans around the railroad station. He felt as if he were in a foreign country. After a while he saw several men of his nationality, one of whom he engaged to carry his luggage to a hotel. They walked up a wide, well-lighted street lined with buildings in which were bright windows. Of the many people encountered by Gale most were Mexicans. His guide explained that the smaller half of Casita lay in Arizona, the other half in Mexico, and of several thousand inhabitants the majority belonged on the southern side of the street, which was the boundary line. He also said that rebels had entered the town that day, causing a good deal of excitement.

Gale was almost at the end of his financial resources, which fact occasioned him to turn away from a pretentious hotel and to ask his guide for a cheaper lodging-house. When this was found, a sight of the loungers in the office, and also a desire for comfort, persuaded Gale to change his traveling-clothes for rough outing garb and boots.

"Well, I'm almost broke," he soliloquized, thoughtfully. "The governor said I wouldn't make any money. He's right—so far. And he said I'd be coming home beaten. There he's wrong. I've got a hunch that something 'll happen to me in this Greaser town."

He went out into a wide, whitewashed, high-ceiled corridor, and from that into an immense room which, but for pool tables, bar, benches, would have been like a courtyard. The floor was cobblestoned, the walls were of adobe, and the large windows opened like doors. A blue cloud of smoke filled the place. Gale heard the click of pool balls and the clink of glasses along the crowded bar. Bare-legged, sandal-footed Mexicans in white rubbed shoulders with Mexicans mantled in black and red. There were others in tight-fitting blue uniforms with gold fringe or tassels at the shoulders. These men wore belts with heavy, bone-handled guns, and evidently were the rurales, or native policemen. There were black-bearded, coarse-visaged Americans, some gambling round the little tables, others drinking. The pool tables were the center of a noisy

310

crowd of younger men, several of whom were unsteady on their feet. There were khaki-clad cavalrymen strutting in and out.

At one end of the room, somewhat apart from the general meelee, was a group of six men round a little table, four of whom were seated, the other two standing. These last two drew a second glance from Gale. The sharp-featured, bronzed faces and piercing eyes, the tall, slender, loosely jointed bodies, the quiet, easy, reckless air that seemed to be a part of the men—these things would plainly have stamped them as cowboys without the buckled sombreros, the colored scarfs, the high-topped, high-heeled boots with great silver-roweled spurs. Gale did not fail to note, also, that these cowboys wore guns, and this fact was rather a shock to his idea of the modern West. It caused him to give some credence to the rumors of fighting along the border, and he felt a thrill.

He satisfied his hunger in a restaurant adjoining, and as he stepped back into the saloon a man wearing a military cape jostled him. Apologies from both were instant. Gale was moving on when the other stopped short as if startled, and, leaning forward, exclaimed:

"Dick Gale?"

"You've got me," replied Gale, in surprise. "But I don't know you."

He could not see the stranger's face, because it was wholly shaded by a wide-brimmed hat pulled well down.

"By Jove! It's Dick! If this isn't great! Don't you know me?"

"I've heard your voice somewhere," replied Gale. "Maybe I'll recognize you if you come out from under that bonnet."

For answer the man, suddenly manifesting thought of himself, hurriedly drew Gale into the restaurant, where he thrust back his hat to disclose a handsome, sunburned face.

"George Thorne! So help me—"

"'S-s-ssh. You needn't yell," interrupted the other, as he met Gale's outstretched hand. There was a close, hard, straining grip. "I must not be recognized here. There are reasons. I'll explain in a minute. Say, but it's fine to see you! Five years, Dick, five years since I saw you run down University Field and spread-eagle the whole Wisconsin football team."

"Don't recollect that," replied Dick, laughing. "George, I'll bet you I'm gladder to see you than you are to see me. It seems so long. You went into the army, didn't you?"

"I did. I'm here now with the Ninth Cavalry. But—never mind me. What're you doing way down here? Say, I just noticed your togs. Dick, you can't be going in for mining or ranching, not in this God-forsaken desert?"

"On the square, George, I don't know any more why I'm here than—than you know."

"Well, that beats me!" ejaculated Thorne, sitting back in his chair, amaze and concern in his expression. "What the devil's wrong? Your old man's got too much money for you ever to be up against it. Dick, you couldn't have gone to the bad?"

A tide of emotion surged over Gale. How good it was to meet a friend—some one to whom to talk! He had never appreciated his loneliness until that moment.

"George, how I ever drifted down here I don't know. I didn't exactly quarrel with the governor. But—damn it, Dad hurt me—shamed me, and I dug out for the West. It was this way. After leaving college I tried to please him by tackling one thing after another that he set me to do. On the square, I had no head for business. I made a mess of everything. The governor got sore. He kept ramming the harpoon into me till I just couldn't stand it. What little ability I possessed deserted me when I got my back up, and there you are. Dad and I had a rather uncomfortable half hour. When I quit—when I told him straight out that I was going West to fare for myself, why, it wouldn't have been so tough if he hadn't laughed at me. He called me a rich man's son—an idle, easy-going spineless swell. He said I didn't even have character enough to be out and out bad. He said I didn't have sense enough to marry one of the nice girls in my sister's crowd. He said I couldn't get back home unless I sent to him for money. He said he didn't believe I could fight—could really make a fight for anything under the sun. Oh—he—he shot it into me, all right."

Dick dropped his head upon his hands, somewhat ashamed of the smarting dimness in his eyes. He had not meant to say so much. Yet what a relief to let out that long-congested burden!

"Fight!" cried Thorne, hotly. "What's ailing him? Didn't they call you Biff Gale in college? Dick, you were one of the best men Stagg ever developed. I heard him say so—that you were the fastest, one-hundred-and-seventy-five-pound man he'd ever trained, the hardest to stop."

"The governor didn't count football," said Dick. "He didn't mean that kind of fight. When I left home I don't think I had an idea what was wrong with me. But, George, I think I know now. I was a rich man's son—spoiled, dependent, absolutely ignorant of the value of money. I haven't yet discovered any earning capacity in me. I seem to be unable to do anything with my hands. That's the trouble. But I'm at the end of my tether now. And I'm going to punch cattle or be a miner, or do some real stunt—like joining the rebels."

"Aha! I thought you'd spring that last one on me," declared Thorne, wagging his head. "Well, you just forget it. Say, old boy, there's something doing in Mexico. The United States in general doesn't realize it. But across that line there are crazy revolutionists, ill-paid soldiers, guerrilla leaders, raiders, robbers, outlaws, bandits galore, starving peons by the thousand, girls and women in terror. Mexico is like some of her volcanoes—ready to erupt fire and hell! Don't make the awful mistake of joining rebel forces. Americans are hated by Mexicans of the lower class—the fighting class, both rebel and federal. Half the time these crazy Greasers are on one side, then on the other. If you didn't starve or get shot in ambush, or die of thirst, some Greaser would knife you in the back for you belt buckle or boots. There are a good many Americans with the rebels eastward toward Agua, Prieta and Juarez. Orozco is operating in Chihuahua, and I guess he has some idea of warfare. But this is Sonora, a mountainous desert, the home of the slave and the Yaqui. There's unorganized revolt everywhere. The American miners and ranchers, those who could get away, have fled across into the States, leaving property. Those who couldn't or wouldn't come must fight for their lives, are fighting now."

"That's bad," said Gale. "It's news to me. Why doesn't the government take action, do something?"

"Afraid of international complications. Don't want to offend the Maderists, or be criticized by jealous foreign nations. It's a delicate situation, Dick. The Washington officials know the gravity of it, you can bet. But the United States in general is in the dark, and the army—well, you ought to hear the inside talk back at San Antonio. We're patrolling the boundary line. We're making a grand bluff. I could tell you of a dozen instances where cavalry should have pursued raiders on the other side of the line. But we won't do it. The officers are a grouchy lot these days. You see, of course, what significance would attach to United States cavalry going into Mexican territory.

There would simply be hell. My own colonel is the sorest man on the job. We're all sore. It's like sitting on a powder magazine. We can't keep the rebels and raiders from crossing the line. Yet we don't fight. My commission expires soon. I'll be discharged in three months. You can bet I'm glad for more reasons than I've mentioned."

Thorne was evidently laboring under strong, suppressed excitement. His face showed pale under the tan, and his eyes gleamed with a dark fire. Occasionally his delight at meeting, talking with Gale, dominated the other emotions, but not for long. He had seated himself at a table near one of the doorlike windows leading into the street, and every little while he would glance sharply out. Also he kept consulting his watch.

These details gradually grew upon Gale as Thorne talked.

"George, it strikes me that you're upset," said Dick, presently. "I seem to remember you as a cool-headed fellow whom nothing could disturb. Has the army changed you?"

Thorne laughed. It was a laugh with a strange, high note. It was reckless—it hinted of exaltation. He rose abruptly; he gave the waiter money to go for drinks; he looked into the saloon, and then into the street. On this side of the house there was a porch opening on a plaza with trees and shrubbery and branches. Thorne peered out one window, then another. His actions were rapid. Returning to the table, he put his hands upon it and leaned over to look closely into Gale's face.

"I'm away from camp without leave," he said.

"Isn't that a serious offense?" asked Dick.

"Serious? For me, if I'm discovered, it means ruin. There are rebels in town. Any moment we might have trouble. I ought to be ready for duty—within call. If I'm discovered it means arrest. That means delay—the failure of my plans—ruin."

Gale was silenced by his friend's intensity. Thorne bent over closer with his dark eyes searching bright.

"We were old pals—once?"

"Surely," replied Dick.

"What would you say, Dick Gale, if I told you that you're the one man I'd rather have had come along than any other at this crisis of my life?"

The earnest gaze, the passionate voice with its deep tremor drew Dick upright, thrilling and eager, conscious of strange, unfamiliar impetuosity.

"Thorne, I should say I was glad to be the fellow," replied Dick.

Their hands locked for a moment, and they sat down again with heads close over the table.

"Listen," began Thorne, in low, swift whisper, "a few days, a week ago—it seems like a year!—I was of some assistance to refugees fleeing from Mexico into the States. They were all women, and one of them was dressed as a nun. Quite by accident I saw her face. It was that of a beautiful girl. I observed she kept aloof from the others. I suspected a disguise, and, when opportunity afforded, spoke to her, offered my services. She replied to my poor efforts at Spanish in fluent English. She had fled in terror from her home, some place down in Sinaloa. Rebels are active there. Her father was captured and held for ransom. When the ransom was paid the rebels killed him. The leader of these rebels was a bandit named Rojas. Long before the revolution began he had been feared by people of class—loved by the peons. Bandits are worshiped by the peons. All of the famous bandits have robbed the rich and given to the poor.

Rojas saw the daughter, made off with her. But she contrived to bribe her guards, and escaped almost immediately before any harm befell her. She hid among friends. Rojas nearly tore down the town in his efforts to find her. Then she disguised herself, and traveled by horseback, stage, and train to Casita.

"Her story fascinated me, and that one fleeting glimpse I had of her face I couldn't forget. She had no friends here, no money. She knew Rojas was trailing her. This talk I had with her was at the railroad station, where all was bustle and confusion. No one noticed us, so I thought. I advised her to remove the disguise of a nun before she left the waiting-room. And I got a boy to guide her. But he fetched her to his house. I had promised to come in the evening to talk over the situation with her.

"I found her, Dick, and when I saw her—I went stark, staring, raving mad over her. She is the most beautiful, wonderful girl I ever saw. Her name is Mercedes Castaneda, and she belongs to one of the old wealthy Spanish families. She has lived abroad and in Havana. She speaks French as well as English. She is—but I must be brief.

"Dick, think, think! With Mercedes also it was love at first sight. My plan is to marry her and get her farther to the interior, away from the border. It may not be easy. She's watched. So am I. It was impossible to see her without the women of this house knowing. At first, perhaps, they had only curiosity—an itch to gossip. But the last two days there has been a change. Since last night there's some powerful influence at work. Oh, these Mexicans are subtle, mysterious! After all, they are Spaniards. They work in secret, in the dark. They are dominated first by religion, then by gold, then by passion for a woman. Rojas must have got word to his friends here; yesterday his gang of cutthroat rebels arrived, and to-day he came. When I learned that, I took my chance and left camp. I hunted up a priest. He promised to come here. It's time he's due. But I'm afraid he'll be stopped."

"Thorne, why don't you take the girl and get married without waiting, without running these risks?" said Dick.

"I fear it's too late now. I should have done that last night. You see, we're over the line—"

"Are we in Mexican territory now?" queried Gale, sharply.

"I guess yes, old boy. That's what complicates it. Rojas and his rebels have Casita in their hands. But Rojas without his rebels would be able to stop me, get the girl, and make for his mountain haunts. If Mercedes is really watched—if her identity is known, which I am sure is the case—we couldn't get far from this house before I'd be knifed and she seized."

"Good Heavens! Thorne, can that sort of thing happen less than a stone's throw from the United States line?" asked Gale, incredulously.

"It can happen, and don't you forget it. You don't seem to realize the power these guerrilla leaders, these rebel captains, and particularly these bandits, exercise over the mass of Mexicans. A bandit is a man of honor in Mexico. He is feared, envied, loved. In the hearts of the people he stands next to the national idol—the bull-fighter, the matador. The race has a wild, barbarian, bloody strain. Take Quinteros, for instance. He was a peon, a slave. He became a famous bandit. At the outbreak of the revolution he proclaimed himself a leader, and with a band of followers he devastated whole counties. The opposition to federal forces was only a blind to rob and riot and carry off women. The motto of this man and his followers was: 'Let us enjoy ourselves while we may!'

"There are other bandits besides Quinteros, not so famous or such great leaders, but just as bloodthirsty. I've seen Rojas. He's a handsome, bold sneering devil, vainer than any peacock. He decks himself in gold lace and sliver trappings, in all the finery he can steal. He was one of the rebels who helped sack Sinaloa and carry off half a million in money and valuables. Rojas spends gold like he spills blood. But he is chiefly famous for abducting women. The peon girls consider it an honor to be ridden off with. Rojas has shown a penchant for girls of the better class."

Thorne wiped the perspiration from his pale face and bent a dark gaze out of the window before he resumed his talk.

"Consider what the position of Mercedes really is. I can't get any help from our side of the line. If so, I don't know where. The population on that side is mostly Mexican, absolutely in sympathy with whatever actuates those on this side. The whole caboodle of Greasers on both sides belong to the class in sympathy with the rebels, the class that secretly respects men like Rojas, and hates an aristocrat like Mercedes. They would conspire to throw her into his power. Rojas can turn all the hidden underground influences to his ends. Unless I thwart him he'll get Mercedes as easily as he can light a cigarette. But I'll kill him or some of his gang or her before I let him get her.... This is the situation, old friend. I've little time to spare. I face arrest for desertion. Rojas is in town. I think I was followed to this hotel. The priest has betrayed me or has been stopped. Mercedes is here alone, waiting, absolutely dependent upon me to save her from—from.... She's the sweetest, loveliest girl!... In a few moments—sooner or later there'll be hell here! Dick, are you with me?"

Dick Gale drew a long, deep breath. A coldness, a lethargy, an indifference that had weighed upon him for months had passed out of his being. On the instant he could not speak, but his hand closed powerfully upon his friend's. Thorne's face changed wonderfully, the distress, the fear, the appeal all vanishing in a smile of passionate gratefulness.

Then Dick's gaze, attracted by some slight sound, shot over his friend's shoulder to see a face at the window—a handsome, bold, sneering face, with glittering dark eyes that flashed in sinister intentness.

Dick stiffened in his seat. Thorne, with sudden clenching of hands, wheeled toward the window.

"Rojas!" he whispered.

II

MERCEDES CASTANEDA

THE dark face vanished. Dick Gale heard footsteps and the tinkle of spurs. He strode to the window, and was in time to see a Mexican swagger into the front door of the saloon. Dick had only a glimpse; but in that he saw a huge black sombrero with a gaudy band, the back of a short, tight-fitting jacket, a heavy pearl-handled gun swinging with a fringe of sash, and close-fitting trousers spreading wide at the bottom. There were men passing in the street, also several Mexicans lounging against the hitching-rail at the curb.

"Did you see him? Where did he go?" whispered Thorne, as he joined Gale. "Those Greasers out there with the cartridge belts crossed over their breasts—they are rebels."

"I think he went into the saloon," replied Dick. "He had a gun, but for all I can see the Greasers out there are unarmed."

"Never believe it! There! Look, Dick! That fellow's a guard, though he seems so unconcerned. See, he has a short carbine, almost concealed.... There's another Greaser farther down the path. I'm afraid Rojas has the house spotted."

"If we could only be sure."

"I'm sure, Dick. Let's cross the hall; I want to see how it looks from the other side of the house."

Gale followed Thorne out of the restaurant into the high-ceiled corridor which evidently divided the hotel, opening into the street and running back to a patio. A few dim, yellow lamps flickered. A Mexican with a blanket round his shoulders stood in the front entrance. Back toward the patio there were sounds of boots on the stone floor. Shadows flitted across that end of the corridor. Thorne entered a huge chamber which was even more poorly lighted than the hall. It contained a table littered with papers, a few high-backed chairs, a couple of couches, and was evidently a parlor.

"Mercedes has been meeting me here," said Thorne. "At this hour she comes every moment or so to the head of the stairs there, and if I am here she comes down. Mostly there are people in this room a little later. We go out into the plaza. It faces the dark side of the house, and that's the place I must slip out with her if there's any chance at all to get away."

They peered out of the open window. The plaza was gloomy, and at first glance apparently deserted. In a moment, however, Gale made out a slow-pacing dark form on the path. Farther down there was another. No particular keenness was required to see in these forms a sentinel-like stealthiness.

Gripping Gale's arm, Thorne pulled back from the window.

"You saw them," he whispered. "It's just as I feared. Rojas has the place surrounded. I should have taken Mercedes away. But I had no time—no chance! I'm bound!... There's Mercedes now! My God!... Dick, think—think if there's a way to get her out of this trap!"

Gale turned as his friend went down the room. In the dim light at the head of the stairs stood the slim, muffled figure of a woman. When she saw Thorne she flew noiselessly down the stairway to him. He caught her in his arms. Then she spoke softly, brokenly, in a low, swift voice. It was a mingling of incoherent Spanish and English; but to Gale it was mellow, deep, unutterably tender, a voice full of joy, fear, passion, hope, and love. Upon Gale it had an unaccountable effect. He found himself thrilling, wondering.

Thorne led the girl to the center of the room, under the light where Gale stood. She had raised a white hand, holding a black-laced mantilla half aside. Dick saw a small, dark head, proudly held, an oval face half hidden, white as a flower, and magnificent black eyes.

Then Thorne spoke.

"Mercedes—Dick Gale, an old friend—the best friend I ever had."

She swept the mantilla back over her head, disclosing a lovely face, strange and striking to Gale in its pride and fire, its intensity.

"Senor Gale—ah! I cannot speak my happiness. His friend!"

"Yes, Mercedes; my friend and yours," said Thorne, speaking rapidly. "We'll have need of him. Dear, there's bad news and no time to break it gently. The priest did not come. He must have been detained. And listen—be brave, dear Mercedes—Rojas is here!"

She uttered an inarticulate cry, the poignant terror of which shook Gale's nerve, and swayed as if she would faint. Thorne caught her, and in husky voice importuned her to bear up.

"My darling! For God's sake don't faint—don't go to pieces! We'd be lost! We've got a chance. We'll think of something. Be strong! Fight!"

It was plain to Gale that Thorne was distracted. He scarcely knew what he was saying. Pale and shaking, he clasped Mercedes to him. Her terror had struck him helpless. It was so intense— it was so full of horrible certainty of what fate awaited her.

She cried out in Spanish, beseeching him; and as he shook his head, she changed to English:

"Senor, my lover, I will be strong—I will fight—I will obey. But swear by my Virgin, if need be to save me from Rojas—you will kill me!"

"Mercedes! Yes, I'll swear," he replied hoarsely. "I know—I'd rather have you dead than— But don't give up. Rojas can't be sure of you, or he wouldn't wait. He's in there. He's got his men there—all around us. But he hesitates. A beast like Rojas doesn't stand idle for nothing. I tell you we've a chance. Dick, here, will think of something. We'll slip away. Then he'll take you somewhere. Only—speak to him—show him you won't weaken. Mercedes, this is more than love and happiness for us. It's life or death."

She became quiet, and slowly recovered control of herself.

Suddenly she wheeled to face Gale with proud dark eyes, tragic sweetness of appeal, and exquisite grace.

"Senor, you are an American. You cannot know the Spanish blood—the peon bandit's hate and cruelty. I wish to die before Rojas's hand touches me. If he takes me alive, then the hour, the little day that my life lasts afterward will be tortured—torture of hell. If I live two days his brutal men will have me. If I live three, the dogs of his camp... Senor, have you a sister whom you love? Help Senor Thorne to save me. He is a soldier. He is bound. He must not betray his honor, his duty, for me.... Ah, you two splendid Americans—so big, so strong, so fierce! What is that little black half-breed slave Rojas to such men? Rojas is a coward. Now, let me waste no more precious time. I am ready. I will be brave."

She came close to Gale, holding out her white hands, a woman all fire and soul and passion. To Gale she was wonderful. His heart leaped. As he bent over her hands and kissed them he seemed to feel himself renewed, remade.

"Senorita," he said, "I am happy to be your servant. I can conceive of no greater pleasure than giving the service you require."

"And what is that?" inquired Thorne, hurriedly.

"That of incapacitating Senor Rojas for to-night, and perhaps several nights to come," replied Gale.

"Dick, what will you do?" asked Thorne, now in alarm.

"I'll make a row in that saloon," returned Dick, bluntly. "I'll start something. I'll rush Rojas and his crowd. I'll—"

"Lord, no; you mustn't, Dick—you'll be knifed!" cried Thorne. He was in distress, yet his eyes were shining.

"I'll take a chance. Maybe I can surprise that slow Greaser bunch and get away before they know what's happened.... You be ready watching at the window. When the row starts those fellows out there in the plaza will run into the saloon. Then you slip out, go straight through the plaza down the street. It's a dark street, I remember. I'll catch up with you before you get far."

Thorne gasped, but did not say a word. Mercedes leaned against him, her white hands now at her breast, her great eyes watching Gale as he went out.

In the corridor Gale stopped long enough to pull on a pair of heavy gloves, to muss his hair, and disarrange his collar. Then he stepped into the restaurant, went through, and halted in the door leading into the saloon. His five feet eleven inches and one hundred and eighty pounds were more noticeable there, and it was part of his plan to attract attention to himself. No one, however, appeared to notice him. The pool-players were noisily intent on their game, the same crowd of motley-robed Mexicans hung over the reeking bar. Gale's roving glance soon fixed upon the man he took to be Rojas. He recognized the huge, high-peaked, black sombrero with its ornamented band. The Mexican's face was turned aside. He was in earnest, excited colloquy with a dozen or more comrades, most of whom were sitting round a table. They were listening, talking, drinking. The fact that they wore cartridge belts crossed over their breasts satisfied that these were the rebels. He had noted the belts of the Mexicans outside, who were apparently guards. A waiter brought more drinks to this group at the table, and this caused the leader to turn so Gale could see his face. It was indeed the sinister, sneering face of the bandit Rojas. Gale gazed at the man with curiosity. He was under medium height, and striking in appearance only because of his dandified dress and evil visage. He wore a lace scarf, a tight, bright-buttoned jacket, a buckskin vest embroidered in red, a sash and belt joined by an enormous silver clasp. Gale saw again the pearl-handled gun swinging at the bandit's hip. Jewels flashed in his scarf. There were gold rings in his ears and diamonds on his fingers.

Gale became conscious of an inward fire that threatened to overrun his coolness. Other emotions harried his self-control. It seemed as if sight of the man liberated or created a devil in Gale. And at the bottom of his feelings there seemed to be a wonder at himself, a strange satisfaction for the something that had come to him.

He stepped out of the doorway, down the couple of steps to the floor of the saloon, and he staggered a little, simulating drunkenness. He fell over the pool tables, jostled Mexicans at the bar, laughed like a maudlin fool, and, with his hat slouched down, crowded here and there. Presently his eye caught sight of the group of cowboys whom he had before noticed with such interest.

They were still in a corner somewhat isolated. With fertile mind working, Gale lurched over to them. He remembered his many unsuccessful attempts to get acquainted with cowboys. If he were to get any help from these silent aloof rangers it must be by striking fire from them in one swift stroke. Planting himself squarely before the two tall cowboys who were standing, he looked straight into their lean, bronzed faces. He spared a full moment for that keen cool gaze before he spoke.

"I'm not drunk. I'm throwing a bluff, and I mean to start a rough house. I'm going to rush that damned bandit Rojas. It's to save a girl—to give her lover, who is my friend, a chance to escape with her. When I start a row my friend will try to slip out with her. Every door and window is watched. I've got to raise hell to draw the guards in.... Well, you're my countrymen. We're in Mexico. A beautiful girl's honor and life are at stake. Now, gentlemen, watch me!"

One cowboy's eyes narrowed, blinking a little, and his lean jaw dropped; the other's hard face rippled with a fleeting smile.

Gale backed away, and his pulse leaped when he saw the two cowboys, as if with one purpose, slowly stride after him. Then Gale swerved, staggering along, brushed against the tables, kicked over the empty chairs. He passed Rojas and his gang, and out of the tail of his eye saw that the bandit was watching him, waving his hands and talking fiercely. The hum of the many voices grew louder, and when Dick lurched against a table, overturning it and spilling glasses into the laps of several Mexicans, there arose a shrill cry. He had succeeded in attracting attention; almost every face turned his way. One of the insulted men, a little tawny fellow, leaped up to confront Gale, and in a frenzy screamed a volley of Spanish, of which Gale distinguished "Gringo!" The Mexican stamped and made a threatening move with his right hand. Dick swung his leg and with a swift side kick knocked the fellows feet from under him, whirling him down with a thud.

The action was performed so suddenly, so adroitly, it made the Mexican such a weakling, so like a tumbled tenpin, that the shrill jabbering hushed. Gale knew this to be the significant moment.

Wheeling, he rushed at Rojas. It was his old line-breaking plunge. Neither Rojas nor his men had time to move. The black-skinned bandit's face turned a dirty white; his jaw dropped; he would have shrieked if Gale had not hit him. The blow swept him backward against his men. Then Gale's heavy body, swiftly following with the momentum of that rush, struck the little group of rebels. They went down with table and chairs in a sliding crash.

Gale carried by his plunge, went with them. Like a cat he landed on top. As he rose his powerful hands fastened on Rojas. He jerked the little bandit off the tangled pile of struggling, yelling men, and, swinging him with terrific force, let go his hold. Rojas slid along the floor, knocking over tables and chairs. Gale bounded back, dragged Rojas up, handling him as if he were a limp sack.

A shot rang out above the yells. Gale heard the jingle of breaking glass. The room darkened perceptibly. He flashed a glance backward. The two cowboys were between him and the crowd of frantic rebels. One cowboy held two guns low down, level in front of him. The other had his gun raised and aimed. On the instant it spouted red and white. With the crack came the crashing of glass, another darkening shade over the room. With a cry Gale slung the bleeding Rojas from him. The bandit struck a table, toppled over it, fell, and lay prone.

Another shot made the room full of moving shadows, with light only back of the bar. A white-clad figure rushed at Gale. He tripped the man, but had to kick hard to disengage himself from grasping hands. Another figure closed in on Gale. This one was dark, swift. A blade glinted—described a circle aloft. Simultaneously with a close, red flash the knife wavered; the man wielding it stumbled backward. In the din Gale did not hear a report, but the Mexican's fall was significant. Then pandemonium broke loose. The din became a roar. Gale heard shots that sounded like dull spats in the distance. The big lamp behind the bar seemingly split, then sputtered and went out, leaving the room in darkness.

Gale leaped toward the restaurant door, which was outlined faintly by the yellow light within. Right and left he pushed the groping men who jostled with him. He vaulted a pool table, sent tables and chairs flying, and gained the door, to be the first of a wedging mob to squeeze through. One sweep of his arm knocked the restaurant lamp from its stand; and he ran out, leaving darkness behind him. A few bounds took him into the parlor. It was deserted. Thorne had gotten away with Mercedes.

It was then Gale slowed up. For the space of perhaps sixty seconds he had been moving with startling velocity. He peered cautiously out into the plaza. The paths, the benches, the shady places under the trees contained no skulking men. He ran out, keeping to the shade, and did not go into the path till he was halfway through the plaza. Under a street lamp at the far end of the path he thought he saw two dark figures. He ran faster, and soon reached the street. The uproar back in the hotel began to diminish, or else he was getting out of hearing. The few people he saw close at hand were all coming his way, and only the foremost showed any excitement. Gale walked swiftly, peering ahead for two figures. Presently he saw them—one tall, wearing a cape; the other slight, mantled. Gale drew a sharp breath of relief. Thorne and Mercedes were not far ahead.

From time to time Thorne looked back. He strode swiftly, almost carrying Mercedes, who clung closely to him. She, too, looked back. Once Gale saw her white face flash in the light of a street lamp. He began to overhaul them; and soon, when the last lamp had been passed and the street was dark, he ventured a whistle. Thorne heard it, for he turned, whistled a low reply, and went on. Not for some distance beyond, where the street ended in open country, did they halt to wait. The desert began here. Gale felt the soft sand under his feet and saw the grotesque forms of cactus. Then he came up with the fugitives.

"Dick! Are you—all right?" panted Thorne, grasping Gale.

"I'm—out of breath—but—O.K.," replied Gale.

"Good! Good!" choked Thorne. "I was scared—helpless.... Dick, it worked splendidly. We had no trouble. What on earth did you do?"

"I made the row, all right," said Dick.

"Good Heavens! It was like a row I once heard made by a mob. But the shots, Dick—were they at you? They paralyzed me. Then the yells. What happened? Those guards of Rojas ran round in front at the first shot. Tell me what happened."

"While I was rushing Rojas a couple of cowboys shot out the lamplights. A Mexican who pulled a knife on me got hurt, I guess. Then I think there was some shooting from the rebels after the room was dark."

"Rushing Rojas?" queried Thorne, leaning close to Dick. His voice was thrilling, exultant, deep with a joy that yet needed confirmation. "What did you do to him?"

"I handed him one off side, tackled, then tried a forward pass," replied Dick, lightly speaking the football vernacular so familiar to Thorne.

Thorne leaned closer, his fine face showing fierce and corded in the starlight. "Tell me straight," he demanded, in thick voice.

Gale then divined something of the suffering Thorne had undergone—something of the hot, wild, vengeful passion of a lover who must have brutal truth.

It stilled Dick's lighter mood, and he was about to reply when Mercedes pressed close to him, touched his hands, looked up into his face with wonderful eyes. He thought he would not soon forget their beauty—the shadow of pain that had been, the hope dawning so fugitively.

"Dear lady," said Gale, with voice not wholly steady, "Rojas himself will hound you no more to-night, nor for many nights."

She seemed to shake, to thrill, to rise with the intelligence. She pressed his hand close over her heaving breast. Gale felt the quick throb of her heart.

"Senor! Senor Dick!" she cried. Then her voice failed. But her hands flew up; quick as a flash she raised her face—kissed him. Then she turned and with a sob fell into Thorne's arms.

There ensued a silence broken only by Mercedes' sobbing. Gale walked some paces away. If he were not stunned, he certainly was agitated. The strange, sweet fire of that girl's lips remained with him. On the spur of the moment he imagined he had a jealousy of Thorne. But presently this passed. It was only that he had been deeply moved—stirred to the depths during the last hour—had become conscious of the awakening of a spirit. What remained with him now was the splendid glow of gladness that he had been of service to Thorne. And by the intensity of Mercedes' abandon of relief and gratitude he measured her agony of terror and the fate he had spared her.

"Dick, Dick, come here!" called Thorne softly. "Let's pull ourselves together now. We've got a problem yet. What to do? Where to go? How to get any place? We don't dare risk the station—the corrals where Mexicans hire out horses. We're on good old U.S. ground this minute, but we're not out of danger."

As he paused, evidently hoping for a suggestion from Gale, the silence was broken by the clear, ringing peal of a bugle. Thorne gave a violent start. Then he bent over, listening. The beautiful notes of the bugle floated out of the darkness, clearer, sharper, faster.

"It's a call, Dick! It's a call!" he cried.

Gale had no answer to make. Mercedes stood as if stricken. The bugle call ended. From a distance another faintly pealed. There were other sounds too remote to recognize. Then scattering shots rattled out.

"Dick, the rebels are fighting somebody," burst out Thorne, excitedly. "The little federal garrison still holds its stand. Perhaps it is attacked again. Anyway, there's something doing over the line. Maybe the crazy Greasers are firing on our camp. We've feared it—in the dark.... And here I am, away without leave—practically a deserter!"

"Go back! Go back, before you're too late!" cried Mercedes.

"Better make tracks, Thorne," added Gale. "It can't help our predicament for you to be arrested. I'll take care of Mercedes."

"No, no, no," replied Thorne. "I can get away—avoid arrest."

"That'd be all right for the immediate present. But it's not best for the future. George, a deserter is a deserter!... Better hurry. Leave the girl to me till tomorrow."

Mercedes embraced her lover, begged him to go. Thorne wavered.

"Dick, I'm up against it," he said. "You're right. If only I can get back in time. But, oh, I hate to leave her! Old fellow, you've saved her! I already owe you everlasting gratitude. Keep out of Casita, Dick. The U.S. side might be safe, but I'm afraid to trust it at night. Go out in the desert, up in the mountains, in some safe place. Then come to me in camp. We'll plan. I'll have to confide in Colonel Weede. Maybe he'll help us. Hide her from the rebels—that's all."

He wrung Dick's hand, clasped Mercedes tightly in his arms, kissed her, and murmured low over her, then released her to rush off into the darkness. He disappeared in the gloom. The sound of his dull footfalls gradually died away.

For a moment the desert silence oppressed Gale. He was unaccustomed to such strange stillness. There was a low stir of sand, a rustle of stiff leaves in the wind. How white the stars burned! Then a coyote barked, to be bayed by a dog. Gale realized that he was between the edge of an unknown desert and the edge of a hostile town. He had to choose the desert, because, though he had no doubt that in Casita there were many Americans who might befriend him, he could not chance the risks of seeking them at night.

He felt a slight touch on his arm, felt it move down, felt Mercedes slip a trembling cold little hand into his. Dick looked at her. She seemed a white-faced girl now, with staring, frightened black eyes that flashed up at him. If the loneliness, the silence, the desert, the unknown dangers of the night affected him, what must they be to this hunted, driven girl? Gale's heart swelled. He was alone with her. He had no weapon, no money, no food, no drink, no covering, nothing except his two hands. He had absolutely no knowledge of the desert, of the direction or whereabouts of the boundary line between the republics; he did not know where to find the railroad, or any road or trail, or whether or not there were towns near or far. It was a critical, desperate situation. He thought first of the girl, and groaned in spirit, prayed that it would be given him to save her. When he remembered himself it was with the stunning consciousness that he could conceive of no situation which he would have exchanged for this one—where fortune had set him a perilous task of loyalty to a friend, to a helpless girl.

"Senor, senor!" suddenly whispered Mercedes, clinging to him. "Listen! I hear horses coming!"

III

A FLIGHT INTO THE DESERT

UNEASY and startled, Gale listened and, hearing nothing, wondered if Mercedes's fears had not worked upon her imagination. He felt a trembling seize her, and he held her hands tightly.

"You were mistaken, I guess," he whispered.

"No, no, senor."

Dick turned his ear to the soft wind. Presently he heard, or imagined he heard, low beats. Like the first faint, far-off beats of a drumming grouse, they recalled to him the Illinois forests of his boyhood. In a moment he was certain the sounds were the padlike steps of hoofs in yielding sand. The regular tramp was not that of grazing horses.

On the instant, made cautious and stealthy by alarm, Gale drew Mercedes deeper into the gloom of the shrubbery. Sharp pricks from thorns warned him that he was pressing into a cactus growth, and he protected Mercedes as best he could. She was shaking as one with a severe chill. She breathed with little hurried pants and leaned upon him almost in collapse. Gale ground his teeth in helpless rage at the girl's fate. If she had not been beautiful she might still have been free and happy in her home. What a strange world to live in—how unfair was fate!

The sounds of hoofbeats grew louder. Gale made out a dark moving mass against a background of dull gray. There was a line of horses. He could not discern whether or not all the horses carried riders. The murmur of a voice struck his ear—then a low laugh. It made him tingle, for it sounded American. Eagerly he listened. There was an interval when only the hoofbeats could be heard.

"It shore was, Laddy, it shore was," came a voice out of the darkness. "Rough house! Laddy, since wire fences drove us out of Texas we ain't seen the like of that. An' we never had such a call."

"Call? It was a burnin' roast," replied another voice. "I felt low down. He vamoosed some sudden, an' I hope he an' his friends shook the dust of Casita. That's a rotten town Jim."

Gale jumped up in joy. What luck! The speakers were none other than the two cowboys whom he had accosted in the Mexican hotel.

"Hold on, fellows," he called out, and strode into the road.

The horses snorted and stamped. Then followed swift rustling sounds—a clinking of spurs, then silence. The figures loomed clearer in the gloom.. Gale saw five or six horses, two with riders, and one other, at least, carrying a pack. When Gale got within fifteen feet of the group the foremost horseman said:

"I reckon that's close enough, stranger."

Something in the cowboy's hand glinted darkly bright in the starlight.

"You'd recognize me, if it wasn't so dark," replied Gale, halting. "I spoke to you a little while ago—in the saloon back there."

"Come over an' let's see you," said the cowboy curtly.

Gale advanced till he was close to the horse. The cowboy leaned over the saddle and peered into Gale's face. Then, without a word, he sheathed the gun and held out his hand. Gale met a grip of steel that warmed his blood. The other cowboy got off his nervous, spirited horse and threw the bridle. He, too, peered closely into Gale's face.

"My name's Ladd," he said. "Reckon I'm some glad to meet you again."

Gale felt another grip as hard and strong as the other had been. He realized he had found friends who belonged to a class of men whom he had despaired of ever knowing.

"Gale—Dick Gale is my name," he began, swiftly. "I dropped into Casita to-night hardly knowing where I was. A boy took me to that hotel. There I met an old friend whom I had not seen for years. He belongs to the cavalry stationed here. He had befriended a Spanish girl— fallen in love with her. Rojas had killed this girl's father—tried to abduct her.... You know what took place at the hotel. Gentlemen, if it's ever possible, I'll show you how I appreciate what you did for me there. I got away, found my friend with the girl. We hurried out here beyond the edge of town. Then Thorne had to make a break for camp. We heard bugle calls, shots, and he was away without leave. That left the girl with me. I don't know what to do. Thorne swears Casita is no place for Mercedes at night."

"The girl ain't no peon, no common Greaser?" interrupted Ladd.

"No. Her name is Castaneda. She belongs to an old Spanish family, once rich and influential."

"Reckoned as much," replied the cowboy. "There's more than Rojas's wantin' to kidnap a pretty girl. Shore he does that every day or so. Must be somethin' political or feelin' against class. Well, Casita ain't no place for your friend's girl at night or day, or any time. Shore, there's Americans who'd take her in an' fight for her, if necessary. But it ain't wise to risk that. Lash, what do you say?"

"It's been gettin' hotter round this Greaser corral for some weeks," replied the other cowboy. "If that two-bit of a garrison surrenders, there's no tellin' what'll happen. Orozco is headin' west from Agua Prieta with his guerrillas. Campo is burnin' bridges an' tearin' up the railroad south of Nogales. Then there's all these bandits callin' themselves revolutionists just for an excuse to steal, burn, kill, an' ride off with women. It's plain facts, Laddy, an' bein' across the U.S. line a few inches or so don't make no hell of a difference. My advice is, don't let Miss Castaneda ever set foot in Casita again."

"Looks like you've shore spoke sense," said Ladd. "I reckon, Gale, you an' the girl ought to come with us. Casita shore would be a little warm for us to-morrow. We didn't kill anybody, but I shot a Greaser's arm off, an' Lash strained friendly relations by destroyin' property. We know people who'll take care of the senorita till your friend can come for her."

Dick warmly spoke his gratefulness, and, inexpressibly relieved and happy for Mercedes, he went toward the clump of cactus where he had left her. She stood erect, waiting, and, dark as it was, he could tell she had lost the terror that had so shaken her.

"Senor Gale, you are my good angel," she said, tremulously.

"I've been lucky to fall in with these men, and I'm glad with all my heart," he replied. "Come."

He led her into the road up to the cowboys, who now stood bareheaded in the starlight. They seemed shy, and Lash was silent while Ladd made embarrassed, unintelligible reply to Mercedes's thanks.

There were five horses—two saddled, two packed, and the remaining one carried only a blanket. Ladd shortened the stirrups on his mount, and helped Mercedes up into the saddle. From the way she settled herself and took the few restive prances of the mettlesome horse Gale judged that she could ride. Lash urged Gale to take his horse. But this Gale refused to do.

"I'll walk," he said. "I'm used to walking. I know cowboys are not."

They tried again to persuade him, without avail. Then Ladd started off, riding bareback. Mercedes fell in behind, with Gale walking beside her. The two pack animals came next, and Lash brought up the rear.

Once started with protection assured for the girl and a real objective point in view, Gale relaxed from the tense strain he had been laboring under. How glad he would have been to acquaint Thorne with their good fortune! Later, of course, there would be some way to get word to the cavalryman. But till then what torments his friend would suffer!

It seemed to Dick that a very long time had elapsed since he stepped off the train; and one by one he went over every detail of incident which had occurred between that arrival and the present moment. Strange as the facts were, he had no doubts. He realized that before that night he had never known the deeps of wrath undisturbed in him; he had never conceived even a passing idea that it was possible for him to try to kill a man. His right hand was swollen stiff, so sore that he could scarcely close it. His knuckles were bruised and bleeding, and ached with a sharp pain. Considering the thickness of his heavy glove, Gale was of the opinion that so to bruise his hand he must have struck Rojas a powerful blow. He remembered that for him to give or take a blow had been nothing. This blow to Rojas, however, had been a different matter. The hot wrath which had been his motive was not puzzling; but the effect on him after he had cooled off, a subtle difference, something puzzled and eluded him. The more it baffled him the more he pondered. All those wandering months of his had been filled with dissatisfaction, yet he had been too apathetic to understand himself. So he had not been much of a person to try. Perhaps it had not been the blow to Rojas any more than other things that had wrought some change in him.

His meeting with Thorne; the wonderful black eyes of a Spanish girl; her appeal to him; the hate inspired by Rojas, and the rush, the blow, the action; sight of Thorne and Mercedes hurrying safely away; the girl's hand pressing his to her heaving breast; the sweet fire of her kiss; the fact of her being alone with him, dependent upon him—all these things Gale turned over and over in his mind, only to fail of any definite conclusion as to which had affected him so remarkably, or to tell what had really happened to him.

Had he fallen in love with Thorne's sweetheart? The idea came in a flash. Was he, all in an instant, and by one of those incomprehensible reversals of character, jealous of his friend? Dick was almost afraid to look up at Mercedes. Still he forced himself to do so, and as it chanced Mercedes was looking down at him. Somehow the light was better, and he clearly saw her white face, her black and starry eyes, her perfect mouth. With a quick, graceful impulsiveness she put her hand upon his shoulder. Like her appearance, the action was new, strange, striking to Gale; but it brought home suddenly to him the nature of gratitude and affection in a girl of her blood. It was sweet and sisterly. He knew then that he had not fallen in love with her. The feeling that was akin to jealousy seemed to be of the beautiful something for which Mercedes stood in Thorne's life. Gale then grasped the bewildering possibilities, the infinite wonder of what a girl could mean to a man.

The other haunting intimations of change seemed to be elusively blended with sensations—the heat and thrill of action, the sense of something done and more to do, the utter vanishing of an old weary hunt for he knew not what. Maybe it had been a hunt for work, for energy, for spirit, for love, for his real self. Whatever it might be, there appeared to be now some hope of finding it.

The desert began to lighten. Gray openings in the border of shrubby growths changed to paler hue. The road could be seen some rods ahead, and it had become a stony descent down, steadily down. Dark, ridged backs of mountains bounded the horizon, and all seemed near at hand, hemming in the plain. In the east a white glow grew brighter and brighter, reaching up to a line of cloud, defined sharply below by a rugged notched range. Presently a silver circle rose behind the black mountain, and the gloom of the desert underwent a transformation. From a gray mantle it changed to a transparent haze. The moon was rising.

"Senor I am cold," said Mercedes.

Dick had been carrying his coat upon his arm. He had felt warm, even hot, and had imagined that the steady walk had occasioned it. But his skin was cool. The heat came from an inward burning. He stopped the horse and raised the coat up, and helped Mercedes put it on.

"I should have thought of you," he said. "But I seemed to feel warm... The coat's a little large; we might wrap it round you twice."

Mercedes smiled and lightly thanked him in Spanish. The flash of mood was in direct contrast to the appealing, passionate, and tragic states in which he had successively viewed her; and it gave him a vivid impression of what vivacity and charm she might possess under happy conditions. He was about to start when he observed that Ladd had halted and was peering ahead in evident caution. Mercedes' horse began to stamp impatiently, raised his ears and head, and acted as if he was about to neigh.

A warning "hist!" from Ladd bade Dick to put a quieting hand on the horse. Lash came noiselessly forward to join his companion. The two then listened and watched.

An uneasy yet thrilling stir ran through Gale's veins. This scene was not fancy. These men of the ranges had heard or seen or scented danger. It was all real, as tangible and sure as the touch of Mercedes's hand upon his arm. Probably for her the night had terrors beyond Gale's power to comprehend. He looked down into the desert, and would have felt no surprise at anything hidden away among the bristling cactus, the dark, winding arroyos, the shadowed rocks with their moonlit tips, the ragged plain leading to the black bold mountains. The wind appeared to blow softly, with an almost imperceptible moan, over the desert. That was a new sound to Gale. But he heard nothing more.

Presently Lash went to the rear and Ladd started ahead. The progress now, however, was considerably slower, not owing to a road—for that became better—but probably owing to caution exercised by the cowboy guide. At the end of a half hour this marked deliberation changed, and the horses followed Ladd's at a gait that put Gale to his best walking-paces.

Meanwhile the moon soared high above the black corrugated peaks. The gray, the gloom, the shadow whitened. The clearing of the dark foreground appeared to lift a distant veil and show endless aisles of desert reaching down between dim horizon-bounding ranges.

Gale gazed abroad, knowing that as this night was the first time for him to awake to consciousness of a vague, wonderful other self, so it was one wherein he began to be aware of an encroaching presence of physical things—the immensity of the star-studded sky, the soaring moon, the bleak, mysterious mountains, and limitless slope, and plain, and ridge, and valley. These things in all their magnificence had not been unnoticed by him before; only now they spoke a different meaning. A voice that he had never heard called him to see, to feel the vast hard externals of heaven and earth, all that represented the open, the free, silence and solitude and space.

Once more his thoughts, like his steps, were halted by Ladd's actions. The cowboy reined in his horse, listened a moment, then swung down out of the saddle. He raised a cautioning hand to the others, then slipped into the gloom and disappeared. Gale marked that the halt had been made in a ridged and cut-up pass between low mesas. He could see the columns of cactus standing out black against the moon-white sky. The horses were evidently tiring, for they showed no impatience. Gale heard their panting breaths, and also the bark of some animal—a dog or a coyote. It sounded like a dog, and this led Gale to wonder if there was any house near at hand. To the right, up under the ledges some distance away, stood two square black objects, too uniform, he thought, to be rocks. While he was peering at them, uncertain what to think, the shrill whistle of a horse pealed out, to be followed by the rattling of hoofs on hard stone. Then a dog barked. At the same moment that Ladd hurriedly appeared in the road a light shone out and danced before one of the square black objects.

"Keep close an' don't make no noise," he whispered, and led his horse at right angles off the road.

Gale followed, leading Mercedes's horse. As he turned he observed that Lash also had dismounted.

To keep closely at Ladd's heels without brushing the cactus or stumbling over rocks and depressions was a task Gale found impossible. After he had been stabbed several times by the bayonetlike spikes, which seemed invisible, the matter of caution became equally one of self-preservation. Both the cowboys, Dick had observed, wore leather chaps. It was no easy matter to lead a spirited horse through the dark, winding lanes walled by thorns. Mercedes horse often balked and had to be coaxed and carefully guided. Dick concluded that Ladd was making a wide detour. The position of certain stars grown familiar during the march veered round from one side to another. Dick saw that the travel was fast, but by no means noiseless. The pack animals at times crashed and ripped through the narrow places. It seemed to Gale that any one within a mile could have heard these sounds. From the tops of knolls or ridges he looked back, trying to locate the mesas where the light had danced and the dog had barked alarm. He could not distinguish these two rocky eminences from among many rising in the background.

Presently Ladd let out into a wider lane that appeared to run straight. The cowboy mounted his horse, and this fact convinced Gale that they had circled back to the road. The march proceeded then once more at a good, steady, silent walk. When Dick consulted his watch he was amazed to see that the hour was still early. How much had happened in little time! He now began to be aware that the night was growing colder; and, strange to him, he felt something damp that in a country he knew he would have recognized as dew. He had not been aware there was dew on the desert. The wind blew stronger, the stars shone whiter, the sky grew darker, and the moon climbed toward the zenith. The road stretched level for miles, then crossed arroyos and ridges, wound between mounds of broken ruined rock, found a level again, and then began a long ascent. Dick asked Mercedes if she was cold, and she answered that she was, speaking especially of her feet, which were growing numb. Then she asked to be helped down to walk awhile. At first she was cold and lame, and accepted the helping hand Dick proffered. After a little, however, she recovered and went on without assistance. Dick could scarcely believe his eyes, as from time to time he stole a sidelong glance at this silent girl, who walked with lithe and rapid stride. She was wrapped in his long coat, yet it did not hide her slender grace. He could not see her face, which was concealed by the black mantle.

A low-spoken word from Ladd recalled Gale to the question of surroundings and of possible dangers. Ladd had halted a few yards ahead. They had reached the summit of what was evidently a high ridge which sloped with much greater steepness on the far side. It was only after a few more forward steps, however, that Dick could see down the slope. Then full in view flashed a bright campfire around which clustered a group of dark figures. They were encamped in a wide arroyo, where horses could be seen grazing in black patches of grass between clusters of trees. A second look at the campers told Gale they were Mexicans. At this moment Lash came forward to join Ladd, and the two spent a long, uninterrupted moment studying the arroyo. A hoarse laugh, faint yet distinct, floated up on the cool wind.

"Well, Laddy, what're you makin' of that outfit?" inquired Lash, speaking softly.

"Same as any of them raider outfits," replied Ladd. "They're across the line for beef. But they'll run off any good stock. As hoss thieves these rebels have got 'em all beat. That outfit is waitin' till it's late. There's a ranch up the arroyo."

Gale heard the first speaker curse under his breath.

"Sure, I feel the same," said Ladd. "But we've got a girl an' the young man to look after, not to mention our pack outfit. An' we're huntin' for a job, not a fight, old hoss. Keep on your chaps!"

"Nothin' to it but head south for the Rio Forlorn."

"You're talkin' sense now, Jim. I wish we'd headed that way long ago. But it ain't strange I'd want to travel away from the border, thinkin' of the girl. Jim, we can't go round this Greaser outfit an' strike the road again. Too rough. So we'll have to give up gettin' to San Felipe."

"Perhaps it's just as well, Laddy. Rio Forlorn is on the border line, but it's country where these rebels ain't been yet."

"Wait till they learn of the oasis an' Beldin's hosses!" exclaimed Laddy. "I'm not anticipatin' peace anywhere along the border, Jim. But we can't go ahead; we can't go back."

"What'll we do, Laddy? It's a hike to Beldin's ranch. An' if we get there in daylight some Greaser will see the girl before Beldin' can hide her. It'll get talked about. The news'll travel to Casita like sage balls before the wind."

"Shore we won't ride into Rio Forlorn in the daytime. Let's slip the packs, Jim. We can hid them off in the cactus an' come back after them. With the young man ridin' we—"

The whispering was interrupted by a loud ringing neigh that whistled up from the arroyo. One of the horses had scented the travelers on the ridge top. The indifference of the Mexicans changed to attention.

Ladd and Lash turned back and led the horses into the first opening on the south side of the road. There was nothing more said at the moment, and manifestly the cowboys were in a hurry.

Gale had to run in the open places to keep up. When they did stop it was welcome to Gale, for he had begun to fall behind.

The packs were slipped, securely tied and hidden in a mesquite clump. Ladd strapped a blanket around one of the horses. His next move was to take off his chaps.

"Gale, you're wearin' boots, an' by liftin' your feet you can beat the cactus," he whispered. "But the—the—Miss Castaneda, she'll be torn all to pieces unless she puts these on. Please tell her—an' hurry."

Dick took the caps, and, going up to Mercedes, he explained the situation. She laughed, evidently at his embarrassed earnestness, and slipped out of the saddle.

"Senor, chapparejos and I are not strangers," she said.

Deftly and promptly she equipped herself, and then Gale helped her into the saddle, called to her horse, and started off. Lash directed Gale to mount the other saddled horse and go next.

Dick had not ridden a hundred yards behind the trotting leaders before he had sundry painful encounters with reaching cactus arms. The horse missed these by a narrow margin. Dick's knees appeared to be in line, and it became necessary for him to lift them high and let his boots take the onslaught of the spikes. He was at home in the saddle, and the accomplishment was about the only one he possessed that had been of any advantage during his sojourn in the West.

Ladd pursued a zigzag course southward across the desert, trotting down the aisles, cantering in wide, bare patches, walking through the clumps of cacti. The desert seemed all of a sameness to Dick—a wilderness of rocks and jagged growths hemmed in by lowering ranges, always looking close, yet never growing any nearer. The moon slanted back toward the west, losing its white radiance, and the gloom of the earlier evening began to creep into the washes and to darken under the mesas. By and by Ladd entered an arroyo, and here the travelers turned and twisted with the meanderings of a dry stream bed. At the head of a canyon they had to take once more to the rougher ground. Always it led down, always it grew rougher, more rolling, with wider bare spaces, always the black ranges loomed close.

Gale became chilled to the bone, and his clothes were damp and cold. His knees smarted from the wounds of the poisoned thorns, and his right hand was either swollen stiff or too numb to move. Moreover, he was tiring. The excitement, the long walk, the miles on miles of jolting trot—these had wearied him. Mercedes must be made of steel, he thought, to stand all that she had been subjected to and yet, when the stars were paling and dawn perhaps not far away, stay in the saddle.

So Dick Gale rode on, drowsier for each mile, and more and more giving the horse a choice of ground. Sometimes a prod from a murderous spine roused Dick. A grayness had blotted out the waning moon in the west and the clear, dark, starry sky overhead. Once when Gale, thinking to fight his weariness, raised his head, he saw that one of the horses in the lead was riderless. Ladd was carrying Mercedes. Dick marveled that her collapse had not come sooner. Another time, rousing himself again, he imagined they were now on a good hard road.

It seemed that hours passed, though he knew only little time had elapsed, when once more he threw off the spell of weariness. He heard a dog bark. Tall trees lined the open lane down which he was riding. Presently in the gray gloom he saw low, square houses with flat roofs. Ladd turned off to the left down another lane, gloomy between trees. Every few rods there was one of the squat houses. This lane opened into wider, lighter space. The cold air bore a sweet perfume—whether of flowers or fruit Dick could not tell. Ladd rode on for perhaps a quarter of a mile, though it seemed interminably long to Dick. A grove of trees loomed dark in the gray morning. Ladd entered it and was lost in the shade. Dick rode on among trees. Presently he heard voices, and soon another house, low and flat like the others, but so long he could not see the farther end, stood up blacker than the trees. As he dismounted, cramped and sore, he could scarcely stand. Lash came alongside. He spoke, and some one with a big, hearty voice replied to him. Then it seemed to Dick that he was led into blackness like pitch, where, presently, he felt blankets thrown on him and then his drowsy faculties faded.

IV

FORLORN RIVER

WHEN Dick opened his eyes a flood of golden sunshine streamed in at the open window under which he lay. His first thought was one of blank wonder as to where in the world he happened to be. The room was large, square, adobe-walled. It was littered with saddles, harness, blankets. Upon the floor was a bed spread out upon a tarpaulin. Probably this was where some one had slept. The sight of huge dusty spurs, a gun belt with sheath and gun, and a pair of leather chaps bristling with broken cactus thorns recalled to Dick the cowboys, the ride, Mercedes, and the whole strange adventure that had brought him there.

He did not recollect having removed his boots; indeed, upon second thought, he knew he had not done so. But there they stood upon the floor. Ladd and Lash must have taken them off when he was so exhausted and sleepy that he could not tell what was happening. He felt a dead weight of complete lassitude, and he did not want to move. A sudden pain in his hand caused him to hold it up. It was black and blue, swollen to almost twice its normal size, and stiff as a board. The knuckles were skinned and crusted with dry blood. Dick soliloquized that it was the worst-looking hand he had seen since football days, and that it would inconvenience him for some time.

A warm, dry, fragrant breeze came through the window. Dick caught again the sweet smell of flowers or fruit. He heard the fluttering of leaves, the murmur of running water, the twittering of birds, then the sound of approaching footsteps and voices. The door at the far end of the room was open. Through it he saw poles of peeled wood upholding a porch roof, a bench, rose bushes in bloom, grass, and beyond these bright-green foliage of trees.

"He shore was sleepin' when I looked in an hour ago," said a voice that Dick recognized as Ladd's.

"Let him sleep," came the reply in deep, good-natured tones. "Mrs. B. says the girl's never moved. Must have been a tough ride for them both. Forty miles through cactus!"

"Young Gale hoofed darn near half the way," replied Ladd. "We tried to make him ride one of our hosses. If we had, we'd never got here. A walk like that'd killed me an' Jim."

"Well, Laddy, I'm right down glad to see you boys, and I'll do all I can for the young couple," said the other. "But I'm doing some worry here; don't mistake me."

"About your stock?"

"I've got only a few head of cattle at the oasis now, I'm worrying some, mostly about my horses. The U. S. is doing some worrying, too, don't mistake me. The rebels have worked west and north as far as Casita. There are no cavalrymen along the line beyond Casita, and there can't be. It's practically waterless desert. But these rebels are desert men. They could cross the line beyond the Rio Forlorn and smuggle arms into Mexico. Of course, my job is to keep tab on Chinese and Japs trying to get into the U.S. from Magdalena Bay. But I'm supposed to patrol the border line. I'm going to hire some rangers. Now, I'm not so afraid of being shot up, though out in this lonely place there's danger of it; what I'm afraid of most is losing that bunch of horses. If any rebels come this far, or if they ever hear of my horses, they're going to raid me. You know what those guerrilla Mexicans will do for horses. They're crazy on horse flesh. They know fine horses. They breed the finest in the world. So I don't sleep nights any more."

"Reckon me an' Jim might as well tie up with your for a spell, Beldin'. We've been ridin' up an' down Arizona tryin' to keep out of sight of wire fences."

"Laddy, it's open enough around Forlorn River to satisfy even an old-time cowpuncher like you," laughed Belding. "I'd take your staying on as some favor, don't mistake me. Perhaps I can persuade the young man Gale to take a job with me."

"That's shore likely. He said he had no money, no friends. An' if a scrapper's all you're lookin' for he'll do," replied Ladd, with a dry chuckle.

"Mrs. B. will throw some broncho capers round this ranch when she hears I'm going to hire a stranger."

"Why?"

"Well, there's Nell— And you said this Gale was a young American. My wife will be scared to death for fear Nell will fall in love with him."

Laddy choked off a laugh, then evidently slapped his knee or Belding's, for there was a resounding smack.

"He's a fine-spoken, good-looking chap, you said?" went on Belding.

"Shore he is," said Laddy, warmly. "What do you say, Jim?"

By this time Dick Gale's ears began to burn and he was trying to make himself deaf when he wanted to hear every little word.

"Husky young fellow, nice voice, steady, clear eyes, kinda proud, I thought, an' some handsome, he was," replied Jim Lash.

"Maybe I ought to think twice before taking a stranger into my family," said Belding, seriously. "Well, I guess he's all right, Laddy, being the cavalryman's friend. No bum or lunger? He must be all right?"

"Bum? Lunger? Say, didn't I tell you I shook hands with this boy an' was plumb glad to meet him?" demanded Laddy, with considerable heat. Manifestly he had been affronted. "Tom Beldin', he's a gentleman, an' he could lick you in—in half a second. How about that, Jim?"

"Less time," replied Lash. "Tom, here's my stand. Young Gale can have my hoss, my gun, anythin' of mine."

"Aw, I didn't mean to insult you, boys, don't mistake me," said Belding. "Course he's all right."

The object of this conversation lay quiet upon his bed, thrilling and amazed at being so championed by the cowboys, delighted with Belding's idea of employing him, and much amused with the quaint seriousness of the three.

"How's the young man?" called a woman's voice. It was kind and mellow and earnest.

Gale heard footsteps on flagstones.

"He's asleep yet, wife," replied Belding. "Guess he was pretty much knocked out.... I'll close the door there so we won't wake him."

There were slow, soft steps, then the door softly closed. But the fact scarcely made a perceptible difference in the sound of the voices outside.

"Laddy and Jim are going to stay," went on Belding. "It'll be like the old Panhandle days a little. I'm powerful glad to have the boys, Nellie. You know I meant to sent to Casita to ask them. We'll see some trouble before the revolution is ended. I think I'll make this young man Gale an offer."

"He isn't a cowboy?" asked Mrs. Belding, quickly.

"No."

"Shore he'd make a darn good one," put in Laddy.

"What is he? Who is he? Where did he come from? Surely you must be—"

"Laddy swears he's all right," interrupted the husband. "That's enough reference for me. Isn't it enough for you?"

"Humph! Laddy knows a lot about young men, now doesn't he, especially strangers from the East?... Tom, you must be careful!"

"Wife, I'm only too glad to have a nervy young chap come along. What sense is there in your objection, if Jim and Laddy stick up for him?"

"But, Tom—he'll fall in love with Nell!" protested Mrs. Belding.

"Well, wouldn't that be regular? Doesn't every man who comes along fall in love with Nell? Hasn't it always happened? When she was a schoolgirl in Kansas didn't it happen? Didn't she have a hundred moon-eyed ninnies after her in Texas? I've had some peace out here in the desert, except when a Greaser or a prospector or a Yaqui would come along. Then same old story—in love with Nell!"

"But, Tom, Nell might fall in love with this young man!" exclaimed the wife, in distress.

"Laddy, Jim, didn't I tell you?" cried Belding. "I knew she'd say that.... My dear wife, I would be simply overcome with joy if Nell did fall in love once. Real good and hard! She's wilder than any antelope out there on the desert. Nell's nearly twenty now, and so far as we know she's never cared a rap for any fellow. And she's just as gay and full of the devil as she was at fourteen. Nell's as good and lovable as she is pretty, but I'm afraid she'll never grow into a woman while we live out in this lonely land. And you've always hated towns where there was a chance for the girl—just because you were afraid she'd fall in love. You've always been strange, even silly, about that. I've done my best for Nell—loved her as if she were my own daughter. I've changed many business plans to suit your whims. There are rough times ahead, maybe. I need men. I'll hire this chap Gale if he'll stay. Let Nell take her chance with him, just as she'll have to take chances with men when we get out of the desert. She'll be all the better for it."

"I hope Laddy's not mistaken in his opinion of this newcomer," replied Mrs. Belding, with a sigh of resignation.

"Shore I never made a mistake in my life figger'n' people," said Laddy, stoutly.

"Yes, you have, Laddy," replied Mrs. Belding. "You're wrong about Tom.... Well, supper is to be got. That young man and the girl will be starved. I'll go in now. If Nell happens around don't—don't flatter her, Laddy, like you did at dinner. Don't make her think of her looks."

Dick heard Mrs. Belding walk away.

"Shore she's powerful particular about that girl," observed Laddy. "Say, Tom, Nell knows she's pretty, doesn't she?"

"She's liable to find it out unless you shut up, Laddy. When you visited us out here some weeks ago, you kept paying cowboy compliments to her."

"An' it's your idea that cowboy compliments are plumb bad for girls?"

"Downright bad, Laddy, so my wife says."

"I'll be darned if I believe any girl can be hurt by a little sweet talk. It pleases 'em.... But say, Beldin', speaking of looks, have you got a peek yet at the Spanish girl?"

"Not in the light."

"Well, neither have I in daytime. I had enough by moonlight. Nell is some on looks, but I'm regretful passin' the ribbon to the lady from Mex. Jim, where are you?"

"My money's on Nell," replied Lash. "Gimme a girl with flesh an' color, an' blue eyes a-laughin'. Miss Castaneda is some peach, I'll not gainsay. But her face seemed too white. An' when she flashed those eyes on me, I thought I was shot! When she stood up there at first, thankin' us, I felt as if a—a princess was round somewhere. Now, Nell is kiddish an' sweet an'—"

"Chop it," interrupted Belding. "Here comes Nell now."

Dick's tingling ears took in the pattering of light footsteps, the rush of some one running.

"Here you are," cried a sweet, happy voice. "Dad, the Senorita is perfectly lovely. I've been peeping at her. She sleeps like—like death. She's so white. Oh, I hope she won't be ill."

"Shore she's only played out," said Laddy. "But she had spunk while it lasted.... I was just arguin' with Jim an' Tom about Miss Castaneda."

"Gracious! Why, she's beautiful. I never saw any one so beautiful.... How strange and sad, that about her! Tell me more, Laddy. You promised. I'm dying to know. I never hear anything in this awful place. Didn't you say the Senorita had a sweetheart?"

"Shore I did."

"And he's a cavalryman?"

"Yes."

"Is he the young man who came with you?"

"Nope. That fellow's the one who saved the girl from Rojas."

"Ah! Where is he, Laddy?"

"He's in there asleep."

"Is he hurt?"

"I reckon not. He walked about fifteen miles."

"Is he—nice, Laddy?"

"Shore."

"What is he like?"

"Well, I'm not long acquainted, never saw him by day, but I was some tolerable took with him. An' Jim here, Jim says the young man can have his gun an' his hoss."

"Wonderful! Laddy, what on earth did this stranger do to win you cowboys in just one night?"

"I'll shore have to tell you. Me an' Jim were watchin' a game of cards in the Del Sol saloon in Casita. That's across the line. We had acquaintances—four fellows from the Cross Bar outfit, where we worked a while back. This Del Sol is a billiard hall, saloon, restaurant, an' the like. An' it was full of Greasers. Some of Camp's rebels were there drinkin' an' playin' games. Then pretty soon in come Rojas with some of his outfit. They were packin' guns an' kept to themselves off to one side. I didn't give them a second look till Jim said he reckoned there was somethin' in the wind. Then, careless-like, I began to peek at Rojas. They call Rojas the 'dandy rebel,' an' he shore looked the part. It made me sick to see him in all that lace an' glitter, knowin' him to be the cutthroat robber he is. It's no oncommon sight to see excited Greasers. They're all crazy. But this bandit was shore some agitated. He kept his men in a tight bunch round a table. He talked an' waved his hands. He was actually shakin'. His eyes had a wild glare. Now I figgered that trouble was brewin', most likely for the little Casita garrison. People seemed to think Campo an' Rojas would join forces to oust the federals. Jim thought Rojas's excitement was at the hatchin' of some plot. Anyway, we didn't join no card games, an' without pretendin' to, we was some watchful.

"A little while afterward I seen a fellow standin' in the restaurant door. He was a young American dressed in corduroys and boots, like a prospector. You know it's no onusual fact to see prospectors in these parts. What made me think twice about this one was how big he seemed, how he filled up that door. He looked round the saloon, an' when he spotted Rojas he sorta jerked up. Then he pulled his slouch hat lopsided an' began to stagger down, down the steps. First off I made shore he was drunk. But I remembered he didn't seem drunk before. It was some queer. So I watched that young man.

"He reeled around the room like a fellow who was drunker'n a lord. Nobody but me seemed to notice him. Then he began to stumble over pool-players an' get his feet tangled up in chairs an' bump against tables. He got some pretty hard looks. He came round our way, an' all of a sudden he seen us cowboys. He gave another start, like the one when he first seen Rojas, then he made for us. I tipped Jim off that somethin' was doin'.

"When he got close he straightened up, put back his slouch hat, an' looked at us. Then I saw his face. It sorta electrified yours truly. It was white, with veins standin' out an' eyes flamin'—a face of fury. I was plumb amazed, didn't know what to think. Then this queer young man shot some cool, polite words at me an' Jim.

"He was only bluffin' at bein' drunk—he meant to rush Rojas, to start a rough house. The bandit was after a girl. This girl was in the hotel, an' she was the sweetheart of a soldier, the young fellow's friend. The hotel was watched by Rojas's guards, an' the plan was to make a fuss an' get the girl away in the excitement. Well, Jim an' me got a hint of our bein' Americans—that cowboys generally had a name for loyalty to women. Then this amazin' chap—you can't imagine how scornful—said for me an' Jim to watch him.

"Before I could catch my breath an' figger out what he meant by 'rush' an' 'rough house' he had knocked over a table an' crowded some Greaser half off the map. One little funny man leaped up like a wild monkey an' began to screech. An' in another second he was in the air upside down. When he lit, he laid there. Then, quicker'n I can tell you, the young man dove at Rojas. Like a mad steer on the rampage he charged Rojas an' his men. The whole outfit went down—smash! I figgered then what 'rush' meant. The young fellow came up out of the pile with Rojas, an' just like I'd sling an empty sack along the floor he sent the bandit. But swift as that went he was on top of Rojas before the chairs an' tables had stopped rollin'.

"I woke up then, an' made for the center of the room. Jim with me. I began to shoot out the lamps. Jim threwed his guns on the crazy rebels, an' I was afraid there'd be blood spilled before I could get the room dark. Bein's shore busy, I lost sight of the young fellow for a second or so, an' when I got an eye free for him I seen a Greaser about to knife him. Think I was some considerate of the Greaser by only shootin' his arm off. Then I cracked the last lamp, an' in the hullabaloo me an' Jim vamoosed.

"We made tracks for our hosses an' packs, an' was hittin' the San Felipe road when we run right plumb into the young man. Well, he said his name was Gale—Dick Gale. The girl was with him safe an' well; but her sweetheart, the soldier, bein' away without leave, had to go back sudden. There shore was some trouble, for Jim an' me heard shootin'. Gale said he had no money, no friends, was a stranger in a desert country; an' he was distracted to know how to help the girl. So me an' Jim started off with them for San Felipe, got switched, and' then we headed for the Rio Forlorn."

"Oh, I think he was perfectly splendid!" exclaimed the girl.

"Shore he was. Only, Nell, you can't lay no claim to bein' the original discoverer of that fact."

"But, Laddy, you haven't told me what he looks like."

At this juncture Dick Gale felt it absolutely impossible for him to play the eavesdropper any longer. Quietly he rolled out of bed. The voices still sounded close outside, and it was only by effort that he kept from further listening. Belding's kindly interest, Laddy's blunt and sincere cowboy eulogy, the girl's sweet eagerness and praise—these warmed Gale's heart. He had fallen among simple people, into whose lives the advent of an unknown man was welcome. He found himself in a singularly agitated mood. The excitement, the thrill, the difference felt in himself, experienced the preceding night, had extended on into his present. And the possibilities suggested by the conversation he had unwittingly overheard added sufficiently to the other feelings to put him into a peculiarly receptive state of mind. He was wild to be one of the Belding rangers. The idea of riding a horse in the open desert, with a dangerous duty to perform, seemed to strike him with an appealing force. Something within him went out to the cowboys, to this blunt and kind Belding. He was afraid to meet the girl. If every man who came along fell in love with this sweet-voiced Nell, then what hope had he to escape—now, when his whole inner awakening betokened a change of spirit, hope, a finding of real worth, real good, real power in himself? He did not understand wholly, yet he felt ready to ride, to fight, to love the desert, to love these outdoor men, to love a woman. That beautiful Spanish girl had spoken to something dead in him and it had quickened to life. The sweet voice of an audacious, unseen girl warned him that presently a still more wonderful thing would happen to him.

Gale imagined he made noise enough as he clumsily pulled on his boots, yet the voices, split by a merry laugh, kept on murmuring outside the door. It was awkward for him, having only one hand available to lace up his boots. He looked out of the window. Evidently this was at the end of the house. There was a flagstone walk, beside which ran a ditch full of swift, muddy water. It made a pleasant sound. There were trees strange of form and color to to him. He heard bees, birds, chickens, saw the red of roses and green of grass. Then he saw, close to the wall, a tub full of water, and a bench upon which lay basin, soap, towel, comb, and brush. The window was also a door, for under it there was a step.

Gale hesitated a moment, then went out. He stepped naturally, hoping and expecting that the cowboys would hear him. But nobody came. Awkwardly, with left hand, he washed his face. Upon a nail in the wall hung a little mirror, by the aid of which Dick combed and brushed his hair. He imagined he looked a most haggard wretch. With that he faced forward, meaning to go round the corner of the house to greet the cowboys and these new-found friends.

Dick had taken but one step when he was halted by laugher and the patter of light feet.

From close around the corner pealed out that sweet voice. "Dad, you'll have your wish, and mama will be wild!"

Dick saw a little foot sweep into view, a white dress, then the swiftly moving form of a girl. She was looking backward.

"Dad, I shall fall in love with your new ranger. I will—I have—"

Then she plumped squarely into Dick's arms.

She started back violently.

Dick saw a fair face and dark-blue, audaciously flashing eyes. Swift as lightning their expression changed to surprise, fear, wonder. For an instant they were level with Dick's grave questioning. Suddenly, sweetly, she blushed.

"Oh-h!" she faltered.

Then the blush turned to a scarlet fire. She whirled past him, and like a white gleam was gone.

Dick became conscious of the quickened beating of his heart. He experienced a singular exhilaration. That moment had been the one for which he had been ripe, the event upon which strange circumstances had been rushing him.

With a couple of strides he turned the corner. Laddy and Lash were there talking to a man of burly form. Seen by day, both cowboys were gray-haired, red-skinned, and weather-beaten, with lean, sharp features, and gray eyes so much alike that they might have been brothers.

"Hello, there's the young fellow," spoke up the burly man. "Mr. Gale, I'm glad to meet you. My name's Belding."

His greeting was as warm as his handclasp was long and hard. Gale saw a heavy man of medium height. His head was large and covered with grizzled locks. He wore a short-cropped mustache and chin beard. His skin was brown, and his dark eyes beamed with a genial light.

The cowboys were as cordial as if Dick had been their friend for years.

"Young man, did you run into anything as you came out?" asked Belding, with twinkling eyes.

"Why, yes, I met something white and swift flying by," replied Dick.

"Did she see you?" asked Laddy.

"I think so; but she didn't wait for me to introduce myself."

"That was Nell Burton, my girl—step-daughter, I should say," said Belding. "She's sure some whirlwind, as Laddy calls her. Come, let's go in and meet the wife."

The house was long, like a barracks, with porch extending all the way, and doors every dozen paces. When Dick was ushered into a sitting-room, he was amazed at the light and comfort. This room had two big windows and a door opening into a patio, where there were luxuriant grass, roses in bloom, and flowering trees. He heard a slow splashing of water.

In Mrs. Belding, Gale found a woman of noble proportions and striking appearance. Her hair was white. She had a strong, serious, well-lined face that bore haunting evidences of past beauty. The gaze she bent upon him was almost piercing in its intensity. Her greeting, which seemed to Dick rather slow in coming, was kind though not cordial. Gale's first thought, after he had thanked these good people for their hospitality, was to inquire about Mercedes. He was informed that the Spanish girl had awakened with a considerable fever and nervousness. When, however, her anxiety had been allayed and her thirst relieved, she had fallen asleep again. Mrs. Belding said the girl had suffered no great hardship, other than mental, and would very soon be rested and well.

"Now, Gale," said Belding, when his wife had excused herself to get supper, "the boys, Jim and Laddy, told me about you and the mix-up at Casita. I'll be glad to take care of the girl till it's safe for your soldier friend to get her out of the country. That won't be very soon, don't mistake me.... I don't want to seem over-curious about you—Laddy has interested me in you—and straight out I'd like to know what you propose to do now."

"I haven't any plans," replied Dick; and, taking the moment as propitious, he decided to speak frankly concerning himself. "I just drifted down here. My home is in Chicago. When I left school some years ago—I'm twenty-five now—I went to work for my father. He's—he has business interests there. I tried all kinds of inside jobs. I couldn't please my father. I guess I put no real heart in my work. The fact was I didn't know how to work. The governor and I didn't exactly quarrel; but he hurt my feelings, and I quit. Six months or more ago I came West, and have knocked about from Wyoming southwest to the border. I tried to find congenial work, but nothing came my way. To tell you frankly, Mr. Belding, I suppose I didn't much care. I believe, though, that all the time I didn't know what I wanted. I've learned—well, just lately—"

"What do you want to do?" interposed Belding.

"I want a man's job. I want to do things with my hands. I want action. I want to be outdoors."

Belding nodded his head as if he understood that, and he began to speak again, cut something short, then went on, hesitatingly:

"Gale—you could go home again—to the old man—it'd be all right?"

"Mr. Belding, there's nothing shady in my past. The governor would be glad to have me home. That's the only consolation I've got. But I'm not going. I'm broke. I won't be a tramp. And it's up to me to do something."

"How'd you like to be a border ranger?" asked Belding, laying a hand on Dick's knee. "Part of my job here is United States Inspector of Immigration. I've got that boundary line to patrol—to keep out Chinks and Japs. This revolution has added complications, and I'm looking for smugglers and raiders here any day. You'll not be hired by the U. S. You'll simply be my ranger, same as Laddy and Jim, who have promised to work for me. I'll pay you well, give you a room here, furnish everything down to guns, and the finest horse you ever saw in your life. Your job won't be safe and healthy, sometimes, but it'll be a man's job—don't mistake me! You can gamble on having things to do outdoors. Now, what do you say?"

"I accept, and I thank you—I can't say how much," replied Gale, earnestly.

"Good! That's settled. Let's go out and tell Laddy and Jim."

Both boys expressed satisfaction at the turn of affairs, and then with Belding they set out to take Gale around the ranch. The house and several outbuildings were constructed of adobe, which, according to Belding, retained the summer heat on into winter, and the winter cold on into summer. These gray-red mud habitations were hideous to look at, and this fact, perhaps, made their really comfortable interiors more vividly a contrast. The wide grounds were covered with luxuriant grass and flowers and different kinds of trees. Gale's interest led him to ask about fig trees and pomegranates, and especially about a beautiful specimen that Belding called palo verde.

Belding explained that the luxuriance of this desert place was owing to a few springs and the dammed-up waters of the Rio Forlorn. Before he had come to the oasis it had been inhabited by a Papago Indian tribe and a few peon families. The oasis lay in an arroyo a mile wide, and sloped southwest for some ten miles or more. The river went dry most of the year; but enough water was stored in flood season to irrigate the gardens and alfalfa fields.

"I've got one never-failing spring on my place," said Belding. "Fine, sweet water! You know what that means in the desert. I like this oasis. The longer I live here the better I like it. There's not a spot in southern Arizona that'll compare with this valley for water or grass or wood. It's beautiful and healthy. Forlorn and lonely, yes, especially for women like my wife and Nell; but I like it.... And between you and me, boys, I've got something up my sleeve. There's gold dust in the arroyos, and there's mineral up in the mountains. If we only had water! This hamlet has steadily grown since I took up a station here. Why, Casita is no place beside Forlorn River. Pretty soon the Southern Pacific will shoot a railroad branch out here. There are possibilities, and I want you boys to stay with me and get in on the ground floor. I wish this rebel war was over.... Well, here are the corrals and the fields. Gale, take a look at that bunch of horses!"

Belding's last remark was made as he led his companions out of shady gardens into the open. Gale saw an adobe shed and a huge pen fenced by strangely twisted and contorted branches or trunks of mesquite, and, beyond these, wide, flat fields, green—a dark, rich green—and dotted with beautiful horses. There were whites and blacks, and bays and grays. In his admiration Gale searched his memory to see if he could remember the like of these magnificent animals, and had to admit that the only ones he could compare with them were the Arabian steeds.

"Every ranch loves his horses," said Belding. "When I was in the Panhandle I had some fine stock. But these are Mexican. They came from Durango, where they were bred. Mexican horses are the finest in the world, bar none."

"Shore I reckon I savvy why you don't sleep nights," drawled Laddy. "I see a Greaser out there—no, it's an Indian."

"That's my Papago herdsman. I keep watch over the horses now day and night. Lord, how I'd hate to have Rojas or Salazar—any of those bandit rebels—find my horses!... Gale, can you ride?"

Dick modestly replied that he could, according to the Eastern idea of horsemanship.

"You don't need to be half horse to ride one of that bunch. But over there in the other field I've iron-jawed broncos I wouldn't want you to tackle—except to see the fun. I've an outlaw I'll gamble even Laddy can't ride."

"So. How much'll you gamble?" asked Laddy, instantly.

The ringing of a bell, which Belding said was a call to supper, turned the men back toward the house. Facing that way, Gale saw dark, beetling ridges rising from the oasis and leading up to bare, black mountains. He had heard Belding call them No Name Mountains, and somehow the appellation suited those lofty, mysterious, frowning peaks.

It was not until they reached the house and were about to go in that Belding chanced to discover Gale's crippled hand.

"What an awful hand!" he exclaimed. "Where the devil did you get that?"

"I stove in my knuckles on Rojas," replied Dick.

"You did that in one punch? Say, I'm glad it wasn't me you hit! Why didn't you tell me? That's a bad hand. Those cuts are full of dirt and sand. Inflammation's setting in. It's got to be dressed. Nell!" he called.

There was no answer. He called again, louder.

"Mother, where's the girl?"

"She's there in the dining-room," replied Mrs. Belding.

"Did she hear me?" he inquired, impatiently.

"Of course."

"Nell!" roared Belding.

This brought results. Dick saw a glimpse of golden hair and a white dress in the door. But they were not visible longer than a second.

"Dad, what's the matter?" asked a voice that was still as sweet as formerly, but now rather small and constrained.

"Bring the antiseptics, cotton, bandages—and things out here. Hurry now."

Belding fetched a pail of water and a basin from the kitchen. His wife followed him out, and, upon seeing Dick's hand, was all solicitude. Then Dick heard light, quick footsteps, but he did not look up.

"Nell, this is Mr. Gale—Dick Gale, who came with the boys last last night," said Belding. "He's got an awful hand. Got it punching that greaser Rojas. I want you to dress it.... Gale, this is my step-daughter, Nell Burton, of whom I spoke. She's some good when there's somebody sick or hurt. Shove out your fist, my boy, and let her get at it. Supper's nearly ready."

Dick felt that same strange, quickening heart throb, yet he had never been cooler in his life. More than anything else in the world he wanted to look at Nell Burton; however, divining that the situation might be embarrassing to her, he refrained from looking up. She began to bathe his injured knuckles. He noted the softness, the deftness of her touch, and then it seemed her fingers were not quite as steady as they might have been. Still, in a moment they appeared to become surer in their work. She had beautiful hands, not too large, though certainly not small, and they were strong, brown, supple. He observed next, with stealthy, upward-stealing glance, that she had rolled up her sleeves, exposing fine, round arms graceful in line. Her skin was brown—no, it was more gold than brown. It had a wonderful clear tint. Dick stoically lowered his eyes then, putting off as long as possible the alluring moment when he was to look into her face. That would be a fateful moment. He played with a certain strange joy of anticipation. When, however, she sat down beside him and rested his injured hand in her lap as she cut bandages, she was so thrillingly near that he yielded to an irrepressible desire to look up. She had a sweet, fair face warmly tinted with that same healthy golden-brown sunburn. Her hair was light gold and abundant, a waving mass. Her eyes were shaded by long, downcast lashes, yet through them he caught a gleam of blue.

Despite the stir within him, Gale, seeing she was now absorbed in her task, critically studied her with a second closer gaze. She was a sweet, wholesome, joyous, pretty girl.

"Shore it musta hurt?" replied Laddy, who sat an interested spectator.

"Yes, I confess it did," replied Dick, slowly, with his eyes on Nell's face. "But I didn't mind."

The girl's lashes swept up swiftly in surprise. She had taken his words literally. But the dark-blue eyes met his for only a fleeting second. Then the warm tint in her cheeks turned as red as her lips. Hurriedly she finished tying the bandage and rose to her feet.

"I thank you," said Gale, also rising.

With that Belding appeared in the doorway, and finding the operation concluded, called them in to supper. Dick had the use of only one arm, and he certainly was keenly aware of the shy, silent girl across the table; but in spite of these considerable handicaps he eclipsed both hungry cowboys in the assault upon Mrs. Belding's bounteous supper. Belding talked, the cowboys talked more or less. Mrs. Belding put in a word now and then, and Dick managed to find brief intervals when it was possible for him to say yes or no. He observed gratefully that no one round the table seemed to be aware of his enormous appetite.

After supper, having a favorable opportunity when for a moment no one was at hand, Dick went out through the yard, past the gardens and fields, and climbed the first knoll. From that vantage point he looked out over the little hamlet, somewhat to his right, and was surprised at its extent, its considerable number of adobe houses. The overhanging mountains, ragged and darkening, a great heave of splintered rock, rather chilled and affronted him.

Westward the setting sun gilded a spiked, frost-colored, limitless expanse of desert. It awed Gale. Everywhere rose blunt, broken ranges or isolated groups of mountains. Yet the desert stretched away down between and beyond them. When the sun set and Gale could not see so far, he felt a relief.

That grand and austere attraction of distance gone, he saw the desert nearer at hand—the valley at his feet. What a strange gray, somber place! There was a lighter strip of gray winding down between darker hues. This he realized presently was the river bed, and he saw how the pools of water narrowed and diminished in size till they lost themselves in gray sand. This was the rainy season, near its end, and here a little river struggled hopelessly, forlornly to live in the desert. He received a potent impression of the nature of that blasted age-worn waste which he had divined was to give him strength and work and love.

V

A DESERT ROSE

BELDING assigned Dick to a little room which had no windows but two doors, one opening into the patio, the other into the yard on the west side of the house. It contained only the barest necessities for comfort. Dick mentioned the baggage he had left in the hotel at Casita, and it was Belding's opinion that to try to recover his property would be rather risky; on the moment Richard Gale was probably not popular with the Mexicans at Casita. So Dick bade good-by to fine suits of clothes and linen with a feeling that, as he had said farewell to an idle and useless past, it was just as well not to have any old luxuries as reminders. As he possessed, however, not a thing save the clothes on his back, and not even a handkerchief, he expressed regret that he had come to Forlorn River a beggar.

"Beggar hell!" exploded Belding, with his eyes snapping in the lamplight. "Money's the last thing we think of out here. All the same, Gale, if you stick you'll be rich."

"It wouldn't surprise me," replied Dick, thoughtfully. But he was not thinking of material wealth. Then, as he viewed his stained and torn shirt, he laughed and said "Belding, while I'm getting rich I'd like to have some respectable clothes."

"We've a little Mex store in town, and what you can't get there the women folks will make for you."

When Dick lay down he was dully conscious of pain and headache, that he did not feel well. Despite this, and a mind thronging with memories and anticipations, he succumbed to weariness and soon fell asleep.

It was light when he awoke, but a strange brightness seen through what seemed blurred eyes. A moment passed before his mind worked clearly, and then he had to make an effort to think. He was dizzy. When he essayed to lift his right arm, an excruciating pain made him desist. Then he discovered that his arm was badly swollen, and the hand had burst its bandages. The injured member was red, angry, inflamed, and twice its normal size. He felt hot all over, and a raging headache consumed him.

Belding came stamping into the room.

"Hello, Dick. Do you know it's late? How's the busted fist this morning?"

Dick tried to sit up, but his effort was a failure. He got about half up, then felt himself weakly sliding back.

"I guess—I'm pretty sick," he said.

He saw Belding lean over him, feel his face, and speak, and then everything seemed to drift, not into darkness, but into some region where he had dim perceptions of gray moving things, and of voices that were remote. Then there came an interval when all was blank. He knew not whether it was one of minutes or hours, but after it he had a clearer mind. He slept, awakened during night-time, and slept again. When he again unclosed his eyes the room was sunny, and cool with a fragrant breeze that blew through the open door. Dick felt better; but he had no particular desire to move or talk or eat. He had, however, a burning thirst. Mrs. Belding visited him often; her husband came in several times, and once Nell slipped in noiselessly. Even this last event aroused no interest in Dick.

On the next day he was very much improved.

"We've been afraid of blood poisoning," said Belding. "But my wife thinks the danger's past. You'll have to rest that arm for a while."

Ladd and Jim came peeping in at the door.

"Come in, boys. He can have company—the more the better—if it'll keep him content. He mustn't move, that's all."

The cowboys entered, slow, easy, cool, kind-voiced.

"Shore it's tough," said Ladd, after he had greeted Dick. "You look used up."

Jim Lash wagged his half-bald, sunburned head, "Musta been more'n tough for Rojas."

"Gale, Laddy tells me one of our neighbors, fellow named Carter, is going to Casita," put in Belding. "Here's a chance to get word to your friend the soldier."

"Oh, that will be fine!" exclaimed Dick. "I declare I'd forgotten Thorne.... How is Miss Castaneda? I hope—"

"She's all right, Gale. Been up and around the patio for two days. Like all the Spanish—the real thing—she's made of Damascus steel. We've been getting acquainted. She and Nell made friends at once. I'll call them in."

He closed the door leading out into the yard, explaining that he did not want to take chances of Mercedes's presence becoming known to neighbors. Then he went to the patio and called.

Both girls came in, Mercedes leading. Like Nell, she wore white, and she had a red rose in her hand. Dick would scarcely have recognized anything about her except her eyes and the way she carried her little head, and her beauty burst upon him strange and anew. She was swift, impulsive in her movements to reach his side.

"Senor, I am so sorry you were ill—so happy you are better."

Dick greeted her, offering his left hand, gravely apologizing for the fact that, owing to a late infirmity, he could not offer the right. Her smile exquisitely combined sympathy, gratitude, admiration. Then Dick spoke to Nell, likewise offering his hand, which she took shyly. Her reply was a murmured, unintelligible one; but her eyes were glad, and the tint in her cheeks threatened to rival the hue of the rose she carried.

Everybody chatted then, except Nell, who had apparently lost her voice. Presently Dick remembered to speak of the matter of getting news to Thorne.

"Senor, may I write to him? Will some one take a letter?... I shall hear from him!" she said; and her white hands emphasized her words.

"Assuredly. I guess poor Thorne is almost crazy. I'll write to him.... No, I can't with this crippled hand."

"That'll be all right, Gale," said Belding. "Nell will write for you. She writes all my letters."

So Belding arranged it; and Mercedes flew away to her room to write, while Nell fetched pen and paper and seated herself beside Gale's bed to take his dictation.

What with watching Nell and trying to catch her glance, and listening to Belding's talk with the cowboys, Dick was hard put to it to dictate any kind of a creditable letter. Nell met his gaze once, then no more. The color came and went in her cheeks, and sometimes, when he told her to write so and so, there was a demure smile on her lips. She was laughing at him. And Belding was talking over the risks involved in a trip to Casita.

"Shore I'll ride in with the letters," Ladd said.

"No you won't," replied Belding. "That bandit outfit will be laying for you."

"Well, I reckon if they was I wouldn't be oncommon grieved."

"I'll tell you, boys, I'll ride in myself with Carter. There's business I can see to, and I'm curious to know what the rebels are doing. Laddy, keep one eye open while I'm gone. See the horses are locked up.... Gale, I'm going to Casita myself. Ought to get back tomorrow some time. I'll be ready to start in an hour. Have your letter ready. And say—if you want to write home it's a chance. Sometimes we don't go to the P. O. in a month."

He tramped out, followed by the tall cowboys, and then Dick was enabled to bring his letter to a close. Mercedes came back, and her eyes were shining. Dick imagined a letter received from her would be something of an event for a fellow. Then, remembering Belding's suggestion, he decided to profit by it.

"May I trouble you to write another for me?" asked Dick, as he received the letter from Nell.

"It's no trouble, I'm sure—I'd be pleased," she replied.

That was altogether a wonderful speech of hers, Dick thought, because the words were the first coherent ones she had spoken to him.

"May I stay?" asked Mercedes, smiling.

"By all means," he answered, and then he settled back and began.

Presently Gale paused, partly because of genuine emotion, and stole a look from under his hand at Nell. She wrote swiftly, and her downcast face seemed to be softer in its expression of sweetness. If she had in the very least been drawn to him— But that was absurd—impossible!

When Dick finished dictating, his eyes were upon Mercedes, who sat smiling curious and sympathetic. How responsive she was! He heard the hasty scratch of Nell's pen. He looked at Nell. Presently she rose, holding out his letter. He was just in time to see a wave of red recede from her face. She gave him one swift gaze, unconscious, searching, then averted it and turned away. She left the room with Mercedes before he could express his thanks.

But that strange, speaking flash of eyes remained to haunt and torment Gale. It was indescribably sweet, and provocative of thoughts that he believed were wild without warrant. Something within him danced for very joy, and the next instant he was conscious of wistful doubt, a gravity that he could not understand. It dawned upon him that for the brief instant when Nell had met his gaze she had lost her shyness. It was a woman's questioning eyes that had pierced through him.

During the rest of the day Gale was content to lie still on his bed thinking and dreaming, dozing at intervals, and watching the lights change upon the mountain peaks, feeling the warm, fragrant desert wind that blew in upon him. He seemed to have lost the faculty of estimating time. A long while, strong in its effect upon him, appeared to have passed since he had met Thorne. He accepted things as he felt them, and repudiated his intelligence. His old inquisitive habit of mind returned. Did he love Nell? Was he only attracted for the moment? What was the use of worrying about her or himself? He refused to answer, and deliberately gave himself up to dreams of her sweet face and of that last dark-blue glance.

Next day he believed he was well enough to leave his room; but Mrs. Belding would not permit him to do so. She was kind, soft-handed, motherly, and she was always coming in to minister to his comfort. This attention was sincere, not in the least forced; yet Gale felt that the friendliness so manifest in the others of the household did not extend to her. He was conscious of something that a little thought persuaded him was antagonism. It surprised and hurt him. He had never been much of a success with girls and young married women, but their mothers and old people had generally been fond of him. Still, though Mrs. Belding's hair was snow-white, she did not impress him as being old. He reflected that there might come a time when it would be desirable, far beyond any ground of every-day friendly kindliness, to have Mrs. Belding be well disposed toward him. So he thought about her, and pondered how to make her like him. It did not take very long for Dick to discover that he liked her. Her face, except when she smiled, was thoughtful and sad. It was a face to make one serious. Like a haunting shadow, like a phantom of happier years, the sweetness of Nell's face was there, and infinitely more of beauty than had been transmitted to the daughter. Dick believed Mrs. Belding's friendship and motherly love were worth striving to win, entirely aside from any more selfish motive. He decided both would be hard to get. Often he felt her deep, penetrating gaze upon him; and, though this in no wise embarrassed him—for he had no shameful secrets of past or present—it showed him how useless it would be to try to conceal anything from her. Naturally, on first impulse, he wanted to hide his interest in the daughter; but he resolved to be absolutely frank and true, and through that win or lose. Moreover, if Mrs. Belding asked him any questions about his home, his family, his connections, he would not avoid direct and truthful answers.

Toward evening Gale heard the tramp of horses and Belding's hearty voice. Presently the rancher strode in upon Gale, shaking the gray dust from his broad shoulders and waving a letter.

"Hello, Dick! Good news and bad!" he said, putting the letter in Dick's hand. "Had no trouble finding your friend Thorne. Looked like he'd been drunk for a week! Say, he nearly threw a fit. I never saw a fellow so wild with joy. He made sure you and Mercedes were lost in the desert. He wrote two letters which I brought. Don't mistake me, boy, it was some fun with Mercedes just now. I teased her, wouldn't give her the letter. You ought to have seen her eyes. If ever you see a black-and-white desert hawk swoop down upon a quail, then you'll know how Mercedes pounced upon her letter... Well, Casita is one hell of a place these days. I tried to get your baggage, and I think I made a mistake. We're going to see travel toward Forlorn River. The federal garrison got reinforcements from somewhere, and is holding out. There's been fighting for three days. The rebels have a string of flat railroad cars, all iron, and they ran this up within range of the barricades. They've got some machine guns, and they're going to lick the federals sure. There are dead soldiers in the ditches, Mexican non-combatants lying dead in the streets— and buzzards everywhere! It's reported that Campo, the rebel leader, is on the way up from Sinaloa, and Huerta, a federal general, is coming to relieve the garrison. I don't take much stock in reports. But there's hell in Casita, all right."

"Do you think we'll have trouble out here?" asked Dick, excitedly.

"Sure. Some kind of trouble sooner or later," replied Belding, gloomily. "Why, you can stand on my ranch and step over into Mexico. Laddy says we'll lose horses and other stock in night raids. Jim Lash doesn't look for any worse. But Jim isn't as well acquainted with Greasers as I am. Anyway, my boy, as soon as you can hold a bridle and a gun you'll be on the job, don't mistake me."

"With Laddy and Jim?" asked Dick, trying to be cool.

"Sure. With them and me, and by yourself."

Dick drew a deep breath, and even after Belding had departed he forgot for a moment about the letter in his hand. Then he unfolded the paper and read:

Dear Dick,—You've more than saved my life. To the end of my days you'll be the one man to whom I owe everything. Words fail to express my feelings.

This must be a brief note. Belding is waiting, and I used up most of the time writing to Mercedes. I like Belding. He was not unknown to me, though I never met or saw him before. You'll be interested to learn that he's the unadulterated article, the real Western goods. I've heard of some of his stunts, and they made my hair curl. Dick, your luck is staggering. The way Belding spoke of you was great. But you deserve it, old man.

I'm leaving Mercedes in your charge, subject, of course, to advice from Belding. Take care of her, Dick, for my life is wrapped up in her. By all means keep her from being seen by Mexicans. We are sitting tight here—nothing doing. If some action doesn't come soon, it'll be darned strange. Things are centering this way. There's scrapping right along, and people have begun to move. We're still patrolling the line eastward of Casita. It'll be impossible to keep any tab on the line west of Casita, for it's too rough. That cactus desert is awful. Cowboys or rangers with desert-bred horses might keep raiders and smugglers from crossing. But if cavalrymen could stand that waterless wilderness, which I doubt much, their horses would drop under them.

If things do quiet down before my commission expires, I'll get leave of absence, run out to Forlorn River, marry my beautiful Spanish princess, and take her to a civilized country, where, I opine, every son of a gun who sees her will lose his head, and drive me mad. It's my great luck, old pal, that you are a fellow who never seemed to care about pretty girls. So you won't give me the double cross and run off with Mercedes—carry her off, like the villain in the play, I mean.

That reminds me of Rojas. Oh, Dick, it was glorious! You didn't do anything to the Dandy Rebel! Not at all! You merely caressed him—gently moved him to one side. Dick, harken to these glad words: Rojas is in the hospital. I was interested to inquire. He had a smashed finger, a dislocated collar bone, three broken ribs, and a fearful gash on his face. He'll be in the hospital for a month. Dick, when I meet that pig-headed dad of yours I'm going to give him the surprise of his life.

Send me a line whenever any one comes in from F. R., and inclose Mercedes's letter in yours. Take care of her, Dick, and may the future hold in store for you some of the sweetness I know now!

Faithfully yours, Thorne.

Dick reread the letter, then folded it and placed it under his pillow.

"Never cared for pretty girls, huh?" he soliloquized. "George, I never saw any till I struck Southern Arizona! Guess I'd better make up for lost time."

While he was eating his supper, with appetite rapidly returning to normal, Ladd and Jim came in, bowing their tall heads to enter the door. Their friendly advances were singularly welcome to

Gale, but he was still backward. He allowed himself to show that he was glad to see them, and he listened. Jim Lash had heard from Belding the result of the mauling given to Rojas by Dick. And Jim talked about what a grand thing that was. Ladd had a good deal to say about Belding's horses. It took no keen judge of human nature to see that horses constituted Ladd's ruling passion.

"I've had wimmen go back on me, but never no hoss!" declared Ladd, and manifestly that was a controlling truth with him.

"Shore it's a cinch Beldin' is agoin' to lose some of them hosses," he said. "You can search me if I don't think there'll be more doin' on the border here than along the Rio Grande. We're just the same as on Greaser soil. Mebbe we don't stand no such chance of bein' shot up as we would across the line. But who's goin' to give up his hosses without a fight? Half the time when Beldin's stock is out of the alfalfa it's grazin' over the line. He thinks he's careful about them hosses, but he ain't."

"Look a-here, Laddy; you cain't believe all you hear," replied Jim, seriously. "I reckon we mightn't have any trouble."

"Back up, Jim. Shore you're standin' on your bridle. I ain't goin' much on reports. Remember that American we met in Casita, the prospector who'd just gotten out of Sonora? He had some story, he had. Swore he'd killed seventeen Greasers breakin' through the rebel line round the mine where he an' other Americans were corralled. The next day when I met him again, he was drunk, an' then he told me he'd shot thirty Greasers. The chances are he did kill some. But reports are exaggerated. There are miners fightin' for life down in Sonora, you can gamble on that. An' the truth is bad enough. Take Rojas's harryin' of the Senorita, for instance. Can you beat that? Shore, Jim, there's more doin' than the raidin' of a few hosses. An' Forlorn River is goin' to get hers!"

Another dawn found Gale so much recovered that he arose and looked after himself, not, however, without considerable difficulty and rather disheartening twinges of pain.

Some time during the morning he heard the girls in the patio and called to ask if he might join them. He received one response, a mellow, "Si, Senor." It was not as much as he wanted, but considering that it was enough, he went out. He had not as yet visited the patio, and surprise and delight were in store for him. He found himself lost in a labyrinth of green and rose-bordered walks. He strolled around, discovering that the patio was a courtyard, open at an end; but he failed to discover the young ladies. So he called again. The answer came from the center of the square. After stooping to get under shrubs and wading through bushes he entered an open sandy circle, full of magnificent and murderous cactus plants, strange to him. On the other side, in the shade of a beautiful tree, he found the girls. Mercedes sitting in a hammock, Nell upon a blanket.

"What a beautiful tree!" he exclaimed. "I never saw one like that. What is it?"

"Palo verde," replied Nell.

"Senor, palo verde means 'green tree,'" added Mercedes.

This desert tree, which had struck Dick as so new and strange and beautiful, was not striking on account of size, for it was small, scarcely reaching higher than the roof; but rather because of its exquisite color of green, trunk and branch alike, and owing to the odd fact that it seemed not to possess leaves. All the tree from ground to tiny flat twigs was a soft polished green. It bore no thorns.

Right then and there began Dick's education in desert growths; and he felt that even if he had not had such charming teachers he would still have been absorbed. For the patio was full of desert wonders. A twisting-trunked tree with full foliage of small gray leaves Nell called a mesquite. Then Dick remembered the name, and now he saw where the desert got its pale-gray color. A huge, lofty, fluted column of green was a saguaro, or giant cactus. Another oddshaped cactus, resembling the legs of an inverted devil-fish, bore the name ocatillo. Each branch rose high and symmetrical, furnished with sharp blades that seemed to be at once leaves and thorns. Yet another cactus interested Gale, and it looked like a huge, low barrel covered with green-ribbed cloth and long thorns. This was the bisnaga, or barrel cactus. According to Nell and Mercedes, this plant was a happy exception to its desert neighbors, for it secreted water which had many times saved the lives of men. Last of the cacti to attract Gale, and the one to make him shiver, was a low plant, consisting of stem and many rounded protuberances of a frosty, steely white, and covered with long murderous spikes. From this plant the desert got its frosty glitter. It was as stiff, as unyielding as steel, and bore the name *choya*.

Dick's enthusiasm was contagious, and his earnest desire to learn was flattering to his teachers. When it came to assimilating Spanish, however, he did not appear to be so apt a pupil. He managed, after many trials, to acquire "buenos dias" and "buenos tardes," and "senorita" and "gracias," and a few other short terms. Dick was indeed eager to get a little smattering of Spanish, and perhaps he was not really quite so stupid as he pretended to be. It was delightful to be taught by a beautiful Spaniard who was so gracious and intense and magnetic of personality, and by a sweet American girl who moment by moment forgot her shyness. Gale wished to prolong the lessons.

So that was the beginning of many afternoons in which he learned desert lore and Spanish verbs, and something else that he dared not name.

Nell Burton had never shown to Gale that daring side of her character which had been so suggestively defined in Belding's terse description and Ladd's encomiums, and in her own audacious speech and merry laugh and flashing eye of that never-to-be-forgotten first meeting. She might have been an entirely different girl. But Gale remembered; and when the ice had been somewhat broken between them, he was always trying to surprise her into her real self. There were moments that fairly made him tingle with expectation. Yet he saw little more than a ghost of her vivacity, and never a gleam of that individuality which Belding had called a devil. On the few occasions that Dick had been left alone with her in the patio Nell had grown suddenly unresponsive and restrained, or she had left him on some transparent pretext. On the last occasion Mercedes returned to find Dick staring disconsolately at the rose-bordered path, where Nell had evidently vanished. The Spanish girl was wonderful in her divination.

"Senor Dick!" she cried.

Dick looked at her, soberly nodded his head, and then he laughed. Mercedes had seen through him in one swift glance. Her white hand touched his in wordless sympathy and thrilled him. This Spanish girl was all fire and passion and love. She understood him, she was his friend, she pledged him what he felt would be the most subtle and powerful influence.

Little by little he learned details of Nell's varied life. She had lived in many places. As a child she remembered moving from town to town, of going to school among schoolmates whom she never had time to know. Lawrence, Kansas, where she studied for several years, was the later exception to this changeful nature of her schooling. Then she moved to Stillwater, Oklahoma, from there to Austin, Texas, and on to Waco, where her mother met and married Belding. They lived in New Mexico awhile, in Tucson, Arizona, in Douglas, and finally had come to lonely Forlorn River.

"Mother could never live in one place any length of time," said Nell. "And since we've been in the Southwest she has never ceased trying to find some trace of her father. He was last heard of in Nogales fourteen years ago. She thinks grandfather was lost in the Sonora Desert.... And every place we go is worse. Oh, I love the desert. But I'd like to go back to Lawrence—or to see Chicago or New York—some of the places Mr. Gale speaks of.... I remember the college at Lawrence, though I was only twelve. I saw races—and once real football. Since then I've read magazines and papers about big football games, and I was always fascinated .... Mr. Gale, of course, you've seen games?

"Yes, a few," replied Dick; and he laughed a little. It was on his lips then to tell her about some of the famous games in which he had participated. But he refrained from exploiting himself. There was little, however, of the color and sound and cheer, of the violent action and rush and battle incidental to a big college football game that he did not succeed in making Mercedes and Nell feel just as if they had been there. They hung breathless and wide-eyed upon his words.

Some one else was present at the latter part of Dick's narrative. The moment he became aware of Mrs. Belding's presence he remembered fancying he had heard her call, and now he was certain she had done so. Mercedes and Nell, however, had been and still were oblivious to everything except Dick's recital. He saw Mrs. Belding cast a strange, intent glance upon Nell, then turn and go silently through the patio. Dick concluded his talk, but the brilliant beginning was not sustained.

Dick was haunted by the strange expression he had caught on Mrs. Belding's face, especially the look in her eyes. It had been one of repressed pain liberated in a flash of certainty. The mother had seen just as quickly as Mercedes how far he had gone on the road of love. Perhaps she had seen more—even more than he dared hope. The incident roused Gale. He could not understand Mrs. Belding, nor why that look of hers, that seeming baffled, hopeless look of a woman who saw the inevitable forces of life and could not thwart them, should cause him perplexity and distress. He wanted to go to her and tell her how he felt about Nell, but fear of absolute destruction of his hopes held him back. He would wait. Nevertheless, an instinct that was perhaps akin to self-preservation prompted him to want to let Nell know the state of his mind. Words crowded his brain seeking utterance. Who and what he was, how he loved her, the work he expected to take up soon, his longings, hopes, and plans—there was all this and more. But something checked him. And the repression made him so thoughtful and quiet, even melancholy, that he went outdoors to try to throw off the mood. The sun was yet high, and a dazzling white light enveloped valleys and peaks. He felt that the wonderful sunshine was the dominant feature of that arid region. It was like white gold. It had burned its color in a face he knew. It was going to warm his blood and brown his skin. A hot, languid breeze, so dry that he felt his lips shrink with its contact, came from the desert; and it seemed to smell of wide-open, untainted places where sand blew and strange, pungent plants gave a bitter-sweet tang to the air.

When he returned to the house, some hours later, his room had been put in order. In the middle of the white coverlet on his table lay a fresh red rose. Nell had dropped it there. Dick picked it up, feeling a throb in his breast. It was a bud just beginning to open, to show between its petals a dark-red, unfolding heart. How fragrant it was, how exquisitely delicate, how beautiful its inner hue of red, deep and dark, the crimson of life blood!

Had Nell left it there by accident or by intent? Was it merely kindness or a girl's subtlety? Was it a message couched elusively, a symbol, a hope in a half-blown desert rose?

VI

THE YAQUI

TOWARD evening of a lowering December day, some fifty miles west of Forlorn River, a horseman rode along an old, dimly defined trail. From time to time he halted to study the lay of the land ahead. It was bare, somber, ridgy desert, covered with dun-colored greasewood and stunted prickly pear. Distant mountains hemmed in the valley, raising black spurs above the round lomas and the square-walled mesas.

This lonely horseman bestrode a steed of magnificent build, perfectly white except for a dark bar of color running down the noble head from ears to nose. Sweatcaked dust stained the long flanks. The horse had been running. His mane and tail were laced and knotted to keep their length out of reach of grasping cactus and brush. Clumsy home-made leather shields covered the front of his forelegs and ran up well to his wide breast. What otherwise would have been muscular symmetry of limb was marred by many a scar and many a lump. He was lean, gaunt, worn, a huge machine of muscle and bone, beautiful only in head and mane, a weight-carrier, a horse strong and fierce like the desert that had bred him.

The rider fitted the horse as he fitted the saddle. He was a young man of exceedingly powerful physique, wide-shouldered, long-armed, big-legged. His lean face, where it was not red, blistered and peeling, was the hue of bronze. He had a dark eye, a falcon gaze, roving and keen. His jaw was prominent and set, mastiff-like; his lips were stern. It was youth with its softness not yet quite burned and hardened away that kept the whole cast of his face from being ruthless.

This young man was Dick Gale, but not the listless traveler, nor the lounging wanderer who, two months before, had by chance dropped into Casita. Friendship, chivalry, love—the deep-seated, unplumbed emotions that had been stirred into being with all their incalculable power for spiritual change, had rendered different the meaning of life. In the moment almost of their realization the desert had claimed Gale, and had drawn him into its crucible. The desert had multiplied weeks into years. Heat, thirst, hunger, loneliness, toil, fear, ferocity, pain—he knew them all. He had felt them all—the white sun, with its glazed, coalescing, lurid fire; the caked split lips and rasping, dry-puffed tongue; the sickening ache in the pit of his stomach; the insupportable silence, the empty space, the utter desolation, the contempt of life; the weary ride, the long climb, the plod in sand, the search, search, search for water; the sleepless night alone, the watch and wait, the dread of ambush, the swift flight; the fierce pursuit of men wild as Bedouins and as fleet, the willingness to deal sudden death, the pain of poison thorn, the stinging tear of lead through flesh; and that strange paradox of the burning desert, the cold at night, the piercing icy wind, the dew that penetrated to the marrow, the numbing desert cold of the dawn.

Beyond any dream of adventure he had ever had, beyond any wild story he had ever read, had been his experience with those hard-riding rangers, Ladd and Lash. Then he had traveled alone the hundred miles of desert between Forlorn River and the Sonoyta Oasis. Ladd's prophecy of trouble on the border had been mild compared to what had become the actuality. With rebel occupancy of the garrison at Casita, outlaws, bandits, raiders in rioting bands had spread westward. Like troops of Arabs, magnificently mounted, they were here, there, everywhere along the line; and if murder and worse were confined to the Mexican side, pillage and raiding were perpetrated across the border. Many a dark-skinned raider bestrode one of Belding's fast horses, and indeed all except his selected white thoroughbreds had been stolen. So the job of the rangers had become more than a patrolling of the boundary line to keep Japanese and Chinese from being smuggled into the United States. Belding kept close at home to protect his family and to hold his property. But the three rangers, in fulfilling their duty had incurred risks on their own side of the line, had been outraged, robbed, pursued, and injured on the other. Some of the few waterholes that had to be reached lay far across the border in Mexican territory. Horses had to drink, men had to drink; and Ladd and Lash were not of the stripe that forsook a task because of danger. Slow to wrath at first, as became men who had long lived peaceful lives, they had at length revolted; and desert vultures could have told a gruesome story. Made a comrade and ally of these bordermen, Dick Gale had leaped at the desert action and strife with an intensity of heart and a rare physical ability which accounted for the remarkable fact that he had not yet fallen by the way.

On this December afternoon the three rangers, as often, were separated. Lash was far to the westward of Sonoyta, somewhere along Camino del Diablo, that terrible Devil's Road, where many desert wayfarers had perished. Ladd had long been overdue in a prearranged meeting with Gale. The fact that Ladd had not shown up miles west of the Papago Well was significant.

The sun had hidden behind clouds all the latter part of that day, an unusual occurrence for that region even in winter. And now, as the light waned suddenly, telling of the hidden sunset, a cold dry, penetrating wind sprang up and blew in Gale's face. Not at first, but by imperceptible degrees it chilled him. He untied his coat from the back of the saddle and put it on. A few cold drops of rain touched his cheek.

He halted upon the edge of a low escarpment. Below him the narrowing valley showed bare, black ribs of rock, long, winding gray lines leading down to a central floor where mesquite and cactus dotted the barren landscape. Moving objects, diminutive in size, gray and white in color, arrested Gale's roving sight. They bobbed away for a while, then stopped. They were antelope, and they had seen his horse. When he rode on they started once more, keeping to the lowest level. These wary animals were often desert watchdogs for the ranger, they would betray the proximity of horse or man. With them trotting forward, he made better time for some miles across the valley. When he lost them, caution once more slowed his advance.

The valley sloped up and narrowed, to head into an arroyo where grass began to show gray between the clumps of mesquite. Shadows formed ahead in the hollows, along the walls of the arroyo, under the trees, and they seemed to creep, to rise, to float into a veil cast by the background of bold mountains, at last to claim the skyline. Night was not close at hand, but it was there in the east, lifting upward, drooping downward, encroaching upon the west.

Gale dismounted to lead his horse, to go forward more slowly. He had ridden sixty miles since morning, and he was tired, and a not entirely healed wound in his hip made one leg drag a little. A mile up the arroyo, near its head, lay the Papago Well. The need of water for his horse entailed a risk that otherwise he could have avoided. The well was on Mexican soil. Gale distinguished a faint light flickering through the thin, sharp foliage. Campers were at the well, and, whoever they were, no doubt they had prevented Ladd from meeting Gale. Ladd had gone back to the next waterhole, or maybe he was hiding in an arroyo to the eastward, awaiting developments.

Gale turned his horse, not without urge of iron arm and persuasive speech, for the desert steed scented water, and plodded back to the edge of the arroyo, where in a secluded circle of mesquite he halted. The horse snorted his relief at the removal of the heavy, burdened saddle and accoutrements, and sagging, bent his knees, lowered himself with slow heave, and plunged down to roll in the sand. Gale poured the contents of his larger canteen into his hat and held it to the horse's nose.

"Drink, Sol," he said.

It was but a drop for a thirsty horse. However, Blanco Sol rubbed a wet muzzle against Gale's hand in appreciation. Gale loved the horse, and was loved in return. They had saved each other's lives, and had spent long days and nights of desert solitude together. Sol had known other masters, though none so kind as this new one; but it was certain that Gale had never before known a horse.

The spot of secluded ground was covered with bunches of galleta grass upon which Sol began to graze. Gale made a long halter of his lariat to keep the horse from wandering in search of water. Next Gale kicked off the cumbersome chapparejos, with their flapping, tripping folds of leather over his feet, and drawing a long rifle from its leather sheath, he slipped away into the shadows.

The coyotes were howling, not here and there, but in concerted volume at the head of the arroyo. To Dick this was no more reassuring than had been the flickering light of the campfire. The wild desert dogs, with their characteristic insolent curiosity, were baying men round a campfire. Gale proceeded slowly, halting every few steps, careful not to brush against the stiff greasewood. In the soft sand his steps made no sound. The twinkling light vanished occasionally, like a Jack-o'lantern, and when it did show it seemed still a long way off. Gale was not seeking trouble or inviting danger. Water was the thing that drove him. He must see who these campers were, and then decide how to give Blanco Sol a drink.

A rabbit rustled out of brush at Gale's feet and thumped away over the sand. The wind pattered among dry, broken stalks of dead ocatilla. Every little sound brought Gale to a listening pause. The gloom was thickening fast into darkness. It would be a night without starlight. He moved forward up the pale, zigzag aisles between the mesquite. He lost the light for a while, but the coyotes' chorus told him he was approaching the campfire. Presently the light danced through the black branches, and soon grew into a flame. Stooping low, with bushy mesquites between him and the fire, Gale advanced. The coyotes were in full cry. Gale heard the tramping, stamping thumps of many hoofs. The sound worried him. Foot by foot he advanced, and finally began to crawl. The wind favored his position, so that neither coyotes nor horses could scent him. The nearer he approached the head of the arroyo, where the well was located, the thicker grew the desert vegetation. At length a dead palo verde, with huge black clumps of its parasite mistletoe thick in the branches, marked a distance from the well that Gale considered close enough. Noiselessly he crawled here and there until he secured a favorable position, and then rose to peep from behind his covert.

He saw a bright fire, not a cooking-fire, for that would have been low and red, but a crackling blaze of mesquite. Three men were in sight, all close to the burning sticks. They were Mexicans and of the coarse type of raiders, rebels, bandits that Gale expected to see. One stood up, his back to the fire; another sat with shoulders enveloped in a blanket, and the third lounged in the sand, his feet almost in the blaze. They had cast off belts and weapons. A glint of steel caught Gale's eye. Three short, shiny carbines leaned against a rock. A little to the left, within the circle of light, stood a square house made of adobe bricks. Several untrimmed poles upheld a roof of brush, which was partly fallen in. This house was a Papago Indian habitation, and a month before had been occupied by a family that had been murdered or driven off by a roving band of outlaws. A rude corral showed dimly in the edge of firelight, and from a black mass within came the snort and stamp and whinney of horses.

Gale took in the scene in one quick glance, then sank down at the foot of the mesquite. He had naturally expected to see more men. But the situation was by no means new. This was one, or part of one, of the raider bands harrying the border. They were stealing horses, or driving a herd already stolen. These bands were more numerous than the waterholes of northern Sonora; they never camped long at one place; like Arabs, they roamed over the desert all the way from Nogales to Casita. If Gale had gone peaceably up to this campfire there were a hundred chances that the raiders would kill and rob him to one chance that they might not. If they recognized him as a ranger comrade of Ladd and Lash, if they got a glimpse of Blanco Sol, then Gale would have no chance.

These Mexicans had evidently been at the well some time. Their horses being in the corral meant that grazing had been done by day. Gale revolved questions in mind. Had this trio of outlaws run across Ladd? It was not likely, for in that event they might not have been so comfortable and care-free in camp. Were they waiting for more members of their gang? That was very probable. With Gale, however, the most important consideration was how to get his horse to water. Sol must have a drink if it cost a fight. There was stern reason for Gale to hurry eastward along the trail. He thought it best to go back to where he had left his horse and not make any decisive move until daylight.

With the same noiseless care he had exercised in the advance, Gale retreated until it was safe for him to rise and walk on down the arroyo. He found Blanco Sol contentedly grazing. A heavy dew was falling, and, as the grass was abundant, the horse did not show the usual restlessness and distress after a dry and exhausting day. Gale carried his saddle blankets and bags into the lee of a little greasewood-covered mound, from around which the wind had cut the soil, and here, in a wash, he risked building a small fire. By this time the wind was piercingly cold. Gale's hands were numb and he moved them to and fro in the little blaze. Then he made coffee in a cup, cooked some slices of bacon on the end of a stick, and took a couple of hard biscuits from a saddlebag. Of these his meal consisted. After that he removed the halter from Blanco Sol, intending to leave him free to graze for a while.

Then Gale returned to his little fire, replenished it with short sticks of dead greasewood and mesquite, and, wrapping his blanket round his shoulders he sat down to warm himself and to wait till it was time to bring in the horse and tie him up.

The fire was inadequate and Gale was cold and wet with dew. Hunger and thirst were with him. His bones ached, and there was a dull, deep-seated pain throbbing in his unhealed wound.

For days unshaven, his beard seemed like a million pricking needles in his blistered skin. He was so tired that once having settled himself, he did not move hand or foot. The night was dark, dismal, cloudy, windy, growing colder. A moan of wind in the mesquite was occasionally pierced by the high-keyed yelp of a coyote. There were lulls in which the silence seemed to be a thing of stifling, encroaching substance—a thing that enveloped, buried the desert.

Judged by the great average of ideals and conventional standards of life, Dick Gale was a starved, lonely, suffering, miserable wretch. But in his case the judgment would have hit only externals, would have missed the vital inner truth. For Gale was happy with a kind of strange, wild glory in the privations, the pains, the perils, and the silence and solitude to be endured on this desert land. In the past he had not been of any use to himself or others; and he had never know what it meant to be hungry, cold, tired, lonely. He had never worked for anything. The needs of the day had been provided, and to-morrow and the future looked the same. Danger, peril, toil—these had been words read in books and papers.

In the present he used his hands, his senses, and his wits. He had a duty to a man who relied on his services. He was a comrade, a friend, a valuable ally to riding, fighting rangers. He had spent endless days, weeks that seemed years, alone with a horse, trailing over, climbing over, hunting over a desert that was harsh and hostile by nature, and perilous by the invasion of savage men. That horse had become human to Gale. And with him Gale had learned to know the simple needs of existence. Like dead scales the superficialities, the falsities, the habits that had once meant all of life dropped off, useless things in this stern waste of rock and sand.

Gale's happiness, as far as it concerned the toil and strife, was perhaps a grim and stoical one. But love abided with him, and it had engendered and fostered other undeveloped traits— romance and a feeling for beauty, and a keen observation of nature. He felt pain, but he was never miserable. He felt the solitude, but he was never lonely.

As he rode across the desert, even though keen eyes searched for the moving black dots, the rising puffs of white dust that were warnings, he saw Nell's face in every cloud. The clean-cut mesas took on the shape of her straight profile, with its strong chin and lips, its fine nose and forehead. There was always a glint of gold or touch of red or graceful line or gleam of blue to remind him of her. Then at night her face shone warm and glowing, flushing and paling, in the campfire.

To-night, as usual, with a keen ear to the wind, Gale listened as one on guard; yet he watched the changing phantom of a sweet face in the embers, and as he watched he thought. The desert developed and multiplied thought. A thousand sweet faces glowed in the pink and white ashes of his campfire, the faces of other sweethearts or wives that had gleamed for other men. Gale was happy in his thought of Nell, for Nell, for something, when he was alone this way in the wilderness, told him she was near him, she thought of him, she loved him. But there were many men alone on that vast southwestern plateau, and when they saw dream faces, surely for some it was a fleeting flash, a gleam soon gone, like the hope and the name and the happiness that had been and was now no more. Often Gale thought of those hundreds of desert travelers, prospectors, wanderers who had ventured down the Camino del Diablo, never to be heard of again. Belding had told him of that most terrible of all desert trails—a trail of shifting sands. Lash had traversed it, and brought back stories of buried waterholes, of bones bleaching white in the sun, of gold mines as lost as were the prospectors who had sought them, of the merciless

Yaqui and his hatred for the Mexican. Gale thought of this trail and the men who had camped along it. For many there had been one night, one campfire that had been the last. This idea seemed to creep in out of the darkness, the loneliness, the silence, and to find a place in Gale's mind, so that it had strange fascination for him. He knew now as he had never dreamed before how men drifted into the desert, leaving behind graves, wrecked homes, ruined lives, lost wives and sweethearts. And for every wanderer every campfire had a phantom face. Gale measured the agony of these men at their last campfire by the joy and promise he traced in the ruddy heart of his own.

By and by Gale remembered what he was waiting for; and, getting up, he took the halter and went out to find Blanco Sol. It was pitch-dark now, and Gale could not see a rod ahead. He felt his way, and presently as he rounded a mesquite he saw Sol's white shape outlined against the blackness. The horse jumped and wheeled, ready to run. It was doubtful if any one unknown to Sol could ever have caught him. Gale's low call reassured him, and he went on grazing. Gale haltered him in the likeliest patch of grass and returned to his camp. There he lifted his saddle into a protected spot under a low wall of the mound, and, laying one blanket on the sand, he covered himself with the other and stretched himself for the night.

Here he was out of reach of the wind; but he heard its melancholy moan in the mesquite. There was no other sound. The coyotes had ceased their hungry cries. Gale dropped to sleep, and slept soundly during the first half of the night; and after that he seemed always to be partially awake, aware of increasing cold and damp. The dark mantle turned gray, and then daylight came quickly. The morning was clear and nipping cold. He threw off the wet blanket and got up cramped and half frozen. A little brisk action was all that was necessary to warm his blood and loosen his muscles, and then he was fresh, tingling, eager. The sun rose in a golden blaze, and the descending valley took on wondrous changing hues. Then he fetched up Blanco Sol, saddled him, and tied him to the thickest clump of mesquite.

"Sol, we'll have a drink pretty soon," he said, patting the splendid neck.

Gale meant it. He would not eat till he had watered his horse. Sol had gone nearly forty-eight hours without a sufficient drink, and that was long enough, even for a desert-bred beast. No three raiders could keep Gale away from that well. Taking his rifle in hand, he faced up the arroyo. Rabbits were frisking in the short willows, and some were so tame he could have kicked them. Gale walked swiftly for a goodly part of the distance, and then, when he saw blue smoke curling up above the trees, he proceeded slowly, with alert eye and ear. From the lay of the land and position of trees seen by daylight, he found an easier and safer course that the one he had taken in the dark. And by careful work he was enabled to get closer to the well, and somewhat above it.

The Mexicans were leisurely cooking their morning meal. They had two fires, one for warmth, the other to cook over. Gale had an idea these raiders were familiar to him. It seemed all these border hawks resembled one another—being mostly small of build, wiry, angular, swarthy-faced, and black-haired, and they wore the oddly styled Mexican clothes and sombreros. A slow wrath stirred in Gale as he watched the trio. They showed not the slightest indication of breaking camp. One fellow, evidently the leader, packed a gun at his hip, the only weapon in sight. Gale noted this with speculative eyes. The raiders had slept inside the little adobe house, and had not yet brought out the carbines. Next Gale swept his gaze to the corral, in which he saw more than a dozen horses, some of them fine animals. They were stamping and whistling, fighting one another, and pawing the dirt. This was entirely natural behavior for desert horses penned in when they wanted to get at water and grass.

But suddenly one of the blacks, a big, shaggy fellow, shot up his ears and pointed his nose over the top of the fence. He whistled. Other horses looked in the same direction, and their ears went up, and they, too, whistled. Gale knew that other horses or men, very likely both, were approaching. But the Mexicans did not hear the alarm, or show any interest if they did. These mescal-drinking raiders were not scouts. It was notorious how easily they could be surprised or ambushed. Mostly they were ignorant, thick-skulled peons. They were wonderful horsemen, and could go long without food or water; but they had not other accomplishments or attributes calculated to help them in desert warfare. They had poor sight, poor hearing, poor judgment, and when excited they resembled crazed ants running wild.

Gale saw two Indians on burros come riding up the other side of the knoll upon which the adobe house stood; and apparently they were not aware of the presence of the Mexicans, for they came on up the path. One Indian was a Papago. The other, striking in appearance for other reasons than that he seemed to be about to fall from the burro, Gale took to be a Yaqui. These travelers had absolutely nothing for an outfit except a blanket and a half-empty bag. They came over the knoll and down the path toward the well, turned a corner of the house, and completely surprised the raiders.

Gale heard a short, shrill cry, strangely high and wild, and this came from one of the Indians. It was answered by hoarse shouts. Then the leader of the trio, the Mexican who packed a gun, pulled it and fired point-blank. He missed once—and again. At the third shot the Papago shrieked and tumbled off his burro to fall in a heap. The other Indian swayed, as if the taking away of the support lent by his comrade had brought collapse, and with the fourth shot he, too, slipped to the ground.

The reports had frightened the horses in the corral; and the vicious black, crowding the rickety bars, broke them down. He came plunging out. Two of the Mexicans ran for him, catching him by nose and mane, and the third ran to block the gateway.

Then, with a splendid vaulting mount, the Mexican with the gun leaped to the back of the horse. He yelled and waved his gun, and urged the black forward. The manner of all three was savagely jocose. They were having sport. The two on the ground began to dance and jabber. The mounted leader shot again, and then stuck like a leech upon the bare back of the rearing black. It was a vain show of horsemanship. Then this Mexican, by some strange grip, brought the horse down, plunging almost upon the body of the Indian that had fallen last.

Gale stood aghast with his rifle clutched tight. He could not divine the intention of the raider, but suspected something brutal. The horse answered to that cruel, guiding hand, yet he swerved and bucked. He reared aloft, pawing the air, wildly snorting, then he plunged down upon the prostrate Indian. Even in the act the intelligent animal tried to keep from striking the body with his hoofs. But that was not possible. A yell, hideous in its passion, signaled this feat of horsemanship.

The Mexican made no move to trample the body of the Papago. He turned the black to ride again over the other Indian. That brought into Gale's mind what he had heard of a Mexican's hate for a Yaqui. It recalled the barbarism of these savage peons, and the war of extermination being waged upon the Yaquis.

Suddenly Gale was horrified to see the Yaqui writhe and raise a feeble hand. The action brought renewed and more savage cries from the Mexicans. The horse snorted in terror.

Gale could bear no more. He took a quick shot at the rider. He missed the moving figure, but hit the horse. There was a bound, a horrid scream, a mighty plunge, then the horse went down, giving the Mexican a stunning fall. Both beast and man lay still.

Gale rushed from his cover to intercept the other raiders before they could reach the house and their weapons. One fellow yelled and ran wildly in the opposite direction; the other stood stricken in his tracks. Gale ran in close and picked up the gun that had dropped from the raider leader's hand. This fellow had begun to stir, to come out of his stunned condition. Then the frightened horses burst the corral bars, and in a thundering, dust-mantled stream fled up the arroyo.

The fallen raider sat up, mumbling to his saints in one breath, cursing in his next. The other Mexican kept his stand, intimidated by the threatening rifle.

"Go, Greasers! Run!" yelled Gale. Then he yelled it in Spanish. At the point of his rifle he drove the two raiders out of the camp. His next move was to run into the house and fetch out the carbines. With a heavy stone he dismantled each weapon. That done, he set out on a run for his horse. He took the shortest cut down the arroyo, with no concern as to whether or not he would encounter the raiders. Probably such a meeting would be all the worse for them, and they knew it. Blanco Sol heard him coming and whistled a welcome, and when Gale ran up the horse was snorting war. Mounting, Gale rode rapidly back to the scene of the action, and his first thought, when he arrived at the well, was to give Sol a drink and to fill his canteens.

Then Gale led his horse up out of the waterhole, and decided before remounting to have a look at the Indians. The Papago had been shot through the heart, but the Yaqui was still alive. Moreover, he was conscious and staring up at Gale with great, strange, somber eyes, black as volcanic slag.

"Gringo good—no kill," he said, in husky whisper.

His speech was not affirmative so much as questioning.

"Yaqui, you're done for," said Gale, and his words were positive. He was simply speaking aloud his mind.

"Yaqui—no hurt—much," replied the Indian, and then he spoke a strange word—repeated it again and again.

An instinct of Gale's, or perhaps some suggestion in the husky, thick whisper or dark face, told Gale to reach for his canteen. He lifted the Indian and gave him a drink, and if ever in all his life he saw gratitude in human eyes he saw it then. Then he examined the injured Yaqui, not forgetting for an instant to send wary, fugitive glances on all sides. Gale was not surprised. The Indian had three wounds—a bullet hole in his shoulder, a crushed arm, and a badly lacerated leg. What had been the matter with him before being set upon by the raider Gale could not be certain.

The ranger thought rapidly. This Yaqui would live unless left there to die or be murdered by the Mexicans when they found courage to sneak back to the well. It never occurred to Gale to abandon the poor fellow. That was where his old training, the higher order of human feeling, made impossible the following of any elemental instinct of self-preservation. All the same, Gale knew he multiplied his perils a hundredfold by burdening himself with a crippled Indian. Swiftly he set to work, and with rifle ever under his hand, and shifting glance spared from his task, he bound up the Yaqui's wounds. At the same time he kept keen watch.

The Indians' burros and the horses of the raiders were all out of sight. Time was too valuable for Gale to use any in what might be a vain search. Therefore, he lifted the Yaqui upon Sol's broad shoulders and climbed into the saddle. At a word Sol dropped his head and started eastward up the trail, walking swiftly, without resentment for his double burden.

Far ahead, between two huge mesas where the trail mounted over a pass, a long line of dust clouds marked the position of the horses that had escaped from the corral. Those that had been stolen would travel straight and true for home, and perhaps would lead the others with them. The raiders were left on the desert without guns or mounts.

Blanco Sol walked or jog-trotted six miles to the hour. At that gait fifty miles would not have wet or turned a hair of his dazzling white coat. Gale, bearing in mind the ever-present possibility of encountering more raiders and of being pursued, saved the strength of the horse. Once out of sight of Papago Well, Gale dismounted and walked beside the horse, steadying with one firm hand the helpless, dangling Yaqui.

The sun cleared the eastern ramparts, and the coolness of morning fled as if before a magic foe. The whole desert changed. The grays wore bright; the mesquites glistened; the cactus took the silver hue of frost, and the rocks gleamed gold and red. Then, as the heat increased, a wind rushed up out of the valley behind Gale, and the hotter the sun blazed down the swifter rushed the wind. The wonderful transparent haze of distance lost its bluish hue for one with tinge of yellow. Flying sand made the peaks dimly outlined.

Gale kept pace with his horse. He bore the twinge of pain that darted through his injured hip at every stride. His eye roved over the wide, smoky prospect seeking the landmarks he knew. When the wild and bold spurs of No Name Mountains loomed through a rent in flying clouds of sand he felt nearer home. Another hour brought him abreast of a dark, straight shaft rising clear from a beetling escarpment. This was a monument marking the international boundary line. When he had passed it he had his own country under foot. In the heat of midday he halted in the shade of a rock, and, lifting the Yaqui down, gave him a drink. Then, after a long, sweeping survey of the surrounding desert, he removed Sol's saddle and let him roll, and took for himself a welcome rest and a bite to eat.

The Yaqui was tenacious of life. He was still holding his own. For the first time Gale really looked at the Indian to study him. He had a large head nobly cast, and a face that resembled a shrunken mask. It seemed chiseled in the dark-red, volcanic lava of his Sooner wilderness. The Indian's eyes were always black and mystic, but this Yaqui's encompassed all the tragic desolation of the desert. They were fixed on Gale, moved only when he moved. The Indian was short and broad, and his body showed unusual muscular development, although he seemed greatly emaciated from starvation or illness.

Gale resumed his homeward journey. When he got through the pass he faced a great depression, as rough as if millions of gigantic spikes had been driven by the hammer of Thor into a seamed and cracked floor. This was Altar Valley. It was a chaos of arroyo's, canyons, rocks, and ridges all mantled with cactus, and at its eastern end it claimed the dry bed of Forlorn River and water when there was any.

With a wounded, helpless man across the saddle, this stretch of thorny and contorted desert was practically impassable. Yet Gale headed into it unflinchingly. He would carry the Yaqui as far as possible, or until death make the burden no longer a duty. Blanco Sol plodded on over the dragging sand, up and down the steep, loose banks of washes, out on the rocks, and through the rows of white-toothed *choyas*.

The sun sloped westward, bending fiercer heat in vengeful, parting reluctance. The wind slackened. The dust settled. And the bold, forbidding front of No Name Mountains changed to red and gold. Gale held grimly by the side of the tireless, implacable horse, holding the Yaqui on the saddle, taking the brunt of the merciless thorns. In the end it became heartrending toil. His heavy chaps dragged him down; but he dared not go on without them, for, thick and stiff as they were, the terrible, steel-bayoneted spikes of the *choyas* pierced through to sting his legs.

To the last mile Gale held to Blanco Sol's gait and kept ever-watchful gaze ahead on the trail. Then, with the low, flat houses of Forlorn River shining red in the sunset, Gale flagged and rapidly weakened. The Yaqui slipped out of the saddle and dropped limp in the sand. Gale could not mount his horse. He clutched Sol's long tail and twisted his hand in it and staggered on.

Blanco Sol whistled a piercing blast. He scented cool water and sweet alfalfa hay. Twinkling lights ahead meant rest. The melancholy desert twilight rapidly succeeded the sunset. It accentuated the forlorn loneliness of the gray, winding river of sand and its grayer shores. Night shadows trooped down from the black and looming mountains.

VII

WHITE HORSES

"A CRIPPLED Yaqui! Why the hell did you saddle yourself with him?" roared Belding, as he laid Gale upon the bed.

Belding had grown hard these late, violent weeks.

"Because I chose," whispered Gale, in reply. "Go after him—he dropped in the trail—across the river—near the first big saguaro."

Belding began to swear as he fumbled with matches and the lamp; but as the light flared up he stopped short in the middle of a word.

"You said you weren't hurt?" he demanded, in sharp anxiety, as he bent over Gale.

"I'm only—all in.... Will you go—or send some one—for the Yaqui?"

"Sure, Dick, sure," Belding replied, in softer tones. Then he stalked out; his heels rang on the flagstones; he opened a door and called: "Mother—girls, here's Dick back. He's done up.... Now—no, no, he's not hurt or in bad shape. You women!... Do what you can to make him comfortable. I've got a little job on hand."

There were quick replies that Gale's dulling ears did not distinguish. Then it seemed Mrs. Belding was beside his bed, her presence so cool and soothing and helpful, and Mercedes and Nell, wide-eyed and white-faced, were fluttering around him. He drank thirstily, but refused food. He wanted rest. And with their faces drifting away in a kind of haze, with the feeling of gentle hands about him, he lost consciousness.

He slept twenty hours. Then he arose, thirsty, hungry, lame, overworn, and presently went in search of Belding and the business of the day.

"Your Yaqui was near dead, but guess we'll pull him through," said Belding. "Dick, the other day that Indian came here by rail and foot and Lord only knows how else, all the way from New Orleans! He spoke English better than most Indians, and I know a little Yaqui. I got some of his story and guessed the rest. The Mexican government is trying to root out the Yaquis. A year ago his tribe was taken in chains to a Mexican port on the Gulf. The fathers, mothers, children, were separated and put in ships bound for Yucatan. There they were made slaves on the great henequen plantations. They were driven, beaten, starved. Each slave had for a day's rations a hunk of sour dough, no more. Yucatan is low, marshy, damp, hot. The Yaquis were bred on the high, dry Sonoran plateau, where the air is like a knife. They dropped dead in the henequen fields, and their places were taken by more. You see, the Mexicans won't kill outright in their war of extermination of the Yaquis. They get use out of them. It's a horrible thing.... Well, this Yaqui you brought in escaped from his captors, got aboard ship, and eventually reached New Orleans. Somehow he traveled way out here. I gave him a bag of food, and he went off with a Papago Indian. He was a sick man then. And he must have fallen foul of some Greasers."

Gale told of his experience at Papago Well.

"That raider who tried to grind the Yaqui under a horse's hoofs—he was a hyena!" concluded Gale, shuddering. "I've seen some blood spilled and some hard sights, but that inhuman devil took my nerve. Why, as I told you, Belding, I missed a shot at him—not twenty paces!"

"Dick, in cases like that the sooner you clean up the bunch the better," said Belding, grimly. "As for hard sights—wait till you've seen a Yaqui do up a Mexican. Bar none, that is the limit! It's blood lust, a racial hate, deep as life, and terrible. The Spaniards crushed the Aztecs four or five hundred years ago. That hate has had time to grow as deep as a cactus root. The Yaquis are mountain Aztecs. Personally, I think they are noble and intelligent, and if let alone would be peaceable and industrious. I like the few I've known. But they are a doomed race. Have you any idea what ailed this Yaqui before the raider got in his work?"

"No, I haven't. I noticed the Indian seemed in bad shape; but I couldn't tell what was the matter with him."

"Well, my idea is another personal one. Maybe it's off color. I think that Yaqui was, or is, for that matter, dying of a broken heart. All he wanted was to get back to his mountains and die. There are no Yaquis left in that part of Sonora he was bound for."

"He had a strange look in his eyes," said Gale, thoughtfully.

"Yes, I noticed that. But all Yaquis have a wild look. Dick, if I'm not mistaken, this fellow was a chief. It was a waste of strength, a needless risk for you to save him, pack him back here. But, damn the whole Greaser outfit generally, I'm glad you did!"

Gale remembered then to speak of his concern for Ladd.

"Laddy didn't go out to meet you," replied Belding. "I knew you were due in any day, and, as there's been trouble between here and Casita, I sent him that way. Since you've been out our friend Carter lost a bunch of horses and a few steers. Did you get a good look at the horses those raiders had at Papago Well?"

Dick had learned, since he had become a ranger, to see everything with keen, sure, photographic eye; and, being put to the test so often required of him, he described the horses as a dark-colored drove, mostly bays and blacks, with one spotted sorrel.

"Some of Carter's—sure as you're born!" exclaimed Belding. "His bunch has been split up, divided among several bands of raiders. He has a grass ranch up here in Three Mile Arroyo. It's a good long ride in U. S. territory from the border."

"Those horses I saw will go home, don't you think?" asked Dick.

"Sure. They can't be caught or stopped."

"Well, what shall I do now?"

"Stay here and rest," bluntly replied Belding. "You need it. Let the women fuss over you—doctor you a little. When Jim gets back from Sonoyta I'll know more about what we ought to do. By Lord! it seems our job now isn't keeping Japs and Chinks out of the U. S. It's keeping our property from going into Mexico."

"Are there any letters for me?" asked Gale.

"Letters! Say, my boy, it'd take something pretty important to get me or any man here back Casita way. If the town is safe these days the road isn't. It's a month now since any one went to Casita."

Gale had received several letters from his sister Elsie, the last of which he had not answered. There had not been much opportunity for writing on his infrequent returns to Forlorn River; and, besides, Elsie had written that her father had stormed over what he considered Dick's falling into wild and evil ways.

"Time flies," said Dick. "George Thorne will be free before long, and he'll be coming out. I wonder if he'll stay here or try to take Mercedes away?"

"Well, he'll stay right here in Forlorn River, if I have any say," replied Belding. "I'd like to know how he'd ever get that Spanish girl out of the country now, with all the trails overrun by rebels and raiders. It'd be hard to disguise her. Say, Dick, maybe we can get Thorne to stay here. You know, since you've discovered the possibility of a big water supply, I've had dreams of a future for Forlorn River.... If only this war was over! Dick, that's what it is—war—scattered war along the northern border of Mexico from gulf to gulf. What if it isn't our war? We're on the fringe. No, we can't develop Forlorn River until there's peace."

The discovery that Belding alluded to was one that might very well lead to the making of a wonderful and agricultural district of Altar Valley. While in college Dick Gale had studied engineering, but he had not set the scientific world afire with his brilliance. Nor after leaving college had he been able to satisfy his father that he could hold a job. Nevertheless, his smattering of engineering skill bore fruit in the last place on earth where anything might have been expected of it—in the desert. Gale had always wondered about the source of Forlorn River. No white man or Mexican, or, so far as known, no Indian, had climbed those mighty broken steps of rock called No Name Mountains, from which Forlorn River was supposed to come. Gale had discovered a long, narrow, rock-bottomed and rock-walled gulch that could be dammed at the lower end by the dynamiting of leaning cliffs above. An inexhaustible supply of water could be stored there. Furthermore, he had worked out an irrigation plan to bring the water down for mining uses, and to make a paradise out of that part of Altar Valley which lay in the United States. Belding claimed there was gold in the arroyos, gold in the gulches, not in quantities to make a prospector rejoice, but enough to work for. And the soil on the higher levels of Altar Valley needed only water to make it grow anything the year round. Gale, too, had come to have dreams of a future for Forlorn River.

On the afternoon of the following day Ladd unexpectedly appeared leading a lame and lathered horse into the yard. Belding and Gale, who were at work at the forge, looked up and were surprised out of speech. The legs of the horse were raw and red, and he seemed about to drop. Ladd's sombrero was missing; he wore a bloody scarf round his head; sweat and blood and dust had formed a crust on his face; little streams of powdery dust slid from him; and the lower half of his scarred chaps were full of broken white thorns.

"Howdy, boys," he drawled. "I shore am glad to see you all."

"Where'n hell's your hat?" demanded Belding, furiously. It was a ridiculous greeting. But Belding's words signified little. The dark shade of worry and solicitude crossing his face told more than his black amaze.

The ranger stopped unbuckling the saddle girths, and, looking at Belding, broke into his slow, cool laugh.

"Tom, you recollect that whopper of a saguaro up here where Carter's trail branches off the main trail to Casita? Well, I climbed it an' left my hat on top for a woodpecker's nest."

"You've been running—fighting?" queried Belding, as if Ladd had not spoken at all.

"I reckon it'll dawn on you after a while," replied Ladd, slipping the saddle.

"Laddy, go in the house to the women," said Belding. "I'll tend to your horse."

"Shore, Tom, in a minute. I've been down the road. An' I found hoss tracks an' steer tracks goin' across the line. But I seen no sign of raiders till this mornin'. Slept at Carter's last night. That raid the other day cleaned him out. He's shootin' mad. Well, this mornin' I rode plumb into a bunch of Carter's hosses, runnin' wild for home. Some Greasers were tryin' to head them round an' chase them back across the line. I rode in between an' made matters embarrassin'. Carter's hosses got away. Then me an' the Greasers had a little game of hide an' seek in the cactus. I was on the wrong side, an' had to break through their line to head toward home. We run some. But I had a closer call than I'm stuck on havin'."

"Laddy, you wouldn't have any such close calls if you'd ride one of my horses," expostulated Belding. "This broncho of yours can run, and Lord knows he's game. But you want a big, strong horse, Mexican bred, with cactus in his blood. Take one of the bunch—Bull, White Woman, Blanco Jose."

"I had a big, fast horse a while back, but I lost him," said Ladd. "This bronch ain't so bad. Shore Bull an' that white devil with his Greaser name—they could run down my bronch, kill him in a mile of cactus. But, somehow, Tom, I can't make up my mind to take one of them grand white hosses. Shore I reckon I'm kinda soft. An' mebbe I'd better take one before the raiders clean up Forlorn River."

Belding cursed low and deep in his throat, and the sound resembled muttering thunder. The shade of anxiety on his face changed to one of dark gloom and passion. Next to his wife and daughter there was nothing so dear to him as those white horses. His father and grandfather—all his progenitors of whom he had trace—had been lovers of horses. It was in Belding's blood.

"Laddy, before it's too late can't I get the whites away from the border?"

"Mebbe it ain't too late; but where can we take them?"

"To San Felipe?"

"No. We've more chance to hold them here."

"To Casita and the railroad?"

"Afraid to risk gettin' there. An' the town's full of rebels who need hosses."

"Then straight north?"

"Shore man, you're crazy. Ther's no water, no grass for a hundred miles. I'll tell you, Tom, the safest plan would be to take the white bunch south into Sonora, into some wild mountain valley. Keep them there till the raiders have traveled on back east. Pretty soon there won't be any rich pickin' left for these Greasers. An' then they'll ride on to new ranges."

"Laddy, I don't know the trails into Sonora. An' I can't trust a Mexican or a Papago. Between you and me, I'm afraid of this Indian who herds for me."

"I reckon we'd better stick here, Tom.... Dick, it's some good to see you again. But you seem kinda quiet. Shore you get quieter all the time. Did you see any sign of Jim out Sonoyta way?"

Then Belding led the lame horse toward the watering-trough, while the two rangers went toward the house, Dick was telling Ladd about the affair at Papago Well when they turned the corner under the porch. Nell was sitting in the door. She rose with a little scream and came flying toward them.

"Now I'll get it," whispered Ladd. "The women'll make a baby of me. An' shore I can't help myself."

"Oh, Laddy, you've been hurt!" cried Nell, as with white cheeks and dilating eyes she ran to him and caught his arm.

"Nell, I only run a thorn in my ear."

"Oh, Laddy, don't lie! You've lied before. I know you're hurt. Come in to mother."

"Shore, Nell, it's only a scratch. My bronch throwed me."

"Laddy, no horse every threw you." The girl's words and accusing eyes only hurried the ranger on to further duplicity.

"Mebbe I got it when I was ridin' hard under a mesquite, an' a sharp snag—"

"You've been shot!... Mama, here's Laddy, and he's been shot!.... Oh, these dreadful days we're having! I can't bear them! Forlorn River used to be so safe and quiet. Nothing happened. But now! Jim comes home with a bloody hole in him—then Dick—then Laddy!.... Oh, I'm afraid some day they'll never come home."

The morning was bright, still, and clear as crystal. The heat waves had not yet begun to rise from the desert.

A soft gray, white, and green tint perfectly blended lay like a mantle over mesquite and sand and cactus. The canyons of distant mountain showed deep and full of lilac haze.

Nell sat perched high upon the topmost bar of the corral gate. Dick leaned beside her, now with his eyes on her face, now gazing out into the alfalfa field where Belding's thoroughbreds grazed and pranced and romped and whistled. Nell watched the horses. She loved them, never tired of watching them. But her gaze was too consciously averted from the yearning eyes that tried to meet hers to be altogether natural.

A great fenced field of dark velvety green alfalfa furnished a rich background for the drove of about twenty white horses. Even without the horses the field would have presented a striking contrast to the surrounding hot, glaring blaze of rock and sand. Belding had bred a hundred or more horses from the original stock he had brought up from Durango. His particular interest was in the almost unblemished whites, and these he had given especial care. He made a good deal of money selling this strain to friends among the ranchers back in Texas. No mercenary consideration, however, could have made him part with the great, rangy white horses he had gotten from the Durango breeder. He called them Blanco Diablo (White Devil), Blanco Sol (White Sun), Blanca Reina (White Queen), Blanca Mujer (White Woman), and El Gran Toro Blanco (The Big White Bull). Belding had been laughed at by ranchers for preserving the sentimental Durango names, and he had been unmercifully ridiculed by cowboys. But the names had never been changed.

Blanco Diablo was the only horse in the field that was not free to roam and graze where he listed. A stake and a halter held him to one corner, where he was severely let alone by the other horses. He did not like this isolation. Blanco Diablo was not happy unless he was running, or fighting a rival. Of the two he would rather fight. If anything white could resemble a devil, this horse surely did. He had nothing beautiful about him, yet he drew the gaze and held it. The look of him suggested discontent, anger, revolt, viciousness. When he was not grazing or prancing, he held his long, lean head level, pointing his nose and showing his teeth. Belding's favorite was almost all the world to him, and he swore Diablo could stand more heat and thirst and cactus than any other horse he owned, and could run down and kill any horse in the Southwest. The fact that Ladd did not agree with Belding on these salient points was a great disappointment, and also a perpetual source for argument. Ladd and Lash both hated Diablo; and Dick Gale, after one or two narrow escapes from being brained, had inclined to the cowboys' side of the question.

El Gran Toro Blanco upheld his name. He was a huge, massive, thick-flanked stallion, a kingly mate for his full-bodied, glossy consort, Blanca Reina. The other mare, Blanca Mujer, was dazzling white, without a spot, perfectly pointed, racy, graceful, elegant, yet carrying weight and brawn and range that suggested her relation to her forebears.

The cowboys admitted some of Belding's claims for Diablo, but they gave loyal and unshakable allegiance to Blanco Sol. As for Dick, he had to fight himself to keep out of arguments, for he sometimes imagined he was unreasonable about the horse. Though he could not understand himself, he knew he loved Sol as a man loved a friend, a brother. Free of heavy saddle and the clumsy leg shields, Blanco Sol was somehow all-satisfying to the eyes of the rangers. As long and big as Diablo was, Sol was longer and bigger. Also, he was higher, more powerful. He looked more a thing for action—speedier. At a distance the honorable scars and lumps that marred his muscular legs were not visible. He grazed aloof from the others, and did not cavort nor prance; but when he lifted his head to whistle, how wild he appeared, and proud and splendid! The dazzling whiteness of the desert sun shone from his coat; he had the fire and spirit of the desert in his noble head, its strength and power in his gigantic frame.

"Belding swears Sol never beat Diablo," Dick was saying.

"He believes it," replied Nell. "Dad is queer about that horse."

"But Laddy rode Sol once—made him beat Diablo. Jim saw the race."

Nell laughed. "I saw it, too. For that matter, even I have made Sol put his nose before Dad's favorite."

"I'd like to have seen that. Nell, aren't you ever going to ride with me?"

"Some day—when it's safe."

"Safe!"

"I—I mean when the raiders have left the border."

"Oh, I'm glad you mean that," said Dick, laughing. "Well, I've often wondered how Belding ever came to give Blanco Sol to me."

"He was jealous. I think he wanted to get rid of Sol."

"No? Why, Nell, he'd give Laddy or Jim one of the whites any day."

"Would he? Not Devil or Queen or White Woman. Never in this world! But Dad has lots of fast horses the boys could pick from. Dick, I tell you Dad wants Blanco Sol to run himself out—lose his speed on the desert. Dad is just jealous for Diablo."

"Maybe. He surely has strange passion for horses. I think I understand better than I used to. I owned a couple of racers once. They were just animals to me, I guess. But Blanco Sol!"

"Do you love him?" asked Nell; and now a warm, blue flash of eyes swept his face.

"Do I? Well, rather."

"I'm glad. Sol has been finer, a better horse since you owned him. He loves you, Dick. He's always watching for you. See him raise his head. That's for you. I know as much about horses as Dad or Laddy any day. Sol always hated Diablo, and he never had much use for Dad."

Dick looked up at her.

"It'll be—be pretty hard to leave Sol—when I go away."

Nell sat perfectly still.

"Go away?" she asked, presently, with just the faintest tremor in her voice.

"Yes. Sometimes when I get blue—as I am to-day—I think I'll go. But, in sober truth, Nell, it's not likely that I'll spend all my life here."

There was no answer to this. Dick put his hand softly over hers; and, despite her half-hearted struggle to free it, he held on.

"Nell!"

Her color fled. He saw her lips part. Then a heavy step on the gravel, a cheerful, complaining voice interrupted him, and made him release Nell and draw back. Belding strode into view round the adobe shed.

"Hey, Dick, that darned Yaqui Indian can't be driven or hired or coaxed to leave Forlorn River. He's well enough to travel. I offered him horse, gun, blanket, grub. But no go."

"That's funny," replied Gale, with a smile. "Let him stay—put him to work."

"It doesn't strike me funny. But I'll tell you what I think. That poor, homeless, heartbroken Indian has taken a liking to you, Dick. These desert Yaquis are strange folk. I've heard strange stories about them. I'd believe 'most anything. And that's how I figure his case. You saved his life. That sort of thing counts big with any Indian, even with an Apache. With a Yaqui maybe it's of deep significance. I've heard a Yaqui say that with his tribe no debt to friend or foe ever went unpaid. Perhaps that's what ails this fellow."

"Dick, don't laugh," said Nell. "I've noticed the Yaqui. It's pathetic the way his great gloomy eyes follow you."

"You've made a friend," continued Belding. "A Yaqui could be a real friend on this desert. If he gets his strength back he'll be of service to you, don't mistake me. He's welcome here. But you're responsible for him, and you'll have trouble keeping him from massacring all the Greasers in Forlorn River."

The probability of a visit from the raiders, and a dash bolder than usual on the outskirts of a ranch, led Belding to build a new corral. It was not sightly to the eye, but it was high and exceedingly strong. The gate was a massive affair, swinging on huge hinges and fastening with heavy chains and padlocks. On the outside it had been completely covered with barb wire, which would make it a troublesome thing to work on in the dark.

At night Belding locked his white horses in this corral. The Papago herdsman slept in the adobe shed adjoining. Belding did not imagine that any wooden fence, however substantially built, could keep determined raiders from breaking it down. They would have to take time, however, and make considerable noise; and Belding relied on these facts. Belding did not believe a band of night raiders would hold out against a hot rifle fire. So he began to make up some of the sleep he had lost. It was noteworthy, however, that Ladd did not share Belding's sanguine hopes.

Jim Lash rode in, reporting that all was well out along the line toward the Sonoyta Oasis. Days passed, and Belding kept his rangers home. Nothing was heard of raiders at hand. Many of the newcomers, both American and Mexican, who came with wagons and pack trains from Casita stated that property and life were cheap back in that rebel-infested town.

One January morning Dick Gale was awakened by a shrill, menacing cry. He leaped up bewildered and frightened. He heard Belding's booming voice answering shouts, and rapid steps on flagstones. But these had not awakened him. Heavy breaths, almost sobs, seemed at his very door. In the cold and gray dawn Dick saw something white. Gun in hand, he bounded across the room. Just outside his door stood Blanco Sol.

It was not unusual for Sol to come poking his head in at Dick's door during daylight. But now in the early dawn, when he had been locked in the corral, it meant raiders—no less. Dick called softly to the snorting horse; and, hurriedly getting into clothes and boots, he went out with a gun in each hand. Sol was quivering in every muscle. Like a dog he followed Dick around the house. Hearing shouts in the direction of the corrals, Gale bent swift steps that way.

He caught up with Jim Lash, who was also leading a white horse.

"Hello, Jim! Guess it's all over but the fireworks," said Dick.

"I cain't say just what has come off," replied Lash. "I've got the Bull. Found him runnin' in the yard."

They reached the corral to find Belding shaking, roaring like a madman. The gate was open, the corral was empty. Ladd stooped over the ground, evidently trying to find tracks.

"I reckon we might jest as well cool off an' wait for daylight," suggested Jim.

"Shore. They've flown the coop, you can gamble on that. Tom, where's the Papago?" said Ladd.

"He's gone, Laddy—gone!"

"Double-crossed us, eh? I see here's a crowbar lyin' by the gatepost. That Indian fetched it from the forge. It was used to pry out the bolts an' steeples. Tom, I reckon there wasn't much time lost forcin' that gate."

Belding, in shirt sleeves and barefooted, roared with rage. He said he had heard the horses running as he leaped out of bed.

"What woke you?" asked Laddy.

"Sol. He came whistling for Dick. Didn't you hear him before I called you?"

"Hear him! He came thunderin' right under my window. I jumped up in bed, an' when he let out that blast Jim lit square in the middle of the floor, an' I was scared stiff. Dick, seein' it was your room he blew into, what did you think?"

"I couldn't think. I'm shaking yet, Laddy."

"Boys, I'll bet Sol spilled a few raiders if any got hands on him," said Jim. "Now, let's sit down an' wait for daylight. It's my idea we'll find some of the hosses runnin' loose. Tom, you go an' get some clothes on. It's freezin' cold. An' don't forget to tell the women folks we're all right."

Daylight made clear some details of the raid. The cowboys found tracks of eight raiders coming up from the river bed where their horses had been left. Evidently the Papago had been false to his trust. His few personal belongings were gone. Lash was correct in his idea of finding more horses loose in the fields. The men soon rounded up eleven of the whites, all more or less frightened, and among the number were Queen and Blanca Mujer. The raiders had been unable to handle more than one horse for each man. It was bitter irony of fate that Belding should lose his favorite, the one horse more dear to him than all the others. Somewhere out on the trail a raider was fighting the iron-jawed savage Blanco Diablo.

"I reckon we're some lucky," observed Jim Lash.

"Lucky ain't enough word," replied Ladd. "You see, it was this way. Some of the raiders piled over the fence while the others worked on the gate. Mebbe the Papago went inside to pick out the best hosses. But it didn't work except with Diablo, an' how they ever got him I don't know. I'd have gambled it'd take all of eight men to steal him. But Greasers have got us skinned on handlin' hosses."

Belding was unconsolable. He cursed and railed, and finally declared he was going to trail the raiders.

"Tom, you just ain't agoin' to do nothin' of the kind," said Ladd coolly.

Belding groaned and bowed his head.

"Laddy, you're right," he replied, presently. "I've got to stand it. I can't leave the women and my property. But it's sure tough. I'm sore way down deep, and nothin' but blood would ever satisfy me."

"Leave that to me an' Jim," said Ladd.

"What do you mean to do?" demanded Belding, starting up.

"Shore I don't know yet.... Give me a light for my pipe. An' Dick, go fetch out your Yaqui."

VIII

THE RUNNING OF BLANCO SOL

THE Yaqui's strange dark glance roved over the corral, the swinging gate with its broken fastenings, the tracks in the road, and then rested upon Belding.

"Malo," he said, and his Spanish was clear.

"Shore Yaqui, about eight bad men, an' a traitor Indian," said Ladd.

"I think he means my herder," added Belding. "If he does, that settles any doubt it might be decent to have—Yaqui—malo Papago—Si?"

The Yaqui spread wide his hands. Then he bent over the tracks in the road. They led everywhither, but gradually he worked out of the thick net to take the trail that the cowboys had followed down to the river. Belding and the rangers kept close at his heels. Occasionally Dick lent a helping hand to the still feeble Indian. He found a trampled spot where the raiders had left their horses. From this point a deeply defined narrow trail led across the dry river bed.

Belding asked the Yaqui where the raiders would head for in the Sonora Desert. For answer the Indian followed the trail across the stream of sand, through willows and mesquite, up to the level of rock and cactus. At this point he halted. A sand-filled, almost obliterated trail led off to the left, and evidently went round to the east of No Name Mountains. To the right stretched the road toward Papago Well and the Sonoyta Oasis. The trail of the raiders took a southeasterly course over untrodden desert. The Yaqui spoke in his own tongue, then in Spanish.

"Think he means slow march," said Belding. "Laddy, from the looks of that trail the Greasers are having trouble with the horses."

"Tom, shore a boy could see that," replied Laddy. "Ask Yaqui to tell us where the raiders are headin', an' if there's water."

It was wonderful to see the Yaqui point. His dark hand stretched, he sighted over his stretched finger at a low white escarpment in the distance. Then with a stick he traced a line in the sand, and then at the end of that another line at right angles. He made crosses and marks and holes, and as he drew the rude map he talked in Yaqui, in Spanish; with a word here and there in English. Belding translated as best he could. The raiders were heading southeast toward the railroad that ran from Nogales down into Sonora. It was four days' travel, bad trail, good sure waterhole one day out; then water not sure for two days. Raiders traveling slow; bothered by too many horses, not looking for pursuit; were never pursued, could be headed and ambushed that night at the first waterhole, a natural trap in a valley.

The men returned to the ranch. The rangers ate and drank while making hurried preparations for travel. Blanco Sol and the cowboys' horses were fed, watered, and saddled. Ladd again refused to ride one of Belding's whites. He was quick and cold.

"Get me a long-range rifle an' lots of shells. Rustle now," he said.

"Laddy, you don't want to be weighted down?" protested Belding.

"Shore I want a gun that'll outshoot the dinky little carbines an' muskets used by the rebels. Trot one out an' be quick."

"I've got a .405, a long-barreled heavy rifle that'll shoot a mile. I use it for mountain sheep. But Laddy, it'll break that bronch's back."

"His back won't break so easy.... Dick, take plenty of shells for your Remington. An' don't forget your field glass."

In less than an hour after the time of the raid the three rangers, heavily armed and superbly mounted on fresh horses, rode out on the trail. As Gale turned to look back from the far bank of Forlorn River, he saw Nell waving a white scarf. He stood high in his stirrups and waved his sombrero. Then the mesquites hid the girl's slight figure, and Gale wheeled grim-faced to follow the rangers.

They rode in single file with Ladd in the lead. He did not keep to the trail of the raiders all the time. He made short cuts. The raiders were traveling leisurely, and they evinced a liking for the most level and least cactus-covered stretches of ground. But the cowboy took a bee-line course for the white escarpment pointed out by the Yaqui; and nothing save deep washes and impassable patches of cactus or rocks made him swerve from it. He kept the broncho at a steady walk over the rougher places and at a swinging Indian canter over the hard and level ground. The sun grew hot and the wind began to blow. Dust clouds rolled along the blue horizon. Whirling columns of sand, like water spouts at sea, circled up out of white arid basins, and swept away and spread aloft before the wind. The escarpment began to rise, to change color, to show breaks upon its rocky face.

Whenever the rangers rode out on the brow of a knoll or ridge or an eminence, before starting to descend, Ladd required of Gale a long, careful, sweeping survey of the desert ahead through the field glass. There were streams of white dust to be seen, streaks of yellow dust, trailing low clouds of sand over the glistening dunes, but no steadily rising, uniformly shaped puffs that would tell a tale of moving horses on the desert.

At noon the rangers got out of the thick cactus. Moreover, the gravel-bottomed washes, the low weathering, rotting ledges of yellow rock gave place to hard sandy rolls and bare clay knolls. The desert resembled a rounded hummocky sea of color. All light shades of blue and pink and yellow and mauve were there dominated by the glaring white sun. Mirages glistened, wavered, faded in the shimmering waves of heat. Dust as fine as powder whiffed up from under the tireless hoofs.

The rangers rode on and the escarpment began to loom. The desert floor inclined perceptibly upward. When Gale got an unobstructed view of the slope of the escarpment he located the raiders and horses. In another hour's travel the rangers could see with naked eyes a long, faint moving streak of black and white dots.

"They're headin' for that yellow pass," said Ladd, pointing to a break in the eastern end of the escarpment. "When they get out of sight we'll rustle. I'm thinkin' that waterhole the Yaqui spoke of lays in the pass."

The rangers traveled swiftly over the remaining miles of level desert leading to the ascent of the escarpment. When they achieved the gateway of the pass the sun was low in the west. Dwarfed mesquite and greasewood appeared among the rocks. Ladd gave the word to tie up horses and go forward on foot.

The narrow neck of the pass opened and descended into a valley half a mile wide, perhaps twice that in length. It had apparently unscalable slopes of weathered rock leading up to beetling walls. With floor bare and hard and white, except for a patch of green mesquite near the far end it was a lurid and desolate spot, the barren bottom of a desert bowl.

"Keep down, boys" said Ladd. "There's the waterhole an' hosses have sharp eyes. Shore the Yaqui figgered this place. I never seen its like for a trap."

Both white and black horses showed against the green, and a thin curling column of blue smoke rose lazily from amid the mesquites.

"I reckon we'd better wait till dark, or mebbe daylight," said Jim Lash.

"Let me figger some. Dick, what do you make of the outlet to this hole? Looks rough to me."

With his glass Gale studied the narrow construction of walls and roughened rising floor.

"Laddy, it's harder to get out at that end than here," he replied.

"Shore that's hard enough. Let me have a look.... Well, boys, it don't take no figgerin' for this job. Jim, I'll want you at the other end blockin' the pass when we're ready to start."

"When'll that be?" inquired Jim.

"Soon as it's light enough in the mornin'. That Greaser outfit will hang till to-morrow. There's no sure water ahead for two days, you remember."

"I reckon I can slip through to the other end after dark," said Lash, thoughtfully. "It might get me in bad to go round."

The rangers stole back from the vantage point and returned to their horses, which they untied and left farther round among broken sections of cliff. For the horses it was a dry, hungry camp, but the rangers built a fire and had their short though strengthening meal.

The location was high, and through a break in the jumble of rocks the great colored void of desert could be seen rolling away endlessly to the west. The sun set, and after it had gone down the golden tips of mountains dulled, their lower shadows creeping upward.

Jim Lash rolled in his saddle blanket, his feet near the fire, and went to sleep. Ladd told Gale to do likewise while he kept the fire up and waited until it was late enough for Jim to undertake circling round the raiders. When Gale awakened the night was dark, cold, windy. The stars shone with white brilliance. Jim was up saddling his horse, and Ladd was talking low. When Gale rose to accompany them both rangers said he need not go. But Gale wanted to go because that was the thing Ladd or Jim would have done.

With Ladd leading, they moved away into the gloom. Advance was exceedingly slow, careful, silent. Under the walls the blackness seemed impenetrable. The horse was as cautious as his master. Ladd did not lose his way, nevertheless he wound between blocks of stone and clumps of mesquite, and often tried a passage to abandon it. Finally the trail showed pale in the gloom, and eastern stars twinkled between the lofty ramparts of the pass.

The advance here was still as stealthily made as before, but not so difficult or slow. When the dense gloom of the pass lightened, and there was a wide space of sky and stars overhead, Ladd halted and stood silent a moment.

"Luck again!" he whispered. "The wind's in your face, Jim. The horses won't scent you. Go slow. Don't crack a stone. Keep close under the wall. Try to get up as high as this at the other end. Wait till daylight before riskin' a loose slope. I'll be ridin' the job early. That's all."

Ladd's cool, easy speech was scarcely significant of the perilous undertaking. Lash moved very slowly away, leading his horse. The soft pads of hoofs ceased to sound about the time the gray shape merged into the black shadows. Then Ladd touched Dick's arm, and turned back up the trail.

But Dick tarried a moment. He wanted a fuller sense of that ebony-bottomed abyss, with its pale encircling walls reaching up to the dusky blue sky and the brilliant stars. There was absolutely no sound.

He retraced his steps down, soon coming up with Ladd; and together they picked a way back through the winding recesses of cliff. The campfire was smoldering. Ladd replenished it and lay down to get a few hours' sleep, while Gale kept watch. The after part of the night wore on till the paling of stars, the thickening of gloom indicated the dark hour before dawn. The spot was secluded from wind, but the air grew cold as ice. Gale spent the time stripping wood from a dead mesquite, in pacing to and fro, in listening. Blanco Sol stamped occasionally, which sound was all that broke the stilliness. Ladd awoke before the faintest gray appeared. The rangers ate and drank. When the black did lighten to gray they saddled the horses and led them out to the pass and down to the point where they had parted with Lash. Here they awaited daylight.

To Gale it seemed long in coming. Such a delay always aggravated the slow fire within him. He had nothing of Ladd's patience. He wanted action. The gray shadow below thinned out, and the patch of mesquite made a blot upon the pale valley. The day dawned.

Still Ladd waited. He grew more silent, grimmer as the time of action approached. Gale wondered what the plan of attack would be. Yet he did not ask. He waited ready for orders.

The valley grew clear of gray shadow except under leaning walls on the eastern side. Then a straight column of smoke rose from among the mesquites. Manifestly this was what Ladd had been awaiting. He took the long .405 from its sheath and tried the lever. Then he lifted a cartridge belt from the pommel of his saddle. Every ring held a shell and these shells were four inches long. He buckled the belt round him.

"Come on, Dick."

Ladd led the way down the slope until he reached a position that commanded the rising of the trail from a level. It was the only place a man or horse could leave the valley for the pass.

"Dick, here's your stand. If any raider rides in range take a crack at him.... Now I want the lend of your hoss."

"Blanco Sol!" exclaimed Gale, more in amazement that Ladd should ask for the horse than in reluctance to lend him.

"Will you let me have him?" Ladd repeated, almost curtly.

"Certainly, Laddy."

A smile momentarily chased the dark cold gloom that had set upon the ranger's lean face.

"Shore I appreciate it, Dick. I know how you care for that hoss. I guess mebbe Charlie Ladd has loved a hoss! An' one not so good as Sol. I was only tryin' your nerve, Dick, askin' you without tellin' my plan. Sol won't get a scratch, you can gamble on that! I'll ride him down into the valley an' pull the greasers out in the open. They've got short-ranged carbines. They can't keep out of range of the .405, an' I'll be takin' the dust of their lead. Sabe, senor?"

"Laddy! You'll run Sol away from the raiders when they chase you? Run him after them when they try to get away?"

"Shore. I'll run all the time. They can't gain on Sol, an' he'll run them down when I want. Can you beat it?"

"No. It's great!... But suppose a raider comes out on Blanco Diablo?"

"I reckon that's the one weak place in my plan. I'm figgerin' they'll never think of that till it's too late. But if they do, well, Sol can outrun Diablo. An' I can always kill the white devil!"

Ladd's strange hate of the horse showed in the passion of his last words, in his hardening jaw and grim set lips.

Gale's hand went swiftly to the ranger's shoulder.

"Laddy. Don't kill Diablo unless it's to save your life."

"All right. But, by God, if I get a chance I'll make Blanco Sol run him off his legs!"

He spoke no more and set about changing the length of Sol's stirrups. When he had them adjusted to suit he mounted and rode down the trail and out upon the level. He rode leisurely as if merely going to water his horse. The long black rifle lying across his saddle, however, was ominous.

Gale securely tied the other horse to a mesquite at hand, and took a position behind a low rock over which he could easily see and shoot when necessary. He imagined Jim Lash in a similar position at the far end of the valley blocking the outlet. Gale had grown accustomed to danger and the hard and fierce feelings peculiar to it. But the coming drama was so peculiarly different in promise from all he had experienced, that he waited the moment of action with thrilling intensity. In him stirred long, brooding wrath at these border raiders—affection for Belding, and keen desire to avenge the outrages he had suffered—warm admiration for the cold, implacable Ladd and his absolute fearlessness, and a curious throbbing interest in the old, much-discussed and never-decided argument as to whether Blanco Sol was fleeter, stronger horse than Blanco Diablo. Gale felt that he was to see a race between these great rivals—the kind of race that made men and horses terrible.

Ladd rode a quarter of a mile out upon the flat before anything happened. Then a whistle rent the still, cold air. A horse had seen or scented Blanco Sol. The whistle was prolonged, faint, but clear. It made the blood thrum in Gale's ears. Sol halted. His head shot up with the old, wild, spirited sweep. Gale leveled his glass at the patch of mesquites. He saw the raiders running to an open place, pointing, gesticulating. The glass brought them so close that he saw the dark faces. Suddenly they broke and fled back among the trees. Then he got only white and dark gleams of moving bodies. Evidently that moment was one of boots, guns, and saddles for the raiders.

Lowering the glass, Gale saw that Blanco Sol had started forward again. His gait was now a canter, and he had covered another quarter of a mile before horses and raiders appeared upon the outskirts of the mesquites. Then Blanco Sol stopped. His shrill, ringing whistle came distinctly to Gale's ears. The raiders were mounted on dark horses, and they stood abreast in a motionless line. Gale chuckled as he appreciated what a puzzle the situation presented for them. A lone horseman in the middle of the valley did not perhaps seem so menacing himself as the possibilities his presence suggested.

Then Gale saw a raider gallop swiftly from the group toward the farther outlet of the valley. This might have been owing to characteristic cowardice; but it was more likely a move of the raiders to make sure of retreat. Undoubtedly Ladd saw this galloping horseman. A few waiting moments ensued. The galloping horseman reached the slope, began to climb. With naked eyes Gale saw a puff of white smoke spring out of the rocks. Then the raider wheeled his plunging horse back to the level, and went racing wildly down the valley.

The compact bunch of bays and blacks seemed to break apart and spread rapidly from the edge of the mesquites. Puffs of white smoke indicated firing, and showed the nature of the raiders' excitement. They were far out of ordinary range, but they spurred toward Ladd, shooting as they rode. Ladd held his ground; the big white horse stood like a rock in his tracks. Gale saw little spouts of dust rise in front of Blanco Sol and spread swift as sight to his rear. The raiders' bullets, striking low, were skipping along the hard, bare floor of the valley. Then Ladd raised the long rifle. There was no smoke, but three high, spanging reports rang out. A gap opened in the dark line of advancing horsemen; then a riderless steed sheered off to the right. Blanco Sol seemed to turn as on a pivot and charged back toward the lower end of the valley. He circled over to Gale's right and stretched out into his run. There were now five raiders in pursuit, and they came sweeping down, yelling and shooting, evidently sure of their quarry. Ladd reserved his fire. He kept turning from back to front in his saddle.

Gale saw how the space widened between pursuers and pursued, saw distinctly when Ladd eased up Sol's running. Manifestly Ladd intended to try to lead the raiders round in front of Gale's position, and, presently, Gale saw he was going to succeed. The raiders, riding like vaqueros, swept on in a curve, cutting off what distance they could. One fellow, a small, wiry rider, high on his mount's neck like a jockey, led his companions by many yards. He seemed to be getting the range of Ladd, or else he shot high, for his bullets did not strike up the dust behind Sol. Gale was ready to shoot. Blanco Sol pounded by, his rapid, rhythmic hoofbeats plainly to be heard. He was running easily.

Gale tried to still the jump of heart and pulse, and turned his eye again on the nearest pursuer. This raider was crossing in, his carbine held muzzle up in his right hand, and he was coming swiftly. It was a long shot, upward of five hundred yards. Gale had not time to adjust the sights of the Remington, but he knew the gun and, holding coarsely upon the swiftly moving blot, he began to shoot. The first bullet sent up a great splash of dust beneath the horse's nose, making him leap as if to hurdle a fence. The rifle was automatic; Gale needed only to pull the trigger. He saw now that the raiders behind were in line. Swiftly he worked the trigger. Suddenly the leading horse leaped convulsively, not up nor aside, but straight ahead, and then he crashed to the ground throwing his rider like a catapult, and then slid and rolled. He half got up, fell back, and kicked; but his rider never moved.

The other raiders sawed the reins of plunging steeds and whirled to escape the unseen battery. Gale slipped a fresh clip into the magazine of his rifle. He restrained himself from useless firing and gave eager eye to the duel below. Ladd began to shoot while Sol was running. The .405 rang out sharply—then again. The heavy bullets streaked the dust all the way across the valley. Ladd aimed deliberately and pulled slowly, unmindful of the kicking dust-puffs behind Sol, and to the side. The raiders spurred madly in pursuit, loading and firing. They shot ten times while Ladd shot once, and all in vain; and on Ladd's sixth shot a raider topped backward, threw his carbine and fell with his foot catching in a stirrup. The frightened horse plunged away, dragging him in a path of dust.

Gale had set himself to miss nothing of that fighting race, yet the action passed too swiftly for clear sight of all. Ladd had emptied a magazine, and now Blanco Sol quickened and lengthened his running stride. He ran away from his pursuers. Then it was that the ranger's ruse was divined by the raiders. They hauled sharply up and seemed to be conferring. But that was a fatal mistake.

Blanco Sol was seen to break his gait and slow down in several jumps, then square away and stand stockstill. Ladd fired at the closely grouped raiders. An instant passed. Then Gale heard the spat of a bullet out in front, saw a puff of dust, then heard the lead strike the rocks and go whining away. And it was after this that one of the raiders fell prone from his saddle. The steel-jacketed .405 had gone through him on its uninterrupted way to hum past Gale's position.

The remaining two raiders frantically spurred their horses and fled up the valley. Ladd sent Sol after them. It seemed to Gale, even though he realized his excitement, that Blanco Sol made those horses seem like snails. The raiders split, one making for the eastern outlet, the other circling back of the mesquites. Ladd kept on after the latter. Then puffs of white smoke and rifle shots faintly crackling told Jim Lash's hand in the game. However, he succeeded only in driving the raider back into the valley. But Ladd had turned the other horseman, and now it appeared the two raiders were between Lash above on the stony slope and Ladd below on the level. There was desperate riding on part of the raiders to keep from being hemmed in closer. Only one of them got away, and he came riding for life down under the eastern wall. Blanco Sol settled into his graceful, beautiful swing. He gained steadily, though he was far from extending himself. By Gale's actual count the raider fired eight times in that race down the valley, and all his bullets went low and wide. He pitched the carbine away and lost all control in headlong flight.

Some few hundred rods to the left of Gale the raider put his horse to the weathered slope. He began to climb. The horse was superb, infinitely more courageous than his rider. Zigzag they went up and up, and when Ladd reached the edge of the slope they were high along the cracked and guttered rampart. Once—twice Ladd raised the long rifle, but each time he lowered it. Gale divined that the ranger's restraint was not on account of the Mexican, but for that valiant and faithful horse. Up and up he went, and the yellow dust clouds rose, and an avalanche rolled rattling and cracking down the slope. It was beyond belief that a horse, burdened or unburdened, could find footing and hold it upon that wall of narrow ledges and inverted, slanting gullies. But he climbed on, sure-footed as a mountain goat, and, surmounting the last rough steps, he stood a moment silhouetted against the white sky. Then he disappeared. Ladd sat astride Blanco Sol gazing upward. How the cowboy must have honored that raider's brave steed!

Gale, who had been too dumb to shout the admiration he felt, suddenly leaped up, and his voice came with a shriek:

"LOOK OUT, LADDY!"

A big horse, like a white streak, was bearing down to the right of the ranger. Blanco Diablo! A matchless rider swung with the horse's motion. Gale was stunned. Then he remembered the first raider, the one Lash had shot at and driven away from the outlet. This fellow had made for the mesquite and had put a saddle on Belding's favorite. In the heat of the excitement, while Ladd had been intent upon the climbing horse, this last raider had come down with the speed of the wind straight for the western outlet. Perhaps, very probably, he did not know Gale was there to block it; and certainly he hoped to pass Ladd and Blanco Sol.

A touch of the spur made Sol lunge forward to head off the raider. Diablo was in his stride, but the distance and angle favored Sol. The raider had no carbine. He held aloft a gun ready to level it and fire. He sat the saddle as if it were a stationary seat. Gale saw Ladd lean down and drop the .405 in the sand. He would take no chances of wounding Belding's best-loved horse.

Then Gale sat transfixed with suspended breath watching the horses thundering toward him. Blanco Diablo was speeding low, fleet as an antelope, fierce and terrible in his devilish action, a horse for war and blood and death. He seemed unbeatable. Yet to see the magnificently running Blanco Sol was but to court a doubt. Gale stood spellbound. He might have shot the raider; but he never thought of such a thing. The distance swiftly lessened. Plain it was the raider could not make the opening ahead of Ladd. He saw it and swerved to the left, emptying his six-shooter as he turned. His dark face gleamed as he flashed by Gale.

Blanco Sol thundered across. Then the race became straight away up the valley. Diablo was cold and Sol was hot; therein lay the only handicap and vantage. It was a fleet, beautiful, magnificent race. Gale thrilled and exulted and yelled as his horse settled into a steadily swifter run and began to gain. The dust rolled in a funnel-shaped cloud from the flying hoofs. The raider wheeled with gun puffing white, and Ladd ducked low over the neck of his horse.

The gap between Diablo and Sol narrowed yard by yard. At first it had been a wide one. The raider beat his mount and spurred, beat and spurred, wheeled round to shoot, then bent forward again. In his circle at the upper end of the valley he turned far short of the jumble of rocks.

All the devil that was in Blanco Diablo had its running on the downward stretch. The strange, cruel urge of bit and spur, the crazed rider who stuck like a burr upon him, the shots and smoke added terror to his natural violent temper. He ran himself off his feet. But he could not elude that relentless horse behind him. The running of Blanco Sol was that of a sure, remorseless driving power—steadier—stronger—swifter with every long and wonderful stride.

The raider tried to sheer Diablo off closer under the wall, to make the slope where his companion had escaped. But Diablo was uncontrollable. He was running wild, with breaking gait. Closer and closer crept that white, smoothly gliding, beautiful machine of speed.

Then, like one white flash following another, the two horses gleamed down the bank of a wash and disappeared in clouds of dust.

Gale watched with strained and smarting eyes. The thick throb in his ears was pierced by faint sounds of gunshots. Then he waited in almost unendurable suspense.

Suddenly something whiter than the background of dust appeared above the low roll of valley floor. Gale leveled his glass. In the clear circle shone Blanco Sol's noble head with its long black bar from ears to nose. Sol's head was drooping now. Another second showed Ladd still in the saddle.

The ranger was leading Blanco Diable—spent—broken—dragging—riderless.

IX

AN INTERRUPTED SIESTA

NO man ever had a more eloquent and beautiful pleader for his cause than had Dick Gale in Mercedes Castaneda. He peeped through the green, shining twigs of the palo verde that shaded his door. The hour was high noon, and the patio was sultry. The only sounds were the hum of bees in the flowers and the low murmur of the Spanish girl's melodious voice. Nell lay in the hammock, her hands behind her head, with rosy cheeks and arch eyes. Indeed, she looked rebellious. Certain it was, Dick reflected, that the young lady had fully recovered the wilful personality which had lain dormant for a while. Equally certain it seemed that Mercedes's earnestness was not apparently having the effect it should have had.

Dick was inclined to be rebellious himself. Belding had kept the rangers in off the line, and therefore Dick had been idle most of the time, and, though he tried hard, he had been unable to stay far from Nell's vicinity. He believed she cared for him; but he could not catch her alone long enough to verify his tormenting hope. When alone she was as illusive as a shadow, as quick as a flash, as mysterious as a Yaqui. When he tried to catch her in the garden or fields, or corner her in the patio, she eluded him, and left behind a memory of dark-blue, haunting eyes. It was that look in her eyes which lent him hope. At other times, when it might have been possible for Dick to speak, Nell clung closely to Mercedes. He had long before enlisted the loyal Mercedes in his cause; but in spite of this Nell had been more than a match for them both.

Gale pondered over an idea he had long revolved in mind, and which now suddenly gave place to a decision that made his heart swell and his cheek burn. He peeped again through the green branches to see Nell laughing at the fiery Mercedes.

"Qui'en sabe," he called, mockingly, and was delighted with Nell's quick, amazed start.

Then he went in search of Mrs. Belding, and found her busy in the kitchen. The relation between Gale and Mrs. Belding had subtly and incomprehensively changed. He understood her less than when at first he divined an antagonism in her. If such a thing were possible she had retained the antagonism while seeming to yield to some influence that must have been fondness for him. Gale was in no wise sure of her affection, and he had long imagined she was afraid of him, or of something that he represented. He had gone on, openly and fairly, though discreetly, with his rather one-sided love affair; and as time passed he had grown less conscious of what had seemed her unspoken opposition. Gale had come to care greatly for Nell's mother. Not only was she the comfort and strength of her home, but also of the inhabitants of Forlorn River. Indian, Mexican, American were all the same to her in trouble or illness; and then she was nurse, doctor, peacemaker, helper. She was good and noble, and there was not a child or grownup in Forlorn River who did not love and bless her. But Mrs. Belding did not seem happy. She was brooding, intense, deep, strong, eager for the happiness and welfare of others; and she was dominated by a worship of her daughter that was as strange as it was pathetic. Mrs. Belding seldom smiled, and never laughed. There was always a soft, sad, hurt look in her eyes. Gale often wondered if there had been other tragedy in her life than the supposed loss of her father in the desert. Perhaps it was the very unsolved nature of that loss which made it haunting.

Mrs. Belding heard Dick's step as he entered the kitchen, and, looking up, greeted him.

"Mother," began Dick, earnestly. Belding called her that, and so did Ladd and Lash, but it was the first time for Dick. "Mother—I want to speak to you."

The only indication Mrs. Belding gave of being started was in her eyes, which darkened, shadowed with multiplying thought.

"I love Nell," went on Dick, simply, "and I want you to let me ask her to be my wife."

Mrs. Belding's face blanched to a deathly white. Gale, thinking with surprise and concern that she was going to faint, moved quickly toward her, took her arm.

"Forgive me. I was blunt.... But I thought you knew."

"I've known for a long time," replied Mrs. Belding. Her voice was steady, and there was no evidence of agitation except in her pallor. "Then you—you haven't spoken to Nell?"

Dick laughed. "I've been trying to get a chance to tell her. I haven't had it yet. But she knows. There are other ways besides speech. And Mercedes has told her. I hope, I almost believe Nell cares a little for me."

"I've known that, too, for a long time," said Mrs. Belding, low almost as a whisper.

"You know!" cried Dick, with a glow and rush of feeling.

"Dick, you must be very blind not to see what has been plain to all of us.... I guess—it couldn't have been helped. You're a splendid fellow. No wonder she loves you."

"Mother! You'll give her to me?"

She drew him to the light and looked with strange, piercing intentness into his face. Gale had never dreamed a woman's eyes could hold such a world of thought and feeling. It seemed all the sweetness of life was there, and all the pain.

"Do you love her?" she asked.

"With all my heart."

"You want to marry her?"

"Ah, I want to! As much as I want to live and work for her."

"When would you marry her?"

"Why!... Just as soon as she will do it. To-morrow!" Dick gave a wild, exultant little laugh.

"Dick Gale, you want my Nell? You love her just as she is—her sweetness—her goodness? Just herself, body and soul?... There's nothing could change you—nothing?"

"Dear Mrs. Belding, I love Nell for herself. If she loves me I'll be the happiest of men. There's absolutely nothing that could make any difference in me."

"But your people? Oh, Dick, you come of a proud family. I can tell. I—I once knew a young man like you. A few months can't change pride—blood. Years can't change them. You've become a ranger. You love the adventure—the wild life. That won't last. Perhaps you'll settle down to ranching. I know you love the West. But, Dick, there's your family—"

"If you want to know anything about my family, I'll tell you," interrupted Dick, with strong feeling. "I've not secrets about them or myself. My future and happiness are Nell's to make. No one else shall count with me."

"Then, Dick—you may have her. God—bless—you—both."

Mrs. Belding's strained face underwent a swift and mobile relaxation, and suddenly she was weeping in strangely mingled happiness and bitterness.

"Why, mother!" Gale could say no more. He did not comprehend a mood seemingly so utterly at variance with Mrs. Belding's habitual temperament. But he put his arm around her. In another moment she had gained command over herself, and, kissing him, she pushed him out of the door.

"There! Go tell her, Dick... And have some spunk about it!"

Gale went thoughtfully back to his room. He vowed that he would answer for Nell's happiness, if he had the wonderful good fortune to win her. Then remembering the hope Mrs. Belding had given him, Dick lost his gravity in a flash, and something began to dance and ring within him. He simply could not keep his steps turned from the patio. Every path led there. His blood was throbbing, his hopes mounting, his spirit soaring. He knew he had never before entered the patio with that inspirited presence.

"Now for some spunk!" he said, under his breath.

Plainly he meant his merry whistle and his buoyant step to interrupt this first languorous stage of the siesta which the girls always took during the hot hours. Nell had acquired the habit long before Mercedes came to show how fixed a thing it was in the life of the tropics. But neither girl heard him. Mercedes lay under the palo verde, her beautiful head dark and still upon a cushion. Nell was asleep in the hammock. There was an abandonment in her deep repose, and a faint smile upon her face. Her sweet, red lips, with the soft, perfect curve, had always fascinated Dick, and now drew him irresistibly. He had always been consumed with a desire to kiss her, and now he was overwhelmed with his opportunity. It would be a terrible thing to do, but if she did not awaken at once— No, he would fight the temptation. That would be more than spunk. It would— Suddenly an ugly green fly sailed low over Nell, appeared about to alight on her. Noiselessly Dick stepped close to the hammock bent under the tree, and with a sweep of his hand chased the intruding fly away. But he found himself powerless to straighten up. He was close to her—bending over her face—near the sweet lips. The insolent, dreaming smile just parted them. Then he thought he was lost. But she stirred—he feared she would awaken.

He had stepped back erect when she opened her eyes. They were sleepy, yet surprised until she saw him. Then she was wide awake in a second, bewildered, uncertain.

"Why—you here?" she asked, slowly.

"Large as life!" replied Dick, with unusual gayety.

"How long have you been here?"

"Just got here this fraction of a second," he replied, lying shamelessly.

It was evident that she did not know whether or not to believe him, and as she studied him a slow blush dyed her cheek.

"You are absolutely truthful when you say you just stepped there?"

"Why, of course," answered Dick, right glad he did not have to lie about that.

"I thought—I was—dreaming," she said, and evidently the sound of her voice reassured her.

"Yes, you looked as if you were having pleasant dreams," replied Dick. "So sorry to wake you. I can't see how I came to do it, I was so quiet. Mercedes didn't wake. Well, I'll go and let you have your siesta and dreams."

But he did not move to go. Nell regarded him with curious, speculative eyes.

"Isn't it a lovely day?" queried Dick.

"I think it's hot."

"Only ninety in the shade. And you've told me the mercury goes to one hundred and thirty in midsummer. This is just a glorious golden day."

"Yesterday was finer, but you didn't notice it."

"Oh, yesterday was somewhere back in the past—the inconsequential past."

Nell's sleepy blue eyes opened a little wider. She did not know what to make of this changed young man. Dick felt gleeful and tried hard to keep the fact from becoming manifest.

"What's the inconsequential past? You seem remarkably happy to-day."

"I certainly am happy. Adios. Pleasant dreams."

Dick turned away then and left the patio by the opening into the yard. Nell was really sleepy, and when she had fallen asleep again he would return. He walked around for a while. Belding and the rangers were shoeing a broncho. Yaqui was in the field with the horses. Blanco Sol grazed contently, and now and then lifted his head to watch. His long ears went up at sight of his master, and he whistled. Presently Dick, as if magnet-drawn, retraced his steps to the patio and entered noiselessly.

Nell was now deep in her siesta. She was inert, relaxed, untroubled by dreams. Her hair was damp on her brow.

Again Nell stirred, and gradually awakened. Her eyes unclosed, humid, shadowy, unconscious. They rested upon Dick for a moment before they became clear and comprehensive. He stood back fully ten feet from her, and to all outside appearances regarded her calmly.

"I've interrupted your siesta again," he said. "Please forgive me. I'll take myself off."

He wandered away, and when it became impossible for him to stay away any longer he returned to the patio.

The instant his glance rested upon Nell's face he divined she was feigning sleep. The faint rose-blush had paled. The warm, rich, golden tint of her skin had fled. Dick dropped upon his knees and bent over her. Though his blood was churning in his veins, his breast laboring, his mind whirling with the wonder of that moment and its promise, he made himself deliberate. He wanted more than anything he had ever wanted in his life to see if she would keep up that pretense of sleep and let him kiss her. She must have felt his breath, for her hair waved off her brow. Her cheeks were now white. Her breast swelled and sank. He bent down closer—closer. But he must have been maddeningly slow, for as he bent still closer Nell's eyes opened, and he caught a swift purple gaze of eyes as she whirled her head. Then, with a little cry, she rose and fled.

X

ROJAS

NO word from George Thorne had come to Forlorn River in weeks. Gale grew concerned over the fact, and began to wonder if anything serious could have happened to him. Mercedes showed a slow, wearing strain.

Thorne's commission expired the end of January, and if he could not get his discharge immediately, he surely could obtain leave of absence. Therefore, Gale waited, not without growing anxiety, and did his best to cheer Mercedes. The first of February came bringing news of rebel activities and bandit operations in and around Casita, but not a word from the cavalryman.

Mercedes became silent, mournful. Her eyes were great black windows of tragedy. Nell devoted herself entirely to the unfortunate girl; Dick exerted himself to persuade her that all would yet come well; in fact, the whole household could not have been kinder to a sister or a daughter. But their united efforts were unavailing. Mercedes seemed to accept with fatalistic hopelessness a last and crowning misfortune.

A dozen times Gale declared he would ride in to Casita and find out why they did not hear from Thorne; however, older and wiser heads prevailed over his impetuosity. Belding was not sanguine over the safety of the Casita trail. Refugees from there arrived every day in Forlorn River, and if tales they told were true, real war would have been preferable to what was going on along the border. Belding and the rangers and the Yaqui held a consultation. Not only had the Indian become a faithful servant to Gale, but he was also of value to Belding. Yaqui had all the craft of his class, and superior intelligence. His knowledge of Mexicans was second only to his hate of them. And Yaqui, who had been scouting on all the trails, gave information that made Belding decide to wait some days before sending any one to Casita. He required promises from his rangers, particularly Gale, not to leave without his consent.

It was upon Gale's coming from this conference that he encountered Nell. Since the interrupted siesta episode she had been more than ordinarily elusive, and about all he had received from her was a tantalizing smile from a distance. He got the impression now, however, that she had awaited him. When he drew close to her he was certain of it, and he experienced more than surprise.

"Dick," she began, hurriedly. "Dad's not going to send any one to see about Thorne?"

"No, not yet. He thinks it best not to. We all think so. I'm sorry. Poor Mercedes!"

"I knew it. I tried to coax him to send Laddy or even Yaqui. He wouldn't listen to me. Dick, Mercedes is dying by inches. Can't you see what ails her? It's more than love or fear. It's uncertainty—suspense. Oh, can't we find out for her?"

"Nell, I feel as badly as you about her. I wanted to ride in to Casita. Belding shut me up quick, the last time."

Nell came close to Gale, clasped his arm. There was no color in her face. Her eyes held a dark, eager excitement.

"Dick, will you slip off without Dad's consent? Risk it! Go to Casita and find out what's happened to Thorne—at least if he ever started for Forlorn River?"

"No, Nell, I won't do that."

She drew away from him with passionate suddenness.

"Are you afraid?"

This certainly was not the Nell Burton that Gale knew.

"No, I'm not afraid," Gale replied, a little nettled.

"Will you go—for my sake?" Like lightning her mood changed and she was close to him again, hands on his, her face white, her whole presence sweetly alluring.

"Nell, I won't disobey Belding," protested Gale. "I won't break my word."

"Dick, it'll not be so bad as that. But—what if it is?... Go, Dick, if not for poor Mercedes's sake, then for mine—to please me. I'll—I'll... you won't lose anything by going. I think I know how Mercedes feels. Just a word from Thorne or about him would save her. Take Blanco Sol and go, Dick. What rebel outfit could ever ride you down on that horse? Why, Dick, if I was up on Sol I wouldn't be afraid of the whole rebel army."

"My dear girl, it's not a question of being afraid. It's my word—my duty to Belding."

"You said you loved me. If you love me you will go... You don't love me!"

Gale could only stare at this transformed girl.

"Dick, listen!... If you go—if you fetch some word of Thorne to comfort Mercedes, you—well, you will have your reward."

"Nell!"

Her dangerous sweetness was as amazing as this newly revealed character.

"Dick, will you go?"

"No-no!" cried Gale, in violence, struggling with himself. "Nell Burton, I'll tell you this. To have the reward I want would mean pretty near heaven for me. But not even for that will I break my word to your father."

She seemed the incarnation of girlish scorn and wilful passion.

"Gracias, senor," she replied, mockingly. "Adios." Then she flashed out of his sight.

Gale went to his room at once, disturbed and thrilling, and did not soon recover from that encounter.

The following morning at the breakfast table Nell was not present. Mrs. Belding evidently considered the fact somewhat unusual, for she called out into the patio and then into the yard. Then she went to Mercedes's room. But Nell was not there, either.

"She's in one of her tantrums lately," said Belding. "Wouldn't speak to me this morning. Let her alone, mother. She's spoiled enough, without running after her. She's always hungry. She'll be on hand presently, don't mistake me."

Notwithstanding Belding's conviction, which Gale shared, Nell did not appear at all during the hour. When Belding and the rangers went outside, Yaqui was eating his meal on the bench where he always sat.

"Yaqui—Lluvia d' oro, si?" asked Belding, waving his hand toward the corrals. The Indian's beautiful name for Nell meant "shower of gold," and Belding used it in asking Yaqui if he had seen her. He received a negative reply.

Perhaps half an hour afterward, as Gale was leaving his room, he saw the Yaqui running up the path from the fields. It was markedly out of the ordinary to see the Indian run. Gale wondered what was the matter. Yaqui ran straight to Belding, who was at work at his bench under the wagon shed. In less than a moment Belding was bellowing for his rangers. Gale got to him first, but Ladd and Lash were not far behind.

"Blanco Sol gone!" yelled Belding, in a rage.

"Gone? In broad daylight, with the Indian a-watch-in?" queried Ladd.

"It happened while Yaqui was at breakfast. That's sure. He'd just watered Sol."

"Raiders!" exclaimed Jim Lash.

"Lord only knows. Yaqui says it wasn't raiders."

"Mebbe Sol's just walked off somewheres."

"He was haltered in the corral."

"Send Yaqui to find the hoss's trail, an' let's figger," said Ladd. "Shore this 's no raider job."

In the swift search that ensued Gale did not have anything to say; but his mind was forming a conclusion. When he found his old saddle and bridle missing from the peg in the barn his conclusion became a positive conviction, and it made him, for the moment, cold and sick and speechless.

"Hey, Dick, don't take it so much to heart," said Belding. "We'll likely find Sol, and if we don't, there's other good horses."

"I'm not thinking of Sol," replied Gale.

Ladd cast a sharp glance at Gale, snapped his fingers, and said:

"Damn me if I ain't guessed it, too!"

"What's wrong with you locoed gents?" bluntly demanded Belding.

"Nell has slipped away on Sol," answered Dick.

There was a blank pause, which presently Belding broke.

"Well, that's all right, if Nell's on him. I was afraid we'd lost the horse."

"Belding, you're trackin' bad," said Ladd, wagging his head.

"Nell has started for Casita," burst out Gale. "She has gone to fetch Mercedes some word about Thorne. Oh, Belding, you needn't shake your head. I know she's gone. She tried to persuade me to go, and was furious when I wouldn't."

"I don't believe it," replied Belding, hoarsely. "Nell may have her temper. She's a little devil at times, but she always had good sense."

"Tom, you can gamble she's gone," said Ladd.

"Aw, hell, no! Jim, what do you think?" implored Belding.

"I reckon Sol's white head is pointed level an' straight down the Casita trail. An' Nell can ride. We're losing' time."

That roused Belding to action.

"I say you're all wrong," he yelled, starting for the corrals. "She's only taking a little ride, same as she's done often. But rustle now. Find out. Dick, you ride cross the valley. Jim, you hunt up and down the river. I'll head up San Felipe way. And you, Laddy, take Diablo and hit the Casita trail. If she really has gone after Thorne you can catch her in an hour or so."

"Shore I'll go," replied Ladd. "But, Beldin', if you're not plumb crazy you're close to it. That big white devil can't catch Sol. Not in an hour or a day or a week! What's more, at the end of any runnin' time, with an even start, Sol will be farther in the lead. An' now Sol's got an hour's start."

"Laddy, you mean to say Sol is a faster horse than Diablo?" thundered Belding, his face purple.

"Shore. I mean to tell you just that there," replied the ranger.

"I'll—I'll bet a—"

"We're wastin' time," curtly interrupted Ladd. "You can gamble on this if you want to. I'll ride your Blanco Devil as he never was rid before, 'cept once when a damn sight better hossman than I am couldn't make him outrun Sol."

Without more words the men saddled and were off, not waiting for the Yaqui to come in with possible information as to what trail Blanco Sol had taken. It certainly did not show in the clear sand of the level valley where Gale rode to and fro. When Gale returned to the house he found Belding and Lash awaiting him. They did not mention their own search, but stated that Yaqui had found Blanco Sol's tracks in the Casita trail. After some consultation Belding decided to send Lash along after Ladd.

The interminable time that followed contained for Gale about as much suspense as he could well bear. What astonished him and helped him greatly to fight off actual distress was the endurance of Nell's mother.

Early on the morning of the second day, Gale, who had acquired an unbreakable habit of watching, saw three white horses and a bay come wearily stepping down the road. He heard Blanco Sol's familiar whistle, and he leaped up wild with joy. The horse was riderless. Gale's sudden joy received a violent check, then resurged when he saw a limp white form in Jim Lash's arms. Ladd was supporting a horseman who wore a military uniform.

Gale shouted with joy and ran into the house to tell the good news. It was the ever-thoughtful Mrs. Belding who prevented him from rushing in to tell Mercedes. Then he hurried out into the yard, closely followed by the Beldings.

Lash handed down a ragged, travel-stained, wan girl into Belding's arms.

"Dad! Mama!"

It was indeed a repentant Nell, but there was spirit yet in the tired blue eyes. Then she caught sight of Gale and gave him a faint smile.

"Hello—Dick."

"Nell!" Gale reached for her hand, held it tightly, and found speech difficult.

"You needn't worry—about your old horse," she said, as Belding carried her toward the door. "Oh, Dick! Blanco Sol is—glorious!"

Gale turned to greet his friend. Indeed, it was but a haggard ghost of the cavalryman. Thorne looked ill or wounded. Gale's greeting was also a question full of fear.

Thorne's answer was a faint smile. He seemed ready to drop from the saddle. Gale helped Ladd hold Thorne upon the horse until they reached the house. Belding came out again. His welcome was checked as he saw the condition of the cavalryman. Thorne reeled into Dick's arms. But he was able to stand and walk.

"I'm not—hurt. Only weak—starved," he said. "Is Mercedes— Take me to her."

"She'll be well the minute she sees him," averred Belding, as he and Gale led the cavalryman to Mercedes's room. There they left him; and Gale, at least, felt his ears ringing with the girl's broken cry of joy.

When Belding and Gale hurried forth again the rangers were tending the tired horses. Upon returning to the house Jim Lash calmly lit his pipe, and Ladd declared that, hungry as he was, he had to tell his story.

"Shore, Beldin'," began Ladd, "that was funny about Diablo catchin' Blanco Sol. Funny ain't the word. I nearly laughed myself to death. Well, I rode in Sol's tracks all the way to Casita. Never seen a rebel or a raider till I got to town. Figgered Nell made the trip in five hours. I went straight to the camp of the cavalrymen, an' found them just coolin' off an' dressin' down their hosses after what looked to me like a big ride. I got there too late for the fireworks.

"Some soldier took me to an officer's tent. Nell was there, some white an' all in. She just said, 'Laddy!' Thorne was there, too, an' he was bein' worked over by the camp doctor. I didn't ask no questions, because I seen quiet was needed round that tent. After satisfying myself that Nell was all right, an' Thorne in no danger, I went out.

"Shore there was so darn many fellers who wanted to an' tried to tell me what'd come off, I thought I'd never find out. But I got the story piece by piece. An' here's what happened.

"Nell rode Blanco Sol a-tearin' into camp, an' had a crowd round her in a jiffy. She told who she was, where she'd come from, an' what she wanted. Well, it seemed a day or so before Nell got there the cavalrymen had heard word of Thorne. You see, Thorne had left camp on leave of absence some time before. He was shore mysterious, they said, an' told nobody where he was goin'. A week or so after he left camp some Greaser give it away that Rojas had a prisoner in a dobe shack near his camp. Nobody paid much attention to what the Greaser said. He wanted money for mescal. An' it was usual for Rojas to have prisoners. But in a few more days it turned out pretty sure that for some reason Rojas was holdin' Thorne.

"Now it happened when this news came Colonel Weede was in Nogales with his staff, an' the officer left in charge didn't know how to proceed. Rojas's camp was across the line in Mexico, an' ridin' over there was serious business. It meant a whole lot more than just scatterin' one Greaser camp. It was what had been botherin' more'n one colonel along the line. Thorne's feller soldiers was anxious to get him out of a bad fix, but they had to wait for orders.

"When Nell found out Thorne was bein' starved an' beat in a dobe shack no more'n two mile across the line, she shore stirred up that cavalry camp. Shore! She told them soldiers Rojas was holdin' Thorne—torturin' him to make him tell where Mercedes was. She told about Mercedes—how sweet an' beautiful she was—how her father had been murdered by Rojas—how she had been hounded by the bandit—how ill an' miserable she was, waitin' for her lover. An' she begged the cavalrymen to rescue Thorne.

"From the way it was told to me I reckon them cavalrymen went up in the air. Fine, fiery lot of young bloods, I thought, achin' for a scrap. But the officer in charge, bein' in a ticklish place, still held out for higher orders.

"Then Nell broke loose. You-all know Nell's tongue is sometimes like a *choya* thorn. I'd have give somethin' to see her work up that soldier outfit. Nell's never so pretty as when she's mad. An' this last stunt of hers was no girly tantrum, as Beldin' calls it. She musta been ragin' with all the hell there's in a woman.... Can't you fellers see her on Blanco Sol with her eyes turnin' black?"

Ladd mopped his sweaty face with his dusty scarf. He was beaming. He was growing excited, hurried in his narrative.

"Right out then Nell swore she'd go after Thorne. If them cavalrymen couldn't ride with a Western girl to save a brother American—let them hang back! One feller, under orders, tried to stop Blanco Sol. An' that feller invited himself to the hospital. Then the cavalrymen went flyin' for their hosses. Mebbe Nell's move was just foxy—woman's cunnin'. But I'm thinkin' as she felt then she'd have sent Blanco Sol straight into Rojas's camp, which, I'd forgot to say, was in plain sight.

"It didn't take long for every cavalryman in that camp to get wind of what was comin' off. Shore they musta been wild. They strung out after Nell in a thunderin' troop.

"Say, I wish you fellers could see the lane that bunch of hosses left in the greasewood an' cactus. Looks like there'd been a cattle stampede on the desert.... Blanco Sol stayed out in front, you can gamble on that. Right into Rojas's camp! Sabe, you senors? Gawd Almighty! I never had grief that 'd hold a candle to this one of bein' too late to see Nell an' Sol in their one best race.

"Rojas an' his men vamoosed without a shot. That ain't surprisin'. There wasn't a shot fired by anybody. The cavalrymen soon found Thorne an' hurried with him back on Uncle Sam's land. Thorne was half naked, black an' blue all over, thin as a rail. He looked mighty sick when I seen him first. That was a little after midday. He was given food an' drink. Shore he seemed a starved man. But he picked up wonderful, an' by the time Jim came along he was wantin' to start for Forlorn River. So was Nell. By main strength as much as persuasion we kept the two of them quiet till next evenin' at dark.

"Well, we made as sneaky a start in the dark as Jim an' me could manage, an' never hit the trail till we was miles from town. Thorne's nerve held him up for a while. Then all at once he tumbled out of his saddle. We got him back, an' Lash held him on. Nell didn't give out till daybreak."

As Ladd paused in his story Belding began to stutter, and finally he exploded. His mighty utterances were incoherent. But plainly the wrath he had felt toward the wilful girl was forgotten. Gale remained gripped by silence.

"I reckon you'll all be some surprised when you see Casita," went on Ladd. "It's half burned an' half tore down. An' the rebels are livin' fat. There was rumors of another federal force on the road from Casa Grandes. I seen a good many Americans from interior Mexico, an' the stories they told would make your hair stand up. They all packed guns, was fightin' mad at Greasers, an' sore on the good old U. S. But shore glad to get over the line! Some were waitin' for trains, which don't run reg'lar no more, an' others were ready to hit the trails north."

"Laddy, what knocks me is Rojas holding Thorne prisoner, trying to make him tell where Mercedes had been hidden," said Belding.

"Shore. It 'd knock anybody."

"The bandit's crazy over her. That's the Spanish of it," replied Belding, his voice rolling. "Rojas is a peon. He's been a slave to the proud Castilian. He loves Mercedes as he hates her. When I was down in Durango I saw something of these peons' insane passions. Rojas wants this girl only to have her, then kill her. It's damn strange, boys, and even with Thorne here our troubles have just begun."

"Tom, you spoke correct," said Jim Ladd, in his cool drawl.

"Shore I'm not sayin' what I think," added Ladd. But the look of him was not indicative of a tranquil optimism.

Thorne was put to bed in Gale's room. He was very weak, yet he would keep Mercedes's hand and gaze at her with unbelieving eyes. Mercedes's failing hold on hope and strength seemed to have been a fantasy; she was again vivid, magnetic, beautiful, shot through and through with intense and throbbing life. She induced him to take food and drink. Then, fighting sleep with what little strength he had left, at last he succumbed.

For all Dick could ascertain his friend never stirred an eyelash nor a finger for twenty-seven hours. When he awoke he was pale, weak, but the old Thorne.

"Hello, Dick; I didn't dream it then," he said. "There you are, and my darling with the proud, dark eyes—she's here?"

"Why, yes, you locoed cavalryman."

"Say, what's happened to you? It can't be those clothes and a little bronze on your face.... Dick, you're older—you've changed. You're not so thickly built. By Gad, if you don't look fine!"

"Thanks. I'm sorry I can't return the compliment. You're about the seediest, hungriest-looking fellow I ever saw.... Say, old man, you must have had a tough time."

A dark and somber fire burned out the happiness in Thorne's eyes.

"Dick, don't make me—don't let me think of that fiend Rojas!.... I'm here now. I'll be well in a day or two. Then!..."

Mercedes came in, radiant and soft-voiced. She fell upon her knees beside Thorne's bed, and neither of them appeared to see Nell enter with a tray. Then Gale and Nell made a good deal of unnecessary bustle in moving a small table close to the bed. Mercedes had forgotten for the moment that her lover had been a starving man. If Thorne remembered it he did not care. They held hands and looked at each other without speaking.

"Nell, I thought I had it bad," whispered Dick. "But I'm not—"

"Hush. It's beautiful," replied Nell, softly; and she tried to coax Dick from the room.

Dick, however, thought he ought to remain at least long enough to tell Thorne that a man in his condition could not exist solely upon love.

Mercedes sprang up blushing with pretty, penitent manner and moving white hands eloquent of her condition.

"Oh, Mercedes—don't go!" cried Thorne, as she stepped to the door.

"Senor Dick will stay. He is not mucha malo for you—as I am."

Then she smiled and went out.

"Good Lord!" exclaimed Thorne. "How I love her. Dick, isn't she the most beautiful, the loveliest, the finest—"

"George, I share your enthusiasm," said Dick, dryly, "but Mercedes isn't the only girl on earth."

Manifestly this was a startling piece of information, and struck Thorne in more than one way.

"George," went on Dick, "did you happen to observe the girl who saved your life—who incidentally just fetched in your breakfast?"

"Nell Burton! Why, of course. She's brave, a wonderful girl, and really nice-looking."

"You long, lean, hungry beggar! That was the young lady who might answer the raving eulogy you just got out of your system.... I—well, you haven't cornered the love market!"

Thorne uttered some kind of a sound that his weakened condition would not allow to be a whoop.

"Dick! Do you mean it?"

"I shore do, as Laddy says."

"I'm glad, Dick, with all my heart. I wondered at the changed look you wear. Why, boy, you've got a different front.... Call the lady in, and you bet I'll look her over right. I can see better now."

"Eat your breakfast. There's plenty of time to dazzle you afterward."

Thorne fell to upon his breakfast and made it vanish with magic speed. Meanwhile Dick told him something of a ranger's life along the border.

"You needn't waste your breath," said Thorne. "I guess I can see. Belding and those rangers have made you the real thing—the real Western goods.... What I want to know is all about the girl."

"Well, Laddy swears she's got your girl roped in the corral for looks."

"That's not possible. I'll have to talk to Laddy.... But she must be a wonder, or Dick Gale would never have fallen for her.... Isn't it great, Dick? I'm here! Mercedes is well—safe! You've got a girl! Oh!.... But say, I haven't a dollar to my name. I had a lot of money, Dick, and those robbers stole it, my watch—everything. Damn that little black Greaser! He got Mercedes's letters. I wish you could have seen him trying to read them. He's simply nutty over her, Dick. I could have borne the loss of money and valuables—but those beautiful, wonderful letters— they're gone!"

"Cheer up. You have the girl. Belding will make you a proposition presently. The future smiles, old friend. If this rebel business was only ended!"

"Dick, you're going to be my savior twice over.... Well, now, listen to me." His gay excitement changed to earnest gravity. "I want to marry Mercedes at once. Is there a padre here?"

"Yes. But are you wise in letting any Mexican, even a priest, know Mercedes is hidden in Forlorn River?"

"It couldn't be kept much longer."

Gale was compelled to acknowledge the truth of this statement.

"I'll marry her first, then I'll face my problem. Fetch the padre, Dick. And ask our kind friends to be witnesses at the ceremony."

Much to Gale's surprise neither Belding nor Ladd objected to the idea of bringing a padre into the household, and thereby making known to at least one Mexican the whereabouts of Mercedes Castaneda. Belding's caution was wearing out in wrath at the persistent unsettled condition of the border, and Ladd grew only the cooler and more silent as possibilities of trouble multiplied.

Gale fetched the padre, a little, weazened, timid man who was old and without interest or penetration. Apparently he married Mercedes and Thorne as he told his beads or mumbled a prayer. It was Mrs. Belding who kept the occasion from being a merry one, and she insisted on not exciting Thorne. Gale marked her unusual pallor and the singular depth and sweetness of her voice.

"Mother, what's the use of making a funeral out of a marriage?" protested Belding. "A chance for some fun doesn't often come to Forlorn River. You're a fine doctor. Can't you see the girl is what Thorne needed? He'll be well to-morrow, don't mistake me."

"George, when you're all right again we'll add something to present congratulations," said Gale.

"We shore will," put in Ladd.

So with parting jests and smiles they left the couple to themselves.

Belding enjoyed a laugh at his good wife's expense, for Thorne could not be kept in bed, and all in a day, it seemed, he grew so well and so hungry that his friends were delighted, and Mercedes was radiant. In a few days his weakness disappeared and he was going the round of the fields and looking over the ground marked out in Gale's plan of water development. Thorne was highly enthusiastic, and at once staked out his claim for one hundred and sixty acres of land adjoining that of Belding and the rangers. These five tracts took in all the ground necessary for their operations, but in case of the success of the irrigation project the idea was to increase their squatter holdings by purchase of more land down the valley. A hundred families had lately moved to Forlorn River; more were coming all the time; and Belding vowed he could see a vision of the whole Altar Valley green with farms.

Meanwhile everybody in Belding's household, except the quiet Ladd and the watchful Yaqui, in the absence of disturbance of any kind along the border, grew freer and more unrestrained, as if anxiety was slowly fading in the peace of the present. Jim Lash made a trip to the Sonoyta Oasis, and Ladd patrolled fifty miles of the line eastward without incident or sight of raiders. Evidently all the border hawks were in at the picking of Casita.

The February nights were cold, with a dry, icy, penetrating coldness that made a warm fire most comfortable. Belding's household usually congregated in the sitting-room, where burning mesquite logs crackled in the open fireplace. Belding's one passion besides horses was the game of checkers, and he was always wanting to play. On this night he sat playing with Ladd, who never won a game and never could give up trying. Mrs. Belding worked with her needle, stopping from time to time to gaze with thoughtful eyes into the fire. Jim Lash smoked his pipe by the hearth and played with the cat on his knee. Thorne and Mercedes were at the table with pencil and paper; and he was trying his best to keep his attention from his wife's beautiful, animated face long enough to read and write a little Spanish. Gale and Nell sat in a corner watching the bright fire.

There came a low knock on the door. It may have been an ordinary knock, for it did not disturb the women; but to Belding and his rangers it had a subtle meaning.

"Who's that?" asked Belding, as he slowly pushed back his chair and looked at Ladd.

"Yaqui," replied the ranger.

"Come in," called Belding.

The door opened, and the short, square, powerfully built Indian entered. He had a magnificent head, strangely staring, somber black eyes, and very darkly bronzed face. He carried a rifle and strode with impressive dignity.

"Yaqui, what do you want?" asked Belding, and repeated his question in Spanish.

"Senor Dick," replied the Indian.

Gale jumped up, stifling an exclamation, and he went outdoors with Yaqui. He felt his arm gripped, and allowed himself to be led away without asking a question. Yaqui's presence was always one of gloom, and now his stern action boded catastrophe. Once clear of trees he pointed to the level desert across the river, where a row of campfires shone bright out of the darkness.

"Raiders!" ejaculated Gale.

Then he cautioned Yaqui to keep sharp lookout, and, hurriedly returning to the house, he called the men out and told them there were rebels or raiders camping just across the line.

Ladd did not say a word. Belding, with an oath, slammed down his cigar.

"I knew it was too good to last.... Dick, you and Jim stay here while Laddy and I look around."

Dick returned to the sitting-room. The women were nervous and not to be deceived. So Dick merely said Yaqui had sighted some lights off in the desert, and they probably were campfires. Belding did not soon return, and when he did he was alone, and, saying he wanted to consult with the men, he sent Mrs. Belding and the girls to their rooms. His gloomy anxiety had returned.

"Laddy's gone over to scout around and try to find out who the outfit belongs to and how many are in it," said Belding.

"I reckon if they're raiders with bad intentions we wouldn't see no fires," remarked Jim, calmly.

"It 'd be useless, I suppose, to send for the cavalry," said Gale. "Whatever's coming off would be over before the soldiers could be notified, let alone reach here."

"Hell, fellows! I don't look for an attack on Forlorn River," burst out Belding. "I can't believe that possible. These rebel-raiders have a little sense. They wouldn't spoil their game by pulling U. S. soldiers across the line from Yuma to El Paso. But, as Jim says, if they wanted to steal a few horses or cattle they wouldn't build fires. I'm afraid it's—"

Belding hesitated and looked with grim concern at the cavalryman.

"What?" queried Thorne.

"I'm afraid it's Rojas."

Thorne turned pale but did not lose his nerve.

"I thought of that at once. If true, it'll be terrible for Mercedes and me. But Rojas will never get his hands on my wife. If I can't kill him, I'll kill her!... Belding, this is tough on you—this risk we put upon your family. I regret—"

"Cut that kind of talk," replied Belding, bluntly. "Well, if it is Rojas he's acting damn strange for a raider. That's what worries me. We can't do anything but wait. With Laddy and Yaqui out there we won't be surprised. Let's take the best possible view of the situation until we know more. That'll not likely be before to-morrow."

The women of the house might have gotten some sleep that night, but it was certain the men did not get any. Morning broke cold and gray, the 19th of February. Breakfast was prepared earlier than usual, and an air of suppressed waiting excitement pervaded the place. Otherwise the ordinary details of the morning's work continued as on any other day. Ladd came in hungry and cold, and said the Mexicans were not breaking camp. He reported a good-sized force of rebels, and was taciturn as to his idea of forthcoming events.

About an hour after sunrise Yaqui ran in with the information that part of the rebels were crossing the river.

"That can't mean a fight yet," declared Belding. "But get in the house, boys, and make ready anyway. I'll meet them."

"Drive them off the place same as if you had a company of soldiers backin' you," said Ladd. "Don't give them an inch. We're in bad, and the bigger bluff we put up the more likely our chance."

"Belding, you're an officer of the United States. Mexicans are much impressed by show of authority. I've seen that often in camp," said Thorne.

"Oh, I know the white-livered Greasers better than any of you, don't mistake me," replied Belding. He was pale with rage, but kept command over himself.

The rangers, with Yaqui and Thorne, stationed themselves at the several windows of the sitting-room. Rifles and smaller arms and boxes of shells littered the tables and window seats. No small force of besiegers could overcome a resistance such as Belding and his men were capable of making.

"Here they come, boys," called Gale, from his window.

"Rebel-raiders I should say, Laddy."

"Shore. An' a fine outfit of buzzards!"

"Reckon there's about a dozen in the bunch," observed the calm Lash. "Some hosses they're ridin'. Where 'n the hell do they get such hosses, anyhow?"

"Shore, Jim, they work hard an' buy 'em with real silver pesos," replied Ladd, sarcastically.

"Do any of you see Rojas?" whispered Thorne.

"Nix. No dandy bandit in that outfit."

"It's too far to see," said Gale.

The horsemen halted at the corrals. They were orderly and showed no evidence of hostility. They were, however, fully armed. Belding stalked out to meet them. Apparently a leader wanted to parley with him, but Belding would hear nothing. He shook his head, waved his arms, stamped to and fro, and his loud, angry voice could be heard clear back at the house. Whereupon the detachment of rebels retired to the bank of the river, beyond the white post that marked the boundary line, and there they once more drew rein. Belding remained by the corrals watching them, evidently still in threatening mood. Presently a single rider left the troop and trotted his horse back down the road. When he reached the corrals he was seen to halt and pass something to Belding. Then he galloped away to join his comrades.

Belding looked at whatever it was he held in his hand, shook his burley head, and started swiftly for the house. He came striding into the room holding a piece of soiled paper.

"Can't read it and don't know as I want to," he said, savagely.

"Beldin', shore we'd better read it," replied Ladd. "What we want is a line on them Greasers. Whether they're Campo's men or Salazar's, or just a wanderin' bunch of rebels—or Rojas's bandits. Sabe, senor?"

Not one of the men was able to translate the garbled scrawl.

"Shore Mercedes can read it," said Ladd.

Thorne opened a door and called her. She came into the room followed by Nell and Mrs. Belding. Evidently all three divined a critical situation.

"My dear, we want you to read what's written on this paper," said Thorne, as he led her to the table. "It was sent in by rebels, and—and we fear contains bad news for us."

Mercedes gave the writing one swift glance, then fainted in Thorne's arms. He carried her to a couch, and with Nell and Mrs. Belding began to work over her.

Belding looked at his rangers. It was characteristic of the man that, now when catastrophe appeared inevitable, all the gloom and care and angry agitation passed from him.

"Laddy, it's Rojas all right. How many men has he out there?"

"Mebbe twenty. Not more."

"We can lick twice that many Greasers."

"Shore."

Jim Lash removed his pipe long enough to speak.

"I reckon. But it ain't sense to start a fight when mebbe we can avoid it."

"What's your idea?"

"Let's stave the Greaser off till dark. Then Laddy an' me an' Thorne will take Mercedes an' hit the trail for Yuma."

"Camino del Diablo! That awful trail with a woman! Jim, do you forget how many hundreds of men have perished on the Devil's Road?"

"I reckon I ain't forgettin' nothin'," replied Jim. "The waterholes are full now. There's grass, an' we can do the job in six days."

"It's three hundred miles to Yuma."

"Beldin', Jim's idea hits me pretty reasonable," interposed Ladd. "Lord knows that's about the only chance we've got except fightin'."

"But suppose we do stave Rojas off, and you get safely away with Mercedes. Isn't Rojas going to find it out quick? Then what'll he try to do to us who're left here?"

"I reckon he'd find out by daylight," replied Jim. "But, Tom, he ain't agoin' to start a scrap then. He'd want time an' hosses an' men to chase us out on the trail. You see, I'm figgerin' on the crazy Greaser wantin' the girl. I reckon he'll try to clean up here to get her. But he's too smart to fight you for nothin'. Rojas may be nutty about women, but he's afraid of the U. S. Take my word for it he'd discover the trail in the mornin' an' light out on it. I reckon with ten hours' start we could travel comfortable."

Belding paced up and down the room. Jim and Ladd whispered together. Gale walked to the window and looked out at the distant group of bandits, and then turned his gaze to rest upon Mercedes. She was conscious now, and her eyes seemed all the larger and blacker for the whiteness of her face. Thorne held her hands, and the other women were trying to still her tremblings.

No one but Gale saw the Yaqui in the background looking down upon the Spanish girl. All of Yaqui's looks were strange; but this singularly so. Gale marked it, and felt he would never forget. Mercedes's beauty had never before struck him as being so exquisite, so alluring as now when she lay stricken. Gale wondered if the Indian was affected by her loveliness, her helplessness, or her terror. Yaqui had seen Mercedes only a few times, and upon each of these he had appeared to be fascinated. Could the strange Indian, because his hate for Mexicans was so great, be gloating over her misery? Something about Yaqui—a noble austerity of countenance—made Gale feel his suspicion unjust.

Presently Belding called his rangers to him, and then Thorne.

"Listen to this," he said, earnestly. "I'll go out and have a talk with Rojas. I'll try to reason with him; tell him to think a long time before he sheds blood on Uncle Sam's soil. That he's now after an American's wife! I'll not commit myself, nor will I refuse outright to consider his demands, nor will I show the least fear of him. I'll play for time. If my bluff goes through... well and good.... After dark the four of you, Laddy, Jim, Dick, and Thorne, will take Mercedes and my best white horses, and, with Yaqui as guide, circle round through Altar Valley to the trail, and head for Yuma.... Wait now, Laddy. Let me finish. I want you to take the white horses for two reasons—to save them and to save you. Savvy? If Rojas should follow on my horses he'd be likely to catch you. Also, you can pack a great deal more than on the bronchs. Also, the big horses can travel faster and farther on little grass and water. I want you to take the Indian, because in a case of this kind he'll be a godsend. If you get headed or lost or have to circle off the trail, think what it 'd mean to have Yaqui with you. He knows Sonora as no Greaser knows it. He could hide you, find water and grass, when you would absolutely believe it impossible. The Indian is loyal. He has his debt to pay, and he'll pay it, don't mistake me. When you're gone I'll hide Nell so Rojas won't see her if he searches the place. Then I think I could sit down and wait without any particular worry."

The rangers approved of Belding's plan, and Thorne choked in his effort to express his gratitude.

"All right, we'll chance it," concluded Belding. "I'll go out now and call Rojas and his outfit over... Say, it might be as well for me to know just what he said in that paper."

Thorne went to the side of his wife.

"Mercedes, we've planned to outwit Rojas. Will you tell us just what he wrote?"

The girl sat up, her eyes dilating, and with her hands clasping Thorne's. She said:

"Rojas swore—by his saints and his virgin—that if I wasn't given—to him—in twenty-four hours—he would set fire to the village—kill the men—carry off the women—hang the children on cactus thorns!"

A moment's silence followed her last halting whisper.

"By his saints an' his virgin!" echoed Ladd. He laughed—a cold, cutting, deadly laugh—significant and terrible.

Then the Yaqui uttered a singular cry. Gale had heard this once before, and now he remembered it was at the Papago Well.

"Look at the Indian," whispered Belding, hoarsely. "Damn if I don't believe he understood every word Mercedes said. And, gentlemen, don't mistake me, if he ever gets near Senor Rojas there'll be some gory Aztec knife work."

Yaqui had moved close to Mercedes, and stood beside her as she leaned against her husband. She seemed impelled to meet the Indian's gaze, and evidently it was so powerful or hypnotic that it wrought irresistibly upon her. But she must have seen or divined what was beyond the others, for she offered him her trembling hand. Yaqui took it and laid it against his body in a strange motion, and bowed his head. Then he stepped back into the shadow of the room.

Belding went outdoors while the rangers took up their former position at the west window. Each had his own somber thoughts, Gale imagined, and knew his own were dark enough. A slow fire crept along his veins. He saw Belding halt at the corrals and wave his hand. Then the rebels mounted and came briskly up the road, this time to rein in abreast.

Wherever Rojas had kept himself upon the former advance was not clear; but he certainly was prominently in sight now. He made a gaudy, almost a dashing figure. Gale did not recognize the white sombrero, the crimson scarf, the velvet jacket, nor any feature of the dandy's costume; but their general effect, the whole ensemble, recalled vividly to mind his first sight of the bandit. Rojas dismounted and seemed to be listening. He betrayed none of the excitement Gale had seen in him that night at the Del Sol. Evidently this composure struck Ladd and Lash as unusual in a Mexican supposed to be laboring under stress of feeling. Belding made gestures, vehemently bobbed his big head, appeared to talk with his body as much as with his tongue. Then Rojas was seen to reply, and after that it was clear that the talk became painful and difficult. It ended finally in what appeared to be mutual understanding. Rojas mounted and rode away with his men, while Belding came tramping back to the house.

As he entered the door his eyes were shining, his big hands were clenched, and he was breathing audibly.

"You can rope me if I'm not locoed!" he burst out. "I went out to conciliate a red-handed little murderer, and damn me if I didn't meet a—a—well, I've not suitable name handy. I started my bluff and got along pretty well, but I forgot to mention that Mercedes was Thorne's wife. And what do you think? Rojas swore he loved Mercedes—swore he'd marry her right here in Forlorn River—swore he would give up robbing and killing people, and take her away from Mexico. He has gold—jewels. He swore if he didn't get her nothing mattered. He'd die anyway without her.... And here's the strange thing. I believe him! He was cold as ice, and all hell inside. Never saw a Greaser like him. Well, I pretended to be greatly impressed. We got to talking friendly, I suppose, though I didn't understand half he said, and I imagine he gathered less what I said. Anyway, without my asking he said for me to think it over for a day and then we'd talk again."

"Shore we're born lucky!" ejaculated Ladd.

"I reckon Rojas'll be smart enough to string his outfit across the few trails leadin' out of Forlorn River," remarked Jim.

"That needn't worry us. All we want is dark to come," replied Belding. "Yaqui will slip through. If we thank any lucky stars let it be for the Indian.... Now, boys, put on your thinking caps. You'll take eight horses, the pick of my bunch. You must pack all that's needed for a possible long trip. Mind, Yaqui may lead you down into some wild Sonora valley and give Rojas the slip. You may get to Yuma in six days, and maybe in six weeks. Yet you've got to pack light—a small pack in saddles—larger ones on the two free horses. You may have a big fight. Laddy, take the .405. Dick will pack his Remington. All of you go gunned heavy. But the main thing is a pack that 'll be light enough for swift travel, yet one that 'll keep you from starving on the desert."

The rest of that day passed swiftly. Dick had scarcely a word with Nell, and all the time, as he chose and deliberated and worked over his little pack, there was a dull pain in his heart.

The sun set, twilight fell, then night closed down fortunately a night slightly overcast. Gale saw the white horses pass his door like silent ghosts. Even Blanco Diablo made no sound, and that fact was indeed a tribute to the Yaqui. Gale went out to put his saddle on Blanco Sol. The horse rubbed a soft nose against his shoulder. Then Gale returned to the sitting-room. There was nothing more to do but wait and say good-by. Mercedes came clad in leather chaps and coat, a slim stripling of a cowboy, her dark eyes flashing. Her beauty could not be hidden, and now hope and courage had fired her blood.

Gale drew Nell off into the shadow of the room. She was trembling, and as she leaned toward him she was very different from the coy girl who had so long held him aloof. He took her into his arms.

"Dearest, I'm going—soon.... And maybe I'll never—"

"Dick, do—don't say it," sobbed Nell, with her head on his breast.

"I might never come back," he went on, steadily. "I love you—I've loved you ever since the first moment I saw you. Do you care for me—a little?"

"Dear Dick—de-dear Dick, my heart is breaking," faltered Nell, as she clung to him.

"It might be breaking for Mercedes—for Laddy and Jim. I want to hear something for myself. Something to have on long marches—round lonely campfires. Something to keep my spirit alive. Oh, Nell, you can't imagine that silence out there—that terrible world of sand and stone!... Do you love me?"

"Yes, yes. Oh, I love you so! I never knew it till now. I love you so. Dick, I'll be safe and I'll wait—and hope and pray for your return."

"If I come back—no—when I come back, will you marry me?"

"I—I—oh yes!" she whispered, and returned his kiss.

Belding was in the room speaking softly.

"Nell, darling, I must go," said Dick.

"I'm a selfish little coward," cried Nell. "It's so splendid of you all. I ought to glory in it, but I can't. ... Fight if you must, Dick. Fight for that lovely persecuted girl. I'll love you—the more.... Oh! Good-by! Good-by!"

With a wrench that shook him Gale let her go. He heard Belding's soft voice.

"Yaqui says the early hour's best. Trust him, Laddy. Remember what I say—Yaqui's a godsend."

Then they were all outside in the pale gloom under the trees. Yaqui mounted Blanco Diablo; Mercedes was lifted upon White Woman; Thorne climbed astride Queen; Jim Lash was already upon his horse, which was as white as the others but bore no name; Ladd mounted the stallion Blanco Torres, and gathered up the long halters of the two pack horses; Gale came last with Blanco Sol.

As he toed the stirrup, hand on mane and pommel, Gale took one more look in at the door. Nell stood in the gleam of light, her hair shining, face like ashes, her eyes dark, her lips parted, her arms outstretched. That sweet and tragic picture etched its cruel outlines into Gale's heart. He waved his hand and then fiercely leaped into the saddle.

Blanco Sol stepped out.

Before Gale stretched a line of moving horses, white against dark shadows. He could not see the head of that column; he scarcely heard a soft hoofbeat. A single star shone out of a rift in thin clouds. There was no wind. The air was cold. The dark space of desert seemed to yawn. To the left across the river flickered a few campfires. The chill night, silent and mystical, seemed to close in upon Gale; and he faced the wide, quivering, black level with keen eyes and grim intent, and an awakening of that wild rapture which came like a spell to him in the open desert.

XI

ACROSS CACTUS AND LAVA

BLANCO SOL showed no inclination to bend his head to the alfalfa which swished softly about his legs. Gale felt the horse's sensitive, almost human alertness. Sol knew as well as his master the nature of that flight.

At the far corner of the field Yaqui halted, and slowly the line of white horses merged into a compact mass. There was a trail here leading down to the river. The campfires were so close that the bright blazes could be seen in movement, and dark forms crossed in front of them. Yaqui slipped out of his saddle. He ran his hand over Diablo's nose and spoke low, and repeated this action for each of the other horses. Gale had long ceased to question the strange Indian's behavior. There was no explaining or understanding many of his manoeuvers. But the results of them were always thought-provoking. Gale had never seen horse stand so silently as in this instance; no stamp—no champ of bit—no toss of head—no shake of saddle or pack—no heave or snort! It seemed they had become imbued with the spirit of the Indian.

Yaqui moved away into the shadows as noiselessly as if he were one of them. The darkness swallowed him. He had taken a parallel with the trail. Gale wondered if Yaqui meant to try to lead his string of horses by the rebel sentinels. Ladd had his head bent low, his ear toward the trail. Jim's long neck had the arch of a listening deer. Gale listened, too, and as the slow, silent moments went by his faculty of hearing grew more acute from strain. He heard Blanco Sol breathe; he heard the pound of his own heart; he heard the silken rustle of the alfalfa; he heard a faint, far-off sound of voice, like a lost echo. Then his ear seemed to register a movement of air, a disturbance so soft as to be nameless. Then followed long, silent moments.

Yaqui appeared as he had vanished. He might have been part of the shadows. But he was there. He started off down the trail leading Diablo. Again the white line stretched slowly out. Gale fell in behind. A bench of ground, covered with sparse greasewood, sloped gently down to the deep, wide arroyo of Forlorn River. Blanco Sol shied a few feet out of the trail. Peering low with keen eyes, Gale made out three objects—a white sombrero, a blanket, and a Mexican lying face down. The Yaqui had stolen upon this sentinel like a silent wind of death. Just then a desert coyote wailed, and the wild cry fitted the darkness and the Yaqui's deed.

Once under the dark lee of the river bank Yaqui caused another halt, and he disappeared as before. It seemed to Gale that the Indian started to cross the pale level sandbed of the river, where stones stood out gray, and the darker line of opposite shore was visible. But he vanished, and it was impossible to tell whether he went one way or another. Moments passed. The horses held heads up, looked toward the glimmering campfires and listened. Gale thrilled with the meaning of it all—the night—the silence—the flight—and the wonderful Indian stealing with the slow inevitableness of doom upon another sentinel. An hour passed and Gale seemed to have become deadened to all sense of hearing. There were no more sounds in the world. The desert was as silent as it was black. Yet again came that strange change in the tensity of Gale's ear-strain, a check, a break, a vibration—and this time the sound did not go nameless. It might have been moan of wind or wail of far-distant wolf, but Gale imagined it was the strangling death-cry of another guard, or that strange, involuntary utterance of the Yaqui. Blanco Sol trembled in all his great frame, and then Gale was certain the sound was not imagination.

That certainty, once for all, fixed in Gale's mind the mood of his flight. The Yaqui dominated the horses and the rangers. Thorne and Mercedes were as persons under a spell. The Indian's strange silence, the feeling of mystery and power he seemed to create, all that was incomprehensible about him were emphasized in the light of his slow, sure, and ruthless action. If he dominated the others, surely he did more for Gale—colored his thoughts—presage the wild and terrible future of that flight. If Rojas embodied all the hatred and passion of the peon— scourged slave for a thousand years—then Yaqui embodied all the darkness, the cruelty, the white, sun-heated blood, the ferocity, the tragedy of the desert.

Suddenly the Indian stalked out of the gloom. He mounted Diablo and headed across the river. Once more the line of moving white shadows stretched out. The soft sand gave forth no sound at all. The glimmering campfires sank behind the western bank. Yaqui led the way into the willows, and there was faint swishing of leaves; then into the mesquite, and there was faint rustling of branches. The glimmering lights appeared again, and grotesque forms of saguaros loomed darkly. Gale peered sharply along the trail, and, presently, on the pale sand under a cactus, there lay a blanketed form, prone, outstretched, a carbine clutched in one hand, a cigarette, still burning, in the other.

The cavalcade of white horses passed within five hundred yards of campfires, around which dark forms moved in plain sight. Soft pads in sand, faint metallic tickings of steel on thorns, low, regular breathing of horses—these were all the sounds the fugitives made, and they could not have been heard at one-fifth the distance. The lights disappeared from time to time, grew dimmer, more flickering, and at last they vanished altogether. Belding's fleet and tireless steeds were out in front; the desert opened ahead wide, dark, vast. Rojas and his rebels were behind, eating, drinking, careless. The somber shadow lifted from Gale's heart. He held now an unquenchable faith in the Yaqui. Belding would be listening back there along the river. He would know of the escape. He would tell Nell, and then hide her safely. As Gale accepted a strange and fatalistic foreshadowing of toil, blood, and agony in this desert journey, so he believed in Mercedes's ultimate freedom and happiness, and his own return to the girl who had grown dearer than life.

A cold, gray dawn was fleeing before a rosy sun when Yaqui halted the march at Papago Well. The horses were taken to water, then led down the arroyo into the grass. Here packs were slipped, saddles removed. Mercedes was cold, lame, tired, but happy. It warmed Gale's blood to look at her. The shadow of fear still lay in her eyes, but it was passing. Hope and courage shone there, and affection for her ranger protectors and the Yaqui, and unutterable love for the cavalryman. Jim Lash remarked how cleverly they had fooled the rebels.

"Shore they'll be comin' along," replied Ladd.

They built a fire, cooked and ate. The Yaqui spoke only one word: "Sleep." Blankets were spread. Mercedes dropped into a deep slumber, her head on Thorne's shoulder. Excitement kept Thorne awake. The two rangers dozed beside the fire. Gale shared the Yaqui's watch. The sun began to climb and the icy edge of dawn to wear away. Rabbits bobbed their cotton tails under the mesquite. Gale climbed a rocky wall above the arroyo bank, and there, with command over the miles of the back-trail, he watched.

It was a sweeping, rolling, wrinkled, and streaked range of desert that he saw, ruddy in the morning sunlight, with patches of cactus and mesquite rough-etched in shimmering gloom. No Name Mountains split the eastern sky, towering high, gloomy, grand, with purple veils upon their slopes. They were forty miles away and looked five. Gale thought of the girl who was there under their shadow.

Yaqui kept the horses bunched, and he led them from one little park of galleta grass to another. At the end of three hours he took them to water. Upon his return Gale clambered down from his outlook, the rangers grew active. Mercedes was awakened; and soon the party faced westward, their long shadows moving before them. Yaqui led with Blanco Diablo in a long, easy lope. The arroyo washed itself out into flat desert, and the greens began to shade into gray, and then the gray into red. Only sparse cactus and weathered ledges dotted the great low roll of a rising escarpment. Yaqui suited the gait of his horse to the lay of the land, and his followers accepted his pace. There were canter and trot, and swift walk and slow climb, and long swing— miles up and down and forward. The sun soared hot. The heated air lifted, and incoming currents from the west swept low and hard over the barren earth. In the distance, all around the horizon, accumulations of dust seemed like ranging, mushrooming yellow clouds.

Yaqui was the only one of the fugitives who never looked back. Mercedes did it the most. Gale felt what compelled her, he could not resist it himself. But it was a vain search. For a thousand puffs of white and yellow dust rose from that backward sweep of desert, and any one of them might have been blown from under horses' hoofs. Gale had a conviction that when Yaqui gazed back toward the well and the shining plain beyond, there would be reason for it. But when the sun lost its heat and the wind died down Yaqui took long and careful surveys westward from the high points on the trail. Sunset was not far off, and there in a bare, spotted valley lay Coyote Tanks, the only waterhole between Papago Well and the Sonoyta Oasis. Gale used his glass, told Yaqui there was no smoke, no sign of life; still the Indian fixed his falcon eyes on distant spots looked long. It was as if his vision could not detect what reason or cunning or intuition, perhaps an instinct, told him was there. Presently in a sheltered spot, where blown sand had not obliterated the trail, Yaqui found the tracks of horses. The curve of the iron shoes pointed westward. An intersecting trail from the north came in here. Gale thought the tracks either one or two days old. Ladd said they were one day. The Indian shook his head.

No farther advance was undertaken. The Yaqui headed south and traveled slowly, climbing to the brow of a bold height of weathered mesa. There he sat his horse and waited. No one questioned him. The rangers dismounted to stretch their legs, and Mercedes was lifted to a rock, where she rested. Thorne had gradually yielded to the desert's influence for silence. He spoke once or twice to Gale, and occasionally whispered to Mercedes. Gale fancied his friend would soon learn that necessary speech in desert travel meant a few greetings, a few words to make real the fact of human companionship, a few short, terse terms for the business of day or night, and perhaps a stern order or a soft call to a horse.

The sun went down, and the golden, rosy veils turned to blue and shaded darker till twilight was there in the valley. Only the spurs of mountains, spiring the near and far horizon, retained their clear outline. Darkness approached, and the clear peaks faded. The horses stamped to be on the move.

"Malo!" exclaimed the Yaqui.

He did not point with arm, but his falcon head was outstretched, and his piercing eyes gazed at the blurring spot which marked the location of Coyote Tanks.

"Jim, can you see anything?" asked Ladd.

"Nope, but I reckon he can."

Darkness increased momentarily till night shaded the deepest part of the valley.

Then Ladd suddenly straightened up, turned to his horse, and muttered low under his breath.

"I reckon so," said Lash, and for once his easy, good-natured tone was not in evidence. His voice was harsh.

Gale's eyes, keen as they were, were last of the rangers to see tiny, needle-points of light just faintly perceptible in the blackness.

"Laddy! Campfires?" he asked, quickly.

"Shore's you're born, my boy."

"How many?"

Ladd did not reply; but Yaqui held up his hand, his fingers wide. Five campfires! A strong force of rebels or raiders or some other desert troop was camping at Coyote Tanks.

Yaqui sat his horse for a moment, motionless as stone, his dark face immutable and impassive. Then he stretched wide his right arm in the direction of No Name Mountains, now losing their last faint traces of the afterglow, and he shook his head. He made the same impressive gesture toward the Sonoyta Oasis with the same somber negation.

Thereupon he turned Diablo's head to the south and started down the slope. His manner had been decisive, even stern. Lash did not question it, nor did Ladd. Both rangers hesitated, however, and showed a strange, almost sullen reluctance which Gale had never seen in them before. Raiders were one thing, Rojas was another; Camino del Diablo still another; but that vast and desolate and unwatered waste of cactus and lava, the Sonora Desert, might appall the stoutest heart. Gale felt his own sink—felt himself flinch.

"Oh, where is he going?" cried Mercedes. Her poignant voice seemed to break a spell.

"Shore, lady, Yaqui's goin' home," replied Ladd, gently. "An' considerin' our troubles I reckon we ought to thank God he knows the way."

They mounted and rode down the slope toward the darkening south.

Not until night travel was obstructed by a wall of cactus did the Indian halt to make a dry camp. Water and grass for the horses and fire to cook by were not to be had. Mercedes bore up surprisingly; but she fell asleep almost the instant her thirst had been allayed. Thorne laid her upon a blanket and covered her. The men ate and drank. Diablo was the only horse that showed impatience; but he was angry, and not in distress. Blanco Sol licked Gale's hand and stood patiently. Many a time had he taken his rest at night without a drink. Yaqui again bade the men sleep. Ladd said he would take the early watch; but from the way the Indian shook his head and settled himself against a stone, it appeared if Ladd remained awake he would have company. Gale lay down weary of limb and eye. He heard the soft thump of hoofs, the sough of wind in the cactus—then no more.

When he awoke there was bustle and stir about him. Day had not yet dawned, and the air was freezing cold. Yaqui had found a scant bundle of greasewood which served to warm them and to cook breakfast. Mercedes was not aroused till the last moment.

Day dawned with the fugitives in the saddle. A picketed wall of cactus hedged them in, yet the Yaqui made a tortuous path, that, zigzag as it might, in the main always headed south. It was wonderful how he slipped Diablo through the narrow aisles of thorns, saving the horse and saving himself. The others were torn and clutched and held and stung. The way was a flat, sandy pass between low mountain ranges. There were open spots and aisles and squares of sand; and hedging rows of prickly pear and the huge spider-legged ocatillo and hummocky masses of clustered bisnagi. The day grew dry and hot. A fragrant wind blew through the pass. Cactus flowers bloomed, red and yellow and magenta. The sweet, pale Ajo lily gleamed in shady corners.

Ten miles of travel covered the length of the pass. It opened wide upon a wonderful scene, an arboreal desert, dominated by its pure light green, yet lined by many merging colors. And it rose slowly to a low dim and dark-red zone of lava, spurred, peaked, domed by volcano cones, a wild and ragged region, illimitable as the horizon.

The Yaqui, if not at fault, was yet uncertain. His falcon eyes searched and roved, and became fixed at length at the southwest, and toward this he turned his horse. The great, fluted saguaros, fifty, sixty feet high, raised columnal forms, and their branching limbs and curving lines added a grace to the desert. It was the low-bushed cactus that made the toil and pain of travel. Yet these thorny forms were beautiful.

In the basins between the ridges, to right and left along the floor of low plains the mirage glistened, wavered, faded, vanished—lakes and trees and clouds. Inverted mountains hung suspended in the lilac air and faint tracery of white-walled cities.

At noon Yaqui halted the cavalcade. He had selected a field of bisnagi cactus for the place of rest. Presently his reason became obvious. With long, heavy knife he cut off the tops of these barrel-shaped plants. He scooped out soft pulp, and with stone and hand then began to pound the deeper pulp into a juicy mass. When he threw this out there was a little water left, sweet, cool water which man and horse shared eagerly. Thus he made even the desert's fiercest growths minister to their needs.

But he did not halt long. Miles of gray-green spiked walls lay between him and that line of ragged, red lava which manifestly he must reach before dark. The travel became faster, straighter. And the glistening thorns clutched and clung to leather and cloth and flesh. The horses reared, snorted, balked, leaped—but they were sent on. Only Blanco Sol, the patient, the plodding, the indomitable, needed no goad or spur. Waves and scarfs and wreaths of heat smoked up from the sand. Mercedes reeled in her saddle. Thorne bade her drink, bathed her face, supported her, and then gave way to Ladd, who took the girl with him on Torre's broad back. Yaqui's unflagging purpose and iron arm were bitter and hateful to the proud and haughty spirit of Blanco Diablo. For once Belding's great white devil had met his master. He fought rider, bit, bridle, cactus, sand—and yet he went on and on, zigzagging, turning, winding, crashing through the barbed growths. The middle of the afternoon saw Thorne reeling in his saddle, and then, wherever possible, Gale's powerful arm lent him strength to hold his seat.

The giant cactus came to be only so in name. These saguaros were thinning out, growing stunted, and most of them were single columns. Gradually other cactus forms showed a harder struggle for existence, and the spaces of sand between were wider. But now the dreaded, glistening *choya* began to show pale and gray and white upon the rising slope. Round-topped hills, sunset-colored above, blue-black below, intervened to hide the distant spurs and peaks. Mile and mile long tongues of red lava streamed out between the hills and wound down to stop abruptly upon the slope.

The fugitives were entering a desolate, burned-out world. It rose above them in limitless, gradual ascent and spread wide to east and west. Then the waste of sand began to yield to cinders. The horses sank to their fetlocks as they toiled on. A fine, choking dust blew back from the leaders, and men coughed and horses snorted. The huge, round hills rose smooth, symmetrical, colored as if the setting sun was shining on bare, blue-black surfaces. But the sun was now behind the hills. In between ran the streams of lava. The horsemen skirted the edge between slope of hill and perpendicular ragged wall. This red lava seemed to have flowed and hardened there only yesterday. It was broken sharp, dull rust color, full of cracks and caves and crevices, and everywhere upon its jagged surface grew the white-thorned *choya*.

Again twilight encompassed the travelers. But there was still light enough for Gale to see the constricted passage open into a wide, deep space where the dull color was relieved by the gray of gnarled and dwarfed mesquite. Blanco Sol, keenest of scent, whistled his welcome herald of water. The other horses answered, quickened their gait. Gale smelled it, too, sweet, cool, damp on the dry air.

Yaqui turned the corner of a pocket in the lava wall. The file of white horses rounded the corner after him. And Gale, coming last, saw the pale, glancing gleam of a pool of water beautiful in the twilight.

Next day the Yaqui's relentless driving demand on the horses was no longer in evidence. He lost no time, but he did not hasten. His course wound between low cinder dunes which limited their view of the surrounding country. These dunes finally sank down to a black floor as hard as flint with tongues of lava to the left, and to the right the slow descent into the cactus plain. Yaqui was now traveling due west. It was Gale's idea that the Indian was skirting the first sharp-toothed slope of a vast volcanic plateau which formed the western half of the Sonora Desert and extended to the Gulf of California. Travel was slow, but not exhausting for rider or beast. A little sand and meager grass gave a grayish tinge to the strip of black ground between lava and plain.

That day, as the manner rather than the purpose of the Yaqui changed, so there seemed to be subtle differences in the others of the party. Gale himself lost a certain sickening dread, which had not been for himself, but for Mercedes and Nell, and Thorne and the rangers. Jim, good-natured again, might have been patrolling the boundary line. Ladd lost his taciturnity and his gloom changed to a cool, careless air. A mood that was almost defiance began to be manifested in Thorne. It was in Mercedes, however, that Gale marked the most significant change. Her collapse the preceding day might never have been. She was lame and sore; she rode her saddle sidewise, and often she had to be rested and helped; but she had found a reserve fund of strength, and her mental condition was not the same that it had been. Her burden of fear had been lifted. Gale saw in her the difference he always felt in himself after a few days in the desert. Already

Mercedes and he, and all of them, had begun to respond to the desert spirit. Moreover, Yaqui's strange influence must have been a call to the primitive.

Thirty miles of easy stages brought the fugitives to another waterhole, a little round pocket under the heaved-up edge of lava. There was spare, short, bleached grass for the horses, but no wood for a fire. This night there was question and reply, conjecture, doubt, opinion, and conviction expressed by the men of the party. But the Indian, who alone could have told where they were, where they were going, what chance they had to escape, maintained his stoical silence. Gale took the early watch, Ladd the midnight one, and Lash that of the morning.

The day broke rosy, glorious, cold as ice. Action was necessary to make useful benumbed hands and feet. Mercedes was fed while yet wrapped in blankets. Then, while the packs were being put on and horses saddled, she walked up and down, slapping her hands, warming her ears. The rose color of the dawn was in her cheeks, and the wonderful clearness of desert light in her eyes. Thorne's eyes sought her constantly. The rangers watched her. The Yaqui bent his glance upon her only seldom; but when he did look it seemed that his strange, fixed, and inscrutable face was about to break into a smile. Yet that never happened. Gale himself was surprised to find how often his own glance found the slender, dark, beautiful Spaniard. Was this because of her beauty? he wondered. He thought not altogether. Mercedes was a woman. She represented something in life that men of all races for thousands of years had loved to see and own, to revere and debase, to fight and die for.

It was a significant index to the day's travel that Yaqui should keep a blanket from the pack and tear it into strips to bind the legs of the horses. It meant the dreaded *choya* and the knife-edged lava. That Yaqui did not mount Diablo was still more significant. Mercedes must ride; but the others must walk.

The Indian led off into one of the gray notches between the tumbled streams of lava. These streams were about thirty feet high, a rotting mass of splintered lava, rougher than any other kind of roughness in the world. At the apex of the notch, where two streams met, a narrow gully wound and ascended. Gale caught sight of the dim, pale shadow of a one-time trail. Near at hand it was invisible; he had to look far ahead to catch the faint tracery. Yaqui led Diablo into it, and then began the most laborious and vexatious and painful of all slow travel.

Once up on top of that lava bed, Gale saw stretching away, breaking into millions of crests and ruts, a vast, red-black field sweeping onward and upward, with ragged, low ridges and mounds and spurs leading higher and higher to a great, split escarpment wall, above which dim peaks shone hazily blue in the distance.

He looked no more in that direction. To keep his foothold, to save his horse, cost him all energy and attention. The course was marked out for him in the tracks of the other horses. He had only to follow. But nothing could have been more difficult. The disintegrating surface of a lava bed was at once the roughest, the hardest, the meanest, the cruelest, the most deceitful kind of ground to travel.

It was rotten, yet it had corners as hard and sharp as pikes. It was rough, yet as slippery as ice. If there was a foot of level surface, that space would be one to break through under a horse's hoofs. It was seamed, lined, cracked, ridged, knotted iron. This lava bed resembled a tremendously magnified clinker. It had been a running sea of molten flint, boiling, bubbling, spouting, and it had burst its surface into a million sharp facets as it hardened. The color was dull, dark, angry red, like no other red, inflaming to the eye. The millions of minute crevices were dominated by deep fissures and holes, ragged and rough beyond all comparison.

The fugitives made slow progress. They picked a cautious, winding way to and fro in little steps here and there along the many twists of the trail, up and down the unavoidable depressions, round and round the holes. At noon, so winding back upon itself had been their course, they appeared to have come only a short distance up the lava slope.

It was rough work for them; it was terrible work for the horses. Blanco Diablo refused to answer to the power of the Yaqui. He balked, he plunged, he bit and kicked. He had to be pulled and beaten over many places. Mercedes's horse almost threw her, and she was put upon Blanco Sol. The white charger snorted a protest, then, obedient to Gale's stern call, patiently lowered his noble head and pawed the lava for a footing that would hold.

The lava caused Gale toil and worry and pain, but he hated the *choyas*. As the travel progressed this species of cactus increased in number of plants and in size. Everywhere the red lava was spotted with little round patches of glistening frosty white. And under every bunch of *choya*, along and in the trail, were the discarded joints, like little frosty pine cones covered with spines. It was utterly impossible always to be on the lookout for these, and when Gale stepped on one, often as not the steel-like thorns pierced leather and flesh. Gale came almost to believe what he had heard claimed by desert travelers—that the *choya* was alive and leaped at man or beast. Certain it was when Gale passed one, if he did not put all attention to avoiding it, he was hooked through his chaps and held by barbed thorns. The pain was almost unendurable. It was like no other. It burned, stung, beat—almost seemed to freeze. It made useless arm or leg. It made him bite his tongue to keep from crying out. It made the sweat roll off him. It made him sick.

Moreover, bad as the *choya* was for man, it was infinitely worse for beast. A jagged stab from this poisoned cactus was the only thing Blanco Sol could not stand. Many times that day, before he carried Mercedes, he had wildly snorted, and then stood trembling while Gale picked broken thorns from the muscular legs. But after Mercedes had been put upon Sol Gale made sure no *choya* touched him.

The afternoon passed like the morning, in ceaseless winding and twisting and climbing along this abandoned trail. Gale saw many waterholes, mostly dry, some containing water, all of them catch-basins, full only after rainy season. Little ugly bunched bushes, that Gale scarcely recognized as mesquites, grew near these holes; also stunted greasewood and prickly pear. There was no grass, and the *choya* alone flourished in that hard soil.

Darkness overtook the party as they unpacked beside a pool of water deep under an overhanging shelf of lava. It had been a hard day. The horses drank their fill, and then stood patiently with drooping heads. Hunger and thirst appeased, and a warm fire cheered the weary and foot-sore fugitives. Yaqui said, "Sleep." And so another night passed.

Upon the following morning, ten miles or more up the slow-ascending lava slope, Gale's attention was called from his somber search for the less rough places in the trail.

"Dick, why does Yaqui look back?" asked Mercedes.

Gale was startled.

"Does he?"

"Every little while," replied Mercedes.

Gale was in the rear of all the other horses, so as to take, for Mercedes's sake, the advantage of the broken trail. Yaqui was leading Diablo, winding around a break. His head was bent as he stepped slowly and unevenly upon the lava. Gale turned to look back, the first time in several days. The mighty hollow of the desert below seemed wide strip of red—wide strip of green—wide strip of gray—streaking to purple peaks. It was all too vast, too mighty to grasp any little details. He thought, of course, of Rojas in certain pursuit; but it seemed absurded to look for him.

Yaqui led on, and Gale often glanced up from his task to watch the Indian. Presently he saw him stop, turn, and look back. Ladd did likewise, and then Jim and Thorne. Gale found the desire irresistible. Thereafter he often rested Blanco Sol, and looked back the while. He had his field-glass, but did not choose to use it.

"Rojas will follow," said Mercedes.

Gale regarded her in amaze. The tone of her voice had been indefinable. If there were fear then he failed to detect it. She was gazing back down the colored slope, and something about her, perhaps the steady, falcon gaze of her magnificent eyes, reminded him of Yaqui.

Many times during the ensuing hour the Indian faced about, and always his followers did likewise. It was high noon, with the sun beating hot and the lava radiating heat, when Yaqui halted for a rest. The place selected was a ridge of lava, almost a promontory, considering its outlook. The horses bunched here and drooped their heads. The rangers were about to slip the packs and remove saddles when Yaqui restrained them.

He fixed a changeless, gleaming gaze on the slow descent; but did not seem to look afar.

Suddenly he uttered his strange cry—the one Gale considered involuntary, or else significant of some tribal trait or feeling. It was incomprehensible, but no one could have doubted its potency. Yaqui pointed down the lava slope, pointed with finger and arm and neck and head—his whole body was instinct with direction. His whole being seemed to have been animated and then frozen. His posture could not have been misunderstood, yet his expression had not altered. Gale had never seen the Indian's face change its hard, red-bronze calm. It was the color and the flintiness and the character of the lava at his feet.

"Shore he sees somethin'," said Ladd. "But my eyes are not good."

"I reckon I ain't sure of mine," replied Jim. "I'm bothered by a dim movin' streak down there."

Thorne gazed eagerly down as he stood beside Mercedes, who sat motionless facing the slope. Gale looked and looked till he hurt his eyes. Then he took his glass out of its case on Sol's saddle.

There appeared to be nothing upon the lava but the innumerable dots of *choya* shining in the sun. Gale swept his glass slowly forward and back. Then into a nearer field of vision crept a long white-and-black line of horses and men. Without a word he handed the glass to Ladd. The ranger used it, muttering to himself.

"They're on the lava fifteen miles down in an air line," he said, presently. "Jim, shore they're twice that an' more accordin' to the trail."

Jim had his look and replied: "I reckon we're a day an' a night in the lead."

"Is it Rojas?" burst out Thorne, with set jaw.

"Yes, Thorne. It's Rojas and a dozen men or more," replied Gale, and he looked up at Mercedes.

She was transformed. She might have been a medieval princess embodying all the Spanish power and passion of that time, breathing revenge, hate, unquenchable spirit of fire. If her beauty had been wonderful in her helpless and appealing moments, now, when she looked back white-faced and flame-eyed, it was transcendant.

Gale drew a long, deep breath. The mood which had presaged pursuit, strife, blood on this somber desert, returned to him tenfold. He saw Thorne's face corded by black veins, and his teeth exposed like those of a snarling wolf. These rangers, who had coolly risked death many times, and had dealt it often, were white as no fear or pain could have made them. Then, on the moment, Yaqui raised his hand, not clenched or doubled tight, but curled rigid like an eagle's claw; and he shook it in a strange, slow gesture which was menacing and terrible.

It was the woman that called to the depths of these men. And their passion to kill and to save was surpassed only by the wild hate which was yet love, the unfathomable emotion of a peon slave. Gale marveled at it, while he felt his whole being cold and tense, as he turned once more to follow in the tracks of his leaders. The fight predicted by Belding was at hand. What a fight that must be! Rojas was traveling light and fast. He was gaining. He had bought his men with gold, with extravagant promises, perhaps with offers of the body and blood of an aristocrat hateful to their kind. Lastly, there was the wild, desolate environment, a tortured wilderness of jagged lava and poisoned *choya*, a lonely, fierce, and repellant world, a red stage most somberly and fittingly colored for a supreme struggle between men.

Yaqui looked back no more. Mercedes looked back no more. But the others looked, and the time came when Gale saw the creeping line of pursuers with naked eyes.

A level line above marked the rim of the plateau. Sand began to show in the little lava pits. On and upward toiled the cavalcade, still very slowly advancing. At last Yaqui reached the rim. He stood with his hand on Blanco Diablo; and both were silhouetted against the sky. That was the outlook for a Yaqui. And his great horse, dazzlingly white in the sunlight, with head wildly and proudly erect, mane and tail flying in the wind, made a magnificent picture. The others toiled on and upward, and at last Gale led Blanco Sol over the rim. Then all looked down the red slope.

But shadows were gathering there and no moving line could be seen.

Yaqui mounted and wheeled Diablo away. The others followed. Gale saw that the plateau was no more than a vast field of low, ragged circles, levels, mounds, cones, and whirls of lava. The lava was of a darker red than that down upon the slope, and it was harder than flint. In places fine sand and cinders covered the uneven floor. Strange varieties of cactus vied with the omnipresent *choya*. Yaqui, however, found ground that his horse covered at a swift walk.

But there was only an hour, perhaps, of this comparatively easy going. Then the Yaqui led them into a zone of craters. The top of the earth seemed to have been blown out in holes from a few rods in width to large craters, some shallow, others deep, and all red as fire. Yaqui circled close to abysses which yawned sheer from a level surface, and he appeared always to be turning upon his course to avoid them.

The plateau had now a considerable dip to the west. Gale marked the slow heave and ripple of the ocean of lava to the south, where high, rounded peaks marked the center of this volcanic region. The uneven nature of the slope westward prevented any extended view, until suddenly the fugitives emerged from a rugged break to come upon a sublime and awe-inspiring spectacle.

They were upon a high point of the western slope of the plateau. It was a slope, but so many leagues long in its descent that only from a height could any slant have been perceptible. Yaqui and his white horse stood upon the brink of a crater miles in circumference, a thousand feet deep, with its red walls patched in frost-colored spots by the silvery *choya*. The giant tracery of lava streams waved down the slope to disappear in undulating sand dunes. And these bordered a seemingly endless arm of blue sea. This was the Gulf of California. Beyond the Gulf rose dim, bold mountains, and above them hung the setting sun, dusky red, flooding all that barren empire with a sinister light.

It was strange to Gale then, and perhaps to the others, to see their guide lead Diablo into a smooth and well-worn trail along the rim of the awful crater. Gale looked down into that red chasm. It resembled an inferno. The dark cliffs upon the opposite side were veiled in blue haze that seemed like smoke. Here Yaqui was at home. He moved and looked about him as a man coming at last into his own. Gale saw him stop and gaze out over that red-ribbed void to the Gulf.

Gale devined that somewhere along this crater of hell the Yaqui would make his final stand; and one look into his strange, inscrutable eyes made imagination picture a fitting doom for the pursuing Rojas.

XII

THE CRATER OF HELL

THE trail led along a gigantic fissure in the side of the crater, and then down and down into a red-walled, blue hazed labyrinth.

Presently Gale, upon turning a sharp corner, was utterly amazed to see that the split in the lava sloped out and widened into an arroyo. It was so green and soft and beautiful in all the angry, contorted red surrounding that Gale could scarcely credit his sight. Blanco Sol whistled his welcome to the scent of water. Then Gale saw a great hole, a pit in the shiny lava, a dark, cool, shady well. There was evidence of the fact that at flood seasons the water had an outlet into the arroyo. The soil appeared to be a fine sand, in which a reddish tinge predominated; and it was abundantly covered with a long grass, still partly green. Mesquites and palo verdes dotted the arroyo and gradually closed in thickets that obstructed the view.

"Shore it all beats me," exclaimed Ladd. "What a place to hole-up in! We could have hid here for a long time. Boys, I saw mountain sheep, the real old genuine Rocky Mountain bighorn. What do you think of that?"

"I reckon it's a Yaqui hunting-ground," replied Lash. "That trail we hit must be hundreds of years old. It's worn deep and smooth in iron lava."

"Well, all I got to say is—Beldin' was shore right about the Indian. An' I can see Rojas's finish somewhere up along that awful hell-hole."

Camp was made on a level spot. Yaqui took the horses to water, and then turned them loose in the arroyo. It was a tired and somber group that sat down to eat. The strain of suspense equaled the wearing effects of the long ride. Mercedes was calm, but her great dark eyes burned in her white face. Yaqui watched her. The others looked at her with unspoken pride. Presently Thorne wrapped her in his blankets, and she seemed to fall asleep at once. Twilight deepened. The campfire blazed brighter. A cool wind played with Mercedes's black hair, waving strands across her brow.

Little of Yaqui's purpose or plan could be elicited from him. But the look of him was enough to satisfy even Thorne. He leaned against a pile of wood, which he had collected, and his gloomy gaze pierced the campfire, and at long intervals strayed over the motionless form of the Spanish girl.

The rangers and Thorne, however, talked in low tones. It was absolutely impossible for Rojas and his men to reach the waterhole before noon of the next day. And long before that time the fugitives would have decided on a plan of defense. What that defense would be, and where it would be made, were matters over which the men considered gravely. Ladd averred the Yaqui would put them into an impregnable position, that at the same time would prove a death-trap for their pursuers. They exhausted every possibility, and then, tired as they were, still kept on talking.

"What stuns me is that Rojas stuck to our trail," said Thorne, his lined and haggard face expressive of dark passion. "He has followed us into this fearful desert. He'll lose men, horses, perhaps his life. He's only a bandit, and he stands to win no gold. If he ever gets out of here it 'll be by herculean labor and by terrible hardship. All for a poor little helpless woman—just a woman! My God, I can't understand it."

"Shore—just a woman," replied Ladd, solemnly nodding his head.

Then there was a long silence during which the men gazed into the fire. Each, perhaps, had some vague conception of the enormity of Rojas's love or hate—some faint and amazing glimpse of the gulf of human passion. Those were cold, hard, grim faces upon which the light flickered.

"Sleep," said the Yaqui.

Thorne rolled in his blanket close beside Mercedes. Then one by one the rangers stretched out, feet to the fire. Gale found that he could not sleep. His eyes were weary, but they would not stay shut; his body ached for rest, yet he could not lie still. The night was so somber, so gloomy, and the lava-encompassed arroyo full of shadows. The dark velvet sky, fretted with white fire, seemed to be close. There was an absolute silence, as of death. Nothing moved—nothing outside of Gale's body appeared to live. The Yaqui sat like an image carved out of lava. The others lay prone and quiet. Would another night see any of them lie that way, quiet forever? Gale felt a ripple pass over him that was at once a shudder and a contraction of muscles. Used as he was to the desert and its oppression, why should he feel to-night as if the weight of its lava and the burden of its mystery were bearing him down?

He sat up after a while and again watched the fire. Nell's sweet face floated like a wraith in the pale smoke—glowed and flushed and smiled in the embers. Other faces shone there—his sister's—that of his mother. Gale shook off the tender memories. This desolate wilderness with its forbidding silence and its dark promise of hell on the morrow—this was not the place to unnerve oneself with thoughts of love and home. But the torturing paradox of the thing was that this was just the place and just the night for a man to be haunted.

By and by Gale rose and walked down a shadowy aisle between the mesquites. On his way back the Yaqui joined him. Gale was not surprised. He had become used to the Indian's strange guardianship. But now, perhaps because of Gale's poignancy of thought, the contending tides of love and regret, the deep, burning premonition of deadly strife, he was moved to keener scrutiny of the Yaqui. That, of course, was futile. The Indian was impenetrable, silent, strange. But suddenly, inexplicably, Gale felt Yaqui's human quality. It was aloof, as was everything about this Indian; but it was there. This savage walked silently beside him, without glance or touch or word. His thought was as inscrutable as if mind had never awakened in his race. Yet Gale was conscious of greatness, and, somehow, he was reminded of the Indian's story. His home had been desolated, his people carried off to slavery, his wife and children separated from him to die. What had life meant to the Yaqui? What had been in his heart? What was now in his mind? Gale could not answer these questions. But the difference between himself and Yaqui, which he had vaguely felt as that between savage and civilized men, faded out of his mind forever. Yaqui might have considered he owed Gale a debt, and, with a Yaqui's austere and noble fidelity to honor, he meant to pay it. Nevertheless, this was not the thing Gale found in the Indian's silent presence. Accepting the desert with its subtle and inconceivable influence, Gale felt that the savage and the white man had been bound in a tie which was no less brotherly because it could not be comprehended.

Toward dawn Gale managed to get some sleep. Then the morning broke with the sun hidden back of the uplift of the plateau. The horses trooped up the arroyo and snorted for water. After a hurried breakfast the packs were hidden in holes in the lava. The saddles were left where they were, and the horses allowed to graze and wander at will. Canteens were filled, a small bag of food was packed, and blankets made into a bundle. Then Yaqui faced the steep ascent of the lava slope.

The trail he followed led up on the right side of the fissure, opposite to the one he had come down. It was a steep climb, and encumbered as the men were they made but slow progress. Mercedes had to be lifted up smooth steps and across crevices. They passed places where the rims of the fissure were but a few yards apart. At length the rims widened out and the red, smoky crater yawned beneath. Yaqui left the trail and began clambering down over the rough and twisted convolutions of lava which formed the rim. Sometimes he hung sheer over the precipice. It was with extreme difficulty that the party followed him. Mercedes had to be held on narrow, foot-wide ledges. The *choya* was there to hinder passage. Finally the Indian halted upon a narrow bench of flat, smooth lava, and his followers worked with exceeding care and effort down to his position.

At the back of this bench, between bunches of *choya*, was a niche, a shallow cave with floor lined apparently with mold. Ladd said the place was a refuge which had been inhabited by mountain sheep for many years. Yaqui spread blankets inside, left the canteen and the sack of food, and with a gesture at once humble, yet that of a chief, he invited Mercedes to enter. A few more gestures and fewer words disclosed his plan. In this inaccessible nook Mercedes was to be hidden. The men were to go around upon the opposite rim, and block the trail leading down to the waterhole.

Gale marked the nature of this eyrie. It was the wildest and most rugged place he had ever stepped upon. Only a sheep could have climbed up the wall above or along the slanting shelf of lava beyond. Below glistened a whole bank of *choya*, frosty in the sunlight, and it overhung an apparently bottomless abyss.

Ladd chose the smallest gun in the party and gave it to Mercedes.

"Shore it's best to go the limit on bein' ready," he said, simply. "The chances are you'll never need it. But if you do—"

He left off there, and his break was significant. Mercedes answered him with a fearless and indomitable flash of eyes. Thorne was the only one who showed any shaken nerve. His leave-taking of his wife was affecting and hurried. Then he and the rangers carefully stepped in the tracks of the Yaqui.

They climbed up to the level of the rim and went along the edge. When they reached the fissure and came upon its narrowest point, Yaqui showed in his actions that he meant to leap it. Ladd restrained the Indian. They then continued along the rim till they reached several bridges of lava which crossed it. The fissures was deep in some parts, choked in others. Evidently the crater had no direct outlet into the arroyo below. Its bottom, however, must have been far beneath the level of the waterhole.

After the fissure was crossed the trail was soon found. Here it ran back from the rim. Yaqui waved his hand to the right, where along the corrugated slope of the crater there were holes and crevices and coverts for a hundred men. Yaqui strode on up the trail toward a higher point, where presently his dark figure stood motionless against the sky. The rangers and Thorne selected a deep depression, out of which led several ruts deep enough for cover. According to Ladd it was as good a place as any, perhaps not so hidden as others, but freer from the dreaded *choya*. Here the men laid down rifles and guns, and, removing their heavy cartridge belts, settled down to wait.

Their location was close to the rim wall and probably five hundred yards from the opposite rim, which was now seen to be considerably below them. The glaring red cliff presented a deceitful and baffling appearance. It had a thousand ledges and holes in its surfaces, and one moment it looked perpendicular and the next there seemed to be a long slant. Thorne pointed out where he thought Mercedes was hidden; Ladd selected another place, and Lash still another. Gale searched for the bank of *choya* he had seen under the bench where Mercedes's retreat lay, and when he found it the others disputed his opinion. Then Gale brought his field glass into requisition, proving that he was right. Once located and fixed in sight, the white patch of *choya*, the bench, and the sheep eyrie stood out from the other features of that rugged wall. But all the men were agreed that Yaqui had hidden Mercedes where only the eyes of a vulture could have found her.

Jim Lash crawled into a little strip of shade and bided the time tranquilly. Ladd was restless and impatient and watchful, every little while rising to look up the far-reaching slope, and then to the right, where Yaqui's dark figure stood out from a high point of the rim. Thorne grew silent, and seemed consumed by a slow, sullen rage. Gale was neither calm nor free of a gnawing suspense nor of a waiting wrath. But as best he could he put the pending action out of mind.

It came over him all of a sudden that he had not grasped the stupendous nature of this desert setting. There was the measureless red slope, its lower ridges finally sinking into white sand dunes toward the blue sea. The cold, sparkling light, the white sun, the deep azure of sky, the feeling of boundless expanse all around him—these meant high altitude. Southward the barren red simply merged into distance. The field of craters rose in high, dark wheels toward the dominating peaks. When Gale withdrew his gaze from the magnitude of these spaces and heights the crater beneath him seemed dwarfed. Yet while he gazed it spread and deepened and multiplied its ragged lines. No, he could not grasp the meaning of size or distance here. There was too much to stun the sight. But the mood in which nature had created this convulsed world of lava seized hold upon him.

Meanwhile the hours passed. As the sun climbed the clear, steely lights vanished, the blue hazes deepened, and slowly the glistening surfaces of lava turned redder. Ladd was concerned to discover that Yaqui was missing from his outlook upon the high point. Jim Lash came out of the shady crevice, and stood up to buckle on his cartridge belt. His narrow, gray glance slowly roved from the height of lava down along the slope, paused in doubt, and then swept on to resurvey the whole vast eastern dip of the plateau.

"I reckon my eyes are pore," he said. "Mebbe it's this damn red glare. Anyway, what's them creepin' spots up there?"

"Shore I seen them. Mountain sheep," replied Ladd.

"Guess again, Laddy. Dick, I reckon you'd better flash the glass up the slope."

Gale adjusted the field glass and began to search the lava, beginning close at hand and working away from him. Presently the glass became stationary.

"I see half a dozen small animals, brown in color. They look like sheep. But I couldn't distinguish mountain sheep from antelope."

"Shore they're bighorn," said Laddy.

"I reckon if you'll pull around to the east an' search under that long wall of lava—there—you'll see what I see," added Jim.

The glass climbed and circled, wavered an instant, then fixed steady as a rock. There was a breathless silence.

"Fourteen horses—two packed—some mounted—others without riders, and lame," said Gale, slowly.

Yaqui appeared far up the trail, coming swiftly. Presently he saw the rangers and halted to wave his arms and point. Then he vanished as if the lava had opened beneath him.

"Lemme that glass," suddenly said Jim Lash. "I'm seein' red, I tell you.... Well, pore as my eyes are they had it right. Rojas an' his outfit have left the trail."

"Jim, you ain't meanin' they've taken to that awful slope?" queried Ladd.

"I sure do. There they are—still comin', but goin' down, too."

"Mebbe Rojas is crazy, but it begins to look like he—"

"Laddy, I'll be danged if the Greaser bunch hasn't vamoosed. Gone out of sight! Right there not a half mile away, the whole caboodle—gone!"

"Shore they're behind a crust or have gone down into a rut," suggested Ladd. "They'll show again in a minute. Look sharp, boys, for I'm figgerin' Rojas 'll spread his men."

Minutes passed, but nothing moved upon the slope. Each man crawled up to a vantage point along the crest of rotting lava. The watchers were careful to peer through little notches or from behind a spur, and the constricted nature of their hiding-place kept them close together. Ladd's muttering grew into a growl, then lapsed into the silence that marked his companions. From time to time the rangers looked inquiringly at Gale. The field glass, however, like the naked sight, could not catch the slightest moving object out there upon the lava. A long hour of slow, mounting suspense wore on.

"Shore it's all goin' to be as queer as the Yaqui," said Ladd.

Indeed, the strange mien, the silent action, the somber character of the Indian had not been without effect upon the minds of the men. Then the weird, desolate, tragic scene added to the vague sense of mystery. And now the disappearance of Rojas's band, the long wait in the silence, the boding certainty of invisible foes crawling, circling closer and closer, lent to the situation a final touch that made it unreal.

"I'm reckonin' there's a mind behind them Greasers," replied Jim. "Or mebbe we ain't done Rojas credit... If somethin' would only come off!"

That Lash, the coolest, most provokingly nonchalant of men in times of peril, should begin to show a nervous strain was all the more indicative of a subtle pervading unreality.

"Boys, look sharp!" suddenly called Lash. "Low down to the left—mebbe three hundred yards. See, along by them seams of lava—behind the *choyas*. First off I thought it was a sheep. But it's the Yaqui!... Crawlin' swift as a lizard! Can't you see him?"

It was a full moment before Jim's companions could locate the Indian. Flat as a snake Yaqui wound himself along with incredible rapidity. His advance was all the more remarkable for the fact that he appeared to pass directly under the dreaded *choyas*. Sometimes he paused to lift his head and look. He was directly in line with a huge whorl of lava that rose higher than any point on the slope. This spur was a quarter of a mile from the position of the rangers.

"Shore he's headin' for that high place," said Ladd. "He's goin' slow now. There, he's stopped behind some *choyas*. He's gettin' up—no, he's kneelin'.... Now what the hell!"

"Laddy, take a peek at the side of that lava ridge," sharply called Jim. "I guess mebbe somethin' ain't comin' off. See! There's Rojas an' his outfit climbin'. Don't make out no hosses.... Dick, use your glass an' tell us what's doin'. I'll watch Yaqui an' tell you what his move means."

Clearly and distinctly, almost as if he could have touched them, Gale had Rojas and his followers in sight. They were toiling up the rough lava on foot. They were heavily armed. Spurs, chaps, jackets, scarfs were not in evidence. Gale saw the lean, swarthy faces, the black, straggly hair, the ragged, soiled garments which had once been white.

"They're almost up now," Gale was saying. "There! They halt on top. I see Rojas. He looks wild. By ——! fellows, an Indian!... It's a Papago. Belding's old herder!... The Indian points—this way—then down. He's showing Rojas the lay of the trail."

"Boys, Yaqui's in range of that bunch," said Jim, swiftly. "He's raisin' his rifle slow—Lord, how slow he is!... He's covered some one. Which one I can't say. But I think he'll pick Rojas."

"The Yaqui can shoot. He'll pick Rojas," added Gale, grimly.

"Rojas—yes—yes!" cried Thorne, in passion of suspense.

"Not on your life!" Ladd's voice cut in with scorn. "Gentlemen, you can gamble Yaqui 'll kill the Papago. That traitor Indian knows these sheep haunts. He's tellin' Rojas—"

A sharp rifle shot rang out.

"Laddy's right," called Gale. "The Papago's hit—his arm falls—There, he tumbles!"

More shots rang out. Yaqui was seen standing erect firing rapidly at the darting Mexicans. For all Gale could make out no second bullet took effect. Rojas and his men vanished behind the bulge of lava. Then Yaqui deliberately backed away from his position. He made no effort to run or hide. Evidently he watched cautiously for signs of pursuers in the ruts and behind the *choyas*. Presently he turned and came straight toward the position of the rangers, sheered off perhaps a hundred paces below it, and disappeared in a crevice. Plainly his intention was to draw pursuers within rifle shot.

"Shore, Jim, you had your wish. Somethin' come off," said Ladd. "An' I'm sayin' thank God for the Yaqui! That Papago 'd have ruined us. Even so, mebbe he's told Rojas more'n enough to make us sweat blood."

"He had a chance to kill Rojas," cried out the drawn-faced, passionate Thorne. "He didn't take it!... He didn't take it!"

Only Ladd appeared to be able to answer the cavalryman's poignant cry.

"Listen, son," he said, and his voice rang. "We-all know how you feel. An' if I'd had that one shot never in the world could I have picked the Papago guide. I'd have had to kill Rojas. That's the white man of it. But Yaqui was right. Only an Indian could have done it. You can gamble the Papago alive meant slim chance for us. Because he'd led straight to where Mercedes is hidden, an' then we'd have left cover to fight it out... When you come to think of the Yaqui's hate for Greasers, when you just seen him pass up a shot at one—well, I don't know how to say what I mean, but damn me, my som-brer-ro is off to the Indian!"

"I reckon so, an' I reckon the ball's opened," rejoined Lash, and now that former nervous impatience so unnatural to him was as if it had never been. He was smilingly cool, and his voice had almost a caressing note. He tapped the breech of his Winchester with a sinewy brown hand, and he did not appear to be addressing any one in particular. "Yaqui's opened the ball. Look up your pardners there, gents, an' get ready to dance."

Another wait set in then, and judging by the more direct rays of the sun and a receding of the little shadows cast by the *choyas*, Gale was of the opinion that it was a long wait. But it seemed short. The four men were lying under the bank of a half circular hole in the lava. It was notched and cracked, and its rim was fringed by *choyas*. It sloped down and opened to an unobstructed view of the crater. Gale had the upper position, fartherest to the right, and therefore was best shielded from possible fire from the higher ridges of the rim, some three hundred yards distant. Jim came next, well hidden in a crack. The positions of Thorne and Ladd were most exposed. They kept sharp lookout over the uneven rampart of their hiding-place.

The sun passed the zenith, began to slope westward, and to grow hotter as it sloped. The men waited and waited. Gale saw no impatience even in Thorne. The sultry air seemed to be laden with some burden or quality that was at once composed of heat, menace, color, and silence. Even the light glancing up from the lava seemed red and the silence had substance. Sometimes Gale felt that it was unbearable. Yet he made no effort to break it.

Suddenly this dead stillness was rent by a shot, clear and stinging, close at hand. It was from a rifle, not a carbine. With startling quickness a cry followed—a cry that pierced Gale—it was so thin, so high-keyed, so different from all other cries. It was the involuntary human shriek at death.

"Yaqui's called out another pardner," said Jim Lash, laconically.

Carbines began to crack. The reports were quick, light, like sharp spats without any ring. Gale peered from behind the edge of his covert. Above the ragged wave of lava floated faint whitish clouds, all that was visible of smokeless powder. Then Gale made out round spots, dark against the background of red, and in front of them leaped out small tongues of fire. Ladd's .405 began to "spang" with its beautiful sound of power. Thorne was firing, somewhat wildly Gale thought. Then Jim Lash pushed his Winchester over the rim under a *choya*, and between shots Gale could hear him singing: "Turn the lady, turn—turn the lady, turn!... Alaman left!... Swing your pardners!... Forward an' back!... Turn the lady, turn!" Gale got into the fight himself, not so sure that he hit any of the round, bobbing objects he aimed at, but growing sure of himself as action liberated something forced and congested within his breast.

Then over the position of the rangers came a hail of steel bullets. Those that struck the lava hissed away into the crater; those that came biting through the *choyas* made a sound which resembled a sharp ripping of silk. Bits of cactus stung Gale's face, and he dreaded the flying thorns more than he did the flying bullets.

"Hold on, boys," called Ladd, as he crouched down to reload his rifle. "Save your shells. The greasers are spreadin' on us, some goin' down below Yaqui, others movin' up for that high ridge. When they get up there I'm damned if it won't be hot for us. There ain't room for all of us to hide here."

Ladd raised himself to peep over the rim. Shots were now scattering, and all appeared to come from below. Emboldened by this he rose higher. A shot from in front, a rip of bullet through the *choya*, a spat of something hitting Ladd's face, a steel missle hissing onward—these inseparably blended sounds were all registered by Gale's sensitive ear.

With a curse Ladd tumbled down into the hole. His face showed a great gray blotch, and starting blood. Gale felt a sickening assurance of desperate injury to the ranger. He ran to him calling: "Laddy! Laddy!"

"Shore I ain't plugged. It's a damn *choya* burr. The bullet knocked it in my face. Pull it out!"

The oval, long-spiked cone was firmly imbedded in Ladd's cheek. Blood streamed down his face and neck. Carefully, yet with no thought of pain to himself, Gale tried to pull the cactus joint away. It was as firm as if it had been nailed there. That was the damnable feature of the barbed thorns: once set, they held on as that strange plant held to its desert life. Ladd began to writhe, and sweat mingled with the blood on his face. He cursed and raved, and his movements made it almost impossible for Gale to do anything.

"Put your knife-blade under an' tear it out!" shouted Ladd, hoarsely.

Thus ordered, Gale slipped a long blade in between the imbedded thorns, and with a powerful jerk literally tore the *choya* out of Ladd's quivering flesh. Then, where the ranger's face was not red and raw, it certainly was white.

A volley of shots from a different angle was followed by the quick ring of steel bullets striking the lava all around Gale. His first idea, as he heard the projectiles sing and hum and whine away into the air, was that they were coming from above him. He looked up to see a number of low, white and dark knobs upon the high point of lava. They had not been there before. Then he saw little, pale, leaping tongues of fire. As he dodged down he distinctly heard a bullet strike Ladd. At the same instant he seemed to hear Thorne cry out and fall, and Lash's boots scrape rapidly away.

Ladd fell backward still holding the .405. Gale dragged him into the shelter of his own position, and dreading to look at him, took up the heavy weapon. It was with a kind of savage strength that he gripped the rifle; and it was with a cold and deadly intent that he aimed and fired. The first Greaser huddled low, let his carbine go clattering down, and then crawled behind the rim. The second and third jerked back. The fourth seemed to flop up over the crest of lava. A dark arm reached for him, clutched his leg, tried to drag him up. It was in vain. Wildly grasping at the air the bandit fell, slid down a steep shelf, rolled over the rim, to go hurtling down out of sight.

Fingering the hot rifle with close-pressed hands, Gale watched the sky line along the high point of lava. It remained unbroken. As his passion left him he feared to look back at his companions, and the cold chill returned to his breast.

"Shore—I'm damn glad—them Greasers ain't usin' soft-nose bullets," drawled a calm voice.

Swift as lightning Gale whirled.

"Laddy! I thought you were done for," cried Gale, with a break in his voice.

"I ain't a-mindin' the bullet much. But that *choya* joint took my nerve, an' you can gamble on it. Dick, this hole's pretty high up, ain't it?"

The ranger's blouse was open at the neck, and on his right shoulder under the collar bone was a small hole just beginning to bleed.

"Sure it's high, Laddy," replied Gale, gladly. "Went clear through, clean as a whistle!"

He tore a handkerchief into two parts, made wads, and pressing them close over the wounds he bound them there with Ladd's scarf.

"Shore it's funny how a bullet can floor a man an' then not do any damage," said Ladd. "I felt a zip of wind an' somethin' like a pat on my chest an' down I went. Well, so much for the small caliber with their steel bullets. Supposin' I'd connected with a .405!"

"Laddy, I—I'm afraid Thorne's done for," whispered Gale. "He's lying over there in that crack. I can see part of him. He doesn't move."

"I was wonderin' if I'd have to tell you that. Dick, he went down hard hit, fallin', you know, limp an' soggy. It was a moral cinch one of us would get it in this fight; but God! I'm sorry Thorne had to be the man."

"Laddy, maybe he's not dead," replied Gale. He called aloud to his friend. There was no answer.

Ladd got up, and, after peering keenly at the height of lava, he strode swiftly across the space. It was only a dozen steps to the crack in the lava where Thorne had fallen head first. Ladd bent over, went to his knees, so that Gale saw only his head. Then he appeared rising with arms round the cavalryman. He dragged him across the hole to the sheltered corner that alone afforded protection. He had scarcely reached it when a carbine cracked and a bullet struck the flinty lava, striking sparks, then singing away into the air.

Thorne was either dead or unconscious, and Gale, with a contracting throat and numb heart, decided for the former. Not so Ladd, who probed the bloody gash on Thorne's temple, and then felt his breast.

"He's alive an' not bad hurt. That bullet hit him glancin'. Shore them steel bullets are some lucky for us. Dick, you needn't look so glum. I tell you he ain't bad hurt. I felt his skull with my finger. There's no hole in it. Wash him off an' tie— Wow! did you get the wind of that one? An' mebbe it didn't sing off the lava!... Dick, look after Thorne now while I—"

The completion of his speech was the stirring ring of the .405, and then he uttered a laugh that was unpleasant.

"Shore, Greaser, there's a man's size bullet for you. No slim, sharp-pointed, steel-jacket nail! I'm takin' it on me to believe you're appreciatin' of the .405, seein' as you don't make no fuss."

It was indeed a joy to Gale to find that Thorne had not received a wound necessarily fatal, though it was serious enough. Gale bathed and bound it, and laid the cavalryman against the slant of the bank, his head high to lessen the probability of bleeding.

As Gale straightened up Ladd muttered low and deep, and swung the heavy rifle around to the left. Far along the slope a figure moved. Ladd began to work the lever of the Winchester and to shoot. At every shot the heavy firearm sprang up, and the recoil made Ladd's shoulder give back. Gale saw the bullets strike the lava behind, beside, before the fleeing Mexican, sending up dull puffs of dust. On the sixth shot he plunged down out of sight, either hit or frightened into seeking cover.

"Dick, mebbe there's one or two left above; but we needn't figure much on it," said Ladd, as, loading the rifle, he jerked his fingers quickly from the hot breech. "Listen! Jim an' Yaqui are hittin' it up lively down below. I'll sneak down there. You stay here an' keep about half an eye peeled up yonder, an' keep the rest my way."

Ladd crossed the hole, climbed down into the deep crack where Thorne had fallen, and then went stooping along with only his head above the level. Presently he disappeared. Gale, having little to fear from the high ridge, directed most of his attention toward the point beyond which Ladd had gone. The firing had become desultory, and the light carbine shots outnumbered the sharp rifle shots five to one. Gale made a note of the fact that for some little time he had not heard the unmistakable report of Jim Lash's automatic. Then ensued a long interval in which the desert silence seemed to recover its grip. The .405 ripped it asunder—spang—spang—spang. Gale fancied he heard yells. There were a few pattering shots still farther down the trail. Gale had an uneasy conviction that Rojas and some of his band might go straight to the waterhole. It would be hard to dislodge even a few men from that retreat.

There seemed a lull in the battle. Gale ventured to stand high, and screened behind *choyas*, he swept the three-quarter circle of lava with his glass. In the distance he saw horses, but no riders. Below him, down the slope along the crater rim and the trail, the lava was bare of all except tufts of *choya*. Gale gathered assurance. It looked as if the day was favoring his side. Then Thorne, coming partly to consciousness, engaged Gale's care. The cavalryman stirred and moaned, called for water, and then for Mercedes. Gale held him back with a strong hand, and presently he was once more quiet.

For the first time in hours, as it seemed, Gale took note of the physical aspect of his surroundings. He began to look upon them without keen gaze strained for crouching form, or bobbing head, or spouting carbine. Either Gale's sense of color and proportion had become deranged during the fight, or the encompassing air and the desert had changed. Even the sun had changed. It seemed lowering, oval in shape, magenta in hue, and it had a surface that gleamed like oil on water. Its red rays shone through red haze. Distances that had formerly been clearly outlined were now dim, obscured. The yawning chasm was not the same. It circled wider, redder, deeper. It was a weird, ghastly mouth of hell. Gale stood fascinated, unable to tell how much he saw was real, how much exaggeration of overwrought emotions. There was no beauty here, but an unparalleled grandeur, a sublime scene of devastation and desolation which might have had its counterpart upon the burned-out moon. The mood that gripped Gale now added to its somber portent an unshakable foreboding of calamity.

He wrestled with the spell as if it were a physical foe. Reason and intelligence had their voices in his mind; but the moment was not one wherein these things could wholly control. He felt life strong within his breast, yet there, a step away, was death, yawning, glaring, smoky, red. It was a moment—an hour for a savage, born, bred, developed in this scarred and blasted place of jagged depths and red distances and silences never meant to be broken. Since Gale was not a savage he fought that call of the red gods which sent him back down the long ages toward his primitive day. His mind combated his sense of sight and the hearing that seemed useless; and his mind did not win all the victory. Something fatal was here, hanging in the balance, as the red haze hung along the vast walls of that crater of hell.

Suddenly harsh, prolonged yells brought him to his feet, and the unrealities vanished. Far down the trails where the crater rims closed in the deep fissure he saw moving forms. They were three in number. Two of them ran nimbly across the lava bridge. The third staggered far behind. It was Ladd. He appeared hard hit. He dragged at the heavy rifle which he seemed unable to raise. The yells came from him. He was calling the Yaqui.

Gale's heart stood still momentarily. Here, then, was the catastrophe! He hardly dared sweep that fissure with his glass. The two fleeing figures halted—turned to fire at Ladd. Gale recognized the foremost one—small, compact, gaudy. Rojas! The bandit's arm was outstretched. Puffs of white smoke rose, and shots rapped out. When Ladd went down Rojas threw his gun aside and with a wild yell bounded over the lava. His companion followed.

A tide of passion, first hot as fire, then cold as ice, rushed over Gale when he saw Rojas take the trail toward Mercedes's hiding-place. The little bandit appeared to have the sure-footedness of a mountain sheep. The Mexican following was not so sure or fast. He turned back. Gale heard the trenchant bark of the .405. Ladd was kneeling. He shot again—again. The retreating bandit seemed to run full into an invisible obstacle, then fell lax, inert, lifeless. Rojas sped on unmindful of the spurts of dust about him. Yaqui, high above Ladd, was also firing at the bandit. Then both rifles were emptied. Rojas turned at a high break in the trail. He shook a defiant hand, and his exulting yell pealed faintly to Gale's ears. About him there was something desperate, magnificent. Then he clambered down the trail.

Ladd dropped the .405, and rising, gun in hand, he staggered toward the bridge of lava. Before he had crossed it Yaqui came bounding down the slope, and in one splendid leap he cleared the fissure. He ran beyond the trail and disappeared on the lava above. Rojas had not seen this sudden, darting move of the Indian.

Gale felt himself bitterly powerless to aid in that pursuit. He could only watch. He wondered, fearfully, what had become of Lash. Presently, when Rojas came out of the cracks and ruts of lava there might be a chance of disabling him by a long shot. His progress was now slow. But he was making straight for Mercedes's hiding-place. What was it leading him there—an eagle eye, or hate, or instinct? Why did he go on when there could be no turning back for him on that trail? Ladd was slow, heavy, staggering on the trail; but he was relentless. Only death could stop the ranger now. Surely Rojas must have known that when he chose the trail. From time to time Gale caught glimpses of Yaqui's dark figure stealing along the higher rim of the crater. He was making for a point above the bandit.

Moments—endless moments dragged by. The lowering sun colored only the upper half of the crater walls. Far down the depths were murky blue. Again Gale felt the insupportable silence. The red haze became a transparent veil before his eyes. Sinister, evil, brooding, waiting, seemed that yawning abyss. Ladd staggered along the trail, at times he crawled. The Yaqui gained; he might have had wings; he leaped from jagged crust to jagged crust; his sure-footedness was a wonderful thing.

But for Gale the marvel of that endless period of watching was the purpose of the bandit Rojas. He had now no weapon. Gale's glass made this fact plain. There was death behind him, death below him, death before him, and though he could not have known it, death above him. He never faltered—never made a misstep upon the narrow, flinty trail. When he reached the lower end of the level ledge Gale's poignant doubt became a certainty. Rojas had seen Mercedes. It was incredible, yet Gale believed it. Then, his heart clamped as in an icy vise, Gale threw forward the Remington, and sinking on one knee, began to shoot. He emptied the magazine. Puffs of dust near Rojas did not even make him turn.

As Gale began to reload he was horror-stricken by a low cry from Thorne. The cavalryman had recovered consciousness. He was half raised, pointing with shaking hand at the opposite ledge. His distended eyes were riveted upon Rojas. He was trying to utter speech that would not come.

Gale wheeled, rigid now, steeling himself to one last forlorn hope—that Mercedes could defend herself. She had a gun. He doubted not at all that she would use it. But, remembering her terror of this savage, he feared for her.

Rojas reached the level of the ledge. He halted. He crouched. It was the act of a panther. Manifestly he saw Mercedes within the cave. Then faint shots patted the air, broke in quick echo. Rojas went down as if struck a heavy blow. He was hit. But even as Gale yelled in sheer madness the bandit leaped erect. He seemed too quick, too supple to be badly wounded. A slight, dark figure flashed out of the cave. Mercedes! She backed against the wall. Gale saw a puff of white—heard a report. But the bandit lunged at her. Mercedes ran, not to try to pass him, but straight for the precipice. Her intention was plain. But Rojas outstripped her, even as she reached the verge. Then a piercing scream pealed across the crater—a scream of despair.

Gale closed his eyes. He could not bear to see more.

Thorne echoed Mercedes's scream. Gale looked round just in time to leap and catch the cavalryman as he staggered, apparently for the steep slope. And then, as Gale dragged him back, both fell. Gale saved his friend, but he plunged into a *choya*. He drew his hands away full of the great glistening cones of thorns.

"For God's sake, Gale, shoot! Shoot! Kill her! Kill her!... Can't—you—see—Rojas—"

Thorne fainted.

Gale, stunned for the instant, stood with uplifted hands, and gazed from Thorne across the crater. Rojas had not killed Mercedes. He was overpowering her. His actions seemed slow, wearing, purposeful. Hers were violent. Like a trapped she-wolf, Mercedes was fighting. She tore, struggled, flung herself.

Rojas's intention was terribly plain.

In agony now, both mental and physical, cold and sick and weak, Gale gripped his rifle and aimed at the struggling forms on the ledge. He pulled the trigger. The bullet struck up a cloud of red dust close to the struggling couple. Again Gale fired, hoping to hit Rojas, praying to kill Mercedes. The bullet struck high. A third—fourth—fifth time the Remington spoke—in vain! The rifle fell from Gale's racked hands.

How horribly plain that fiend's intention! Gale tried to close his eyes, but could not. He prayed wildly for a sudden blindness—to faint as Thorne had fainted. But he was transfixed to the spot with eyes that pierced the red light.

Mercedes was growing weaker, seemed about to collapse.

"Oh, Jim Lash, are you dead?" cried Gale. "Oh, Laddy!... Oh, Yaqui!"

Suddenly a dark form literally fell down the wall behind the ledge where Rojas fought the girl. It sank in a heap, then bounded erect.

"Yaqui!" screamed Gale, and he waved his bleeding hands till the blood bespattered his face. Then he choked. Utterance became impossible.

The Indian bent over Rojas and flung him against the wall. Mercedes, sinking back, lay still. When Rojas got up the Indian stood between him and escape from the ledge. Rojas backed the other way along the narrowing shelf of lava. His manner was abject, stupefied. Slowly he stepped backward.

It was then that Gale caught the white gleam of a knife in Yaqui's hand. Rojas turned and ran. He rounded a corner of wall where the footing was precarious. Yaqui followed slowly. His figure was dark and menacing. But he was not in a hurry. When he passed off the ledge Rojas was edging farther and farther along the wall. He was clinging now to the lava, creeping inch by inch. Perhaps he had thought to work around the buttress or climb over it. Evidently he went as far as possible, and there he clung, an unscalable wall above, the abyss beneath.

The approach of the Yaqui was like a slow dark shadow of gloom. If it seemed so to the stricken Gale what must it have been to Rojas? He appeared to sink against the wall. The Yaqui stole closer and closer. He was the savage now, and for him the moment must have been glorified. Gale saw him gaze up at the great circling walls of the crater, then down into the depths. Perhaps the red haze hanging above him, or the purple haze below, or the deep caverns in the lava, held for Yaqui spirits of the desert, his gods to whom he called. Perhaps he invoked shadows of his loved ones and his race, calling them in this moment of vengeance.

Gale heard—or imagined he heard—that wild, strange Yaqui cry.

Then the Indian stepped close to Rojas, and bent low, keeping out of reach. How slow were his motions! Would Yaqui never—never end it?... A wail drifted across the crater to Gale's ears.

Rojas fell backward and plunged sheer. The bank of white *choyas* caught him, held him upon their steel spikes. How long did the dazed Gale sit there watching Rojas wrestling and writhing in convulsive frenzy? The bandit now seemed mad to win the delayed death.

When he broke free he was a white patched object no longer human, a ball of *choya* burrs, and he slipped off the bank to shoot down and down into the purple depths of the crater.

XIII

CHANGES AT FORLORN RIVER

THE first of March saw the federal occupation of the garrison at Casita. After a short, decisive engagement the rebels were dispersed into small bands and driven eastward along the boundary line toward Nogales.

It was the destiny of Forlorn River, however, never to return to the slow, sleepy tenor of its former existence. Belding's predictions came true. That straggling line of home-seekers was but a forerunner of the real invasion of Altar Valley. Refugees from Mexico and from Casita spread the word that water and wood and grass and land were to be had at Forlorn River; and as if by magic the white tents and red adobe houses sprang up to glisten in the sun.

Belding was happier than he had been for a long time. He believed that evil days for Forlorn River, along with the apathy and lack of enterprise, were in the past. He hired a couple of trustworthy Mexicans to ride the boundary line, and he settled down to think of ranching and irrigation and mining projects. Every morning he expected to receive some word form Sonoyta or Yuma, telling him that Yaqui had guided his party safely across the desert.

Belding was simple-minded, a man more inclined to action than reflection. When the complexities of life hemmed him in, he groped his way out, never quite understanding. His wife had always been a mystery to him. Nell was sunshine most of the time, but, like the sun-dominated desert, she was subject to strange changes, wilful, stormy, sudden. It was enough for Belding now to find his wife in a lighter, happier mood, and to see Nell dreamily turning a ring round and round the third finger of her left hand and watching the west. Every day both mother and daughter appeared farther removed from the past darkly threatening days. Belding was hearty in his affections, but undemonstrative. If there was any sentiment in his make-up it had an outlet in his memory of Blanco Diablo and a longing to see him. Often Belding stopped his work to gaze out over the desert toward the west. When he thought of his rangers and Thorne and Mercedes he certainly never forgot his horse. He wondered if Diablo was running, walking, resting; if Yaqui was finding water and grass.

In March, with the short desert winter over, the days began to grow warm. The noon hours were hot, and seemed to give promise of the white summer blaze and blasting furnace wind soon to come. No word was received from the rangers. But this caused Belding no concern, and it seemed to him that his women folk considered no news good news.

Among the many changes coming to pass in Forlorn River were the installing of post-office service and the building of a mescal drinking-house. Belding had worked hard for the post office, but he did not like the idea of a saloon for Forlorn River. Still, that was an inevitable evil. The Mexicans would have mescal. Belding had kept the little border hamlet free of an establishment for distillation of the fiery cactus drink. A good many Americans drifted into Forlorn River—miners, cowboys, prospectors, outlaws, and others of nondescript character; and these men, of course, made the saloon, which was also an inn, their headquarters. Belding, with Carter and other old residents, saw the need of a sheriff for Forlorn River.

One morning early in this spring month, while Belding was on his way from the house to the corrals, he saw Nell running Blanco Jose down the road at a gait that amazed him. She did not take the turn of the road to come in by the gate. She put Jose at a four-foot wire fence, and came clattering into the yard.

"Nell must have another tantrum," said Belding. "She's long past due."

Blanco Jose, like the other white horses, was big of frame and heavy, and thunder rolled from under his great hoofs. Nell pulled him up, and as he pounded and slid to a halt in a cloud of dust she swung lightly down.

It did not take more than half an eye for Belding to see that she was furious.

"Nell, what's come off now?" asked Belding.

"I'm not going to tell you," she replied, and started away, leading Jose toward the corral.

Belding leisurely followed. She went into the corral, removed Jose's bridle, and led him to the watering-trough. Belding came up, and without saying anything began to unbuckle Jose's saddle girths. But he ventured a look at Nell. The red had gone from her face, and he was surprised to see her eyes brimming with tears. Most assuredly this was not one of Nell's tantrums. While taking off Jose's saddle and hanging it in the shed Belding pondered in his slow way. When he came back to the corral Nell had her face against the bars, and she was crying. He slipped a big arm around her and waited. Although it was not often expressed, there was a strong attachment between them.

"Dad, I don't want you to think me a—a baby any more," she said. "I've been insulted."

With a specific fact to make clear thought in Belding's mind he was never slow.

"I knew something unusual had come off. I guess you'd better tell me."

"Dad, I will, if you promise."

"What?"

"Not to mention it to mother, not to pack a gun down there, and never, never tell Dick."

Belding was silent. Seldom did he make promises readily.

"Nell, sure something must have come off, for you to ask all that."

"If you don't promise I'll never tell, that's all," she declared, firmly.

Belding deliberated a little longer. He knew the girl.

"Well, I promise not to tell mother," he said, presently; "and seeing you're here safe and well, I guess I won't go packing a gun down there, wherever that is. But I won't promise to keep anything from Dick that perhaps he ought to know."

"Dad, what would Dick do if—if he were here and I were to tell him I'd—I'd been horribly insulted?"

"I guess that 'd depend. Mostly, you know, Dick does what you want. But you couldn't stop him—nobody could—if there was reason, a man's reason, to get started. Remember what he did to Rojas!... Nell, tell me what's happened."

Nell, regaining her composure, wiped her eyes and smoothed back her hair.

"The other day, Wednesday," she began, "I was coming home, and in front of that mescal drinking-place there was a crowd. It was a noisy crowd. I didn't want to walk out into the street or seem afraid. But I had to do both. There were several young men, and if they weren't drunk they certainly were rude. I never saw them before, but I think they must belong to the mining company that was run out of Sonora by rebels. Mrs. Carter was telling me. Anyway, these young fellows were Americans. They stretched themselves across the walk and smiled at me. I had to go out in the road. One of them, the rudest, followed me. He was a big fellow, red-faced, with prominent eyes and a bold look. He came up beside me and spoke to me. I ran home. And as I ran I heard his companions jeering.

"Well, to-day, just now, when I was riding up the valley road I came upon the same fellows. They had instruments and were surveying. Remembering Dick, and how he always wished for an instrument to help work out his plan for irrigation, I was certainly surprised to see these strangers surveying—and surveying upon Laddy's plot of land. It was a sandy road there, and Jose happened to be walking. So I reined in and asked these engineers what they were doing. The leader, who was that same bold fellow who had followed me, seemed much pleased at being addressed. He was swaggering—too friendly; not my idea of a gentleman at all. He said he was glad to tell me he was going to run water all over Altar Valley. Dad, you can bet that made me wild. That was Dick's plan, his discovery, and here were surveyors on Laddy's claim.

"Then I told him that he was working on private land and he'd better get off. He seemed to forget his flirty proclivities in amazement. Then he looked cunning. I read his mind. It was news to him that all the land along the valley had been taken up.

"He said something about not seeing any squatters on the land, and then he shut up tight on that score. But he began to be flirty again. He got hold of Jose's bridle, and before I could catch my breath he said I was a peach, and that he wanted to make a date with me, that his name was Chase, that he owned a gold mine in Mexico. He said a lot more I didn't gather, but when he called me 'Dearie' I—well, I lost my temper.

"I jerked on the bridle and told him to let go. He held on and rolled his eyes at me. I dare say he imagined he was a gentlemen to be infatuated with. He seemed sure of conquest. One thing certain, he didn't know the least bit about horses. It scared me the way he got in front of Jose. I thanked my stars I wasn't up on Blanco Diablo. Well, Dad, I'm a little ashamed now, but I was mad. I slashed him across the face with my quirt. Jose jumped and knocked Mr. Chase into the sand. I didn't get the horse under control till I was out of sight of those surveyors, and then I let him run home."

"Nell, I guess you punished the fellow enough. Maybe he's only a conceited softy. But I don't like that sort of thing. It isn't Western. I guess he won't be so smart next time. Any fellow would remember being hit by Blanco Jose. If you'd been up on Diablo we'd have to bury Mr. Chase."

"Thank goodness I wasn't! I'm sorry now, Dad. Perhaps the fellow was hurt. But what could I do? Let's forget all about it, and I'll be careful where I ride in the future.... Dad, what does it mean, this surveying around Forlorn River?"

"I don't know, Nell," replied Belding, thoughtfully. "It worries me. It looks good for Forlorn River, but bad for Dick's plan to irrigate the valley. Lord, I'd hate to have some one forestall Dick on that!"

"No, no, we won't let anybody have Dick's rights," declared Nell.

"Where have I been keeping myself not to know about these surveyors?" muttered Belding. "They must have just come."

"Go see Mrs. Cater. She told me there were strangers in town, Americans, who had mining interests in Sonora, and were run out by Orozco. Find out what they're doing, Dad."

Belding discovered that he was, indeed, the last man of consequence in Forlorn River to learn of the arrival of Ben Chase and son, mineowners and operators in Sonora. They, with a force of miners, had been besieged by rebels and finally driven off their property. This property was not destroyed, but held for ransom. And the Chases, pending developments, had packed outfits and struck for the border. Casita had been their objective point, but, for some reason which Belding did not learn, they had arrived instead at Forlorn River. It had taken Ben Chase just one day to see the possibilities of Altar Valley, and in three days he had men at work.

Belding returned home without going to see the Chases and their operations. He wanted to think over the situation. Next morning he went out to the valley to see for himself. Mexicans were hastily erecting adobe houses upon Ladd's one hundred and sixty acres, upon Dick Gale's, upon Jim Lash's and Thorne's. There were men staking the valley floor and the river bed. That was sufficient for Belding. He turned back toward town and headed for the camp of these intruders.

In fact, the surroundings of Forlorn River, except on the river side, reminded Belding of the mushroom growth of a newly discovered mining camp. Tents were everywhere; adobe shacks were in all stages of construction; rough clapboard houses were going up. The latest of this work was new and surprising to Belding, all because he was a busy man, with no chance to hear village gossip. When he was directed to the headquarters of the Chase Mining Company he went thither in slow-growing wrath.

He came to a big tent with a huge canvas fly stretched in front, under which sat several men in their shirt sleeves. They were talking and smoking.

"My name's Belding. I want to see this Mr. Chase," said Belding, gruffly.

Slow-witted as Belding was, and absorbed in his own feelings, he yet saw plainly that his advent was disturbing to these men. They looked alarmed, exchanged glances, and then quickly turned to him. One of them, a tall, rugged man with sharp face and shrewd eyes and white hair, got up and offered his hand.

"I'm Chase, senior," he said. "My son Radford Chase is here somewhere. You're Belding, the line inspector, I take it? I meant to call on you."

He seemed a rough-and-ready, loud-spoken man, withal cordial enough.

"Yes, I'm the inspector," replied Belding, ignoring the proffered hand, "and I'd like to know what in the hell you mean by taking up land claims—staked ground that belongs to my rangers?"

"Land claims?" slowly echoed Chase, studying his man. "We're taking up only unclaimed land."

"That's a lie. You couldn't miss the stakes."

"Well, Mr. Belding, as to that, I think my men did run across some staked ground. But we recognize only squatters. If your rangers think they've got property just because they drove a few stakes in the ground they're much mistaken. A squatter has to build a house and live on his land so long, according to law, before he owns it."

This argument was unanswerable, and Belding knew it.

"According to law!" exclaimed Belding. "Then you own up; you've jumped our claims."

"Mr. Belding, I'm a plain business man. I come along. I see a good opening. Nobody seems to have tenable grants. I stake out claims, locate squatters, start to build. It seems to me your rangers have overlooked certain precautions. That's unfortunate for them. I'm prepared to hold my claim and to back all the squatters who work for me. If you don't like it you can carry the matter to Tucson. The law will uphold me."

"The law? Say, on this southwest border we haven't any law except a man's word and a gun."

"Then you'll find United States law has come along with Ben Chase," replied the other, snapping his fingers. He was still smooth, outspoken, but his mask had fallen.

"You're not a Westerner?" queried Belding.

"No, I'm from Illinois."

"I thought the West hadn't bred you. I know your kind. You'd last a long time on the Texas border; now, wouldn't you? You're one of the land and water hogs that has come to root in the West. You're like the timber sharks—take it all and leave none for those who follow. Mr. Chase, the West would fare better and last longer if men like you were driven out."

"You can't drive me out."

"I'm not so sure of that. Wait till my rangers come back. I wouldn't be in your boots. Don't mistake me. I don't suppose you could be accused of stealing another man's ideas or plan, but sure you've stolen these four claims. Maybe the law might uphold you. But the spirit, not the letter, counts with us bordermen."

"See here, Belding, I think you're taking the wrong view of the matter. I'm going to develop this valley. You'd do better to get in with me. I've a proposition to make you about that strip of land of yours facing the river."

"You can't make any deals with me. I won't have anything to do with you."

Belding abruptly left the camp and went home. Nell met him, probably intended to question him, but one look into his face confirmed her fears. She silently turned away. Belding realized he was powerless to stop Chase, and he was sick with disappointment for the ruin of Dick's hopes and his own.

XIV

A LOST SON

TIME passed. The population of Forlorn River grew apace. Belding, who had once been the head of the community, found himself a person of little consequence. Even had he desired it he would not have had any voice in the selection of postmaster, sheriff, and a few other officials. The Chases divided their labors between Forlorn River and their Mexican gold mine, which had been restored to them. The desert trips between these two places were taken in automobiles. A month's time made the motor cars almost as familiar a sight in Forlorn River as they had been in Casita before the revolution.

Belding was not so busy as he had been formerly. As he lost ambition he began to find less work to do. His wrath at the usurping Chases increased as he slowly realized his powerlessness to cope with such men. They were promoters, men of big interests and wide influence in the Southwest. The more they did for Forlorn River the less reason there seemed to be for his own grievance. He had to admit that it was personal; that he and Gale and the rangers would never have been able to develop the resources of the valley as these men were doing it.

All day long he heard the heavy booming blasts and the rumble of avalanches up in the gorge. Chase's men were dynamiting the cliffs in the narrow box canyon. They were making the dam just as Gale had planned to make it. When this work of blasting was over Belding experienced a relief. He would not now be continually reminded of his and Gale's loss. Resignation finally came to him. But he could not reconcile himself to misfortune for Gale.

Moreover, Belding had other worry and strain. April arrived with no news of the rangers. From Casita came vague reports of raiders in the Sonoyta country—reports impossible to verify until his Mexican rangers returned. When these men rode in, one of them, Gonzales, an intelligent and reliable halfbreed, said he had met prospectors at the oasis. They had just come in on the Camino del Diablo, reported a terrible trip of heat and drought, and not a trace of the Yaqui's party.

"That settles it," declared Belding. "Yaqui never went to Sonoyta. He's circled round to the Devil's Road, and the rangers, Mercedes, Thorne, the horses—they—I'm afraid they have been lost in the desert. It's an old story on Camino del Diablo."

He had to tell Nell that, and it was an ordeal which left him weak.

Mrs. Belding listened to him, and was silent for a long time while she held the stricken Nell to her breast. Then she opposed his convictions with that quiet strength so characteristic of her arguments.

"Well, then," decided Belding, "Rojas headed the rangers at Papago Well or the Tanks."

"Tom, when you are down in the mouth you use poor judgment," she went on. "You know only by a miracle could Rojas or anybody have headed those white horses. Where's your old stubborn confidence? Yaqui was up on Diablo. Dick was up on Sol. And there were the other horses. They could not have been headed or caught. Miracles don't happen."

"All right, mother, it's sure good to hear you," said Belding. She always cheered him, and now he grasped at straws. "I'm not myself these days, don't mistake that. Tell us what you think. You always say you feel things when you really don't know them."

"I can say little more than what you said yourself the night Mercedes was taken away. You told Laddy to trust Yaqui, that he was a godsend. He might go south into some wild Sonora valley. He might lead Rojas into a trap. He would find water and grass where no Mexican or American could."

"But mother, they're gone seven weeks. Seven weeks! At the most I gave them six weeks. Seven weeks in the desert!"

"How do the Yaquis live?" she asked.

Belding could not reply to that, but hope revived in him. He had faith in his wife, though he could not in the least understand what he imagined was something mystic in her.

"Years ago when I was searching for my father I learned many things about this country," said Mrs. Belding. "You can never tell how long a man may live in the desert. The fiercest, most terrible and inaccessible places often have their hidden oasis. In his later years my father became a prospector. That was strange to me, for he never cared for gold or money. I learned that he was often gone in the desert for weeks, once for months. Then the time came when he never came back. That was years before I reached the southwest border and heard of him. Even then I did not for long give up hope of his coming back, I know now—something tells me—indeed, it seems his spirit tells me—he was lost. But I don't have that feeling for Yaqui and his party. Yaqui has given Rojas the slip or has ambushed him in some trap. Probably that took time and a long journey into Sonora. The Indian is too wise to start back now over dry trails. He'll curb the rangers; he'll wait. I seem to know this, dear Nell, so be brave, patient. Dick Gale will come back to you."

"Oh, mother!" cried Nell. "I can't give up hope while I have you."

That talk with the strong mother worked a change in Nell and Belding. Nell, who had done little but brood and watch the west and take violent rides, seemed to settle into a waiting patience that was sad, yet serene. She helped her mother more than ever; she was a comfort to Belding; she began to take active interest in the affairs of the growing village. Belding, who had been breaking under the strain of worry, recovered himself so that to outward appearance he was his old self. He alone knew, however, that his humor was forced, and that the slow burning wrath he felt for the Chases was flaming into hate.

Belding argued with himself that if Ben Chase and his son, Radford, had turned out to be big men in other ways than in the power to carry on great enterprises he might have become reconciled to them. But the father was greedy, grasping, hard, cold; the son added to those traits an overbearing disposition to rule, and he showed a fondness for drink and cards. These men were developing the valley, to be sure, and a horde of poor Mexicans and many Americans were benefiting from that development; nevertheless, these Chases were operating in a way which proved they cared only for themselves.

Belding shook off a lethargic spell and decided he had better set about several by no means small tasks, if he wanted to get them finished before the hot months. He made a trip to the Sonoyta Oasis. He satisfied himself that matters along the line were favorable, and that there was absolutely no trace of his rangers. Upon completing this trip he went to Casita with a number of his white thoroughbreds and shipped them to ranchers and horse-breeders in Texas. Then, being near the railroad, and having time, he went up to Tucson. There he learned some interesting particulars about the Chases. They had an office in the city; influential friends in the Capitol. They were powerful men in the rapidly growing finance of the West. They had interested the Southern Pacific Railroad, and in the near future a branch line was to be constructed from San Felipe to Forlorn River. These details of the Chase development were insignificant when compared to a matter striking close home to Belding. His responsibility had been subtly attacked. A doubt had been cast upon his capability of executing the duties of immigration inspector to the best advantage of the state. Belding divined that this was only an entering wedge. The Chases were bent upon driving him out of Forlorn River; but perhaps to serve better their own ends, they were proceeding at leisure. Belding returned home consumed by rage. But he controlled it. For the first time in his life he was afraid of himself. He had his wife and Nell to think of; and the old law of the West had gone forever.

"Dad, there's another Rojas round these diggings," was Nell's remark, after the greetings were over and the usual questions and answers passed.

Belding's exclamation was cut short by Nell's laugh. She was serious with a kind of amused contempt.

"Mr. Radford Chase!"

"Now Nell, what the—" roared Belding.

"Hush, Dad! Don't swear," interrupted Nell. "I only meant to tease you."

"Humph! Say, my girl, that name Chase makes me see red. If you must tease me hit on some other way. Sabe, senorita?"

"Si, si, Dad."

"Nell, you may as well tell him and have it over," said Mrs. Belding, quietly.

"You promised me once, Dad, that you'd not go packing a gun off down there, didn't you?"

"Yes, I remember," replied Belding; but he did not answer her smile.

"Will you promise again?" she asked, lightly. Here was Nell with arch eyes, yet not the old arch eyes, so full of fun and mischief. Her lips were tremulous; her cheeks seemed less round.

"Yes," rejoined Belding; and he knew why his voice was a little thick.

"Well, if you weren't such a good old blind Dad you'd have seen long ago the way Mr. Radford Chase ran round after me. At first it was only annoying, and I did not want to add to your worries. But these two weeks you've been gone I've been more than annoyed. After that time I struck Mr. Chase with my quirt he made all possible efforts to meet me. He did meet me wherever I went. He sent me letters till I got tired of sending them back.

"When you left home on your trips I don't know that he grew bolder, but he had more opportunity. I couldn't stay in the house all the time. There were mama's errands and sick people and my Sunday school, and what not. Mr. Chase waylaid me every time I went out. If he works any more I don't know when, unless it's when I'm asleep. He followed me until it was less embarassing for me to let him walk with me and talk his head off. He made love to me. He begged me to marry him. I told him I was already in love and engaged to be married. He said that didn't make any difference. Then I called him a fool.

"Next time he saw me he said he must explain. He meant I was being true to a man who, everybody on the border knew, had been lost in the desert. That—that hurt. Maybe—maybe it's true. Sometimes it seems terribly true. Since then, of course, I have stayed in the house to avoid being hurt again.

"But, Dad, a little thing like a girl sticking close to her mother and room doesn't stop Mr. Chase. I think he's crazy. Anyway, he's a most persistent fool. I want to be charitable, because the man swears he loves me, and maybe he does, but he is making me nervous. I don't sleep. I'm afraid to be in my room at night. I've gone to mother's room. He's always hanging round. Bold! Why, that isn't the thing to call Mr. Chase. He's absolutely without a sense of decency. He bribes our servants. He comes into our patio. Think of that! He makes the most ridiculous excuses. He bothers mother to death. I feel like a poor little rabbit holed by a hound. And I daren't peep out."

Somehow the thing struck Belding as funny, and he laughed. He had not had a laugh for so long that it made him feel good. He stopped only at sight of Nell's surprise and pain. Then he put his arms round her.

"Never mind, dear. I'm an old bear. But it tickled me, I guess. I sure hope Mr. Radford Chase has got it bad... Nell, it's only the old story. The fellows fall in love with you. It's your good looks, Nell. What a price women like you and Mercedes have to pay for beauty! I'd a d——— a good deal rather be ugly as a mud fence."

"So would I, Dad, if—if Dick would still love me."

"He wouldn't, you can gamble on that, as Laddy says. ... Well, the first time I catch this locoed Romeo sneaking round here I'll—I'll—"

"Dad, you promised."

"Confound it, Nell, I promised not to pack a gun. That's all. I'll only shoo this fellow off the place, gently, mind you, gently. I'll leave the rest for Dick Gale!"

"Oh, Dad!" cried Nell; and she clung to him wistful, frightened, yet something more.

"Don't mistake me, Nell. You have your own way, generally. You pull the wool over mother's eyes, and you wind me round your little finger. But you can't do either with Dick Gale. You're tender-hearted; you overlook the doings of this hound, Chase. But when Dick comes back, you just make up your mind to a little hell in the Chase camp. Oh, he'll find it out. And I sure want to be round when Dick hands Mr. Radford the same as he handed Rojas!"

Belding kept a sharp lookout for young Chase, and then, a few days later, learned that both son and father had gone off upon one of their frequent trips to Casa Grandes, near where their mines were situated.

April grew apace, and soon gave way to May. One morning Belding was called from some garden work by the whirring of an automobile and a "Holloa!" He went forward to the front yard and there saw a car he thought resembled one he had seen in Casita. It contained a familiar-looking driver, but the three figures in gray coats and veils were strange to him. By the time he had gotten to the road he decided two were women and the other a man. At the moment their faces were emerging from dusty veils. Belding saw an elderly, sallow-faced, rather frail-appearing man who was an entire stranger to him; a handsome dark-eyed woman whose hair showed white through her veil; and a superbly built girl, whose face made Belding at once think of Dick Gale.

"Is this Mr. Tom Belding, inspector of immigration?" inquired the gentleman, courteously.

"I'm Belding, and I know who you are," replied Belding in hearty amaze, as he stretched forth his big hand. "You're Dick Gale's Dad—the Governor, Dick used to say. I'm sure glad to meet you."

"Thank you. Yes, I'm Dick's governor, and here, Mr. Belding—Dick's mother and his sister Elsie."

Beaming his pleasure, Belding shook hands with the ladies, who showed their agitation clearly.

"Mr. Belding, I've come west to look up my lost son," said Mr. Gale. "His sister's letters were unanswered. We haven't heard from him in months. Is he still here with you?"

"Well, now, sure I'm awful sorry," began Belding, his slow mind at work. "Dick's away just now—been away for a considerable spell. I'm expecting him back any day.... Won't you come in? You're all dusty and hot and tired. Come in, and let mother and Nell make you comfortable. Of course you'll stay. We've a big house. You must stay till Dick comes back. Maybe that 'll be— Aw, I guess it won't be long.... Let me handle the baggage, Mr. Gale.... Come in. I sure am glad to meet you all."

Eager, excited, delighted, Belding went on talking as he ushered the Gales into the sitting-room, presenting them in his hearty way to the astounded Mrs. Belding and Nell. For the space of a few moments his wife and daughter were bewildered. Belding did not recollect any other occasion when a few callers had thrown them off their balance. But of course this was different. He was a little flustered himself—a circumstance that dawned upon him with surprise. When the Gales had been shown to rooms, Mrs. Belding gained the poise momentarily lost; but Nell came rushing back, wilder than a deer, in a state of excitement strange even for her.

"Oh! Dick's mother, his sister!" whispered Nell.

Belding observed the omission of the father in Nell's exclamation of mingled delight and alarm.

"His mother!" went on Nell. "Oh, I knew it! I always guessed it! Dick's people are proud, rich; they're somebody. I thought I'd faint when she looked at me. She was just curious—curious, but so cold and proud. She was wondering about me. I'm wearing his ring. It was his mother's, he said. I won't—I can't take it off. And I'm scared.... But the sister—oh, she's lovely and sweet— proud, too. I felt warm all over when she looked at me. I—I wanted to kiss her. She looks like Dick when he first came to us. But he's changed. They'll hardly recognize him.... To think they've come! And I had to be looking a fright, when of all times on earth I'd want to look my best."

Nell, out of breath, ran away evidently to make herself presentable, according to her idea of the exigency of the case. Belding caught a glimpse of his wife's face as she went out, and it wore a sad, strange, anxious expression. Then Belding sat alone, pondering the contracting emotions of his wife and daughter. It was beyond his understanding. Women were creatures of feeling. Belding saw reason to be delighted to entertain Dick's family; and for the time being no disturbing thought entered his mind.

Presently the Gales came back into the sitting-room, looking very different without the long gray cloaks and veils. Belding saw distinction and elegance. Mr. Gale seemed a grave, troubled, kindly person, ill in body and mind. Belding received the same impression of power that Ben Chase had given him, only here it was minus any harshness or hard quality. He gathered that Mr.

Gale was a man of authority. Mrs. Gale rather frightened Belding, but he could not have told why. The girl was just like Dick as he used to be.

Their manner of speaking also reminded Belding of Dick. They talked of the ride from Ash Fork down to the border, of the ugly and torn-up Casita, of the heat and dust and cactus along the trail. Presently Nell came in, now cool and sweet in white, with a red rose at her breast. Belding had never been so proud of her. He saw that she meant to appear well in the eyes of Dick's people, and began to have a faint perception of what the ordeal was for her. Belding imagined the sooner the Gales were told that Dick was to marry Nell the better for all concerned, and especially for Nell. In the general conversation that ensued he sought for an opening in which to tell this important news, but he was kept so busy answering questions about his position on the border, the kind of place Forlorn River was, the reason for so many tents, etc., that he was unable to find opportunity.

"It's very interesting, very interesting," said Mr. Gale. "At another time I want to learn all you'll tell me about the West. It's new to me. I'm surprised, amazed, sir, I may say.... But, Mr. Belding, what I want to know most is about my son. I'm broken in health. I've worried myself ill over him. I don't mind telling you, sir, that we quarreled. I laughed at his threats. He went away. And I've come to see that I didn't know Richard. I was wrong to upbraid him. For a year we've known nothing of his doings, and now for almost six months we've not heard from him at all. Frankly, Mr. Belding, I weakened first, and I've come to hunt him up. My fear is that I didn't start soon enough. The boy will have a great position some day—God knows, perhaps soon! I should not have allowed him to run over this wild country for so long. But I hoped, though I hardly believed, that he might find himself. Now I'm afraid he's—"

Mr. Gale paused and the white hand he raised expressively shook a little.

Belding was not so thick-witted where men were concerned. He saw how the matter lay between Dick Gale and his father.

"Well, Mr. Gale, sure most young bucks from the East go to the bad out here," he said, bluntly.

"I've been told that," replied Mr. Gale; and a shade overspread his worn face.

"They blow their money, then go punching cows, take to whiskey."

"Yes," rejoined Mr. Gale, feebly nodding.

"Then they get to gambling, lose their jobs," went on Belding.

Mr. Gale lifted haggard eyes.

"Then it's bumming around, regular tramps, and to the bad generally." Belding spread wide his big arms, and when one of them dropped round Nell, who sat beside him, she squeezed his hand tight. "Sure, it's the regular thing," he concluded, cheerfully.

He rather felt a little glee at Mr. Gale's distress, and Mrs. Gale's crushed I-told-you-so woe in no wise bothered him; but the look in the big, dark eyes of Dick's sister was too much for Belding.

He choked off his characteristic oath when excited and blurted out, "Say, but Dick Gale never went to the bad!... Listen!"

Belding had scarcely started Dick Gale's story when he perceived that never in his life had he such an absorbed and breathless audience. Presently they were awed, and at the conclusion of that story they sat white-faced, still, amazed beyond speech. Dick Gale's advent in Casita, his rescue of Mercedes, his life as a border ranger certainly lost no picturesque or daring or even noble detail in Belding's telling. He kept back nothing but the present doubt of Dick's safety.

Dick's sister was the first of the three to recover herself.

"Oh, father!" she cried; and there was a glorious light in her eyes. "Deep down in my heart I knew Dick was a man!"

Mr. Gale rose unsteadily from his chair. His frailty was now painfully manifest.

"Mr. Belding, do you mean my son—Richard Gale—has done all that you told us?" he asked, incredulously.

"I sure do," replied Belding, with hearty good will.

"Martha, do you hear?" Mr. Gale turned to question his wife. She could not answer. Her face had not yet regained its natural color.

"He faced that bandit and his gang alone—he fought them?" demanded Mr. Gale, his voice stronger.

"Dick mopped up the floor with the whole outfit!"

"He rescued a Spanish girl, went into the desert without food, weapons, anything but his hands? Richard Gale, whose hands were always useless?"

Belding nodded with a grin.

"He's a ranger now—riding, fighting, sleeping on the sand, preparing his own food?"

"Well, I should smile," rejoined Belding.

"He cares for his horse, with his own hands?" This query seemed to be the climax of Mr. Gale's strange hunger for truth. He had raised his head a little higher, and his eye was brighter.

Mention of a horse fired Belding's blood.

"Does Dick Gale care for his horse? Say, there are not many men as well loved as that white horse of Dick's. Blanco Sol he is, Mr. Gale. That's Mex for White Sun. Wait till you see Blanco Sol! Bar one, the whitest, biggest, strongest, fastest, grandest horse in the Southwest!"

"So he loves a horse! I shall not know my own son.... Mr. Belding, you say Richard works for you. May I ask, at what salary?"

"He gets forty dollars, board and outfit," replied Belding, proudly.

"Forty dollars?" echoed the father. "By the day or week?"

"The month, of course," said Belding, somewhat taken aback.

"Forty dollars a month for a young man who spent five hundred in the same time when he was at college, and who ran it into thousands when he got out!"

Mr. Gale laughed for the first time, and it was the laugh of a man who wanted to believe what he heard yet scarcely dared to do it.

"What does he do with so much money—money earned by peril, toil, sweat, and blood? Forty dollars a month!"

"He saves it," replied Belding.

Evidently this was too much for Dick Gale's father, and he gazed at his wife in sheer speechless astonishment. Dick's sister clapped her hands like a little child.

Belding saw that the moment was propitious.

"Sure he saves it. Dick's engaged to marry Nell here. My stepdaughter, Nell Burton."

"Oh-h, Dad!" faltered Nell; and she rose, white as her dress.

How strange it was to see Dick's mother and sister rise, also, and turn to Nell with dark, proud, searching eyes. Belding vaguely realized some blunder he had made. Nell's white, appealing face gave him a pang. What had he done? Surely this family of Dick's ought to know his relation to Nell. There was a silence that positively made Belding nervous.

Then Elsie Gale stepped close to Nell.

"Miss Burton, are you really Richard's betrothed?"

Nell's tremulous lips framed an affirmative, but never uttered it. She held out her hand, showing the ring Dick had given her. Miss Gale's recognition was instant, and her response was warm, sweet, gracious.

"I think I am going to be very, very glad," she said, and kissed Nell.

"Miss Burton, we are learning wonderful things about Richard," added Mr. Gale, in an earnest though shaken voice. "If you have had to do with making a man of him—and now I begin to see, to believe so—may God bless you!... My dear girl, I have not really looked at you. Richard's fiancee!... Mother, we have not found him yet, but I think we've found his secret. We believed him a lost son. But here is his sweetheart!"

It was only then that the pride and hauteur of Mrs. Gale's face broke into an expression of mingled pain and joy. She opened her arms. Nell, uttering a strange little stifled cry, flew into them.

Belding suddenly discovered an unaccountable blur in his sight. He could not see perfectly, and that was why, when Mrs. Belding entered the sitting-room, he was not certain that her face was as sad and white as it seemed.

XV

BOUND IN THE DESERT

FAR away from Forlorn River Dick Gale sat stunned, gazing down into the purple depths where Rojas had plunged to his death. The Yaqui stood motionless upon the steep red wall of lava from which he had cut the bandit's hold. Mercedes lay quietly where she had fallen. From across the depths there came to Gale's ear the Indian's strange, wild cry.

Then silence, hollow, breathless, stony silence enveloped the great abyss and its upheaved lava walls. The sun was setting. Every instant the haze reddened and thickened.

Action on the part of the Yaqui loosened the spell which held Gale as motionless as his surroundings. The Indian was edging back toward the ledge. He did not move with his former lithe and sure freedom. He crawled, slipped, dragged himself, rested often, and went on again. He had been wounded. When at last he reached the ledge where Mercedes lay Gale jumped to his feet, strong and thrilling, spurred to meet the responsibility that now rested upon him.

Swiftly he turned to where Thorne lay. The cavalryman was just returning to consciousness. Gale ran for a canteen, bathed his face, made him drink. The look in Thorne's eyes was hard to bear.

"Thorne! Thorne! it's all right, it's all right!" cried Gale, in piercing tones. "Mercedes is safe! Yaqui saved her! Rojas is done for! Yaqui jumped down the wall and drove the bandit off the ledge. Cut him loose from the wall, foot by foot, hand by hand! We've won the fight, Thorne."

For Thorne these were marvelous strength-giving words. The dark horror left his eyes, and they began to dilate, to shine. He stood up, dizzily but unaided, and he gazed across the crater. Yaqui had reached the side of Mercedes, was bending over her. She stirred. Yaqui lifted her to her feet. She appeared weak, unable to stand alone. But she faced across the crater and waved her hand. She was unharmed. Thorne lifted both arms above head, and from his lips issued a cry. It was neither call nor holloa nor welcome nor answer. Like the Yaqui's, it could scarcely be named. But it was deep, husky, prolonged, terribly human in its intensity. It made Gale shudder and made his heart beat like a trip hammer. Mercedes again waved a white hand. The Yaqui waved, too, and Gale saw in the action an urgent signal.

Hastily taking up canteen and rifles, Gale put a supporting arm around Thorne.

"Come, old man. Can you walk? Sure you can walk! Lean on me, and we'll soon get out of this. Don't look across. Look where you step. We've not much time before dark. Oh, Thorne, I'm afraid Jim has cashed in! And the last I saw of Laddy he was badly hurt."

Gale was keyed up to a high pitch of excitement and alertness. He seemed to be able to do many things. But once off the ragged notched lava into the trail he had not such difficulty with Thorne, and could keep his keen gaze shifting everywhere for sight of enemies.

"Listen, Thorne! What's that?" asked Gale, halting as they came to a place where the trail led down through rough breaks in the lava. The silence was broken by a strange sound, almost unbelieveable considering the time and place. A voice was droning: "Turn the lady, turn! Turn the lady, turn! Alamon left. All swing; turn the lady, turn!"

434

"Hello, Jim," called Gale, dragging Thorne round the corner of lava. "Where are you? Oh, you son of a gun! I thought you were dead. Oh, I'm glad to see you! Jim, are you hurt?"

Jim Lash stood in the trail leaning over the butt of his rifle, which evidently he was utilizing as a crutch. He was pale but smiling. His hands were bloody. A scarf had been bound tightly round his left leg just above the knee. The leg hung limp, and the foot dragged.

"I reckon I ain't injured much," replied Him. "But my leg hurts like hell, if you want to know."

"Laddy! Oh, where's Laddy?"

"He's just across the crack there. I was trying to get to him. We had it hot an' heavy down here. Laddy was pretty bad shot up before he tried to head Rojas off the trail.... Dick, did you see the Yaqui go after Rojas?"

"Did I!" exclaimed Gale, grimly.

"The finish was all that saved me from runnin' loco plumb over the rim. You see I was closer'n you to where Mercedes was hid. When Rojas an' his last Greaser started across, Laddy went after them, but I couldn't. Laddy did for Rojas's man, then went down himself. But he got up an' fell, got up, went on, an' fell again. Laddy kept doin' that till he dropped for good. I reckon our chances are against findin' him alive.... I tell you, boys, Rojas was hell-bent. An' Mercedes was game. I saw her shoot him. But mebbe bullets couldn't stop him then. If I didn't sweat blood when Mercedes was fightin' him on the cliff! Then the finish! Only a Yaqui could have done that.... Thorne, you didn't miss it?"

"Yes, I was down and out," replied the cavalryman.

"It's a shame. Greatest stunt I ever seen! Thorne, you're standin' up pretty fair. How about you? Dick, is he bad hurt?"

"No, he's not. A hard knock on the skull and a scalp wound," replied Dick. "Here, Jim, let me help you over this place."

Step by step Gale got the two injured men down the uneven declivity and then across the narrow lava bridge over the fissure. Here he bade them rest while he went along the trail on that side to search for Laddy. Gale found the ranger stretched out, face downward, a reddened hand clutching a gun. Gale thought he was dead. Upon examination, however, it was found that Ladd still lived, though he had many wounds. Gale lifted him and carried him back to the others.

"He's alive, but that's all," said Dick, as he laid the ranger down. "Do what you can. Stop the blood. Laddy's tough as cactus, you know. I'll hurry back for Mercedes and Yaqui."

Gale, like a fleet, sure-footed mountain sheep, ran along the trail. When he came across the Mexican, Rojas's last ally, Gale had evidence of the terrible execution of the .405. He did not pause. On the first part of that descent he made faster time than had Rojas. But he exercised care along the hard, slippery, ragged slope leading to the ledge. Presently he came upon Mercedes and the Yaqui. She ran right into Dick's arms, and there her strength, if not her courage, broke, and she grew lax.

"Mercedes, you're safe! Thorne's safe. It's all right now."

"Rojas!" she whispered.

"Gone! To the bottom of the crater! A Yaqui's vengeance, Mercedes."

He heard the girl whisper the name of the Virgin. Then he gathered her up in his arms.

"Come, Yaqui."

The Indian grunted. He had one hand pressed close over a bloody place in his shoulder. Gale looked keenly at him. Yaqui was inscrutable, as of old, yet Gale somehow knew that wound meant little to him. The Indian followed him.

Without pausing, moving slowly in some places, very carefully in others, and swiftly on the smooth part of the trail, Gale carried Mercedes up to the rim and along to the the others. Jim Lash worked awkwardly over Ladd. Thorne was trying to assist. Ladd, himself, was conscious, but he was a pallid, apparently a death-stricken man. The greeting between Mercedes and Thorne was calm—strangely so, it seemed to Gale. But he was calm himself. Ladd smiled at him, and evidently would have spoken had he the power. Yaqui then joined the group, and his piercing eyes roved from one to the other, lingering longest over Ladd.

"Dick, I'm figger'n hard," said Jim, faintly. "In a minute it 'll be up to you an' Mercedes. I've about shot my bolt.... Reckon you'll do— best by bringin' up blankets—water—salt—firewood. Laddy's got—one chance—in a hundred. Fix him up—first. Use hot salt water. If my leg's broke—set it best you can. That hole in Yaqui—only 'll bother him a day. Thorne's bad hurt... Now rustle—Dick, old—boy."

Lash's voice died away in a husky whisper, and he quietly lay back, stretching out all but the crippled leg. Gale examined it, assured himself the bones had not been broken, and then rose ready to go down the trail.

"Mercedes, hold Thorne's head up, in your lap—so. Now I'll go."

On the moment Yaqui appeared to have completed the binding of his wounded shoulder, and he started to follow Gale. He paid no attention to Gale's order for him to stay back. But he was slow, and gradually Gale forged ahead. The lingering brightness of the sunset lightened the trail, and the descent to the arroyo was swift and easy. Some of the white horses had come in for water. Blanco Sol spied Gale and whistled and came pounding toward him. It was twilight down in the arroyo. Yaqui appeared and began collecting a bundle of mesquite sticks. Gale hastily put together the things he needed; and, packing them all in a tarpaulin, he turned to retrace his steps up the trail.

Darkness was setting in. The trail was narrow, exceedingly steep, and in some places fronted on precipices. Gale's burden was not very heavy, but its bulk made it unwieldy, and it was always overbalancing him or knocking against the wall side of the trail. Gale found it necessary to wait for Yaqui to take the lead. The Indian's eyes must have seen as well at night as by day. Gale toiled upward, shouldering, swinging, dragging the big pack; and, though the ascent of the slope was not really long, it seemed endless. At last they reached a level, and were soon on the spot with Mercedes and the injured men.

Gale then set to work. Yaqui's part was to keep the fire blazing and the water hot, Mercedes's to help Gale in what way she could. Gale found Ladd had many wounds, yet not one of them was directly in a vital place. Evidently, the ranger had almost bled to death. He remained unconscious through Gale's operations. According to Jim Lash, Ladd had one chance in a hundred, but Gale considered it one in a thousand. Having done all that was possible for the ranger, Gale slipped blankets under and around him, and then turned his attention to Lash.

Jim came out of his stupor. A mushrooming bullet had torn a great hole in his leg. Gale, upon examination, could not be sure the bones had been missed, but there was no bad break. The application of hot salt water made Jim groan. When he had been bandaged and laid beside Ladd,

Gale went on to the cavalryman. Thorne was very weak and scarcely conscious. A furrow had been plowed through his scalp down to the bone. When it had been dressed, Mercedes collapsed. Gale laid her with the three in a row and covered them with blankets and the tarpaulin.

Then Yaqui submitted to examination. A bullet had gone through the Indian's shoulder. To Gale it appeared serious. Yaqui said it was a flea bite. But he allowed Gale to bandage it, and obeyed when he was told to lie quiet in his blanket beside the fire.

Gale stood guard. He seemed still calm, and wondered at what he considered a strange absence of poignant feeling. If he had felt weariness it was now gone. He coaxed the fire with as little wood as would keep it burning; he sat beside it; he walked to and fro close by; sometimes he stood over the five sleepers, wondering if two of them, at least, would ever awaken.

Time had passed swiftly, but as the necessity for immediate action had gone by, the hours gradually assumed something of their normal length. The night wore on. The air grew colder, the stars brighter, the sky bluer, and, if such could be possible, the silence more intense. The fire burned out, and for lack of wood could not be rekindled. Gale patrolled his short beat, becoming colder and damper as dawn approached. The darkness grew so dense that he could not see the pale faces of the sleepers. He dreaded the gray dawn and the light. Slowly the heavy black belt close to the lava changed to a pale gloom, then to gray, and after that morning came quickly.

The hour had come for Dick Gale to face his great problem. It was natural that he hung back a little at first; natural that when he went forward to look at the quiet sleepers he did so with a grim and stern force urging him. Yaqui stirred, roused, yawned, got up; and, though he did not smile at Gale, a light shone swiftly across his dark face. His shoulder drooped and appeared stiff, otherwise he was himself. Mercedes lay in deep slumber. Thorne had a high fever, and was beginning to show signs of restlessness. Ladd seemed just barely alive. Jim Lash slept as if he was not much the worse for his wound.

Gale rose from his examination with a sharp breaking of his cold mood. While there was life in Thorne and Ladd there was hope for them. Then he faced his problem, and his decision was instant.

He awoke Mercedes. How wondering, wistful, beautiful was that first opening flash of her eyes! Then the dark, troubled thought came. Swiftly she sat up.

"Mercedes—come. Are you all right? Laddy is alive Thorne's not—not so bad. But we've got a job on our hands! You must help me."

She bent over Thorne and laid her hands on his hot face. Then she rose—a woman such as he had imagined she might be in an hour of trial.

Gale took up Ladd as carefully and gently as possible.

"Mercedes, bring what you can carry and follow me," he said. Then, motioning for Yaqui to remain there, he turned down the slope with Ladd in his arms.

Neither pausing nor making a misstep nor conscious of great effort, Gale carried the wounded man down into the arroyo. Mercedes kept at his heels, light, supple, lithe as a panther. He left her with Ladd and went back. When he had started off with Thorne in his arms he felt the tax on his strength. Surely and swiftly, however, he bore the cavalryman down the trail to lay him beside Ladd. Again he started back, and when he began to mount the steep lava steps he was hot, wet, breathing hard. As he reached the scene of that night's camp a voice greeted him. Jim Lash was sitting up.

"Hello, Dick. I woke some late this mornin'. Where's Laddy? Dick, you ain't a-goin' to say—"

"Laddy's alive—that's about all," replied Dick.

"Where's Thorne an' Mercedes? Look here, man. I reckon you ain't packin' this crippled outfit down that awful trail?"

"Had to, Jim. An hour's sun—would kill—both Laddy and Thorne. Come on now."

For once Jim Lash's cool good nature and careless indifference gave precedence to amaze and concern.

"Always knew you was a husky chap. But, Dick, you're no hoss! Get me a crutch an' give me a lift on one side."

"Come on," replied Gale. "I've no time to monkey."

He lifted the ranger, called to Yaqui to follow with some of the camp outfit, and once more essayed the steep descent. Jim Lash was the heaviest man of the three, and Gale's strength was put to enormous strain to carry him on that broken trail. Nevertheless, Gale went down, down, walking swiftly and surely over the bad places; and at last he staggered into the arroyo with bursting heart and red-blinded eyes. When he had recovered he made a final trip up the slope for the camp effects which Yaqui had been unable to carry.

Then he drew Jim and Mercedes and Yaqui, also, into an earnest discussion of ways and means whereby to fight for the life of Thorne. Ladd's case Gale now considered hopeless, though he meant to fight for him, too, as long as he breathed.

In the labor of watching and nursing it seemed to Gale that two days and two nights slipped by like a few hours. During that time the Indian recovered from his injury, and became capable of performing all except heavy tasks. Then Gale succumbed to weariness. After his much-needed rest he relieved Mercedes of the care and watch over Thorne which, up to that time, she had absolutely refused to relinquish. The cavalryman had high fever, and Gale feared he had developed blood poisoning. He required constant attention. His condition slowly grew worse, and there came a day which Gale thought surely was the end. But that day passed, and the night, and the next day, and Thorne lived on, ghastly, stricken, raving. Mercedes hung over him with jealous, passionate care and did all that could have been humanly done for a man. She grew wan, absorbed, silent. But suddenly, and to Gale's amaze and thanksgiving, there came an abatement of Thorne's fever. With it some of the heat and redness of the inflamed wound disappeared. Next morning he was conscious, and Gale grasped some of the hope that Mercedes had never abandoned. He forced her to rest while he attended to Thorne. That day he saw that the crisis was past. Recovery for Thorne was now possible, and would perhaps depend entirely upon the care he received.

Jim Lash's wound healed without any aggravating symptoms. It would be only a matter of time until he had the use of his leg again. All these days, however, there was little apparent change in Ladd's condition unless it was that he seemed to fade away as he lingered. At first his wounds remained open; they bled a little all the time outwardly, perhaps internally also; the blood did not seem to clot, and so the bullet holes did not close. Then Yaqui asked for the care of Ladd. Gale yielded it with opposing thoughts—that Ladd would waste slowly away till life ceased, and that there never was any telling what might lie in the power of this strange Indian. Yaqui absented himself from camp for a while, and when he returned he carried the roots and leaves of desert plants unknown to Gale. From these the Indian brewed an ointment. Then he stripped the bandages from Ladd and applied the mixture to his wounds. That done, he let him lie with the wounds exposed to the air, at night covering him. Next day he again exposed the wounds to the warm, dry air. Slowly they closed, and Ladd ceased to bleed externally.

Days passed and grew into what Gale imagined must have been weeks. Yaqui recovered fully. Jim Lash began to move about on a crutch; he shared the Indian's watch over Ladd. Thorne lay haggard, emaciated ghost of his rugged self, but with life in the eyes that turned always toward Mercedes. Ladd lingered and lingered. The life seemingly would not leave his bullet-pierced body. He faded, withered, shrunk till he was almost a skeleton. He knew those who worked and watched over him, but he had no power of speech. His eyes and eyelids moved; the rest of him seemed stone. All those days nothing except water was given him. It was marvelous how tenaciously, however feebly, he clung to life. Gale imagined it was the Yaqui's spirit that held back death. That tireless, implacable, inscrutable savage was ever at the ranger's side. His great somber eyes burned. At length he went to Gale, and, with that strange light flitting across the hard bronzed face, he said Ladd would live.

The second day after Ladd had been given such thin nourishment as he could swallow he recovered the use of his tongue.

"Shore—this's—hell," he whispered.

That was a characteristic speech for the ranger, Gale thought; and indeed it made all who heard it smile while their eyes were wet.

From that time forward Ladd gained, but he gained so immeasurably slowly that only the eyes of hope could have seen any improvement. Jim Lash threw away his crutch, and Thorne was well, if still somewhat weak, before Ladd could lift his arm or turn his head. A kind of long, immovable gloom passed, like a shadow, from his face. His whispers grew stronger. And the day arrived when Gale, who was perhaps the least optimistic, threw doubt to the winds and knew the ranger would get well. For Gale that joyous moment of realization was one in which he seemed to return to a former self long absent. He experienced an elevation of soul. He was suddenly overwhelmed with gratefulness, humility, awe. A gloomy black terror had passed by. He wanted to thank the faithful Mercedes, and Thorne for getting well, and the cheerful Lash, and Ladd himself, and that strange and wonderful Yaqui, now such a splendid figure. He thought of home and Nell. The terrible encompassing red slopes lost something of their fearsomeness, and there was a good spirit hovering near.

"Boys, come round," called Ladd, in his low voice. "An' you, Mercedes. An' call the Yaqui."

Ladd lay in the shade of the brush shelter that had been erected. His head was raised slightly on a pillow. There seemed little of him but long lean lines, and if it had not been for his keen, thoughtful, kindly eyes, his face would have resembled a death mask of a man starved.

"Shore I want to know what day is it an' what month?" asked Ladd.

Nobody could answer him. The question seemed a surprise to Gale, and evidently was so to the others.

"Look at that cactus," went on Ladd.

Near the wall of lava a stunted saguaro lifted its head. A few shriveled blossoms that had once been white hung along the fluted column.

"I reckon according to that giant cactus it's somewheres along the end of March," said Jim Lash, soberly.

"Shore it's April. Look where the sun is. An' can't you feel it's gettin' hot?"

"Supposin' it is April?" queried Lash slowly.

"Well, what I'm drivin' at is it's about time you all was hittin' the trail back to Forlorn River, before the waterholes dry out."

"Laddy, I reckon we'll start soon as you're able to be put on a hoss."

"Shore that 'll be too late."

A silence ensued, in which those who heard Ladd gazed fixedly at him and then at one another. Lash uneasily shifted the position of his lame leg, and Gale saw him moisten his lips with his tongue.

"Charlie Ladd, I ain't reckonin' you mean we're to ride off an' leave you here?"

"What else is there to do? The hot weather's close. Pretty soon most of the waterholes will be dry. You can't travel then.... I'm on my back here, an' God only knows when I could be packed out. Not for weeks, mebbe. I'll never be any good again, even if I was to get out alive.... You see, shore this sort of case comes round sometimes in the desert. It's common enough. I've heard of several cases where men had to go an' leave a feller behind. It's reasonable. If you're fightin' the desert you can't afford to be sentimental... Now, as I said, I'm all in. So what's the sense of you waitin' here, when it means the old desert story? By goin' now mebbe you'll get home. If you wait on a chance of takin' me, you'll be too late. Pretty soon this lava 'll be one roastin' hell. Shore now, boys, you'll see this the right way? Jim, old pard?"

"No, Laddy, an' I can't figger how you could ever ask me."

"Shore then leave me here with Yaqui an' a couple of the hosses. We can eat sheep meat. An' if the water holds out—"

"No!" interrupted Lash, violently.

Ladd's eyes sought Gale's face.

"Son, you ain't bull-headed like Jim. You'll see the sense of it. There's Nell a-waitin' back at Forlorn River. Think what it means to her! She's a damn fine girl, Dick, an' what right have you to break her heart for an old worn-out cowpuncher? Think how she's watchin' for you with that sweet face all sad an' troubled, an' her eyes turnin' black. You'll go, son, won't you?"

Dick shook his head.

The ranger turned his gaze upon Thorne, and now the keen, glistening light in his gray eyes had blurred.

"Thorne, it's different with you. Jim's a fool, an' young Gale has been punctured by *choya* thorns. He's got the desert poison in his blood. But you now—you've no call to stick—you can find that trail out. It's easy to follow, made by so many shod hosses. Take your wife an' go.... Shore you'll go, Thorne?"

Deliberately and without an instant's hesitation the cavalryman replied "No."

Ladd then directed his appeal to Mercedes. His face was now convulsed, and his voice, though it had sunk to a whisper, was clear, and beautiful with some rich quality that Gale had never heard in it.

"Mercedes, you're a woman. You're the woman we fought for. An' some of us are shore goin' to die for you. Don't make it all for nothin'. Let us feel we saved the woman. Shore you can make

Thorne go. He'll have to go if you say. They'll all have to go. Think of the years of love an' happiness in store for you. A week or so an' it 'll be too late. Can you stand for me seein' you?... Let me tell you, Mercedes, when the summer heat hits the lava we'll all wither an' curl up like shavin's near a fire. A wind of hell will blow up this slope. Look at them mesquites. See the twist in them. That's the torture of heat an' thirst. Do you want me or all us men seein' you like that?... Mercedes, don't make it all for nothin'. Say you'll persuade Thorne, if not the others."

For all the effect his appeal had to move her Mercedes might have possessed a heart as hard and fixed as the surrounding lava.

"Never!"

White-faced, with great black eyes flashing, the Spanish girl spoke the word that bound her and her companions in the desert.

The subject was never mentioned again. Gale thought that he read a sinister purpose in Ladd's mind. To his astonishment, Lash came to him with the same fancy. After that they made certain there never was a gun within reach of Ladd's clutching, clawlike hands.

Gradually a somber spell lifted from the ranger's mind. When he was entirely free of it he began to gather strength daily. Then it was as if he had never known patience—he who had shown so well how to wait. He was in a frenzy to get well. He appetite could not be satisfied.

The sun climbed higher, whiter, hotter. At midday a wind from gulfward roared up the arroyo, and now only palos verdes and the few saguaros were green. Every day the water in the lava hole sank an inch.

The Yaqui alone spent the waiting time in activity. He made trips up on the lava slope, and each time he returned with guns or boots or sombreros, or something belonging to the bandits that had fallen. He never fetched in a saddle or bridle, and from that the rangers concluded Rojas's horses had long before taken their back trail. What speculation, what consternation those saddled horses would cause if they returned to Forlorn River!

As Ladd improved there was one story he had to hear every day. It was the one relating to what he had missed—the sight of Rojas pursued and plunged to his doom. The thing had a morbid fascination for the sick ranger. He reveled in it. He tortured Mercedes. His gentleness and consideration, heretofore so marked, were in abeyance to some sinister, ghastly joy. But to humor him Mercedes racked her soul with the sensations she had suffered when Rojas hounded her out on the ledge; when she shot him; when she sprang to throw herself over the precipice; when she fought him; when with half-blinded eyes she looked up to see the merciless Yaqui reaching for the bandit. Ladd fed his cruel longing with Thorne's poignant recollections, with the keen, clear, never-to-be-forgotten shocks to Gale's eye and ear. Jim Lash, for one at least, never tired of telling how he had seen and heard the tragedy, and every time in the telling it gathered some more tragic and gruesome detail. Jim believed in satiating the ranger. Then in the twilight, when the campfire burned, Ladd would try to get the Yaqui to tell his side of the story. But this the Indian would never do. There was only the expression of his fathomless eyes and the set passion of his massive face.

Those waiting days grew into weeks. Ladd gained very slowly. Nevertheless, at last he could walk about, and soon he averred that, strapped to a horse, he could last out the trip to Forlorn River.

There was rejoicing in camp, and plans were eagerly suggested. The Yaqui happened to be absent. When he returned the rangers told him they were now ready to undertake the journey back across lava and cactus.

Yaqui shook his head. They declared again their intention.

"No!" replied the Indian, and his deep, sonorous voice rolled out upon the quiet of the arroyo. He spoke briefly then. They had waited too long. The smaller waterholes back in the trail were dry. The hot summer was upon them. There could be only death waiting down in the burning valley. Here was water and grass and wood and shade from the sun's rays, and sheep to be killed on the peaks. The water would hold unless the season was that dreaded ano seco of the Mexicans.

"Wait for rain," concluded Yaqui, and now as never before he spoke as one with authority. "If no rain—" Silently he lifted his hand.

XVI

MOUNTAIN SHEEP

WHAT Gale might have thought an appalling situation, if considered from a safe and comfortable home away from the desert, became, now that he was shut in by the red-ribbed lava walls and great dry wastes, a matter calmly accepted as inevitable. So he imagined it was accepted by the others. Not even Mercedes uttered a regret. No word was spoken of home. If there was thought of loved one, it was locked deep in their minds. In Mercedes there was no change in womanly quality, perhaps because all she had to love was there in the desert with her.

Gale had often pondered over this singular change in character. He had trained himself, in order to fight a paralyzing something in the desert's influence, to oppose with memory and thought an insidious primitive retrogression to what was scarcely consciousness at all, merely a savage's instinct of sight and sound. He felt the need now of redoubled effort. For there was a sheer happiness in drifting. Not only was it easy to forget, it was hard to remember. His idea was that a man laboring under a great wrong, a great crime, a great passion might find the lonely desert a fitting place for either remembrance or oblivion, according to the nature of his soul. But an ordinary, healthy, reasonably happy mortal who loved the open with its blaze of sun and sweep of wind would have a task to keep from going backward to the natural man as he was before civilization.

By tacit agreement Ladd again became the leader of the party. Ladd was a man who would have taken all the responsibility whether or not it was given him. In moments of hazard, of uncertainty, Lash and Gale, even Belding, unconsciously looked to the ranger. He had that kind of power.

The first thing Ladd asked was to have the store of food that remained spread out upon a tarpaulin. Assuredly, it was a slender enough supply. The ranger stood for long moments gazing down at it. He was groping among past experiences, calling back from his years of life on range and desert that which might be valuable for the present issue. It was impossible to read the gravity of Ladd's face, for he still looked like a dead man, but the slow shake of his head told Gale much. There was a grain of hope, however, in the significance with which he touched the bags of salt and said, "Shore it was sense packin' all that salt!"

Then he turned to face his comrades.

"That's little grub for six starvin' people corralled in the desert. But the grub end ain't worryin' me. Yaqui can get sheep up the slopes. Water! That's the beginnin' and middle an' end of our case."

"Laddy, I reckon the waterhole here never goes dry," replied Jim.

"Ask the Indian."

Upon being questioned, Yaqui repeated what he had said about the dreaded ano seco of the Mexicans. In a dry year this waterhole failed.

"Dick, take a rope an' see how much water's in the hole."

Gale could not find bottom with a thirty foot lasso. The water was as cool, clear, sweet as if it had been kept in a shaded iron receptacle.

Ladd welcomed this information with surprise and gladness.

"Let's see. Last year was shore pretty dry. Mebbe this summer won't be. Mebbe our wonderful good luck'll hold. Ask Yaqui if he thinks it 'll rain."

Mercedes questioned the Indian.

"He says no man can tell surely. But he thinks the rain will come," she replied.

"Shore it 'll rain, you can gamble on that now," continued Ladd. "If there's only grass for the hosses! We can't get out of here without hosses. Dick, take the Indian an' scout down the arroyo. To-day I seen the hosses were gettin' fat. Gettin' fat in this desert! But mebbe they've about grazed up all the grass. Go an' see, Dick. An' may you come back with more good news!"

Gale, upon the few occasions when he had wandered down the arroyo, had never gone far. The Yaqui said there was grass for the horses, and until now no one had given the question more consideration. Gale found that the arroyo widened as it opened. Near the head, where it was narrow, the grass lined the course of the dry stream bed. But farther down this stream bed spread out. There was every indication that at flood seasons the water covered the floor of the arroyo. The farther Gale went the thicker and larger grew the gnarled mesquites and palo verdes, the more cactus and greasewood there were, and other desert growths. Patches of gray grass grew everywhere. Gale began to wonder where the horses were. Finally the trees and brush thinned out, and a mile-wide gray plain stretched down to reddish sand dunes. Over to one side were the white horses, and even as Gale saw them both Blanco Diablo and Sol lifted their heads and, with white manes tossing in the wind, whistled clarion calls. Here was grass enough for many horses; the arroyo was indeed an oasis.

Ladd and the others were awaiting Gale's report, and they received it with calmness, yet with a joy no less evident because it was restrained. Gale, in his keen observation at the moment, found that he and his comrades turned with glad eyes to the woman of the party.

"Senor Laddy, you think—you believe—we shall—" she faltered, and her voice failed. It was the woman in her, weakening in the light of real hope, of the happiness now possible beyond that desert barrier.

"Mercedes, no white man can tell what'll come to pass out here," said Ladd, earnestly. "Shore I have hopes now I never dreamed of. I was pretty near a dead man. The Indian saved me. Queer notions have come into my head about Yaqui. I don't understand them. He seems when you look at him only a squalid, sullen, vengeful savage. But Lord! that's far from the truth. Mebbe Yaqui's different from most Indians. He looks the same, though. Mebbe the trouble is we white folks never knew the Indian. Anyway, Beldin' had it right. Yaqui's our godsend. Now as to the future, I'd like to know mebbe as well as you if we're ever to get home. Only bein' what I am, I say, Quien sabe? But somethin' tells me Yaqui knows. Ask him, Mercedes. Make him tell. We'll all be the better for knowin'. We'd be stronger for havin' more'n our faith in him. He's silent Indian, but make him tell."

Mercedes called to Yaqui. At her bidding there was always a suggestion of hurry, which otherwise was never manifest in his actions. She put a hand on his bared muscular arm and began to speak in Spanish. Her voice was low, swift, full of deep emotion, sweet as the sound of a bell. It thrilled Gale, though he understood scarcely a word she said. He did not need translation to know that here spoke the longing of a woman for life, love, home, the heritage of a woman's heart.

Gale doubted his own divining impression. It was that the Yaqui understood this woman's longing. In Gale's sight the Indian's stoicism, his inscrutability, the lavalike hardness of his face, although they did not change, seemed to give forth light, gentleness, loyalty. For an instant Gale seemed to have a vision; but it did not last, and he failed to hold some beautiful illusive thing.

"Si!" rolled out the Indian's reply, full of power and depth.

Mercedes drew a long breath, and her hand sought Thorne's.

"He says yes," she whispered. "He answers he'll save us; he'll take us all back—he knows!"

The Indian turned away to his tasks, and the silence that held the little group was finally broken by Ladd.

"Shore I said so. Now all we've got to do is use sense. Friends, I'm the commissary department of this outfit, an' what I say goes. You all won't eat except when I tell you. Mebbe it'll not be so hard to keep our health. Starved beggars don't get sick. But there's the heat comin', an' we can all go loco, you know. To pass the time! Lord, that's our problem. Now if you all only had a hankerin' for checkers. Shore I'll make a board an' make you play. Thorne, you're the luckiest. You've got your girl, an' this can be a honeymoon. Now with a few tools an' little material see what a grand house you can build for your wife. Dick, you're lucky, too. You like to hunt, an' up there you'll find the finest bighorn huntin' in the West. Take Yaqui and the .405. We need the meat, but while you're gettin' it have your sport. The same chance will never come again. I wish we all was able to go. But crippled men can't climb the lava. Shore you'll see some country from the peaks. There's no wilder place on earth, except the poles. An' when you're older, you an' Nell, with a couple of fine boys, think what it'll be to tell them about bein' lost in the lava, an' huntin' sheep with a Yaqui. Shore I've hit it. You can take yours out in huntin' an' thinkin'. Now if I had a girl like Nell I'd never go crazy. That's your game, Dick. Hunt, an' think of Nell, an' how you'll tell those fine boys about it all, an' about the old cowman you knowed, Laddy, who'll by then be long past the divide. Rustle now, son. Get some enthusiasm. For shore you'll need it for yourself an' us."

Gale climbed the lava slope, away round to the right of the arroyo, along an old trail that Yaqui said the Papagos had made before his own people had hunted there. Part way it led through spiked, crested, upheaved lava that would have been almost impassable even without its silver coating of *choya* cactus. There were benches and ledges and ridges bare and glistening in the sun. From the crests of these Yaqui's searching falcon gaze roved near and far for signs of sheep, and Gale used his glass on the reaches of lava that slanted steeply upward to the corrugated peaks, and down over endless heave and roll and red-waved slopes. The heat smoked up from the lava, and this, with the red color and the shiny *choyas*, gave the impression of a world of smoldering fire.

Farther along the slope Yaqui halted and crawled behind projections to a point commanding a view over an extraordinary section of country. The peaks were off to the left. In the foreground were gullies, ridges, and canyons, arroyos, all glistening with *choyas* and some other and more numerous white bushes, and here and there towered a green cactus. This region was only a splintered and more devastated part of the volcanic slope, but it was miles in extent. Yaqui peeped over the top of a blunt block of lava and searched the sharp-billowed wilderness. Suddenly he grasped Gale and pointed across a deep wide gully.

With the aid of his glass Gale saw five sheep. They were much larger than he had expected, dull brown in color, and two of them were rams with great curved horns. They were looking in his direction. Remembering what he had heard about the wonderful eyesight of these mountain animals, Gale could only conclude that they had seen the hunters.

Then Yaqui's movements attracted and interested him. The Indian had brought with him a red scarf and a mesquite branch. He tied the scarf to the stick, and propped this up in a crack of the lava. The scarf waved in the wind. That done, the Indian bade Gale watch.

Once again he leveled the glass at the sheep. All five were motionless, standing like statues, heads pointed across the gully. They were more than a mile distant. When Gale looked without his glass they merged into the roughness of the lava. He was intensely interested. Did the sheep see the red scarf? It seemed incredible, but nothing else could account for that statuesque alertness. The sheep held this rigid position for perhaps fifteen minutes. Then the leading ram started to approach. The others followed. He took a few steps, then halted. Always he held his head up, nose pointed.

"By George, they're coming!" exclaimed Gale. "They see that flag. They're hunting us. They're curious. If this doesn't beat me!"

Evidently the Indian understood, for he grunted.

Gale found difficulty in curbing his impatience. The approach of the sheep was slow. The advances of the leader and the intervals of watching had a singular regularity. He worked like a machine. Gale followed him down the opposite wall, around holes, across gullies, over ridges. Then Gale shifted the glass back to find the others. They were coming also, with exactly the same pace and pause of their leader. What steppers they were! How sure-footed! What leaps they made! It was thrilling to watch them. Gale forgot he had a rifle. The Yaqui pressed a heavy hand down upon his shoulder. He was to keep well hidden and to be quiet. Gale suddenly conceived the idea that the sheep might come clear across to investigate the puzzling red thing fluttering in the breeze. Strange, indeed, would that be for the wildest creatures in the world.

The big ram led on with the same regular persistence, and in half an hour's time he was in the bottom of the great gulf, and soon he was facing up the slope. Gale knew then that the alluring scarf had fascinated him. It was no longer necessary now for Gale to use his glass. There was a short period when an intervening crest of lava hid the sheep from view. After that the two rams and their smaller followers were plainly in sight for perhaps a quarter of an hour. Then they disappeared behind another ridge. Gale kept watching sure they would come out farther on. A tense period of waiting passed, then a suddenly electrifying pressure of Yaqui's hand made Gale tremble with excitement.

Very cautiously he shifted his position. There, not fifty feet distant upon a high mound of lava, stood the leader of the sheep. His size astounded Gale. He seemed all horns. But only for a moment did the impression of horns overbalancing body remain with Gale. The sheep was graceful, sinewy, slender, powerfully built, and in poise magnificent. As Gale watched, spellbound, the second ram leaped lightly upon the mound, and presently the three others did likewise.

Then, indeed, Gale feasted his eyes with a spectacle for a hunter. It came to him suddenly that there had been something he expected to see in this Rocky Mountain bighorn, and it was lacking. They were beautiful, as wonderful as even Ladd's encomiums had led him to suppose. He thought perhaps it was the contrast these soft, sleek, short-furred, graceful animals afforded to what he imagined the barren, terrible lava mountains might develop.

The splendid leader stepped closer, his round, protruding amber eyes, which Gale could now plainly see, intent upon that fatal red flag. Like automatons the other four crowded into his tracks. A few little slow steps, then the leader halted.

At this instant Gale's absorbed attention was directed by Yaqui to the rifle, and so to the purpose of the climb. A little cold shock affronted Gale's vivid pleasure. With it dawned a realization of what he had imagined was lacking in these animals. They did not look wild! The so-called wildest of wild creatures appeared tamer than sheep he had followed on a farm. It would be little less than murder to kill them. Gale regretted the need of slaughter. Nevertheless, he could not resist the desire to show himself and see how tame they really were.

He reached for the .405, and as he threw a shell into the chamber the slight metallic click made the sheep jump. Then Gale rose quickly to his feet.

The noble ram and his band simply stared at Gale. They had never seen a man. They showed not the slightest indication of instinctive fear. Curiosity, surprise, even friendliness, seemed to mark their attitude of attention. Gale imagined that they were going to step still closer. He did not choose to wait to see if this were true. Certainly it already took a grim resolution to raise the heavy .405.

His shot killed the big leader. The others bounded away with remarkable nimbleness. Gale used up the remaining four shells to drop the second ram, and by the time he had reloaded the others were out of range.

The Yaqui's method of hunting was sure and deadly and saving of energy, but Gale never would try it again. He chose to stalk the game. This entailed a great expenditure of strength, the eyes and lungs of a mountaineer, and, as Gale put it to Ladd, the need of seven-league boots. After being hunted a few times and shot at, the sheep became exceedingly difficult to approach. Gale learned to know that their fame as the keenest-eyed of all animals was well founded. If he worked directly toward a flock, crawling over the sharp lava, always a sentinel ram espied him before he got within range. The only method of attack that he found successful was to locate sheep with his glass, work round to windward of them, and then, getting behind a ridge or buttress, crawl like a lizard to a vantage point. He failed often. The stalk called forth all that was in him of endurance, cunning, speed. As the days grew hotter he hunted in the early morning hours and a while before the sun went down. More than one night he lay out on the lava, with the great stars close overhead and the immense void all beneath him. This pursuit he learned to love. Upon those scarred and blasted slopes the wild spirit that was in him had free rein. And like a shadow the faithful Yaqui tried ever to keep at his heels.

One morning the rising sun greeted him as he surmounted the higher cone of the volcano. He saw the vastness of the east aglow with a glazed rosy whiteness, like the changing hue of an ember. At this height there was a sweeping wind, still cool. The western slopes of lava lay dark, and all that world of sand and gulf and mountain barrier beyond was shrouded in the mystic cloud of distance. Gale had assimilated much of the loneliness and the sense of ownership and the love of lofty heights that might well belong to the great condor of the peak. Like this wide-winged bird, he had an unparalleled range of vision. The very corners whence came the winds seemed pierced by Gale's eyes.

Yaqui spied a flock of sheep far under the curved broken rim of the main crater. Then began the stalk. Gale had taught the Yaqui something—that speed might win as well as patient cunning. Keeping out of sight, Gale ran over the spike-crusted lava, leaving the Indian far behind. His feet were magnets, attracting supporting holds and he passed over them too fast to fall. The wind, the keen air of the heights, the red lava, the boundless surrounding blue, all seemed to have something to do with his wildness. Then, hiding, slipping, creeping, crawling, he closed in upon his quarry until the long rifle grew like stone in his grip, and the whipping "spang" ripped the silence, and the strange echo boomed deep in the crater, and rolled around, as if in hollow mockery at the hopelessness of escape.

Gale's exultant yell was given as much to free himself of some bursting joy of action as it was to call the slower Yaqui. Then he liked the strange echoes. It was a maddening whirl of sound that bored deeper and deeper along the whorled and caverned walls of the crater. It was as if these aged walls resented the violating of their silent sanctity. Gale felt himself a man, a thing alive, something superior to all this savage, dead, upflung world of iron, a master even of all this grandeur and sublimity because he had a soul.

He waited beside his quarry, and breathed deep, and swept the long slopes with searching eyes of habit.

When Yaqui came up they set about the hardest task of all, to pack the best of that heavy sheep down miles of steep, ragged, *choya*-covered lava. But even in this Gale rejoiced. The heat was nothing, the millions of little pits which could hold and twist a foot were nothing; the blade-edged crusts and the deep fissures and the choked canyons and the tangled, dwarfed mesquites, all these were as nothing but obstacles to be cheerfully overcome. Only the *choya* hindered Dick Gale.

When his heavy burden pulled him out of sure-footedness, and he plunged into a *choya*, or when the strange, deceitful, uncanny, almost invisible frosty thorns caught and pierced him, then there was call for all of fortitude and endurance. For this cactus had a malignant power of torture. Its pain was a stinging, blinding, burning, sickening poison in the blood. If thorns pierced his legs he felt the pain all over his body; if his hands rose from a fall full of the barbed joints, he was helpless and quivering till Yaqui tore them out.

But this one peril, dreaded more than dizzy height of precipice or sunblindness on the glistening peak, did not daunt Gale. His teacher was the Yaqui, and always before him was an example that made him despair of a white man's equality. Color, race, blood, breeding—what were these in the wilderness? Verily, Dick Gale had come to learn the use of his hands.

So in a descent of hours he toiled down the lava slope, to stalk into the arroyo like a burdened giant, wringing wet, panting, clear-eyed and dark-faced, his ragged clothes and boots white with *choya* thorns.

The gaunt Ladd rose from his shaded seat, and removed his pipe from smiling lips, and turned to nod at Jim, and then looked back again.

The torrid summer heat came imperceptibly, or it could never have been borne by white men. It changed the lives of the fugitives, making them partly nocturnal in habit. The nights had the balmy coolness of spring, and would have been delightful for sleep, but that would have made the blazing days unendurable.

The sun rose in a vast white flame. With it came the blasting, withering wind from the gulf. A red haze, like that of earlier sunsets, seemed to come sweeping on the wind, and it roared up the arroyo, and went bellowing into the crater, and rushed on in fury to lash the peaks.

During these hot, windy hours the desert-bound party slept in deep recesses in the lava; and if necessity brought them forth they could not remain out long. The sand burned through boots, and a touch of bare hand on lava raised a blister.

A short while before sundown the Yaqui went forth to build a campfire, and soon the others came out, heat-dazed, half blinded, with parching throats to allay and hunger that was never satisfied. A little action and a cooling of the air revived them, and when night set in they were comfortable round the campfire.

As Ladd had said, one of their greatest problems was the passing of time. The nights were interminably long, but they had to be passed in work or play or dream—anything except sleep. That was Ladd's most inflexible command. He gave no reason. But not improbably the ranger thought that the terrific heat of the day spend in slumber lessened a wear and strain, if not a real danger of madness.

Accordingly, at first the occupations of this little group were many and various. They worked if they had something to do, or could invent a pretext. They told and retold stories until all were wearisome. They sang songs. Mercedes taught Spanish. They played every game they knew. They invented others that were so trivial children would scarcely have been interested, and these they played seriously. In a word, with intelligence and passion, with all that was civilized and human, they fought the ever-infringing loneliness, the savage solitude of their environment.

But they had only finite minds. It was not in reason to expect a complete victory against this mighty Nature, this bounding horizon of death and desolation and decay. Gradually they fell back upon fewer and fewer occupations, until the time came when the silence was hard to break.

Gale believed himself the keenest of the party, the one who thought most, and he watched the effect of the desert upon his companions. He imagined that he saw Ladd grow old sitting round the campfire. Certain it was that the ranger's gray hair had turned white. What had been at times hard and cold and grim about him had strangely vanished in sweet temper and a vacant-mindedness that held him longer as the days passed. For hours, it seemed, Ladd would bend over his checkerboard and never make a move. It mattered not now whether or not he had a partner. He was always glad of being spoken to, as if he were called back from vague region of mind. Jim Lash, the calmest, coolest, most nonchalant, best-humored Westerner Gale had ever met, had by slow degrees lost that cheerful character which would have been of such infinite good to his companions, and always he sat brooding, silently brooding. Jim had no ties, few memories, and the desert was claiming him.

Thorne and Mercedes, however, were living, wonderful proof that spirit, mind, and heart were free—free to soar in scorn of the colossal barrenness and silence and space of that terrible hedging prison of lava. They were young; they loved; they were together; and the oasis was almost a paradise. Gale believe he helped himself by watching them. Imagination had never pictured real happiness to him. Thorne and Mercedes had forgotten the outside world. If they had been existing on the burned-out desolate moon they could hardly have been in a harsher, grimmer, lonelier spot than this red-walled arroyo. But it might have been a statelier Eden than that of the primitive day.

Mercedes grew thinner, until she was a slender shadow of her former self. She became hard, brown as the rangers, lithe and quick as a panther. She seemed to live on water and the air—perhaps, indeed, on love. For of the scant fare, the best of which was continually urged upon her, she partook but little. She reminded Gale of a wild brown creature, free as the wind on the lava slopes. Yet, despite the great change, her beauty remained undiminished. Her eyes, seeming so much larger now in her small face, were great black, starry gulfs. She was the life of that camp. Her smiles, her rapid speech, her low laughter, her quick movements, her playful moods with the rangers, the dark and passionate glance, which rested so often on her lover, the whispers in the dusk as hand in hand they paced the campfire beat—these helped Gale to retain his loosening hold on reality, to resist the lure of a strange beckoning life where a man stood free in the golden open, where emotion was not, nor trouble, nor sickness, nor anything but the savage's rest and sleep and action and dream.

Although the Yaqui was as his shadow, Gale reached a point when he seemed to wander alone at twilight, in the night, at dawn. Far down the arroyo, in the deepening red twilight, when the heat rolled away on slow-dying wind, Blanco Sol raised his splendid head and whistled for his master. Gale reproached himself for neglect of the noble horse. Blanco Sol was always the same. He loved four things—his master, a long drink of cool water, to graze at will, and to run. Time and place, Gale thought, meant little to Sol if he could have those four things. Gale put his arm over the great arched neck and laid his cheek against the long white mane, and then even as he stood there forgot the horse. What was the dull, red-tinged, horizon-wide mantle creeping up the slope? Through it the copper sun glowed, paled, died. Was it only twilight? Was it gloom? If he thought about it he had a feeling that it was the herald of night and the night must be a vigil, and that made him tremble.

At night he had formed a habit of climbing up the lava slope as far as the smooth trail extended, and there on a promontory he paced to and fro, and watched the stars, and sat stone-still for hours looking down at the vast void with its moving, changing shadows. From that promontory he gazed up at a velvet-blue sky, deep and dark, bright with millions of cold, distant, blinking stars, and he grasped a little of the meaning of infinitude. He gazed down into the shadows, which, black as they were and impenetrable, yet have a conception of immeasurable space.

Then the silence! He was dumb, he was awed, he bowed his head, he trembled, he marveled at the desert silence. It was the one thing always present. Even when the wind roared there seemed to be silence. But at night, in this lava world of ashes and canker, he waited for this terrible strangeness of nature to come to him with the secret. He seemed at once a little child and a strong man, and something very old. What tortured him was the incomprehensibility that the vaster the space the greater the silence! At one moment Gale felt there was only death here, and that was the secret; at another he heard the slow beat of a mighty heart.

He came at length to realize that the desert was a teacher. He did not realize all that he had learned, but he was a different man. And when he decided upon that, he was not thinking of the slow, sure call to the primal instincts of man; he was thinking that the desert, as much as he had experienced and no more, would absolutely overturn the whole scale of a man's values, break old habits, form new ones, remake him. More of desert experience, Gale believe, would be too much for intellect. The desert did not breed civilized man, and that made Gale ponder over a strange thought: after all, was the civilized man inferior to the savage?

Yaqui was the answer to that. When Gale acknowledged this he always remembered his present strange manner of thought. The past, the old order of mind, seemed as remote as this desert world was from the haunts of civilized men. A man must know a savage as Gale knew Yaqui before he could speak authoritatively, and then something stilled his tongue. In the first stage of Gale's observation of Yaqui he had marked tenaciousness of life, stoicism, endurance, strength. These were the attributes of the desert. But what of that second stage wherein the Indian had loomed up a colossal figure of strange honor, loyalty, love? Gale doubted his convictions and scorned himself for doubting.

There in the gloom sat the silent, impassive, inscrutable Yaqui. His dark face, his dark eyes were plain in the light of the stars. Always he was near Gale, unobtrusive, shadowy, but there. Why? Gale absolutely could not doubt that the Indian had heart as well as mind. Yaqui had from the very first stood between Gale and accident, toil, peril. It was his own choosing. Gale could not change him or thwart him. He understood the Indian's idea of obligation and sacred duty. But there was more, and that baffled Gale. In the night hours, alone on the slope, Gale felt in Yaqui, as he felt the mighty throb of that desert pulse, a something that drew him irresistibly to the Indian. Sometimes he looked around to find the Indian, to dispel these strange, pressing thoughts of unreality, and it was never in vain.

Thus the nights passed, endlessly long, with Gale fighting for his old order of thought, fighting the fascination of the infinite sky, and the gloomy insulating whirl of the wide shadows, fighting for belief, hope, prayer, fighting against that terrible ever-recurring idea of being lost, lost, lost in the desert, fighting harder than any other thing the insidious, penetrating, tranquil, unfeeling self that was coming between him and his memory.

He was losing the battle, losing his hold on tangible things, losing his power to stand up under this ponderous, merciless weight of desert space and silence.

He acknowledged it in a kind of despair, and the shadows of the night seemed whirling fiends. Lost! Lost! Lost! What are you waiting for? Rain!... Lost! Lost! Lost in the desert! So the shadows seemed to scream in voiceless mockery.

At the moment he was alone on the promontory. The night was far spent. A ghastly moon haunted the black volcanic spurs. The winds blew silently. Was he alone? No, he did not seem to be alone. The Yaqui was there. Suddenly a strange, cold sensation crept over Gale. It was new. He felt a presence. Turning, he expected to see the Indian, but instead, a slight shadow, pale, almost white, stood there, not close nor yet distant. It seemed to brighten. Then he saw a woman who resembled a girl he had seemed to know long ago. She was white-faced, golden-haired, and her lips were sweet, and her eyes were turning black. Nell! He had forgotten her. Over him flooded a torrent of memory. There was tragic woe in this sweet face. Nell was holding out her arms—she was crying aloud to him across the sand and the cactus and the lava. She was in trouble, and he had been forgetting.

That night he climbed the lava to the topmost cone, and never slipped on a ragged crust nor touched a *choya* thorn. A voice called to him. He saw Nell's eyes in the stars, in the velvet blue of sky, in the blackness of the engulfing shadows. She was with him, a slender shape, a spirit, keeping step with him, and memory was strong, sweet, beating, beautiful. Far down in the west, faintly golden with light of the sinking moon, he saw a cloud that resembled her face. A cloud on the desert horizon! He gazed and gazed. Was that a spirit face like the one by his side? No—he did not dream.

In the hot, sultry morning Yaqui appeared at camp, after long hours of absence, and he pointed with a long, dark arm toward the west. A bank of clouds was rising above the mountain barrier.

"Rain!" he cried; and his sonorous voice rolled down the arroyo.

Those who heard him were as shipwrecked mariners at sight of a distant sail.

Dick Gale, silent, grateful to the depths of his soul, stood with arm over Blanco Sol and watched the transforming west, where clouds of wonderous size and hue piled over one another, rushing, darkening, spreading, sweeping upward toward that white and glowing sun.

When they reached the zenith and swept round to blot out the blazing orb, the earth took on a dark, lowering aspect. The red of sand and lava changed to steely gray. Vast shadows, like ripples on water, sheeted in from the gulf with a low, strange moan. Yet the silence was like death. The desert was awaiting a strange and hated visitation—storm! If all the endless torrid days, the endless mystic nights had seemed unreal to Gale, what, then, seemed this stupendous spectacle?

"Oh! I felt a drop of rain on my face!" cried Mercedes; and whispering the name of a saint, she kissed her husband.

The white-haired Ladd, gaunt, old, bent, looked up at the maelstrom of clouds, and he said, softly, "Shore we'll get in the hosses, an' pack light, an' hit the trail, an' make night marches!"

Then up out of the gulf of the west swept a bellowing wind and a black pall and terrible flashes of lightning and thunder like the end of the world—fury, blackness, chaos, the desert storm.

XVII

THE WHISTLE OF A HORSE

AT the ranch-house at Forlorn River Belding stood alone in his darkened room. It was quiet there and quiet outside; the sickening midsummer heat, like a hot heavy blanket, lay upon the house.

He took up the gun belt from his table and with slow hands buckled it around his waist. He seemed to feel something familiar and comfortable and inspiring in the weight of the big gun against his hip. He faced the door as if to go out, but hesitated, and then began a slow, plodding walk up and down the length of the room. Presently he halted at the table, and with reluctant hands he unbuckled the gun belt and laid it down.

The action did not have an air of finality, and Belding knew it. He had seen border life in Texas in the early days; he had been a sheriff when the law in the West depended on a quickness of wrist; he had seen many a man lay down his gun for good and all. His own action was not final. Of late he had done the same thing many times and this last time it seemed a little harder to do, a little more indicative of vacillation. There were reasons why Belding's gun held for him a gloomy fascination.

The Chases, those grasping and conscienceless agents of a new force in the development of the West, were bent upon Belding's ruin, and so far as his fortunes at Forlorn River were concerned, had almost accomplished it. One by one he lost points for which he contended with them. He carried into the Tucson courts the matter of the staked claims, and mining claims, and water claims, and he lost all. Following that he lost his government position as inspector of immigration; and this fact, because of what he considered its injustice, had been a hard blow. He had been made to suffer a humiliation equally as great. It came about that he actually had to pay the Chases for water to irrigate his alfalfa fields. The never-failing spring upon his land answered for the needs of household and horses, but no more.

These matters were unfortunate for Belding, but not by any means wholly accountable for his worry and unhappiness and brooding hate. He believed Dick Gale and the rest of the party taken into the desert by the Yaqui had been killed or lost. Two months before a string of Mexican horses, riderless, saddled, starved for grass and wild for water, had come in to Forlorn River. They were a part of the horses belonging to Rojas and his band. Their arrival complicated the mystery and strengthened convictions of the loss of both pursuers and pursued. Belding was wont to say that he had worried himself gray over the fate of his rangers.

Belding's unhappiness could hardly be laid to material loss. He had been rich and was now poor, but change of fortune such as that could not have made him unhappy. Something more somber and mysterious and sad than the loss of Dick Gale and their friends had come into the lives of his wife and Nell. He dated the time of this change back to a certain day when Mrs. Belding recognized in the elder Chase an old schoolmate and a rejected suitor. It took time for slow-thinking Belding to discover anything wrong in his household, especially as the fact of the Gales lingering there made Mrs. Belding and Nell, for the most part, hide their real and deeper feelings. Gradually, however, Belding had forced on him the fact of some secret cause for grief other than Gale's loss. He was sure of it when his wife signified her desire to make a visit to her old home back in Peoria. She did not give many reasons, but she did show him a letter that had found its way from old friends. This letter contained news that may or may not have been authentic; but it was enough, Belding thought, to interest his wife. An old prospector had returned to Peoria, and he had told relatives of meeting Robert Burton at the Sonoyta Oasis fifteen years before, and that Burton had gone into the desert never to return. To Belding this was no surprise, for he had heard that before his marriage. There appeared to have been no doubts as to the death of his wife's first husband. The singular thing was that both Nell's father and grandfather had been lost somewhere in the Sonora Desert.

Belding did not oppose his wife's desire to visit her old home. He thought it would be a wholesome trip for her, and did all in his power to persuade Nell to accompany her. But Nell would not go.

It was after Mrs. Belding's departure that Belding discovered in Nell a condition of mind that amazed and distressed him. She had suddenly become strangely wretched, so that she could not conceal it from even the Gales, who, of all people, Belding imagined, were the ones to make Nell proud. She would tell him nothing. But after a while, when he had thought it out, he dated this further and more deplorable change in Nell back to a day on which he had met Nell with Radford Chase. This indefatigable wooer had not in the least abandoned his suit. Something about the fellow made Belding grind his teeth. But Nell grew not only solicitously, but now strangely, entreatingly earnest in her importunities to Belding not to insult or lay a hand on Chase. This had bound Belding so far; it had made him think and watch. He had never been a man to interfere with his women folk. They could do as they liked, and usually that pleased him. But a slow surprise gathered and grew upon him when he saw that Nell, apparently, was accepting young Chase's attentions. At least, she no longer hid from him. Belding could not account for this, because he was sure Nell cordially despised the fellow. And toward the end he divined, if he did not actually know, that these Chases possessed some strange power over Nell, and were using it. That stirred a hate in Belding—a hate he had felt at the very first and had manfully striven against, and which now gave him over to dark brooding thoughts.

Midsummer passed, and the storms came late. But when they arrived they made up for tardiness. Belding did not remember so terrible a storm of wind and rain as that which broke the summer's drought.

In a few days, it seemed, Altar Valley was a bright and green expanse, where dust clouds did not rise. Forlorn River ran, a slow, heavy, turgid torrent. Belding never saw the river in flood that it did not give him joy; yet now, desert man as he was, he suffered a regret when he thought of the great Chase reservoir full and overflowing. The dull thunder of the spillway was not pleasant. It was the first time in his life that the sound of falling water jarred upon him.

Belding noticed workmen once more engaged in the fields bounding his land. The Chases had extended a main irrigation ditch down to Belding's farm, skipped the width of his ground, then had gone on down through Altar Valley. They had exerted every influence to obtain right to connect these ditches by digging through his land, but Belding had remained obdurate. He refused to have any dealings with them. It was therefore with some curiosity and suspicion that he saw a gang of Mexicans once more at work upon these ditches.

At daylight next morning a tremendous blast almost threw Belding out of his bed. It cracked the adobe walls of his house and broke windows and sent pans and crockery to the floor with a crash. Belding's idea was that the store of dynamite kept by the Chases for blasting had blown up. Hurriedly getting into his clothes, he went to Nell's room to reassure her; and, telling her to have a thought for their guests, he went out to see what had happened.

The villagers were pretty badly frightened. Many of the poorly constructed adobe huts had crumbled almost into dust. A great yellow cloud, like smoke, hung over the river. This appeared to be at the upper end of Belding's plot, and close to the river. When he reached his fence the smoke and dust were so thick he could scarcely breathe, and for a little while he was unable to see what had happened. Presently he made out a huge hole in the sand just about where the irrigation ditch had stopped near his line. For some reason or other, not clear to Belding, the Mexicans had set off an extraordinarily heavy blast at that point.

Belding pondered. He did not now for a moment consider an accidental discharge of dynamite. But why had this blast been set off? The loose sandy soil had yielded readily to shovel; there were no rocks; as far as construction of a ditch was concerned such a blast would have done more harm than good.

Slowly, with reluctant feet, Belding walked toward a green hollow, where in a cluster of willows lay the never-failing spring that his horses loved so well, and, indeed, which he loved no less. He was actually afraid to part the drooping willows to enter the little cool, shady path that led to the spring. Then, suddenly seized by suspense, he ran the rest of the way.

He was just in time to see the last of the water. It seemed to sink as in quicksand. The shape of the hole had changed. The tremendous force of the blast in the adjoining field had obstructed or diverted the underground stream of water.

Belding's never-failing spring had been ruined. What had made this little plot of ground green and sweet and fragrant was now no more. Belding's first feeling was for the pity of it. The pale Ajo lilies would bloom no more under those willows. The willows themselves would soon wither and die. He thought how many times in the middle of hot summer nights he had come down to the spring to drink. Never again!

Suddenly he thought of Blanco Diablo. How the great white thoroughbred had loved this spring! Belding straightened up and looked with tear-blurred eyes out over the waste of desert to the west. Never a day passed that he had not thought of the splendid horse; but this moment, with its significant memory, was doubly keen, and there came a dull pang in his breast.

"Diablo will never drink here again!" muttered Belding.

The loss of Blanco Diablo, though admitted and mourned by Belding, had never seemed quite real until this moment.

The pall of dust drifting over him, the din of the falling water up at the dam, diverted Belding's mind to the Chases. All at once he was in the harsh grip of a cold certainty. The blast had been set off intentionally to ruin his spring. What a hellish trick! No Westerner, no Indian or Mexican, no desert man could have been guilty of such a crime. To ruin a beautiful, clear, cool, never-failing stream of water in the desert!

It was then that Belding's worry and indecision and brooding were as if they had never existed. As he strode swiftly back to the house, his head, which had long been bent thoughtfully and sadly, was held erect. He went directly to his room, and with an air that was now final he buckled on his gun belt. He looked the gun over and tried the action. He squared himself and walked a little more erect. Some long-lost individuality had returned to Belding.

"Let's see," he was saying. "I can get Carter to send the horses I've left back to Waco to my brother. I'll make Nell take what money there is and go hunt up her mother. The Gales are ready to go—to-day, if I say the word. Nell can travel with them part way East. That's your game, Tom Belding, don't mistake me."

As he went out he encountered Mr. Gale coming up the walk. The long sojourn at Forlorn River, despite the fact that it had been laden with a suspense which was gradually changing to a sad certainty, had been of great benefit to Dick's father. The dry air, the heat, and the quiet had made him, if not entirely a well man, certainly stronger than he had been in many years.

"Belding, what was that terrible roar?" asked Mr. Gale. "We were badly frightened until Miss Nell came to us. We feared it was an earthquake."

"Well, I'll tell you, Mr. Gale, we've had some quakes here, but none of them could hold a candle to this jar we just had."

Then Belding explained what had caused the explosion, and why it had been set off so close to his property.

"It's an outrage, sir, an unspeakable outrage," declared Mr. Gale, hotly. "Such a thing would not be tolerated in the East. Mr. Belding, I'm amazed at your attitude in the face of all this trickery."

"You see—there was mother and Nell," began Belding, as if apologizing. He dropped his head a little and made marks in the sand with the toe of his boot. "Mr. Gale, I've been sort of half hitched, as Laddy used to say. I'm planning to have a little more elbow room round this ranch. I'm going to send Nell East to her mother. Then I'll— See here, Mr. Gale, would you mind having Nell with you part way when you go home?"

"We'd all be delighted to have her go all the way and make us a visit," replied Mr. Gale.

"That's fine. And you'll be going soon? Don't take that as if I wanted to—" Belding paused, for the truth was that he did want to hurry them off.

"We would have been gone before this, but for you," said Mr. Gale. "Long ago we gave up hope of—of Richard ever returning. And I believe, now we're sure he was lost, that we'd do well to go home at once. You wished us to remain until the heat was broken—till the rains came to make traveling easier for us. Now I see no need for further delay. My stay here has greatly benefited my health. I shall never forget your hospitality. This Western trip would have made me a new man if—only—Richard—"

"Sure. I understand," said Belding, gruffly. "Let's go in and tell the women to pack up."

Nell was busy with the servants preparing breakfast. Belding took her into the sitting-room while Mr. Gale called his wife and daughter.

"My girl, I've some news for you," began Belding. "Mr. Gale is leaving to-day with his family. I'm going to send you with them—part way, anyhow. You're invited to visit them. I think that 'd be great for you—help you to forget. But the main thing is—you're going East to join mother."

Nell gazed at him, white-faced, without uttering a word.

"You see, Nell, I'm about done in Forlorn River," went on Belding. "That blast this morning sank my spring. There's no water now. It was the last straw. So we'll shake the dust of Forlorn River. I'll come on a little later—that's all."

"Dad, you're packing your gun!" exclaimed Nell, suddenly pointing with a trembling finger. She ran to him, and for the first time in his life Belding put her away from him. His movements had lost the old slow gentleness.

"Why, so I am," replied Belding, coolly, as his hand moved down to the sheath swinging at his hip. "Nell, I'm that absent-minded these days!"

"Dad!" she cried.

"That'll do from you," he replied, in a voice he had never used to her. "Get breakfast now, then pack to leave Forlorn River."

"Leave Forlorn River!" whispered Nell, with a thin white hand stealing up to her breast. How changed the girl was! Belding reproached himself for his hardness, but did not speak his thought aloud. Nell was fading here, just as Mercedes had faded before the coming of Thorne.

Nell turned away to the west window and looked out across the desert toward the dim blue peaks in the distance. Belding watched her; likewise the Gales; and no one spoke. There ensued a long silence. Belding felt a lump rise in his throat. Nell laid her arm against the window frame, but gradually it dropped, and she was leaning with her face against the wood. A low sob broke from her. Elsie Gale went to her, embraced her, took the drooping head on her shoulder.

"We've come to be such friends," she said. "I believe it'll be good for you to visit me in the city. Here—all day you look out across that awful lonely desert.... Come, Nell."

Heavy steps sounded outside on the flagstones, then the door rattled under a strong knock. Belding opened it. The Chases, father and son, stood beyond the threshold.

"Good morning, Belding," said the elder Chase. "We were routed out early by that big blast and came up to see what was wrong. All a blunder. The Greaser foreman was drunk yesterday, and his ignorant men made a mistake. Sorry if the blast bothered you."

"Chase, I reckon that's the first of your blasts I was ever glad to hear," replied Belding, in a way that made Chase look blank.

"So? Well, I'm glad you're glad," he went on, evidently puzzled. "I was a little worried—you've always been so touchy—we never could get together. I hurried over, fearing maybe you might think the blast—you see, Belding—"

"I see this, Mr. Ben Chase," interrupted Belding, in curt and ringing voice. "That blast was a mistake, the biggest you ever made in your life."

"What do you mean?" demanded Chase.

"You'll have to excuse me for a while, unless you're dead set on having it out right now. Mr. Gale and his family are leaving, and my daughter is going with them. I'd rather you'd wait a little."

"Nell going away!" exclaimed Radford Chase. He reminded Belding of an overgrown boy in disappointment.

"Yes. But—Miss Burton to you, young man—"

"Mr. Belding, I certainly would prefer a conference with you right now," interposed the elder Chase, cutting short Belding's strange speech. "There are other matters—important matters to discuss. They've got to be settled. May we step in, sir?"

"No, you may not," replied Belding, bluntly. "I'm sure particular who I invite into my house. But I'll go with you."

Belding stepped out and closed the door. "Come away from the house so the women won't hear the—the talk."

The elder Chase was purple with rage, yet seemed to be controlling it. The younger man looked black, sullen, impatient. He appeared not to have a thought of Belding. He was absolutely blind to the situation, as considered from Belding's point of view. Ben Chase found his voice about the time Belding halted under the trees out of earshot from the house.

"Sir, you've insulted me—my son. How dare you? I want you to understand that you're—"

"Chop that kind of talk with me, you —— —— —— ——!" interrupted Belding. He had always been profane, and now he certainly did not choose his language. Chase turned livid, gasped, and seemed about to give way to fury. But something about Belding evidently exerted a powerful quieting influence. "If you talk sense I'll listen," went on Belding.

Belding was frankly curious. He did not think any argument or inducement offered by Chase could change his mind on past dealings or his purpose of the present. But he believed by listening he might get some light on what had long puzzled him. The masterly effort Chase put forth to conquer his aroused passions gave Belding another idea of the character of this promoter.

"I want to make a last effort to propitiate you," began Chase, in his quick, smooth voice. That was a singular change to Belding—the dropping instantly into an easy flow of speech. "You've had losses here, and naturally you're sore. I don't blame you. But you can't see this thing from my side of the fence. Business is business. In business the best man wins. The law upheld those transactions of mine the honesty of which you questioned. As to mining and water claims, you lost on this technical point—that you had nothing to prove you had held them for five years. Five years is the time necessary in law. A dozen men might claim the source of Forlorn River, but if they had no house or papers to prove their squatters' rights any man could go in and fight them for the water. .... Now I want to run that main ditch along the river, through your farm. Can't we make a deal? I'm ready to be liberal—to meet you more than halfway. I'll give you an interest in the company. I think I've influence enough up at the Capitol to have you reinstated as inspector. A little reasonableness on your part will put you right again in Forlorn River, with a chance of growing rich. There's a big future here.... My interest, Belding, has become personal. Radford is in love with your step-daughter. He wants to marry her. I'll admit now if I had foreseen this situation I wouldn't have pushed you so hard. But we can square the thing. Now let's get together not only in business, but in a family way. If my son's happiness depends upon having this girl, you may rest assured I'll do all I can to get her for him. I'll absolutely make good all your losses. Now what do you say?"

"No," replied Belding. "Your money can't buy a right of way across my ranch. And Nell doesn't want your son. That settles that."

"But you could persuade her."

"I won't, that's all."

"May I ask why?" Chases's voice was losing its suave quality, but it was even swifter than before.

"Sure. I don't mind your asking," replied Belding in slow deliberation. "I wouldn't do such a low-down trick. Besides, if I would, I'd want it to be a man I was persuading for. I know Greasers—I know a Yaqui I'd rather give Nell to than your son."

Radford Chase began to roar in inarticulate rage. Belding paid no attention to him; indeed, he never glanced at the young man. The elder Chase checked a violent start. He plucked at the collar of his gray flannel shirt, opened it at the neck.

"My son's offer of marriage is an honor—more an honor, sir, than you perhaps are aware of."

Belding made no reply. His steady gaze did not turn from the long lane that led down to the river. He waited coldly, sure of himself.

"Mrs. Belding's daughter has no right to the name of Burton," snapped Chase. "Did you know that?"

"I did not," replied Belding, quietly.

"Well, you know it now," added Chase, bitingly.

"Sure you can prove what you say?" queried Belding, in the same cool, unemotional tone. It struck him strangely at the moment what little knowledge this man had of the West and of Western character.

"Prove it? Why, yes, I think so, enough to make the truth plain to any reasonable man. I come from Peoria—was born and raised there. I went to school with Nell Warren. That was your wife's maiden name. She was a beautiful, gay girl. All the fellows were in love with her. I knew Bob Burton well. He was a splendid fellow, but wild. Nobody ever knew for sure, but we all supposed he was engaged to marry Nell. He left Peoria, however, and soon after that the truth about Nell came out. She ran away. It was at least a couple of months before Burton showed up in Peoria. He did not stay long. Then for years nothing was heard of either of them. When word did come Nell was in Oklahoma, Burton was in Denver. There's chance, of course, that Burton followed Nell and married her. That would account for Nell Warren taking the name of Burton. But it isn't likely. None of us ever heard of such a thing and wouldn't have believed it if we had. The affair seemed destined to end unfortunately. But Belding, while I'm at it, I want to say that Nell Warren was one of the sweetest, finest, truest girls in the world. If she drifted to the Southwest and kept her past a secret that was only natural. Certainly it should not be held against her. Why, she was only a child—a girl—seventeen—eighteen years old.... In a moment of amazement—when I recognized your wife as an old schoolmate—I blurted the thing out to Radford. You see now how little it matters to me when I ask your stepdaughter's hand in marriage for my son."

Belding stood listening. The genuine emotion in Chase's voice was as strong as the ring of truth. Belding knew truth when he heard it. The revelation did not surprise him. Belding did not soften, for he devined that Chase's emotion was due to the probing of an old wound, the recalling of a past both happy and painful. Still, human nature was so strange that perhaps kindness and sympathy might yet have a place in this Chase's heart. Belding did not believe so, but he was willing to give Chase the benefit of the doubt.

"So you told my wife you'd respect her secret—keep her dishonor from husband and daughter?" demanded Belding, his dark gaze sweeping back from the lane.

"What! I—I" stammered Chase.

"You made your son swear to be a man and die before he'd hint the thing to Nell?" went on Belding, and his voice rang louder.

Ben Chase had no answer. The red left his face. His son slunk back against the fence.

"I say you never held this secret over the heads of my wife and her daughter?" thundered Belding.

He had his answer in the gray faces, in the lips that fear made mute. Like a flash Belding saw the whole truth of Mrs. Belding's agony, the reason for her departure; he saw what had been driving Nell; and it seemed that all the dogs of hell were loosed within his heart. He struck out blindly, instinctively in his pain, and the blow sent Ben Chase staggering into the fence corner. Then he stretched forth a long arm and whirled Radford Chase back beside his father.

"I see it all now," went on Belding, hoarsely. "You found the woman's weakness—her love for the girl. You found the girl's weakness—her pride and fear of shame. So you drove the one and hounded the other. God, what a base thing to do! To tell the girl was bad enough, but to threaten her with betrayal; there's no name for that!"

Belding's voice thickened, and he paused, breathing heavily. He stepped back a few paces; and this, an ominous action for an armed man of his kind, instead of adding to the fear of the Chases, seemed to relieve them. If there had been any pity in Belding's heart he would have felt it then.

"And now, gentlemen," continued Belding, speaking low and with difficulty, "seeing I've turned down your proposition, I suppose you think you've no more call to keep your mouths shut?"

The elder Chase appeared fascinated by something he either saw or felt in Belding, and his gray face grew grayer. He put up a shaking hand. Then Radford Chase, livid and snarling, burst out: "I'll talk till I'm black in the face. You can't stop me!"

"You'll go black in the face, but it won't be from talking," hissed Belding.

His big arm swept down, and when he threw it up the gun glittered in his hand. Simultaneously with the latter action pealed out a shrill, penetrating whistle.

The whistle of a horse! It froze Belding's arm aloft. For an instant he could not move even his eyes. The familiarity of that whistle was terrible in its power to rob him of strength. Then he heard the rapid, heavy pound of hoofs, and again the piercing whistle.

"Blanco Diablo!" he cried, huskily.

He turned to see a huge white horse come thundering into the yard. A wild, gaunt, terrible horse; indeed, the loved Blanco Diablo. A bronzed, long-haired Indian bestrode him. More white horses galloped into the yard, pounded to a halt, whistling home. Belding saw a slim shadow of a girl who seemed all great black eyes.

Under the trees flashed Blanco Sol, as dazzling white, as beautiful as if he had never been lost in the desert. He slid to a halt, then plunged and stamped. His rider leaped, throwing the bridle. Belding saw a powerful, spare, ragged man, with dark, gaunt face and eyes of flame.

Then Nell came running from the house, her golden hair flying, her hands outstretched, her face wonderful.

"Dick! Dick! Oh-h-h, Dick!" she cried. Her voice seemed to quiver in Belding's heart.

Belding's eyes began to blur. He was not sure he saw clearly. Whose face was this now close before him—a long thin, shrunken face, haggard, tragic in its semblance of torture, almost of death? But the eyes were keen and kind. Belding thought wildly that they proved he was not dreaming.

"I shore am glad to see you all," said a well-remembered voice in a slow, cool drawl.

XVIII

REALITY AGAINST DREAMS

LADD, Lash, Thorne, Mercedes, they were all held tight in Belding's arms. Then he ran to Blanco Diablo. For once the great horse was gentle, quiet, glad. He remembered this kindest of masters and reached for him with warm, wet muzzle.

Dick Gale was standing bowed over Nell's slight form, almost hidden in his arms. Belding hugged them both. He was like a boy. He saw Ben Chase and his son slip away under the trees, but the circumstances meant nothing to him then.

"Dick! Dick!" he roared. "Is it you?... Say, who do you think's here—here, in Forlorn River?"

Gale gripped Belding with a hand as rough and hard as a file and as strong as a vise. But he did not speak a word. Belding thought Gale's eyes would haunt him forever.

It was then three more persons came upon the scene—Elsie Gale, running swiftly, her father assisting Mrs. Gale, who appeared about to faint.

"Belding! Who on earth's that?" cried Dick hoarsely.

"Quien sabe, my son," replied Belding; and now his voice seemed a little shaky. "Nell, come here. Give him a chance."

Belding slipped his arm round Nell, and whispered in her ear. "This 'll be great!"

Elsie Gale's face was white and agitated, a face expressing extreme joy.

"Oh, brother! Mama saw you—Papa saw you, and never knew you! But I knew you when you jumped quick—that way—off your horse. And now I don't know you. You wild man! You giant! You splendid barbarian!... Mama, Papa, hurry! It is Dick! Look at him. Just look at him! Oh-h, thank God!"

Belding turned away and drew Nell with him. In another second she and Mercedes were clasped in each other's arms. Then followed a time of joyful greetings all round.

The Yaqui stood leaning against a tree watching the welcoming home of the lost. No one seemed to think of him, until Belding, ever mindful of the needs of horses, put a hand on Blanco Diablo and called to Yaqui to bring the others. They led the string of whites down to the barn, freed them of wet and dusty saddles and packs, and turned them loose in the alfalfa, now breast-high. Diablo found his old spirit; Blanco Sol tossed his head and whistled his satisfaction; White Woman pranced to and fro; and presently they all settled down to quiet grazing. How good it was for Belding to see those white shapes against the rich background of green! His eyes glistened. It was a sight he had never expected to see again. He lingered there many moments when he wanted to hurry back to his rangers.

At last he tore himself away from watching Blanco Diablo and returned to the house. It was only to find that he might have spared himself the hurry. Jim and Ladd were lying on the beds that had not held them for so many months. Their slumber seemed as deep and quiet as death. Curiously Belding gazed down upon them. They had removed only boots and chaps. Their clothes were in tatters. Jim appeared little more than skin and bones, a long shape, dark and hard as iron. Ladd's appearance shocked Belding. The ranger looked an old man, blasted, shriveled, starved. Yet his gaunt face, though terrible in its records of tortures, had something fine and noble, even beautiful to Belding, in its strength, its victory.

Thorne and Mercedes had disappeared. The low murmur of voices came from Mrs. Gale's room, and Belding concluded that Dick was still with his family. No doubt he, also, would soon seek rest and sleep. Belding went through the patio and called in at Nell's door. She was there sitting by her window. The flush of happiness had not left her face, but she looked stunned, and a shadow of fear lay dark in her eyes. Belding had intended to talk. He wanted some one to listen to him. The expression in Nell's eyes, however, silenced him. He had forgotten. Nell read his thought in his face, and then she lost all her color and dropped her head. Belding entered, stood beside her with a hand on hers. He tried desperately hard to think of the right thing to say, and realized so long as he tried that he could not speak at all.

"Nell—Dick's back safe and sound," he said, slowly. "That's the main thing. I wish you could have seen his eyes when he held you in his arms out there.... Of course, Dick's coming knocks out your trip East and changes plans generally. We haven't had the happiest time lately. But now it'll be different. Dick's as true as a Yaqui. He'll chase that Chase fellow, don't mistake me.... Then mother will be home soon. She'll straighten out this—this mystery. And Nell—however it turns out—I know Dick Gale will feel just the same as I feel. Brace up now, girl."

Belding left the patio and traced thoughtful steps back toward the corrals. He realized the need of his wife. If she had been at home he would not have come so close to killing two men. Nell would never have fallen so low in spirit. Whatever the real truth of the tragedy of his wife's life, it would not make the slightest difference to him. What hurt him was the pain mother and daughter had suffered, were suffering still. Somehow he must put an end to that pain.

He found the Yaqui curled up in a corner of the barn in as deep a sleep as that of the rangers. Looking down at him, Belding felt again the rush of curious thrilling eagerness to learn all that had happened since the dark night when Yaqui had led the white horses away into the desert. Belding curbed his impatience and set to work upon tasks he had long neglected. Presently he was interrupted by Mr. Gale, who came out, beside himself with happiness and excitement. He flung a hundred questions at Belding and never gave him time to answer one, even if that had been possible. Finally, when Mr. Gale lost his breath, Belding got a word in. "See here, Mr. Gale, you know as much as I know. Dick's back. They're all back—a hard lot, starved, burned, torn to pieces, worked out to the limit I never saw in desert travelers, but they're alive—alive and well, man! Just wait. Just gamble I won't sleep or eat till I hear that story. But they've got to sleep and eat."

Belding gathered with growing amusement that besides the joy, excitement, anxiety, impatience expressed by Mr. Gale there was something else which Belding took for pride. It pleased him. Looking back, he remembered some of the things Dick had confessed his father thought of him. Belding's sympathy had always been with the boy. But he had learned to like the old man, to find him kind and wise, and to think that perhaps college and business had not brought out the best in Richard Gale. The West had done that, however, as it had for many a wild youngster; and Belding resolved to have a little fun at the expense of Mr. Gale. So he began by making a few remarks that appeared to rob Dick's father of both speech and breath.

"And don't mistake me," concluded Belding, "just keep out of earshot when Laddy tells us the story of that desert trip, unless you're hankering to have your hair turn pure white and stand curled on end and freeze that way."

About the middle of the forenoon on the following day the rangers hobbled out of the kitchen to the porch.

"I'm a sick man, I tell you," Ladd was complaining, "an' I gotta be fed. Soup! Beef tea! That ain't so much as wind to me. I want about a barrel of bread an' butter, an' a whole platter of mashed potatoes with gravy an' green stuff—all kinds of green stuff—an' a whole big apple pie. Give me everythin' an' anythin' to eat but meat. Shore I never, never want to taste meat again, an' sight of a piece of sheep meat would jest about finish me.... Jim, you used to be a human bein' that stood up for Charlie Ladd."

"Laddy, I'm lined up beside you with both guns," replied Jim, plaintively. "Hungry? Say, the smell of breakfast in that kitchen made my mouth water so I near choked to death. I reckon we're gettin' most onhuman treatment."

"But I'm a sick man," protested Ladd, "an' I'm agoin' to fall over in a minute if somebody doesn't feed me. Nell, you used to be fond of me."

"Oh, Laddy, I am yet," replied Nell.

"Shore I don't believe it. Any girl with a tender heart just couldn't let a man starve under her eyes... Look at Dick, there. I'll bet he's had something to eat, mebbe potatoes an' gravy, an' pie an'—"

"Laddy, Dick has had no more than I gave you—indeed, not nearly so much."

"Shore he's had a lot of kisses then, for he hasn't hollered onct about this treatment."

"Perhaps he has," said Nell, with a blush; "and if you think that—they would help you to be reasonable I might—I'll—"

"Well, powerful fond as I am of you, just now kisses 'll have to run second to bread an' butter."

"Oh, Laddy, what a gallant speech!" laughed Nell. "I'm sorry, but I've Dad's orders."

"Laddy," interrupted Belding, "you've got to be broke in gradually to eating. Now you know that. You'd be the severest kind of a boss if you had some starved beggars on your hands."

"But I'm sick—I'm dyin'," howled Ladd.

"You were never sick in your life, and if all the bullet holes I see in you couldn't kill you, why, you never will die."

"Can I smoke?" queried Ladd, with sudden animation. "My Gawd, I used to smoke. Shore I've forgot. Nell, if you want to be reinstated in my gallery of angels, just find me a pipe an' tobacco."

"I've hung onto my pipe," said Jim, thoughtfully. "I reckon I had it empty in my mouth for seven years or so, wasn't it, Laddy? A long time! I can see the red lava an' the red haze, an' the red twilight creepin' up. It was hot an' some lonely. Then the wind, and always that awful silence! An' always Yaqui watchin' the west, an' Laddy with his checkers, an' Mercedes burnin' up, wastin' away to nothin' but eyes! It's all there—I'll never get rid—"

"Chop that kind of talk," interrupted Belding, bluntly. "Tell us where Yaqui took you—what happened to Rojas—why you seemed lost for so long."

"I reckon Laddy can tell all that best; but when it comes to Rojas's finish I'll tell what I seen, an' so'll Dick an' Thorne. Laddy missed Rojas's finish. Bar none, that was the—"

"I'm a sick man, but I can talk," put in Ladd, "an' shore I don't want the whole story exaggerated none by Jim."

Ladd filled the pipe Nell brought, puffed ecstatically at it, and settled himself upon the bench for a long talk. Nell glanced appealingly at Dick, who tried to slip away. Mercedes did go, and was followed by Thorne. Mr. Gale brought chairs, and in subdued excitement called his wife and daughter. Belding leaned forward, rendered all the more eager by Dick's reluctance to stay, the memory of the quick tragic change in the expression of Mercedes's beautiful eyes, by the strange gloomy cast stealing over Ladd's face.

The ranger talked for two hours—talked till his voice weakened to a husky whisper. At the conclusion of his story there was an impressive silence. Then Elsie Gale stood up, and with her hand on Dick's shoulder, her eyes bright and warm as sunlight, she showed the rangers what a woman thought of them and of the Yaqui. Nell clung to Dick, weeping silently. Mrs. Gale was overcome, and Mr. Gale, very white and quiet, helped her up to her room.

"The Indian! the Indian!" burst out Belding, his voice deep and rolling. "What did I tell you? Didn't I say he'd be a godsend? Remember what I said about Yaqui and some gory Aztec knifework? So he cut Rojas loose from that awful crater wall, foot by foot, finger by finger, slow and terrible? And Rojas didn't hang long on the *choya* thorns? Thank the Lord for that!... Laddy, no story of Camino del Diablo can hold a candle to yours. The flight and the fight were jobs for men. But living through this long hot summer and coming out—that's a miracle. Only the Yaqui could have done it. The Yaqui! The Yaqui!"

"Shore. Charlie Ladd looks up at an Indian these days. But Beldin', as for the comin' out, don't forget the hosses. Without grand old Sol an' Diablo, who I don't hate no more, an' the other Blancos, we'd never have got here. Yaqui an' the hosses, that's my story!"

Early in the afternoon of the next day Belding encountered Dick at the water barrel.

"Belding, this is river water, and muddy at that," said Dick. "Lord knows I'm not kicking. But I've dreamed some of our cool running spring, and I want a drink from it."

"Never again, son. The spring's gone, faded, sunk, dry as dust."

"Dry!" Gale slowly straightened. "We've had rains. The river's full. The spring ought to be overflowing. What's wrong? Why is it dry?"

"Dick, seeing you're interested, I may as well tell you that a big charge of nitroglycerin choked my spring."

"Nitroglycerin?" echoed Gale. Then he gave a quick start. "My mind's been on home, Nell, my family. But all the same I felt something was wrong here with the ranch, with you, with Nell... Belding, that ditch there is dry. The roses are dead. The little green in that grass has come with the rains. What's happened? The ranch's run down. Now I look around I see a change."

"Some change, yes," replied Belding, bitterly. "Listen, son."

Briefly, but not the less forcibly for that, Belding related his story of the operations of the Chases.

Astonishment appeared to be Gale's first feeling. "Our water gone, our claims gone, our plans forestalled! Why, Belding, it's unbelievable. Forlorn River with promoters, business, railroad, bank, and what not!"

Suddenly he became fiery and suspicious. "These Chases—did they do all this on the level?"

"Barefaced robbery! Worse than a Greaser holdup," replied Belding, grimly.

"You say the law upheld them?"

"Sure. Why, Ben Chase has a pull as strong as Diablo's on a down grade. Dick, we're jobbed, outfigured, beat, tricked, and we can't do a thing."

"Oh, I'm sorry, Belding, most of all for Laddy," said Gale, feelingly. "He's all in. He'll never ride again. He wanted to settle down here on the farm he thought he owned, grow grass and raise horses, and take it easy. Oh, but it's tough! Say, he doesn't know it yet. He was just telling me he'd like to go out and look the farm over. Who's going to tell him? What's he going to do when he finds out about this deal?"

"Son, that's made me think some," replied Belding, with keen eyes fast upon the young man. "And I was kind of wondering how you'd take it."

"I? Well, I'll call on the Chases. Look here, Belding, I'd better do some forestalling myself. If Laddy gets started now there'll be blood spilled. He's not just right in his mind yet. He talks in his sleep sometimes about how Yaqui finished Rojas. If it's left to him—he'll kill these men. But if I take it up—"

"You're talking sense, Dick. Only here, I'm not so sure of you. And there's more to tell. Son, you've Nell to think of and your mother."

Belding's ranger gave him a long and searching glance.

"You can be sure of me," he said.

"All right, then; listen," began Belding. With deep voice that had many a beak and tremor he told Gale how Nell had been hounded by Radford Chase, how her mother had been driven by Ben Chase—the whole sad story.

"So that's the trouble! Poor little girl!" murmured Gale, brokenly. "I felt something was wrong. Nell wasn't natural, like her old self. And when I begged her to marry me soon, while Dad was here, she couldn't talk. She could only cry."

"It was hard on Nell," said Belding, simply. "But it 'll be better now you're back. Dick, I know the girl. She'll refuse to marry you and you'll have a hard job to break her down, as hard as the one you just rode in off of. I think I know you, too, or I wouldn't be saying—"

"Belding, what 're you hinting at?" demanded Gale. "Do you dare insinuate that—that—if the thing were true it'd make any difference to me?"

"Aw, come now, Dick; I couldn't mean that. I'm only awkward at saying things. And I'm cut pretty deep—"

"For God's sake, you don't believe what Chase said?" queried Gale, in passionate haste. "It's a lie. I swear it's a lie. I know it's a lie. And I've got to tell Nell this minute. Come on in with me. I want you, Belding. Oh, why didn't you tell me sooner?"

Belding felt himself dragged by an iron arm into the sitting-room out into the patio, and across that to where Nell sat in her door. At sight of them she gave a little cry, drooped for an instant, then raised a pale, still face, with eyes beginning to darken.

"Dearest, I know now why you are not wearing my mother's ring," said Gale, steadily and low-voiced.

"Dick, I am not worthy," she replied, and held out a trembling hand with the ring lying in the palm.

Swift as light Gale caught her hand and slipped the ring back upon the third finger.

"Nell! Look at me. It is your engagement ring.... Listen. I don't believe this—this thing that's been torturing you. I know it's a lie. I am absolutely sure your mother will prove it a lie. She must have suffered once—perhaps there was a sad error—but the thing you fear is not true. But, hear me, dearest; even if it was true it wouldn't make the slightest difference to me. I'd promise you on my honor I'd never think of it again. I'd love you all the more because you'd suffered. I want you all the more to be my wife—to let me make you forget—to—"

She rose swiftly with the passionate abandon of a woman stirred to her depths, and she kissed him.

"Oh, Dick, you're good—so good! You'll never know—just what those words mean to me. They've saved me—I think."

"Then, dearest, it's all right?" Dick questioned, eagerly. "You will keep your promise? You will marry me?"

The glow, the light faded out of her face, and now the blue eyes were almost black. She drooped and shook her head.

"Nell!" exclaimed Gale, sharply catching his breath.

"Don't ask me, Dick. I—I won't marry you."

"Why?"

"You know. It's true that I—"

"It's a lie," interrupted Gale, fiercely. "But even if it's true—why—why won't you marry me? Between you and me love is the thing. Love, and nothing else! Don't you love me any more?"

They had forgotten Belding, who stepped back into the shade.

"I love you with my whole heart and soul. I'd die for you," whispered Nell, with clenching hands. "But I won't disgrace you."

"Dear, you have worried over this trouble till you're morbid. It has grown out of all proportion. I tell you that I'll not only be the happiest man on earth, but the luckiest, if you marry me."

"Dick, you give not one thought to your family. Would they receive me as your wife?"

"They surely would," replied Gale, steadily.

"No! oh no!"

"You're wrong, Nell. I'm glad you said that. You give me a chance to prove something. I'll go this minute and tell them all. I'll be back here in less than—"

"Dick, you will not tell her—your mother?" cried Nell, with her eyes streaming. "You will not? Oh, I can't bear it! She's so proud! And Dick, I love her. Don't tell her! Please, please don't! She'll be going soon. She needn't ever know—about me. I want her always to think well of me. Dick, I beg of you. Oh, the fear of her knowing has been the worst of all! Please don't go!"

"Nell, I'm sorry. I hate to hurt you. But you're wrong. You can't see things clearly. This is your happiness I'm fighting for. And it's my life.... Wait here, dear. I won't be long."

Gale ran across the patio and disappeared. Nell sank to the doorstep, and as she met the question in Belding's eyes she shook her head mournfully. They waited without speaking. It seemed a long while before Gale returned. Belding thrilled at sight of him. There was more boy about him than Belding had ever seen. Dick was coming swiftly, flushed, glowing, eager, erect, almost smiling.

"I told them. I swore it was a lie, but I wanted them to decide as if it were true. I didn't have to waste a minute on Elsie. She loves you, Nell. The Governor is crazy about you. I didn't have to waste two minutes on him. Mother used up the time. She wanted to know all there was to tell. She is proud, yes; but, Nell, I wish you could have seen how she took the—the story about you. Why, she never thought of me at all, until she had cried over you. Nell, she loves you, too. They all love you. Oh, it's so good to tell you. I think mother realizes the part you have had in the—what shall I call it?—the regeneration of Richard Gale. Doesn't that sound fine? Darling, mother not only consents, she wants you to be my wife. Do you hear that? And listen—she had me in a corner and, of course, being my mother, she put on the screws. She made me promise that we'd live in the East half the year. That means Chicago, Cape May, New York—you see, I'm not exactly the lost son any more. Why, Nell, dear, you'll have to learn who Dick Gale really is. But I always want to be the ranger you helped me become, and ride Blanco Sol, and see a little of the desert. Don't let the idea of big cities frighten you. W'ell always love the open places best. Now, Nell, say you'll forget this trouble. I know it'll come all right. Say you'll marry me soon.... Why, dearest, you're crying.... Nell!"

"My—heart—is broken," sobbed Nell, "for—I—I—can't marry you."

The boyish brightness faded out of Gale's face. Here, Belding saw, was the stern reality arrayed against his dreams.

"That devil Radford Chase—he'll tell my secret," panted Nell. "He swore if you ever came back and married me he'd follow us all over the world to tell it."

Belding saw Gale grow deathly white and suddenly stand stock-still.

"Chase threatened you, then?" asked Dick; and the forced naturalness of his voice struck Belding.

"Threatened me? He made my life a nightmare," replied Nell, in a rush of speech. "At first I wondered how he was worrying mother sick. But she wouldn't tell me. Then when she went away he began to hint things. I hated him all the more. But when he told me—I was frightened, shamed. Still I did not weaken. He was pretty decent when he was sober. But when he was half drunk he was the devil. He laughed at me and my pride. I didn't dare shut the door in his face. After a while he found out that your mother loved me and that I loved her. Then he began to threaten me. If I didn't give in to him he'd see she learned the truth. That made me weaken. It nearly killed me. I simply could not bear the thought of Mrs. Gale knowing. But I couldn't marry him. Besides, he got so half the time, when he was drunk, he didn't want or ask me to be his wife. I was about ready to give up and go mad when you—you came home."

She ended in a whisper, looking up wistfully and sadly at him. Belding was a raging fire within, cold without. He watched Gale, and believed he could foretell that young man's future conduct. Gale gathered Nell up into his arms and held her to his breast for a long moment.

"Dear Nell, I'm sure the worst of your trouble is over," he said gently. "I will not give you up. Now, won't you lie down, try to rest and calm yourself. Don't grieve any more. This thing isn't so bad as you make it. Trust me. I'll shut Mr. Radford Chase's mouth."

As he released her she glanced quickly up at him, then lifted appealing hands.

"Dick, you won't hunt for him—go after him?"

Gale laughed, and the laugh made Belding jump.

"Dick, I beg of you. Please don't make trouble. The Chases have been hard enough on us. They are rich, powerful. Dick, say you will not make matters worse. Please promise me you'll not go to him."

"You ask me that?" he demanded.

"Yes. Oh yes!"

"But you know it's useless. What kind of a man do you want me to be?"

"It's only that I'm afraid. Oh, Dick, he'd shoot you in the back."

"No, Nell, a man of his kind wouldn't have nerve enough even for that."

"You'll go?" she cried wildly.

Gale smiled, and the smile made Belding cold.

"Dick, I cannot keep you back?"

"No," he said.

Then the woman in her burst through instinctive fear, and with her eyes blazing black in her white face she lifted parted quivering lips and kissed him.

Gale left the patio, and Belding followed closely at his heels. They went through the sitting-room. Outside upon the porch sat the rangers, Mr. Gale, and Thorne. Dick went into his room without speaking.

"Shore somethin's comin' off," said Ladd, sharply; and he sat up with keen eyes narrowing.

Belding spoke a few words; and, remembering an impression he had wished to make upon Mr. Gale, he made them strong. But now it was with grim humor that he spoke.

"Better stop that boy," he concluded, looking at Mr. Gale. "He'll do some mischief. He's wilder'n hell."

"Stop him? Why, assuredly," replied Mr. Gale, rising with nervous haste.

Just then Dick came out of his door. Belding eyed him keenly. The only change he could see was that Dick had put on a hat and a pair of heavy gloves.

"Richard, where are you going?" asked his father.

"I'm going over here to see a man."

"No. It is my wish that you remain. I forbid you to go," said Mr. Gale, with a hand on his son's shoulder.

Dick put Mr. Gale aside gently, respectfully, yet forcibly. The old man gasped.

"Dad, I haven't gotten over my bad habit of disobeying you. I'm sorry. Don't interfere with me now. And don't follow me. You might see something unpleasant."

"But my son! What are you going to do?"

"I'm going to beat a dog."

Mr. Gale looked helplessly from this strangely calm and cold son to the restless Belding. Then Dick strode off the porch.

"Hold on!" Ladd's voice would have stopped almost any man. "Dick, you wasn't agoin' without me?"

"Yes, I was. But I'm thoughtless just now, Laddy."

"Shore you was. Wait a minute, Dick. I'm a sick man, but at that nobody can pull any stunts round here without me."

He hobbled along the porch and went into his room. Jim Lash knocked the ashes out of his pipe, and, humming his dance tune, he followed Ladd. In a moment the rangers appeared, and both were packing guns.

Not a little of Belding's grim excitement came from observation of Mr. Gale. At sight of the rangers with their guns the old man turned white and began to tremble.

"Better stay behind," whispered Belding. "Dick's going to beat that two-legged dog, and the rangers get excited when they're packing guns."

"I will not stay behind," replied Mr. Gale, stoutly. "I'll see this affair through. Belding, I've guessed it. Richard is going to fight the Chases, those robbers who have ruined you."

"Well, I can't guarantee any fight on their side," returned Belding, dryly. "But maybe there'll be Greasers with a gun or two."

Belding stalked off to catch up with Dick, and Mr. Gale came trudging behind with Thorne.

"Where will we find these Chases?" asked Dick of Belding.

"They've got a place down the road adjoining the inn. They call it their club. At this hour Radford will be there sure. I don't know about the old man. But his office is now just across the way."

They passed several houses, turned a corner into the main street, and stopped at a wide, low adobe structure. A number of saddled horses stood haltered to posts. Mexicans lolled around the wide doorway.

"There's Ben Chase now over on the corner," said Belding to Dick. "See, the tall man with the white hair, and leather band on his hat. He sees us. He knows there's something up. He's got men with him. They'll come over. We're after the young buck, and sure he'll be in here."

They entered. The place was a hall, and needed only a bar to make it a saloon. There were two rickety pool tables. Evidently Chase had fitted up this amusement room for his laborers as well as for the use of his engineers and assistants, for the crowd contained both Mexicans and Americans. A large table near a window was surrounded by a noisy, smoking, drinking circle of card-players.

"Point out this Radford Chase to me," said Gale.

"There! The big fellow with the red face. His eyes stick out a little. See! He's dropped his cards and his face isn't red any more."

Dick strode across the room.

Belding grasped Mr. Gale and whispered hoarsely: "Don't miss anything. It'll be great. Watch Dick and watch Laddy! If there's any gun play, dodge behind me."

Belding smiled with a grim pleasure as he saw Mr. Gales' face turn white.

Dick halted beside the table. His heavy boot shot up, and with a crash the table split, and glasses, cards, chips flew everywhere. As they rattled down and the chairs of the dumfounded players began to slide Dick called out: "My name is Gale. I'm looking for Mr. Radford Chase."

A tall, heavy-shouldered fellow rose, boldly enough, even swaggeringly, and glowered at Gale.

"I'm Radford Chase," he said. His voice betrayed the boldness of his action.

It was over in a few moments. The tables and chairs were tumbled into a heap; one of the pool tables had been shoved aside; a lamp lay shattered, with oil running dark upon the floor. Ladd leaned against a post with a smoking gun in his hand. A Mexican crouched close to the wall moaning over a broken arm. In the far corner upheld by comrades another wounded Mexican cried out in pain. These two had attempted to draw weapons upon Gale, and Ladd had crippled them.

In the center of the room lay Radford Chase, a limp, torn, hulking, bloody figure. He was not seriously injured. But he was helpless, a miserable beaten wretch, who knew his condition and felt the eyes upon him. He sobbed and moaned and howled. But no one offered to help him to his feet.

Backed against the door of the hall stood Ben Chase, for once stripped of all authority and confidence and courage. Gale confronted him, and now Gale's mien was in striking contrast to the coolness with which he had entered the place. Though sweat dripped from his face, it was as white as chalk. Like dark flames his eyes seemed to leap and dance and burn. His lean jaw hung down and quivered with passion. He shook a huge gloved fist in Chase's face.

"Your gray hairs save you this time. But keep out of my way! And when that son of yours comes to, tell him every time I meet him I'll add some more to what he got to-day!"

XIX

THE SECRET OF FORLORN RIVER

IN the early morning Gale, seeking solitude where he could brood over his trouble, wandered alone. It was not easy for him to elude the Yaqui, and just at the moment when he had cast himself down in a secluded shady corner the Indian appeared, noiseless, shadowy, mysterious as always.

"Malo," he said, in his deep voice.

"Yes, Yaqui, it's bad—very bad," replied Gale.

The Indian had been told of the losses sustained by Belding and his rangers.

"Go—me!" said Yaqui, with an impressive gesture toward the lofty lilac-colored steps of No Name Mountains.

He seemed the same as usual, but a glance on Gale's part, a moment's attention, made him conscious of the old strange force in the Yaqui. "Why does my brother want me to climb the nameless mountains with him?" asked Gale.

"Lluvia d'oro," replied Yaqui, and he made motions that Gale found difficult of interpretation.

"Shower of Gold," translated Gale. That was the Yaqui's name for Nell. What did he mean by using it in connection with a climb into the mountains? Were his motions intended to convey an idea of a shower of golden blossoms from that rare and beautiful tree, or a golden rain? Gale's listlessness vanished in a flash of thought. The Yaqui meant gold. Gold! He meant he could retrieve the fallen fortunes of the white brother who had saved his life that evil day at the Papago Well. Gale thrilled as he gazed piercingly into the wonderful eyes of this Indian. Would Yaqui never consider his debt paid?

"Go—me?" repeat the Indian, pointing with the singular directness that always made this action remarkable in him.

"Yes, Yaqui."

Gale ran to his room, put on hobnailed boots, filled a canteen, and hurried back to the corral. Yaqui awaited him. The Indian carried a coiled lasso and a short stout stick. Without a word he led the way down the lane, turned up the river toward the mountains. None of Belding's household saw their departure.

What had once been only a narrow mesquite-bordered trail was now a well-trodden road. A deep irrigation ditch, full of flowing muddy water, ran parallel with the road. Gale had been curious about the operations of the Chases, but bitterness he could not help had kept him from going out to see the work. He was not surprised to find that the engineers who had constructed the ditches and dam had anticipated him in every particular. The dammed-up gulch made a magnificent reservoir, and Gale could not look upon the long narrow lake without a feeling of gladness. The dreaded ano seco of the Mexicans might come again and would come, but never to the inhabitants of Forlorn River. That stone-walled, stone-floored gulch would never leak, and already it contained water enough to irrigate the whole Altar Valley for two dry seasons.

Yaqui led swiftly along the lake to the upper end, where the stream roared down over unscalable walls. This point was the farthest Gale had ever penetrated into the rough foothills, and he had Belding's word for it that no white man had ever climbed No Name Mountains from the west.

But a white man was not an Indian. The former might have stolen the range and valley and mountain, even the desert, but his possessions would ever remain mysteries. Gale had scarcely faced the great gray ponderous wall of cliff before the old strange interest in the Yaqui seized him again. It recalled the tie that existed between them, a tie almost as close as blood. Then he was eager and curious to see how the Indian would conquer those seemingly insurmountable steps of stone.

Yaqui left the gulch and clambered up over a jumble of weathered slides and traced a slow course along the base of the giant wall. He looked up and seemed to select a point for ascent. It was the last place in that mountainside where Gale would have thought climbing possible. Before him the wall rose, leaning over him, shutting out the light, a dark mighty mountain mass. Innumerable cracks and crevices and caves roughened the bulging sides of dark rock.

Yaqui tied one end of his lasso to the short, stout stick and, carefully disentangling the coils, he whirled the stick round and round and threw it almost over the first rim of the shelf, perhaps thirty feet up. The stick did not lodge. Yaqui tried again. This time it caught in a crack. He pulled hard. Then, holding to the lasso, he walked up the steep slant, hand over hand on the rope. When he reached the shelf he motioned for Gale to follow. Gale found that method of scaling a wall both quick and easy. Yaqui pulled up the lasso, and threw the stick aloft into another crack. He climbed to another shelf, and Gale followed him. The third effort brought them to a more rugged bench a hundred feet above the slides. The Yaqui worked round to the left, and turned into a dark fissure. Gale kept close to his heels. They came out presently into lighter space, yet one that restricted any extended view. Broken sections of cliff were on all sides.

Here the ascent became toil. Gale could distance Yaqui going downhill; on the climb, however, he was hard put to it to keep the Indian in sight. It was not a question of strength or lightness of foot. These Gale had beyond the share of most men. It was a matter of lung power, and the Yaqui's life had been spent scaling the desert heights. Moreover, the climbing was infinitely slow, tedious, dangerous. On the way up several times Gale imagined he heard a dull roar of falling water. The sound seemed to be under him, over him to this side and to that. When he was certain he could locate the direction from which it came then he heard it no more until he had gone on. Gradually he forgot it in the physical sensations of the climb. He burned his hands and knees. He grew hot and wet and winded. His heart thumped so that it hurt, and there were instants when his sight was blurred. When at last he had toiled to where the Yaqui sat awaiting him upon the rim of that great wall, it was none too soon.

Gale lay back and rested for a while without note of anything except the blue sky. Then he sat up. He was amazed to find that after that wonderful climb he was only a thousand feet or so above the valley. Judged by the nature of his effort, he would have said he had climbed a mile. The village lay beneath him, with its new adobe structures and tents and buildings in bright contrast with the older habitations. He saw the green alfalfa fields, and Belding's white horses, looking very small and motionless. He pleased himself by imagining he could pick out Blanco Sol. Then his gaze swept on to the river.

Indeed, he realized now why some one had named it Forlorn River. Even at this season when it was full of water it had a forlorn aspect. It was doomed to fail out there on the desert—doomed never to mingle with the waters of the Gulf. It wound away down the valley, growing wider and shallower, encroaching more and more on the gray flats, until it disappeared on its sad journey toward Sonoyta. That vast shimmering, sun-governed waste recognized its life only at this flood season, and was already with parched tongue and insatiate fire licking and burning up its futile waters.

Yaqui put a hand on Gale's knee. It was a bronzed, scarred, powerful hand, always eloquent of meaning. The Indian was listening. His bent head, his strange dilating eyes, his rigid form, and that close-pressing hand, how these brought back to Gale the terrible lonely night hours on the lava!

"What do you hear, Yaqui?" asked Gale. He laughed a little at the mood that had come over him. But the sound of his voice did not break the spell. He did not want to speak again. He yielded to Yaqui's subtle nameless influence. He listened himself, heard nothing but the scream of an eagle. Often he wondered if the Indian could hear things that made no sound. Yaqui was beyond understanding.

Whatever the Indian had listened to or for, presently he satisfied himself, and, with a grunt that might mean anything, he rose and turned away from the rim. Gale followed, rested now and eager to go on. He saw that the great cliff they had climbed was only a stairway up to the huge looming dark bulk of the plateau above.

Suddenly he again heard the dull roar of falling water. It seemed to have cleared itself of muffled vibrations. Yaqui mounted a little ridge and halted. The next instant Gale stood above a bottomless cleft into which a white stream leaped. His astounded gaze swept backward along this narrow swift stream to its end in a dark, round, boiling pool. It was a huge spring, a bubbling well, the outcropping of an underground river coming down from the vast plateau above.

Yaqui had brought Gale to the source of Forlorn River.

Flashing thoughts in Gale's mind were no swifter than the thrills that ran over him. He would stake out a claim here and never be cheated out of it. Ditches on the benches and troughs on the steep walls would carry water down to the valley. Ben Chase had build a great dam which would be useless if Gale chose to turn Forlorn River from its natural course. The fountain head of that mysterious desert river belonged to him.

His eagerness, his mounting passion, was checked by Yaqui's unusual action. The Indian showed wonder, hesitation, even reluctance. His strange eyes surveyed this boiling well as if they could not believe the sight they saw. Gale divined instantly that Yaqui had never before seen the source of Forlorn River. If he had ever ascended to this plateau, probably it had been to some other part, for the water was new to him. He stood gazing aloft at peaks, at lower ramparts of the mountain, and at nearer landmarks of prominence. Yaqui seemed at fault. He was not sure of his location.

Then he strode past the swirling pool of dark water and began to ascend a little slope that led up to a shelving cliff. Another object halted the Indian. It was a pile of stones, weathered, crumbled, fallen into ruin, but still retaining shape enough to prove it had been built there by the hands of men. Round and round this the Yaqui stalked, and his curiosity attested a further uncertainty. It was as if he had come upon something surprising. Gale wondered about the pile of stones. Had it once been a prospector's claim?

"Ugh!" grunted the Indian; and, though his exclamation expressed no satisfaction, it surely put an end to doubt. He pointed up to the roof of the sloping yellow shelf of stone. Faintly outlined there in red were the imprints of many human hands with fingers spread wide. Gale had often seen such paintings on the walls of the desert caverns. Manifestly these told Yaqui he had come to the spot for which he had aimed.

Then his actions became swift—and Yaqui seldom moved swiftly. The fact impressed Gale. The Indian searched the level floor under the shelf. He gathered up handfuls of small black stones, and thrust them at Gale. Their weight made Gale start, and then he trembled. The Indian's next move was to pick up a piece of weathered rock and throw it against the wall. It broke. He snatched up parts, and showed the broken edges to Gale. They contained yellow steaks, dull glints, faint tracings of green. It was gold.

Gale found his legs shaking under him; and he sat down, trying to take all the bits of stone into his lap. His fingers were all thumbs as with knife blade he dug into the black pieces of rock. He found gold. Then he stared down the slope, down into the valley with its river winding forlornly away into the desert. But he did not see any of that. Here was reality as sweet, as wonderful, as saving as a dream come true. Yaqui had led him to a ledge of gold. Gale had learned enough about mineral to know that this was a rich strike. All in a second he was speechless with the joy of it. But his mind whirled in thought about this strange and noble Indian, who seemed never to be able to pay a debt. Belding and the poverty that had come to him! Nell, who had wept over the loss of a spring! Laddy, who never could ride again! Jim Lash, who swore he would always look after his friend! Thorne and Mercedes! All these people, who had been good to him and whom he loved, were poor. But now they would be rich. They would one and all be his partners. He had discovered the source of Forlorn River, and was rich in water. Yaqui had made him rich in gold. Gale wanted to rush down the slope, down into the valley, and tell his wonderful news.

Suddenly his eyes cleared and he saw the pile of stones. His blood turned to ice, then to fire. That was the mark of a prospector's claim. But it was old, very old. The ledge had never been worked, the slope was wild. There was not another single indication that a prospector had ever been there. Where, then, was he who had first staked this claim? Gale wondered with growing hope, with the fire easing, with the cold passing.

The Yaqui uttered the low, strange, involuntary cry so rare with him, a cry somehow always associated with death. Gale shuddered.

The Indian was digging in the sand and dust under the shelving wall. He threw out an object that rang against the stone. It was a belt buckle. He threw out old shrunken, withered boots. He came upon other things, and then he ceased to dig.

The grave of desert prospectors! Gale had seen more than one. Ladd had told him many a story of such gruesome finds. It was grim, hard fact.

Then the keen-eyed Yaqui reached up to a little projecting shelf of rock and took from it a small object. He showed no curiosity and gave the thing to Gale.

How strangely Gale felt when he received into his hands a flat oblong box! Was it only the influence of the Yaqui, or was there a nameless and unseen presence beside that grave? Gale could not be sure. But he knew he had gone back to the old desert mood. He knew something hung in the balance. No accident, no luck, no debt-paying Indian could account wholly for that moment. Gale knew he held in his hands more than gold.

The box was a tin one, and not all rusty. Gale pried open the reluctant lid. A faint old musty odor penetrated his nostrils. Inside the box lay a packet wrapped in what once might have been oilskin. He took it out and removed this covering. A folded paper remained in his hands.

It was growing yellow with age. But he descried a dim tracery of words. A crabbed scrawl, written in blood, hard to read! He held it more to the light, and slowly he deciphered its content.

"We, Robert Burton and Jonas Warren, give half of this gold claim to the man who finds it and half to Nell Burton, daughter and granddaughter."

Gasping, with a bursting heart, overwhelmed by an unutterable joy of divination, Gale fumbled with the paper until he got it open.

It was a certificate twenty-one years old, and recorded the marriage of Robert Burton and Nellie Warren.

XX

DESERT GOLD

A SUMMER day dawned on Forlorn River, a beautiful, still, hot, golden day with huge sail clouds of white motionless over No Name Peaks and the purple of clear air in the distance along the desert horizon.

Mrs. Belding returned that day to find her daughter happy and the past buried forever in two lonely graves. The haunting shadow left her eyes. Gale believed he would never forget the sweetness, the wonder, the passion of her embrace when she called him her boy and gave him her blessing.

The little wrinkled padre who married Gale and Nell performed the ceremony as he told his beads, without interest or penetration, and went his way, leaving happiness behind.

"Shore I was a sick man," Ladd said, "an' darn near a dead one, but I'm agoin' to get well. Mebbe I'll be able to ride again someday. Nell, I lay it to you. An' I'm agoin' to kiss you an' wish you all the joy there is in this world. An', Dick, as Yaqui says, she's shore your Shower of Gold."

He spoke of Gale's finding love—spoke of it with the deep and wistful feeling of the lonely ranger who had always yearned for love and had never known it. Belding, once more practical, and important as never before with mining projects and water claims to manage, spoke of Gale's great good fortune in finding of gold—he called it desert gold.

"Ah, yes. Desert Gold!" exclaimed Dick's father, softly, with eyes of pride. Perhaps he was glad Dick had found the rich claim; surely he was happy that Dick had won the girl he loved. But it seemed to Dick himself that his father meant something very different from love and fortune in his allusion to desert gold.

That beautiful happy day, like life or love itself, could not be wholly perfect.

Yaqui came to Dick to say good-by. Dick was startled, grieved, and in his impulsiveness forgot for a moment the nature of the Indian. Yaqui was not to be changed.

Belding tried to overload him with gifts. The Indian packed a bag of food, a blanket, a gun, a knife, a canteen, and no more. The whole household went out with him to the corrals and fields from which Belding bade him choose a horse—any horse, even the loved Blanco Diablo. Gale's heart was in his throat for fear the Indian might choose Blanco Sol, and Gale hated himself for a selfishness he could not help. But without a word he would have parted with the treasured Sol.

Yaqui whistled the horses up—for the last time. Did he care for them? It would have been hard to say. He never looked at the fierce and haughty Diablo, nor at Blanco Sol as he raised his noble head and rang his piercing blast. The Indian did not choose one of Belding's whites. He caught a lean and wiry broncho, strapped a blanket on him, and fastened on the pack.

Then he turned to these friends, the same emotionless, inscrutable dark and silent Indian that he had always been. This parting was nothing to him. He had stayed to pay a debt, and now he was going home.

He shook hands with the men, swept a dark fleeting glance over Nell, and rested his strange eyes upon Mercedes's beautiful and agitated face. It must have been a moment of intense feeling for the Spanish girl. She owed it to him that she had life and love and happiness. She held out those speaking slender hands. But Yaqui did not touch them. Turning away, he mounted the broncho and rode down the trail toward the river.

"He's going home," said Belding.

"Home!" whispered Ladd; and Dick knew the ranger felt the resurging tide of memory. Home—across the cactus and lava, through solemn lonely days, the silent, lonely nights, into the vast and red-hazed world of desolation.

"Thorne, Mercedes, Nell, let's climb the foothill yonder and watch him out of sight," said Dick.

They climbed while the others returned to the house. When they reached the summit of the hill Yaqui was riding up the far bank of the river.

"He will turn to look—to wave good-by?" asked Nell.

"Dear he is an Indian," replied Gale.

From that height they watched him ride through the mesquites, up over the river bank to enter the cactus. His mount showed dark against the green and white, and for a long time he was plainly in sight. The sun hung red in a golden sky. The last the watchers saw of Yaqui was when he rode across a ridge and stood silhouetted against the gold of desert sky—a wild, lonely, beautiful picture. Then he was gone.

Strangely it came to Gale then that he was glad. Yaqui had returned to his own—the great spaces, the desolation, the solitude—to the trails he had trodden when a child, trails haunted now by ghosts of his people, and ever by his gods. Gale realized that in the Yaqui he had known the spirit of the desert, that this spirit had claimed all which was wild and primitive in him.

Tears glistened in Mercedes's magnificent black eyes, and Thorne kissed them away—kissed the fire back to them and the flame to her cheeks.

That action recalled Gale's earlier mood, the joy of the present, and he turned to Nell's sweet face. The desert was there, wonderful, constructive, ennobling, beautiful, terrible, but it was not for him as it was for the Indian. In the light of Nell's tremulous returning smile that strange, deep, clutching shadow faded, lost its hold forever; and he leaned close to her, whispering: "Lluvia d'oro"—"Shower of Gold."

FEB 2018

CPSIA information can be obtained
at www.ICGtesting.com
Printed in the USA
LVOW04s0753210118
563411LV00003B/99/P